THE WEST COUNTRY TRILOGY

Complete Series

THE WEST COUNTRY TRILOGY

Complete Series

JOHANNA CRAVEN

CONTENTS

"These superstitions have their origin in the purest feelings of the heart… They are the shadowings forth of love, tinctured with the melancholy dyes of that fear which is born of mystery."

Robert Hunt
Popular Romances of the West of England

PREQUEL

MOONSHINE

MIDNIGHT

Cornwall, England

1726

The moon is high. Just past midnight.

Isaac Bailey peers through the window of his cottage. Sparsely spread lamps build shadows in the street. Beyond them, the darkness is thick. He opens the door a crack. Hears the sea sigh, the wind push through the trees. No sound of human life. The village sleeps.

Now or never.

Isaac slides on his coat and slings a pack over his shoulder. He looks at his sister. Scarlett stares up at him, dark eyes enormous beneath the hood of her cloak.

He takes her hand. "Quiet now. Not a word."

She nods.

And into the dark they go, pulling closed the cottage door. Closing the door on memories of his mother's lullabies, his father's adventure tales. Memories, Isaac finds, that now hurt to remember.

He walks down the hill towards the beach, relying on his mind's eye to navigate the dark. He's been away from this place for four years, but his body remembers the village's twists and turns instinctively, surely, as though he'd never left.

Beside him, Scarlett's footsteps are soundless. Her fingers cling to his, thin and cold.

A strange sort of goodbye. He'd farewelled the place as the sun went down, knowing he'd see little as they made their escape in the dark. He is grateful to be leaving this miserable adult life that has been thrust upon him. But there's a sentimentality he is unable to shake off; an unavoidable love for his childhood of ghost stories and moonlight, caves filled with contraband, barefooted summers of sand and sea.

Here is the beach. Isaac can hear it; the *slash, slash* of the ocean. From here they will take the cliff path and feel their way to the next village. And then the next, the next. Feel their way to freedom.

But then, footsteps. Not his own. Too heavy to be Scarlett's.

The click of a pistol.

Isaac stops walking.

"Yes." A man's voice. "Wise."

Isaac hears the cold snap of flint. Lantern light spills over the sand. Scarlett squints and presses herself against her brother's hip.

The smugglers' banker holds the pistol, the lamp.

"Reuben had you follow us," Isaac says bitterly.

The banker slides the pistol into his belt. "Follow you, no. Wait for you, rather. He knew you'd try something like this. Assumed you untrustworthy. Like your father."

Isaac grits his teeth. "Let us go."

"I'll let you go. You'll walk back up that hill to your house and ensure you're at the harbour to meet Charles Reuben tomorrow morning."

"And if I don't? Will you shoot me in front of a child?"

"Is that something you wish to find out?"

Isaac glances up at the path snaking along the clifftop. It will take them to Polperro where they'll find either a boat or carriage out of Cornwall. He and Scarlett have spent their childhoods racing across the path. They could make it in the dark. Easy.

The man won't shoot. The thugs working for Reuben are little more than well-paid footmen. Surely not the type to kill a man in front of his child sister.

He glances down at Scarlett. "Run," he murmurs.

Her eyes are fixed on the pistol. She shakes her head.

"The girl is wise," says the banker. "I assure you, Mr Bailey, if you try and run I will pull the trigger."

Isaac draws in his breath. Presses a hand to Scarlett's shoulder and walks back up the hill. Back to the cottage with the memories and the dark.

LIQUOR BENEATH THE SEA

Isaac looks down at the ledger Charles Reuben has pressed into his hand.

Brandy, wine, Rotterdam gin. Ivory tobacco rasp for the eccentric Mr Smith who lives on Talland Hill.

This has been a shore of brandy, wine and Rotterdam gin for as long as Isaac can remember. Ankers buried in caves and liquor beneath the sea.

This free trading game was supposed to be the domain of other, more foolish men.

Isaac had left the west country four years ago, sure, even at seventeen, that he didn't want his life to be one of smuggling brandy, wine and gin.

"My agent is expecting you in Saint Peter Port," Reuben tells him, pacing the edge of the harbour. He folds his arms across his gold-threaded waistcoat. "I trust you'll not be making any more ill-advised escape attempts."

Isaac says nothing.

His father, Jacob, had been the leader of the Talland smuggling syndicate; the man taking the ledger from Charles Reuben's fist. Buying goods from the tax-free Channel Islands and selling them to penny-poor locals. A decent cut of the proceeds in his pocket, but Jacob had wanted more.

He had made his own contacts in Saint Helier. Made his own plans to sell behind Reuben's back. Purchased his own haul and overloaded the ship. In heavy seas, Reuben's cutter had rolled; the ship and its cargo diving to the bottom of the Channel.

Isaac had returned to Talland after four years of merchant service. Instead of the welcome he'd been expecting from his parents, he had found their graves.

His father swallowed by the sea. Mother taken by an illness everyone called grief. His seven-year-old sister waiting to be rescued from the children's home by her mysterious brother who sailed the seas. And Charles Reuben waiting at the door with a ledger in his fist.

Isaac had known nothing of this man who stood on the doorstep in a powdered wig and velvet coat. Knew nothing of the overloaded ship or the cargo destroyed by his father.

But there was a debt to be settled.

"I paid for that vessel out of my own pocket," said Reuben. "Her cargo too, of course. I expect repayment."

Isaac had no money, but he had a sailor's brain, a sailor's body. The right man to captain Reuben's lugger to Saint Peter Port and complete the free trading transactions.

Repayment, Charles Reuben had said when he had arrived at Isaac's door. Repayment for the ship, the cargo, the interest accumulated since Jacob's death.

Isaac shoves the ledger into his pocket. Since Reuben's appearance, he has done nothing but think of ways out of this life bestowed upon him by his father. His efforts have come to nothing. In six days' time, he is to make his first voyage to Guernsey. No longer can he claim that free trading is the domain of more foolish men.

He looks past Reuben to where the two masts of the lugger sway on the silvery water. Feels something turn over in his stomach. "I need to see the vessel."

Hugging the slope above the western beach, the Mariner's Arms languishes in shadow; its bar rotting and disused. The cellar is cluttered with broken furniture, walls hatched by mice's claws.

No liquor flowing at the inn. No stories told. No drunkards or traders or overnight guests. Just the village charmer and her snowy-haired daughter.

Healer, Meg Lucas calls herself, opening the doors of the inn to the sick and needy people of Talland. *Wise woman.*

But her daughter, Flora, has been watching Meg through critical, seventeen-year-old eyes. And she has calculated that most of the ill who stumble into her mother's parlour do not end up healed. They end up dead.

Flora has grown up with the smell of burning herbs and fragrant tea. Grown up among shelves lined with witch bottles and animal hearts in jars. And she has grown up with a parade of cursed and coughing villagers traipsing through her home. Here in Talland they are twenty miles from the nearest physician. Two hundred miles from London where curses belong only in fairy tales. What choice do these people have but to put their faith in potions and prayers?

She tries, her mother. Bless her. But smallpox cannot be healed with enchanted stones. Typhus, immune to herbal tea. The more people that die on Meg's watch, the more Flora feels her own faith fading.

She lets herself into the inn. Walks through the abandoned bar and up the stairs to the living area. She can hear her mother chatting in the parlour with Martha Francis from the village.

Springtime. Meg's business flourishes as wildflowers colour the cliffs. Each day for weeks, Flora has returned home from her job at the charity school to find her mother in the parlour with another of the villagers.

A charm for the spring. Magic words written on parchment. Lengths of hangman's rope crammed in bags to be worn around the neck. A fresh dose of good luck to see them through the year.

Martha leaves, clutching a small pouch to her chest. Flora returns her smile stiffly.

She finds her mother at the table with an array of greenery spread in front of her. The sweet aroma is overpowering.

Meg smiles at Flora as she enters. "How was your day? Those little ones behave themselves for you?"

Flora kisses her mother's cheek. "The children were fine." She sits at the table and gathers up a bundle of flowers. Ties a length of twine around the stems.

"Elderflower," says Meg, hanging a bunch above the hearth to dry. "For…?"

"Coughs and colds."

"Angelica?"

"Protection against the devil's magic." Flora is unenthused.

"Good girl." Meg nods towards the black glass hand mirror sitting on the sideboard. "Take a look. Tell me what you see."

Flora hesitates. The black mirror. Peer into it and the future's secrets will show themselves. Show themselves, of course, to believers only.

"Not now, Mamm. I'm tired."

"Good. Then your mind will still more freely." She picks up the mirror and presses it into her daughter's hand.

Flora glances at the dark surface. Sees her own eyes flickering back at her. She lowers the mirror.

"You're not even trying," says Meg.

Flora puts the mirror back on the table.

"What's gotten into you? You had the knack for this as a girl."

Had she? She remembers staring into the glass and relaying visions of snow storms and ships from foreign lands. But had it been anything more than imagination? A child trying to please her mother? She can't recall any of her visions actually coming true.

"It's foolish," she says. "A glass cannot tell the future. Only time can do such a thing."

Meg's eyes harden. "And when did you get so wise? There's far more mystery in the world than can be understood by a scrap of seventeen." She yanks the twine around the flower stems. "This is who you are, child. This is to be your calling, just as it was my mother's before me."

Flora feels the weight of it swing towards her. She says nothing.

"Where will this poor village be if you choose to abandon the craft? Who will take care of them when I'm gone?"

Flora concentrates on bundling the flowers, avoiding her mother's eyes. "I didn't say I was to abandon it. I just…" She sighs. "If this is to be my life, I suppose I just need more to go on than your word. I need proof that there's more to this than wishful thinking."

Meg doesn't look at her. She finishes bundling the flowers in silence. "Proof," she snorts finally. "You're an arrogant girl, Flora Lucas. Our craft is a sacred thing and it's not for you to doubt it." She hears a faint tremor in her mother's voice. "To question it is to question God."

In the morning, Flora escapes to the market. She walks the cliff path to Polperro, letting the sun thaw her body after the eternal winter. The clifftops are a carpet of purple and yellow, the sea a marbled blue grey. The sound of the waves follows her down the hill and into the market.

Kalash. Kalash.

Has she ever in her life not been able to hear the sea?

She fills her basket. Potatoes. Bread. Mead. There is something comforting about the weight of the food in her arms. Something earthly. Solid.

When she sees Isaac by the baker's stall, her heart springs into her throat. He is taller than she remembers. Shoulders broader. He wears rolled-up shirtsleeves and a faded blue waistcoat. His dark hair is tied back, his queue reaching past his shoulders.

She had heard of his return, of course. In a world where they breathe each other's air, news travels fast. She had thought to visit. But no. She is sure he has far too much on his mind to bother making small talk with a girl from the long-gone past.

She glances at him again. He had been seventeen when he'd left Talland to join the merchant service. Now he has the look of a man who has seen more of the world than this unchanging pocket. Flora feels heat prickle the back of her neck.

Isaac has always had an air about him. An appeal that both draws her to him and makes her nervous to approach. A worry, perhaps, that he'll not be pleased to see her. Or worse, that he'll not remember her.

She sucks in her breath. Begins to walk back towards the cliff path.

"Flora," he calls.

She turns abruptly. Feels suddenly hot and anxious. She pushes her nerves away. She is a woman now. Will not behave like some fluff-brained idiot.

Isaac towers over her. He tilts his head. What does he see? That freckled, white-haired girl of thirteen she'd been when he had left? Can he smell elderflower on her? Angelica for protection against dark magic? The smell of ignorance and superstition.

He hovers for a moment, as though unsure how to approach her. When last he'd been here, they'd greeted each other by tossing stones at the window and hurling playful insults. But when last he'd been here, they'd been children with sandy feet and knotted hair.

Hesitantly, Flora extends her hand. But Isaac lurches forward and pulls her into his arms. Her basket bumps against his side.

"I'm glad to see you," he says, close to her ear. "So glad you're still here." He releases her suddenly, as though feeling disapproving eyes on him. The sandy-footed children have become unmarried adults.

Flora smiles. "I'm still here, ayes. Little changes in this place." She feels a stab of regret the moment she speaks. Plenty has changed for Isaac.

Scarlett races up to them with a basket in her hands. "I got fish and potatoes. What else?"

Isaac hesitates. Looks down in slight bewilderment at the tangle-haired child bouncing in front of him.

How foreign this must be to him; a world of market shopping and meal times.

"Flour," Flora tells Scarlett. "Milk and eggs. Then you'll come for a visit and Mamm will teach you to make starrygazy pie."

Scarlett grins and bounds back into the market.

Isaac gives Flora a small smile. "Thank you."

"Quite a change for you, I'm sure."

He sucks in his breath. "Better way I get used to it."

They watch Scarlett hold out the basket for the milk bottle.

"They all know her," says Isaac. "The stall owners. She tells them a story and they give her the food for cheap. So she says." He chuckles, but the laughter is forced.

Flora can feel a heaviness about him. She wishes she could do more than offer a miserable cooking lesson. "She's a sweet thing," she says, watching Scarlett in animated conversation with the milkman.

Isaac folds his arms. "She has a temper that could scare off a hurricane." He looks at Flora. "Walk back to Talland with us."

Scarlett hands her brother the basket and scrambles onto the cliff path ahead of them. A faint breeze skims through the wildflowers. Clouds billow across the sun.

For a long time, they walk in a silence halfway between uncomfortable and pleasant. Isaac has always been this way. Tight-fisted with words. Flora churns through potential topics of conversation. The Easter sun dance, the latest hunt, Anne Martin's wedding. Each seems trivial for a man whose life has been upturned the way Isaac's has. Her world is small and uninspiring, Flora realises flatly.

"Busy time for your mamm," he says after a while. "She's plenty of visitors this time of year, I'm sure."

"Indeed," says Flora. "The inn is just full of desperate souls."

Isaac laughs.

"She wishes I help, of course. She's grooming me to follow in her path."

"I don't see you following your mother's path," he says bluntly. "You've too much intelligence for that."

Flora smiles.

"Forgive me. That was—"

"It's all right. I'm ashamed to admit I've thought it too."

Isaac chuckles. He looks down. "I'm to sail for Charles Reuben," he says after a moment.

"Trading?"

"Ayes. It seems my father died in a great deal of debt to the man." His voice is cold with resentment.

Flora looks at her feet. "I'm sorry. Truly. I know you never wanted to get caught up in free trade."

She'd heard rumours of Jacob's debt. Hoped for Isaac's sake it was little more than gossip.

"Perhaps you ought to leave," she says. "Take Scarlett and disappear in the night."

"I thought to do it. But Reuben has men with eyes on us. Found us before we'd passed the beach and put a pistol to my head." He digs his hand into the pocket of his breeches. "I see little choice but to do what Reuben wants. He's too powerful. I can't put my sister in danger like that again."

"Perhaps for now you have little choice. But prove yourself trustworthy to Reuben and the chance for escape will come."

Isaac looks ahead to where Scarlett is zag-zagging across the path. "What of her? I can't leave her alone while I sail to Guernsey."

Flora walks close beside him as the path narrows. Impulsively, she takes his arm. Is relived when he doesn't pull away. "Scarlett will come to us," she tells him. "Mamm will teach her about starrygazy pies and charms for desperate souls."

TRADERS

The night is still pink when Isaac and his crew slide out of Polperro harbour. Reuben's lugger is new, fast. If this breeze keeps up, they will make Saint Peter Port before dawn.

He'd planted Scarlett at the door of the Mariner's Arms, sulky and dejected.

"I don't want you to go to sea," she said, hugging her wooden court doll to her chest.

He'd heard it from her before; that plaintive voice, begging him to keep his feet on dry land.

What if the sea spirits take you?

Or the merrymaids or the monsters or the ghosts of drowned sailors?

He understands, of course. The sea has their father. How can Scarlett's young mind help but populate the ocean with unseen horrors?

Stories, he wants to say. *Tall tales.*

Don't be afraid.

This black-eyed scrap is all the family he has now.

He remembers his other siblings with varying degrees of clarity. There were those who had died in the cradle, others who'd lived long enough to have stories told about them. The brother who had stolen the cake from the market, the sister who could sing. But disease had been a constant in their draughty, overcrowded cottage. When Isaac had left Talland, he and Scarlett had been the only children left.

He doesn't want his sister to grow up believing in the horror stories that make this village shake in the night. These people have spent their lives watching waves eat away at the cliffs, watching shadows move the surface of the sea. Ghosts and monsters may be invisible, but they are undeniable. The villagers pray to the sea spirits more often than to God.

Isaac's secluded existence had broken away when his merchant ship had first barrelled out of the Celtic Sea. He had found a world clamouring for knowledge. A world where science overrules superstition.

One day he will make sure Scarlett sees it too.

"There's no such things as merrymaids," he had said, lifting the brass knocker on the door of the inn. Footsteps sounded down the stairs. Isaac found himself hoping Flora would answer the door and not her smoke-scented mother.

"I've seen them," Scarlett said defiantly. Her doll peered up at Isaac; its painted eyebrows chipped and scornful.

"Where?"

"Tasik showed me once when he took me to sea. Said they was as real as the boat beneath our feet."

Polperro disappears into the darkness, the sea swelling as the lugger slides into the Channel.

Isaac and his crew say little beyond the workings of the ship.

He feels the eyes of the men on him. Cautious. Untrusting. He doesn't blame them, of course. These five fishermen had crewed his father's smuggling runs. He is the son of the man who had near sent them to the bottom of the sea.

He thinks to tell them he has none of his father's greed, no dreams of crossing Reuben and lining his pockets with gold. He wants nothing more than to be free of this mess of watchful eyes and moonshine. Wants nothing more than for his life to go back to being his own.

Scarlett charges through the Mariner's Arms like a cat let loose in a chicken coop. She has been inside before, of course, clamped to her mother's hip while the village healer fawned over her sick brothers and sisters. But with the run of the place she is all wide eyes and curious fingers, a torrent of unintelligible chatter.

Flora tries to see the inn as a seven-year-old might. The disused bar with its gaping black hearth and long-hardened candle stumps. Guest rooms strung with drying herbs, fragrant smoke scenting the hallways.

Magic, of course.

Meg follows Scarlett through the inn, answering her barrage of questions.

What's this? A wand of hazel.

And this? Hangman's rope.

Down there? The cellar, of course. Full of rats.

Flora abandons the tour and goes to the parlour to light the fire. The sun has dipped below the horizon and a chill has settled over the sprawling stone building.

When they return to the parlour, Scarlett is clutching the hand mirror. She hovers by the hearth and peers into it curiously. "Why is it black?"

"It's a special mirror," says Meg. "Lets you see far more than your reflection."

Flora shifts uncomfortably. "Mamm," she murmurs.

"What? I'm just teaching the girl the ways of the world."

Ways of this world or another? Flora is not sure Isaac will be pleased if his sister runs home blathering about telling fortunes.

"Mamm, she needs to learn how to cook. Not how to see the future."

Meg huffs. "All right, child. We'll get to the cooking."

"Isaac won't like it."

Her mother gives a short laugh. "Ah. That's what this is about then, is it? A man?"

Flora's ears burn.

Meg lowers her voice. "You can forget that right now. I'll not see you married to Isaac Bailey."

She feels a sudden flash of anger. "He's a good man."

"He's a slave to Charles Reuben. And penniless, I'll warrant. And what about this one?" Meg nods towards Scarlett. "You want a child latched to you before you're eighteen? No. I'll not have it. Your father wouldn't like it and nor do I. A girl like you can do far better." She sits at the table and gestures to Scarlett to join her. "Come, *cheel-vean*. Let's see what the future wants to show us."

The girl clambers onto a chair with the mirror in her hand. Flora folds her arms across her chest, hot and angry. She regrets lighting the fire.

"Look into the glass," Meg tells Scarlett. "Let your eyes relax. Let the pictures show themselves. What do you see?"

Scarlett frowns in concentration. "Fire," she says after a moment.

"What fire?"

"Here."

Flora sighs and takes the glass from Scarlett's hand. Nods to the logs flickering in the grate. "She's seeing the reflection of the flames, Mamm. This isn't good for her." She ushers Scarlett from the chair. "Come on. I'll show you how to make that pie."

Charles Reuben emerges from his palatial house on the hill above Polperro. Buttons his coat to his neck. Even on the edge of summer, the wind has a chill. He trudges down the winding path, remembering why he sends other men into the night to do his work for him.

The village is quiet, save for the pocket of noise spilling from the Three Pilchards. A metallic clatter as the wind skims through the forest of masts in the harbour.

Light glows inside the customs house. Reuben eyes it warily.

Before he had taken over, the Polperro free trade had been a shamble. Small-scale, disorganised. Capital pooled by liquored-up villagers and goods sold for meagre profits.

Reuben had seen opportunity. Knew himself the right man to turn this farce into an endless stream of profit. He has always had a brain for business. First, an accountant, then a distributor. Investor in the aptly named Good Fortune mine.

He likes the solidity of numbers. Mathematics can be relied upon when the world bends with the weight of superstition and story. His business brain had seen him through when he had buried his wife and child. There's a thrill in seeing the numbers climb, the profits grow.

A business-brained man sees the problem: a nation reliant on taxing overseas trade. He sees demand in the public houses, in mines filled with thirsty workers. And a business-brained man creates a solution.

In Jacob Bailey, Reuben had believed he'd found the right man to lead his ring. A good sailor. Hardworking, well-liked. He'd not counted on the greedy streak that hid beneath the surface.

He hopes he has acted wisely, entrusting the ring to Jacob's son. Isaac has a seriousness about him his father had not had. An anger bubbling below the surface. Reuben can't blame him, of course. He appreciates the hell he's tossed Isaac Bailey into. Still, it is a fair thing to expect the boy to pay his father's debts. A fair thing, if without compassion. A business-brained man has no room for compassion.

Reuben trudges out of the village towards the house of Elias Smith, the man with a desperate need for a hand-carved tobacco rasp.

The street lamps disappear behind a curve in the road and Reuben relies on his lantern to navigate the inky hill behind the town. He's promised Smith the rasp the moment the men land. Top price for a quick delivery.

Smith's house is crooked and dark. A board covers one window and the door hangs ajar; warped and groaning. The wrong house, perhaps? This hardly seems the dwellings of a man who can afford handcrafted ivory. He's followed the directions Smith had given him when they'd met in the Ship Inn. Half way up the hill, the house with the crooked chimney, last in the line of three.

Reuben knocks. He wants payment before that precious rasp gets close to this hovel.

Smith opens the door. He is wearing a long, discoloured nightshirt and stockings, his hair a voluminous white cloud. Reuben purses his lips and tries not to show his distaste. The man had seemed an oddity in the inn, decked out in a patched purple frock coat. But at least he had been clothed.

Smith leans on the creaking door. "You have the rasp?"

"I need payment first. You'll have it once the men land."

Smith hesitates. "I'll pay half now. The other half on delivery. A fair deal, I'm sure you'll find." He leans forward. Reuben smells tobacco and rosewater. Underneath, the odour of unwashed skin. "You are fond of a fair deal, are you not, Mr Reuben? I've heard that about you."

"Very well. Half now. But I wish to see the rest of the money."

Smith chuckles to himself. He vanishes inside and reappears with a pouch jangling with coins. Pulls out a handful of banknotes and counts Reuben's sum. He slides the rest back into the pouch. "I trust that will suppress your doubts. You'll have the rasp for me the minute the men land."

Reuben pockets the money. "Why such urgency?"

"Because I don't trust it in the hands of your men."

Reuben sighs. "My ship is due tomorrow evening. One of the men will bring it as soon as possible."

Smith manages a faint smile. "I'll look forward to it."

Reuben is not alone on his walk back to the village. Riding officers surround him; a thunder of hooves, a parade of blue and gold. "Good evening, Mr Reuben."

He glances up at them. Keeps walking. "Gentlemen."

The horses pace beside him.

"What's your business this evening?"

Reuben smiles wryly to himself. "Is this how the preventative service is operating these days? Accosting innocent men out visiting friends?" His digs his hands into his pockets. "Your ineptitude never ceases to amaze me."

He is edgy as he makes his way back to the house. As his syndicate expands, word spreads. For better or worse, he is building a name for himself. The riding officers will be on alert, having seen him walking the hills at night. Foolish to have visited Smith himself. He sees that now. But even after four years in this game, he still struggles to trust his own men.

Will the riding officers be prowling these hills tomorrow night? There's a good chance of it.

He eyes the customs station. He needs a man on the inside. It is no secret that corruption runs rife in the preventative service. Surely he can find a man willing to share information in exchange for a piece of his wealth.

But such a thing will take patience. Testing and grooming to find the right man. Open his mouth too early and he risks exposing the whole ring.

He lets himself into the house and paces across the parlour in his coat and boots. With the revenue men on alert, making the run to smith's house is a gamble. He needs a solution before tomorrow night's landing.

Flora and Scarlett return from the charity school to find a young woman in the parlour of the Mariner's Arms.

"Ah, Flora," says Meg. "I'm glad you're back. I've to go to Polruan. This woman's poor mother is asking for me."

"Says she's been ill-wished by her neighbour," the woman says. "She's in a right state."

Meg takes three jars from above the hearth and places them carefully into a basket.

"You'll not make it back by dark," says Flora. "It's a dangerous road at night."

The young woman flashes her a smile. "Your mamm is welcome to stay with us tonight, Miss Lucas. My mother will be glad of it. I'll see her home in the morning."

Meg laces her cloak and turns to Flora. "You and the girl will be all right here?"

"Of course." Flora kisses her cheek. "Go."

It is late afternoon when the men come to the door. The thud of the brass knocker echoes through the house. Flora puts down her fork and stands up from the table. She peers out the parlour window.

"Who's there?" Scarlett asks, a chunk of potato half way to her mouth.

Flora has seen these men before. One is Reuben's footman, the other, the traders' banker. She steps hurriedly away from the window. Crawls towards the hearth, careful to stay hidden. "Let's finish our supper on the floor. Like a picnic."

Scarlett drops to the floor obediently. But her raised eyebrows tell Flora she is not about to believe the rubbish about the picnic. "Who's at the door?"

"Just men I don't wish to speak to."

"They sound angry."

"Ayes, well. We'll ignore them and they'll go away."

They knock again. Louder. "Open the door or we'll break it down."

Scarlett looks at Flora with frightened eyes. Another knock. And a louder, angrier thump. Are they kicking the door? Flora grabs Scarlett's hand and hurries into the hall. She pushes open the door of one of the empty guest rooms. "Hide."

Scarlett wriggles under the bed and peers out at Flora. "Don't let them in," she hisses. "Please."

Flora pulls the door closed and edges onto the stairs. Another kick at the door. It rattles loudly against its frame. The men will force their way inside. Surely they will be calmer if she lets them in herself.

She opens the door, heart pounding. "Pardon me," she says stiffly. "I was washing."

"Charles Reuben wants the Bailey girl," says the banker.

"She's not here."

"Don't lie to me. We saw her come back from Polperro with you."

"You're mistaken. I'm sorry." Flora can hear the tremor in her voice. "Please leave."

A fist comes towards her. And then darkness.

SIGNAL FIRE

Charles Reuben waits in the parlour. He paces, watching out the window as night falls over the village. Footsteps sound down the hall. Two of his men lead the girl into the room. She has food down the front of her coverall, her dark hair a tangled mess. She glares at him with hard, dry eyes.

He almost laughs. He had been gifted that look many times by Jacob. There is something vaguely humorous about seeing the same glare from his seven-year-old daughter.

"Scarlett," he says.

She narrows her eyes.

Reuben sits and gestures to the armchair beside him. "Sit down, please."

She climbs into the chair.

"I have cake. Would you like some?"

She shakes her head stiffly. Something behind her eyes makes Reuben shift uncomfortably. Then he gives a short chuckle. He likes this girl.

He nods to his housekeeper. Cake and sweet tea. She will bend.

"We have a very important job for you, Scarlett. Can you help us?"

She doesn't answer.

"It will be a big help to Isaac. I know you'd like to help your brother."

She nods.

"Good. He'll be grateful." Reuben leans towards her. "You're good at climbing the hills, I'm sure. Even without the path."

She eyes him. "I can climb the hills."

"I thought so. And I imagine you're good at hiding. I'm sure you could climb those hills without anyone seeing you."

She nods.

Reuben flashes her a smile. A risk to put the fragile rasp in the girl's hand? Perhaps. But she will be faster, quieter than any of his men. Send her up the side of the hill and the riding officers will have no way of following her. A risk worth taking.

"Give me your cloak," he says.

Scarlett hesitates.

"It's all right. Margaret's going to stitch a pocket on the inside for you." He smiles at her conspiratorially. "You see, I've a package for a man who lives on the hill. I need you to take it to him. You'll hide it in your pocket." He looks up as the maid approaches with a tray of cake and tea. "Here, look. Something to eat and drink. Eat now and we will talk some more once you're finished."

Scarlett glances at the cake, then back to Reuben. "Where's Flora?"

Reuben tries on his warmest smile. "She's at home at the inn. She'll be waiting for you when you're done."

Flora opens her eyes. Her head is pounding. She sits, nausea turning her stomach. The tavern is lightless. She hears mice scuttle beneath the bar. She touches a swelling on the side of her head.

She scrambles to her feet, gripping the bar to keep her balance. Dizziness washes over her. "Scarlett?" She stumbles up the stairs. "Scarlett? Are you here?"

The building creaks in response.

Flora lights a lamp and rushes through the inn, searching the guest rooms, the cellar, the kitchen.

Nothing but shadows.

She sits. Tries to steady her thoughts.

Reuben's men have Scarlett. Why? Does he plan to use her for the landing?

She needs to go to the authorities. Send dragoons to Reuben's house to set Scarlett free. But tonight, the lugger will slide into Polperro with a haul of contraband. Expose Charles Reuben and she will expose Isaac as well.

She snatches her cloak and hurries from the inn.

She slows as she walks the cliff path; her legs tentative beneath her. The lamps of Reuben's house glow on the hill.

When she reaches Polperro, she stops, hunching as a fresh wave of dizziness swings over her.

"Do you need help, mistress?"

She whirls around. A customs officer stands before her, his young face creased in concern.

Flora straightens. Forces a smile. "No. Thank you. I'm well."

"You don't look well."

"I fell, that's all. I'm on my way home now. To rest."

He eyes her. Does he recognise her? Flora, the witch's daughter?

"Perhaps I could see you home."

"That's not necessary." Her voice is clipped. "But thank you."

She hurries towards the house on the hill. Reuben's mansion is a great brick monstrosity, festooned with chimneys and mock turrets. She has passed it countless times. Has always been vaguely curious as to what lies inside. But as she charges up the winding front path, her curiosity is replaced with a burning anger.

She knocks loudly. A young woman in a cloth cap and white apron lets her inside.

"Miss Lucas?" Reuben appears at the top of the stairs. He wears shirtsleeves and an embroidered waistcoat, his balding head without its customary white wig. He makes his way downstairs.

Flora pushes past the maid. "Where's Scarlett?"

Reuben frowns at the pink swelling on the side of her face. "Did my men do this?"

"You sound surprised."

Something passes across Reuben's eyes. Regret? "I'm deeply sorry. That was not my intention. Rest assured they will be punished."

She glares at him. "What have you done with Scarlett?"

"You need not worry yourself. The girl is safe. We need her for tonight's delivery is all. You must come and sit down. Rest. I insist. I'll have Margaret bring you some tea."

"I don't want tea," she snaps. "I want to take Scarlett home. You've already got Isaac under your command. You don't need his sister too."

"She's a necessary part of the operation," says Reuben. "But I'll see no harm comes to her."

"Is she here?"

"No."

"Take me to her."

"That's not a good idea. You've been hurt."

Flora glares at him. "Isaac Bailey put me in charge of his sister and I don't intend on letting him down. Take me to Scarlett, or I'll have no choice but to run around looking for her in the midst of a landing."

Reuben sighs. Nods faintly. "My carriage is outside."

The coach rolls down the hill towards the harbour. Lamplight glows on the clifftop beside the huers' watch houses.

"Up there," Reuben tells Flora.

She leaps from the carriage and hurries up the narrow path, Reuben trudging behind her. Men from the landing party are gathered on the cliff, watching the sea for any sign of Isaac's lugger. Watching the village for any sign of the revenue men. Scarlett hovers behind them, entwining her hands in the hem of her cloak.

Flora kneels beside her. "Scarlett? Have these men hurt you?"

She shakes her head. "I'm going to help Isaac."

Flora forces a smile. "He'll be glad of it, I'm sure." She grips the girl's shoulders. "Tell me what they've asked you to do."

A late-night delivery. Lightless and soundless. A child to slip beneath the eyes of the riding officers.

Flora turns to Reuben. "Let me go in her place."

Reuben smiles. "It's hardly an appropriate thing for a young woman to be doing now, is it." He turns to look out over the water. "I want Scarlett, Miss Lucas. She's smaller and faster. Far less likely to draw attention to herself. You want to be of use, you can be an extra pair of eyes against the riding officers."

"The last thing I want is to be of use to you," Flora hisses.

Reuben doesn't look at her. "Free trade is a noble business. A girl from these parts ought to know that. It's been a part of this life long before you or I were born and it will continue long after we die. I suggest you do not attempt to fight it."

"I've no thought of fighting free trade. I just want to see Scarlett home safely." Flora glances around her. The landing party line the cliff like soldiers in battle. Isaac is right. Reuben's men have eyes everywhere. She is sure he had only agreed to bring her here so she could see how futile it is to fight. She pulls her cloak around her tightly and glares. "What kind of man sends a child to do his bidding?"

As the lights of Polperro push through the darkness, a hush falls over the lugger.

Isaac remembers his father speaking of the thrill and tension of the approach to the coast.

Is there a thrill to this? Perhaps a small one, behind the shame. He ought to focus on it. If this is to be his life, he'd best find the part that makes him glad to be living it.

He has always known what his father was. Always known him to be knee-deep in free trade. Isaac had never thought much of it. In these parts, every second man has boots soaked in moonshine. Dishonest? Perhaps. But the people look to smuggling as a virtuous business. The trade that defies the government and brings power to the poorest of men.

Regardless, Isaac had wanted more from his life. His travels have shown him a world of sun and spices, new ideas and languages. A world he is not even close to finished exploring.

But his reality has become bleak and black and damp. He feels a surge of fresh resentment for his greedy, drowned father.

He has spent the day walking in Jacob's footsteps. Shouldering through crowds along the cobbles of Saint Peter Port. Handing Reuben's money to his agent, triple-checking the ledger. Supervising the chain of whisky ankers being loaded onto his lugger. The ivory rasp for Elias Smith he had kept in his own pocket, to whispers and glares from his crew.

Ought we trust him with that?

Wouldn't trust his father.

Isaac had met their critical eyes. "I'm not my father. It's time you understood that."

Half way back to Polperro, he had brought a brandy bottle from the saloon and poured a shot for each of the men. "I don't like this any more than you do," he told them. "But it's the way things are. Better way we learn to deal with it."

A bank of cloud blows in, obscuring the moon. The spotsman stands at the bow of the ship, guiding them through the dark water. In the faint light, Isaac can make out the curve in the rock face that will shield them from the customs station. He will hide the lugger in that blind circle of sea. The landing party will bring their boats. Unload the whisky from his hold and bury it deep within the cliffs.

Isaac turns to his first mate. "Signal the lander."

The first mate raises a pistol loaded only with powder. The snap of the trigger sends a flash of blue light into the sky.

Isaac watches the cliffs for the wink of the signalling lanterns. Instead, a sudden burst of flame shoots into the sky. He feels his shoulders tighten.

Try as he has to keep his distance from free trade, the language of the watchmen is ingrained in him.

Lantern light: a clear coast. Beacon of fire: revenue men.

Douse the beacon and the clifftop is plunged into darkness. The men are still, silent. Flora holds Scarlett by the wrist.

The dark is inky, fragrant with smoke and sea. The landing party surrounds them; an invisible barricade of murmurs and breath. Flora squints into the night, trying to make out the path. Even if she and Scarlett manage to escape the men, where can she go? Return to the inn and Reuben will know exactly where to find them. She can't go to the authorities. And everyone in the village knows better than to cross Charles Reuben. They could hide in the cellar, perhaps, until Isaac and the other men return from sea. But then they will face Reuben's wrath. And what if her mother were to return from Polruan to find the traders' banker at their door again?

The sky opens. The rain is cold against Flora's cheeks.

Her stomach turns over with the hopelessness of it. This is Isaac's world, she realises sickly. What choice does he have but to fall into line with Reuben's plans? What choice do any of them have?

Isaac watches the flame on the cliff disappear. His heart quickens. He feels the eyes of the men on him, awaiting instruction.

"Slip the tubs," he orders, hoping his voice doesn't betray his uncertainty.

String up the barrels with sinking stones and send the cargo into shallow water. Slide into the harbour as a mere passenger vessel. Return the next night with grappling hooks and haul the whisky from the sea.

The plan makes him edgy, though he knows his father had done the same many times. He's drunk more than one glass of rum tainted with shrub cordial to mask the taste of seeping seawater.

The crew doesn't argue. They tie up the ankers of liquor wordlessly. Slide them into the sea.

Isaac's thoughts are racing by the time they return to the harbour. He slips the tobacco rasp into his first mate's hand as the customs officials board the lugger. Once the passenger manifest has been confirmed, the first mate slides from the ship to deliver the rasp into Reuben's hands.

The run has been clumsy, fraught with danger. They've come far too close to capture. There has to be a better way. Riding officers are a regular fixture on this coast. They can't rely on burning furze to deceive them.

If this is to be his life, he will do things wisely. Slipping the cargo is time consuming, hazardous. They risk losing the liquor, losing money.

The lugger can be altered. A false bottom. Hidden bulkheads. Means to glide contraband past customs' eyes.

He doesn't trust the caves as a hiding place either. He'd spent his childhood exploring them. Stumbled upon water-damaged ankers more than once. The caves are too shallow, too susceptible to the tides. For this ring to prosper—for him to have any chance of earning enough to prise himself free of Reuben—they will need proper methods of storage. He will not run these voyages in the haphazard way his father had. Jacob had been greedy. Lacked intelligence. Little wonder things had played out the way they had.

SILENT AS SLEEP

Reuben takes Scarlett by the wrist and leads her down the cliff towards the harbour. A ship has returned. Her brother's? She squints in the pale lamplight. Sees men moving about on the deck. She can't make out their faces.

Reuben returns and hands Scarlett the tobacco grinder. "Put it in your pocket. Quickly now. Take it straight to Mr Smith. The house with the crooked chimney."

Yes, yes. She looks at him witheringly. He has repeated his instructions at least five times. Does he think her brainless as a fly?

The rasp heavy in the pocket stitched into her cloak, she darts through the village and out to the hills.

No light around but the faint smoulder of the moon. Lamps winking in the houses on Talland Hill.

She has never been afraid of the dark. Has always liked the peace of it, the silence, the secrets. Its ability to make this wild world disappear.

Rain runs down the back of her neck. She can feel the earth turning to mud beneath her boots. Through the trees. Through the tangled undergrowth. Fast. Quiet. Isaac will be impressed. Reuben will be impressed.

She crawls over the edge of the embankment and onto the path, her cloak waterlogged and heavy. She pulls the rasp from her sodden pocket and holds it against her chest.

She stares down the path. It is narrow and muddy, cottages spread sparsely along it.

The last house in the row of three. She turns right. Walks slowly, uncertainly, squinting through the sheets of rain.

A voice in the darkness makes her start. "You there."

She turns, heart thudding. A man is watching from his doorway, a lamp in hand. Rain mists around the light.

"Come inside, maid."

Scarlett shakes her head.

"It's raining. Come on now. Dry yourself by the fire."

Inside the house, she can see the orange glow of the flames. She shivers. Ahead of her, the path is wet and lightless.

She slips through the door. The house is thick with shadow, lit only by the blaze in the grate. A crooked table sits in one corner, sleeping pallet by the hearth. She smells piss and fire.

The man is tall, hair hanging loose to his shoulders. His beard is grey, cut close to his chin, the way her father's had been the last time she had seen him.

He looks at the tobacco grinder pressed to her chest. "What you got there?"

"I'm not supposed to say."

"You're Jacob's girl, ayes? I was wondering how long it would be before Reuben got to you."

Rain pelts the windows. Scarlett shivers, her fingers numb. She slides the rasp back into her pocket and edges towards the fire.

The man nods. "That's it, maid. Warm yourself." He sits at the table. "Who's your package for? That cuckoo Elias Smith?"

She hesitates.

"You're not supposed to say."

A nod.

"What's Reuben want with you, then? An innocent face to slide under the riding officers' noses?"

"I'm good at climbing the hills," says Scarlett.

He chuckles. "I'm sure you are." He goes to the shelf in the corner of the room and returns brandishing a pocket knife. Scarlett's heart speeds.

Run.

Her legs feel suddenly heavy.

The man kneels in front of her, eyes level with hers. He holds out the knife. "Have you ever used one of these?"

She shakes her head. Can't pull her eyes from the flames reflecting on the blade.

He presses it into her hand. "Take it."

She wraps her hand around it hesitantly.

"I knew Jacob, you see. I know your *tasik* would not want his girl running goods without protection." He folds his leathery hand over hers. Guides the blade towards his stomach. "Here. A man comes at you, you strike him here. Then you drive it upwards. Under the ribs." He jerks her hand in a swift, upwards motion. Scarlett feels a sudden rush of energy. She imagines digging her knife into the men who had carried her from the Mariner's Arms.

Fast. Upwards. Under the ribs.

"Show me," says the man.

Scarlett grips the knife. She holds the blade against his stomach. Copies his movement. Swift, angry.

"Good. Put it by your stockings, ayes. Carry it with you always."

She slides it into her garter. The feel of it against her thigh makes her stomach swirl.

She feels old, strong. Can't wait to show Isaac.

She grins.

The man returns her smile. "Go on then. The rain is stopping. Elias Smith is two houses along the road."

Scarlett knocks on Smith's crooked door. Drizzle patters in the puddles dinted across the path.

She thinks of the knife at her knee. Feels a tingle of excitement.

The man who answers the door is white-haired and hunched. Surprise in his eyes.

She is not afraid. Can he tell? She likes the feeling of power the knife gives her.

The man looks down at her. "Who are you?"

She looks him in the eye. "Scarlett Bailey."

"Did Reuben send you?"

"Ayes."

"You got something for me then?"

She reaches into her cloak and produces the rasp. The man takes it. Mutters to himself.

"Stay here." He disappears into the house and returns with a pouch heavy with coin. "Put this in your cloak. Take it straight to Reuben, you understand? Lose it and I'll be after you."

Scarlett takes the pouch and slides it into her pocket.

"Go on now. Get out of here." Smith closes the door, leaving a thin thread of light peeking beneath it.

Scarlett turns to look out over the black expanse of the hills. With the lights behind her, her bearings are tangled. Which way back to Polperro? The path will take her to the village, but Reuben has forbidden her from using it in case the riding officers return.

She shivers. She's had enough of being useful now. She wants to find Flora. Wants to go back to the inn and eat lamb and potatoes.

She stands in the middle of the path with her hand in her pocket, clutching Smith's money. Watches the dark until she hears horses approach. Riding officers' lanterns appear over the curve of the hill. The man who had given her the knife bursts from his cottage. He wraps an arm around her chest and hauls her inside. A beam of light glides over their faces before he can slam the door. The thunder of hooves grows louder. And stops.

A thump at the door.

The man hisses at Scarlett: "Hide."

She crawls beneath the table, finding the shadows. Curls into a ball and peeks out over her knees.

She sees the men's feet: the ragged cloth shoes of the man who had given her the knife. Two pairs of black riding boots with buckles at the calves.

"Where's the girl?" one of the officers asks.

"There's no girl. I live alone."

"Don't lie. We saw her. What's she doing out here? Running goods?"

Scarlett bites her lip, tries to stop her noisy breath from giving her away.

"You've no proof of anything. Get the hell out of my house."

"Search the place," says one of the officers.

The man grabs the fire poker. "I told you to get out of my house."

Scarlett sees the cloth shoes and the boots move towards the door.

The man says it again, angrier. *Get out of my house.*

"Put down your weapon," an officer tells him. "Or we'll shoot."

The man snorts. "Shoot me? For what? You got no right to search me. Corrupt bastards."

The voices grow more distant. Scarlett catches fragments of their conversation.

Trading run.

Thieves.

Liar.

And she hears the pistol shot. Feels the muscles around her spine tighten. Her throat clamps and she buries her face against her knee to stop her cry of shock.

Mumbled words from the officers. Horses, galloping, fading.

The fire pops loudly.

When the silence thickens, Scarlett crawls out from beneath the table. The door hangs open, letting a stream of cold air inside. She shivers in her wet clothes. Edges out into the street.

The rain has eased to a faint drizzle. The moon peeks out from behind a bank of cloud. In its white light, Scarlett sees the face of the man who had given her the knife. His eyes are open, glassy. His head is turned to the side, as though trying to catch one last glimpse inside his home. A dark stain creeps across his chest and runs into the mud on the path. The fire poker lies by his side.

Scarlett feels suddenly, violently angry. Angry at those black riding boots, those thundering, escaping hooves.

She hears herself breathe loud and fast, feels rage rising from her stomach, into her throat. She wants to scream, wants to cry, wants to take the knife from her garter and show the riding officers *fast, upwards, under the ribs.*

She hears a throaty cry escape her. Covers her mouth hurriedly.

Don't make a sound.

She feels the anger push around inside her. It escapes as a scream. A hand is clamped suddenly over her mouth and her anger gives way to fear.

"It's all right, Scarlett." Isaac is breathless. "Calm down now. Not a sound."

He releases her and she whirls around to face him.

Why is he here? Did Reuben send him after her? Do the men not think her capable of doing as she is asked?

"I did my job," she hisses, her insides hot. "I did it just as he asked. He didn't need to send you."

"Don't be foolish," Isaac whispers. "Reuben doesn't know I'm here. Flora found me. Told me you were up here." He gulps down his breath. "Are you all right?"

She nods. Realises she is glad to see him. She grabs a fistful of his damp greatcoat and presses her shoulder against his side. He holds his big hand to the top of her head. The anger inside her begins to fade. "Where's Flora?" she asks.

"I told her to go back to the inn." Isaac looks down at the body. "Did you see who did this?"

"The men," she says. "With the horses."

"The riding officers?"

"Ayes."

"What did he do?"

She shrugs. Nudges the fire poker with her toe. "Why did they just leave him?"

"Because they're corrupt bastards, Scarlett. Probably killed the poor fellow with no good reason." He catches her staring into the man's glassy eyes. Leans down and closes them. "Did you deliver the rasp?" he asks.

She nods. Takes the money from her cloak.

"Give it to me."

She hands it to him. He looks down at it, says nothing. Finally, he tucks it into the pocket of his coat.

Where is *thank you*? Where is *well done*? They'd all said he'd be glad of her help. Reuben had promised. Flora had promised.

She wants to tell him of the way she had climbed the hill in the dark. Wants to tell him of how she had found the man's house, had hidden from the soldiers. Wants to lift her coverall and show him the blade at her knee. Show him *fast, upwards, under the ribs.*

But something in his eyes stops her.

She nods to the man on the road. His blood is running towards her boots. "He's dead," she says.

"Ayes. He is."

She hears more voices, more hooves. The wet clatter of wagon wheels in the mud. Isaac grabs her hand and pulls her from the path. They lie on their fronts on the side of the hill, blanketed by tangled, dripping vines. Scarlett feels water soak through her stockings. Feels the cold blade of the knife.

On the path in front of them, the wagon stops. A man leaps from the box seat to inspect the body.

Beside her, Isaac is silent, motionless. Scarlett digs her fingers into the earth to steady herself. Lies just as quiet. Just as still.

Once, before her parents had died, the riding officers had come to the door. Her father had hidden a bag of tobacco beneath her sleeping pallet and laid her on top of it.

Quiet now. Not a sound. As silent as sleep.

"He's dead," the coachman calls to his passenger. "Looks as though he's been shot. We ought to go back to the village and report it."

His lantern passes over Scarlett's face as he turns. She doesn't move. Silent as sleep.

The wagon disappears. Isaac climbs to his feet. Grabs her hand and leads her back down the hill towards Polperro.

With each step, she feels the knife move against her knee. Thinks of the rush of energy when she'd held that blade in her hand. Thinks of the officers with black buckled boots and the lifeless eyes of the man in the road.

Fast, she thinks. *Upwards. Under the ribs and dead.*

Suddenly the idea terrifies her. She squeezes Isaac's hand and pushes the thought away.

The banker is waiting by the harbour. He looks at Scarlett. Ignores Isaac. "Do you have the money?"

"Where's Reuben?" Isaac demands.

"Home," says the banker. "I need that money from Smith. Does your sister have it or not?"

Isaac pushes past him. "We'll take it to Reuben ourselves."

He strides towards the mansion on the hill, Scarlett running to keep up with him. "I want to speak to Reuben," he says when the maid answers the door. She nods, disappears inside.

Scarlett looks up at Isaac with her saucer eyes. Her clothes are wet and muddy.

He feels something lurch inside him. He wants to hold her tight and promise her that next time he will do a better job. Next time she won't be cold or afraid or angry enough for that temper in her to tear itself free. But he can't promise this, of course. Can't promise a thing. Not safety, or security, or a life without free trade.

"Wait here," he tells her, emotion thickening his voice. He charges into the entrance hall.

Reuben meets him at the bottom of the stairs, his banyan robe unbuttoned and his head bare. Isaac shoves hard against his chest, pins him to the wall.

Reuben exhales sharply. "Don't be foolish, Mr Bailey. What do you think my men would do if you tried anything?"

"Use me," Isaac hisses. "But not my sister. Put her in danger like that again and I'll kill you. Do you hear me?"

Reuben smiles thinly. "You're in no position to bargain. Your father made sure of that." He shoves him away. "Where's the money from Elias Smith?"

Reluctantly, Isaac pulls the pouch from his pocket and hands it to Reuben. "I want payment."

Reuben reaches into the pouch. Rifles through the banknotes and gold before pressing a little into Isaac's hand.

He looks down at the silver. "Five shillings? What kind of dog are you?"

Reuben slides the pouch into his pocket. "I promised wages enough to keep you and Scarlett clothed and fed. Nothing more. The rest of your payment will go towards recovering the costs of the ship and cargo lost by your father." He buttons his robe. "We agreed to this, Mr Bailey. I don't know why you're suddenly so antagonistic."

Isaac's stomach turns over. He feels trapped. Useless.

Flora is right. His only hope of getting out of this is to build Reuben's trust. Slowly, surely. Convince himself that one day the chance for freedom will come.

LET HIM COME TO TRUST

Mallow leaves for bruising. Mix with a spoon of lard.

Flora tears at the green fronds, simmering with frustration, anger at her own failure. The first hint of sun peeks through the parlour windows. It illuminates streams of dust and abandoned plates of potatoes.

Flora puts down the mallow leaves. Carries the plates into the kitchen and empties them into the trough with violent, angry scrapes. She walks wearily down the passage to her bedroom, eyes stinging with sleeplessness. A day at the charity school ahead of her. In spite of her exhaustion, she is glad to be going. Grateful for the chance to fill children's heads with words and numbers instead of magic charms and smuggling plots. Grateful for the chance to be of use.

Her movements are sluggish. Fresh clothes, she thinks. Wash face. Comb hair.

She leans over the wash stand and splashes her cheeks, letting the chill of the water awaken her slightly. She pins her blonde hair neatly at the base of her neck. Peers into the mirror at the purple bruising on the side of her face.

Seventeen years in Talland and she had never before seen free trade up so close. Had she been lucky? Or just blind?

A warren of empty rooms in the tavern around her. A lightless cellar. A path to the sea. Had her father ever opened these doors to the smugglers? Had the cellar once been loaded with brandy and wine? What plans had been made over these counters when the inn's doors were open? Believing the Mariner's Arms was a law-abiding place suddenly seems the greatest of naiveties.

Flora ties her bonnet. She is early, but she needs to check on Scarlett. Needs to face Isaac. And, she realises, she needs to escape the Mariner's Arms with its herb-scented smugglers' hideouts. Needs to escape the mallow leaves and the drying flowers and the life as the village charmer her mother has laid at her feet.

Isaac lights the fire. He pulls Scarlett's wet cloak from her shoulders and drapes it across the table.

"I have school," she says.

"You're not going to school today. Go to bed."

She nods. Disappears into her bedroom.

Isaac pulls a bottle of brandy from the shelf and pours a glass. He slides a chair to the fire and swallows in one mouthful. Watches the flames dance before his heavy eyes.

Movement outside the window. He turns, sees Flora approaching the cottage. The sight of her brings a strange twist to his stomach, as it had the day at the market.

He opens the door before she knocks. "Forgive me," he says. "I ought to have come to check on you. Made sure you got home safely."

"Don't be foolish. You had far more important things to worry about. Scarlett. Is she safe?"

"Ayes. She's safe. For now."

Flora clasps her hands. "I'm so sorry, Isaac. You trusted her with me."

Her ushers her inside. "Those men are bastards. There's nothing you could have done." He frowns. Pushes back her bonnet. The side of her face is dark with bruising. "Hell. Did Reuben's men do this? I'm the one who ought to be sorry. Dragging you into this mess." He touches her cheek gently, thoughtlessly. Hurriedly pulls away.

"I ought to go," she says. "I'm sure you could use a little peace."

Isaac catches her wrist. "Stay. Please. We'll have tea."

She smiles faintly. "I've to be at the charity school in an hour."

He drops her wrist. "Of course." For the best, no doubt. Look at this sagging, windswept cottage. This life of servitude, of instant, clumsy fatherhood. What right does he have inviting a woman in for tea?

Flora straightens her bonnet. "Perhaps I'll see you at the market again. I'll be about."

He feels a smile in the corner of his mouth. He will be about too, of course. Modifying the lugger, finding secure, reliable storage for the contraband. Taking men across the Channel.

Beneath the resentment he feels something strangely, darkly close to excitement. Let Reuben see his brains, his ingenuity. Let Reuben foolishly come to trust.

Isaac watches Flora as she leaves the cottage and walks towards the cliff path. She is there beside him, he realises, when he pictures he and Scarlett breaking free of this life. She is there with her snowy, windswept hair, clutching his hand in the boat as they sail free of Reuben, of the smuggling ring, of the battered, smoke-stained inn. He feels an unexpected thrill at the challenge.

He goes out to the street. It is quiet in the early morning. He hears the sigh of the sea, a distant animal moan.

He takes in the village with fresh eyes.

The Miller family's barn. The cellar of the Mariner's Arms. The empty hut behind the manor house. All places he could load with brandy, wine, Rotterdam gin.

He peers through the trees to the spire of the church.

Even better.

Customs will never dare raid a house of the Lord.

Isaac feels a faint smile in the corner of his mouth. He will be patient. He will build that trust. And when he finally breaks free, he will send Reuben's world toppling.

BOOK ONE

BRIDLES LANE

DEAD WRECK

Cornwall, England.
1740

There gunshots.

Ship in the bay.

A woman crouches in the churchyard. She grips a lantern and peers over the cliff at the sea thrashing the headland. Behind her, a little to the right, her family lies; their coffins crumbling and their bones becoming earth.

But there is a living brother, in a whisky-laden lugger, past where her eyes can reach. Scarlett Bailey has tossed a bunch of heather down to the sea spirits.

Bring him safely home.

She has been waiting here since dusk; signalling lantern in hand. A bundle of furze sits at her side, ready to be set ablaze if riding officers appear.

A flash of the lamp for an empty beach. Fire for prying eyes and revenue men.

Instead of Isaac's ship, this beast of a brig had come seesawing around the point, mainsail thudding. It would strike the cliffs for certain. Be wrecked upon their beach.

One, two, three shots of the banker's pistol and the villagers had poured onto the sand. Men and women, barefooted children, arms laden with rope and axes.

Wake up! Ship in the bay.

Scarlett tucks the lantern behind a headstone. There'll be no need for it tonight. The crowd will pillage the wreck; tear it clean. Isaac and his crew won't land their goods with such an audience.

The path from the churchyard down to the beach is steep and slick. Scarlett grabs her skirts in her fist and runs it with the certain legs of a native.

The ship plunges. Its yardarms strike the headland, hull into rock. Mast lamps dance wildly; one plunging into the sea.

No shouts. No cries for help. No-one struggling for escape. The strange stillness makes Scarlett's breathing quicken.

Men launch themselves into the sea. A whaleboat pulls towards the brig's starboard side. Men working for Charles Reuben, Scarlett is sure. Following orders while Reuben stands on the cliff and counts his fortune.

The ship writhes against the land like a wounded beast. Scarlett tucks her skirts up and clambers over the rocks at the edge of the beach. She will board the ship from her port side and get her hands to a little of the cargo.

Look what I found, she will tell Isaac. *Are you proud of me?*

The cold sea steals her breath. She lurches towards the ship's ladder, a sudden swell slamming her legs. She snatches the rungs and pulls herself from the water. Climbs tentatively over the gunwale.

The wreck is dark. Spars groan and glass shatters. Lifeboats sway on their davits. The boats look untouched. No attempt made to use them.

In the moonlight, Scarlett sees dark beads staining the boards. Blood? Perhaps.

Dark blood.

Old blood.

It leads from the hatch to the gunwale and disappears into the sea.

She ought to leave.

No. She cannot go to Isaac empty-handed. To hell if she will let Reuben's men take everything.

The hatch opens with a creak. She climbs below and feels her way, sightless, through the dark passage.

There is no sound of life here in the crew's quarters. But nor is there anything in the darkness to hint at the presence of the dead.

She feels an indentation beneath her hand. Traces a finger along the carving in the bulkhead. A crooked crucifix is scrawled into the wood.

She can hear Reuben's men raiding the hold. She can't hope to compete with them. But she will find plenty in the captain's quarters. Trinkets and navigation tools, no doubt. Coin if she is lucky. Enough to put food on their table for a few nights at least.

The ship groans. The sea thunders into a distant cavity.

Scarlett stumbles down the passage, water at her ankles. She shoves open the door of the captain's cabin. The sea swirls around her knees. Lamplight from shore glows through the shattered porthole.

She wades towards the desk and tugs open the drawers.

Empty.

No trinkets, no tools, no coin.

She goes to the cupboard in the corner of the cabin.

Empty.

Dead wreck, they call the ships that are flung onto their shores with no living soul left aboard. But here is a skeleton; a wreck already plundered.

Lifeboats untouched.

Scarlett's mind goes to freak waves, to sirens, to hidden monsters and mutinies.

The rising water chases her from of the cabin. Soon this ship will rot on the floor of their bay. She hurries back to the deck, clutching the corner of the pilot house to keep her balance.

She hears movement, groaning. She crouches, reaching into the dark. Her fingers find something hot and wet. Blood.

And this dead wreck, she realises, is still breathing.

He feels fingers work across his neck, searching for a pulse. Sharp pain at the side of his head. Blood runs over his ear.

He makes out the shape of the person leaning over him. A young woman.

Her hand on his forearm eases him into sitting. Nausea turns his stomach. He hears the sea battering into unwelcome places.

He shifts, his hand finding the pool of blood on the pilot house floor.

The woman tears at her underskirt and presses the fabric against the cut on his scalp.

"Listen." Her voice is a sharp whisper. "There are men plundering your ship. They'll want this to be a dead wreck so they can legally claim her cargo. If they see you, they'll want you killed."

Asher stands, stumbles. He hears voices and footsteps. Life. But these voices are unfamiliar.

"Nothing down there but a few ankers," a man says.

"Take them ashore."

The woman darts out of the pilot house, leaving Asher alone in the darkness.

"What are you doing here, girl?" says a gravelly voice on the other side of the door.

"I thought to bring something back before you get your greedy hands to everything." Fear shakes her words. "You found cargo?"

"A little. Half the hold is underwater."

"The rest of the ship is empty," she says. "Was this Reuben's doing?"

A laugh. "Not everything untoward is Reuben's doing."

She snorts.

"Get off the ship, Miss Bailey. We're setting her alight before the riding officers find her."

The men's footsteps disappear.

The woman throws open the door. "Come with me," she tells Asher.

He grips the bulkhead to keep his balance. "What's your name?"

She glances over her shoulder. "Is it important?" A flash of light illuminates her face. Thin and pale, dominated by large charcoal eyes. Tangled black hair clings to her cheeks.

"Your name." Urgency in his voice.

"Scarlett. Scarlett Bailey."

Asher's heart quickens at the impossibility of it. He says nothing.

She clamps a hand around the top of his arm. "Come on now. Lean on me." She crouches, edging her way across the violent slope of the deck. The sea swells over the gunwale and the ship's ladder vanishes.

Asher grapples with the deck's smooth surface. Finds nothing to steady himself. He reaches instinctively for a fistful of Scarlett's dress.

Her eyes scan the sea for a path back to the rocks. "This way."

Dark water sweeps over the deck, licking Asher's boots. He breathes hard, tightens his handful of her skirts.

"Can you swim?" he asks, his mouth dry.

"Ayes. I can swim. But the water's shallow. We'll not need to."

With a deep, undersea groan, the deck shifts further. Scarlett pulls her skirts free from Asher's grip and laces her fingers through his. She moves with sudden urgency towards the shore. He stumbles behind, blood running into his eye.

And the ship is gone from beneath his feet. Water on all sides. He panics, thrashes until his toes find the rocky sea bed. Scarlett looks back at him, gripping his hand tightly. Water swells around their shoulders. Asher feels the sea tug him back towards the wreck. He keeps wading, keeps stumbling. Finally, the water becomes shallow and he drops to his knees on the rocky outcrop beside the beach.

Orange light flares on the edge of his vision. He glances over his shoulder to see flames shooting up the limp, tangled sails. Smoke plumes, melting into the blue dawn.

A crowd is gathered on the sand. Their murmurs carry on the cold air.

An empty wreck?

The boats untouched.

"Stay back," Scarlett hisses. "Don't let them see you."

Ghost ship.

A sight he must be with his matted hair and his shirt black with blood.

Keeping his back pressed to the cliffs, he edges around the point behind Scarlett. At the top of the hill, a church spire is silhouetted against the lightening sky.

Talland.

Oh, this village. How he despises it. And yet what twisted joy he feels to have been flung onto her shore.

Scarlett follows his gaze. "You can't go to the church. No one there will help you. Come with me." She leads him up the steep path from the beach. By the first bend in the road sits a dark stone building.

She thumps on the door. "Flora! Quickly! Let us in!"

And then there is a woman in the doorway; pale hair falling over her shoulders and lamplight flickering on her cheeks. Her eyebrows shoot up as she takes in Asher's bloodied clothes, Scarlett's wet skirts. She takes his other arm and leads him into a world of shadows and flickering orange light.

He is in the village tavern, Asher realises. A dark wooded room lit only by the lamp in the blonde woman's hand. The bar is empty of both people and liquor. Crooked shelves, stacked stools, tables lined up against the wall. A great black hearth sits cold and empty.

The noise from the beach has disappeared, replaced by the loud, fast thud of his heart beating in his ears. His legs give way. The dark closes in.

BELL HOUSE

'My dear brother Dodge,

I have ventured to trouble you, at the earnest request of the people of my parish with a matter which ... is causing much terror in my neighbourhood.'

Taken from a letter to Rev. Richard Dodge from Mr Gryllis,
Rector of Lanreath
1725

Isaac Bailey trudges up the hill to the church, legs weighted with exhaustion. The service is filling. He slips onto the end of a pew.

How glad he is to see them; Caroline with her brilliant gold-flecked eyes, Mary wriggling in her mother's arms, Gabriel marching toy soldiers across his knees.

His wife eyes him.

He's a mess. He smells of sweat and sea. His hair is dishevelled, his greatcoat flecked with salt. He has left a trail of wet footprints down the aisle. He pushes dark strands of hair behind his ears and rubs his eyes.

Caroline twitches her lips, considering. "Has something happened?"

He reaches for her hand. "A late night is all."

Gabriel lurches across his mother's lap. "Tasik, did you bring us a gift from the ship?" He grins and Isaac sees himself thirty years ago.

A quick smile. "Hush, boy. A good sailor knows when to keep things to himself."

They had returned to Talland with a lugger full of French whisky. Fresh from the hold of a merchant moored in the Channel. Give us your best price.

Isaac had not seen the wrecked ship until he was about to enter the bay. A brig, dancing like a madman. He'd had no doubt it would be wrecked. Had cursed at missed opportunities. A wreck about to be handed to them and he'd been stuck at sea with a lugger full of contraband. There would be no landing in Talland that night. The wreck would bring a crowd. A circus of treasure hunters and paupers. Revenue men perhaps.

Isaac had taken his load to Polperro and unloaded in the caves that burrow into the cliffs.

Scarlett slides into the pew behind him and pokes her head over his shoulder. "Did you see it? The wreck?"

Isaac nods. "From a distance."

"I went aboard. Tried to get my hands on something before Reuben's men got to it all. But it were the strangest thing. The ship was near empty."

Isaac turns to face his sister. "You went aboard? Alone? That was foolish."

"You'd not be saying that if I'd brought us back a fortune. Anyway, did you not hear what I said? The ship was empty. No crew. No bodies. Reuben's men found a few ankers of brandy in the hold but the rest of the cargo was gone."

"Lifeboats?"

"Not been touched."

Talk of the ship is everywhere, Isaac realises.

A dead wreck, say the villagers; shoulder to shoulder in the pews.

A twisted gift from the sea spirits.

No bodies.

How does a ship sail the seas without a man on board?

Lord protect us. For we all know a wreck brings a curse.

The vicar shuffles towards the pulpit, spine bowed with age. The black sleeves of his gown stream behind him, face weathered beneath his powdered white wig.

Reverend Dodge has inhabited this church for as long as Isaac can remember. He had listened to the vicar's sermons as a boy; lectures of ghosts and demons and otherworlds. Back then, Dodge's words had been truth, told in candlelight and gloom as the wind tore across the clifftop. Isaac had only been able to see the vicar's eccentricities once his travels had returned him to Talland with adult eyes.

Dodge leans forward, hunching over the pulpit. Caterpillar brows obscure his eyes. A hush falls.

"Let us pray."

The prayer echoes in the candlelit church. A hymn swells; fervent, nervous voices.

"Many of you have come to me afeared," says Dodge. "Afeared of the ghostly ship washed up upon our shore last night. Afeared this community has been ill-wished."

A murmur ripples through the congregation.

Isaac swaps a smile of amusement with Caroline.

Such is the value of eccentricity, he thinks. Tell tall stories with conviction and breed believers.

Caroline pockets Gabriel's toy soldiers that have walked their way to the top of the pew. The baby fidgets and gurgles. Isaac blinks, fighting off a wave of exhaustion.

"I remind you in times like this of what we hear in Corinthians, chapter four, verse four: 'In whom the god of this world hath blinded the minds of them which believe not, lest the light of the glorious gospel of Christ, who is the image of God, should shine unto them'." He leans forward, wiry, speckled hands gripping the pulpit. "We have been tested before. And now the devil is testing us again by bringing this phantom ship to our shores." Dodge's voice rises as he gathers momentum. "But have no fear, good people. We will remain believers. Have faith in the Lord and He will deliver you from the evil around us."

Charles Reuben waits outside the church, arms folded across his thick chest. In his powdered wig and crimson justacorps, he is a sight among the sea-stained greatcoats of Talland. When he sees Isaac, he raises his eyebrows expectantly. "Where are the goods?"

"In the cave at Polperro."

"Everything?"

Isaac nods. "They'll be brought to the church tonight."

"Any water damage will be taken from your cut."

Scarlett huffs loudly behind them. Isaac hadn't realised she was there.

"Water damage," she snaps. "How was he to land with half the country on the beach last night?"

Reuben ignores her. Scarlett's eyes flash and harden at the slight.

When he was twenty-one, Isaac had come home to Talland for the first time in four years. His merchant voyages had shown him Europe, then taken him to the East Indies, where the air was damp and fragrant and England was easily forgotten.

He walked the cliff path from Polperro with a pack on his back, waiting to see his parents' faces when he burst through the door.

The house was swathed in cobwebs and dust. A strange stillness about the place.

He couldn't make sense of it. The place felt odd, like he'd stepped off the ship at the wrong port and this village just bore a passing resemblance to his childhood home.

He went to see Martha Francis who lived in the neighbouring cottage.

"Oh." She looked at her feet. "Isaac."

Their graves were in the churchyard, she said. Isaac realised he must have walked past them minutes earlier. A shipwreck. An illness. Both taken within months of each other.

He looked over his shoulder at the empty cottage, unsure what to do. His parents had been dead for almost two years. It seemed too late for goodbyes. He stood staring at the house until Martha said:

"And there's Scarlett, of course."

Scarlett was not an *of course*. She was a distant, supporting character in Isaac's life. He'd left home when he was seventeen; his sister all of three.

There had been other siblings that had come and gone as he had grown up. An ever-expanding row of headstones like crooked teeth in that graveyard atop the cliff. Isaac had given little thought to Scarlett, assuming perhaps, that the same fate would befall her. She was a stranger. Little more than a name and a fading, outdated image. But an outdated image, he learned, who was waiting for him at the children's home in Polperro.

He ought to leave. There was nothing for him here. Scarlett could stay at the children's home. She was an orphan now. It was where she belonged.

He began to walk through the drizzle, climbing higher and higher up the cliff path until the expanse of white sky was matched by a churning grey sea. Isaac kept walking. He was heading for the harbour, he realised. Board the first ship leaving for who cared where. But he found himself knocking on the children's home door.

"Yes, yes, Mr Bailey. Scarlett will be so excited to see you."

Isaac followed the woman down the hall, their footsteps echoing in the cavernous passage. Children peered at him with vague, saucer eyes. Children everywhere; tangled hair and snotty noses. Mouths gawping like they had questions to ask but couldn't find the words. Which of these children was he to take with him? He had no idea which was his sister. He tried to swallow, but his mouth was dry.

The woman pointed to a girl kneeling by the window. Her back was to them as she crouched over a pile of jacks.

"That's her?" Isaac asked throatily.

"Ayes. That's her." The woman padded over to the girl. She bent and put a gentle hand on her shoulder.

He ought to leave. His sister would be better off here. The woman caring for her seemed loving and kind. More of a parent than he would ever be.

Scarlett rose from the floor and turned to face him. She was small and dirty, clad in a blue pinafore that had slipped off one shoulder. Her black hair hung loose past her shoulders. Eyes dark like his own. Isaac saw their mother in Scarlett's high cheekbones and sharp chin. His stomach twisted.

"Are you Isaac?" she asked.

He nodded.

What did she see in him, he wondered? Was she disappointed in this tatty, sea-hardened man who had come to claim her? Had she been expecting something better?

Her lips curled up. "Are we going home now?"

He managed a nod. "Get your things."

She grinned and disappeared down the hall.

The gravity of the situation swung at him suddenly. He was a sailor. How was he to earn a living now he was shackled to the land by this pitiful creature? He had a sudden urge to throw himself at the woman with the kind eyes.

Help me.

"I don't know how to care for her," he said huskily. "I can barely care for myself."

The woman reached up and held his shoulders. "I know you'll do right. It's the best thing for her to be around her family."

"Family." He exhaled sharply. "She don't know me from the next man."

The woman smiled gently. "She will."

They walked back along the cliff path, Scarlett clutching her cloak and a chipped wooden court doll. Isaac's mind raced. He had no food or clothing for her. Little money. He'd not even thought to explore the house before he'd plucked her from the children's home. Were there any bedclothes? Firewood? Pots and pans? Hell, even if there were, his cooking skills extended as far as opening a jar of pickled fish.

He realised he wasn't breathing.

He felt her hand at his wrist. She smiled up at him. Giant eyes. "Do you want to hear a story?"

And among the cobwebs that had taken over the house after their parents' deaths, they began to cobble together a life.

Each morning, a walk across the cliffs to Polperro. Isaac would sail into the Channel with the fishermen. Scarlett; walk to the charity school with the court doll tucked beneath her arm. After her lessons, she would wait with the women of the pilchard palace, learning to salt and press. Practice her crooked letters in the mud.

There was strength in his sister, Isaac realised. Resilience. He was a terrible parent, but Scarlett would not curl up and die from a diet of salted fish. Wouldn't crumble when the world shook beneath her.

Sometimes she'd look to him like he were her father.

Yes, bedtime. Agreed.

Other times they'd fight like the siblings they were, the fourteen years between them insignificant.

She was full of stories, this little creature who had upturned his world.

Giants and fairies and merrymaids. The chirruping bird who had accompanied their mother to Heaven.

Tales to placate the horrors that had filled her seven years of life.

Were the horrors to blame for her temper? Isaac couldn't be sure.

Wild, unpredictable rage would seize her without warning. A poison that crept up from behind. It would steal the stories and the smiles and the warm-hearted sister he was coming to know.

The first time, it was cold stew. Scarlett leapt from her chair and hurled the tin plate against the wall, contents splattering. She screeched, unintelligible. Her eyes shone wild in the lamplight. Who was this child, Isaac wondered? Where had she been hiding? She kicked, pulled at her hair. Knocked over the chair and tore at her clothes like something savage had crawled inside her.

He blew out the lamp. Didn't know why. Just felt, somehow, that the darkness would soothe her. He crouched on the floor. Said nothing. Watched as that rage disappeared with the light. Watched as his sunny sister returned to him.

Scarlett sat as his side, breathing hard.

He looked through the darkness to find her eyes. "What's this about then?"

She peered back at him, confused. Trying to place her anger? Trying to remember it? She opened her mouth to speak but said nothing.

Isaac lit the lamp. Nodded to the stew running down the wall. "Clean it."

She nodded. Cleaned. Bewildered.

He came to see they were both survivors. Saw why they had not been buried among their other siblings in the graveyard on the cliff.

They'd been together a week when Charles Reuben appeared at the door.

"Ah, the young Mr Bailey. I'm most happy to see you." His smile reached his eyes, but the sting of it made Isaac wary.

"Who are you?"

And there on the doorstep, Reuben proceeded to tell the whole miserable story.

A smuggling run to Guernsey. Reuben's cutter captained by Isaac's father, Jacob. With the ship full of French tobacco, the cutter had detoured to Saint Helier. A sly, secret journey.

Jacob Bailey had made free trading contacts of his own. An agent starting out in the business. Jacob had invested his own money, arranged his own buyers. Loaded Reuben's ship with additional contraband until the bulkheads groaned.

Overloaded and unbalanced, the cutter had rolled; the ship and her cargo sucked into the whirlpooling sea. Jacob had crawled into a lifeboat and watched his dreams of wealth disappear. Fishermen had ferried he and the crew back to Talland and the critical eyes of Charles Reuben.

Less than two years later, Jacob had been wrecked again. This time there had been no fishermen to save him and he had faced the critical eyes of God.

Reuben handed Isaac a scrawled ledger. "I paid for that vessel out of my own pocket. Her cargo too, of course. I expect repayment."

Isaac glanced at the ledger. His hand clenched around the door frame. "Does it look like I've that sort of money?" He screwed up the page and tossed it in the mud.

Reuben smiled, unperturbed by the rain drizzling down his collar. "I'm quite sure you don't. You'll work for me. You're a sailor, I hear. Just the man I need to captain a lugger to Saint Peter Port once a month. I put up the capital and liaise with my agent. You get the lugger there and back. Complete the transactions. I'll provide you with enough of the profits to keep you and your sister clothed and fed. The rest of your cut will go towards paying off your father's debts, and the interest accumulated."

Isaac's stomach tightened. The world seemed to lose its colour. "This is criminal."

"It's not criminal. It's business. The repayment plan was drawn up by my banker. You'll find it a fair deal, I'm sure."

"Go to hell," Isaac spat. "I left this place so I'd not get caught up in free trade."

Reuben smiled thinly. "A shame your father didn't have your sense."

"Your business was with Jacob, not me. I'm not willing to take on his debts."

"But you're willing to take on his property, his land. I'm sorry, Mr Bailey, but this isn't your choice."

Isaac closed his eyes. "Take the house and the land. Leave us be."

"A sailor is of far more value to me. I'm glad you turned up when you did. I was beginning to think I'd have to have your little sister hawk for us."

Isaac felt suddenly, fiercely protective. "Stay the hell away from Scarlett."

Reuben plucked the ledger from the mud and shoved it against Isaac's chest. "I've made arrangements with my agent for you to be in Saint Peter Port in a week."

Isaac clenched his jaw. "I've no boat."

"Lucky for you, I'm in a generous mood. I've recently taken ownership of a new lugger. Purpose-built out of Mevagissey. In the right hands, she can cross the Channel in eight hours. You'll meet me at Polperro harbour tomorrow morning. Get to know your new vessel."

That night, Isaac stuffed their few belongings into a pack and bundled Scarlett's cloak around her shoulders. They made it as far as the landing beach before the smugglers' banker found them and put a gun to their heads. Reuben had eyes all over the village, Isaac realised. To try and leave would be the end of them.

He had never been close to his father. Even as a boy, he had seen something in Jacob that had made him wary. His sailing lessons had been interspersed with tours of cliffs and coves; this beach good for a landing in low tide, that cave a perfect hideout. Instructions on how to rope up the barrels and hide them in shallow water. How to use a grappling hook to haul them from the sea.

He was determined that this would not be his life; this endless, oppressive crawl beneath the revenue men's eyes.

There was an entire world out there, beyond the village, beyond the Channel. A world of which Isaac knew nothing, but of which he longed to know everything. The urge to leave was overpowering.

He packed his bags the day after his seventeenth birthday, desperate to escape the pull of Jacob's smuggling ring.

His father stood at the front door with his arms folded across his chest. Watched Isaac kiss his mother's cheek. Watched him swing his pack onto his back with poorly hidden enthusiasm.

"So this is your choice then."

"Ayes, this is my choice. Forgive me, Tas."

His father didn't speak again, just pulled the door closed with a dejected sigh.

In the end, Jacob had gotten what he wanted; his son following in his footsteps.

His legacy is heavy on Isaac's shoulders. Captain of a smuggling lugger. Errand boy for the wealthy landowner who controls the region's free trade.

It has been fourteen years since Reuben had appeared at their door. Fourteen years since Isaac had stood in the rain and listened to the story of his father and the lost cutter.

He feels this will be his entire life.

Charles Reuben is past fifty, but he is a wealthy man with high-placed connections. Could find himself a wife without trouble. Produce an heir to hold the debt over Isaac's family for another generation.

No. He won't—can't—let such a thing happen. Can't give his children the life his father had given him.

"Has the vicar been informed you will be loading the church tonight?" Reuben asks.

"He's been informed." Isaac touches Scarlett's elbow, ushering her towards the gate. "I'm sure the spirits are trembling as we speak."

SAILOR

Asher opens his eyes. Candlelight flickers over the cellar walls. He smells earth and clay. He lies on his side with a flimsy cushion beneath his head, a blanket tossed over him. His legs and head ache, tight strapping around his skull. His hair feels matted and brittle. His breeches are stiff with salt and blood, chest bare.

He looks around for his coat. Finds it draped across a barrel in the corner of the cellar. His bloodstained shirt is nowhere to be seen. He crawls towards the coat. Checks the inner pocket. The letter is there, sodden, but intact. He shoves it into the pocket of his breeches.

He hears footsteps and the creak of stairs. Shuffles back to his makeshift bed. His blurred vision makes out two women; one dark, one fair. The blonde woman carries a lantern and a bottle.

"He's awake," she says.

The dark-haired woman comes towards him. Scarlett. She is younger than the other; barely twenty, perhaps. Dishevelled, but faintly pretty with high cheekbones and pale skin. Wildness at her edges.

She had been a child when last he had set foot in this village. Asher had been the age Scarlett is now. Had brimmed with similar impulsiveness.

She kneels. Tilts her head so their eyes meet at the same angle. She takes the bottle from the blonde woman and holds it to Asher's lips. He gulps the water as it drizzles down his cheek. He sits, head thumping.

Scarlett lifts the strapping around his head and peers at the wound. "Bleeding's stopped." She jabs his skull.

"Don't go poking the poor fellow, Scarlett. He's not a pudding." The blonde woman's voice is lyrical, gentle. She winds the strapping around his head again. "How do you feel?"

Feel? He feels a constant prickling beneath his skin at being in this place again. Feels impatient, wary, frustrated by his injuries.

He squints. The woman's face is familiar. Her hair is eerily, unnaturally pale. So blonde it is almost without colour. Her eyes blaze deep-sea blue.

He hopes she has no recollection of him.

"Where am I?" he asks.

"In the cellar of the Mariner's Arms," says Scarlett. "Flora's inn."

She sits close. She has questions for him. And Asher answers, because of who she is and what she might know.

Yes, the wrecked *Avalon* was a merchant ship. London to Penzance. A cargo of liquor and lace embroidered with gold anchors.

A tragedy, yes. No, I remember little.

"The ship was empty but for you and a few ankers of brandy," Scarlett tells him. "We found no bodies. The lifeboats were still aboard. The village is in a panic because they've never seen such a thing. A ghost ship washed up on our very shore. They fear it has cursed us."

He chuckles to himself. Fools.

He tries to stand.

Flora's hand shoots out and finds his arm. "Stay down. You need to recover. I'm sorry for such miserable lodgings, but it's important no one sees you. If customs see fit to investigate, the men who plundered your ship will ensure it was a dead wreck."

Investigate? He almost laughs. There will be no investigation. The ship has been burned. And this is Charles Reuben's trading territory. Asher is sure they have the protection of the revenue men. How deep does the rot go, he wonders? Has Scarlett Bailey taken up the family business?

She pokes and preens, easing him back to the bed of blankets. They have cheese for him. Tea, stale bread.

He takes the food. Eats.

"I'll stay with him," Scarlett says, giving Flora a look that clearly says she wants her to leave. And Flora does, letting the door close with a creak and thud.

There is a gaping hole hacked into the wall of the cellar. It has been boarded up with rough planks. He crawls towards it, curious. The planks have been hammered crookedly, hurriedly.

"You can't get out that way," says Scarlett.

"What is it? A smuggling tunnel?"

She straightens his blankets. "What's your name?"

He tells her: "Asher Hales." The name he has adopted. The name the world will one day come to know. He tells her again: "My name is Asher Hales." He likes the sound his new name makes as it rolls off his tongue.

Asher Hales is a shipwreck survivor. He is a man who prospers when life hands him a rough deal. A man who rises above the rest.

Scarlett smiles. "A pleasure to meet you, Mr Hales."

He takes her outstretched hand. Squeezes it gently and looks into her eyes until her cheeks flush and she pulls away. He allows himself a faint smile.

Asher Hales recognises opportunity. When he is pulled from a sinking ship by Jacob Bailey's daughter, he will draw her close and not let go.

EXORCISM

'I will ... recount to you the whole of this strange story as it has reached my ears, for as yet I have not satisfied my eyes of its truth. It has been told me by men of honest and good report ... with such strong assurances that it behoves us to look more closely into the matter.'

Taken from a letter to Rev. Richard Dodge from Mr Gryllis,
Rector of Lanreath
1725

The vicar paces, a whip in his fist. A lamp hangs by the door of the church. It sways in the wind, making shadows dance.

A laying of the spirits. Behold the great ghost hunter, Reverend Dodge.

Onlookers huddle at the edge of the lane. Women entangle themselves in shawls while men pace, trying to hide their unease. Whispering, peering, shuffling. Residents of the surrounding villages braving the darkness and demons to witness a spectacle.

"You ought not be here!" Dodge tells the crowd.

Flora snorts. Heaven forbid the vicar's theatrics go unobserved.

In the cove below, the boats of Isaac's landing party pull towards the shore. Flora hears faint voices floating up to the clifftop, the sigh of oars in sea.

She ushers her daughter, Bessie, towards the church. "Go on now. I'll not be long."

Bessie clutches a book to her chest and scurries through the crooked gravestones.

"We have again been challenged by evil," Dodge booms. "A ghost ship washed up upon our shore. But we will not let Satan defeat us, will we, Mrs Kelly?" He whirls around to face Flora.

"No," she mumbles. "We will not let Satan defeat us."

A woman grabs her husband's arm and tugs him back up the lane. The rest of the pack draws closer.

Dodge paces across the churchyard, hurling the whip into the darkness.

Crack and the onlookers jump. Huddle closer.

Crack. Can you see the demons hiding in the dark?

Out onto Bridles Lane. *Crack.*

"The holy water, Mrs Kelly."

Flora hands Dodge the bowl.

He circles the cemetery again, droplets of water flying from his fingertips.

A final word to God.

"Amen," Flora echoes. The insincerity in her voice is so blatant she is sure the crowd can sense it.

She has done this with Dodge; this sham, a thousand times.

A solemn prayer, a flick of his wrists and Bridles Lane will be clear of prying eyes. Free for the landing party to carry their haul to the church.

The vicar had singled Flora out, asking for her assistance long before she'd married Jack. An extra voice to send away the demons. An extra set of eyes to keep the curious away from the Bridles Lane deliveries. No, she had told Dodge firmly. She'd not involve herself in free trade.

But then there was Jack Kelly, the sailor with a laugh that made Flora's heart skip. Arrived from upcountry and joined the Polperro fishing fleet. He had hair the colour of autumn leaves and eyes full of light. Had been snatched up by the free traders before his first month was through, but Flora had loved him in spite of it.

Married to Jack, there were long, sleepless nights. Nights she lay in bed staring into the dark, her stomach turning over with worry. She became gripped with fear that he would fall into the hands of the revenue men. She needed to be involved, she realised. Needed to be the eyes Dodge had asked her to be.

As a love-drunk young wife, hunting ghosts with the vicar had been a thrill. A joke. She'd cast out the spirits with Dodge, then drink away the night with the traders once the haul was safely stored in the church.

Two years after Jack's death, she is still here. Still traipsing after Dodge on his otherworldly adventures. Here for the paltry pennies the vicar pays for her services. A pittance, of course, when Reuben hands Dodge such a large percentage of the profits from the sales of the contraband.

She has come to hate the scam, the dishonesty. Instilling fear into the villagers for the sake of greed.

He is full of stories, this vicar. A headless horseman banished from Blackadown Moor. The demons of Bridles Lane.

True? Of course they are true.

Yes, yes, Flora says, whenever wide-eyed spectators ask. *I saw that horseman with my own eyes. I saw Reverend Dodge send it back to Hell.*

The tales grow legs. Fairy tales become truths. A haunted coast, the people say. Men refuse to ride Bridles Lane at night. Richard Dodge has become a legend. And Reuben's pockets have grown heavy with smuggling riches.

The vicar watches as the last of the onlookers disappear into the night. "Signal the men," he instructs Flora. "Tell them the lane is clear."

She takes the lamp to the edge of the cliff. Moonlight spills across the sea. The charred skeleton of the *Avalon* juts from the water.

She shines the light to the men below. Bring up your goods. Fill our bell house with liquor.

She pulls her shawl tight around her shoulders. Opens the church door and finds Bessie in a pew at the back of the nave. The girl hunches over a candle, the book in her lap. Her blonde hair glows in the candlelight.

"Come, *cheel-vean.* Time to go."

Bessie blows out the candle and plunges the church into darkness. Her footsteps patter on the flagstones. Hand in hand, she and Flora hurry towards the gate. They keep their heads down, avoiding the vicar.

Flora unlocks the creaking front door of the inn. She lights the lamps and sends Bessie to bed.

She finds Scarlett in the cellar, watching over the shipwrecked sailor. He sleeps on his side in the pile of blankets. She dozes, sitting up against the wall.

Flora shakes her shoulder. "Go home, Scarlett. Get a little sleep. I'll take care of him."

Scarlett hesitates. She glances at the sailor, then at Flora. Finally, she nods and makes her way sleepily up the cellar stairs.

When Scarlett is gone, Flora walks slowly through the empty bar. It creaks and groans like the hull of a ship.

With the money she has earned tonight, she can afford fresh paint for the window sills. She will be able to open the inn's doors again soon. No more exorcising the demons of Dodge's imagination. She'll extract herself from the vicar's grasp. And once the Mariner's Arms is open, she'll keep her feet firmly planted in the land of the living.

The building is old and crooked; a relic from the turn of the previous century. The ceilings are low, lined with beams hauled from faraway forests. The great black hearth gapes and wind whistles down the chimney. The windows are thick, speckled with salt. Even on the brightest days, the Mariner's Arms is a place of candlelight and shadow.

Upstairs, the rooms are dusty and neglected, silent with the voices of guests who had never arrived.

Flora's memory is filled with countless games of hide and seek. First as a daughter, then a mother. Climbing over rickety furniture, hiding in cupboards. Don't sneeze from the dust.

Bessie, I hear you breathing.

One day, she will empty these rooms. Send guests up there to make their own memories. But for now, opening the bar consumes her.

Flora's family had owned the tavern, though it has not been a public house since her grandfather had closed its doors some forty years earlier. For all Flora's life, the tables have been nothing more than dust collectors, the cellar cluttered with broken furniture. Neither of her parents had had any interest in bringing the tavern back to life.

But this place had been Jack's dream. On the death of Flora's mother, three years ago, he had inherited the property. Had struggled to hide his excitement beneath the obligatory grief over his mother-in-law's passing.

He'd taken Flora by the hand and walked her through the building.

The bar here, guest rooms there, a rocking horse for Bessie and a great curtained bed for us. Fit for a king and queen.

Flora is determined to see his dream come to life.

She brings out a pot of beeswax from beneath the bar and dips in a rag. She polishes until her arms ache and the counter begins to shine.

Soon people will sit at this bar and speak of hurling matches. Speak of changing winds and stolen kisses. They'll spill ale on the counter and never notice how much it shines.

She can't wait for it.

A knock at the door makes her start. There is Isaac, the wind whipping his dark hair around stubbled cheeks. Dawn is creeping over the horizon.

"I saw the lamp lit," he says.

Flora ushers him inside. She gestures to the polish. "I'll sleep once the inn is open."

Isaac digs into his pocket. A seashell. Pink and white and perfect. "I found it in the cave. Thought it a good fit for your collection."

Flora takes the shell and turns it over in her hands. She runs a finger over its pearly surface. "It's beautiful." She places it among the shells that sit upon the window ledge. "Thank you."

Isaac runs a hand across the polished surface of the bar. He looks up at the shelves behind the counter. One has worked free from the wall and slopes like a see-saw. "You need help with that?"

"I can manage. I don't want to make trouble."

"You know it's no trouble." He grins. "I'll come by tomorrow."

SEASHELLS

Isaac walks the length of the bar, floorboards creaking beneath his boots. Sun struggles through the windows. The inn has been swept free of its eternal layer of dust. The tables are planed and polished, the enormous hearth blacked. New stools are stacked in the corner of the room.

"The place looks grand," he tells Flora. He tilts his head, considering the crooked shelves. "Better way they come down. Start again, I'd say."

"Whatever you think best."

He pulls a hammer from his satchel and sets to work attacking the rotting wood.

Flora watches. Watches him flick his hair from his eyes. Watches his muscles tense beneath rolled-up shirtsleeves. And for a moment, it is Jack with the hammer in hand, his rust-coloured hair as bright as Isaac's is dark.

Her chest tightens.

A delivery tomorrow, he tells her between his hammering. Half the whisky brought in from the run.

"You've buyers already?" Flora asks, attacking the tables with the beeswax polish.

"Ayes. Customs House."

She laughs. "What?"

"I'm to plant the ankers on the moor. Then pay customs a visit. Let them know I found a haul of contraband while I was out riding. Collect a handsome reward." There is light in his eyes.

She gives him a crooked smile. "Your idea, I'm sure. Reuben would never have come up with such a plan."

He chuckles. "And he's to pay me well for my brilliance. Thirty percent. A decent cut for once."

"Seems a bargain for your brains."

He has always been this way; sharp witted and clever. As children, Isaac had been the one full of ideas. Build a raft to sail to the eastern beach. Supper of blackberries from the

51

bushes behind the bell house. A lantern-lit parade into the cave at Polperro to find the ghost of poor drowned Willie Wilcox. Flora had trailed along with her skirts at her knees, doe-eyed and doting.

Even as a boy, Isaac had had an air about him. A dark magnetism that set Flora on edge.

She had been thirteen years old when he had gone to sea. Had thrown her arms around him, then turned away quickly so he wouldn't see her cry. She watched out the parlour window as he disappeared over the clifftops.

She'd been sure then that he had a great life ahead of him. He would see the world, make his fortune. Return to Talland as a sea captain.

But not like this. Not captain of a smuggling lugger whose strings are pulled by another man. The injustice of it burns inside her.

He hammers in the final nails. Steps back to admire his work. "What do you think?"

Flora tosses down her polishing rag. "It's perfect. Thank you."

He presses a hand to her arm; warm and solid. "You'll tell us if you need more help. You're not alone, you know."

"Of course I'm not. I have Bessie." She closes her eyes, instantly regretting her sharpness.

Isaac tucks his tools back into his satchel and wipes his dusty hands on his breeches. "And you've Caroline and I. And Scarlett."

Flora nods stiffly. She can't bear to be seen as the needy widow. Especially not to Isaac and Caroline. "I'm sorry. I didn't mean to be so curt."

His eyes meet hers.

She flushes, ashamed. "The seashells," she manages. "They'll fit perfectly on the top shelf."

Isaac smiles. "I'm glad of it."

She walks him to the door. "You'll be watchful tomorrow night, won't you. You've a fine plan, but it's a dangerous one. I hope you're as careful as you are clever."

"Nothing dangerous about it. Customs are nothing but a bunch of understrappers."

She jabs a finger under his nose. "It's talk like that that'll have you in trouble."

He catches her outstretched finger and gives it a quick squeeze. "We'll watch ourselves. I swear it."

THE HEALING WOMAN

'There is in this neighbourhood a barren bit of moor which had no owner. ... The lords of the adjoining manors debated its ownership between themselves, ... both determined to take it from the other. ... The two litigants contested it with much violence and ... it is said to have hastened [one's] death. If current reports are worthy of credit ... at night-time his apparition is seen on the moor to the great fright of the neighbouring villagers.'

Taken from a letter to Rev. Richard Dodge from Mr Gryllis,
Rector of Lanreath
1725

"Corpse candles," says Isaac's spotsman.

The two men are high on the shadow-bathed moor, the road a narrow ribbon through snarls of gorse. Their wagon creaks beneath the weight of the whisky ankers. Ahead, the sea and sky melt into one another. Specks of blue light glitter on the horizon.

"You see them? The lights?" Isaac's spotsman, George Gibson is a weathered, grey bear of a man. A sailor with a healthy fear of the sea and the spirits who inhabit it.

Corpse candles. Isaac remembers the stories. Told by his father who had lived with one foot in a world of fantasy. The corpse candles were the souls of the dead, Jacob Bailey had said. Ghosts of drowned sailors.

Gibson breathes hard and fast. "They appear right after that cursed ship washes up on our beach. Tell me it don't mean something."

"Forget that ship. It's the best thing for all of us."

"You think it that easy?" Gibson wraps his arms around himself. Stares at the hovering lights. "You know what they say about the corpse candles, ayes? Death is coming for whoever sees them."

Isaac snorts. "You've been listening to too many of the vicar's stories."

While his father had believed wholeheartedly in such things, Isaac sees them for what they are; stories, superstitions. His travels have shown him an enlightened world; a place of reason and rationality where nature lives by laws and the dead stay in their graves. But this county refuses to let go of its ancestors' legends. It has lived in ignorance for far too long. As far as Isaac is concerned, the sooner Cornwall comes to agree with the rest of the country, the better.

"Enough of this," he says. "Help me get these ankers hidden." He leaps from the wagon and tosses aside the thin layer of kelp hiding the whisky. He heaves out the first of the barrels and shoves it into the tangled scrub.

Gibson hides the ankers without speaking; his eyes darting from the wagon to the lights on the horizon.

He will go to the vicar, he announces as they conceal the last of the whisky. Leaps into the box seat and snatches the reins.

Isaac chuckles. "Dodge? What's that mad bastard going to do?"

"Send these spirits away, can't he. We've all seen it. Rid us of the very devil, so he did."

Gibson goads the horse into a trot. The corpse candles disappear behind the curve of the hills.

Isaac lurches for the reins. "You can't go to Dodge. I've to be at Customs House in Fowey in a few hours. Tell them about this whisky."

Gibson tenses. "Stop the wagon. I need to see the vicar. If you'll not take me back, I'll bloody well walk."

"Come," says Dodge. "We've people to see."

Flora grips the doorframe and tugs her shawl around her shoulders. "It's barely dawn. My daughter is sleeping."

"She can sleep in the carriage. George Gibson has requested my help. It seems we were plagued by corpse candles tonight. The man is most unsettled." Dodge shifts impatiently. "Please, Mrs Kelly. We must make haste."

Flora clenches her teeth and hurries upstairs.

Damn George Gibson and his feverish faith. For a man who has spent years loading Dodge's bell house with contraband, he is easily swayed by the vicar's ghost stories.

She pulls on her dress and cloak, then scoops Bessie out of bed, wrapping a blanket around her limp body. She follows Dodge out to the carriage.

The driver pulls away from the inn and they wind up the narrow path towards the top of the hill. The houses lining the road are lightless, lifeless.

"Really Father? Is such a thing necessary at this hour?"

Dodge smiles. "The Lord will protect you, Mrs Kelly. You know that."

"I'm not afraid. I just… I suppose I don't see the point."

Dodge raises his woolly eyebrows. "My people have come to me for help. What kind of man would I be if I did not follow up on their claims?"

The coachman stops the carriage and tethers the horse to a tree. Flora follows Dodge into the orange dawn. They have left the road behind and the carriage stands in the farmland that sprawls across the clifftop. Far below, the sea is agitated and grey.

On the cliff edge, Flora can make out the figures of Gibson and several other men from Isaac's crew, pacing edgily. There are a few others; women from the charity school and an elderly couple wrapped in enormous brown greatcoats.

Flora squints into the rising sun. "I don't see the corpse candles."

"They are there," Gibson says darkly. "That ship brought them with her, I know it. They left with the dawn. But they'll be back."

"We saw them too," the old woman pipes up. "Clear as day. Lost souls, Father. You must cast them out before they bring ill luck to this village."

Dodge squeezes the woman's hands. "I will speak with these uneasy spirits. Draw from them the dread secrets that trouble them." He walks to the edge of the cliff and closes his eyes. Begins to rock back and forth as though entranced.

Flora feels ill.

What is this, this theatrical swaying and murmuring? These prayers howled to the wind? What is it but trickery?

"You have nothing to fear if you put your faith in the Lord," Dodge says finally. People cluster around him, clutching at his gnarled hands.

Flora follows him back to the carriage. "That couple was in the churchyard two nights ago. They watched you cast the demons out of Bridles Lane."

"Indeed. No doubt that is why they have sought my counsel."

"Your exorcisms are beginning to frighten people."

"As well they should! Only a foolish man would not fear the devil!"

"Father, you and I both know these tales of ghosts and demons are a sham to keep the lane clear for the traders."

For several moments, Dodge doesn't reply. "These strange lights," he says finally. "What do you believe them to be?"

"I didn't see any lights."

"Do you think these people lying?"

Flora sighs. "I don't know what these people saw. But I don't believe lights on the horizon are to be feared. And after this wreck…" She pauses. "Perhaps validating the villagers' worries by traipsing out to the clifftops at first light is not in their best interest."

Dodge purses his lips. For a moment, Flora is a child again, cowering in a pew while the vicar pelts out a sermon.

"We will go where we are asked to go. These people need to have faith in their vicar. And faith in the Lord." He looks at Flora pointedly. "As do you, Mrs Kelly. I am surprised to find your mind so closed to the divine. I admit I am shaken by it."

"I'm no fool, Father. Your exorcisms are based on trickery and greed. I'll not be a part of it any longer."

Dodge's eyebrows shoot up. "You cannot just walk away."

"Of course I can. I'll have the inn to run soon. I can't be spending my evenings gallivanting about the clifftops." She glances down at Bessie. "And I want more for my daughter than sleeping in the back of a carriage while her mother chases ghosts."

"Instead she is to sleep above a public house while her mother plies the village with liquor?"

Flora grits her teeth. "Find someone else to accompany you. Any fool could hand you holy water and carry a signalling lantern."

"No. It must be you. It is of utmost importance that I keep you on the path of God."

She sighs. "This is about my mother."

"Yes," Dodge admits. "Your mother darkened her soul by dabbling in witchcraft."

Flora laughs humourlessly. "My mother did nothing more than offer a few herbal remedies. She was just a healing woman. And a mediocre one at that."

"She was a practitioner of dark magic. I tried to bring her back to God, but I failed in my attempts. It is my duty to ensure you do not follow the same path."

"That's what this has been about? That's why you asked for my help? To try and prove God's power to me so I didn't stray?"

"I've proved God's power to you a hundred times over."

"Is that so?"

"How can you be so dismissive after all you've seen?"

"After all I've seen? I've seen nothing. Just you waving your arms about on the clifftops while the smugglers load their haul into your church."

"Perhaps there were a few theatrics for the benefit of the traders. But my exorcisms are based in truth. Evil is all around us, Mrs Kelly. We must be vigilant."

Flora snorts. "You've fallen for your own sham. Stop the carriage," she calls to the coachman. "I can walk the rest of the way."

Dodge waves a bony finger in her face as she pushes open the door. "You'll come to me when your soul is darkened by your mother's legacy. You'll come begging for redemption. You shall see."

Flora hauls Bessie from the carriage and slings her over her shoulder. "I've no intention of darkening my soul, Father. But my days of chasing demons are through."

SEA SPIRITS

The men talk of corpse candles as they sail out of the harbour. George Gibson speaks of Dodge's performance on the clifftops. A banishing of lost souls. A counter to the ill luck cast over the village.

Ill luck? Isaac doesn't see it. He'd made five pounds that morning.

He had led the customs officers out to the moor and watched as his whisky had been hauled from the undergrowth.

Thank you for your vigilance, Mr Bailey. And he'd left with a pocket full of coin.

Much of the money will go to Charles Reuben, another slice divided up between the crew. But there will be a sizeable chunk left in Isaac's hands.

He ought to put the money towards his debts, of course. Chip away at a little of that ugly figure. But he can't help thinking of the things that money could buy. A spinning top for Gabriel. New shawl for Caroline. A boost for Scarlett's paltry dowry.

He allows himself a faint smile.

Today they are honest fishermen, scooping pilchards from the sea. Isaac sails his lugger with Gibson and John Baker, the other boats of the fishing fleet filled with men from his trading ring.

The day is grey and heavy. Isaac is glad to be on the water. Glad for open space and clean air. He does his best to stay away from the men and their endless parade of horror stories.

A shout comes from the huers standing by the watch houses on the cliff.

Pilchard shoals.

The huers wave their sticks, directing the boats towards the dark masses of fish. The men are tiny on the cliff; Gabriel's toy soldiers.

Nets are cast into the water, strung between the three boats. Pilchards swarm beneath them. The fish are hauled aboard, silver and squirming.

Another shoal. Another shout. Another net of fish.

They float now on the edge of the Channel. Polperro has disappeared. There is a dampness about everything. The clouds are low, melting thick and grey into the sea. The boat is heavy with pilchards.

Turn back. Home.

As they come about, the wind blows up, squally and fierce. The swell climbs. The sky blackens.

Isaac buttons his tarred greatcoat, hair whipping around his cheeks. He grabs at the line above his head as the lugger pitches wildly. He peers into the bank of cloud, seeking out the lights of the village. Sees nothing through the wall of mist.

The sky opens. Fat rain blackens the deck and runs down the back of Isaac's neck. The deck seesaws. He glances upwards at the single, shortened sail. Furl it and they'll be swept back into the Channel. Continue to sail and they risk rolling on this wild sea.

He looks to the men. "Hand her in." His shout is swallowed by the roar of water.

The sail thunders as it's furled. The sea curls into mountains. Water sweeps across the deck.

Ocean waves. A deep sea storm.

Isaac has never seen conditions like this; not here on the fringes of the Channel.

He stumbles towards the hatch, water streaming from his coat. They have little choice but to huddle below deck and let themselves be flung about like a cork. Wait for the sea to settle.

He does not even see the wave coming. He feels the deck fly beneath him. Snatches at the gunwale. The baskets of fish tumble; thousands of silver bodies swept back into the ocean. The bare masts arc through the air, lurching until they are horizontal, lying against the sea.

For a moment, Isaac feels the stillness. The ship hanging, hull to the sky. His knuckles whiten. Nothing beneath his feet but air and sea.

No thoughts. Just *hold on*. And *survive*.

And then from deep in his mind come a thousand stories. Angered sea spirits and cursed ships. Ill wishing and omens of death. The names of drowned sailors hummed in the wind.

The lugger rolls back, righting herself. The masts rise from the waves and reel against the grey sky.

Isaac scrambles to his feet. He is dizzy with something. Is it fear? Relief? His breath is hard and fast. His world is solid again. No longer filled with tales told by desperate men.

He says nothing to Scarlett about the knockdown. Underplays the loss of the fish when she runs from the pilchard palace asking questions.

An accident. Clumsiness.

There's an uneasiness in her, he knows. A respect for the sea that borders on fear. Her vivid imagination has populated the ocean floor with monsters. Catch hold of Gibson's *curse* and *lost souls* and she'll be tossing sleepless in her bed for weeks.

She grips his arm tightly as they follow the cliff path back to Talland. Walks pressed to his side until the path becomes too narrow to walk together.

Isaac shivers in his wet clothes. Doesn't let himself think of how close he had come to drowning. Tries not to picture his own memorial stone standing in the churchyard beside his father's.

It's late when the men come to the house. Scarlett has disappeared to Flora's inn and Caroline sits at the table with a needle and thread. Isaac stands close to the fire, his blood cold and fingers stiff.

Gibson knocks loudly and lets himself inside, the other members of Isaac's crew trailing.

Caroline lowers the shift she is hemming. She glances at the men's muddy boots. "Do come in. Make yourselves at home."

Gibson lowers his eyes. "I beg your pardon, Mrs Bailey." He takes off his knitted cap and bundles it into his fist.

He is afeared, he tells Isaac. The men are afeared. Death is coming for them. His speech is garbled and punctuated with phrases like *corpse candles* and *curse*.

But his meaning is clear. The men will not return to sea.

"Don't be so foolish!" Isaac demands. "You can't leave me stranded like this! We've a run to Falmouth in a week. Guernsey in a fortnight. How do you imagine Reuben will react if we don't make it?"

The men won't look at him. Won't look at Caroline. Their eyes are on the fire, on the floor. Reuben is Isaac's concern, of course. How he will react is of little bother to the other men.

"How are we to make a living if you'll not go to sea?" he asks tautly.

"I'll not die in pursuit of making a living," Gibson says. "We could well have drowned today. The corpse candles, you know they foretell death. It nearly were ours."

"And yet here we are."

"I daresay we was only spared because of the fish."

"The fish?"

"We lost them all. Sea spirits took them as a sacrifice. So they let us live."

Isaac curses under his breath. "You're my spotsman, George. You know I need you."

Gibson says nothing.

"I'll increase your cut. Fifteen percent."

"This isn't about money. We value our lives too much. There are mysteries out there, Isaac. You're a fool if you don't respect the sea."

Caroline snorts. "You come in here with these fanciful tales and have the nerve to call my husband a fool?"

"With respect, Mrs Bailey," Gibson says carefully, "you don't come from these parts. We'd not expect a foreigner to understand."

Caroline's eyebrows shoot up. *Foreigner* is barbed after more than a decade in the west country.

Isaac steps towards Gibson threateningly. "I'm no foreigner," he says. "And Caroline is right. You'd do far better if you kept your feet planted in the real world."

HENRY AVERY

Scarlett reports. No word of an investigation. And no one suspects the *Avalon* was anything but a dead wreck. Asher is free to leave.

He sits. The cut on his head is tender, but the searing pain is gone.

"I am a mess," he tells Scarlett.

Her eyes brighten. Clean clothes, yes of course. Boots too, perhaps she can find boots.

"A razor," says Asher.

She hurries from the cellar. Returns with her arms full. She hands him a clean shirt and coat. Breeches. No boots. She is sorry.

She turns her back as he peels off his filthy clothes. He slides the letter into the pocket of the greatcoat. The clothing Scarlett has brought smells musty and neglected. She looks back to see him brushing a layer of dust from the coat's sleeves.

"I'm sorry," she says. "They belonged to Flora's husband. He's not been with us for several years. I'm afraid his things have seen little daylight." She has placed a water bowl and razor on the floor by the lamp. "Sit."

He kneels in front of her. She grips the razor.

"Let me," says Asher.

She shakes her head. "Please."

She has saved him. Nursed him. Wants to see him clean and shorn before she sends him back out into the world. There is something mildly touching about it.

And so he sits motionless and lets her run the blade over the pale stubble on his cheeks. Her strokes are careful, precise. A crease appears between her eyes as she frowns in concentration. Tenderness in her touch.

This girl needs a dog. Or a husband.

She leans close, tilts her head. Trying to place his age, perhaps. His hair is thick and sandy, eyes blue and bright. The creases in his face tell of a difficult life, but not a long one. Her father's age, no. Closer to her brother's.

And what is that look? That light in her eyes? Desire?

Little Scarlett Bailey. What would your father think?

He remembers her. A black-haired child building castles on the beach. Little legs powering up the hill to keep pace with her striding father.

She continues to shave. "George Gibson saw the corpse candles. They say they are the souls of your crew—" She stops. "Forgive me. I'm sure it is difficult to speak of them."

Asher says nothing.

Easy for these people to believe in tales of lost souls. Look at the depth of the darkness. Listen to the shriek as the wind makes twisted wrecks of trees.

Their stories make sense of a wild world. They give these people a beacon in the night.

Corpse candles. Asher had heard of them when he had arrived in Cornwall as a young man. Floating lights, displaced souls. Spoken of in whispers, among words of prayer.

And what might they be, he had wondered, filtering the stories through a mind that had grown up reading Newton, Kepler, Galileo.

The lights had appeared on the edge of the graveyard, following the burial of a local man in Looe. The town became gripped with terror. An omen of death, they said between mumbled prayers.

Asher had walked the abandoned cemetery, seeking answers to satisfy his curious mind.

Blue lights hovering inches above the ground, close to the grave of a newly buried man. A flash of energy, perhaps? A fragment of the dead man's escaping soul? Each time he grew close, the lights would melt into the atmosphere.

Asher had been born to a struggling family in Bristol. His father had spent every penny on educating his son and Asher was determined to make the most of his opportunity. He dreamed with an expansiveness far greater than his station in life. Between endless hours of hauling fishing nets, he consumed as many books as he could manage. His mind was torn open by the riddles of science. Invisible life writhing beneath the glass of a microscope. That unfathomable chain of distant planets and moons.

Why turn to myth when the natural world held so much magic and mystery?

He found himself drawn to the work of the animists and their fascination with the human soul. What was it that separated the living from the inanimate? What was this inexplicable life force? A great, intangible mystery. A mystery Asher wanted solved.

The animists' ideas were controversial. Groundbreaking.

A soul is overactive and illness results. The soul chooses to leave the body and a man will die.

The idea obsessed him.

This would be his life, he decided. He had been blessed with an inquiring mind and he wanted all the world to know it. He would rise above the salt-stained filth of his fishing boots. Somehow, some day, he would make it to university. Study alongside those who shared his passion for knowledge. Seek answers to the questions that puzzled humankind.

For a pilchard fisherman, a university degree was as distant as the moon. But Asher held tight to his dream. One day he would make it reality. He felt certain of it, even if he had no clue as to how he would make it so.

There had to be a solid, scientific explanation to the corpse candles. He wanted to solve the mysteries of the natural world and he would begin with the riddles of the Cornish myths.

But his hunt for the solution led him down the same blind alley as so many of his searches in this place. A futile hunt for answers. A quest for evidence where there was none to be found.

"There." Scarlett puts down the razor and wipes his cheeks with a fresh cloth. "You are most handsome."

Asher runs a hand over his smooth cheek. He feels more like a man and less like something the sea coughed up.

His lifts his chin. Presses his shoulders back.

Behave, they say, like the man you wish to be.

"Take the lane up the hill," Scarlett tells him as they climb from the cellar. The tavern above is empty and dark. "Once you're out of the village you can follow the path into Killigarth or Polperro. Perhaps you'll find someone willing to give you work. Earn enough for passage to Penzance. Or back to London."

He hears sadness in her voice. Aiding his recovery has been her mission. She is not ready to let him go. Perhaps she imagines saving his life might fetter them together for eternity. And that, thinks Asher, would be serve him well.

"The thing is, Miss Bailey," he says, leaning towards her conspiratorially. "I don't want to leave Talland. I'm looking for something. And I believe it to be in these parts."

She leans closer. "Looking for what?"

He has her. "Have you ever heard of Henry Avery?"

"The pirate."

"Yes."

Excitement in her voice. "Of course. He plundered the Grand Moghul ships. Commanded a whole fleet of pirates. Biggest haul ever taken." Her eyes shine. "Hid his jewels somewhere on this coast, so they say." She steps closer. "Is that why you planned to come to Cornwall, Mr Hales? Are you looking for Avery's haul?"

He chuckles. She has been told a glorified version of the tale, he is sure. No word of the torture and rape Avery had inflicted on his victims. No word of the women who had flung themselves into the Persian Sea to avoid his crew's attentions.

Asher keeps the details to himself. Scarlett has fantasised about that hidden haul; he can see it in her face. She has dreamt of stumbling across jewels in the sand. Has glanced into rock pools in case something glittered beneath the surface.

"You think Avery's haul is real?" she asks.

"Far more real than the ghost ship that has your village so afeared." Asher gives a short smile. "Do I believe Avery buried a treasure chest in your landing beach? Of course not. Why would any man be foolish enough to do that? But I have reason to believe a little of that haul made it to these parts."

"What reason?"

"You have an interest in this, I see. Perhaps you might help me with my search."

"Ayes. Of course." She catches his eye. "In exchange for compensation should you find it."

Perhaps her head is not as full of air as he had first thought. He is coming to like this girl, in spite of her father's blood. "Compensation, of course. Perhaps you might start by relaying the stories you heard as a child. It would be a great help to hear these tales as they were told by local men."

Her smile widens. "It would be a pleasure. My father was most intrigued by Henry Avery. We used to dig in the sand and pretend we were looking for his treasure."

Good. Jacob had shared his fascination with Avery with his daughter. Perhaps he had also shared information.

Asher leans close; close enough to smell her honey soap and the salt on her skirts. He says: "This will be our secret, of course."

The rest is easy. He needs a place to sleep. Does she think the innkeeper will mind him curling up on her cellar floor while he begins his search?

"Oh no," says Scarlett. "You cannot stay down there."

And she leads him by the arm, up the hill to the candlelit cottage once owned by Jacob Bailey.

1724

Five men, pipe smoke and brandy. Could have been any night at sea.

Polperro to Saint Peter Port. Round trip, sixteen hours in good conditions.

Asher had completed the voyage several times. Each time, he'd tell himself it would be his last. He was an honest, hardworking fisherman. Soon an honest, hardworking surgeon. Not a man who dirtied his hands with moonshine.

The Cornish, they saw nobility in their free trade. A service that made lives better. But Asher had been born the wrong side of the Tamar to see greatness in the tax evasion and midnight rendezvous. Saw free trade as no more than theft.

But there was money to be made in smuggling. Plenty of it. Asher had dreams of greatness that a life hauling pilchards could not hope to fulfil. And so when Jacob Bailey had sat him down in the Ship Inn and spoken of a free trading run, Asher had listened.

Yes, yes sir, I can sail a cutter. Channel Islands?

A challenging voyage to be certain, but his hands were callused and his sea legs sure. He would make a challenging voyage a hundred times over if it saw his pockets filled with the enticing sum Jacob had promised.

The cutter was owned by the great Charles Reuben, so Jacob said. To Asher, Reuben was no more than a name, a myth. The man who would fill their pockets when the voyage was complete.

His ship held five men and their tankards comfortably when a black-glass Channel had them marooned in their own saloon.

With each emptied glass, the stories grew wilder.

Murmurs of a capsized ship. A debt that would fetter Jacob to Reuben until death.

And then; Henry Avery. Moghuls, pirate fleets, vanished jewels.

Asher snorted into his brandy. The story-teller, Albert Davey, had no family and few friends. A prime candidate for a man loose with the truth.

"I was there," Albert said.

Laughter.

Jacob leant forward. "You're a liar."

"I never lie. I was there, on the *Fancy* with Avery himself. I helped take the *Gunsway* from those Moghul bastards."

"You're a liar," Jacob said again. But Asher could see something behind his eyes. Challenge.

"They say that haul was hidden at Lizard Point," said Asher. "Men went searching for it a few years past. Said they had a letter from Avery himself saying it were hidden in the dunes. Didn't find a thing."

Albert snorted. "Of course they didn't. That letter was a fake. Avery was far too intelligent to hide his fortune in the sand."

"Then where is it?"

"Divided among his men, as the ship's articles dictated."

When the others were snoring around them, Jacob said: "They say it was the richest haul ever taken. If you've a share of it, why do you spend your days free trading for other men?"

"Because the sea is in my blood." Albert reached into his pack. He opened his fist. "My good luck charm."

The coin was rugged and silver; illegible, alien writing spun across its surface. Jacob took it from Albert and held it to the candlelight. Asher reached for it, but Jacob pushed his hand away. Gave Albert a crooked smile.

"Is there more?"

"Of course."

"Where?"

He laughed. "Why should I tell you?"

Neither man said more. But Asher saw something flicker behind Jacob's eyes.

THE MAN FROM THE SEA

She brings home the man from the wreck like a child presenting a crab she'd fished from a rock pool. There is no back slapping, no congratulations, no *well done, Scarlett, for saving a man's life*.

Caroline looks at Asher as though he were dripping with plague. "He cannot stay here," she says with dagger eyes. "We don't know a thing about him. Besides, how are we to feed another mouth?" She paces, slinging the baby from one hip to the other. "Isaac, tell this man to leave at once."

Scarlett feels something sink inside her. She has saved a man's life. Worth a little recognition, surely?

She has always been the one who has needed saving, feeding, scooping from the children's home. Always the burden, never the protector. She had assumed her gallant rescue might warrant at least a smile of approval.

She looks at Isaac, trying for some acknowledgement. He is uncorking a brandy bottle with a level of concentration Scarlett is sure isn't necessary.

"Forgive me, Mrs Bailey," Asher says in a velvety voice, his eyes following Caroline across the room. "I would hate to cause you trouble."

She doesn't look at him.

Finally, Isaac speaks. He has filled a glass and is swirling it in his hand. He stares into the whirlpool of liquid. "You found this man on the wreck? The ship was empty." Amber drops slosh over the side of his glass. "You told everyone it was a dead wreck, Scarlett. Why?"

"I thought it best to keep it a secret," she says. "Keep Mr Hales safe from Reuben."

"Why didn't you tell *me*?"

Why not? Because of the criticism she can see in his eyes. Because of *that was foolish, Scarlett.* And because of the distrust she can see he has for Asher. He is never trusting, her brother. Always waiting to be deceived and double-crossed. Guard always up. He will see a man's faults before he sees goodness.

She is sure he is looking now, wondering if the sailor from the ghost ship has dared touch his sister. And whether his sister has been bold and mad enough to touch the man from the ghost ship.

"We don't keep secrets," Isaac says finally.

Scarlett feels anger stir inside her.

It comes from nowhere, this rage in her blood. The Wild, she calls it. The wild thing that takes her over. Naming it makes it easier. Makes it a thing separate from herself.

It has been with her as long as she can remember. The sudden swings of anger, the blinding rage. Sometimes warranted, sometimes irrational.

When the Wild takes over, she feels she is watching herself from afar. Watches herself scream and curse and destroy. Watches thoughts fly through her head that do not belong to her.

But today she is determined not to let her anger out. Not in front of Asher. She closes her eyes. Inhales until she feels the dark thing within her lose its shape.

"I'm sorry," she tells Isaac, calmly, evenly. "You're right. We don't keep secrets." But the knowledge of Asher's search swirls warmly inside her.

What a thrill it is to be sharing a confidence with the mysterious man from the wreck. The men in her life are sea-stained and rough around the edges. Asher Hales shines among them. She sees an intelligence behind his eyes. The man come to Cornwall to unearth hidden riches.

Sharing his secret, she thinks, sliding the coat from his shoulders, is made even more appealing by the unwelcome reception her heroics have earned from her family.

Isaac empties his glass. Caroline looks at Asher, the extra mouth to feed. Her eyes blaze. She herds Gabriel into the bedroom, the baby warbling beneath her arm. The door slams.

Isaac watches Caroline disappear. He rubs the dark stubble on his chin. Brow creased in thought. He paces. Paces. Paces until Scarlett is mad with it.

"Mr Hales, please, you will take my room," she says, deciding her brother is not going to speak.

"I'll not take your bed. A blanket by the fire will be plenty."

"Please. I insist. You are still injured. I'll be quite fine by the fire. This way." She ushers him towards the bedroom, liking the feel of his arm beneath her fingers. She waits for Isaac to stop her.

"Sailor," he calls. "Can you handle a lugger?"

THE HOUSE ON THE HILL

Flora peers into the mirror and straightens her bonnet. The straw is coming loose in places, ribbons frayed at the edges. Every penny has gone into the Mariner's Arms. No time or money for hats and ribbons.

She straightens her back and lifts her chin. She might not look a successful business owner, but she can damn well act as one.

Charles Reuben's house is a sprawling brick monstrosity overlooking Polperro harbour. The building is cluttered with windows and chimneys, a ridiculous mock turret cobbled to one wall. Wealth, Flora realises, has little bearing on good taste.

Reuben's maid ushers Flora and Bessie into the parlour. The room glitters with gilded mirrors and polished tables. The windows are bathed in crimson curtains.

So this is what Isaac's ventures are funding.

Reuben's boots click against the flagstones. "Good afternoon, Mrs Kelly." He smiles warmly and eases himself into an armchair. "To what do I owe this pleasure?"

"I'm here on business."

"I see."

A black and white dog scurries into the room, its claws tapping rhythmically. Bessie grins and flings herself towards it.

"Bessie! Behave."

Reuben chuckles. "Take him outside, my dear. He could use a good run."

Bessie grins and hurries out to the garden, the dog trotting beside her.

Reuben gestures to an armchair so elaborately embroidered Flora is embarrassed to sit on it. "Please. We'll talk business over a cup of tea."

"I don't plan on staying long."

"Humour me."

She sits reluctantly. Takes off her bonnet and squeezes it between her hands. A clock on the mantle ticks away the seconds.

"I plan to open the Mariner's Arms," she begins.

"So I hear."

"You've a store of liquor in the bell house."

He nods.

"Do you have buyers?"

"Of course," says Reuben. "But that doesn't mean I can't spare enough to get your doors open. Will the Mariner's Arms be a licensed property?"

Flora's mouth is suddenly dry. "I have an ale licence. But as for the liquor…" She looks down, irrationally ashamed. "Well, perhaps in the future I will be able to do things lawfully…"

"So you also want my protection from the excisemen."

"I'm not asking for anything from you other than a sale. I'm willing to take my chances with the excisemen."

Reuben smiles. He laces his hands over his thick, waistcoated middle. "I'll see they don't come near you. If you wish to purchase liquor from me, it's in my best interests to keep your doors open."

The maid returns with a tea tray and pours two cups.

"How much were you hoping to purchase? I've deliveries of whisky going to the Three Pilchards and the Ship Inn." Reuben brings the cup to his lips. "But then there's the brandy from the wreck that unexpectedly fell into my hands the other night. I'm sure we can put some aside for you." He smiles. "That's if you don't mind taking goods from a ship many believe has brought a curse. To be honest, I've had trouble shifting the stuff."

"Then you'll give me a good price."

He chuckles. "Indeed. How much will you take?"

"I've ten pounds." A pitiful sum. Flora reddens.

"Then you'll take all twenty ankers. It's fine stuff. Cognac, I believe."

"I can't take that much. You're selling it to me far too cheaply."

"You can't very well run a public house with less."

Flora hesitates. Bessie flies past the window with the dog, her blonde hair streaming out behind her.

Reuben's cup clinks as he places it on the saucer. "You don't want to be indebted to me like your friend Mr Bailey."

Flora says nothing.

"You'll not owe me a thing, I assure you. Consider it a gift."

"I no more want to accept a gift from you," she says stiffly.

"I simply want to see the Mariner's Arms open, Mrs Kelly. The good people of Talland can't be traipsing over the clifftops every time they want a drink." He runs a finger through his beard. "My footmen will bring the goods to the inn this afternoon. You'll have the money for them then."

FAR-FETCHED TALES

Scarlett can tell her father's stories are useless. *Hmm,* says Asher as she garbles through tales of lost gold and sword-fights too dashing to be true. *I see.*

These are bedtime stories, she realises. Far-fetched tales Jacob had told while she peeked out from beneath her blankets. Whatever her father had known about Henry Avery, he had smoothed the edges for his five-year-old daughter.

The house is quiet. Close to midnight. Tomorrow, they will trade with an East India merchant in Falmouth. Isaac sleeps. Caroline has barely left her bedroom since Asher appeared at the door.

Scarlett pushes the pie she has baked across the table. "Eat. Please." If she cannot aid Asher's search, she can at least feed him. She passes him a fork. Asher Hales, she is sure, is not a man who eats with his hands.

He eyes the pilchard heads poking from the pastry. Then he digs in his fork. Chews slowly. "It's good. You're not eating?"

"You have it. You need a good feed more than I do."

He pushes the plate into the middle of the table. "We'll share. I insist."

Scarlett hesitates. Then, her hunger getting the better of her, she pulls a small piece from the edge of the pie. Asher digs in his fork again. Swallows the fish head-first.

"What are you doing?" she cries. "Eat that way and you'll turn the fish away from our coast. Tail first, if you please."

Asher gives a snort of laughter. But, Scarlett notices, he is careful to eat the tail of the next fish first.

When she has finished her mouthful, she says: "My stories are of no help."

Asher chuckles to himself. "No. They're not."

Her cheeks flush with embarrassment. "What will you do next? Where will you look? You must have your reasons for believing the haul is in this village."

"There was a man," he says, "who once showed me a piece of Avery's silver. A man from these parts. Said there was more. Said he had it well hidden."

"What man?"

"A former crewman of mine. And of Avery's. He died alone, very suddenly. Wherever he hid his wealth, I'll warrant it's still there."

"And if you find it? You will just take it?"

Asher leans close. She sees the faint lines around his eyes, the freckle beside his nose. "It's not theft, Miss Bailey. It's resourcefulness. It's how you rise to the top in this beastly world." He sits back in his chair and folds his arms. "Being a part of the convoy that captured the Moghul ships was this man's greatest achievement. He would have told others of the money. Perhaps hinted at where it was hidden. There may be people in this place who know something."

She will ask, Scarlett tells him. Seek out the wrinkled faces and gnarled hands and old minds who will remember the stories of a man who brought jewels to their shore. If the haul is here, she tells Asher, she will find it. She punctuates her announcement by slamming her tankard onto the table.

"Hush," he hisses, his eyes light with amusement. "You want to wake the witch your brother has married?"

Scarlett laughs.

He leans close. "Forgive me. I have judged her hurriedly."

"You have judged her well." Scarlett grins, buoyed by his nearness. She lowers her voice. "When my father died, he left us in great debt to Charles Reuben. It is a hard thing for Caroline. It is wearing her down after so many years."

"What kind of woman marries into a family with such a debt hanging over them?"

"The money, it never mattered to her. She and Isaac love each other. My brother is a good man, Mr Hales. He would do anything for his family. Caroline is lucky to have him."

For a long time, Asher says nothing. Finally: "Your father left you in quite the position."

Scarlett nods. "I know he couldn't bear it if he knew the life he'd left for us. Sometimes I fear he's not at rest at all."

Asher's eyes fall to the cracked hearth stones, the threadbare curtains. What must he think of this shabby, grey existence?

He points to the brass quadrant that sits on the shelf above the range. "Was that his?"

Scarlett nods. "An offering from a wreck."

"Your father was a wrecker?"

She feels a sudden flush of anger. Pushes it away. "No. My father was a good man. He'd never see a ship wrecked for his own gain. Wrecks happen in these waters, Mr Hales. The shores are rugged and the weather can change in an instant. We treat the ships that come to us as gifts. The food that washes up on our beaches keeps us fed. The wool keeps us warm."

"And what of my ship? What did that bring you?"

"Well." She smiles. "That depends who you ask. My father used to say a wreck would see a place haunted. He was very superstitious. Not that it helped him in the end."

"He was drowned?"

She nods. "He went out fishing in a dory one morning and never came home."

"And your mother?"

"She died not long after my father. Went to sleep one night and never woke up. I suppose she tried to live without him and couldn't. After that it was just me and Isaac." She picks at the pie crust. "The villagers speak of the corpse candles. They believe we have been cursed by the souls of your lost crew. I can tell you have no such beliefs. What do you think happened on your ship?"

Asher slides his chair back from the table. "Let's not speak of it."

"Why not?"

He folds his hands. "Those men were murdered," he says finally.

"Murdered?" Scarlett's stomach turns over.

"My crew were involved in the trade," says Asher. "The night of the wreck they were engaged with smugglers. Selling our cargo for a price. And they paid dearly for involving themselves with such men."

Scarlett shakes her head. "The free traders in these parts are fair men. Not killers."

Asher snorts. "I know of many free traders with blood on their hands."

"You're mistaken. I'm sure of it."

Asher pushes back the sweep of sandy hair that hangs over his eyes. The cut beneath it is still red and raw. He leans towards Scarlett. "This wound was not caused by the wreck. I was struck when I tried to fight the smugglers who boarded our ship. Knocked unconscious."

Scarlett raises her eyebrows. "Why fight them?"

"Because I believed the *Avalon* was a fine British merchant. She deserved better than to be caught up in the trade."

He sits back and ties his hair neatly at his neck. "Once, I was foolish enough to involve myself in smuggling. It near ruined my life. I'd never have signed aboard the *Avalon* if I'd known the sole purpose of the voyage was free trade." His voice hardens. "The men were blatantly flouting the hovering act. Had we been caught, I'd have been as guilty as the rest. I was not willing to risk conviction for something I didn't believe in. I was alone in my protests, of course. I was overpowered and knocked out. When I regained consciousness, I found the smugglers gone and my crew dead."

Scarlett sits back from the table. The pie feels heavy in her stomach. "Why were you spared?"

"Perhaps they believed me already dead."

She clasps her hands tightly in her lap. Asher's story feels cold and raw. "These men. What did they look like? Did you see their ship?"

"I'm sorry. I remember little. But I know I'm lucky to be alive."

Scarlett busies herself carrying the dishes back to the kitchen. "If you despise free trade so, why are you willing to come to Falmouth tomorrow?"

Asher catches hold of her wrist as she passes. Pulls her close. Her heart leaps into her throat. "You are to help me with my search," he says, his fingers moving on her wrist. "It's only fair I help you make your run, wouldn't you agree?"

"Ayes," she mumbles. "I suppose it only fair." She sits back at the table, entwining her fingers in her shawl. "We need to tell Isaac what happened to your crew. If you truly believe they were murdered, he needs to know there are traders out there willing to kill."

"No. You're not to tell anyone. I don't know who I can trust."

"You can trust Isaac."

"I don't know that."

"You trust me, don't you?"

"Yes."

"Then believe me when I say you can trust my brother."

Asher covers her hand with his. Squeezes tightly. Scarlett's heart shoots into her throat.

"This is between you and I. Promise me."

SEA MONSTERS

Here he is, tangled again in free trade. This time, under the command of Jacob's son. The irony is not lost on him.

"I want a guarantee," Asher says to Isaac. "If we're caught, you'll tell the revenue men I was forced into this. I'm willing to help you, but I'll not risk conviction."

Isaac nods faintly. "Ayes. A guarantee."

"And payment, of course. For this voyage and the run to Guernsey. Enough to see me out of this wretched place."

It is late afternoon when they slide out of the harbour towards Falmouth. The sun is dull and low, the sea leathery. A bunch of withered heather floats on the surface; Scarlett's sacrifice to the sea spirits.

Asher says little. He follows instructions, proves himself a knowledgeable sailor.

When the lugger is careening rhythmically along the coast, Scarlett hands him a mug of tea and sits beside him on the afterdeck.

"You know how to sail," he says.

"That surprises you."

"Most women I know would turn green if they even looked at a ship."

"You must know some right boring women." She is dressed in breeches, cinched alluringly at her narrow waist. She wears tall black riding boots, her hair bundled into a knot at her neck. "I've been sailing since I could walk. My father didn't believe I ought to be stuck at home with a needle and thread." She wraps narrow fingers around her mug; fingers Asher is sure have never once held a needle and thread. He can't deny she is intriguing.

Is it worth it, this gamble? His smooth-talking infiltration of the Baileys' world?

Perhaps not. One look at that rickety cottage had told him they had not a scrap of wealth. If Jacob had found the haul, he'd not shared it with his children.

And the stories? He'd been hoping for some clue, some fragment that might point him in the right direction. Jacob had had information about the haul's whereabouts, Asher is sure. But Scarlett's tales had been full of froth and fantasy.

Nevertheless, her trust is a valuable thing.

She will ask the villagers. Dig for tales and clues among those old enough to remember. And those wrinkled faces will look at her and see that poor, innocent maid whose family died around her and they will give up their secrets.

So, in the name of trust, he'd begun to toss out scraps of the story. A most unsettling, pitiable story of murder on the sea.

He had thought of telling Scarlett that he'd known the father she idolises. Thought fleetingly of telling her that first night, when she'd plucked him from the rising water.

But no. If he begins to tell the story of his time with Jacob, he might be unable to stop. She can't know things yet. Not until the desire in her eyes has her clinging on to every word he says.

This game, this girl must be played with care.

His story, of course, will sully her memories of a heroic father with the truth of who Jacob was. The picture of the caring family man she paints is very different from the Jacob Bailey Asher had known. How would she react if she found out the truth, he wonders? How *will* she react?

He'd not even been twenty when he'd stepped aboard Jacob's smuggling cutter. Had become drunk on dreams of the wealth that would see him become an educated, enlightened man.

Within months, his life was destroyed.

He was captured, convicted. Sold to a merchant as an indentured servant and hauled out to New England. Where there had once been reading and learning, there was digging, hauling, building. A decade of exile.

Asher blames it all on Jacob Bailey.

He takes a long mouthful of tea. His insides are shaken. He hates this backward, windblown land. Even at sea, this place is oppressive. A warren of narrow lanes and cramped harbours. Just being in the place, his breathing feels constricted. And yet that hollow promise of riches has drawn him back, as surely as if he were caught on the tide.

He glances sideways at Scarlett. Providence has served him well by wrecking him at her feet.

Seize the opportunity.

When Isaac has disappeared below deck, Asher reaches out and pushes back the strand of hair that has fallen across her eyes. She smiles crookedly, cheeks flushed.

Drawing her close will be easy. And, he thinks, his insides warm from the rare human contact, perhaps he might even enjoy it.

They reach the anchored merchant vessel by dusk. Scarlett stands at the wheel while Isaac climbs aboard the ship, Reuben's ledger in his pocket.

Her eyes are on the horizon. The corpse candles have not been seen in days, but she has no trust for the ocean. She scans the purple expanse of sea and sky.

The men of Isaac's crew are right to be afraid. Scarlett feels it too; an uneasiness inside her as they rise and fall with the sway of the sea. She feels the invisible presence of lost souls and water spirits. Imagines unseen monsters gliding beneath the ship.

The ocean had taken her father. His dory swallowed, body never recovered.

She had been seven years old when Isaac had sat her down and told her he too was to sail to Guernsey. She had been gripped with fear. The sea had taken her father and then, in its own twisted way, her mother. She couldn't bear for it to take her brother too.

No choice, Isaac had said. *Be brave.*

She had clung to his neck. Wrapped her legs around him tightly so she might tether herself to him. She didn't want to be brave. She had had enough of bravery.

Be brave, as she had farewelled her father, then her mother. As Dodge carted her over the cliff to the children's home.

Always, *be brave.*

Isaac's voice was muffled by her hair. "I'll be back soon, I promise."

He couldn't make such promises. Not really. Scarlett was a child, but she knew. Knew a man could promise and plan and pray all he wanted, but the sea chose at will who it would allow home again.

But she recognised sorrow in her brother's eyes as he said: "I'm sorry, Scarlett. I've no choice."

And so she unfurled her arms and legs and let him go.

Be brave, she had thought, when Isaac had told her Gibson and the other men had refused to come to sea.

He had secured Asher's services, but the lugger could not be sailed and loaded with less than three.

"The landing party?" Scarlett had suggested. But no, they were farmers, miners. No use past the bay. And so she said: "I can come with you."

Isaac raised his eyebrows. "I thought you'd be as taken with these ghost stories as the rest of them."

Scarlett laughed it off. Corpse candles? She'd rather deal with phantom lights than the anger of Charles Reuben. "Let me come, Isaac, please. I want to help. You know I can handle the lugger. Besides, I'm good in the dark. I can act as spotsman."

And so, here she is with a cold sky pressing down on her and merrymaids beneath her feet. Perhaps out here there is even a ship full of smugglers who would kill an entire crew.

She can't think of it. Monsters hiding at the bottom of the sea she can handle. But a murderous crew is far too real.

Isaac climbs back aboard the lugger. He and Asher shoulder the crates and barrels passed down from the merchant ship. Whisky, tobacco, tea. A roll of silk the colour of fresh blood. All carried below and hidden beneath the fake bottom of the lugger.

A passenger craft, they will say if customs comes prowling.

Ahead of them, the merchant slides into the dark.

Asher and Isaac heave the lugger's halyards and the sails spill noisily.

Isaac looks at Scarlett across the deck. *All right?*

She nods. She feels emboldened by the knowledge that she is of use. A help, not a hindrance. Today her brother will look at her and see more than the thing that has tied him to Talland and a life under the control of Charles Reuben.

A light on the sea. Her heart jumps— *corpse candles?* — but this is just a ship. "Light," she calls. "Three points to port."

Isaac lifts the spying glass. "It's Tom Leach."

"Revenue men?" Asher's voice is taut.

"They're free traders out of Polruan," Scarlett tells him, marching onto the foredeck. She squints, trying to make out the ship. Leach has decked out his cutter with a black hull and sails to slide undetected into the estuary. "They're thieves and liars. Bring a bad name to the trade." She looks at Isaac. "Should we let them catch us?"

He shakes his head. "Whatever they want I'm not interested."

A voice from Leach's speaking trumpet: "Isaac Bailey! We need to speak."

Isaac keeps the lugger steady. Gives no response. A gunshot splinters the stillness. He shoves Scarlett aside as a bullet flies across their foredeck. "The dogs," he hisses. "Let them catch us."

He stands at the bow as Leach's ship draws closer. Scarlett hovers at his shoulder, bolstered by her brother's nearness.

"That how you're doing things now, Leach?" says Isaac. "A trigger-happy rifleman on your watch?"

Their captain chuckles. "Only way to get your attention." Leach is tall and thin, a dirty black greatcoat hanging from his shoulders and a grey-streaked beard hanging from his chin. His narrow eyes make heat shoot down Scarlett's spine.

Isaac folds his arms. "What do you want?"

"You took the silk from the East India brig." Leach shakes the parchment in his fist. "Our agent placed an order for it. We already got buyers."

"Shame it's in my hold then."

Leach's eyes dart between Asher and Scarlett. "This the only rabble you can get to sail with you these days?"

"Indeed," says Isaac. "And I've still beaten you to the prize."

"Rabble?" Scarlett hisses, rage flaring suddenly.

"Stop," Isaac murmurs.

She grits her teeth. The muscles in her stomach tighten.

"Where are Gibson and the rest of your lot then?" Leach asks. "They been scared off by that wreck that washed up on your beach last week?"

Isaac says nothing.

A chuckle ripples through Leach's crew. Scarlett glances at the pistol in her brother's belt. What a satisfying thing it would be to pull the trigger and see Leach's blood stain his own deck. The vicious thought makes her breath catch. She shoves it away.

"The silk," says Leach. "Give it to me."

"Reuben placed an order for it," Isaac tells him. "If you've a problem, take it up with him. I'm just the runner."

"Ayes. Reuben's errand boy. Always will be."

"You know nothing, Leach!" Scarlett yells suddenly. "Shut your filthy mouth!"

Isaac snatches her wrist. "Enough." He looks over his shoulder at Asher. "Come about." He marches Scarlett towards the hatch. "Get below," he hisses. "Now."

She climbs down into the darkness. Crouches in the saloon with her knees to her chest. Forces herself to breathe deeply.

Somehow, the Wild is afraid of the dark. Somehow, when the light is gone, it takes the rest of the world with it. It takes Leach and the pistol. Takes cold stew, torn stockings, lying men. Takes the anger back to its hiding place. For all the ghosts that wait in the dark, Scarlett fears who she would be without it.

She feels the ship turn, carving its way towards home. Her breathing begins to slow. The violent thoughts fade into the blackness. But she finds herself thinking of wolf-eyed Tom Leach and the wreck coughed up upon their shore.

Dodge has heard the whispers.

Charlatan. Fraud.

He is grateful for the darkness. He can let anger crease his brow and make knots of his fists. More than thirty years he has been vicar of this scrappy parish. More than thirty years of soothing nightmares. Of reminding his people that power lies with God; the hand behind the natural world. And now, at the flickering of lights on the horizon; *charlatan, fraud.*

He had stood upon the clifftops at dawn for these people. Sent away the spirits that haunt them. But George Gibson had returned from his ill-fated fishing trip garbling of bad luck and omens of death. He has stirred up a panic. Cast doubt over the vicar's abilities.

From the cliff, he sees a flash of blue light shoot up from the sea. An empty pistol fired from Isaac Bailey's ship, alerting his men of his arrival. From the cliff at the edge of the churchyard, the lander responds with a flash of his lantern. The path to the church is clear.

Slowly, the landing party trudges up the hill; a paltry cluster of miners and farmers. Some little more than boys. Hunched under the weight of the ankers on their backs, they file into the churchyard and pile their goods into the vestry.

Charles Reuben watches, order papers crammed into his fist. Hidden in the shadows and dressed in his customary black, Dodge feels pleasantly invisible.

Footsteps up the lane. The Baileys have moored their ship and returned to Talland.

"Reuben's here," the girl hisses. "I've got to keep Mr Hales out of sight."

The vicar shifts curiously. He sees Isaac approach Reuben. Sees nothing of the girl, or the stranger of which she speaks.

"Take twelve ankers to the Ship Inn," Reuben tells the men. "Keep the rest in the church for later distribution." He hands Isaac the papers. "I trust you can take care of things here." And he is gone.

Dodge weaves through the crooked headstones. The girl hovers by the gate, a tall, thin man beside her. There is a disturbing, haughty air about the way he lifts his chin. A vague familiarity to him. Dodge cannot place it. Too many people have passed through this place in his time.

"Who is this?" he demands.

The girl starts. "It's no one, Father."

"No one?"

Her brother appears behind them. "He's an extra pair of hands, Father. Nothing more."

"An extra pair of hands from where?"

"It's not important."

Dodge clamps wiry fingers around the top of Isaac's arm. It will do a rattled community no good to find an unfamiliar face hiding among their graves. "Where did this man come from, Mr Bailey? Tell me."

Isaac sighs. "My sister found him on the wreck." He looks the vicar in the eye. "I trust you'll protect a man's life and not tell Reuben."

"Your crew won't like that. They are convinced that ship was cursed. They'll not welcome a man who came from it."

"My crew have given me little choice in the matter." He eyes the vicar. "Is it not your job to allay their fears, Father? They came to you for help and reassurance. And yet they're still afraid."

Dodge pushes away his anger. Anger is not what these people need. "I have asked the Lord's help to cleanse our village of the ill luck that came to us with this ship. And help will come. Perhaps your men would feel more at ease if they remembered that God works in His own time."

"Perhaps the men would feel more at ease if you didn't fill their heads with ghost stories each Sunday." Isaac turns away. Conversation over. "We've enough hands," he tells his sister. "Take Mr Hales back to the house."

THE GIRL WITH THE WHITE RIBBON

It is close to dawn when Isaac returns to the cottage. Light pushes beneath the door of his bedroom. Caroline is perched on the edge of the bed, buttoned into her cloak and riding boots. A worn wooden trunk sits at her feet.

"I can't do this anymore, Isaac," she says. "I can't live this way. Let's just go. Get as far away as we can."

He sits beside her. "Has something happened?"

A cold laugh. "Has something happened? The last decade has happened! All these years of handing everything over to Reuben. And now Scarlett brings home this jetsam from the wreck…" She rubs a hand across her forehead in frustration.

Isaac reaches for her hand. "I've tried leaving before. You know that. Reuben, he has eyes everywhere."

"That was a lifetime ago. You've been loyal to the man for fourteen years. Surely you've built up enough trust that he no longer has men spying on you in the night."

"How can we risk that? How can we put our children in that kind of danger?"

The children weigh on him heavily. A desperate, unconditional love, of course, but a constant, vague sickness in the pit of his stomach. Bringing children into this life? What had he been thinking?

Sometimes, gripped with anxiety, he watches them in their sleep. Gabriel's grubby half-moon fingernails. The veins in Mary's paper-thin eyelids. How can such innocence exist in this world of corruption?

Already, he can see so much of himself in his eight-year-old son. The crooked smile, the dark ribbon of hair tied at his neck. He can only pray he'll not pass on his debts as well.

And rosy, fragile Mary. Will she grow up creeping about in the moonlight like her aunt?

Isaac has already failed to keep Scarlett from dirtying her hands with free trade. The moment he'd begun working for Reuben, she'd had bladders of moonshine quilted into her skirts. He'll die before he sees the same thing happen to his daughter. But he will not risk her life by trying to flee without proper means of escape.

Caroline's cheeks are hot and pink, her eyes glowing. Her hand tightens around his. There is desperation in her touch. Anger.

How blessed Isaac had been to find her. A woman willing to marry into a life of debt to Charles Reuben. Into instant motherhood to a nine-year-old spitfire.

With Scarlett latched to him, Isaac had resigned himself to unmarried life. But then there was Caroline; lighting up the Ship Inn with her bell of a laugh and making Isaac's day hauling fishing nets seem a distant memory.

She sidled up to the bar and stood close enough for her shoulder to graze his. "Buy me a drink," she said, the gold flecks in her eyes lighting as she smiled.

Isaac grinned at her boldness. "How can I turn down such a request?"

"Well. You look a man who has no time for games." Her words were neat and polished beside his own clipped speech.

She wore skirts the colour of daisies; her dark hair tied with a thin white ribbon. Arrived in Polperro from the east, she said. No family. Twenty-one and left to make her own way in the world.

Isaac was taken by her optimism, her bravery. He told her of his own trials and felt not a scrap of shame. Her face was even as she listened without judgement or pity. She stirred in him some long-abandoned hope."

They escaped to a corner of the tavern and sat with their heads bent towards each other to keep out the rest of the world. Told tales of their lives and drank mahogany, until Isaac remembered he'd left Scarlett with a packer from the pilchard palace.

They were married by Dodge two months later; forty ankers of smuggled whisky in the vestry behind them.

She knew it all, of course. The debt, Isaac's role in the smuggling syndicate. Knew he had nothing to give her but love.

That was enough, she'd said. How could she want more?

Before Gabriel had arrived, she had joined him on his voyages to Guernsey. She would stand at the bow with her hair flying and her cheeks pink. Sprawl over his bunk like a siren, her skirts tossed to the floor.

Suddenly, with Caroline, there was hope. There was fireside conversation, arms around him at night. There was more on the supper table than sailors' rations; scraps of vegetables magicked into pies. There was someone to steer Scarlett away from the rudderless life he was providing.

But Caroline's optimism has faded. The spark behind her eyes is gone. How can he blame her? The pressure of debt, the bleakness of their future is enough to extinguish any light.

Isaac aches for her laughter, for her fingers pressing into his arm as the wind sweeps through their hair. He longs for her skirts on the floor of his cabin, her naked body in his bunk. Longs for that distant time when he didn't feel he had failed the woman he loves.

"There has to be an end to it." A waver in her voice. "If we take the lugger—"

"Steal Reuben's ship? We'll be at the mercy of the authorities. They'll hang me if we're caught. In all likelihood, they'll hang you too."

"We need to start taking risks. You say you don't want to put the children in danger by trying to leave, but can't you see it's just as unsafe for them here?"

"Why?" he hisses. "I'd never see any harm come to them."

"But you're willing for them to have the same life you and Scarlett have had?"

"Of course not. But what can I to do? Go behind Reuben's back? Deceive him and earn money on the side like my father tried to do?"

"Yes!" Caroline pulls him towards her. New lines around her eyes. New threads of grey at her temples. "What loyalty do you owe him? What decency? We both know your father's debt will never paid off. Reuben designed it that way. Deceiving him is the only way we will be free of him." She squeezes his hand, too tightly. "You're an intelligent man, Isaac. Hiding that whisky was clever. You've a resourcefulness in you that Reuben doesn't have. You've got to use that."

They've made these plans before. Complete runs behind Reuben's back. Earn enough for passage out of Cornwall. Tickets for a voyage to Scotland, Ireland, anywhere far from Reuben's watchful eyes. For fourteen years, Isaac has plotted and dreamed of ways to free his family. And each of those fourteen years, escape has seemed more distant. The drive to succeed has faded. Because the reality is always there, staring him down.

Once, his father had tried to deceive Charles Reuben. And the world had fallen down around him.

And so he climbs into bed, stepping over his wife's packed trunk. He hears himself mumble his apologies.

Caroline remains perched on the edge of the bed in her cloak and boots. Her eyes are hard in the candlelight. "You're a resourceful man, Isaac," she says finally. "But to hell if you're not full of excuses."

MARINER'S ARMS

'The appearance is said to be that of a man habited in black, driving a carriage drawn by headless horses. This is, I know, very marvellous to believe, but it has had so much credible testimony in my parish that some steps seem necessary to allay the excitement it causes. I have been applied to for this purpose, and my present business is to ask your assistance.'

Taken from a letter to Rev. Richard Dodge from Mr Gryllis,
Rector of Lanreath
1725

A creak of the door and the Mariner's Arms is open. An occasion worthy of the hike from Polperro.

By six, the tavern brims with laughter, chatter, ale-fuelled cursing. Glasses filled with brandy hauled from the ghostly *Avalon*.

George Gibson puts down his cup and scowls at Scarlett. "You're just trying to bait me, maid. This didn't come from that cursed ship."

"Flora says otherwise." Scarlett leans close. "Drink it. Feel the darkness flowing through your veins."

A curse? Perhaps. She's heard of stranger things. Either way, it's a pleasure to stir up grizzly George Gibson. A welcome distraction from Asher's tales of killers in the bay.

Gibson looks across the bar to Flora. "This true, Mrs Kelly? You serving the brandy Reuben's men brought ashore from the wreck?"

Flora plants a hand on her hip. "If you've a problem with it, don't drink it."

"I'm surprised at you, Miss Bailey," he says loudly. "Working for a landlady who's been dealing with Charles Reuben."

Scarlett glances at Flora. She had mentioned nothing of her business with Reuben. Still, Scarlett can hardly claim to be surprised. She shrugs. "A person wants to open a tavern in these parts they've little choice but to deal with Reuben."

Gibson snorts. "And what's he gone and done? Sold her brandy from a cursed wreck."

"What's this about a wreck?" This is Bobby Carter, sidling to the bar with a dimpled grin. He wears the brass buttons of the revenue men and the loose morals of the free traders. Pockets full of smuggling riches in exchange for protection.

Men like Bobby are hauled out of the preventative service regularly. Strung up to cries of *corruption* and *shame*. But Bobby has a decency Scarlett has seen in few men from either side.

"One day, Scarlett Bailey," he'd told her, swanning around the Ship Inn in his blue and yellow uniform, "I'm going to make an honest woman of you."

She had laughed and snatched his glass. Emptied it in one mouthful. "You'll have to make an honest man of yourself first. Weren't it Reuben's money that bought this whisky?"

Bobby winks at Scarlett, his cheeks round and pink. "Never heard of no wreck."

She grins. Pours him a glass from the kettle beneath the bar in which Flora has hidden the liquor. "Indeed you haven't. And that's why we love you."

He tosses back the brandy, blue eyes sparkling. "I can feel the darkness in me already."

She laughs. When Bobby is around, ghost ships and curses fade away.

"You're both asking for trouble," says Gibson. "Making light of such things. The vicar ought to have a word in your ears."

"Thought you'd lost faith in the vicar," says Scarlett.

"I was a fool. God works in His own time, so he does. Dodge will rid us of the lights. He's always come through for us in the past."

"The man's a fraud," Bobby snorts. "Laying ghosts and demons not a soul can see."

Gibson bristles. "Dodge laid the ghosts on Blackadown Moor. There were plenty of souls saw that carriage. Headless horses and all, so they say."

"So they say." Flora smiles crookedly. "Did you see this ghostly carriage, Mr Gibson?"

He slides from his stool. "You don't need to see a thing to know it's real."

"There are no demons in Cornwall," says Flora. "They're too afraid they'll be made into a pie."

Scarlett laughs.

Gibson jabs a finger at her. "Your father knew better." He disappears out the door, leaving his brandy untouched.

Bobby slides onto the vacated stool. He leans across the bar so his face is close to Scarlett's. "They say you're keeping a man from that wreck for your own purposes."

Her cheeks flush. "They're lying."

Bobby tugs at the strand of hair hanging over her cheek. "I hope so. Or I fear my poor heart would break."

Scarlett's eyebrows shoot up as two riding officers walk through the door. "What are you doing bringing the cavalry?" she hisses at Bobby.

"Calm yourself. They're here for a drink, is all. They don't want no trouble." He grins at Flora. "Give them all a serve of shipwrecked brandy."

She empties Gibson's glass and nudges the kettle further beneath the bar. "As far as they're concerned I'm nothing but an alehouse." She fills three glasses from the anker of spiced ale and lines them up along the counter for the riding officers. "Try the lambswool, gentlemen. Specialty of the house."

And here is Charles Reuben, swanning in, nodding to the officers.

Bobby flashes Scarlett a grin. "See? We're all friends here."

Scarlett narrows her eyes at Reuben. "What do you want?"

"Nice to see you making an honest woman of yourself, Miss Bailey." He smiles, more to himself than Scarlett. "Ale, if you please."

She hesitates. Reuben is a man with eyes everywhere. If there is information to be known about the wreck of the *Avalon*, he will have it. She has promised Asher her silence, but the thought of the murders gnaw at her constantly.

She lowers her voice. "What do you know about the crew of that wreck?"

"I asked for an ale," says Reuben. "Fetch it for me, then perhaps I'll answer your question."

Scarlett fills a tankard and tops it with a glob of spittle.

Flora sighs. Takes the glass from Scarlett and empties it into the trough. Gives her a fresh tankard and a warning look.

Scarlett dumps the ale on the bar in front of Reuben. "Tell me what you know."

He sips slowly. "What makes you think I know anything?"

"Because whenever there's something untoward, you've always got your hands in it."

Reuben chuckles. "I've always liked you. That sharp tongue of yours keeps things interesting."

She narrows her eyes. "An entire crew vanished from that ship." Careful words. Nothing that might give away Asher's presence, Asher's theory. "These are free trading waters. Perhaps they were involved in smuggling."

"Very likely. But I can't tell you what happened to those men. If that curious mind of yours is seeking answers, you'll have to look elsewhere."

She eyes him. "Are you lying?"

"You know I don't lie. And you know I've never given you any reason not to trust me. Besides, I don't know why you're asking me. You'd never catch me out at sea. Speak to your brother. Perhaps he's come across some unsavoury creatures in his travels."

"My brother does not associate with unsavoury creatures. He's a good man."

"Just like your father, is that right?" Reuben chuckles. "Ah, Miss Bailey. It never ceases to amaze me you can be so deep in free trade yet see such goodness all around you."

She folds her arms. "I don't see goodness in you."

The lights of the Mariner's Arms glitter in the bend of the road.

The grand opening.

Isaac is glad of it. He needs a drink.

Needs to see Flora.

No, needs a drink.

He'd met with the traders' banker in Polperro. "I want the conditions of my arrangement with Charles Reuben to be rewritten."

"You'll need to speak to Mr Reuben himself."

"You think I've not tried?" Isaac hissed, stifled by the curtain of pipe smoke in the banker's office. "He'll not see me. Told me to speak with you."

He'd take the moral approach, he'd told himself. Going behind Reuben's back was trouble. "I've been loyal to the man for fourteen years. I want terms that will allow my father's debt to repaid. A reduction in interest."

"The terms of repayment were signed by your father before his death. I'm afraid there's little room for negotiation."

Isaac curses to himself as he marches down the hill. He will be forced to go back to Caroline and tell her of his failure. Why has he been condemned to take the moral approach when corruption is all around him?

He shoves open the door of the inn. Inside is hot and noisy. Traders share tables with revenue men. Bobby Carter playing both sides. Reuben in animated conversation with Scarlett.

Bastard. Rather spend his time drinking than be bothered giving his captain an hour of his time. Isaac marches towards him, simmering with frustration.

Flora catches his eye across the room. Her face lights. Isaac feels his anger dissipate. He'll not confront Reuben. Not now. He'll push his own miserable problems aside and be happy for Flora.

He returns her smile and slides onto a stool.

She darts back behind the bar, blue skirts swilling. She is striking; her cheeks pink and eyes alight. Blonde hair swept into a neat knot on top of her head. Isaac finds it hard to look away.

"You made it," she smiles.

"Of course." He leans over the bar to kiss her cheek. "Jack would be very proud."

"Thank you, Isaac. I couldn't have done it without your help." She drops her voice. "Your meeting. Was it a success?"

He glances across the room at Reuben. "Let's not speak of it here."

The door creaks. In come Tom Leach and three of his men. Isaac watches Reuben's face darken.

"Who brought these dogs?" Scarlett says brassily.

Flora leans close to Isaac. "Who are they?"

"Tom Leach and his men. From Polruan."

"Traders?"

He nods. "Ayes. Been making trouble for us."

Scarlett moves towards them, but Isaac grabs her wrist. "Leave him."

"I'll not make trouble," she whispers. "Just want to find out why they're here."

He sighs.

Flora hands him a glass. "She just wants to impress you. You know that, don't you."

He smiles wryly. Holds out a penny.

Flora shakes her head. "Put it away."

Scarlett sashays across the bar towards the men. "Don't you have your own taverns to destroy?"

Leach grins. "We've come all this way just to see you, dearest."

"Are you planning on ordering a drink? If not, you can bloody well get out."

"You hear that, innkeeper?" calls Leach. "Your bar wench is threatening to throw us out on the street!"

Flora raises her eyebrows. "It seems my bar wench is a good judge of character."

Isaac hides a smile.

"Don't you go making out you're the innocent ones," Leach tells Scarlett. "Your brother over there took that French silk we had our names on."

"I'm sorry," she says. "It would have looked most becoming on you."

Leach glares. "This has happened too many times."

"Your issue is with Reuben and his agent. Not with Isaac. Or are you too stupid to know how this game is played?"

He lurches towards her. Isaac leaps from his stool, but Reuben steps in front of Scarlett, pressing a firm hand to Leach's chest.

"She's right," he says. "Your issue is with me. We can discuss it further if you wish."

Leach hovers. Considers further discussion. Then one of the other men pulls him away.

"The bastard ain't worth it," he hisses.

Reuben runs a hand over his shorn chin. Watches them leave. "You ought to be careful who you let through these doors, Mrs Kelly."

Flora shrugs. "Their coin is as good as anyone's."

"They're trouble."

"I can handle them."

"Yes," says Reuben. "I don't doubt that."

Light and laughter spills from the inn. Asher keeps walking. The church is dark and empty. He tries the vicarage.

"Oh no," says the young woman who answers the door. "The reverend doesn't take lodgings here." She points him up the winding hill towards Killigarth.

Asher follows the woman's directions to a manor house on the edge of the village. Knocks. "I need to see the vicar."

The maid leads him into a lamp-lit parlour. Dodge is reclined in an armchair, his stockinged feet stretched towards the fire and a glass of brandy pressed to his chest. Without his wig, thin white hair rises from his head like wisps of smoke. He looks up as Asher approaches. "You're the man from the wreck."

"Yes."

The vicar rubs his chin, considering. After a moment, he gestures to the armchair beside him. Asher perches on the edge.

"Is it your lost crewmates that bring you to me?"

Asher smiles crookedly. His lost crewmates? Those men can stay hidden at the back of his mind until time removes them completely. "I need information," he says. "About a man from this area."

Dodge drums his fingers against his glass. "Which man?"

"Albert Davey."

The vicar makes a noise from the back of his throat. He empties his glass and sets it on the side table. "Why do you seek information on poor Albert Davey?"

"That is my own business."

Dodge's voice darkens. "Leave the past where it is, Mr—"

"Hales."

"Mr Hales. I suggest you leave this place. The people believe your ship has cursed the village. If they see you walking the streets, it is hard to say where their fears will lead them."

"Perhaps to the tales of ghosts and demons you are so fond of?"

"Perhaps." Dodge gives a humourless smile.

Asher chuckles. "I am neither ghost nor demon. Any sane man can see that."

Dodge clasps his wiry hands. "This is a village of believers."

"Because you have made it so."

"Yes."

Asher leans forward. A log shifts and crackles in the grate. "And are you a believer too, Father? Do you believe demons walk Bridles Lane? Or do you believe only in the gold Charles Reuben lines your pockets with?"

Dodge's eyes harden.

"How many of your villagers know their church is full of smuggled goods?" Asher keeps his voice even, controlled. "Such a thing would shake their faith, would it not?"

Dodge breathes heavily, noisily. "The people would not believe a word that came from you."

"Are you so certain of that?"

For a long time, the vicar doesn't speak. The fire pops loudly. Finally, he says: "What do you want?"

Asher smiles faintly. "Albert Davey. Tell me where he lived."

Flora heaves closed the door and slides the key into the lock. Drunken voices disappear up the lane.

Scarlett smiles, reaching for a broom. "Congratulations. A success."

Flora pours two cups of brandy from the kettle. *A success.* She allows herself to savour the words. She paces across the bar with the tin cup in her hand and a faint smile on her lips. Runs a finger along one of the seashells on the shelf. "Sit, Scarlett. Drink. We'll clean later."

Scarlett hesitates.

"In a hurry to leave, are you?" says Flora. "Does this have anything to do with your shipwrecked sailor?"

Scarlett's cheeks flush.

Flora sits, sips her drink. The alcohol softens her aching muscles. "Please be careful. None of us know a thing about him." The man from the wreck has a vague familiarity to him; one she has been unable to place. But he is no stranger to Talland; of that she is sure.

"I trust him," Scarlett says defensively. "I don't want to live my life seeing the worst in people as my brother does."

Flora nods. A difficult case to argue. "Go to him if you wish."

"No. We ought to celebrate." Scarlett takes her cup. "Are you worried about Bobby bringing the revenue men?"

Flora shrugs. "They just want a cheap drink like the rest of them."

"And what if the excisemen were to pay you a visit? What if they catch you serving liquor? Ask to see your licence?"

Flora looks down. She feels oddly reluctant to tell Scarlett she has secured Reuben's protection against the excisemen. Accepting so much help from him feels like a betrayal.

"They'll not be bothering us," she says shortly. "They're easily bought. And with this place open, I've had the last of the vicar and his games."

Scarlett rolls the cup between her hands. "Why did Dodge ask for your help with his exorcisms?"

"I suppose he knew I needed the money. Felt sorry for me, perhaps. After Jack."

"No. You were helping him long before Jack died."

Flora glances down. In the corner of her eye, she can see a grin on Scarlett's face.

"My mamm, she used to come to your mamm. When one of us were sick and the like. I remember her boiling herbs on the range. Making teas that smelled of faraway places. She was a healer, wasn't she. A charmer."

Flora nods.

Scarlett peers over the top of her glass. "Is Dodge keeping you close because he fears you have her abilities? Because he fears it ungodly?"

"I have no abilities. Nor did my mother. The graves of your brothers and sisters ought to tell you that."

Scarlett shrugs. "That were God's way." She leans forward. "Do you ever think of it? Doing as your mother did?"

"No." Flora empties her cup and grabs the broom. "Never."

With Scarlett gone, she climbs upstairs, letting the sudden stillness of the inn wash over her.

"I did it, Jack," she murmurs. "Are you proud?"

Silence, of course. Her heart lurches.

She peeks into Bessie's room. Her daughter is asleep on her back, pale hair fanned out across the pillow. Flora pulls the door closed, too overcharged to sleep.

She carries a lamp into the parlour and lights the fire. Perches on the edge of a chair and stares into the flames. If she is honest with herself, excitement over the inn accounts for only half her jittery state. Scarlett's comments have worked their way beneath her skin.

Her mother the healer. Flora remembers people coming to the inn at all hours.

Fix my cough, my cuts, my curse.

Her talents had done little to help the Baileys, but people had kept coming.

Flora has made no attempt to follow her mother's path. She wants the Mariner's Arms to be the thriving business she and Jack had dreamed of, not a wish house for the desperate souls of Talland. And yet there is a restlessness within her, stirred up by Scarlett's prying.

She leaps suddenly from the chair. Paces down the hall.

When her mother had died, Flora had been unable to part with her belongings. But nor could she bear to look at them. Instead, she had piled them into one of the empty guest rooms on the second floor.

The passage is narrow and crooked. Her bedroom and Bessie's at one end, beside the parlour and kitchen. At the other, the three untouched rooms. A room for her mother. Her father. Her husband. Too many rooms that brim with loss. Too many untouched shrines to the dead.

She will open them all. Go through each locked chest. Keep the good memories and dispose of the bad. Now the tavern is open, she has to look forward. And she will start with her mother's room. Tonight.

She turns the handle slowly. The door sticks, creaks. She shines her lamp around the room. Her mother's things are everywhere; ankle boots crammed beneath the wash stand; a pile of books beside the bed, threadbare cloak hanging from the back of the door. Everything is blanketed in dust.

A scratched wooden chest is hidden in the corner. Flora unlatches the lid. Inside is a jumble of glass bottles and wooden boxes. Pouches crammed with dried herbs. A gold-rimmed hand mirror with a painted black surface.

Flora has told no-one of the hours she and her mother had spent among these bottles and herbs. Told no-one of the days she had spent memorising remedies and incantations.

As a child, such things had been indisputable. But with Jack's arrival, Flora had begun to see the world through adult eyes. Easterner's eyes. Jack had laughed at the rhymes and rituals. Smiled politely at Flora's mother when she spoke of her craft, but there was a humour behind his eyes. Flora had begun to see the humour too. She kept her knowledge of such things a secret from Jack. A fragment of her past she'd become ashamed to admit to.

But Jack is not here to see her now. No one is here to see. She carries the chest back to the parlour and lifts out a tattered cloth bag. The worn fabric in her palms makes her feel suddenly, happily close to her mother. She opens the bag.

A musty floral scent rises into the darkness, plunging her into her childhood. The bag is full of dried flowers and herbs. She lifts out the fragile leaves, one by one.

Groundsel, for fever.

Brambles for a burn.

Out with thee fire and in with thee frost.
In the name of the Father, the Son and the Holy Ghost.

The incantation comes to her like a long-forgotten nursery rhyme.

Now the mirror. Firelight flickers across its black surface; a glimmer in a bottomless pond. Flora stares into the dark glass.

How many times had she watched her mother sit with the glass in her lap, eyes growing vacant as she stared into its surface, waiting for images to appear. Pieces of the future, plucked from the depths of the mirror.

Flora smiles wryly to herself.

Pieces of the future. As real as the demons cowering beneath Dodge's whip.

She puts down the mirror.

Her work with the vicar has left her jaded. She sees the irony. Dodge has kept her close so she might embrace the power of God. But instead she has been left with a world unenchanted.

A pouch of herbs, a jar of animal hair. Black mirror. These things are not cures. These things are just trickery. This is nothing but a chest of false hope. A craft built upon trickery and deceit.

Flora shoves the mirror back in the trunk. She will not involve herself in such things. Not after ridding herself of Dodge's games. Her world may be unenchanted but its edges are clear.

She peers into the chest. Sees her own eyes stare back at her from the depths of the mirror. She hurriedly slams the lid.

FALSE HOPE

Everyone has a tale about Henry Avery.

With each story, the haul gets bigger. Mountains of gold, silks and spices. Enough jewels to bathe in.

Everyone has a theory. The haul stolen, spent, divided. Buried in the sand at Lizard Point.

"Lizard Point?" Scarlett says flippantly, swimming through endless cups of sweet tea. "Oh, how interesting."

No, she tells them, she is asking for no reason. Nothing but curiosity.

After winding her way through Polperro and Killigarth, she ends at the door of her neighbour, Martha Francis.

Martha's eyes light up at the visitor. She tugs Scarlett inside and plies her with saffron cake.

Scarlett sits at the table and eats. For a moment she is a child again, coddled by Martha while Isaac's lugger slides soundlessly to Guernsey.

But: "Henry Avery," Scarlett says and the smile disappears from Martha's lined face.

"Oh Scarlett. There's nothing to those stories."

Scarlett shuffles to the edge of her chair. "Ayes, there is. I can tell by your reaction."

Martha sighs. She looks down, cobwebs of hair falling over her cheeks. "Don't do this, my girl. Your father was convinced that haul was real. For a time, he talked of nothing else. But you can see what it was can't you? It was his way out. He'd find that money and be under Reuben's control no longer." She reaches for Scarlett's hand. "I know things are not easy for you and Isaac. But searching for something that doesn't exist will only bring you disappointment."

"My father believed it was real. Why?"

"It was his desperation talking." Martha squeezes her fingers. "Don't go digging up the past, *cheel-vean*. Please. Don't give yourself false hope."

Scarlett pushes her plate away, her appetite gone.

Martha reaches for her arm as she makes for the door. "Is it true you found a man on the wreck?" Her voice is hushed, though they are the only ones in the house.

"Where did you hear that?"

The old woman shrugs. "Word gets around."

Scarlett sighs. "Dodge."

"Don't be like that. You can trust me. So did he tell you what happened? How did the rest of his crew die? Is there anything strange about him?" Her grey eyes glitter in pitted cheeks.

"The vicar is mistaken. There was no one on that ship. It was a dead wreck." Scarlett feels a pang of guilt at her lies. But there is a wreck in the bay and corpse candles on the horizon. People mumble prayers and speak of approaching death. Every scrap of misfortune is attributed to the curse. Lost cats, burnt bread, broken windows; each the result of the wreck the sea spirits flung upon their shore.

What would the villagers see in the man crawled from the ship? A hint of the devil, perhaps?

There has been talk, of course. In this place, there is always talk. A man from the wreck. A man who had fought off the sea monsters or sirens or the great sweep of the sea. And for such a tale to come from the vicar, well, what can it be but truth?

"No," Scarlett says when people approach her in the street. "The vicar is mistaken."

"Mistaken?" Martha Francis repeats.

Yes, mistaken. She will forget about Avery's haul, she promises, if Martha speaks no more about the man pulled from the sea.

The man pulled from the sea stands outside the house once inhabited by Albert Davey. A pauper's house on the edge of Polperro; cramped and dark, the roof sagging, windows patched. A thin line of smoke rises from the chimney.

Sixteen years, of course, since Davey had lived here, but even without the chipped paint and broken glass, it hardly looks the cottage of a man with a pocket of foreign riches.

Asher peers through the window. The fire is smouldering beneath a black iron pot, underskirts hung over a chair to dry. He feels a faint sinking inside him. No doubt the cottage has been lived in since Davey's death. If he'd hidden his share of the haul here, it would have been found. Still, he has come this far. Prised the information from the vicar. He needs to get inside.

The door is locked. He rattles the wood covering the broken window. It is damp, pliable. Easy to snap.

He glances over his shoulder. The street is empty. He scrambles through the gaping window on his front, landing heavily on his hands. Pain shoots through his wrists. The cut on his head throbs.

He scrambles to his feet. The house smells of wood smoke and wet laundry. The soup pot on the fire is simmering. Whoever lives here could return at any time. Asher glances around. What is he hoping to find?

He thumps on the wall. Solid brick. He walks the length of the room, keeps thumping. Solid brick, solid brick. No hiding places. He tries the floor. Packed earth; dense and unyielding.

He hears voices and footsteps at the back of the house. He scrambles out the window and runs.

When Polperro is behind him, he stops, gasping down his breath. Sweat runs down his back. There is an ache in his knees, reminding him he is no longer the agile teenager he had been last time he'd visited this place.

He sits on the edge of the path and watches the sea roll towards the cliffs. Tries to untangle the emotions swirling inside him.

Disappointment? A little, yes, but he'd known from the beginning that visiting Davey's cottage was unlikely to bring results. He feels strangely invigorated. Perhaps by the charge up the cliff path, or perhaps by the knowledge that he has returned to Albert Davey's world. The knowledge that, although the haul is still hiding, he is closer to it here than he has been for almost two decades.

Or perhaps it is the knowledge that he has Jacob's daughter on his side. He can see now he will need to take his search further afield. Find people from the past, push aside the secrets and lies. How valuable Scarlett will be.

But not yet. She needs to trust. Needs to believe every word that comes from him. Needs not to let go when he turns her world upside down.

SAINTS DAY

Caroline has been busy. Isaac finds the house brimming with scents of lamb and plum cake; a lavish Feasten Sunday supper.

Underneath it is another, earthier scent. Plants. Animals.

Caroline leans over the table, spreading a tray with dark, wet leaves. Gabriel kneels up on a chair, watching his mother with interest.

Isaac slides off his coat. "What is this?"

"The tea you landed the other night." Caroline doesn't look up. "I'm making us a little money."

And he realises at once what she is doing. Soak elder leaves in water seeped with dung. Dry them, bake them, crumble to resemble tea. Mix with the real thing. Half the tainted tea back in Dodge's vestry. The rest in their hands.

Caroline smiles out the corner of her mouth. "I'm sure you could find a gentleman or two interested in purchasing a fine French infusion."

"That tea was hidden in the church," says Isaac. "How did you get your hands on it?"

She shrugs. "Town's going mad. The wind blows the wrong way and everything falls to pieces. Your son and I managed to get our hands on the stuff while the vicar was busy consoling Martha Francis."

"Gabriel stole this?" Isaac feels something twist inside him.

The boy grins. "I sneaked in like a mouse, Tasik. The father never knew I was there."

Isaac forces a smile. Runs hand through Gabriel's knotted hair.

Caroline wipes her hands on her apron. "Don't give me that look, Isaac. I'm doing this for the good of our family. I'm going to earn enough for tickets out of this place. I'm going to get us out of this life. As you ought to be doing."

He hears footsteps come towards the door. "Put the tea away. I don't want Scarlett knowing about it."

"I've not dried it yet."

Scarlett lets the door slam. "What's all this?"

Isaac takes the tray of leaves into the bedroom. "Nothing you need to involve yourself with."

Scarlett goes to the table, the man from the wreck trailing. She peers at the spilled leaves, at the bags of tea leaning against the table leg. Hand on hips, accusingly. "Did you steal those from Reuben?"

"You heard your brother," Caroline says sharply. "It's nothing you need to involve yourself with."

"We shouldn't keep secrets," says Scarlett, infuriating because she is right.

What is that look in her eyes? Disappointment. It hits Isaac hard.

She has always looked up to him. Respected, listened. Never given him this thinly veiled scorn.

Caroline sweeps the stray leaves onto the floor. She spoons boiled potatoes from a pot on the range and sets the bowl on the table. Looks at Asher, then back to Scarlett. "This man is not welcome at our supper."

"Of course he is."

"The saint's day is a sacred occasion. I don't want a stranger at my table. I don't trust him."

"Sacred occasion," Scarlett snorts. "The house smells of sheep dung."

Gabriel giggles and lurches towards the potato bowl.

Scarlett glares at her brother. "I'm no fool, Isaac. I can see what you're doing. I never took you for a thief." She flings her cloak off dramatically. "Mr Hales will stay."

Caroline's eyes meet Asher's. "You are not welcome here," she says again. "Leave."

Asher smiles slightly.

"Isaac!" Scarlett demands. "This man has agreed to come to Guernsey with you! We'd be lost without him! Are you really going to let your wife cast him out of the house?"

Isaac looks at Caroline. Scarlett is right to be angry, of course. This animosity she has towards the man has come from nowhere. And he needs Hales to make the Guernsey run. But he will not, *cannot* disappoint his wife any longer. "You will do as Caroline has asked."

Scarlett huffs and pulls on her cloak.

"Where are you going?" he demands.

"I'll not stay here."

"Caroline has prepared supper for you."

"And I am to be grateful?"

"Ayes," Isaac says tautly. "You are to be grateful."

Scarlett snorts. Her eyes flash.

Isaac walks away, leaving her fuming in the kitchen. He is no mood to deal with her dark streak. If she is to let loose that temper, she can damn well do it in the street.

Scarlett snatches a brandy bottle from the shelf. "Let's leave," she tells Asher. She looks back at Caroline. "Mr Hales has done nothing to you. What a sad life you must lead to be so untrusting."

A sad life, thinks Isaac. Scarlett's words leave a coldness inside him.

Caroline stares after her. "It's time you found that girl a husband. See her settled in a life of her own." She heaves the stew pot from the range. "You've done enough for her, Isaac. It's time you let go a little."

He knows what she really means. Time for them to raise their children without Scarlett's brassy chatter and shipwrecked sailors.

But he finds it hard to let go. Hard to cast his sister out into the world with his questionable parenting behind her. Scarlett has strength, but there is plenty within her that could set her adrift. Her blind naivety. The way she trusts so easily. And that wildness hiding in a corner that twists her into a different woman.

"I promised her she could make her own choice of husband," Isaac tells Caroline.

She laughs coldly. "And look at the choices she's making." She spoons the stew into three bowls. "You're hungry, I hope. No point letting her share go to waste."

"Why not ask Flora and Bess to join us? It seems foolish for us to be celebrating alone."

"The food is on the table, Isaac. I've been cooking all day. I don't want you to eat it cold."

There is more to it, of course. Caroline and Flora barely share a word these days. The four of them had been inseparable when Jack was alive. The men at sea, the women sharing each other's kitchens. Gabriel and Bessie sharing each other's toys.

Now there is guilt, regret. Blame, perhaps.

Caroline had pulled away from Flora after the accident. Couldn't bear to look in her in the eye.

Isaac knows Flora has never held him responsible for Jack's death. But Caroline? Though she has never said a word, Isaac knows there's a part of her that wonders.

"Perhaps it would do you good to see her," he says. "Remember how things were."

Remember that once we were happy.

Caroline sets his bowl in front of him. "Isaac," she says, "will you say the grace?"

He feels an ache deep inside him. The futility of trying to recapture something that can never be restored.

Asher follows Scarlett out of the cottage and up the hill.

Is she angry on his behalf? Or angry that her heroics have not been properly recognised? The brandy bottle swings in her fist. He hears *Caroline* and cursing.

"Dishonest," she hisses. "That's what this is. Stealing Reuben's tea and tainting it for their own gain. It's dishonest thieving, Mr Hales." She storms past the beach. "My brother is not a dishonest thief."

The tea laced with sheep dung would suggest otherwise, Asher thinks.

"And to throw you from the house after all you've done for us? How dare she? How dare *he*?"

He watches her curiously. Energy is exuding from her. Where is sweet-spoken Scarlett who had baked him pilchard pie?

She leads him to the clifftop. The village below is a wash of lamplight. A crowd follows a piper up the street, the guttural melody floating on the wind.

Asher remembers coming here as a young man. Come to think, reflect, dream.

Scarlett uncorks the brandy. Drinks. Passes him the bottle.

He wants to tell her it doesn't matter. He has no desire to sit down for a Feasten supper with Caroline Bailey and her viper tongue. But he is curious to see where Scarlett's anger will take her. How much of her father's blood is running through her?

He takes a gulp of brandy and hands the bottle back to her.

"The village thinks your haul is a myth," she says finally. "Martha Francis tells me my father's interest came only from his desperation."

Asher makes a noise from the back of his throat.

She turns to face him. The brandy and the charge up the cliffs have flushed her cheeks. Dark hair falls across her face. "But you believe the haul is real. And you're not driven by desperation." She looks at him with hot eyes. "What are you driven by, Mr Hales?"

For a moment, he sees himself through her—an enigmatic man arrived on the tides. Older, wiser. Brimming with secrets.

He likes the way he looks through her eyes.

He tells her the truth. He is driven by a desire for the world to one day know his name.

She edges closer. He smells brandy on her breath. Her hand slides towards his; fingers touching.

What is this, an act of defiance? Or an act of desire?

Asher is not sure he cares.

He wants to be the man she sees; this enigma arrived on the tides. Wants to be looked at with blazing eyes.

And his lips are on hers. Is this his doing? He is unsure. The anger in her, he can feel it. Feel it in the hands pulling at his collar, pulling at his hair. Feels it in the way her mouth opens so willingly beneath his. An act of both defiance and desire.

Asher pulls away.

Control.

His blood is hot, thumping inside him. When had he last felt a woman's hands on his body? A part of him would lift Scarlett's skirts and have her here on the weatherworn cliffs. But Asher Hales is careful, calculating. He needs Scarlett to want more from him. Needs her to keep returning.

She lies on her back, eyes on the stars peeking through the cloud. Her hair spills across the earth. Lips flushed, parted. Her breathing heavy.

She reaches for Asher's fingers and tugs him down beside her. Lifts his hand to her chest. He feels her ribs rise and fall.

Asher Hales is careful and calculating. But he feels a striking, unbidden pleasure at feeling someone else's heart beat beside his own.

STORM WINDS

'To the ignorance of men in our age in this particular and mysterious part of philosophy and religion—namely, the communication between spirits and men,—not one scholar out of ten thousand ... knows anything of it, or the way to manage it. This ignorance breeds fear and abhorrence of that which otherwise might be of incomparable benefit to mankind.'

'An Account of an Apparition'
Rev. William Ruddel, Minister in Launceston
1665

The village crawls out from beneath its unease for the saint's day fair.

As a child, Scarlett had loved the feast day celebration; the gypsies and freak shows, charmers with bottled wares. Huntsmen gathering at the church with their horses and dogs.

Today, she is restless.

She had crept back to the house with Asher after midnight. The cottage smelled of cold grease and wood smoke. Scarlett found the remains of a bread loaf. Handed half to Asher. She stood close, feeling the heat of his body. Her fingers roamed, touching his chest, his face, his lips.

This man she had saved.

She lifted her face to his, hoping for another kiss. Hoping for more. Daring Caroline to catch her.

Asher took her arm and eased her away from him.

"I wish you could come to the fair tomorrow," she said.

A laugh. "And what would your villagers make of me? The man pulled from the ghostly wreck? I imagine the sight of me might ruin their celebrations." He pecked her cheek and disappeared into the bedroom without waiting for her response.

Scarlett lay by the fire and replayed the night in her mind.

There have been men in the past. Boys. Spotty-cheeked fishermen and sunburnt farmhands. An uninspiring parade of stolen kisses and sweaty hands. Each nothing but a momentary distraction.

But with Asher, there is more. There are secrets in him. Ambition. Passion simmering below his polished surface. She had felt it, fleetingly, when she had curled up beside him on the cliff top.

She trudges past fruit stalls and gypsy wagons. The sky is punctuated with waterlogged ribbons, strung beneath the trees.

What a feeling it would have been to walk the fair on a handsome man's arm. *Yes*, she would tell people when they asked, *he owes me his life.*

She feels flat and heavy. She closes her eyes and her hearing sharpens. The world is a dissonance of footsteps and voices and hunting horns. Her restlessness makes her heart quicken. She feels it swim inside her, threatening to become rage.

This wild anger that plagues her, she has always felt it a separate entity. She is light and optimism and trust. A victim of the violent thoughts that seize her without warning.

She opens her eyes. A dog gallops from the hunting party and presses its nose against her palm. *Light*, she tells herself. *Optimism. Trust.*

She makes her way to the wrestling ring and watches two men from the landing party fling each other across the grass. A cheer rises from the crowd.

Bobby Carter squeezes his way to her side, a neat figure in his blue uniform.

Scarlett is glad to see him. "I'm surprised you're not involved in this," she says, twisting the buttons on her cloak.

He laughs. "I've too much class to be seen covered in mud and sweat."

She gives him a short smile. "Is that so?"

The farmers shake hands and clamber from the ring. Isaac makes his way into the centre. He pulls off his shirt and slides on the wrestling jacket. He circles his opponent; eyes dark and serious. There is anger in his movements, tension.

He grabs his opponent's jacket and flings him onto his back. The crowd roars.

"I don't like who my brother is becoming," Scarlett tells Bobby. "He and Caroline have been stealing tea from Reuben. Tainting it."

Bobby chuckles. "They could do plenty worse than steal from Charles Reuben."

"Isaac is not a thief. Something has changed in him lately. He's thinking of escape again, I'm sure of it."

"You don't wish to escape?"

"Of course. But I don't want Isaac to become a thief to do it. He'll come to regret it. I know he will."

Bobby presses a hand to her shoulder. "Perhaps a tussle in the ring will do him good."

A thud as the men's bodies collide. Isaac's black hair has come loose from its queue and is plastered to his neck and shoulders. Beneath the jacket, his bare chest is splattered with mud.

Scarlett's lips curl in distaste. She glances across the ring at Caroline. She watches the wrestling with her hand around Gabriel's wrist, Mary on her hip. Does she find this boorish display from Isaac attractive, Scarlett wonders?

She tugs Bobby's arm. "I want to leave."

They walk towards the beach. Wind whips through the street, rolling apples from tables and making flags dance wildly.

"People claim they've seen this man from the wreck," says Bobby. "It's true, isn't it. He's staying at your cottage."

Scarlett looks at her feet. "I'm sorry. I didn't mean to keep things from you. But the village is unsettled. Knowing there's a man from the wreck among us would do the people no good. I don't want to put him in danger."

"You care for this man."

"I just want to help him find out what happened to his crew."

Bobby tucks a strand of hair beneath her woollen bonnet. "You've a kind heart. I wish you'd give me a piece of it."

Scarlett sighs inwardly. Marriage to Bobby has been tossed about since she was seventeen.

A gentle nudge from Isaac. Comments over the supper table.

He's a good man, that Bobby Carter, or *you could do plenty worse.*

Scarlett had laughed it off. "See me married to the revenue service, will you?" Because, yes, Bobby Carter is a good man, but Scarlett had been sure there was someone out there who would make her heart speed and her cheeks flush.

She has been friends with Bobby since her days at the charity school. After their classes they would escape to the beach and bury themselves in the cave. Tell ghost stories until the tide licked their boots.

Scarlett loves him deeply, desperately. Has even allowed herself to consider being his wife during nights when there seemed to be one too many chairs at Isaac and Caroline's supper table. But the thought of climbing into his marriage bed leaves her cold.

A gust of wind sends vegetables tumbling from a cart. A dog gallops towards it and sniffs at spilled cabbages. Onions roll down the hill. A crowd descends, snatching armfuls of food. The stall owner shouts, shoves, curses.

Scarlett feels the Wild shift inside her. She squeezes Bobby's arm. "You don't want my heart," she mumbles. "There's darkness inside it."

Unreason works its way into every space, Flora realises, as she watches clouds roll over the fair. Unreason is dark and damaging; water freezing in cracks and fracturing the rock.

She hears whispers pass through the fair.

Do you hear them in the wind? The voices of the dead?

The wind is strong today, but they are perched on a hill with the sea unfolding beneath them. A strong wind is no anomaly. Not a thing to be feared.

Flora shivers. The wind? No, it's the people who unnerve her.

She pulls her cloak around herself tightly. Voices of the dead in the wind. Calling the name of the next to die.

Jack had laughed at such sailor's superstitions. Over time, she had come to agree with him. Come to see life through his critical, well-travelled eyes. It had been his gift to her, Flora thinks. A solid, reliable world where wind is just wind and the dead have no voice.

She had defied tradition by taking a husband from outside the village. Who would she be if she had married a man whose world extended as far as the Polperro taverns? A man whose worldly knowledge was built on the ghost stories spouted by Dodge each Sunday?

She'd be the village charmer, Flora is sure of it. She'd live by the moon and hear the dead in the wind. Whisper prayers to the sea spirits into her shells.

She watches Gabriel pull Bessie up the road in a rickety cart. The wooden wheels clatter and crunch. Wind howls, streaming the children's hair behind them; Bessie's like snow, Gabriel's dark as coal. For a moment Flora is watching herself and Isaac charge up the street.

The two children had once been inseparable; Bessie trailing Gabriel like the older brother she had never had.

Flora glances at Caroline, who watches the children from the opposite side of the road. They meet each other's eyes. Faint nods. Flora turns away uncomfortably. So much had died with Jack.

Another gust and Bessie's shawl flies from her shoulders, dancing kite-like in the sky. The boats in the bay lurch on the swell. Hawsers groan and ratlines clatter.

Now there are more whispers snaking through the fair.

A body, washed up on the landing beach.

People swarm down the hill. Shouting. Frantic footsteps. A dog barks. Men bowl toward the beach, upturning the children's cart. Bessie shrieks and tumbles to the path. Flora glares as the men charge by, oblivious. She helps Bessie climb to her feet, smooths her hair. "You're all right," she says firmly. "Everything is all right."

She will not let her daughter fall to this madness. Her daughter will have strength. Sense. She will see more clearly than the parade of grown men trekking towards the beach, crying desperate prayers and shouting of curses.

A crowd gathers on the sand. Bessie presses herself against her mother.

A man, they say, spat out of the rotting wreck.

A man with a bullet wound in his chest.

There are questions, many questions.

Who killed this man? Where was he hiding?

"The ship was half underwater." Scarlett's explanation is lost beneath the shouting.

Of course they couldn't search the whole ship, she is saying. More bodies? Yes, perhaps there are more bodies. She shoves her way to the top of the beach. Bobby Carter grips her arm, as though protecting her from the barrage of voices. Flora grabs Scarlett's other hand and pulls her through the crowd.

Scarlett scrambles from the beach and looks back at the wild-eyed mob. Her bonnet has slid from her head and hair whips around her cheeks. She clings to Bobby's arm.

Flora lets her hand fall. There is a face in the crowd with a vague familiarity. Dark, narrow eyes. A long beard splattered with grey.

Yes, she remembers. Tom Leach, the trader. Flora eyes him. A strange thing for a Polruan man to bother with another parish's feast day.

She thinks of Asher Hales, the wrecked sailor. Does he know his ship carried a murdered man?

Bessie tries to push her way through the crowd. "I want to see the man on the beach, Mammik."

Flora catches her arm. "No you don't. Let's go." She tugs her daughter back towards the inn. There will be fears to soothe with brandy. Panic to ease with a tankard of ale. If the village is to crumble beneath the weight of its dread, Flora will use it to her advantage.

"Flora."

She turns at the sound of Martha Francis's voice.

"What do you make of all this? Do you believe this talk of a curse?"

"A curse, no." Flora presses a key into Bessie's hand. "Go home, *cheel-vean*. Quick now. I'll not be long."

Martha watches the girl hurry up the path towards the inn. "They are saying the man was murdered."

"So why do we look to evil spirits instead of evil men?"

Martha glances back at the beach. "Reverend Dodge will have you out here tonight, I'm sure of it."

"I've told the vicar I'll involve myself in his theatrics no longer."

"Theatrics? Is that what you believe them to be?"

"Of course. Look where his tales are leading. Are we to become screaming fools each time the wind blows? I'll not be a part of it. And I've no desire to watch this. I've a tavern to run."

Martha flashes her a smile. "Your mother would be proud of you. Even if you've not embraced her way of life." She walks with Flora towards the inn. "Your mother used to give Henry and I a tonic for our joints. Worked a charm." She smiles wistfully. "I do miss her."

Flora looks down.

"You know there are many people who would find great comfort in having a healer in the village again."

Flora glances over her shoulder at the crowd on the beach. Men are wrapping the body in a hessian bag. Dodge hovers over them, head bowed in prayer. Desperate hands grapple at his greatcoat.

"Camomile flowers," says Flora.

"What?"

"That's what my mother would prescribe for aching joints. Seep them in boiling water and add it to your bath."

Martha squeezes her hand. "Bless you."

Dodge dreams of brandy. Bed. A fire.

The allure of normality is intense.

But a man like him has no luxury of normality. There are souls to soothe, to save. Phantom lights to extinguish and howling dead to silence.

None of these things are new. He has been a man of God for too many decades to be surprised by the things life can fling at him.

Corpse candles had been seen above these waters not long after he had arrived in Talland. A curious thing, for certain, light dancing on the edge of the sea. A thing of mystery. Beauty.

But; *souls of the dead,* the people had cried. And souls of the dead they had become.

Dodge had shouted a prayer from the clifftops. Spouted comforting words to his frightened parishioners. The corpse candles had disappeared after a night and never been seen again.

Dodge had taken the credit. As far as his people were concerned, he had sent those wayward souls into the netherworlds, where they would never haunt the living again. *Yes, my children. You can rely on me.*

And rely on him they have; these needy people of Talland. These sorry souls who live on the edge of a restless sea. He has laid the ghosts haunting their dreams. Exorcised the demons of their imagination. And managed to line his pockets with free trading gold in the process.

But he can feel his control slipping.

Lights on the horizon, voices in the wind. Ghost ships and a murdered man. The truth somewhere between nature and the unknown.

He's heard talk.

Camomile flowers

A strange thing, he thinks with odd detachment, that camomile flowers might strike such fear into his heart.

God is challenging him. Testing his resolve, his influence. He feels the pressure to succeed as a weight upon his chest.

He seeks George Gibson out from the crowd. Bodies are trickling up from the beach, seeking out the illuminated building at the bend in the road.

Gibson is a flushed mess. He clutches at his hair and garbles about the storm winds. "I heard the dead speak my name, Father. The voices in the wind were calling for me. I fear my death is coming."

Death is coming for us all, Dodge wants to say. It is coming faster for a weather-beaten vicar approaching ninety.

Instead, he presses a hand to Gibson's shoulder. The man can be no more than forty, surely, yet his face has become lined and weary in what seems like days.

"These people are making for the Mariner's Arms, are they not?"

Gibson sniffs. "I suspect so, Father."

The Mariner's Arms. Its dark windows and thick stone walls speak of ungodliness. Black mirrors and burning herbs.

"Flora Kelly is offering healing charms to our villagers. What do you make of it?"

Gibson breathes heavily. "It's as you say, Father. The people need God. Not thinly-veiled witchcraft."

Dodge nods. "I wish to speak with her. Fetch her for me."

The vicar paces. Flora slips out of the tavern and folds her arms in greeting.

"You offered herbal charms to Martha Francis," says Dodge.

She doesn't reply.

"I don't want this in my village, do you understand? The people need God, not sorcery."

"You can hardly call a few healing herbs sorcery."

She is not as fragile as she looks; this snowy-haired scrap. Dodge had realised this early on. Had watched her grow, as he has so many of these villagers. Watched her change from a blonde twig of a girl to the woman who so resembles her mother. The village charmer.

He feels a surge of old regret at not being able to save the soul of Flora's mother. The physical ills, they are challenges from God. A thing to be endured. But it is the vicar's job to see his parishioners' souls purified.

Flora's mother had died with an adder stone beneath her pillow and weakness in her lungs. Dodge fears where God will send a woman who dies with an adder stone beneath her pillow.

His anger gives way. "Mrs Kelly, it is not too late. Come back and work with me. God is forgiving of those who lose their way."

"No. I'm sorry. You know my thoughts on this business."

"And how many of my parishioners are you going to drag down with you?"

"Please. I offered the woman a few camomile flowers for her joints."

"Camomile flowers today. What tomorrow? Hemlock and blood magic? I will not have it."

Flora raises her eyebrows. "Are you threatening me?"

"You were not in church last Sunday."

"Does that truly surprise you?"

"I fear for your soul if you choose to abandon the church, Mrs Kelly. And the soul of your daughter."

"Leave my daughter out of this." She turns her back. "If you'll excuse me, Father, I've a tavern to run."

Scarlett returns to the cottage after the fair, her cheeks flushed and her hair wild. Her words are a garble. *A body*, she tells Asher. *Murder* and *Leach*.

Calm down. Tell me again.

So it seems the sea is unable to keep secrets. A body washed from the wreck of the *Avalon*. A body with a bullet in the chest.

Confirmation, Scarlett says, of all Asher has claimed. The crew murdered by smugglers.

There is a loud thump at the front door. "Is he there?" Angry, frightened voices. "The sailor from the wreck? Did he kill the man on the beach?"

"Hide." Scarlett ushers Asher into the bedroom. "There is no sailor from the wreck," he hears her hiss through the door. "Leave me in peace."

When the voices are silent, he emerges to find her pacing by the hearth.

Her brother is not safe, she says. She is not safe. None of them are. She has inhaled a little of the crowd's mania. Caught their disease.

"I want to speak to Tom Leach," she announces.

"Leach? The captain who wanted the silk?"

"He and his men were at the fair. They were on the beach when the body was found. Why were they here, Asher? I need to know."

"Don't be foolish. You think to charge up to these men and accuse them of murder?"

"I can't just do nothing!" She paces. "Did you hear the storm winds? They speak the name of the next man to die."

Asher rubs his eyes. She is tiring him.

"What if it's Isaac? What if my brother is the next man to die?"

He grabs her arm to stop her pacing. "We will confront no one. Do you hear me?"

"Why not? Don't you want answers?"

His grip tightens. "Scarlett, you are to tell no one what I told you."

"Tell no one your crew was murdered? I'm sorry, but I don't think that's a secret any longer. Not after your crewmate washes up on our beach with a bullet in his chest."

"My crewmate was foolish enough to engage in free trade. He deserved all that came to him. I've no desire to hunt down his killer."

Scarlett's eyes flash. "You may not want answers, Asher, but I do. The free traders I know have always worked together. The people against the system. If there are traders out there willing to kill, I need to know who they are."

"If you were to tell everyone what I told you, where would that lead? To an investigation. To this village crawling with the authorities. Is that what you want?"

"Of course not."

"No. And nor do I. Because the revenue men will dig, and they will shine a light on you and your brother. You'll be strung up for smuggling and what use will you be to me then?"

"What *use* will I be to you? Is that all I am? A means to finding your precious haul? Why are you even still here? I've no information for you. No one does." She shoves against his chest. "Leave! Go on! I'm no use to you!"

Oh no, he is far from being done with her. He grabs her wrists.

She says: "Your haul is a myth."

"It's not a myth. I'm sure of it." He holds her until she stills. He stands close, his breath against her ear. "Forgive me," he says smoothly. "You are far more to me than just your father's stories. You are the only goodness in my life. You saved me." And all this, Asher realises, is true.

She pulls away. "Leach and his men took the cliff path to Polperro. I'm going after them." She takes a knife from the kitchen and slides it into her garter.

He watches her go. Watches from the window as she climbs the hill on the men's trail.

Let her go. She is disobedient and rash. Makes his blood heat.

But: *you are more to me than your father's stories.*

Curse on her. He pulls on his coat. Follows her into the village.

Dusk is falling. The whitewashed buildings of Polperro are otherworldly in the lamplight.

Scarlett peers through the window of the Three Pilchards. The tavern is dark and smoky. Leach and his men sit in a corner, talking, laughing, drinks in hand.

She slips inside. Approaches the innkeeper.

He turns away. "I can't be seen talking to you, Miss Bailey. You'd best leave now."

"Can't be seen talking to me? Why not?"

He sighs. "Go home. There's enough trouble about."

"Leach and his men. Have you caught word of what they're saying?"

"Just leave. Please. Those men are dangerous."

"I know they're dangerous. That's why I'm here." She slides onto a chair at Leach's table. "You were in Talland today. Why?"

Leach chuckles, exhaling a cloud of pipe smoke. "Visiting the fair, of course."

Laughter from the men. One pulls his stool closer to Scarlett's. She smells his sweat, old salt in his beard. She tenses, the knife hard against her thigh. "Did you have something to do with the body that came from the wreck?"

"Something to do with the body? What exactly do you mean by that? Did I dive onto the wreck and pull it from the ocean floor? Or did I plant it?"

Her skin is hot and sticky beneath her bodice. "Did you kill him?"

Leach puts down his pipe. "And if I did? You expect me to just admit to it? Absolve my sins by confessing to a little hawker?"

She flushes. "Why not? What power do I have? What authority?"

Leach jabs a finger under her nose. "You've a certain friendship with one of this town's preventative men. That's what power you have."

"I don't know what you're talking about."

Leach gives her a crooked smile. "Miss Bailey. You know how things are among us traders. We tell the truth. There needs to be trust among us. Or else where we be?" He takes a gulp of his ale and holds it out to her.

She shakes her head stiffly.

"A revenue officer on our side is of value to all of us. There need not be a rivalry between your brother's ring and my own. Why can't we work together?"

Scarlett laughs coldly. "You sent a bullet across our bow for the sake of a little silk. And now you want to work together?" She moves to stand, but Leach clamps a hand around her wrist.

"Accusing a man of murder is a serious thing. I don't appreciate it."

She clenches her teeth. "If you behave like a dog it's how you will be treated."

His grip tightens. "One day that tongue of yours is going to get you into trouble."

"Scarlett."

She turns at the sound of Asher's voice.

"Let's go. Come on."

Leach releases her arm. "Is this the mysterious man from the wreck? Everyone is speaking of you. Been press-ganged into Isaac Bailey's miserable cause, have you?"

Asher says nothing. He catches Scarlett's eye.

"I'm not going anywhere," she hisses. She turns back to Leach. "Tell me why you're here. Why were you in Talland when that body was found?"

"Think on it, Miss Bailey. That body was washed up from the wreck. Even if I had killed the man, how was I to know he would be coughed up by the tide today?" He smiles faintly. "You're so eager to be of value, aren't you. You want to be the one to run back to your brother with all the answers." He laughs to himself. "There's nothing quite so pathetic as a maid desperate to please."

Scarlett snatches her knife and leaps to her feet. In a second, Leach is out of his chair, grabbing her wrists and whirling her around. The blade hovers in her fist inches from his face.

Leach leans close. "I've struck a nerve, I see." His breath is stale and smoky. Threads of his beard tickle her skin.

She clenches her teeth.

He eyes the knife. "You know how to use that?"

"Ayes," she hisses. "Under the ribs. Good and fast. You'd be dead in an instant."

He chuckles. "Then it's a good thing your blade is nowhere near my ribs."

"Let go of me!" She kicks against him. Leach slams her back hard against the wall. Pain jolts through her. The knife clatters to the floor. Asher snatches it before the other men reach it.

"Perhaps I ought to be the one questioning you over this man on the beach," Leach tells Scarlett. "Who do you think you are, going about with a blade in your skirts?"

Asher holds out the knife. "Let her go, Leach. She's nothing to you."

Scarlett glances at Asher. There is a tremble in his fist.

Leach shoves her away. Asher grabs her hand hurriedly and pulls her from the inn. They walk in silence towards the cliff path.

They climb steadily, the darkness thickening. Scarlett is jittery, her skin damp with sweat. She hates that Leach can see into her so easily. Hates that Asher has seen her failings. She charges up the path, seeking the calming dark of the clifftop.

Asher hurries after her. "Let me go first."

"Don't be foolish. You don't know the path like I do."

The trail narrows. Careful steps. She runs a hand over the scrub to keep her bearings. A turn to the left here. Now the right. Below her, the sea thunders.

She glances over her shoulder at Asher. She can see only shadows of his face in the moonlight.

"You are a fool," he hisses. "I told you not to go after those men. They could easily have killed you. And then where would I be?"

For a long time, Scarlett says nothing. There is anger in Asher's voice. Is he rattled at the thought of losing her? Or losing a means to his fortune? He is still in Talland for a reason. Perhaps there is more to his search than he is letting on.

She pushes away her distrust. He has risked his life to save her.

"Thank you," she mumbles finally. "For coming for me. I know you were afraid."

"Afraid?" His voice sparks. "You think me afraid?"

She keeps walking.

"Leach is right, isn't he." Asher is close behind. "You want answers so you can go to Isaac and be of worth. So you can be more than just a chain around his neck."

Scarlett grits her teeth. "Leach isn't right about anything."

"Why does it matter so much? You said yourself, your brother is a liar and a thief. Why do you care what he thinks?"

Her throat tightens. "I'm tired of being a burden."

Asher grabs her suddenly. "You don't want to be a burden? Then stop chasing dangerous men in the night."

"I need to find the killers."

He whirls her around until she stands at the edge of the cliff.

Her heart shoots into her throat. "What are you doing?"

Asher hesitates, his fingers digging into the tops of her arms. Wind rushes up from the sea. Finally, he says: "Can I trust you?" His voice is a harsh whisper.

She nods faintly.

"And do you trust me? Because if I share this with you, it's important that we trust each other."

She nods again.

"Do you?" he says. "Truly?"

The wind thunders, whipping her skirts around her legs. She grapples at Asher's forearms, her heart speeding. "Yes." Her voice is thin, trapped in her throat.

"Show me."

She leans forward. Pecks his stony lips.

"No. Show me you really trust me. Take a step back. I'll not let you fall."

She hesitates. Shakes her head stiffly.

"I have most important things I need to share with you. But I need to know we trust each other."

She swallows hard. She is light, optimism, trust. She will see the best in Asher Hales. She will trust him with her life.

Will not let the darkness win.

Slowly, she shuffles backwards. The earth disappears from beneath her heels. Her toes cling to the edge of the path. Below her; air and sea.

She feels her weight teeter. Her fingers dig into Asher's arms. She blinks hard, fighting off a wave of dizziness.

"Are you afraid?" he asks.

"No." She tries to force the tremor from her voice. "You'll not let me fall."

A smile creeps across his face; his eyes warming suddenly. He steps back from the cliff edge, tugging her forward. She stumbles, gulping down her breath. Drops to her knees. Asher sits beside her. He kisses her forehead, her cheek, the edge of her lips. Scarlett tenses. Her breath is hard and fast.

Light, she tells herself. *Optimism. Trust.*

"You'll not find the killers," Asher says, looking out over the water. "The men of the *Avalon* were not killed by free traders. They were killed by me."

UNREASON

Dizziness washes over her. She scrambles away from Asher on hands and knees, afraid to stand in case she pitches into the sea.

Is this to be her reward for fighting the Wild? For daring to trust? To be thrown from the cliffs by a butcher?

He hurries after her. Braces his arms either side of her and presses his chest against her back. She hears herself cry out.

Asher wraps his arm around her middle. "It's all right." His mouth is close to her ear. "It's all right."

Scarlett gulps down her breath.

"Sometimes a man has no choice but to kill," he says, his breath hot against her cheek. "Sometimes his life depends on it." He pulls her into sitting. "Look at me."

She doesn't turn.

"I told you this because we trust each other," he says. "Because I thought you would understand. You know what it's like to need to protect yourself with force. I've seen it."

He runs a hand through her hair. His fingers catch in the tangles and send a jolt through her.

"And I told you this because I don't want you to go looking for the killers again. You'll end up dead. And I couldn't bear that."

Finally, Scarlett turns. His nose is inches from hers. She says: "Tell me what happened."

Asher keeps his hand pressed to her arm. "The *Avalon's* first mate died soon after we left London. A sudden death." In the faint moonlight, Scarlett can see his eyes glowing. "Death is a fascinating thing, don't you agree? The first mate sat among us at supper and the next morning he was gone forever. Where is a dead man's consciousness? What is this force that determines whether a man lives or dies?" A pale smile lightens his face. "It is the greatest of mysteries."

Scarlett shifts uncomfortably. "I have seen too much death to be fascinated by such a thing."

"Is there no curiosity in you? No interest in science?"

"Science? No, Asher, I've no interest in science right now!"

He smiles to himself. "I suppose that's to be expected. From a woman."

Tell me what happened on your ship!" cries Scarlett.

His nose wrinkles with annoyance. After a moment, he says: "The men wanted the first mate's body disposed of hurriedly."

"Why?"

He pushes past her question. "The ceremony was rushed and incomplete. And, well, I'm sure a Cornish girl like yourself knows what they say about sailors who've not been buried properly."

Scarlett's throat is dry. "Their ghosts will walk."

Asher chuckles. "Their ghosts will walk. And superstitious men are immune to reason."

"Your crew saw your first mate's ghost?"

"Your curiosity is here, I see. In your fairy tales."

"They are not fairy tales." She cradles her knees. "If your mind is closed you'll never see the world for what it truly is."

Asher smiles faintly. "You are right, of course. In a strange sort of way, you and I, we believe the same thing."

No, her world is full of different mysteries.

When she was five years old, she had stood on the moor and watched a man disappear. She had gone to her father. Told him of the coldness in the air.

Yes, my girl. Sometimes the dead remain.

And so it has always been.

Asher tilts his head. "The same mysteries perhaps. Viewed through different eyes." He leans close. "There are strange noises on a ship at night. You know that. Shadows move. Sounds distort. It's easy to imagine things that aren't there. Yes, my crew believed they saw the ghost of our first mate. But that was nothing but unreason."

"Unreason."

"Yes. It spreads like plague. Men lose their ability to think rationally. People behave like fools. Like animals. It's a dangerous thing."

Scarlett thinks of the frenzied voices crowding the body on the beach. An odd shiver slides through her. Would unreason carry the villagers as far as it had carried the crew of the *Avalon*?

"The crew convinced themselves the ship was haunted. They were nervous. On edge. They began to speak of demons and dark things. Carried pistols in their belts.

"When I saw the smuggling craft approach, I told the other men to turn around. Told them not to engage with the traders. I found myself being fired upon. Two near misses. The men were manic; their shots wild. I had little choice but to fire back."

He lowers his eyes. "I hoped the shooting would stop after the first death. But it was not to be. I had little choice but to keep firing. I know how lucky I was to escape with my life."

Scarlett knots her fingers. "How many men?"

"Five. Five men. I'm not proud of such a thing. But sometimes we must kill to survive. Sometimes we have no choice."

Her thoughts knock together. "And the smugglers?"

"I stood on deck and told them we no longer wanted to trade. The gun in my hand was enough to convince them. I was left alone on the ship. Nothing to do but dispose of the bodies and try and make port. An impossible thing for a man to do alone, of course. In my panic, I must have left one of the men aboard. The body on the beach."

The story is terrifying. Dramatic. Torn from the pages of an adventure novel. But why lie to her now? Why tell her only half-truths?

She will trust. She will believe. She will have faith in the man who had risked his life to save hers, as she had risked hers to save him. She will not let herself believe the foolish talk of the villagers. Will not believe she has dragged a demon onto their shore.

Unreason. It spreads like plague.

He stands close. "I'm no coward, Scarlett. You can see that, can't you."

"I can see that, Asher. You're no coward." She stares over the edge of the cliff. White water glows in the darkness. "Why are you still here? No one can help you find the haul. There's nothing in this place for you but bad memories."

"That's not true." He traces a finger lightly across the back of her neck. Presses a cold kiss into her shoulder.

She shivers. Begins to walk slowly back to Talland. "Tomorrow Dodge will bury the body of your crewmate. Perhaps you ought to be there. Perhaps it might help you move on."

BURIAL

In the morning, Asher goes to the church. The body lies before the altar beneath its unceremonious sheath. Asher stands at the bottom of the aisle.

It has been several years since he has set foot in a church. Hasn't ventured inside a house of the Lord since his release from servitude. He has no desire to praise God for the rough hand he has been dealt.

Dodge appears behind him. "You."

"I need to see the body," says Asher. "I need to know which of my crewmates has been found."

Dodge hesitates, then nods. Leads him to the altar and pulls back the hessian pall.

As he expected; Peter Barrett, that bastard of a quartermaster. His skin is colourless and waxy, ravaged by undersea claws and mouths.

He lifts the remains of the man's shirt. Bullet wound in the chest. The poor, crazed fool.

The sea-soaked mind, Asher had realised during his days on the *Avalon*, works this way:

A death on board results in a haunted ship.

Men see ghosts in the shadows.

The men talk, tell stories and the tales take on a life of their own.

Ghosts become demons. A ship becomes cursed.

And reason founders. Panic tears through the crew and leads them towards death.

The *Avalon's* first mate was dead before London had slipped over the horizon. A tragedy, of course. But Asher had seen an opportunity to learn. The soul; he knew it responsible for every working of the body. Fever, convulsions, disease; all the result of an overactive life force. And when the soul abandons the body? Would it leave a trail on the affected organs?

If Asher were to look at a lifeless body, would he be able to determine how death had arrived?

A decade of exile had left him hungry for knowledge and learning. Released into the wilds of the New England colonies, he had ached for his cultured homeland.

For three years, he lent his mind to growing New Hampshire. There were bridges to build. Inns, boats, schools. Mills to run and farms to tend to. Three years of back breaking, menial work. But enough to fill his pockets with a fare back to England.

And he was home. His sentence complete. His past beginning to fade.

He left his old, crime-stained name in New Hampshire with his old, crime-stained self. A new name for a new beginning. Asher; his grandfather. Hales; borrowed from the great English scientist.

This new man, Asher Hales, walked the streets of London with his shoulders back and head held high. He frequented the coffeehouses, filling his mind with the new ideas he had been so starved of. He used what little money he had to buy second hand books and the finest clothes he could find at the charity stalls. The shirts were discoloured and the coats worn at the elbows, but it was enough to give him a glimpse of the man he would soon be. A glimpse of the life that awaited him once he found Henry Avery's haul.

He secured a berth on a merchant ship. London to Penzance.

The day before the *Avalon*'s voyage, he stole into the Barber Surgeons' Hall and watched a man dissect a human corpse. He had spent countless hours poring over anatomy plates and drawings, yet the sight of a real body took his breath away. From the back of the theatre, he could see little, but it was enough to make his heart speed.

In contrast to his own racing pulse, the dead man's heart lay still and colourless. Asher craned his neck, trying to see lungs, stomach, bones, skin. Trying to see what clues the departing soul had left behind.

These surgeons would scoff at the animists' ideas, Asher was sure. But the controversy only added to its allure.

There was so much to learn. He needed to see more. Needed to be the man with the scalpel in his hand.

The dead first mate in the *Avalon's* sick bay. A body waiting to be wrapped for burial. Surgeon's tools. Endless hours of ocean.

He would be a fool if he did not grasp this opportunity.

He hunched over a candle. Slid a knife down the man's chest with precision. He felt a shiver of excitement.

There was a faint warmth to the body. Blood beaded on his knife.

Intestines. Lungs. Still heart.

All as he had seen that day in the Barber Surgeons' Hall. All as he had seen in his books. But look at these things he had not seen. These tiny veins and arteries, fine like a web. The puzzle of bones in the man's hand. Fibres of knotted muscle.

There was a beauty to it. A complex machine. But what was this magical element that brought the body to life? Where was the first mate's soul now?

Asher stood in the cabin beside that open body and let the mystery engulf him. Two men. One alive, one dead. What was it that made it so?

Footsteps yanked him from his thoughts. Quartermaster Barrett stood in the doorway, eyes wide. He crossed himself. Cursed and spat. Then he disappeared onto the deck, his footfalls thundering above Asher's head.

And the rest of the men arrived.

Filth, they called Asher as their eyes fell to the gaping body. Wild arms shoved him from the sick bay. The close-minded fools, unable to see beyond the blood to the mysteries begging to be unravelled. Could they not see how lucky they were to be living in this century where scientific discoveries waited around every corner? Could they not see how lucky they were to be living at all?

They wrapped the first mate's body, his insides gaping. Carried him through the dark ship.

Asher chased them through the passage, out onto the deck. There was still so much to discover. So much to learn.

The body left beads of blood across the deck and terror in the men's eyes. They heaved the corpse over the gunwale and watched as it sank, devoid of prayer or ceremony.

Asher turned to leave. He would return to the sick bay. Ponder the things he had learnt before the body had been so rudely been torn away. Dive deeper into the mysteries of life and death that lay before him.

Barrett snatched his collar. Hauled him backwards. His spine slammed against the gunwale.

Filth, the men repeated. *Mad filth.*

"Did you hear me?" said Barrett. "You're mad filth. Nothing more. We ought to throw you off too."

Fear weakened Asher's legs. Barrett was a head taller than him, shoulders far wider. And he had four other men crowded behind him.

In his head, Asher played out the action. Fist to the side of Barrett's face. The man crumpling, blood streaming.

But Asher Hales was not that kind of man. He was a great mind, not a bully, or a criminal. Not mad filth. He would not allow small-minded men to drag him down to their level.

"What do you say?" hissed Barrett. "Ought we throw you over?"

Asher shook his head, his voice caught in his throat. Sweat trickled down the back of his neck.

Barrett released him suddenly and he stumbled towards the pilot house. Asher threw open the hatch and hurried below. He heard the distant voices of the crew.

"A prayer, quickly."

Say a prayer. Hurry now.

"We've done our first mate wrong. Now the poor man's soul will never be at rest."

He hears footsteps behind him.

"Better way you stay in the church, Asher," Scarlett says, entwining her fingers in her shawl. "The villagers have come to witness the burial. I didn't expect it."

He can hear voices in the graveyard. Many voices. A sign of respect? A desperate attempt to soothe their own fears, more likely. See their ill luck buried along with the dead.

Asher looks back at Barrett's body. He needs to see this man buried. It will be a victory to watch the bastard disappear into the earth. He strides from the church. The villagers' eyes fix on him.

A demon, spat from their bell house.

Yes, he's real.

Scarlett stands close as the cursory service begins. Despite all he has told her, she is here by his side, her arm pressing against his. They will criticise her for it, Asher is sure. He feels a sudden rush of gratitude.

It had been a risk of course, telling her of the killings. But Scarlett has bravery in her. Look at her, stumbling backwards on the cliff edge to prove herself a trusting soul. Plenty of bravery, no matter how misdirected. He needs her to see that he is just as brave. Needs her to see he is powerful. Needs her to see that when men like Quartermaster Barrett threaten him, they end up with a bullet in their chest. And he needs to keep seeing himself through her admiring eyes.

The body is lowered into a hurriedly dug grave. Earth tossed over it. The slosh of shovels is loud amongst the wordlessness.

Where are these people's superstitions now? Where are their bells and burial songs? This is no funeral. It's nothing but a disposal of rubbish.

The vicar bows his head. A hurried prayer as the body begins its descent into the earth.

A murmur ripples through the crowd. Now there is just one man left from the ghost ship.

George Gibson stares at the grave as though he is afraid the dead man will break free. He scans the crowd with shadowy eyes. "Where is Flora Kelly? Would she rather play her heathen's games than farewell a murdered man?"

Flora wrenches open the window and lets a salty breeze flutter the curtains. From the second storey of the inn, she can see the crowd in the cemetery.

No, my darling, we will not be going to the church.

She will not subject her daughter to the mania brought about by the burial.

Instead, she has spent the morning among dusty, herb-scented memories, as she cleans out her mother's room. She has been unable to part with much. Has tossed the moth-eaten bedsheets in the fire. Scant pieces of wearable clothing folded up for the charity collection.

In the corner of the room is the wooden chest. She has tucked it away. Unneeded. Unwanted.

But now, with Dodge hollering on the hilltops, the chest does not feel quite so unwanted. Flora opens the lid. Lines up its contents on the floor in front of her.

Pouches and glass vials. Bone rings and a length of hangman's rope. In one jar sits a preserved animal heart. She holds it up to the light, drawn to its grotesque black shape. She remembers her mother using the heart as a counter spell to darkness.

Pierce the heart with pins and draw out the dark.

She allows herself a smile.

Camomile flowers, for aching joints.

Mugwort for a head cold.

Bullock's heart to combat ill-wishing.

Where is the line between nature and the unearthly?

Ground ivy has the power to heal a man's wounds, Flora has seen it many times. Mallow leaves to lighten bruises.

Magic?

And if camomile can ease a man's joints, can a blackened heart ease his terrors?

Healing herbs grow everywhere. A gift from God? Or the lure of the devil?

Flora rubs her eyes. She doesn't want this to be her world. She wants solidity. The clink of glasses and the burn of brandy.

And yet, what gratitude she had seen in Martha Francis's eyes when she had offered a simple herbal remedy.

Had the vicar ever threatened her mother the way he had threatened her? Had she too felt the unreason of the God-fearing?

Flora feels sure of it. And yet her mother had kept on sharing what little knowledge she'd had, kept on trying to bring hope to the desolate. She feels a sudden surge of pride.

Voices filter in the open window as the villagers leave the church. The murdered man is buried. What ghoulish theories has Dodge filled his parishioners' heads with today?

A sudden shattering of glass from downstairs. Flora leaps to her feet.

"Mammik?" Bessie's footsteps thud down the passage.

Flora snatches the fire poker from the parlour. "Stay here."

The stairs creak beneath her feet. Long shadows lie over the bar. Glass crunches beneath her boots. The front window has been shattered, broken edges jutting like teeth.

"Is someone here?"

Silence.

She feels something solid beneath her boot. Looks down. At her feet, a thick wooden cross.

Flora drags Bessie down the street and pounds on Isaac's front door. "You need to stop using the church," she tells him breathlessly. "Stop using Dodge. He can't be trusted."

"What are you talking about? What's happened?"

She shoves the cross beneath his nose. "Someone threw this through my window."

Isaac glances over his shoulder. Caroline and the children sit at the table, bent over steaming soup bowls. He takes Flora's arm and ushers her outside. Pulls the door closed behind them.

"You think this was Dodge?" he asks. "He may be mad, but I've never known him to be violent."

"Dodge threatened me last night," Flora tells him. "He's upset because I'll not follow him blindly any longer. And then he heard me offer a herbal cure to Martha Francis. He thinks I'm going to turn the village away from God. Looks at me like I'm the devil himself."

"You're giving out herbal cures?"

Flora folds her arms. "Is that how you see me too, Isaac? Like the devil himself?"

He touches her elbow. "Show me what happened."

Isaac follows her into the bar. A stream of cold air blows through the gaping window. Shards of glass are strewn across the floor. He folds his arms, hot with anger.

Flora nods at Bessie. "Upstairs, *cheel-vean*." She turns to Isaac. "The cross was thrown after the burial. Perhaps Dodge felt I ought to have been there."

"You weren't there?"

"Nor were you, I see."

"There's madness in the town. I've no desire to surround myself with it." No desire to surround himself with talk of the wreck or the dead man spat from it. No desire to surround himself with childish talk of demons and curses.

He'd sat by the fire and played checkers with Gabriel while nervous chatter from the village floated beneath the door. Had hoped all talk of the *Avalon* might be buried with the dead man.

Flora tosses the crucifix into the fire grate. "You can't have the vicar involved in your operation. He's not trustworthy."

"You've no proof it was Dodge," Isaac says gently.

"Dodge or his supporters. They are one and the same."

"How are we to operate without him? We need the lane clear to bring the goods from the beach. And we need the bell house to store them."

Flora looks down. Her eyes on the floor, she says: "The tunnel."

Isaac's stomach knots. "No."

She clutches his arm. "You and Jack, you were almost through. You can land on the eastern beach. Bring the goods through the tunnel and store them in my cellar. You need not go near Bridles Lane, or the church. You'd not need Dodge." Her fingers knead his bare wrist. "I'd not think of doing it if I weren't desperate. But this frightened me. It frightened my daughter." She sits at a table and squeezes her hands together. "Jack always said there was something not right about the vicar. I know if he were here, he'd not want Dodge involved any longer."

"If he were here? And why is Jack not here, Flora? Because we were foolish enough to try and dig that tunnel." He hears his voice waver with emotion. "I watched him die. And now you're asking me to go back down there? I can't believe you of all people is asking!"

"The cross was a warning, Isaac. A threat. How do you think that makes me feel? I've a daughter to protect! You know exactly what that's like."

"Because of that tunnel, Bess is growing up without a father. Do you want Gabriel and Mary to as well?"

Flora squeezes her eyes closed. She kneels and begins to gather up the broken glass.

Isaac watches her without speaking. Though he's sure she'd be appalled by his pity, he has felt a need to watch out for her since Jack's death. A lifetime of friendship has taught him that her façade of strength is easily chipped. She has buried her grief deeply and he's sure it will one day resurface. The thought of her alone in the inn makes something tighten in his chest.

"I thought you wanted nothing to do with your mother's craft. I thought you didn't believe in such things."

She doesn't look at him. "All I did was offer a woman relief from her aching joints. Is that so terrible?"

"Of course not." He kneels beside her and puts a hand to her wrist. "But, Flora, I can see where the vicar is coming from. People are frightened after this wreck. They see death and demons around every corner. Perhaps Dodge is right. Perhaps a little faith in God will do them good."

"The people are afraid because Dodge wants them to be! Each time you use the bell house, he stirs up the village with one of his sham exorcisms. You saw the way things were at the fair. These people are scared. I fear where it will lead."

Isaac sighs. "Opening the tunnel is not the answer."

"Perhaps it is."

He rubs his eyes. Lets his gaze settle on the cellar door. Sweat prickles the back of his neck. "Please don't ask me to do this."

DELIVERY

Isaac sits by the window of the Mariner's Arms, watching rain slap the glass. The fire crackles. The inn is warm with the smell of wood smoke.

A delivery tonight. Contraband transported to buyers. A late-night parade of candlelight and covered wagons.

The inn is quiet. Isaac is glad of a little stillness.

He has spent the day finding buyers for Caroline's tea. Her tainted brew is convincing, in looks at least. He is not sure how far the ruse will last once the west country's gentry start filling their cups. Still, the sales will make a start towards those elusive tickets out of Reuben's life. Tickets that have been far too many years coming.

He hears footsteps behind him. Flora takes his empty glass and replaces it with a fresh one.

She presses a hand to his shoulder. "Slower this time, ayes? Keep up at that rate and they'll have you in the stocks for drunkenness."

He smiles. She has said no more on the tunnel and Isaac is grateful.

She watches Asher and Scarlett pass the window. "Tell her to be careful. Hales shared his ship with a murdered man. I'm not sure we ought to trust him."

Isaac nods. "I'll tell her."

In truth, he has spoken little to Scarlett since she'd come home to find the house strung with tainted tea. The disappointment in her eyes had been glaring. He has found it hard to face her.

She has always looked up to him. Seen nothing but good in him, even when his arms have been full of smuggled liquor. Is this to be the cost of breaking free of Reuben? The loss of his sister's respect?

Heavy breathing behind him. George Gibson's eyes are underlined with deep shadows. Shoulders hunched as though he is trying to disappear into the earth.

"You look like hell," says Isaac.

Gibson crumples onto a stool beside him. "I heard them. Voices in the storm winds. Heard them hailing my name, clear as day. I'm going to be the next to die." He grabs fistfuls of his snarling grey hair. "I can't get the image of the dead man on the beach out of my head. His face all eaten up like that... I keep imagining it's me rotting there on the sand." He looks at Isaac with watery eyes. "The devil, he keeps us fixated on our mistakes, don't he. I am a good man, Isaac. I've always tried to be a good man."

"Ayes, George. I know." Isaac claps him on the shoulder. "You need a good sleep, is all."

"Sleep? How can I sleep? I'll be gone by week's end, I know it."

"This business with the *Avalon* has been no good for anyone. But we're all best off forgetting it. The man's been buried. It's time to move past it."

"Move past it? You've the sailor from the wreck staying with you."

"What choice have you given me? He's the only man willing to come to sea."

Gibson wrings his hands together. "Coming to shore alone on an abandoned ship. Do you think it's true what they're saying?"

Isaac chuckles. "Do I believe the man is a demon? No. I don't."

Gibson stares at the candle flickering in the centre of the table. Shadows move across his cheeks.

Isaac empties his glass and stands abruptly. "I'm doing my best to forget that ship, George. You ought to do the same."

Scarlett sits beside Asher at the bar of the Three Pilchards. A cloth bag has been placed in the corner of the counter. Asher peers inside.

Scarlett slaps his hand away. "Don't touch that."

"It's full of dirt."

"Earth from a man's grave. A charm against ill luck."

Asher chuckles to himself. The bartender eyes him warily.

"The innkeeper is fearful," says Scarlett. "Ever since Leach paid him a visit he's been convinced trouble is coming." She glances edgily over her shoulder as the door creaks open. "You'll stay here, ayes? Until the delivery is complete?"

Asher smiles wryly. "You don't want me in the cottage with the children. Is this your wish or your brother's?"

She says nothing.

"I'll need coin. I can hardly sit here all night without buying a drink."

Scarlett pulls a penny from her pocket and hands it to him.

"Give me another."

She does, reluctantly. Picks at her fingernails. "If we are to continue our search," she says carefully, "I need to know more. I know nothing of who you are beyond this place."

He has been waiting for this. Can't pretend to be surprised it has come now, after the monstrous revelation he had dropped at her feet the night after the fair.

How to play it?

He could tell her lies of a privileged, law-abiding upbringing. No. She will see through them to the truth of his tattered clothes and empty pockets. Instead, play on her pity. After all, isn't that what this twisted tryst is based on? She sees him as the debonair man who needs her help and at the thought of being useful, she has her skirts around her hips.

And useful she is. Useful for his fragile ego. Useful for his search. Soon Scarlett Bailey will see just how damn useful she is.

Asher waves for the bartender and orders an ale. "Life dealt me a rough hand," he tells Scarlett, wrapping his fingers around the tankard. "One I didn't deserve."

"A rough hand?"

He tells her of his life in broad, undetailed strokes.

A poor upbringing, his years of servitude. All because he'd been deceived by a man he had been foolish enough to trust.

"Which man?"

A nameless man, of course.

She asks about his exile.

He tells her of the orange leaves of New Hampshire and the bridges he'd built with his bare hands. No mention of the attack on the dragoons that had seen him carted from England in chains. And then to claw back any trust he may have lost, he tells his sorry tale of trying to land the empty *Avalon*.

Blackness around him. Creaks and groans and the rumble of the sea. Blood running into his eyes. The wretchedness of it is enough to wipe any scrap of doubt from Scarlett's face.

He had seen the jagged headland in the last of the purple light.

This coast he knew with a sickening familiarity. Sickening, yes, but he'd climbed aboard the *Avalon* in London so he might set foot here again.

He would reach that headland. Reach those stifling villages that dripped with secrets and superstition. The villages hiding Henry Avery's riches.

"You tried to sail the ship alone?" says Scarlett. "Why didn't you come ashore in the lifeboat?"

"How was I to manage the davits singlehandedly? I knew the ship would wreck close to Talland Bay. Exactly where I needed to be. How could that be anything other than providence at work? How could I not have trusted in fate and stayed aboard the ship?"

"You are a man of science," says Scarlett. "A man like you does not believe in fate. A man like you makes his own fate."

He says nothing. Lets her words fall into place.

She twists a coil of hair around her finger. "You could have died."

"Yes. But I didn't. Because of you." This is the way to placate her, of course. Acknowledge her most heroic of deeds. He touches her cheek. She stiffens, but doesn't pull away.

"You would risk your life to find this haul. You must truly believe in it."

"Of course. I've seen it."

"You've seen one coin. For a man who believes in science so, you are relying on faith an awful lot when it comes to Avery's haul."

She is right, of course. There is an element of faith. But one black night on the landing beach, he had seen a smile creep across Jacob Bailey's face. The smile of a man who had uncovered valuable information. The smile of a man who *knew*.

"I need to believe," he says. "I need that money so I can be the person I was always meant to be."

"And who is that?"

A better person than this wreck who sits before her, dressed in a dead man's clothes. A person with his hands in far more noble things than free trade.

Scarlett knots her fingers together. "You know something. Something that tells you the haul is real when everyone around us is convinced it's a myth."

"It's as you said. Faith."

Her eyes harden. "What are you keeping from me?"

"Nothing." He reaches out, covers her hand with his. "Look at me."

She does, reluctantly.

"I've told you what happened on the *Avalon*. I told you I killed those five men. Why would I keep things from you now?"

Close to midnight. The churchyard is lamp-lit, streaked with silver plumes of breath. Isaac feels Flora's brandy warm his insides.

Ankers are passed down a chain of men from the vestry to the wagon by the gate. Scarlett watches them hide the ankers beneath a layer of kelp, arms wrapped around herself to keep out the bitter cold.

"Where's Hales?" Isaac asks her. "Is he out of the cottage?"

"Ayes. He tells me he has no interest in adulterating tea." She catches his eye, trying for a rise from him.

Isaac hands her a package. "Leather gloves and tobacco. Smith has agreed to give you three shillings for it."

She slides the package into the pocket stitched in the lining of her cloak. Pulls the hood up over her dark hair.

"Be careful," says Isaac. Fourteen years have not made it easier to send his sister into the night.

She nods.

He grabs her wrist as she turns to leave. "Be careful with Hales too, Scarlett. Please."

She twitches her lips, considering. "You don't trust him. You're just like Caroline."

"And you? Do you trust him?"

She falters. "Of course." She takes a lantern from beside the gravestones. "I've got to go."

The delivery wagon rattles past her as she begins the walk towards Talland Hill.

Isaac checks the door of the vestry. Locked. He nods at the vicar. Makes his way towards the lane. The clatter of the wagon fades. But something is not right. The sound of hooves is coming towards him as well. Three horses? Perhaps four?

The urgency of the hoof-falls tells Isaac *soldiers. Riding officers.*

Impossible. They have the protection of Bobby Carter. Their runs are scheduled to align with his working hours. Reuben's fortune makes sure of it.

Isaac peers down the dark road. He looks back at Dodge and the other men. "Douse the lights."

Blackness falls over the churchyard.

Isaac hurries to his cottage. Caroline sits by the fire with a mug in her hand, Mary asleep on her shoulder.

"The tea. We need to hide it." He scoops up the bags from beneath the table.

She follows him into the bedroom. "What's happening?"

"Riding officers." He shoves two bags beneath their mattress, the third into the cradle.

Caroline lays the baby in the crib, pulling the blanket over her and the satchel of tea. "Do you think Bobby has betrayed us?"

"I don't know." Isaac goes to the door and peers into the street.

Caroline stands beside him. "Is the church empty?"

He nods. "Gibson has the brandy. He ought to have made it to Polperro by now." He folds his hands behind his head. "Scarlett is out there."

"Scarlett knows what she's doing."

Isaac hears Dodge's voice, faint. "How dare you suggest such a thing! This is a house of God!"

He pulls the door closed. What had he been thinking, allowing Caroline to steal the tea? Allowing her to risk their safety like this? He feels a flush of anger. At her. At himself.

He waits. Her hand tenses around his arm. Neither of them speak. He hears voices from the street. House to house go the officers. Questioning. Searching.

And then a knock at the door.

The two men are dressed in the blue and brass of the preventative service. Bobby Carter is not among them.

"We've received information about a smuggling operation taking place in this village tonight," says one of the officers, striding into the house.

"Mammik?" Gabriel stumbles from the bedroom, his hair tousled and eyes wide. Caroline pulls him into her hip. Wraps her arms around him tightly.

The officers tear through the house, emptying cupboards and chests. Searching the fireplace, the oven, inside pots and pans.

Gabriel watches silently. Knows better than to say a word, Isaac is sure.

Still eyes and silent mouths. He had repeated the same words to his son he'd grown up hearing his parents recite.

Still eyes.

Silent mouths.

"You'll find nothing here," Isaac says darkly. His heart speeds.

"Check the cradle," says one of the officers.

Caroline steps in front of the crib. "Don't you even think about waking my baby." She reaches a protective arm over Mary's body. "You've found nothing. Leave us in peace."

The officer meets her glare. "There are smugglers in this village."

Caroline narrows her eyes. "You've not found them."

Scarlett paces up the lane, her path lit only by the faint circle of light from her lantern. A hand from behind snatches her wrist.

"Asher!" she hisses. "What in hell?" She gulps down her breath. "You followed me?"

"What you're doing is dangerous."

"Dangerous? I've been doing it since I were seven years old."

"That doesn't make it any safer. Where are you going?"

"Talland Hill. I've a package for Elias Smith."

"I'm coming with you."

She eyes him. "All right. But stay out of the way when we reach Smith's house. He's suspicious of his own cat. It's taken years for him to trust me. He'll not like the look of you."

They walk steadily up the hill, the sound of their footsteps lost as wind thrashes the trees.

Scarlett hears a high-pitched grunt. An animal?

She shines her lantern over the edge of the incline. At the bottom, a horse writhes.

"Is anyone there?" She pans the light through the inky shapes of the trees. The beam falls across a crumpled body. Her breath catches. "Someone's down there." She swings her legs over the edge.

Asher pulls her back. "What are you doing? It's too steep."

"We have to help them!"

She hears the steady thunder of hooves. She blows out the candle, plunging them into blackness. Lies on her front among the knotted undergrowth, the package of tobacco heavy at the bottom of her cloak. Beneath them, the horse bellows. Her stomach tightens.

Yellow light spills over the road as the riding officers round the corner. She presses a hand to her mouth to quiet her noisy breathing.

The horses thunder past and disappear up the lane. Scarlett scrambles to her feet.

Asher peers over the edge into the darkness. "You can't go down there."

"I have to."

She slides over the edge of the incline, her boots scrabbling. She grabs at the twisted tree roots that curl through the earth. Moves with careful, sightless movements.

She hears Asher above her, climbing onto the slope. Streams of earth shoot out from beneath his boots and rain down beside her.

She lands heavily at the bottom and hurries to the body. Kneels at the man's side. She leans over him, making out his face in the muted moonlight. Tears tighten her throat. "Perhaps that explains the riding officers," she coughs. "This is Bobby Carter."

TELL ME ABOUT YOUR FATHER

Scarlett kneels over the body. "He's still alive. Help me, Asher. We have to get him back up the cliff."

Asher squints at Bobby's broken figure. Blood is gushing from the back of his head. One of his legs is twisted beneath him. His eyelids are fluttering. Soul close to escape.

"I'm sorry, Scarlett. There's nothing we can do."

She covers her mouth, choking back a sob.

The horse groans loudly. Scarlett reaches beneath her skirt and pulls a knife from her garter. "The horse," she coughs. "Kill it."

Asher wraps his fingers around the handle. Stands over the animal's body. Its legs writhe beneath him. He presses a hand to the horse's head. Feels its heat, its life. He holds the knife against the thick pulsing neck. His own heart is racing, he realises. What power he has right now, holding this great beast's life in his hands. What power to control life and death. He feels a tremor go through him.

The horse is quiet now, as if waiting, submitting.

Asher swallows hard. He drives the knife into its neck. A final cry from the horse. Blood runs hot over his hands. He feels the animal still. Feels himself shudder with the power of it.

Yes, there is a strange beauty in death.

He looks back at Scarlett. She is hunched over the man's body, murmuring words of comfort. Bobby's hand is clasped in both of hers.

He has been where she is, crouching over a dying man, listening to his last groans and confessions.

He pushes away the memory. Can't let himself go back there.

Scarlett's voice is a lullaby: *Tell me about your mother. Your father. Tell me about home.*

Bobby's voice is faint. Unintelligible. Scarlett's shoulders shake with tears.

What if it were himself lying broken on the undergrowth, Asher wonders? Would she cry as the life slipped out of him? Would anyone cry? Or has he gone too far into the darkness for that?

He hovers behind her, clutching the bloodied knife. Wants to step closer to the dying man. Observe that precious moment when the soul slips away. But he feels an intruder.

What had he been thinking, following her out here, digging deeper into her world of free trade? Scarlett Bailey ought to have been nothing but a means to an end. Gaining her trust no more than a necessary— if enjoyable— step towards finding that haul.

But as he had sat in the tavern and watched her disappear onto the cliffs, he had been gripped with apprehension.

He'd felt the need to follow. Chase the woman who sees him as a brave, bright man. Keep her safe. Close.

A sudden cry from Scarlett. She lays her head against Bobby's still chest.

A globe of light at the top of the cliff illuminates the night.

Riding officers: "Stay where you are."

Asher doesn't move. His shirt and breeches are soaked with the horse's blood. Wet linen clings to his skin.

Two officers make their way down the incline. One shines the light in Scarlett's watery eyes, then over Bobby's body. "What happened?"

She sniffs. "He fell... The horse... I saw them from the road."

"Why were you on the road?"

"Is such a thing a crime?" She meets the officer's eyes challengingly.

"On your feet."

She stands, swallowing her tears.

"We know Bobby Carter was working for Charles Reuben. That's why he left Polperro in such a hurry. I daresay that's why he fell."

More light. More voices. Asher looks up. Isaac Bailey and a cluster of men stand at the top of the cliff. His cowardly crew, no doubt.

"Scarlett?" calls Isaac. He and several of the men begin to climb down the slope.

The first officer pulls his pistol. "Stay where you are, all of you."

The men continue to scramble down the cliff.

Isaac looks at the body, at Asher's bloodstained clothes. He turns to his sister. "Are you hurt?"

No.

The first officer looks to the second. He nods towards Scarlett and Asher. "Search them."

Asher stands motionless as the man's hands work across his chest, into his pockets, feel for hidden treasures inside his boots. The officer moves onto Scarlett. He pulls the cloak from her shoulders. Kneels at her feet. His hands slide up her legs, over her bodice, around her waist.

Finally, she slaps him away. "May we go now?"

"No," says the first officer. "I'm no fool. I know well we've interrupted a smuggling run."

"You've found nothing," says Isaac. "You've no grounds to make an arrest."

"We've found a man covered in blood."

"It's the horse's blood!" cries Scarlett. "Can't you see that? He had to put the poor animal out of its misery!"

Isaac steps close to the officer. "Bobby and the horse fell. Any fool can see that. And you've no proof of this smuggling run you're so convinced is taking place. Let them go."

They walk back to the cottage in silence. Scarlett knots her fingers in her cloak and stares at her feet. She hears shouted instructions as the riding officers haul Bobby's body back up the slope.

"I ought to take the tobacco to Mr Smith," she mumbles.

"Not tonight." Isaac ushers them inside the cottage. "The man can wait." He produces a clean shirt and breeches from his bedroom. Tosses them at Asher and nods to the wash stand in the corner of the kitchen. "Clean yourself."

Scarlett sits at the table, staring into the lantern.

Isaac murmurs to Caroline, his words distant.

Bobby dead. A leak. Cover blown.

Scarlett wipes her eyes. "Tom Leach and his men saw me with Bobby at the fair. They know he was working for us." She coughs down a fresh flood of tears. "They did this. I know it. They tipped off the revenue men. Told them about Bobby."

Caroline looks at Asher. "How do you know your shipwrecked sailor wasn't involved?"

He laughs coldly. Sits at the table in her husband's shirt, pale curls of hair escaping out the open neck. "Is there a basis for these wild accusations, Mrs Bailey?"

"Asher had every chance to turn me over to the riding officers," Scarlett hisses. "I trust him." She says it again, to push away her doubts, Isaac's doubts. *I trust him.*

"I don't," says Caroline. "And after all that's happened, a little distrust may well be a good thing. Isn't that right, Isaac?"

Isaac rubs his eyes. "Leave us," he tells Asher.

"As you wish." He disappears from the table, letting the bedroom door slam.

"You're far too trusting, Scarlett. It will be the end of you." A faint tremor in Caroline's voice.

Pots have been flung across the kitchen, Scarlett realises. The tea hidden. Riding officers have been here.

Isaac pulls a bottle of brandy from the shelf. Three glasses. He empties his own in a mouthful. "Customs knows we're using the bell house. There'll be eyes on the lane next time we take the lugger out, you can be sure of it."

Scarlett pulls at the dirt beneath her fingernails. "Flora asked you to open the tunnel."

Isaac doesn't reply.

"You're thinking of it, ayes."

He lowers his eyes. "I saw Jack die in there."

Caroline reaches over and squeezes his wrist. Isaac tenses visibly.

"You'll not let anything like that happen again," she says. "You'll take your time. Shore the walls properly. Take enough men." When he doesn't reply, she says: "I don't see what choice you have. You can't use the church now customs are on your trail."

He pulls away. Weighted silence hangs between the two of them. Scarlett keeps her eyes down.

Finally, Caroline stands. "You will come to bed soon?"

A nod.

She disappears into their bedroom.

Isaac hovers beside Scarlett, his empty glass in his hand.

She waits for a word from him. Waits for a hand against her shoulder. Waits for anything to show her that she does not have to carry her grief alone.

But he disappears into the bedroom without speaking.

Her throat tightens.

She has brought this distance on herself, she knows it. She has been critical and cold towards her brother since discovering the stolen tea. But she can't bear this iciness between them. She wants nothing more than to bury her head in his shoulder and disappear from the world, the way she had when she was a child.

He has always been able to fix things.

Lace from Saint Peter Port for her court doll's torn dress.

A tale of magic lands to keep the ghosts away.

A dimming of the lamp when anger takes her over.

She had spent two years in the Polperro children's home. There was a brother, she knew, out there somewhere, with tar on his hands and salt in his hair. She had no recollection of him, but made her own image, brought to life by her parents' stories.

Isaac, who sailed to faraway places. Who would one day come for her with his salty hair and take her back to that cottage on the hill.

Perhaps, they had told her at the home. For it was a dangerous thing to dream too hard in this world.

And what excitement she had felt the day he had appeared to collect her. Excitement she had been too afraid to express in case her brother vanished the way her parents had.

He and Caroline speak of escape; a conversation that is reignited every few years. But this time feels different. Isaac has a new desperation in him. A desperation that has him stealing from the bell house for his own gain. He is reaching the end of his patience; Scarlett can feel it.

And what is this bubbling beneath her own skin? The rage that lives inside her is simmering in her stomach, set alight by her fury at Tom Leach. She feels it build. Feels her breathing quicken. Feels sweat prickle her neck. Again, she sees herself with a pistol in her hand. Sees Leach crumple in his own blood.

The lamp hisses.

Blow it out.

A dark room will calm her, will send these murderous thoughts fleeing. But she stares into the flame and feels her anger burn.

She thinks of Bobby. His laughter, his sparkling eyes. Their childhood adventures, his loving words.

He wouldn't want this. No anger. No retribution. He'd just want to be remembered.

She blows out the lamp and empties her glass, her throat burning as the dark engulfs her.

Isaac tugs off his coat and shirt and slides tensely into bed. He stares at the rugged beams across the ceiling.

"I'm sorry," Caroline murmurs. "For the tea."

Isaac can't look at her. He feels an invisible barrier between them in the bed. He folds his arms across his chest. "Do you know how hard I've fought to keep the trade out of our home?"

Caroline covers her eyes. "I'm sorry. I wasn't to know the revenue men would storm the place."

"Of course you weren't! How can we ever know? And yet here we are lining our children's beds with stolen tea."

What would they have done had the riding officers lifted Mary's mattress? He'd have been hauled away and impressed into service. Thrown into naval slops and been shipped away to fight the Spanish.

"You're right," Caroline says huskily. "Everything you've said is right. Punish me, husband."

"I don't want to punish you." For all her misjudgements, she has done more to get them out of this life than he has.

Caroline sits up on her knees. "Look at me, Isaac." Her face is lined and shadowy in the candlelight. "I'm sorry. Truly." She presses a hand to his stubbly cheek. His anger fades slightly.

She runs her finger through the beginnings of his beard. "I'll destroy the tea."

He closes his eyes. The tea. Caroline's desperate attempt at freedom. How can he take it from her?

"No," he says. "We'll gain nothing from that. But I don't want it in the house."

After a moment, Caroline mumbles: "Buyers?"

"It's arranged," he says flatly. "We can sell it to the wink in Falmouth."

She keeps stroking. Her hands in his hair now. There is desperation in her touch. As though she is trying to push away her mistakes. Her fingers are hard and fast against his scalp. He reaches up and grabs her hand.

Stop.

She bends over him. The gold flecks in her eyes glisten with tears.

Isaac can't remember when he had last seen her cry. Something tightens in his chest. He pushes away the sweep of brown hair that has fallen across her face. "We were lucky this time. A reprieve."

Her tears spill. "I'm so sorry. For everything."

He nods slightly.

She straddles him suddenly, pressing her lips hard against his.

Isaac hears himself groan. Christ, how he's missed this. How he's missed *her*. But he feels her shaking in his arms. Feels her tears slide over his cheeks.

He turns his head, breaking her deep, desperate kiss. "There's something more. Tell me."

She shakes her head. Slides her shift over her head and presses her bare chest hard against his. "There's nothing more," she breathes. "Nothing more."

THE HEALING WOMAN'S DAUGHTER

Isaac heaves his axe into the wooden planks at the entrance of the tunnel. He had hammered these beams into place himself, the day they'd hauled Jack's body from the rubble.

Ahead of him, the tunnel gapes, black and lightless. He lifts his lamp. The passage is crooked, walls shored with bricks. All as he had left it two years ago. The smell of the earth is painfully familiar.

Flora watches from the cellar stairs. Isaac can't look at her.

The plan had been his from the beginning. Dig a tunnel from the tavern's cellar through to the eastern beach. No more carting barrels up the hill to the church. No more dealings with mad Dodge. The vicar's cut of the takings in their own pockets.

Jack had clapped him on the back. *The men will love it,* he'd said. *We'll be heroes.*

To be a hero was a foreign thing to Isaac. He was a criminal, a petty smuggler under the thumb of Charles Reuben. He longed to be a hero. And so off they went with picks and shovels, carving into the earth beneath the Mariner's Arms. Brimming with confidence and knowledge they didn't have.

Jack had gone ahead, leaving Isaac to shore up the walls. An unexplained weakness in the rock. Isaac had heard the sound in his sleep for months. The rumble and roar of collapsing earth. Jack's screams. And worst, the deathly silence that hung in the tunnel once it was over.

Still, they can't risk using the church again. And he'll not risk water damage by hiding the goods in the caves. Now the revenue men are on their trail, they will need to be smarter than ever.

And so Isaac marches into the tunnel, trailed by John Baker and the men from the landing party. Men with shovels, bricks, hammers. They will do things right this time.

Isaac heaves his pick into the rock. Feels the vibration charge through his body.

Flora climbs from the cellar. Her throat is tight.

She had wanted this, she reminds herself. Had practically forced the pick into Isaac's hand. And yet the emotion of it simmers beneath the surface, threatening to break free.

She can't shake the tension in her shoulders. Can't shake the sense of things shifting, unravelling.

An hour before Isaac had prised open the tunnel, there had been revenue men at the inn. They'd stood with untaxed brandy to their right and a trading tunnel beneath their feet. Pressed her for information on the smuggling run they'd been unable to prove. Information on the dead man, Bobby Carter.

"I barely knew him," Flora had said, sure they could hear the thud of her heart. "Where was I the night of the delivery? Why, here of course, running my inn."

The night of Bobby's death, she had emptied the liquor kettle and lined the brandy ankers up behind the bar. If revenue men came searching, they'd take one look at the kettle and know she was unlicensed. Displaying the liquor is a risk, but it gives her at least the appearance of legality.

The officers stalked through the tavern. Flora felt a line of sweat run down her back.

"You have a licence for the sale of your liquor?"

"Of course." She forced her most law-abiding smile. "But that would be the business of the excisemen, would it not? And when they pay me a visit, I will be happy to show them my paperwork."

She'd bought herself a little time, perhaps.

She takes herself to the parlour and begins unhemming the skirts Bessie has outgrown. Even from the second storey, she can hear the thud of picks and hammers echoing beneath her feet. Had she sat listening to the earth splinter like this the day Jack had died? Had she been alone in the inn, the way she is now?

Her memories of that awful day are hazy. But *thud, thud* and the recollections return in pieces.

The thumping of Jack's pick replaced by the thunder of rock. Cries; Isaac's cries. She had run to the cellar. Found the room swirling with dust. Isaac had stumbled out of the tunnel and grabbed her tightly. Fallen to his knees.

Flora throws down her sewing, her hands trembling and ineffective. She walks down the hallway. Presses her hand to the door of the room containing Jack's things. For a moment, she considers stepping inside. Losing herself among his dust covered clothing.

No. Not today. The ache in her chest is already too intense.

She lets herself into her mother's room. She sits on the bed, pulling her knees to her chest. There is something calming about being here among the memories of her mother. This is where she needs to be while the men carve the tunnel beneath her.

She shivers. Lights the fire in the grate and stares into it, letting her mind still.

And then she has the black mirror in her hands.

She is hearing her mother's voice.

Hold the glass still.

Watch, cheel-vean. *Be patient.*

The black surface is swirling. Her eyes have lost focus, says her rational mind. But just for now, she wants to hear nothing from her rational mind. Her rational mind is the one who thought it best to open the tunnel.

And so she watches the swirling glass. Watches as flames dance across its surface.

She starts at a knock on the door. Throws down the mirror.

A reflection of the fire, of course. Nothing more.

She finds Martha Francis on her doorstep, huddled in a heavy brown cloak.

"Flora. Please. You need to do something to stop the darkness that has fallen over this village. The wreck and that dreadful body… And poor Bobby Carter… How can we deny we have been ill-wished?"

"Bobby Carter was involved in free trade. In all likelihood, the wrecked ship was too. It's a dangerous life. There will always be casualties."

Martha winds the strings of her bonnet around her hand. "There have been corpse candles on our horizon. Storm winds. A tip-off and two dead men. All since that ship was wrecked. Are we truly to put it down to coincidence?" The old woman shivers. A dreary, wet day. Flora thinks to let her inside. But she is sure the hammering will do nothing for Martha's fragile state.

She tugs her shawl tight around her shoulders and steps out into the street.

"My son won't go to sea," Martha tells her.

"No. He's left Isaac in quite the position."

"He'll not fish. He'll not trade. How are we to get by?" She wrings her hands together. "Not that I blame the boy, of course. The vicar's talk of ghosts and demons is very unsettling."

"The vicar's tales are intended to frighten you. Please don't believe everything he says. Man of God or no."

"If he means to frighten us, he is succeeding. It's why I've come to you." Martha's voice softens. "Your mother, she knew what to do at times like this. When you gave me that remedy for my joints, it brought me such joy to know you're choosing to follow in her path."

This had been her mother's skill, Flora realises. Not magic, or prophecy but providing comfort and peace to those around her. Providing a little assurance when the wind blew too hard or the sea surged.

She presses a hand to Martha's arm. "Wait here."

She runs upstairs and rifles through the chest. Finds two black feathers. She has vague memories of her mother using such things as a charm against disease. Perhaps if she speaks with enough conviction, they might also become a charm against fear.

She hurries back to the street and hands them to Martha. "Protection," she says loudly, clearly. "Carry this with you and no ill-luck will find you."

The old woman can see through her lies, surely. She is as much of a fraud as Reverend Dodge.

But Martha's face breaks into a relieved smile.

"And one for your son," says Flora. "Perhaps he might find the courage to return to sea and help Isaac."

"Thank you." Martha squeezes Flora's hand. "Please stop hiding, my dear girl. We need you."

They heave and dig and shore for four hours or more, finally stumbling back to the bar with aching arms and dusty skin. The inn is quiet. Dust dances in the shafts of pearly light. The Mariner's Arms will remain closed tonight, as it has each day since the revenue men had stormed the village.

Isaac feels for Flora. Her joy at finally opening the bar had been short-lived. But with a cellar full of unlicensed liquor, she has little choice but to keep the doors bolted. With the riding officers' eyes fixed to the town, the excisemen will not be far behind.

She comes downstairs at the sound of their footsteps and places a bowl of water on the table. "Clean yourself, Isaac. You're a mess."

The water is cold and bracing. He runs the cloth over his face and neck, washing away the grime, the unease. He steps back from the basin to let the other men wash.

"Are you all right?" Flora asks softly.

He nods. "And you?"

"Opening the tunnel was my idea."

"Still. I know it can't be easy for you."

She looks away. "No," she says finally. "It's not easy. But I'm not about to fall to pieces."

Isaac glances at the men. When they are looking the other way, he stands close to Flora and presses his hand over hers. "No one would blame you if you did."

She gives a faint smile, meeting his eyes. "My husband died a long time ago. I've moved past it."

LEGAL STOCK

Reuben smiles when he sees Flora in his parlour. "Mrs Kelly. You are well, I hope?" He gestures to the armchair.

She remains standing. "I'm well. Despite a visit from the revenue men."

Reuben sits. Opens a tobacco box and fills his pipe. "Did they cause you trouble?"

"No trouble. Not yet. Though I fear the excisemen will be on their tail."

"You ought to hide your liquor. If you need help, I could—"

"I don't need your help. Thank you."

Reuben hums. "I've noticed that about you. Never willing to accept a helping hand. No matter how well-intentioned." He takes a long draw on the pipe and blows a line of smoke towards her. "You want to prove yourself independent, I suppose. Prove yourself a survivor, even without your husband. Show everyone you're not a weakling."

"What is wrong with that?"

"Nothing. But accepting help is not a sign of weakness. Especially when you've a young daughter to protect."

Flora presses her shoulders back. "There is something I need. A copy of a liquor licence."

"Why?"

"You know why."

"You plan to forge it."

She nods.

Reuben sighs heavily. "This is very dangerous. If you're caught, you'll be punished far more severely than if you were merely found to be selling unlicensed liquor."

"I'll not be caught."

Another draw of the pipe. "Run the Mariner's Arms as an alehouse. I will buy the brandy back from you."

"And how long do you think my business will last if I'm selling nothing but lambswool? The inns in Polperro will run me into the ground." She looks Reuben in the eye. "You want to help me. This is what you can do."

He leans back in his armchair. "You've put me in quite the position, Mrs Kelly. Yes, I can get you what you need. But by giving it to you, I would be putting you in serious danger."

"That is not your problem."

"Do you truly think I could wash my hands of your plight so easily?"

"The Mariner's Arms is my life. And until I can afford to run it legally, I'm willing to take my chances." She forces steadiness into her voice. Ignores the thudding of her heart, the trickle of sweat running down her back.

"The preventative service has their eyes on our village," says Reuben.

"Which is why I need the documents." She looks him in the eye. "Do you intend to stop your illegal activities, Mr Reuben?"

"No. But—"

"So why should I?"

"I can see there's no point in arguing."

"You are right. There is no point."

A temporary solution, she tells herself. As soon as she has the money, she will purchase the correct licences. Purchase only legal stock. And once Isaac has broken free of Reuben, she will block up the tunnel. The Mariner's Arms will be a law-abiding place she and her daughter can be proud of.

Reuben sits his pipe in a pewter ashtray and eases himself from the chair. "The licence is typeset. You'll need to find a printer willing to help you."

"I can do that."

He sighs. "Come back and see me this evening. I'll have what you need."

Scarlett pushes open the bedroom door. Asher looks up from the bed. He can see her silhouette in the glowing remains of the fire. Her shoulders are hunched. Hair hangs loose and tangled. She is wearing only her shift; a frayed tartan blanket around her shoulders. She hovers in the doorway like a ghost.

Asher's heart quickens. He had felt her trust slipping, but here she is in her underclothes, stealing towards his bed. Perhaps drawing her close will be easy after all. Perhaps all his work so far has not been a waste after all.

"You can't be in here," he says. "What if your brother were to catch you?"

"I don't care." Her voice is thick with tears. "I don't want to be alone."

She climbs beneath the blankets. "They've opened the tunnel." Her voice is muffled.

"I heard."

"It's no good for them," she sniffs. "For Isaac and Flora. How it must be to go down there after what happened to poor Jack." She presses herself hard against Asher's chest and buries her eyes in his shoulder. "Still, they have no choice I suppose. Not after Bobby."

He feels her tears against his bare shoulder. With Scarlett clinging to him, he feels a bigger, better man. A man of coffeehouses and lecture halls.

It has been many years since he has felt a woman's skin against his own. For the last sixteen years, his life has been lonely one. His drive to succeed has left little room for love.

How different things might have been if he had walked away from Jacob on the beach that night. If he had been happy with all he'd had.

There had been coins in his pocket; a meagre sum, but enough to get by. There had been a woman who had loved him. Had he walked away from the beach, he might be waking each morning to a woman's smile, gentle hands, loving words.

He can feel the heat of Scarlett's body through her thin sleeve. For a fleeting moment, his control leaves him. For a moment, he doesn't want wealth, or acknowledgement, or success. He just wants gentle hands. Loving words. The affection he has been starved of. And it matters little if it come from Jacob Bailey's daughter.

His hand slides up Scarlett's arm to the bare skin on her collarbone. He hears her breath catch in her throat.

It would be all too easy to draw her towards him and feel her skin against his. Feel, just for a few moments, a ghost of that life he could have chosen. He feels his blood heat. His hand slides under her nightshift and finds the hot skin on her thigh.

She shifts suddenly. "Asher, please. I've just lost Bobby." Her voice is thick with tears. "Be the decent man I know you are."

He rolls onto his back. Mumbles an apology. He feels his heart beat through his whole body; vibrating with desire, with humiliation.

But: *a decent man?* He has been a lowly slave, smuggling scum, mad filth. But now; a decent man?

He turns onto his knees and leans over Scarlett's curled body. He grips her wrists tightly. "You think me a decent man? Even after what I did to those men on the ship?"

She opens her eyes. Murmurs: "Sometimes you have no choice but to kill."

Asher smiles to himself. Yes. No choice but to kill a horse writhing in pain at the bottom of a cliff. No choice but to kill the men who have lost all reason and seek to take your life.

Bless this girl who is so easy to sway. Her thoughts so easy to manipulate. Bless her need to see the best in even the most miserable of men.

He kisses her hard, impulsively. She stays motionless for a moment before softening, letting his tongue slide between her lips.

"What I did on the *Avalon*..." Asher says, his nose grazing hers, "the terrible thing I was forced to do... Do you think it courageous?"

Scarlett doesn't answer at once. Asher realises he is holding his breath.

"Courageous," she says finally. "Yes, I'm sure it was courageous."

He rolls onto his side, pushing his head against hers. He needs to be near her; this woman who sees him the way he has always longed to been seen. This child of Jacob's who makes him believe his desperate dreams are in reach.

He holds his lips against her neck. Closes his eyes. Allows himself to forget who she is, whose blood is coursing through her, how deep she is in the trade he so despises.

Her body tenses against his. She digs her fingers into his arm. Grips tighter and tighter until her nails leave flecks of blood on his skin.

POLRUAN

A gathering at the Three Pilchards.

Glasses raised.

To Bobby.

Scarlett sits with her back to the bar, red-rimmed eyes gazing out across the tavern. Isaac had tried to talk her out of coming. Wouldn't hear of it, of course.

He stands at her side, feeling useless. What can he say that might bring a little comfort? Words have never been his strength. He hesitates. "Scarlett—"

She looks at him expectantly.

The door creaks. Leach and his men.

Scarlett leaps from her stool, eyes flashing.

Isaac snatches her arm. "Don't."

She struggles against him. "Let go of me."

He wraps an arm around her waist and pulls her close.

Leach approaches with a faint smile. "We've just come to pay our respects, Miss Bailey. No need to be so aggressive."

"Ignore him," Isaac says, close to her ear. "Don't give him what he wants." He feels her trembling with anger.

Leach and his men make their way to the bar through a gauntlet of wild eyes and cursing. Someone hawks a glob of spittle onto his collar.

"Are you calm?" Isaac murmurs. Scarlett nods faintly. He releases his hold on her and pushes his way to the bar. "Get the hell out of here," he tells Leach. "You've caused enough trouble."

Leach chuckles. "You're damn quick to lay blame."

"We're not fools," says Isaac. "Leave us."

And finally they do, emptying their glasses and walking back through the tavern to the same icy silence they had entered to.

George Gibson appears at Isaac's side. "You've opened the tunnel?"

"Christ, George. Not now."

"Are you mad? Have you learned nothing after Jack? And to do such a thing with a curse upon us…"

Isaac lowers his voice. "We can't use the bell house, ayes? Customs have their eyes on it. And I'm losing whatever fragile faith I had in the vicar."

Gibson snorts. "It's that witch in the inn we can't trust. Is she the one telling you Dodge is untrustworthy?"

"You then was it? The bastard who threw the cross through her window?"

Gibson straightens his shoulders. "A warning, is all. At times like this, we don't need her kind inviting the devil along for the ride."

Isaac glares. "Stay away from her."

"What's it to you?"

Heat prickles his neck. He looks up. "Hell. Where's Scarlett?" He pushes his way through the crowded tavern. Shoves open the door and steps out into the icy night.

He finds her by the side of the building, untying one of the horses drinking from the water trough. "What are you doing?"

She glances at him, then swings herself into the saddle.

Isaac snatches the reins. "This is theft."

"I don't care. I have to go after Leach."

"Go after him? And do what?"

"I don't know. But I can't just let him ride away. Bobby is dead because of him."

"Come on," he says. "Get off the horse."

But she pulls the reins from his hand and disappears up the dark street.

Isaac curses under his breath. He unties the second horse and leaps into the saddle. Unhooks a lantern from the inn's awnings.

He catches up with her on the edge of town. Ahead of the them, the road vanishes into blackness.

Scarlett looks over her shoulder at him. "Go away." Her voice is throaty.

"You know I'm not going to do that." He holds up the lantern. "Besides, you'll need the light."

Polruan is still. The streets are empty, bathed in shadow. The river slaps rhythmically against the harbour walls.

Scarlett asks after Leach at the inn. The bartender eyes them with suspicion, but points them towards a small stone cottage behind the blockhouse.

Isaac climbs from his horse and peers through the window. Leach sits at the table with a red-haired woman. They scoop handfuls of pie from the same dish, laughing in the lamplight.

Isaac feels a strange flush of jealousy.

"That bastard," Scarlett hisses. "Going about his life as if nothing at all has happened." She reaches into her cloak. And Isaac sees it.

A pistol in her belt. His pistol. She must have been carrying it all evening. And for how long before that? He feels the same wrench in his stomach he had hearing Gabriel brag about stealing the tea.

Look at what his family is becoming.

"Give me the gun," he says huskily.

Scarlett slides from her horse.

He blocks her way to the door. "What are you planning to do? Just waltz in there and shoot the man?"

"Why shouldn't I?"

"Because you'll be strung up for murder!"

She opens her mouth to reply, then stops. Begins to pace. "He'll never be punished. The authorities see Bobby's death as an accident. But that's not what it was! He was fleeing Polperro because Leach turned him in."

"I know. Leach is a dog. But if you go in there and shoot him you'll hang for it. And he's sure as hell not worth that."

Scarlett blinks back tears. "It's my fault Bobby's dead."

What can he offer but dull words of comfort? *It's not your fault. Don't blame yourself.*

Once, he'd been able to make things better for her. Frighten away the monsters that hid in the shadows.

Now what? Now the monsters have faces, weapons, brass-buttoned uniforms and deceitful plots.

Now the darkness that has flickered in her since childhood is threatening to force its way out.

He holds out his hand. "Give me my gun." His voice hardens. "Do it. Now."

She shakes her head.

"You're not this person, Scarlett. I know it. Whatever Leach has done, it doesn't matter. You're better than this."

She squeezes her eyes closed. Hands him the pistol. The metal is warm in his hands.

Whatever Leach has done, it doesn't matter.

Ride away.

No. A man is dead. Their informant. Their friend. The safety of his family has been compromised.

He hands Scarlett his horses' reins.

"What are you doing?"

"Leach knew about the delivery. I need to know who told him."

He thumps on the door, hand wrapped around the pistol.

Leach's face breaks into a grin as he answers. Isaac grabs his collar and pulls him into the street. Shoves him hard against the wall of the house.

"How did you do it?" he hisses. "How did you know about the run?"

Leach chuckles. "I've no idea what you're talking about."

Isaac shoves the nose of his pistol into Leach's stomach.

"Tom?" The woman pokes her head out the door, starting at the sight of Isaac and Scarlett. She darts inside and returns brandishing a kitchen knife.

Leach glances at her. "Go inside, Jane. These people aren't worth the time of day. They're just smuggling scum from Talland."

Isaac shoves the pistol harder into Leach's flesh.

He groans. "We tipped off the revenue men. Is that what you wanted to hear? You've an innkeeper in Polperro who can't keep quiet when there's a gun pointed at him. Told us the day of the delivery."

"What were you doing in Talland the day of the fair?"

Leach sucks in his breath. "We had eyes on the Mariner's Arms. But the innkeeper is far too tight with your lot. I knew we'd get nothing out of her." He smiles. "What will you do now, Bailey? What will you do with this knowledge? Shoot me in front of my wife?"

"I ought to," hisses Isaac. "A man is dead because of you."

The faint grin doesn't leave Leach's face.

And suddenly Isaac feels that same rage he had seen in Scarlett's eyes. His finger trembles on the trigger.

You're not this man.

Isn't he?

He has been a man with morals. And what has it gotten him? Unpayable debt. A wife who longs for another existence. Children to which he can offer nothing but this life of servitude he'd been gifted by his own father.

He flings the gun away before he is tempted to use it.

Scarlett snatches it from the cobblestones. She holds it out in front of her, fingers clasped tightly around the grip. Fire behind her eyes. She walks slowly towards Leach. "Bastard," she hisses.

Isaac watches the gun tremble in her hand. Her eyes are coal. Face stony. He knows this look. Knows there is no reaching her. Knows her rage is winning.

He steps in front of the pistol.

"Get out of the way, Isaac!" she cries. "Now! Or I'll bloody well shoot you!"

"No you won't." He grits his teeth. Hopes he is right.

Leach laughs and disappears inside the house.

Scarlett lets out a cry of frustration and fires into the wall of the cottage. She grabs a stone from the side of the road and hurls it through Leach's window. Isaac snatches her wrist and drags her away from the cottage, down into a shadowy alley. Down into the dark. He pushes her back against the wall of a house. "Calm down now."

She closes her eyes. And the fire is gone. Replaced by a flood of tears. She throws her arms around his neck. "I'm sorry," she sobs. "I'm sorry. I can't control it."

"It's all right, ayes?" He holds her until her tears ease. He steps back. "It's all right."

Scarlett sinks to the ground. "It's not all right."

He sits beside her.

"I didn't want you to come here tonight," she says. "I didn't want you to be burdened by me. This is my fight with Leach. I started it by accusing him of killing that man from the wreck."

"You didn't start it, Scarlett. Leach and his men have been looking for a fight for as long as I've known them. They like the thrill of it I suppose."

"They're dogs," she mumbles.

"Ayes. And we'll not lower ourselves to their level, do you understand me?" He is trying to convince himself as much as he is her, Isaac realises.

Scarlett rubs her eyes. "It's my fault you're caught up in this life. You're right to want to get out."

He turns to face her. Her eyes glisten in the faint light. "You think this your fault?"

"Of course. If it weren't for me, you'd never have stayed in Talland. You'd have signed on another merchant voyage and you'd have been free. It's what you ought to have done. Reuben would never have found you."

"I don't regret coming for you, Scarlett. I wouldn't change any of it."

She laughs incredulously.

Isaac puts a hand to her arm. "Listen to me. If I'd left Talland, I'd have no one. But I have you. My children. I have Caroline."

"Caroline?" Scarlett snorts. "I'm no fool, Isaac. Men in happy marriages don't have wandering eyes."

He drops her wrist. Stands. "I've to go for the horses," he says tautly.

Frustration and anger simmer inside him. He feels a need to make someone pay for this twisted slope their lives have begun to career down.

For a fleeting moment, he wishes he had let Scarlett pull the trigger.

For a fleeting moment he wishes he had pulled the trigger.

He collects the horses and leads them back towards the alley. They climb into the saddles and pace without speaking.

Isaac looks out over the harbour. Leach's cutter rocks on the dark surface of the river. And as he watches that boat sway, he is suddenly done with this doomed attempt at decency. Done with trying to shoehorn his life of free trading into a moral existence.

He dismounts and unties a dinghy roped to the moorings.

"What are you doing?"

"Keep watch for the harbour master." He climbs into the boat and pushes away from the moorings. The oars sigh in the water.

His common sense says this will do nothing but cause more trouble.

But he is done listening.

Done listening to Caroline's disapproval and the men's foolish fears. Done following Charles Reuben's orders.

His own inaction sickens him. What intense, crushing uselessness he'd felt when he'd stood beside Scarlett at Bobby's wake. Her grief and guilt had been glaring, and what had he been able to offer her but a miserable glass of brandy?

Now what? He will sink a ship out of retribution and say *here, Bobby's death avenged?*

Don't cry, Leach's cutter is at the bottom of the river.

Sinking Leach's boat will not help Scarlett, of course. But perhaps it might still the restlessness inside him, if only for a moment.

He climbs aboard the cutter and carries his lamp below deck.

There is little in the hold but piles of canvas and old lines.

He takes the rope. Holds it to the lamp until it flares. He lets the flame flicker against the hull. The fire snakes along the coiled rope, blackening, weakening the wood. He kicks hard. The hull cracks, splinters. In comes the first trickle of sea, dousing the smouldering rope. Isaac kicks again. Dark water swells around his boots. With each kick, he feels a dam break inside him.

No longer will he sit by and let Reuben take everything. No longer will he live in fear of the life he will leave his children. To hell with his hapless attempt at decency.

He climbs from the hold, heart thumping with a new, violent enthusiasm.

Water swells around the bottom of the ladder.

Let the river flow in.

A MYTH

Flora pulls open the door of the inn. "Thank you for coming."

Scarlett smiles faintly. "Of course."

Flora pulls her into a tight embrace. "I'm sorry. I know how dear Bobby was to you."

Scarlett plays with the hem of her shawl. She is still humming with nervous energy from the previous night in Polruan. Still feels the pistol in her hand.

The Wild has always been with her. A shadow she has learned to live with. A shadow she has always been afraid to explore. Where does it come from? Why has it chosen her?

The anger steals her reason and, sometimes, her memories. Often, she'll crawl out from behind the shadow and have no recollection of what had triggered it, or what it had made her do.

But there is no haziness to her memories of Polruan.

She had scared herself. What would she have done had Isaac not stepped in front of Leach? For all the wildness that plagues her, she had never truly considered herself capable of murder. Never considered herself capable of the urge to kill that had seized her when she'd stood with a gun pointed at Tom Leach's chest.

"The place needs a sweep and polish," Flora says, leading her into the bar. "I want to reopen as soon as possible, but the place is a mess and Bessie's not well."

Scarlett takes off her cloak and shawl. Reaches for the broom. "You're reopening now? Is that wise?"

"Perhaps not. But I have protection in place. Best if you know no more."

Yes. Best. Scarlett can't fill her head with Flora's troubles too. "Go to Bessie," she says. "I'll see to things down here."

She sweeps and polishes and remains in an ignorance to the workings of the inn that is both necessary and pleasant. Lamplight flickers over the bar and slowly wears away her tension. She feels a little of her warmth creep back.

She thinks of Leach's cutter, lying at the bottom of the river. Fish in the pilot house and weed hanging from the gunwale. She allows herself a faint smile.

Isaac had surprised her. In their fourteen years together, she had never seen him act out in such a way.

A part of her is glad of it. Glad to see him breaking free of his henpecked existence. But a part of her is wary. Leach will come again, for certain, once he discovers his sunken ship.

Isaac had climbed from the dinghy, his clothes thick with the smell of smoke. He slid the pistol into his belt. "Scarlett," he said, not looking at her, "we'll speak of tonight to no one."

When the shelf is lined with glasses and the counter shines, she trudges upstairs to see Flora.

A faint lullaby comes from Bessie's room.

Over thee I keep my lonely watch
Intent thy lightest breath to catch
Oh when thou wakes to see thee smile
And thus my sorrow to beguile

Scarlett goes to the parlour. The fire crackles and casts dancing shadows. On the table lies a black glass mirror.

This mirror, she knows it. She had watched Flora's mother stare into it and pull out pieces of tomorrow.

She picks it up curiously.

She has heard the talk, of course. Flora and her healing herbs. Antidotes for the vicar's tales.

Scarlett stares at her distorted reflection. What have Flora's farsighted eyes seen in this? Can they pull the truth of Avery's haul from a tangle of myths and fairy tales? She longs for a distraction from the constant ache of Bobby's death.

"What are you doing in here?" Flora's voice makes her start.

Scarlett holds out the mirror. "Can you use it?"

Flora takes the glass and places it back on the table.

"Can you find things? Things that are lost?"

"What do you mean? What are you looking for?"

She hesitates. "Mr Hales is looking for Henry Avery's haul."

Flora lets out her breath. "Scarlett—"

"Everyone says it's a myth but—"

"Everyone is right."

"How can you be so sure? Asher knew a man who sailed with Avery when he raided the Moghul fleet. He's seen a coin that came from the haul." Scarlett lifts the mirror again. "Please. I need the distraction. Just let me bring Mr Hales here. You can speak to him about it. And perhaps something may show itself in that mirror."

Flora nods finally. "Very well. Bring him here."

"A mirror?" Asher snorts. "That's ridiculous." He rams his shovel into the earth and leaves it standing up beside the carrot patch.

"Didn't expect to find you in our garden." Scarlett smiles crookedly. "Hoping to impress Caroline were you?"

Asher gives an unenthused laugh. He'd found himself craving the physicality. Craving anything to alleviate his boredom.

Scarlett touches his elbow. "Come and see Flora. She can help with our search. I know it."

He wipes his muddy hands on his breeches. "Men have been searching for this haul for decades. You'll not find it by resorting to cheap parlour tricks."

Scarlett folds her arms. "I respect your beliefs, Asher. Perhaps you ought to do the same for me."

"You will hound me until I agree to go along with your games."

"Yes."

"Very well." He sighs dramatically, marching from the vegetable patch. "Take me to your witch."

His memories of the inn are hazy. He remembers the cold floor of the cellar, the boarded tunnel, the pain in his head. Remembers waking intermittently with Scarlett watching over him.

Flora leads them up the stairs into the parlour. She looks at Asher with cold blue eyes. "Scarlett," she says, "I will take Mr Hales into my mother's room. I will try with the mirror in there."

Scarlett nods, her disappointment at being left out thinly veiled.

Flora gestures for Asher to follow her down the hall. Her footsteps click rhythmically on the floorboards. She pushes open a door and leads him inside. Thin curtains hang over the windows, allowing the last threads of daylight inside. On the bed lies the black mirror.

Flora nods to a chair beside the washstand. *Sit.*

She stands over him. "You'll not find that haul. My family has been in this village for generations. If Avery was ever here, I'd have heard about it. The story is a myth."

"All myths are born from a grain of truth."

Delirious in the cellar, he had been unable to place this woman. But of course. The charmer's daughter.

He dares to look into her eyes. Recognition there too. "You remember me," he says.

Flora nods.

He will not panic. She will remember him as no more than a foolish sailor caught up in free trade. Surely, she knows nothing about what had happened that dreadful night on the landing beach. Asher had been hauled out of the place by dragoons while the moon was still high. Any knowledge the villagers have can be based on nothing more than gossip.

His hand shoots out to cover the mirror. "Don't."

Flora turns the looking glass over so its black surface lies against the bed.

"I don't know how to use that mirror, Mr Hales. You know that, I'm sure. You'd not have come otherwise. Honestly, I don't know if the mirror is anything more than a game." She leans forward. "But I can tell there is fear in you. You're afraid of what I might discover."

Asher's heart quickens. "You're a fraud. You're just trying to scare me."

"For what purpose?"

"Perhaps you know more of Avery than you are letting on."

Flora laughs. "Avery. Forget that myth and leave our village in peace. There is nothing to find."

"I know better than to trust a woman in league with free traders."

Flora raises her eyebrows. "Perhaps that is something you ought to tell Scarlett."

He feels her eyes burn into him.

"You were in league with the Talland free traders once, were you not?" she says.

"Yes. My greatest mistake. And from it, I learned never to trust any of you."

"Well, Mr Hales, I can assure you the feeling of distrust is more than mutual. Scarlett is young and impulsive. She sees the best in people, which is both a blessing and a curse. But there are many of us who will do all they can to protect her."

"I care for Scarlett. I would never see harm come to her."

"Does she know you sailed with her father?"

Asher snorts. "Did you see that in your mirror?"

Flora says nothing.

"I had little to do with the man. I understand he is long dead."

She smiles wryly. "I may not have the abilities this village believes I have, but I can tell when a man is lying." She sits on the bed and folds her hands. "I couldn't place you at first. But now I remember. You made trading voyages with Jacob Bailey. Around the time he became obsessed with Avery's lost wealth."

Asher stares her down.

"Scarlett and Isaac know nothing about what happened with their father that night on the beach. And there is no reason for them to find out, do you understand?"

"That night on the beach," Asher spits. "I've no idea what you're talking about."

Flora doesn't speak, infuriating him. Does she believe him? Impossible to tell.

"This mess over Avery's fortune," she says finally, icily, "it's in the past. Leave it there. For the sake of Jacob's children."

Scarlett hears footsteps thud down the stairs. She races after Asher. He throws open the door and disappears into the purple dusk.

"Let him go," says Flora.

Scarlett whirls around in the doorway. "What happened? Did you see something about the haul?"

Flora sighs. "There is no haul, Scarlett. Please believe me."

"You didn't see that. That's just what you want me to believe."

"Ayes." Flora reaches for her arm. "It's what I want you to believe, because I don't want it to consume you, the way it consumed your father."

Scarlett peers into the dark street. "What did you say to Asher?"

"The same thing I just told you."

"Don't lie to me! Whatever you said has sent him running into the night."

Flora sighs. "Mr Hales is keeping things from you. You ought to involve yourself with him no longer."

For a long time, Scarlett says nothing. "How do you know that?" she mumbles finally.

"It doesn't matter how I know."

Scarlett glares. "He's keeping things from me? Just as you're doing?"

"I'm sorry. It's not my place to tell you any of this." Flora tries to usher her inside, but Scarlett stays planted in the doorway.

"Any of what?" she says icily.

"I'm sorry. I shouldn't have said a thing. But please, just believe me. You can't trust Asher Hales."

Scarlett clenches her teeth. Wind tunnels through the open door and makes the lamp above the stairs flicker.

Flora plants her hands on her hips. "You know I'm right. It's why you brought Mr Hales to me, ayes? Because you're not sure you can trust him?"

"Of course not! I brought him to you to help find Avery's haul." Scarlett looks at her feet, her stomach knotting. She swallows heavily. "I trust Asher. I do. He's not hiding anything."

"You asked me for help because you believe I can see things," says Flora. "This is what I can see."

SEA CHANTEYS AND SHOULDER RIDES

Scarlett sleeps little. She had returned home from the inn and lain awake by the fire, waiting for Asher to return.

He is keeping things from you.

Anything that comes from Flora is difficult to disregard.

When Asher had slipped through the door in the early hours of the morning, Scarlett had been unable to confront him.

She will not let Flora plant doubts. She has lived her life seeing the best in people and that is what she will do for Asher. See good in the world and keep the Wild at bay.

Her sleep had been punctuated with dreams of falling horses and Bobby's lifeless eyes. She wakes to the sinking feeling of reality being as bleak as dreaming.

She leaves for the fishing port without a word. The pilchard palace is quiet without the men at sea, but she busies herself with a mop and polishing rag. Anything to calm the doubts tearing through her mind.

In the evening, she goes to Martha Francis. "Why did you warn me to stop looking for Avery's haul?"

Martha sighs and ushers her inside. "Look at you. You're a mess."

Half her hair has blown loose from her plait and her boots are caked in mud. She is still wearing her fish-stained apron beneath her cloak.

Martha wraps her arms around her anyway. "After what happened to poor Bobby, I can't blame you."

"You told me not to dig up the past. What were you afraid I would find?"

"Scarlett, please. Let's not talk about this now. Not after all that's happened."

"Tell me!"

Martha sinks into a chair at the table. "Sit down."

Scarlett begins to pace. "I'd rather stand."

The old woman sighs. Wrings her hands together. "A man was shot on the landing beach many years ago. Back when you were just a child. When the soldiers arrived, they found a young man crouched over the body. The victim was killed over Avery's haul, this man said." She opens her mouth to say more, then stops.

"What?" Scarlett pushes. "Tell me."

Martha avoids her eyes. "He claimed your father was the killer."

Scarlett's stomach turns over. She feels suddenly hot. Angry. At who?

"It was all lies, of course," Martha says hurriedly. "Your father was no killer. You know that."

"Of course." Her father was sea chanteys and bedtime stories and shoulder rides. And yet the world feels suddenly colourless and unsteady.

Martha bustles to the range and pours a cup of tea from the kettle. She places it on the table and ushers Scarlett into a chair. "Drink this. It'll do you good."

She stares into it, unable to lift it to her lips.

All the people who must know of this. Flora. Dodge. Gibson.

Isaac? He had been away at sea. Has the village let him live in ignorance or has he kept things from her too?

The Wild stirs inside her. She clenches her fist until her hand begins to shake. She cannot let her anger out. Not here, not now.

Her hand flies out and knocks the cup from the table. It shatters on the flagstones, tea splattering up the table legs.

Martha whirls around.

"I'm sorry." Scarlett drops to the floor and gathers up the broken pieces. "I'm so sorry." Her cheeks flush with shame.

Martha bends stiffly and takes Scarlett's arm, ushering her back to her chair. "It's all right, *cheel-vean*. It was just an accident. No bother." She stands over her, holding her tightly. Scarlett lets her head rest against Martha's heaving chest. The old woman smells of musk and baking. Comforting smells. Smells from her childhood. Scarlett closes her eyes and tries to breathe deeply. Lets Martha run a hand through her tangled hair.

At the back of her mind, Scarlett finds a faint memory. Soldiers at the door. Her mother crying, father comforting. *All a mistake. I'm innocent.*

"What happened?" she asks finally.

"Jacob was freed, of course. They found no evidence connecting him to the murder. Your father was a good man, Scarlett. I know you remember that."

"Who was the other man?"

Martha sighs. "A stranger. No one I ever knew."

Scarlett's heart speeds. "Was he found guilty?"

Martha shakes her head faintly. "Of the murder, no. But they say he attacked the officers who came after him. Sent to the colonies. After that we never had word from him again."

DEAD MEN'S CANDLES

Bessie curls up in a corner of her bed, hair clinging to her damp cheeks. Her forehead burns. And then that horrid, growl of a cough that wracks her tiny body.

Flora sits at the bedside, drizzling elderflower tea down her daughter's throat.

A powerful, otherworldly odour.

The scent of the tea draws out her memories.

Flora; seven years old, the age Bessie is now. Sick in bed, feverish and weak. The world tossed upside down by fever. Her mother had bent over her and whispered an incantation.

In the name of the Father, the Son and the Holy Ghost…

Within two days, Flora had been out of bed and running in the street.

She had become well because she had believed.

And this, Flora thinks sadly, wiping a damp cloth over Bessie's forehead, this is why she will never truly follow her mother down the path of the charmer.

Yes, she can bring hope. Help others believe. But she herself cannot see magic. Cannot see healing in a desperately whispered rhyme.

Magic. Another word for trickery. Deception. The vicar's flailing arms to hide a bell house full of liquor.

She bends to kiss Bessie's damp forehead. Leaves her daughter breathing raspily and sets her lamp on the table in the parlour.

Rain pelts the windows. Flora throws a log on the fire. She looks at the pages spread across the table.

Licence for the retailers of spirituous liquors…

The printing is neat, professional, the seal a close replica. Surely only the most alert of excisemen will be able to tell it a fake.

What would Jack make of all this? He had been a free trader to the bottom of his soul, so perhaps he'd have loved the thrill of it. Or perhaps it would sicken him to see the danger Flora is putting herself and their daughter in.

She pulls a flask of brandy from the shelf and pours herself a shallow glass. She sips slowly, feeling it slide hot down her throat. Her heart refuses to slow. Is it the counterfeit licence on her table, or that shipwrecked sailor heaving up the past? Perhaps the growing tunnel that snakes through the earth, clutching the last memories of her husband.

Grief wells inside her. She forces her tears away. How can she hope to show strength in front of others if she cannot even show it to herself?

She finds herself standing at the mouth of the tunnel; the lamp in her hand casting shadows into the gloom.

She has not stepped inside since the day Jack had been killed. Isaac had boarded up the entrance and Flora had done her best to forget the dark chasm that lay beneath her feet.

But tonight she feels drawn inside. Feels the need to be close to her husband. What a cursed thing, that it's here Jack feels closest. Here, where his life had come to a sudden and horrific end. Not beneath the sheets of the bed they had curled up in together during their nine years of marriage.

She steps into the tunnel, trailing a finger along the cold walls. Her footsteps echo. She hears herself say: "Jack?"

Silence, of course.

Her tears resurface and spill.

She has prided herself on holding her life together. On being strong for Bessie. No weakness. No neediness.

She drops to her knees. She longs for him. Longs for his tuneless whistle, his guttural laugh, his hands, his beard, his mouth, his skin.

She has never let herself think *if only*. What good will *if only* do? But now the words churn through her head as though they've spent the past two years gaining momentum.

If only they'd taken their time. If only Jack had been happy with all they had had. For underneath it all, Flora knows the uncomfortable truth: Isaac is a free trader out of necessity. Jack had been one out of greed. And for his greed he had paid dearly.

What is she doing staying here in Talland, ensnaring herself deeper in free trade? Pressing Isaac to reopen the tunnel? Why not just take Bessie and disappear east? Start a new life.

Fine, flighty ideas. But opening the inn has consumed her every thought for the last three years. How can she walk away?

She presses her eyes against her knees. There is more to it, she knows. Hiding in the back of her mind is the fear that perhaps Jack's soul lingers in this place. As much as she longs to believe he is at peace, she fears a man killed in such a terrible accident would rarely be so lucky.

Their souls will walk, her mother had told her when she was a child.

How hard she has tried to silence these ideas. Tried to let her rational mind win. These childish thoughts of ghosts go hand in hand with tales of blackened bullock hearts and blood magic. Things she does not believe in.

But what if she is wrong? What if she has been wrong about all of it?

How can she leave the Mariner's Arms if Jack will be forever unable? How can she leave the Mariner's Arms if there is even a scrap of possibility that her husband is still here?

The idea brings a fresh flood of tears. These are thoughts she has never allowed to take shape. She has gone about her life speaking with Jack since his death—casual asides to allay her loneliness—but she has never allowed herself to truly consider that he might be in the inn with her.

"Jack," she whispers, her voice disappearing. She waits in the silence. Leaps to her feet and hurries back to the land of the living.

Isaac makes his way home from the harbour along the cliff path. Rain pours in runnels down his tarred greatcoat. The path slides beneath his boots.

He is grateful when the earth begins to slope towards the village. Lights from the scattering of houses glow through the mist. And there, at the bend in the road, is an orange glow from the top floor of the Mariner's Arms.

He follows the light; a moth towards a flame.

A rough arm seizes his neck. He swings wildly. Contact. Fist to—what? A man's face? Yes, Tom Leach, spitting, hauling his arm back, ready for the retaliation.

Leach's men surround him. Isaac ducks a wild fist. The second blow makes contact, splitting the skin above his eye.

He'll take a blow to the head for a lost cutter. Dizziness swirls through him, along with a frisson of exhilaration.

He wants to fight.

The men grab his arms. He thrashes against them, outnumbered. The punch to his stomach is hard and fast. Blood runs into his eye. A second blow. He gasps for breath.

Flora throws open the door and charges into the street, something twisted and black in her hand.

"Get away from my inn," she hisses. "I wish to God that good luck never comes to your door." She shoves a needle into the charred ball in her fist. Isaac feels the hands fall from around the tops of his arms.

"Witch," Leach hisses. "We'll see you hanged."

Flora gives a short laugh. "Hanged?" She steps close, holding the black ball to his face. "These are enlightened times, Mr Leach. It is a crime to accuse a woman of witchcraft. This is, after all, nothing but a bullock's heart."

Leach's eyes flash. He and his men turn and hurry up the lane, disappearing into the darkness.

Isaac wipes the blood trickling down the side of his face. "A bullock's heart?"

She laughs. "A rotten potato. But it seems superstitious men will believe anything." She tosses it into the street and takes his arm. "You're soaked through. Come inside and let me fix that cut."

She leads him up to the parlour. Isaac drops onto the rug by the hearth and slides off his sodden coat. He edges close to the flames. After a moment, Flora returns with a basin in her hands. She kneels opposite him, her knees pressing against his. He can see the pale freckles scattered across her nose. She holds a cloth to the cut on his cheek. Her fingers to his skin. Heat courses through him.

"They were the traders from Polruan," she says.

He nods.

"Why did they attack you?"

"I sunk Leach's cutter. Payback for Bobby."

Flora sighs. "Oh Isaac. Please be careful. You're behaving rashly. It's not like you. You're going to get yourself killed." She plunges the cloth back into the bowl and wrings it out. Holds it to his cheek again. "You've always been so careful."

"And what has being careful brought me? I've spent fourteen years being loyal to Reuben. Trying to do things the right way. And I'm no closer to a free man. Every day I look at my son and think of what kind of life he'll have when I'm gone. I have to start taking risks. Do something to get my family out of this life."

"Ayes," says Flora. "You do. But you need to do things wisely. You can't go about sinking ships out of retribution. It's foolish."

"I know. I've just grown tired of decency. Of morality."

She tosses the cloth back into the pink water. "Perhaps you cannot be so moral when you're caught up in this world."

Isaac touches the swelling at the side of his face. "No. Perhaps not."

"Just be careful," she says. "Please. I can't lose you too."

Her eyes are red-rimmed, he notices, feeling his heart lurch. A heaviness had fallen about her the moment he had prised the tunnel open. He reaches out impulsively and clutches her hand.

Flora glances down at their intertwined fingers. "Isn't it Caroline you ought to be speaking to about all this?"

"You're right. I'm sorry." He pulls away. "I shouldn't have burdened you."

"That's not what I meant. I…" She digs a hand into her apron pocket and produces a vial of liquor. Uncorks it and hands it to Isaac.

"What's got you carrying brandy in your pocket?"

Flora snorts. "Fear of the devil. Or the vicar."

Isaac tosses back a mouthful, his throat heating. "Dodge? Is he still threatening you?"

"He has the villagers worked up. He's feeding them these stories so they'll cling tightly to God. I fear where this will lead."

"I hear there are some that are clinging tightly to you. Following in your mother's path, they say. Cursing men with rotten potatoes." He gives her a half smile. "I thought this was no more than offering a woman a remedy for her joints."

"The people need comfort. Dodge is not providing it. Perhaps I can."

Isaac hums noncommittally. He glances at the papers on the table. He stands, looks over them. "A liquor licence? You're reopening the inn?"

She nods.

"Is it—"

"Forged? Ayes. And before you say it, I know it's dangerous. But I have no choice."

Isaac looks at her pointedly. "I'm the one who ought to be telling you to be careful."

Flora hugs her knees and stares into the flames. "This man from the wreck, Asher Hales. Please don't take him to Guernsey with you. I don't trust him."

"I have to take him. I've no one else."

"Aren't you bothered that his crewmate was found with a bullet in his chest?"

"Hales didn't kill that man. I'm sure of it."

"How are you so sure?" She squeezes his arm. "Tell Reuben you can't make the run. He'll understand, surely. After all that's happened."

"Understand? Are we speaking of the same man?"

"Just tell him, Isaac. Please. I don't want you at sea with Hales. Especially not on such a perilous journey."

He hesitates. Sits with his shoulder pressed against Flora's and watches steam rise from his wet shirt. The fire pops suddenly and he leaps to his feet.

"What is it?" She grabs the lamp and chases him downstairs. "What are you doing?"

"I'm going to finish this damn tunnel." He charges through the dark bar and heaves open the cellar door. "The final beams are in place. I just wanted to wait until dark to break through to the beach." He grabs his pick. "Give me the lamp."

Flora grips the lantern. "I want to come."

"Are you sure?"

She nods. Wraps her long fingers around the handle of the shovel and follows Isaac into the dark passage.

Their footsteps are steady, rhythmic. Isaac's heart is fast, as it has been each time he has stepped into the tunnel. But the agitation in him has stilled.

Flora sets the lamp down at the end of the tunnel.

"Listen." Isaac reaches blindly for her wrist.

A sighing. Whispering. The sea.

He sees a faint smile on Flora's face. He runs a hand over the beams he and Baker had pounded into the earth the day before. Sturdy. Solid.

He heaves the pick into the earth, his beaten muscles groaning in protest. His wet shirt clings to his shoulders. Fragments of rock prickle his skin.

Suddenly, a thread of cold air. He swings the pick again and the blade bursts through the surface. Another swing. Showers of dirt rain over them. Isaac tosses down the pick and crawls through the hole. The rain has eased to a fine drizzle. His boots sink into the sand.

Flora wipes the dirt from her face and follows him onto the beach. Faint blue lights glow on the horizon.

Isaac takes a long, slow breath. These lights will spark a fresh wave of chaos. But just for now, there is stillness. There is just he and Flora and the constant ocean.

This hidden eastern beach, accessible only by sea. And now by the secret tunnel he has carved through the rock.

Flora looks out at the corpse candles. She tilts her head, considering.

Isaac watches her out of the corner of his eye. He wants to step closer. Wants to touch that white skin on her neck. Wants to feel her breath against his ear. His heart thuds at the thought of it.

As he shifts his feet, Flora turns to look back at the tunnel. She reaches for his forearm and squeezes tightly. "You did it."

THE GHOST OF ALBERT DAVEY

'Avery came and said, "I am a man of fortune, and must seek my fortune."'

Testimony of David Creagh,
Crewman of Henry Avery
1696

"I've been waiting for you," Asher says, when Scarlett finally returns to the cottage. It's late and cold; the sky dotted with corpse candles. "Where have you been?"

She unlaces her cloak and flings it over the back of a chair. Beneath it, her apron and skirts are grimy. "I thought you'd be asleep." She goes to the kitchen and hacks at a loaf of bread.

Asher hovers. He regrets running from the witch's house. Regrets his anger. Asher Hales is poised and polished; not a fool who tears into the night, mad with rage. What conclusions must Scarlett have drawn?

She pulls the crust from the bread, refusing to look at him. He feels a weight in his stomach. Where is Scarlett who makes him feel a worthy man? When he catches his reflection through these new, cold eyes of hers, he doesn't like what he sees.

He takes the bread from her hand. "Walk with me."

She watches his fingers trying to needle their way between hers. Chews slowly. "Very well. We will walk."

She takes the lead. Straight for the landing beach. And Asher feels his stomach clench. She knows.

They stand beside each other, eyes fixed to the ghostly blue lights. Scarlett wraps her arms around herself. She has left the house without her cloak and she shivers slightly as wind whips up the sand.

The sea is white and restless. The cliffs make shadows. Splintered moonlight falls across the wreck.

The beach is empty. No one will venture here at night now. No one will dare look at the ribs of the *Avalon* emerging with the low tide.

A haunted beach, they say. Plagued by the souls of his lost crew.

The people are right. The past has a way of lasting.

There by the cliff is the patch of sand on which the quartermaster's body had been found. That gift from the twisted wreck of the *Avalon*.

And there, by the river? There is the invisible ghost of Albert Davey, the man who had brought the Moghuls' treasure to Talland.

"A man was once killed here over Avery's haul," Scarlett says to the sea. "Did you know of it?"

"No."

"I know you're lying." She breathes heavily. "They found a man on the beach with the body. Was it you? Were you the man who accused my father?"

Asher pauses.

"Yes," says Scarlett. "Just say it, Asher. Yes. Tell me the truth."

So he says: "Yes."

He waits for the eruption. Waits for her anger to tear itself free.

There was to be a time for these revelations. A time to tell Scarlett of his relationship with her father. She would be trusting, loving. And when the truth knocked her down, she would let him catch her. To hell with that witch in the inn, prying and planting doubts.

But there is no eruption. Scarlett's voice is controlled, even. Sends a chill through him.

"Is that why you didn't tell me you knew him? Because you were afraid I would find out what happened here?"

"Your father is your hero. I can see that. How could I ruin your memories of him?"

Look at her; dishevelled and dirty, her eyes wide and glistening. If he shakes her foundations further, how hard will she fall?

"Please. I'm sure my memories are of little bother to you." She shivers. "Who killed that man, Asher? You or my father?"

He exhales sharply. "How can I answer that? Whatever I say will destroy you."

"How do you answer it? You answer it with the truth!"

The truth.

Jacob Bailey had tried to double-cross Charles Reuben. His penance; an unpayable debt.

To many, Avery's haul was a myth. To Jacob, it was a life raft. One he would pursue by whatever means necessary.

Since the trip to Guernsey when Albert Davey had produced the coin, Jacob had trailed the man like a shadow. Under the guise of friendship, of course, but Asher was sure no one was fooled. Jacob's friendship with Albert was two-faced and laced with threat. Full of questions.

What happened to the rest of Avery's crew?

How much coin was distributed?

Show me more. I want to see more.

Albert was lonely and desperate for friends. Desperate for acceptance. But he was no fool. "I have that money well hidden, Bailey. I'd die before I let you get your hands on it."

A threat Jacob was willing to test. He trailed Albert home from Polperro. Asher followed.

He was in too deep, he knew. What had been a drunken tall tale had become a thing of guns and knives and threats. He wanted to leave. But Jacob was sure Albert would crumble under the pressure of two men. He had promised Asher a share of whatever was uncovered if he would be that second, ruthless man.

Asher had never been a ruthless man. He had been walked over by life, dragged through the mud. But if Albert's stories were true, his share of the haul would be enough to buy the life he longed for. And so he stayed on the beach.

Jacob put forth his case. Albert was an old man with no friends or family. Jacob had a wife and children and a debt hanging over him that darkened their lives. What use did an old man have for a haul of foreign riches?

Albert laughed coldly. "So I ought to hand it over to you so it can line Charles Reuben's pockets? You made your own mistakes, Bailey. Fix them yourself."

More heated words. Asher watched without speaking. Couldn't hear what was being said. Jacob drew a pistol and held it to Albert's chest. More words. And a smile on Jacob's lips.

In that moment, Asher knew. Jacob had information. On the threat of death, Albert Davey had given up the location of the fortune.

Asher let himself think of the learning. The people he would meet. The luxurious life he would build.

And then a pistol shot. Albert Davey fell to the sand. Jacob ran.

Asher dropped to his knees beside the dying man. Pulled off his neck cloth and pressed it uselessly to the bloom of blood creeping across Albert's stomach.

Albert motioned to the knife in his belt. "Kill me."

Asher's stomach tightened. He slid the knife from its holster. A violent tremor struck up in his hand. The man's face was contorted, his cold fingers gripping Asher's forearm. Blood ran from his body, into the stream, into the sea.

And then Albert Davey said no more. His breathing grew shorter, shallow. His eyes glazed.

Asher realised he was watching death. Watching the soul escape. This was the crucial moment. The moment with the answers. He sat the knife beside Albert's head and leant close to the body. He heard the distant clatter of horses. Didn't take his eyes from Albert Davey's quaking chest.

"On your feet."

And only then did Asher look up. Dragoons. They hovered over him on their horses, pistols in hand.

Again: "Stand."

No. Not until the man was dead. Then they could haul him away. But at that moment, following Albert Davey's soul was the only thing that mattered.

The soldiers yanked him to his feet. Asher fought against them, struggled to get back to the body. He pulled an arm free. Snatched Albert's knife from the sand. And with a wild swing, the blade sliced through a coat, through a soldier's forearm.

A pistol was pulled. Asher's hands tied. He was leashed to the back of a horse and marched from the beach before Albert Davey was dead. The priceless opportunity lost.

Asher protested his innocence. The dragoons had been aggressive, he claimed. The attack had been provoked. A misunderstood fisherman, yes. A killer, no.

He named names, of course—what loyalty did he have to the man who had left him on the beach with a murder victim?—but he had nothing linking Jacob to the crime. A Cornish jury would always protect their own.

Asher was an outsider. A foreigner.

Hang by the neck until you are dead.

In the end, the absence of a murder weapon saved him from the scaffold. But his attack on the soldier saw him labelled a criminal. His sentence; half a lifetime of exile in the blazing and bloodstained New England colonies.

But he is a free man now. A new man. And whatever secrets Albert Davey had whispered to Jacob, he will uncover. Wherever that haul hides, he will find it.

"Tell me who killed that man." Scarlett's eyes are critical, cold. He had seen the same look from the men of the *Avalon* when they had found him bloodied beside the first mate's body.

Who is she to look at him this way? How dare she? His anger gives way to self-loathing. She has made him feel worthless. Small. Things he never wanted to feel again. So he will gift her with the truth.

"Your father," he says. "Your father killed that man."

THE MAN WHO SHONE LIKE A STAR

"I must confess the parishioners do not send their children and servants to be instructed in the Catechism as your Lordship expects they would."

From a return made by Rev. Richard Dodge,
Vicar of Talland
1745

Polperro Harbour is strung with mist. The corpse candles have vanished with the dawn. Isaac scrubs, polishes, loads ankers of water and loaves of bread, readying the lugger for tomorrow's voyage.

Caroline wipes the windows of the pilot house, Mary clamped to her hip. Gabriel lies on his stomach across the deck and lines his soldiers up for impending battle.

Caroline speaks in jaded half-sentences as she works. *Apples from the market, your son needs new boots, be careful, be watchful.*

Isaac's responses are habitual, unthinking. Once, these mundane words between he and his wife had been enough. But this talk of escape has made him restless.

Sink the cutter. Break through the cliff. Steal and lie and see the faint, glittering potential of a better life.

He glances sideways at Caroline. Her skirts are grey, cloak grey. Her hair in a lifeless plait down her back. So often these days, she seems devoid of colour. He thinks of her in the Ship Inn so many years ago, dressed in yellow with a white ribbon in her hair. He tries to conjure up that old desire. Tries to find the passion he'd felt when they had curled up in his cabin while the sea writhed beneath them. All he can manage is a kind of muted tolerance.

He disappears below and returns with a packet of finely embroidered lace. A souvenir from a trading run.

He has been waiting for the right time to give it to Caroline. Has come to the conclusion there will not be one.

He hands it to her without speaking.

She sits beside the pilot house and opens the cloth wrapping. "Where did this come from?"

He smiles stiffly. "Never you mind."

She runs her finger over its delicate gold embroidery. "It's beautiful. Thank you."

"You'll wear it at your collar," he says throatily. "In our new life."

A smile flickers in the corner of her mouth.

He kneels over her suddenly. Presses a palm to her cheek. He wants the girl with the white ribbon. "Sleep on the ship tonight."

"What?" She gives a short laugh.

"As we used to." He kisses her neck. Feels her soften slightly.

She hesitates. "What of the children?"

"We'll put Mary in her basket with us. Gabriel can have a hammock in the saloon. He'll think it an adventure." His lips work their way along her jawline. "What do you say?"

Caroline lifts Mary onto her shoulder as she begins to whine. "What's gotten into you, Isaac?"

"I thought it was what you wanted. Things to change."

She smiles faintly. Stands. "Your daughter's hungry," she says, pulling on the hatch.

Isaac grabs her elbow before she disappears. "Sleep on the ship tonight. Please."

"In that cramped little bunk?"

"Ayes. In that cramped little bunk with Mary on the floor beside us."

She sighs, but there is light behind her eyes. "Very well, husband. You want to sleep on your ship, we will sleep on your ship."

Asher wakes from a broken sleep. The house is still. Is he alone? He has not seen Scarlett since she ran from the beach last night.

He pushes open the bedroom door. The kitchen is empty, the fire cold.

He is afraid of her, Asher realises. She has Jacob's blood in her. What is she capable of? How much has the truth of her father shaken her?

He slides on his coat and laces his boots. Fills his pockets with bread and cheese. Takes the handful of coins that sit on the kitchen shelf.

He'll head east. Find work. Reassess and plan where his search goes from here. His head will be clearer once he is free of this place.

He steps into the street. Hears angry voices. A crowd is gathering on the landing beach.

Another body? He finds himself hurrying towards them.

Men and women wade in the shallow water, clambering over rocks like frenzied beasts. They attack the skeleton of the Avalon with axes and hammers, frantic hands. Pieces of charred wood, sunken ropes and gnarled iron are carried back to shore. A pile of debris sits on the sand. Children run across the beach with armfuls of bracken and fling them onto the pile.

The vicar stands on the sand, the thin thread of the river running over his boots.

"What's happening?"

Dodge glances at Asher, then looks back at the crowd. "The people think to burn what's left of your ship. Burn out the spirits that haunt them. They believe it will free them of this curse. The corpse candles were on our horizon again last night."

Eyes are on him, Asher realises. Women frozen at the water's edge. Children whispering. Men with axes.

"You," says George Gibson.

Dodge clears his throat. "As you were, my son."

Gibson hesitates. His body tenses as he stares at Asher. Around him, the procession continues. The pile of debris grows.

Asher turns to leave. An arm is around him suddenly, hurling him backwards. He falls to his knees.

Gibson shoves him onto his back. "What are you then? A demon? You can't be no man to have come from that ship!"

Asher tries to push him away, but Gibson's thick arms pin his shoulders to the sand.

"Ought we throw you to the fire too?"

Asher's heart speeds. "Bloody fools," he spits. These witless men. He has seen their kind before. Seen them walking the decks of the Avalon.

The crowd closes in. Small-minded men with hate in their eyes He feels suddenly hot. The world seems to contort and contract around him.

He hears the voice of Barrett, the quartermaster.

Ought we throw you over?

"Violence will not solve your problem, Mr Gibson," says the vicar.

"And what would you have us do, Father? Sit by and wait for your empty promises to be fulfilled? Sit by and wait to die?" He stands, letting Asher scramble to his feet.

"What do you expect to befall a village who has turned to black magic to cure their ills?" Dodge looks out over the crowd, the wind whipping his white wig. "Yes, I know where your faith is. With the trickery pedalled by Flora Kelly. Do you truly expect the Lord to do your work, when you show faith in nothing but a witch's charms?"

"I had faith in you, Father," Gibson hisses. "But the lights in the sky are still with us. And so is he." He points a grimy finger at Asher. "How can we believe him a normal man when he came to us alone on that cursed wreck? How can we believe him anything but a demon?"

Dodge looks at Asher, his eyes glowing beneath ragged brows. "You are right to fear the demons around us, Mr Gibson. And in such times, only a fool would turn from God."

Asher sees a sudden flash of light. Gibson swings a flaming branch towards his head. He ducks, falls to his knees. He scrambles to his feet, dizzy with fear.

And he runs.

He runs until his lungs blaze. Where is he? Trees fill the land below him, hiding the village. A wild expanse of moorland behind, ocean beyond.

He stumbles out onto the moor.

Space. Openness.

Wind scuds through the grass and the ancient hills look to be breathing. The sky is white and endless. After crawling through the cramped villages, the moor is a deep inhalation.

How beautiful the silence is. How terrifying.

But it isn't really silence, is it. Even on this empty plain, there's the twitter of birdsong, the hiss of the wind.

Emptiness does not mean silence. On an abandoned ship, there is the creaking of spars, waves against the hull, the thunder of sails catching the wind.

Real silence is as rare as gold.

Asher lies on his back. The grass is damp and cold through his coat. He seethes with anger, hatred. For this place. For superstitious men.

Why was he returning to the west country, he had wondered, the night Quartermaster Barrett had threatened to throw him from the ship. What would he find there, but heathens and a land seeped in ancient ways? Why not stay in London among minds lofty like his own? Among people who would see beauty in the human body and the secrets it held.

The thought had been fleeting. Because what choice had he had but to return to Cornwall? Finding that haul is his key to bringing him the life he longs for.

He climbs to his feet. Begins to walk. He needs this openness. This breathing room. He walks across paddocks and unclaimed plains. Through winding villages and over tiny glittering streams. He walks away the day. Walks until his feet ache and the bread in his pocket is gone.

He looks out over the carpet of shadowed green. Boulders are silhouetted in the fading light.

Remnants of the giants' battles. He's heard the tales.

He hears himself laugh, cold and humourless.

Giants. Ghost ships. Curses.

Buried gold.

The realisation swings at him suddenly. Is he the most foolish of the superstitious men? Has he spent his life chasing a myth? Fallen for the bedtime stories Jacob Bailey had told his daughter?

No. He had seen that coin glittering between Albert Davey's wrinkled fingers.

All myths are born of truth.

But truths the size of coins become myths that can consume a desperate man. He thinks of the broken cottage that had housed Albert Davey. The home of a pauper, not a man rich with foreign silver.

That elusive haul, it had been a light in the darkness. He'd seen Jacob Bailey chase those coins to make his life better and to hell if Asher is not doing exactly that.

Sweat prickles his neck. His cheeks burn, then sting with cold.

These fools, he'd thought, clinging to fairy tales that make their dark world glitter. But now he sees with sickening clarity. He has fallen for the myth he had been so desperate to believe.

This is the secret Albert Davey had whispered to Jacob as he'd stood with a pistol pressed to his chest. Asher is certain of it. This is the secret that had made Jacob angry enough to kill.

All a lie. All a myth.

A story poor men clutch at so they might know greatness.

Once he had found Avery's money, Asher had told himself, then the world would come to know him and his great mind. He would travel. London, Paris, Rome. He would learn more, share his ideas. Chase the elusive soul.

Look, the world would say. *Look at this man born with nothing. Look at the way he crawled from the wreckage of his life and shone like a star.*

WHEN GOD STOPS LISTENING

Flora paces. Countless sick children had been brought through these doors while her mother was alive.

Give me hope. A miracle.

Flowers boiled, leaves crushed, spells whispered.

But Flora can see behind the magic. Sees there are no miracles on offer. And yet she feels the desperation shared by so many of the mothers who had carried their children into the Mariner's Arms.

She goes to the parlour and opens the chest.

Herbs have done nothing. She has flooded Bessie with healing teas and elderflower baths. Still her skin burns and her body is wracked with violent coughing.

At the bottom of the chest are the tufts of animal hair, the jars of nail clippings. That grotesque, blackened heart that had inspired her deception of Tom Leach.

Sorcery.

What good will it do? She doesn't believe. Power lies nowhere but with a God she cannot reach.

Illness a trial from the Lord, says Dodge. A thing to be endured. And for days, Flora has prayed and hoped, while Bessie groans and writhes in her bed.

But what happens, she thinks, when God stops listening? Ought they then turn elsewhere for answers?

A memory comes to her.

A charm against the child's-cough.

Spar stones from a running stream. Collect the water. Heat the stones. Brew a healing infusion that will silence the cough.

Flora grabs a jug from the kitchen. A lamp. She runs outside before she changes her mind. The night is cold and solid. She stumbles around the back of the inn to where the stream trickles towards the sea. She fills the jug. Plucks stones from the icy water and shoves them into the pocket of her apron.

She lights the fire in the bar. Lines the stones up along the great black hearth. Holds her numb fingers to the flames to warm them.

A knock at the door. She ignores it.

Again, louder. Insistent.

Go away.

A third knock.

The shipwrecked sailor leans wearily against the doorframe, shivering, despite wearing Jack's greatcoat. His cheeks are flushed and his hair is tangled about his shoulders.

"The inn is closed," says Flora. "I'm sorry."

He holds out a hand, preventing her from closing the door. "It's not real, is it."

"I don't know what you're talking about. Please, just leave, Mr Hales. My daughter is unwell."

"Just tell me. Avery's haul. Is it all a lie?"

"I've no idea."

"You spoke of it before. Tell me what you know!" He slams his hand hard against the door.

Flora glares. "It's a myth, ayes. A story. People cling to it because they need hope."

Asher looks over her shoulder to the stones lined up along the hearth. "Healing stones. Is that what you cling to? I thought you more intelligent than that."

She feels heat rising in her cheeks. "My daughter is very ill. I'm desperate."

"What is wrong with her?"

"The child's-cough. The herbal remedies are not working."

"Hot stones won't cure her. But salted water may."

"Salted water?"

"Yes. There is a new school of thought that believes illness is caused by an overactive soul." His voices catches slightly, then grows louder, imbued with sudden confidence. "The cure, many believe, is to cleanse the body with salted water."

Flora hesitates. This man is a liar. She knows it. But for the first time since he stumbled bloodied into her inn, she sees a sincerity in his eyes.

This is his passion. His life.

She steps back, pulling open the door. "Mr Hales. Please. Will you help my daughter?"

"Is she going to die?" Flora asks Asher.

The girl has kicked off her blankets in her sleep. Her nightgown is tangled around skeletal white legs, blonde hair clinging to her flushed cheeks. Her breathing is shallow and husky.

Asher takes the jug of salted water and drizzles it down her throat. "You'll not cure her with magic stones."

He sees the irony. These scornful words coming from the man who has sailed across the world in search of a fairy tale. And why not? Look at this dying child. This ruined man. This sad, creaking tavern, haunted by lost love. Reality is cold and unforgiving.

"The salted water," says Flora, lacing her fingers through the girl's. "Will it work?"

Truly, he has no idea. His knowledge is built on borrowed books and theory. All his life will allow. He longs to be able to offer cures with conviction.

"Yes," he says. "It will work."

She nods faintly. Looks up at him. "Thank you."

What is that in the witch's eyes? Gratitude. Respect.

Where is the suspicion, the distrust?

For a fleeting moment, Asher catches a glimpse of the man he longs to be. The man with power. Knowledge. Wealth.

The man he will never be.

He lets himself out of the inn. Sees an orange glow from the bonfire as the villagers play out their strange ritual.

A light shines in the church.

He climbs the hill and pushes open the gate. Finds himself wandering among the graves. Albert Davey; is he here? Where does a lonely, murdered man lie?

There; a memorial stone. Jacob Bailey, lost at sea. Asher snorts. Backs away from the marker. The wind whips through the graveyard. He shivers violently and pushes open the door of the vestry.

What is he doing here? He is wise and forward thinking. Not a man who cowers at a priest's feet. And yet, now he sees the haul for what it is, he feels himself unravelling. Begins to see himself for who he truly is.

Begins to see that bold, brave Asher Hales is also a myth.

Dodge looks up from the book in his hand. Squints. "The shipwrecked sailor."

Asher shivers. "Why are you here, Father? It's the middle of the night."

"It seems these villagers could use a watchful eye. Even if it's the eye of a man they no longer trust." He hauls himself to his feet and retrieves a greying blanket from the cupboard. Hands it to Asher. "Sit down, boy."

Asher sits, pulling the blanket around his shoulders.

"You are troubled," says Dodge. "Perhaps you might unburden yourself before God."

Asher tries to slow his breathing.

Unburden yourself.

Yes. He feels the weight of it all; his past, his lies, his secrets. Feels the weight of being so far from the man he ought to be.

"I am lost," he tells Dodge. "I feel as though my world has crumbled beneath me."

The vicar says nothing. Allows Asher to continue.

"I want to be a great man, Father. I have spent my life in pursuit of knowledge. Medicine. The work of the animists. I tell myself I will one day have the greatness I deserve."

"The animists," says Dodge. "You chase the soul."

"Yes. The soul is responsible for all the workings of the body."

"Many would say these are theologians' ideas. Not the ideas of a scientist."

"And why must these two views be exclusive? Why can they not exist in harmony?"

Dodge murmurs indistinctly. His gaze drifts out the window into the lightless churchyard.

Asher sighs. "Men are so terrified of new ideas. So afraid to see the world in a different light. I never understood why. But now I do. Now I see how your entire existence is upturned when you realise you've been believing a lie." He rubs his eyes. "I'm a man of science. But I've spent my life searching for something that isn't real." He looks again at the vicar. Can he see the irony; this gnarled, faded man of God? Can he see they've both spent their lives chasing demons in the dark?

"Searching for what?" Dodge asks.

"A myth. I can tell you no more."

"How do you know it isn't real?"

"Because all the evidence points to the opposite. And a man of science looks to evidence."

"Must a man of science also be devoid of faith? You said yourself, science and religion ought to exist in harmony."

Asher pulls the blanket around himself tightly. Faith has led him to a dead end, he is sure of it. "I believed because I had to. I looked down on these people who hear the dead in a storm and believe themselves cursed. But what difference is there between I and them? I'm far more of a fool than any of the people on that beach. And this life I want, this life of greatness, I can see now it will never be more than an illusion."

He closes his eyes. Sees himself in embroidered waistcoats and monogrammed shirts, drinking wine with men whose work he admires.

Fiction, of course. He is penniless. Hopeless.

But then Asher Hales sees with sudden clarity. Scarlett has led him deep into their world. He knows of the tunnel, the church, the false bottom in the hold of Isaac Bailey's lugger.

He knows, of course, of their run to Guernsey tomorrow. And knows the man who had protected these free traders now lies lifeless in the earth.

Fifty pounds reward for the capture of smugglers.

Nothing on Avery's haul. But Avery's haul is a myth.

Asher leaps from his chair and runs from the church. Tears through the village until he reaches the flickering lights of Polperro. He is breathless when he reaches the customs station.

"A lugger will return to these parts tomorrow night," he says. "They will land a load of contraband in Talland Bay. Intercept them."

FRENCH LACE

Scarlett sits on the edge of the cliff and watches flames colour the sky. Behind her, a little to the right, stands the memorial stone to her father; a path worn through the grass towards it.

She feels its presence, as though Jacob is standing behind her. She can't bring herself to look at it.

Asher's story of the murder on the beach is just that; a story. One that, like tales of ghost ships and curses, she can choose to believe or discard.

Her father a killer? The thought is far more foolish than dead men's voices in the wind.

In truth, she has no knowledge with which to acquit him. She had been five years old when Jacob had died. She has no proof of her father's decency beyond garbled, tinted memories. But it is a matter of faith.

And so here is her choice: Asher Hales is a liar. Asher Hales had kissed her lips and whispered of trust and spoken to her in lies.

Her father had been found not guilty. Why should she believe the word of a convicted man?

Her muscles tighten and her skin prickles. She has always believed the Wild to be separate from her true self. An intruder. But perhaps she has been gifted this darkness by her father. Had Jacob truly stood on the landing beach with a gun in his hand? Had he felt the same anger Scarlett had felt when she'd pointed the pistol at Tom Leach? Had her father left her his darkness as well as his debt?

Asher Hales is a liar, she could say until the words lose their meaning. But the darkness inside her makes it frighteningly easy to picture her father pulling the trigger on another man.

She stands abruptly. She can't be here beside his memorial any longer. She stumbles out of the churchyard. George Gibson is staggering towards the beach with his arms full of branches.

"You're right," Scarlett tells him. "That ship has cursed us."

Perhaps it has not bought ghosts and demons, but it has brought her Asher Hales. Those garbled memories of her father are all she has of him. How dare he chip away at them?

Gibson nods. "Ayes, maid. It will destroy us if we're not vigilant."

"I was a fool," she says. "I trusted him. The man from the wreck."

"Trust?" Gibson steps close, his cheeks streaked with ash. "Don't you know, a demon can work its way inside your head. And when they do that, you'll believe anything."

She lets herself into the cottage and lights the lamp. A scrawled note from Isaac sits on the table. Spending the night on the lugger. No sign of Asher. No doubt he has dropped his tales at her feet and disappeared.

Scarlett's head pounds. She feels like she has lost her father all over again. Has Isaac heard these stories about the murder on the beach? How can she ask? How can she risk darkening his memories of their father too? She feels rattled at her foundations.

What a fool she had been to trust Asher so willingly. She has always fought to see the best in people; her fight back against the anger inside her. But what has she done but open herself up to disappointment?

That night, she had sat at the edge of the churchyard and watched through the window as Asher whimpered before the priest.

Deceiver, she'd thought.

Dodge: *manipulator*.

Look down at the beach.

Gibson: *madman*.

Martha Francis: *secret keeper*.

She hates this bitterness that is taking root inside her. But perhaps it is safer. Perhaps it is closer to the truth. Perhaps bitterness is better than believing a lie.

She hopes Asher has left for good. Hopes there'll be no voyage to Guernsey tomorrow. The Wild is close to the surface. She doubts it will stay silent if they are flung across the sea together.

She moves to blow out the candle, seeking darkness.

She stops.

What is that on the table, beneath her brother's knitted cap? She'd not noticed it when she'd stumbled bleary-eyed into the cottage.

Lace.

She lifts its delicate threads; holds them close to the candle flame. Gold anchors glitter in the light.

Gold anchors.

She has heard Asher speak of this lace. Lace the *Avalon* had been transporting. Lace once carried by vanished men.

Lace that is now in her brother's possession.

Her breathing quickens.

Isaac had made a trading run the night of the wreck. And now she sees. He had been trading with the *Avalon*. Trading with the man who had turned up dead on their landing beach.

Scarlett feels hot and dizzy.

She will not believe it. After all she has learned these past days, she cannot follow this thread.

She looks down at the lace.

Evidence, says the Wild. She had pronounced her father guilty with far less.

Her father is nothing more than distant figure she had moulded into a hero. But Isaac is real. The love she has for him is far more solid than anything she has ever felt for Jacob. She longs for her sunny sham of a world where the men she cares for can do no wrong.

To hell with the *Avalon* and all the trouble that washed up with her. The villagers are right to burn her.

She grips the lace, her hand trembling. Is this where George Gibson's terror has come from? Guilt? Were he and Isaac the ones to put the bullet in the quartermaster's chest?

No. Not her decent, moral brother who had given up everything to raise her.

Her brother who had dug the pistol into Leach's stomach. Sent his ship to the bottom of the river.

She had never imagined her father capable of killing. But with each stir of the darkness inside her, the possibility seems more and more plausible. Is the Wild inside Isaac too?

It has her. It had her father. Why not her brother?

She shoves the lace into her pocket. Blows out the lamp.

VOYAGE

Scarlett stands at the edge of the harbour and stares at her brother's ship. The morning is pink and misty. Her eyes sting with sleeplessness and old smoke.

Through the window of the pilot house, she sees Isaac bending over his log.

How many times has she watched him do this? Ready his ship to be filled with smuggled goods? Land by moonlight, deceive the authorities. And what had she seen in him but decency? An honest man in a life he did not choose.

But she sees now there are pieces she has been missing. The night she had stood on the clifftop and watched the *Avalon* catapult into Talland Bay, Isaac and his men had been on the very same ship. Cleared her of her cargo.

And what of her crew?

She can't bear to confront him. Better to live in doubt. Better to cling to those last threads of optimism.

She glances over her shoulder into the empty street. No sign of Asher. She is glad of it.

If Isaac had been aboard the *Avalon*, Asher's tales of killing the crew are lies. *Sent the smugglers away*, he had told her. And yet her pocket is crammed with smuggled French lace.

Lies for what purpose? What kind of mind tells tales of murdering men?

Gabriel scrambles out of the hatch, trailed by Caroline and Mary. Isaac kisses each of them. One, two, three.

Do they know, Scarlett wonders? Does Caroline know her husband walked the decks of the wrecked ship? Has he seen the faces of the vanished men?

Isaac watches them leave. He leans over the gunwale and calls down to Scarlett. The side of his face is bruised and dark, a cut beside his eye. Reluctantly, she makes her way towards the ship. Reaches for the ladder and climbs aboard.

"Where's Hales?" asks Isaac.

She shrugs.

He nods at her mud-caked skirts. "You can't come to sea dressed like that. There are spare breeches in the cabin."

Scarlett glances down at her skirts. She'd left the house without thinking, dressed in her smoke-stained clothes. She trudges below deck and exchanges her petticoats for Isaac's shirt and breeches. Cinches the waist with a belt and pulls her cloak back over her shoulders.

"You've not slept," says Isaac, when she returns to the deck. "You're in a state. What's happened? Has Hales done something?"

She clenches her teeth. Refuses to look at him.

"I don't want you at sea like this. It's not safe for any of us. Tell me what's happened."

She turns away, her throat tightening. She will see the best in him. Find a forgiving explanation for that lace with gold anchors.

"I'm well," she says huskily.

She hears footsteps. Asher climbs onto the ship. His face is shadowed with sleeplessness, but his eyes are determined. Isaac nods to him wordlessly.

Underway.

Smoke curls through the churchyard.

The vicar trudges down to the beach. The bonfire roars, sparks shooting into the sky. The pile is far too big to be the ruins of the ship. Dodge had watched the fire throughout the night. Burning down, blazing, burning down, reborn. Now the flames lick at... what? Chairs? A table? Is that a man's bed? This fear, he realises has seeped into every part of their lives.

George Gibson watches the flames with wild eyes; his hair loose, shirtsleeves black with ash.

"Go home, Mr Gibson," says Dodge. "Sleep will do you good." He rubs his stinging eyes. "Sleep will do us all good."

"How can I sleep? I can think of nothing but when death will come for me. I'm afraid to close my eyes in case I never open them again."

Dodge presses a hand to the man's arm. Tries to steer him away from the fire. Perhaps with the leader gone, the rest might disperse.

But no, here come more men, trudging down Bridles Lane. Lord protect them. He knows these men. The free traders from Polruan.

"Burning the wreck won't solve your problems," Tom Leach spits. "You've a witch in your village." Such venom in his voice that Dodge feels a run chill through him. "I was cursed by your innkeeper."

The villagers' eyes flash and harden. Voices rise.

No. When we fear the devil, we turn to God. We don't become the very monsters we are running from.

Dodge hollers to the crowd, his words disappearing beneath the clamour. He has tried to create faithful, decent souls. And yet before him is a band of witch-hunters, arming themselves with flaming sticks and axes. George Gibson leads the charge towards the Mariner's Arms. And the vicar sees his own failure.

WITCH

Banging on the door. Violent. Insistent.

Flora peeks through the parlour window. The street is full of men with weapons in their hands. Behind them, smoke darkens the sky.

Her heart thuds. She locks Bessie's bedroom and throws the key in the drawer.

A weapon. She needs a weapon. Had Jack owned a pistol?

She snatches the fire poker. Stands with her back pressed against Bessie's door. She grips the wall to stop the trembling in her hands.

Glass shatters. "Witch!"

She squeezes her eyes closed. Mumbles a hurried prayer.

How many women before her, she wonders, had pleaded to God while *witch* floated through their broken windows?

She hears the thud of boots inside the tavern.

She will meet them. Face them. See they come nowhere near her daughter. Gripping the bannister, she edges downstairs, the poker held in front of her. Six, seven, eight men? Perhaps more. George Gibson at the front, his face flushed and wild. Beside him, Tom Leach.

The men circle her. Grab her arms. The poker clatters to the floor.

"Let go of me!"

They march her from the tavern, towards the funnel of smoke. The people shout all at once, their voices unintelligible. Martha stoops at the edge of the beach, tears rolling down her cheeks. There are those who support her, Flora realises. But the men who don't are stronger.

Gibson looms over her, his wild grey hair grazing her cheek. He smells of sweat and smoke. "You laid a curse on Tom Leach. Do you deny it?"

"It was a trick. Nothing more." Her words tangle with fear.

"A trick?" Leach spits.

"Yes. Nothing more. I swear it."

"Did you curse us by bringing that ship?" Gibson hisses.

179

"The ship? No! I—"

Leach produces a knife and holds it close to Flora's face. Dizziness courses through her. "They say to break a curse, you must bleed the witch."

Her legs weaken. The hands around the tops of her arms yank her back to standing.

Leach presses the knife to her stomach. "Shall we cut the witch here?" Her throat. "Or here?"

"Please," Flora coughs. "My daughter. I'm all she has."

Her eyes fall to the gun in Leach's belt. He jerks suddenly and swipes the knife across her forearm. White-hot pain. She clenches her teeth. Will not give these people the satisfaction of hearing her scream.

The men holding her arm release their grip as blood runs over their fingers. She lurches forward, snatches Leach's pistol. Hands yank her hair, pulling her backwards. She falls onto her side, not releasing the gun. The men circle her. Flora scrambles to her feet, holding out the pistol. Her blood beads on the sand. She backs away. Reaches the top of the beach. And she runs.

Where to go? Bessie is alone at the inn. But she cannot risk the men storming through her windows again.

Help. She needs help.

Isaac and Scarlett are at sea.

Reuben, perhaps, would help her, but she will never make it to Polperro without the men catching her.

Desperation has her knocking on Caroline's door.

Caroline's eyes fall to the blood tricking down Flora's arm. She pulls her inside and locks the door. "What happened?"

Flora gulps down her breath. "They blame me for the wreck. They believe I cursed them."

"Mad fools." Caroline pushes back her bloodstained sleeve. "The cut is deep. It will need stitching."

"Not now. I need you to go to Bessie. Please."

Caroline wraps a cloth tightly around Flora's forearm. "Where will you go?"

"I don't know. But I need to keep those men away from the inn."

"You've a weapon," says Caroline. "You have power over them."

Yes. The pistol is solid in her hand. Real power. Not flimsy incantations whispered in desperation.

Caroline scoops her baby from the cradle, cocooning her in blankets. "We'll go to the inn together. Bessie needs her mother."

Flora glances out the window. Two hundred yards from the cottage to the inn. The street is empty. Perhaps the pistol has kept the crowd away. "We need to go now," she tells Caroline. "Quickly."

They hurry down the hill. The beach is still dotted with people, still murky with smoke.

The door of the tavern hangs open. Broken glass juts from the windows. Flora pushes the door tentatively. A dark figure stands in the bar. She raises the pistol, hands trembling. "Stay where you are."

"Please, Mrs Kelly," says Dodge. "I'm not here to hurt you."

She gulps down her breath. "What do you want?"

He shuffles towards her. Glances at the blood splattered down the front of her dress. "I'm sorry I couldn't keep those animals from coming after you."

Flora snorts. "Did you not send them?"

"I suppose it is to my shame that you would think such a thing."

She pushes past him and hurries upstairs towards Bessie's bedroom. Unlocks the door to find her daughter asleep on her side, her breathing rapid and raspy. Flora straightens the blankets and smooths Bessie's hair.

Dodge joins her, breathless. "Your daughter is unwell?"

Flora says nothing.

"Perhaps I might pray for her."

"You did not come to pray for my daughter. Tell me why you're here."

Dodge begins to pace, the floorboards creaking beneath his boots. "The people of this town are scared. They are divided between the way of God and the old ways your mother once followed. Ways you too have chosen to follow." He grips the foot of Bessie's bed. "Last night I was reminded that perhaps two ways can exist in harmony. Perhaps if the people see you and I working together to end the curse they believe has befallen them, it will restore a sense of peace."

"You expect me to go back out there? I was lucky they didn't kill me."

"You have set yourself up as a healer," says Dodge. "A figure of note. And now people will turn to you in good times and bad."

Flora rubs her eyes. "I just wanted to help them."

"Indeed. I have thought the same many times."

She runs a finger over Bessie's knuckles. "I know how you see me, Father. As a dark witch. And thanks to you, that's how much of the village sees me."

"Thanks to you, much of the village sees me as a fraud who has done nothing but stoke their nightmares." His voice softens slightly. "This town, these people, they cannot survive with such a divide. Look at them tearing themselves apart. They need to see you and I working together."

Flora closes her eyes. Her heart is still racing and the cut on her arm burns. She has no desire to face the crowd again. The hunched and fragile vicar can't protect her. He can barely protect himself. But what are her choices? Barricade herself in the inn until the fire and the fury has burned out? Let the village believe she is responsible for their ills?

She sucks in her breath. Looks up at the vicar. "Very well, Father. As you wish."

He eyes her bloodstained sleeve. "Forgive me. I ought to have done more to help you." He presses a paper-thin hand over hers. "I failed your mother, Mrs Kelly. I don't intend to fail you too."

Flora closes the door on Bessie and ushers Dodge into the parlour. "What do you wish me to do?"

He sits at the table and clasps his speckled hands. "For better or for worse, we have created a village of believers. And we must use that to our advantage."

Flora thinks of Tom Leach fleeing her rotten vegetables. Yes, people can be trained to believe anything.

Chaos and unreason have raged like a disease. She is not without blame. But perhaps now she might spread the antidote.

She carries her mother's chest into the centre of the room. Caroline watches from the doorway.

At the bottom of the trunk is the grotesque, blackened heart. Flora stares at it. It had been enough to strike terror into Tom Leach. Perhaps she can use that fear. Twist it. Convince these frightened people she is fighting a powerful curse with powerful magic.

Pierce the heart with pins and draw out the dark.

She lifts the jar from the chest.

Caroline's lip curls. "What is that?"

"A charm. To break a curse."

She gives a short laugh. "Do you believe in such things?"

"It doesn't matter what I believe. It matters what the people believe." Flora can see this through Caroline's eyes, of course. Can see it through the doubting eyes of a foreigner.

She holds her aching arm close to her body. There is no room for doubting eyes. She must dig into superstition, into faith. Dig into beliefs as old as the land. If she is to calm the unreason, she needs to convince them that she herself believes.

She turns abruptly as footsteps thunder on the stairs.

A LETTER

Saint Peter Port is just as Asher remembers.

Brick houses line the waterfront, the anchorage a forest of masts. The afternoon sun shines off the water, making a silhouette of the castle.

Asher waits with Scarlett by the harbour. The streets are a wash of coloured gowns and carriages. Barefooted slaves trail men in velvet frock coats and sailors stumble bleary-eyed from harbour taverns. Anker-makers heave their wares into waiting coaches.

Scarlett paces the cobbled walkway in boots and breeches, oblivious to passing glances. Her brother has disappeared to the office of Reuben's agent. There is money changing hands, contraband being loaded onto wagons. In a few hours they will return to Talland Bay with a full ship and be swooped upon by revenue men. Revenue men who know the lugger's route, know of her false bulkhead.

Perhaps it will be a strange kind of revenge, to string up Jacob's children.

The lugger will be broken up; her parts sold at auction. Isaac will be thrown into naval slops. He will have a touch rod forced into his hand and he will be ordered to light the cannons against the Spanish.

And what of Scarlett? Perhaps a jail cell. Perhaps a lenient Cornish jury.

If the lugger is full enough, perhaps the hangman.

Will she walk calmly to her death? Or be hauled onto the scaffold a tearful mess?

Asher sees her with a rope around her neck, sees her patched woollen skirts bubble around her as she falls. Black hair a stark contrast to her lifeless white skin.

When would her soul leave her? When would she stop being that starry-eyed person that had seen the good in him?

What does it matter now? Dead or alive, she is no longer that person.

But then something twists inside him. He thinks of her, pink-cheeked upon the clifftops. Thinks of her hauling him from the drowning *Avalon*.

"You can't go back to Talland tonight," he says suddenly. "You can't be on the lugger."

She gives him little more than a passing glance. Keeps pacing. "What are you talking about?"

Here is what a good man would do: tell Scarlett about the revenue men. Tell her it was all a mistake. Have Isaac moor in Guernsey for the night and return to Talland in clear waters.

Scarlett will go free. But Asher will be poor. He will never have that elusive university degree. And he will never again see the gratitude he had seen from the witch when he had proffered a cure for her daughter.

Which man is he to be?

He takes her arm and pulls her from the walkway. Sits on the harbour wall. "It's not safe for you to be on that ship. Isaac and I will return to Talland without you. You'll find passage back on another vessel."

She stands over him and plants her hands on her hips. "Do you think me mad? Why should I trust a word that comes from you?"

Asher opens his mouth to speak. Finds nothing.

"You didn't kill your crew," Scarlett spits. "Your tale of being fired upon by madmen, it was all a lie."

He feels a sudden rush of anger, a sudden rush of fear. "Why do you think me lying?"

"I don't *think* you lying, Asher. I know it! What kind of madman would confess to murders he did not commit?"

He stands to face her. Stares her down. *Madman.* How dare she? He feels a sudden urge to strike her.

She rams her fists into his shoulders. "What happened aboard that ship, Asher? Tell me!"

He forces himself to breathe evenly, though his insides are rattling. "I have told you. I have told you everything."

"Everything you've told me is a lie. You didn't kill your crew. And my father did not kill anyone." She looks at her feet. "My father is a good man."

He hears the tremor in her voice.

Say it again. Convince yourself of its truth.

Asher reaches into the pocket of his coat. Pulls out the yellowing letter he has carried with him for the past sixteen years. "Jacob is a dog, Scarlett. He's deceived you as much as he did me."

She falters. Keeps staring at her boots. Finally, she dares to look up at him. "What did you say?"

He hands her the letter.

Jacob is no longer in Talland. He left this place in his fishing boat, the village believing him drowned. On your return to England, you will find him in Portreath.

The words swim in front of Scarlett's eyes.

She glances at the date. 1724. The year her father had disappeared.

Her throat tightens. "Who wrote this?"

"No one you know."

"This person is lying. My father didn't go to Portreath. My father drowned at sea."

"Did they find his boat? His body?"

She feels a sudden weakness in her legs. "There is never a body. The sea makes sure of it." Yes, it is easy to mould the truth. Make it fit. Make it easy to swallow. If Asher can do it, so can she. "My father is dead. His grave is in our churchyard."

"His grave?"

No. His memorial stone.

She had never questioned it. An honourable dead father, she realises, is so much better than a living man who has abandoned his family in the face of his debts. The world feels colourless. "Whoever wrote this letter is making things up."

"What reason would they have to do that?"

"I don't know, Asher! But you have plenty! That much is obvious!" She screws up the page. But then shoves it into her pocket.

She sees her own foolishness. Trusting, naïve Scarlett who sees the sun before the clouds. Who sees good in the world around her. Sees only what she wants to see.

Bitterness rises in her throat. She drops to her knees at the harbour edge and retches into the water. Nothing comes up. She reaches into the sea and splashes her hot cheeks.

Asher stands behind her. "You were to be my key. I was to take you to Portreath. You would bring Jacob out of hiding for me."

She sits with her back to him, letting droplets of water slide from her chin. She feels the Wild heat her heart, tighten her muscles. "That's why you're here? That's what I am to you? Your key to finding my father?"

For a while, he says nothing. "You were more once," he tells her finally. "You made me believe I could be the man I long to be."

Scarlett turns to look at him. For a long time, she stares at him without speaking.

Deceiver.

Manipulator.

Madman.

Secret keeper.

She lets this new, accurate view of him wash away the last of her love-struck blindness.

She turns suddenly as Isaac leaps from a wagon stacked with crates and barrels. The dinghy bumps against the harbour wall, ready to be loaded and rowed back to the lugger.

Asher climbs into the boat to take the ankers from Isaac.

Scarlett kneels on the wall and looks down at him. His eyes are red and shadowy, his shoulders sunken. A shadow of his polished self. "You planned to take me to Portreath?" she hisses.

"Yes." Asher waits until Isaac has returned to the wagon. "Perhaps your father would tell you his secrets. Tell you all he knows of that haul. But I see now that all Jacob knows is that Avery's haul is a myth."

"A myth," she says. "After all this, you believe it a myth?"

Asher glances at her, then looks away hurriedly. Is that fear in his eyes? Can he see how close the darkness is to the surface? He takes a crate from Isaac and stacks it into the corner of the boat.

"Eventually," he says slowly, "everyone stops believing."

TO THE FIRE

'A public path leads by at no great distance from the spot and on diverse occasions has the labourer returning from his works been scared nigh into lunacy by sights and sounds of a very dreadful character.'

Taken from a letter to Rev. Richard Dodge from Mr Gryllis,
Rector of Lanreath
1725

Flora snatches the pistol from the table. She rushes to the drawer and hands Caroline the key. "Lock Mary in my mother's room."

Men charge into the parlour. Leach grabs the chest and upends it over the floor. He hurls a vial of nail clippings into the cold grate. Spins around to face the other men. "You question why you're ill-wished? How can you be otherwise when you've black magic in the village tavern?"

"Ignorant fool," spits Flora.

Gibson points a grimy finger at Dodge. "You expect loyalty, Father? When we find you here?"

Leach lurches towards Flora. "Give me my gun, witch. What need do you have for such earthly things?" He makes a grab for it, but she darts backwards, clattering into the table.

Dodge shuffles towards them, hand outstretched. "Put the gun down, Mrs Kelly. Please. Before someone is hurt."

Men rifle through the spilled contents of the chest. Glass shatters as jars are flung into the fireplace. Bunches of herbs are kicked across the floor.

"Stop this second!" cries Dodge. "Look at yourselves! Look at what you're becoming!"

A wild arm catches him on the side of the head and he stumbles, landing hard against the sideboard. Flora grabs his arm, the pistol spilling. She kicks it across the room. Caroline darts in from the hallway and snatches it from the floor.

Into the fireplace go feathers and flowers. Gibson reaches for the jar containing the blackened bullock heart.

"Stop," Flora cries, suddenly, instinctively. "Destroy that and you'll have no way of ridding us of this curse."

He lowers the jar. "Are you lying to us, witch?"

She gulps down her breath. "No. I can use the heart to draw out the curse. It's a charm of my mother's. She did such a thing many times."

He steps towards her, his breath hot and stale. "If you have the power to end this, why have you not done it already? Why let that body wash up on our beach? Why let Bobby Carter die?"

Flora looks past Gibson at Leach. "You wish to blame someone for Bobby's death, you ought not be looking at me."

Dodge stands shakily and holds out his hand for the jar. "Give it to me, Mr Gibson. This town has been divided for long enough."

Hesitantly, Gibson hands Dodge the jar. Flora takes it, shoves it into the pocket of her apron.

"We will go now to the beach," says the vicar. "We will see an end to this darkness. This madness." He glances at Flora. "Mrs Kelly?"

She nods. Picks up a crumpled parchment of incantations, scrawled in her mother's flowery hand. She shoves it into her pocket beside the jar. Perhaps carrying a little of her mother's handwriting might help her carry a little of her mother's faith. "Get out of my house," she tells the men. "And then I will come."

The crowd snakes slowly from the parlour. Flora laces her cloak. Helps the vicar shuffle to the stair rail.

Caroline hands her the pistol. "Take it. Just in case."

Flora nods. Slides it into her cloak.

Caroline touches her wrist. "Be careful."

She manages a faint smile.

To the beach. To the fire.

Witch they had called her. So *witch* she will be.

BELIEVERS

They walk together to the beach, the witch and the vicar. Walk to the fire and the frenzied, smoke-stained villagers.

The sun is sinking; the sky orange behind the smoke haze.

"The churchyard," Dodge murmurs. "These people need to see this done beneath the eyes of God."

Flora leads the way, past her inn with its broken windows and snaking tunnel. Up Bridles Lane where the demons gather. Towards the creaking gate of the churchyard.

She hears voices behind her.

Where is she going?

To the bell house.

Sacred ground.

She keeps walking.

Witch. How dare she enter?

She glances over her shoulder.

George Gibson at the front of the crowd. Martha Francis huddled in her cloak. There are the men who had held her arms and dragged her from the inn. Tom Leach stands among them, her blood still staining his knife blade.

Flora stops at the edge of the cemetery. The sea stretches out behind her, grey and white and restless. How many times has she stood here, signalling to the traders at the end of Dodge's exorcisms? She has been as responsible as anyone for sparking the mania that has consumed the village.

"Let us pray." The vicar bows his head. Wind billows up from the sea and makes a cloud of his black robes. "Strengthen us in the power of your might, oh God. Dress us in your armour so we might stand firm against the schemes of the devil." He turns to Flora. "The heart," he murmurs.

She takes the jar from her pocket. A murmur ripples through the churchyard. She feels Tom Leach's eyes on her; dark and hard. Beside him, Gibson is edgy, peering over his shoulder into the shadows of Bridles Lane.

Flora holds the blackened heart in her palm.

"As I pierce this heart," she begins, forcing a steadiness into her voice, "the darkness will be drawn from this place."

Another murmur from the crowd. She can't make out their words.

Fraud? Charlatan?

Witch?

She speaks the incantation loudly, clearly.

In the name of the Father, the Son and the Holy Ghost.

Shoves the first pin into the blackened flesh.

Beside her, she hears Gibson's breathing quicken.

He cries out. "Stop her, Father! Don't you see them? The demons? Her black magic is bringing them to us!"

Dodge presses a hand to Gibson's arm. "Calm yourself, my son. The Lord is with us." He nods at Flora to continue.

Another pin. Another shout from Gibson. He grabs at Flora's elbow. "Stop! Please!" He drops to his knees, clutching fistfuls of her skirts.

She glances at Dodge.

"Keep going," he tells her.

Gibson howls. Points to the shadows in the corner of the churchyard.

His wild cry gives Flora a sudden, violent chill. She stops. Bends over him and looks into his feverish eyes. "This is nothing but a trick, do you understand me? Look." She flings the heart from the cliff. A murmur ripples through the villagers. A woman pushes forward and peers into the sea.

Gibson stumbles, backing towards the edge of the cliff. "Stop them, Father. Please. They're coming for me." Sweat trickles down the side of his face.

Flora grips his shoulders. Drops her voice. "There's nothing in the lane. There never was. You know that, ayes? Our exorcisms, they were just a cover."

Gibson shakes his head. He breathes short and fast. "No. You're wrong. You've closed your mind and now you can't see the world as it truly is." He drops to his knees, burying his eyes in her blood-splattered skirt. "But I can see. They're coming for me. Because of what I did aboard that ship."

And then Flora does see.

Hales didn't kill that man.

How are you so sure?

She pushes Gibson into sitting. Looks him in the eye. "You and Isaac were on the *Avalon*."

The cutter appears like a blot of ink against the sunset.

Asher lifts the spying glass.

Revenue men.

He says nothing.

Scarlett's hands are clenched, her shoulders back. Something is boiling inside her.

She reaches into her cloak. Pulls out a spool of lace and flings it at her brother's feet.

Asher has seen this lace before. He had carried it from the hold of the *Avalon* and stored it in the captain's cabin to protect it from bilge water.

And now it is on Isaac Bailey's ship.

Scarlett glares at her brother. "You were on the *Avalon*."

Asher's heart begins to speed. Isaac Bailey was on his ship. Isaac Bailey and his crew put a bullet in the quartermaster's chest. Somewhere, in a distant pocket of his mind, Asher is aware he ought to feel anger at this. Ought to feel to the need for retribution, the desire for justice on account of his murdered crewmate. But the only thoughts he can manage are these:

Isaac Bailey knows the truth of what happened that night. He knows the weak and miserable man Asher Hales truly is. Sickness rises in his throat.

Isaac says nothing. His eyes lift to the ship on the horizon. He snatches the spying glass.

Yes. Revenue men.

"Was this your doing?" Isaac demands.

His doing? Of course not. Asher knows better than to accept responsibility while Scarlett has such fire in her eyes. This will not be his doing until he is safely aboard the revenue cutter and the Baileys are in chains.

Isaac curses under his breath. "Bring her about," he calls sharply. "We'll try and lose them."

Scarlett stands on the foredeck, staring her brother down.

"Christ, Scarlett!" he cries. "Move! If they catch us, this bastard will tell them where the goods are hidden!"

She kicks the lace towards him.

Isaac charges past her. "I've no time to explain myself to you."

"Make time!"

"To convince you I didn't kill those men? Is that what you want? And why in hell should I have to do that? Why do you see good in everyone but the worst in me?"

Asher glances at Scarlett. Her brother is wrong. That girl who sees the good in everyone is gone.

Isaac turns to leave, then stops. He sees it too, Asher realises. Sees this new depth to his sister's anger.

She steps towards him, not taking her eyes from his. "Tell me what happened."

Isaac looks at the revenue ship. Looks back at his sister. "Reuben arranged a rendezvous with the *Avalon's* captain. We came aboard to buy a shipment of whisky. The crew was mad. Saw ghosts. Wanted to rid themselves of a ship they saw as cursed. They paid me in coin and lace to ferry them ashore."

"Ferry them ashore?" Scarlett's voice is clipped. Disbelieving.

"Yes."

Behind the lies, Asher has always known, of course. Knows the crew of the *Avalon* saw him as a monster. Mad filth, who cut up the body of a dead man.

He was knocked unconscious by his own crew before the smugglers had even boarded. A blow to the head and left to die. How could he have admitted such a thing?

A man abandoned on a plundered merchant ship is not who he wants Asher Hales to be. A man who fights off would-be murderers, yes. Who refuses to be sunk with a wreck, yes. Mad filth, no.

But when he looks up, Asher sees he has become invisible. Scarlett's eyes are flashing, fixed to her brother. "The crew are alive?"

"Does that surprise you, Scarlett?" Ice in Isaac's voice. "Did you have me pegged as a murderer?"

"You left Mr Hales to die."

The rest of the night Asher remembers only in fragments.

His crewmates leaning over him. *Madman.*

His crewmates dragging his body into the cabin so he'd not be seen by the boarding smugglers. Footsteps thundering down the passage as the traders raided the ship. Men climbing onto the deck.

And then, when consciousness returned completely; the impenetrable darkness of an empty ship.

Left to die on account of his great mind.

And as he lay there feeling blood trickle down his neck, he'd had just one thought. No one could ever know of this. No one could know of such shame.

He climbed to his feet, dizzily searching the ship for any leftover life. He found Quartermaster Barrett in the hold. And the thought came to him. One man murdered? No, let the world believe there had been five men killed. Let them see Asher Hales as the brave man who had survived both a shipwreck and a shower of gunfire. Far more commendable than being left to die.

But in pliable, trusting Scarlett he had seen an opportunity to become more than just the man who had survived a murder. With her trust secured, he had become the killer. An act of necessity, of course. Necessity and great bravery. And through her eyes, Asher had seen himself as the man he'd always wanted to be.

But now Scarlett's optimistic eyes see nothing. The man who fought off his five killers is gone. Left to die.

The smugglers who had taken Asher's crew ashore had been nameless. Faceless. But now, when he pictures the men scrambling from the *Avalon* and leaving him to bleed and drown, it is Isaac Bailey at the helm of the rescue ship.

Confront him. Demand answers.

But Asher Hales says nothing. Because beneath the lies and the dreams, he knows he is nothing more than a coward.

Scarlett is watching herself from afar. The world feels hazy. Unfocused. A distant, detached part of her can see Isaac's innocence. But the rage taking her over wants him condemned. "The dead man on the beach. Who killed him?"

The sea streams over the gunwale, soaking her boots. The lugger flies, plunging violently into the waves.

The revenue cutter is faster.

Isaac pushes past her question. "We need to lose the cargo." He looks pointedly at Asher. "Help me."

Scarlett chases the men into the hold. She feels both heavy and alive with energy. Hears herself speak without the thoughts entering her head. "The dead man. Tell me."

And Isaac tells her.

As he hauls the ankers from the hold, he tells her of the fear he had sensed the moment he had stepped aboard the *Avalon*. Tells her of the scrawled crucifixes and the crew red-eyed with sleeplessness. As he heaves the crates through the hatch, he tells her of the current in the air. The way it prickled his skin. The way he had questioned, fleetingly, the solidity of his rational world.

He slams the hatch and tells her of the blood staining the deck of the *Avalon's* sick bay. Their first mate's body carved up by a madman.

Scarlett's thinks of Asher and his fascination with death. She sees him with a knife in his hand. Blood-stained skin.

Isaac tells her more. As they shove the contraband into the sea, he tells her of the unexplained shape passing through the hold.

Ghost, said the men. *Demon.*

And Isaac tells her how quickly fear spreads. He tells her of the panic that rippled through his own men.

The pistol in George Gibson's fist.

The shadow again.

Unreason, it spreads like plague.

Thirty years of Dodge's stories have worked their way beneath the men's skin. Thirty years of ghosts and demons and sea spirits.

Unreason makes it easy to see things on the edge of your vision. To see a ghost where there is only a shadow. To see a demon where there is only a man.

Gibson whirled around. Fired.

The quartermaster fell.

And there was silence.

A cursed ship, said the men of the *Avalon*. They loaded their cargo into the hold of Isaac's lugger. Emptied their cabins.

"Coin and lace. Ferry us ashore."

Let the ship wreck.

Scarlett looks into the sea. The barrels and cases vanish below the surface. Whisky. Tobacco. Wine. Enough to tie them to Reuben for another lifetime.

She doesn't care. The Wild tells her to leave this place, this life. Escape Talland and let her brother carry the debt. His story doesn't vindicate him. His story shows that *we don't keep secrets* is the biggest of lies. Shows that there is trust between them only when Isaac chooses.

Beneath them, the sea thunders. The sea that had brought the *Avalon* to Talland. The sea that has ill-wished them. The sea that brought them Asher Hales, the man who has shattered the pedestal on which she had placed her father, her brother. On which she had placed Asher himself.

Demon, say the villagers. Perhaps there is a little truth to it.

She reaches into her belt. Pulls out the pistol and holds it to Asher's chest.

"Get off the ship," she says.

Send him back to where he came from. To break a curse, a sacrifice must be made.

Gibson's breath is fast and ragged.

Ghosts, he'd told Flora. A bloodstained ship. A terrified crew.

Demons.

He stares into Bridles Lane, eyes glassy with fear.

What does he see? What form has he given these creatures crawled from his nightmares?

Flora squeezes his hands. "There's nothing there. I swear it." Her voice is muted. How can her mumbled words compete with a lifetime of belief?

"I killed that man," Gibson coughs. "And now the demons are coming for me." He pulls at her cloak. Finds the pistol in her pocket. He yanks it out and presses it into her hand. "Shoot me. Before they find me." He clamps his hands over hers, working her finger towards the trigger. She pulls free. Hurls the pistol over the edge of the cliff. Gibson lurches towards her with a cry. His fingers dig into the cut on her arm. Pain shoots through her, blurring her vision.

And she sees the shadows move. Sees, what? A shifting of the darkness in the corner of the churchyard. Arms? Legs? Eyes?

No.

She looks again. The shape is still there, moving in the shadow. A strange, fluid, human form.

She feels suddenly hot. Her ears ring. The world loses colour.

Unreason. Spreads like plague. She will not let it catch her. Will not let Dodge's exorcisms be anything more than theatre. This is her eyes playing tricks, nothing more. This is flames reflecting in the black mirror. This is her stress, her fear, her pain, her grief.

The opening of the tunnel, the counterfeit licence, the revenue men at her door. But for all the clamouring of her rational mind, she can't pull her eyes from that shape in the shadows.

Beside her, Gibson stills. He follows her gaze. Does he see what she sees?

He scrambles towards the cliff edge. With his sudden movement, Flora's world is solid again. She dives after him, clutches desperately at his coat hem. The worn fabric slides through her fingers as he jumps, flying from the edge of the churchyard into the waiting sea.

Scarlett backs Asher towards the gunwale until his spine is hard against the rail. "Get off the ship," she says again.

Isaac edges towards her, hand outstretched. "Scarlett—"

She glances at him. Is that fear in his eyes? What will you do now, Isaac? Douse the lights? The sun is still sinking.

"Give me the pistol," he says. "Please."

When Scarlett remembers her father, he has Isaac's face, Isaac's body. She is sure in reality, her brother is not such a copy of Jacob, but her memories are hazy and she fills the gaps as she can.

She looks at Isaac now and sees Jacob on the landing beach, pistol in hand. She sees a trail of men climb from the *Avalon*. Sees the ravaged body coughed from the wreck. "Why should I listen to you? You're as much of a liar as the others."

"The others? Who are the others?" Isaac steps closer. "Who are the others, Scarlett? Who else has been lying to you?" She hears the control in his voice, the forced composure, the thinly veiled fear.

She turns away. Stares instead at Asher. The man in front of her is dishevelled; his face colourless. His shoulders curl. Hands white around the gunwale.

How had she seen superiority in this pathetic creature? Is he a different man? Or is she seeing through different eyes?

She hears herself say: "Jump."

Asher's eyes flicker. "I can't swim."

Good. Then the sea spirits will take him. He will vanish into the depths and the darkness over the town will be lifted. Perhaps the darkness in herself might also be eased.

She cocks the trigger. A sacrifice to the sea spirits. A sacrifice to the wildness so desperate to see her kill. "Jump."

And Asher does.

The sea rises to meet him. Steals his breath. Cold water closes in over his head, pulling him down, down. Filling his boots, pulling at his coat, making his hair dance around his head. His muscles tighten with shock.

Fitting that he might die in Cornish waters. He has always reserved a special hatred for the place. And the place has reserved the same special hatred for him.

But then he finds himself kicking.

And he remembers himself.

Asher Hales is a man with ambition. Dreams. He will not become these foolish people's sacrifice. He will not drown to appease the dark thing Scarlett Bailey has become. Will not give her the satisfaction of seeing him die.

He opens his eyes beneath the water. Gains little light. He wriggles free of his coat, letting it float to the bottom with the barrels. He kicks again. Feels himself rise.

Kicks again. Again. This time, strong and sure.

Somehow, he will win against a world that has done nothing but beat him down. He will stand before a body with a scalpel in his hand and the crowd will hold their breath in anticipation of his brilliance.

For all his lies, he sees a sudden, brilliant truth. Asher Hales is a survivor. Exile, abandonment, shipwreck, drowning. The crushing reality of the haul's nonexistence.

Today, the revenue men will find an empty ship. But tomorrow he will lead them to the smuggling tunnel, to the landing beach, to the monstrous house in which Charles Reuben directs his troops. He will have customs chip away at the Talland ring until that reward money is safe in his hands.

After all life has thrown at him, he can still see the sun glowing through the surface of the water. He bursts through with a gasp, fills his lungs with frosty air. Asher Hales is a survivor. A great mind. The man who shines like the brightest of stars.

Scarlett watches from the afterdeck as Asher climbs from the sea. She sees him the way the villagers had; a curse casting its shadow over their lives.

This curse brought with the *Avalon*; she sees now it can't be broken. She can't unlearn the things she now knows.

The world feels darker. Heavier.

Clearer.

She pulls Asher's letter from her pocket and holds it over the gunwale. It flutters between her fingers like a flag. Something stops her from letting go. She screws it up. Shoves it back into her pocket.

Isaac watches. "What was that?"

"Nothing." He has kept things from her. And she will do the same.

She walks without speaking towards the hatch. Seeking out the dark.

It won't work, she thinks, feeling the Wild press against her heart. Dark can't bring her peace. How can she feel peace after all she has learned?

But she walks towards the hatch anyway. Perhaps she'll not find peace, but she will find solitude, if only for a moment.

The revenue cutter is growing larger. It will catch them. Board them. Tear through the ship.

Find us, she thinks. *Find us empty. Find us with our wealth at the bottom of the sea.*

Flora drops to her knees. She pulls the parchment from her pocket. Lets it flutter from her fingers and follow George Gibson over the cliff. She stares at the patch of dark sea where he had disappeared.

When such things go wrong, her mother would say, the charmer blames black magic.

What a relief it would be to share her mother's belief. To say, *no, I didn't fail that man.* The man's soul was darkened as he stepped aboard a cursed ship.

Black magic. Not her own failings. What a pleasure it would be to believe.

She glances over her shoulder to where she had seen the shadows move. Nothing, of course. Empty darkness. And yet there is a strange depth to it as though an unseen layer has opened up behind her world.

She feels the eyes of the villagers burning into the back of her. Her arm pulses with pain. Slowly, she climbs to her feet. Dares to face them. Will they see Gibson's death as her doing? Her failing?

But then she hears: "The spirits have been appeased." A small, trembling voice at the back of the churchyard. The words filter through the crowd.

The spirits have been appeased.

And what more powerful thing is there, Flora wonders, than to believe?

Dodge hovers on the edge of the cliff, a prayer for the dead man cast down into the blackness.

"Mrs Kelly?" says the voice. "Tell us the curse has been lifted."

Their eyes are on her. On this sceptical, charlatan of a woman who has done little more than recite incantations she does not believe. On this sceptical, charlatan of a woman who wanted nothing more but to help ease the fear in the air.

She swallows hard, forcing away the sickness in her belly. "Ayes. The curse has been lifted. You may safely return to sea." She fills her words with as much confidence as she can manage, the way she remembers her mother speaking.

Drink this, Flora. And you will be well.

John Baker turns to Dodge. "Father? Is she telling the truth? Will we see the corpse candles again?"

The vicar glances at the sea. "Perhaps the lights will come and go. Perhaps we ought not fear them, but pray for the souls caught between this world and the next."

Enough. Enough madness.

Flora walks towards the gate, weaving through the cluster of people.

Inside the inn, she takes the spar stones from beside the hearth and drops them into the jug of water. She climbs the stairs to Bessie's bedside. Pours a cup and shakes her daughter's shoulder.

Drink this, Bessie. And you will be well.

ANOTHER DAWN

Here is Polperro harbour; misty and still and blue as they had left it. Caroline waits at the docks, the children in her arms. She watches as customs boards the ship. Watches Isaac hand over the passenger list, watches them disappear into the hold.

They are hours late into port. The landing party will have dispersed with the dawn. The tunnel remains unused.

The cargo was lost, Isaac will tell his wife. Will tell her of how the revenue cutter had chased them down. Boarded them to find an empty ship. And perhaps she will say: *you're safe, at least.*

Or perhaps he will just see that familiar coldness in her eyes as she adds the sum of the lost cargo to the unclimbable pile of their debt.

No. Instead, he will tell her of the plans he had set in motion in Saint Peter Port. Plans he had made as he had slipped away from Asher and Scarlett to his new agent's office. Secret, underhand plans that will see them free of this life. An agent of his own. Runs of his own. The takings in his pocket.

Deceive Charles Reuben.

This world of free trade has dragged him far from the man he wants to be. Far from the life he wants for his wife and children. His sister. The only way to break free, he sees now, is to burrow down to the level of Leach and Reuben and the man he became the night he sank the cutter.

Burrow down to the level of his father.

He takes an oar to bring the lugger into her moorings. Scarlett stands over him. Her eyes are shadowed with exhaustion, her skin colourless.

"We don't keep secrets," she says coldly. "That's what you've always said."

He nods, avoiding her eyes. "Ayes. I'm sorry."

Her voice sparks. "Why didn't you tell me what happened on that ship?"

"Because I left a man to die, Scarlett! I left a man to die for a scrap of lace and a few miserable coins! How could I admit that to you?" The guilt flares inside him. "How could I admit that this is the man I am now?"

They had left the quartermaster's body in the hold where he had fallen, both crews desperate to leave the ship. They had loaded the lugger and formed a frantic parade up to the deck, past hurriedly scrawled crucifixes and a sick bay stained with blood.

What else could be done, Isaac had thought? The sea would take the body when the abandoned ship foundered.

How, he had thought later, as Scarlett brought a sailor from the *Avalon* through their door, was he to know they were leaving a second man to die?

She looks down at him. "If the ship's owner comes looking you'll likely hang for what you did."

"There'll be no investigation. The ship is burned. The crew has disappeared."

"Not all of them."

"Asher Hales has no proof of anything. The revenue men will have no choice but to throw out his stories."

Scarlett knits her fingers together. "Did you know he was aboard?"

Isaac's guilt gives way to anger. "Do you truly need to ask that?"

"Yes." Her eyes are coal. "Because I've spent my life being deceived. And I see now I can trust you no more than anyone else."

Isaac exhales sharply, suddenly hot with resentment.

And he lets himself reach the thought he has spent fourteen years avoiding.

What if he had left? What if he had walked past that children's home and sailed away from this place?

For a fleeting moment, he lets himself see that life, that freedom. And a fleeting moment is enough.

When he looks back at Scarlett, he is done with her. Done dimming the lights, done excusing her temper, her tantrums. Done pretending that wildness is the doing of anything other than herself. If his only thanks is to be accused of murder, she can find her own way in the world.

He pulls on the oar. Turns away from her bitter, ungrateful eyes. "Believe what you wish."

Asher stands at the edge of the harbour. Watches Isaac with his family. His son trails him like a shadow as he checks the moorings, scrawls his final entry in the log. He lifts the baby above his head, making her squeal with laughter.

Asher feels something burn inside him as he watches.

Hatred? Strangely, no.

Jealousy? This is closer.

He watches Scarlett disappear towards the cliff path. Waits until Isaac has climbed back aboard the lugger. And Asher stands beside Caroline, close, his shoulder pressed to hers. Her baby stares up at him with her father's dark eyes.

Caroline doesn't turn. "Leave."

Standing so near her, Asher feels something faint stir inside him. He smiles. "How long are we to keep playing this game, Callie?"

"You think this a game?"

"Yes. And a fine one at that."

"If it's a game, I'll not be outplayed." Her eyes are on the lugger, ready to spring away from him if Isaac should reappear. "Leave," she says again. "Avery's haul is nothing but a fairy tale. Have you not you realised that by now?"

"I've realised it, yes. As have you, I see."

"I realised it a long time ago."

The details on her face are just as he remembers them. Freckle beside her nose. The faint cleft in her chin. The neat, expressive arch of her brows. There is something exhilarating about standing close and speaking after so many wordless days in the cottage.

He smiles faintly. "I missed you."

She gives a snort of humourless laughter.

"You think me lying? I thought of you endlessly."

"Well I thought nothing of you."

"That I know is not true."

"Stay away from me." Her eyes flash with an intensity Asher had once known well. "And stay away from Scarlett."

He raises his eyebrows. "I didn't imagine there was any love lost between you and Scarlett."

"Don't pretend to know me," she says bitterly. "Leave this place and don't come back."

Her demands are unsurprising, of course, yet the sting of them feels fresh. "Is that truly what you want, Caroline?"

She looks at him for the first time. "Do you honestly think I could want otherwise?"

He thinks to tell her of his plans to send customs rifling through the Baileys' life. Thinks to tell her of the greatness that awaits him once the money is in his hands. Thinks to say *come with me.*

But her iciness has halted any scrap of the love that had once existed between them.

"Very well," says Asher, his voice controlled and even. "Then I will leave."

Flora unlocks the inn and lets Isaac inside.

He cups her injured arm in his hand. "I heard what happened. Are you all right?"

"Ayes. I think so." She nods at the boarded windows. Needles of pale light hatch the floor. "The place is a mess, but it will be fixed." She speaks softly, the confidence gone from her voice.

"We will mend the windows," says Isaac. But he can tell this new unease comes from far more than broken glass.

She follows him to the fire. Crouches by the hearth, her blue skirts pooling around her. "I feel responsible for George. I know I ought to have left my mother's chest where I found it. But…" She wraps her arms around herself. "Bessie. Her fever … it's less. I don't know why."

Isaac smiles. "It doesn't matter why." He squeezes her shoulder.

"How did Reuben take the news about the goods?" Flora asks.

He exhales sharply. "I need a drink."

"That I can offer." She pours him a glass of brandy. "Why did you not tell me you were on the *Avalon*?" she asks, her back to him.

Isaac's stomach turns over. He'd thought of telling her. Had wanted to the night they'd finished the tunnel. "The men and I swore we'd tell no one. It was foolish, I know. Perhaps if he'd spoken of it, it wouldn't have haunted George as it did."

Flora hands him the glass. Her face gives nothing away.

"I'm sorry," he says.

He looks up as his wife and children enter. He catches a faint smile between Caroline and Flora.

And then the crew. John Baker and Martha Francis's son. Men from the landing party.

Gaping holes, thinks Isaac. George Gibson. Bobby Carter.

Scarlett.

Glasses filled, raised. Toasts to the dead.

Isaac sits with Caroline at a table close to the fire. He edges his chair closer to hers and lifts the baby from her arms. Mary's head feels downy and fragile against his chin. "I've made arrangements with an agent in Saint Peter Port," he says. "He's starting out in the business. I'll invest the money from the tea in a run of my own."

He sees a new light behind Caroline's eyes.

"Reuben will have your head if he catches you."

"Ayes." He is walking in his father's path, he knows. He thinks of the smugglers' banker who had stood on the landing beach and held the gun to his head so many years ago. And he thinks of the rush he'd felt when he had sent Leach's cutter to the bottom of the river. Immorality, he realises, makes him feel alive. "But I have to do it."

Caroline smiles. "Yes. You do. We do." She touches his wrist and tilts her head to catch his eye. "I do love you, Isaac. You know that, don't you?"

He loops his fingers through hers. "Of course."

A gentle squeeze. Caroline glances across the bar at Flora. "I hope you'll always remember it."

Asher trudges up the lane, his lungs hot and straining. Easier to escape this way, than to take the cliff path past the inn full of villagers. He will climb the hill into Killigarth and follow it into Polperro where the customs house waits.

Needles of light pierce the trees. He keeps walking. Higher, higher until the cottages and church have given way to green. His legs burn. The muscles in his arms ache from his battle with the sea. His heart thumps with determination.

Scarlett stands at the top of the lane. She wears a brown woollen dress and riding boots. A pack is tied to her back.

"I thought I would catch you here," she says. "Asher Hales, the greatest of liars." Her eyes are hard, underlined with shadow. She has clamped a fist around the strap of her pack.

Asher's mouth is suddenly dry. He keeps walking. "Let me leave. It's the best thing for both of us."

She snatches his arm. Digs her fingers in with a force that stills him. "You're coming with me. Now. We need to find a carriage."

"I've no money."

She pulls a tangle of white and gold lace from her pocket. "This will get us to Portreath."

Asher's chest tightens. "Portreath? No, Scarlett. I don't think that wise." He tries to shake his arm free.

She hitches her skirt to reveal the silver blade in her garter. "I will decide what's wise, Mr Hales. Take me to see my father."

BOOK TWO

HILLS OF SILVER

EMPTY LAND

He is afraid of her. She can tell.

Scarlett watches Asher as the carriage rattles and thuds. They sit opposite each other on rough-hewn wooden benches, crammed beside wool bales that smell of earth and damp. He is forcing himself to keep his face impassive; jaw tight, lips pressed into a narrow line. His eyes flicker to the knife lying across her lap.

He could overpower her easily. She reaches his shoulder, slim and slight. His muscular sailor's arms could break her like a twig. But Asher Hales, Scarlett has come to realise, is a coward. And as long as she sits with a knife in her lap, he will follow her like a dog.

Once, she'd been drawn to this man. Had been drawn like a lovesick heroine to the fall of his hair, the sharp line of his jaw, his velvet voice and carefully chosen words. She had been drawn to him back in those distant days when her brother could do no wrong and her father's body lay on the sea floor.

Distant days.

They feel it. But it had been only that morning they had boarded the carriage in Polperro. Less than a day since Scarlett had seen behind Asher's velvet voice to the lies that lay beneath. Less than a day since he had produced his letter and everything Scarlett had known to be true had crumbled.

Her new world is harsh. Sharp-edged. She sees in bright colours, bolts of flame. Feels a chill in her chest and a simmering in the rest of her body. But she is glad the lies have been torn away.

Is glad to be seeing through clear eyes.

The carriage rattles, trundling from Polperro towards Portreath where, if the letter Asher has given her is to be believed, her father lives in hiding. The road snakes over balding hills and groves of trees blazing in the autumn. The sea has disappeared, leaving only the rise and fall of the land.

They have passed few others on the road. There is a strange emptiness to the place. An odd stillness between the bawl of the gulls and the rhythmic clatter of wheels through mud. Scarlett feels a deep pang of loneliness.

She shuffles uncomfortably as the carriage lurches. Her shift has bunched beneath her stays and she fidgets in annoyance. Everything is riling her; the shift, the smell of the wet wool, Asher's pathetic, doe-eyed cowardice.

She reaches into her cloak pocket and pulls out the letter. The page is thin and fragile. Sixteen years old.

She has read it so many times, she knows its contents from memory. But she reads it again, as though hoping she might find some hidden meaning, some new scrap of information.

Jacob is no longer in Talland, it says. *He left this place in his fishing boat, the village believing him drowned. On your return to England, you will find him in Portreath…*

Nothing new. Just the same, neat allegations. The father she had idolised had abandoned his children. Gifted them his unpayable debt.

Asher's eyes have shifted from the knife to the discoloured paper in her hand. His cheeks are flushed, the rest of his face ashen as though sickness had fallen over him the moment his dashing persona had been torn away. How can a man manage to be both flushed and pale at the same time, Scarlett wonders distantly? She shakes the letter at him.

"Who gave you this?" she asks again. "Who wrote it?"

Always the same response: "No one you know."

"But you trust this letter. You believe we will find my father in Portreath." Her words are thin as she voices the possibility. If she is to find her father, there will be no great reunion. She will not fly into his arms and lose herself in a flood of happy tears. No, if she finds her father, she will make sure he knows how she and her brother have suffered. The wild anger will rise inside her and she will not do a thing to stop it.

Asher nods slowly. "I trust the letter. Yes." He looks again at the knife. A sign he is lying? Or just a twitch of his nerves?

Scarlett grits her teeth in frustration. Asher Hales is both a liar and a coward. But he is also an intelligent man. A man that plots, plans, manipulates. A man who knows, surely, that keeping his knowledge close to his chest is the way to ensure his survival.

LOYALTY

The plan is sound. Forty ankers of brandy bought by a new agent in Saint Peter Port. Reuben's lugger to collect the shipment in. The Polperro caves in which to hide it.

A small venture, but Isaac hopes it will be a profitable one.

A secret one.

He and his crew hover by the fire at the Mariner's Arms. The tavern is closed to customers, but Flora has left the doors unlocked so they might plan their ventures away from the eyes and ears of Charles Reuben.

The conditions of the debt left to him by his father state Isaac must hand over his earnings to Reuben. And for fourteen years he has done just that; captained a smuggling lugger on an endless zigzag across the Channel, completing the runs and filling Reuben's pockets. Meanwhile, his family languishes in a world of patched clothing and sparrow pie.

He will do it no longer. He has spent far too many years paying for his father's mistakes.

On his last visit to Guernsey, he had met with an agent starting out in the business. A man willing to accept his meagre investment. The money made from this secretive run will buy passage for his family out of Cornwall. North, he thinks. Ireland, Scotland. Anywhere the past can fade, and Reuben cannot find them.

Will he earn enough from the sales of a single run? He can't be sure. He'll need enough for the journey and a roof over their head when they arrive. Enough to live on while he finds work. Enough for five tickets.

Four tickets, perhaps.

Isaac can't think of his sister without his anger blazing. He and Scarlett had parted that morning without speaking. Her last words to him had been ones of accusation, anger. Distrust.

He had given up his freedom to raise his sister. Shackled himself to Talland by plucking her from the children's home. And she repays him with distrust?

She can stay away, he tells himself. He has no desire to see her. And yet, the thought of her charging wildly through an unknown world makes something turn over in his stomach.

He pushes the thoughts of Scarlett aside. She is a grown woman now. Capable of making her own way in the world. He has his own business to attend to. Whether or not she will leave Talland with them is a problem for another day.

He tosses another log onto the fire, sending sparks flying up the chimney. Shadows move inside the empty tavern.

The crew are full of questions.

When? As soon as possible.

How? With Reuben's lugger.

Dangerous?

Reuben has sent pistol-wielding men after him in the past. If he's caught making a run of his own, Isaac is sure shots will be fired.

But to the men, he says: "Thirty percent of the profits divided among you. Tell me you'll get figures like that from Reuben."

He's told just two of his crewmates of the voyage. All he needs to sail and load the lugger. John Baker and Will Francis are young men, good sailors. Trustworthy.

"How do you plan to leave the harbour without being seen?" Baker speaks in a whisper, as though afraid his words might carry up the chimney and drift across the village.

"We'll set sail in the night. Arrive in Guernsey by late morning. Store the goods in the Polperro cave when we return. I'll spread word before we leave that I'm taking the ship for careening."

Isaac catches a glance between the two men. His crew are in the trade for wealth. Smuggling can provide a life of polished boots and fine wine that farmers and miners can only dream of. A cut of thirty percent will have their attention. These men are loyal enough not to spread his secrets, yes. But he does not know whether their loyalty extends far enough for them to risk antagonising Charles Reuben.

"Thirty percent among us, you say?" Baker asks, calculating.

"Ayes. Thirty percent."

Baker holds out a hand. Isaac shakes, giving him a ghost of a smile. After a moment, Will follows. And loyalty, Isaac realises, can be bought by any man willing to pay the right price.

Caroline pushes back the curtain. Watches a line of silver smoke rise from a chimney of the Mariner's Arms.

She pictures her husband by the hearth, telling the crew of his plans in that gravelly half-whisper he uses when he has secrets to share.

She lets the curtain fall. She needs a yes from the crew. Isaac needs a yes. He has spent far too long as a slave to Charles Reuben, scratching at the debt of a father he had cared little for.

A debt, Caroline had said in the bliss of young love, that mattered little to her. She hadn't wanted to be that woman who thought only of silks and laces. That woman who turned away from a good man because of his empty pockets.

But twelve years of debt-ridden marriage have worn her down. Her love is no longer young, but their pockets are still empty. Her skirts are zigzagged with mending, boots patched so many times the soles are almost entirely made of pitch. Her son and daughter wear clothes outgrown by the village's other children.

Mary's smock gathers dust as she crawls across a floor that needs sweeping. She is bright-eyed and chatty. Caroline swings her onto her hip, pulling her smock down over soft pink knees.

"Well," she tells her, "if you'll not sleep, you'll come with me to see what's become of your aunt."

Mary fixes her with dark, knowing eyes.

Caroline pushes open the door of Scarlett's tiny bedroom. Her narrow sleeping pallet lies against one wall, blankets tossed messily across it. A candleholder sits beside the bed, clutching a cold, waxy stump. A stained apron hangs on the back of the door. The storage chest is open.

Caroline looks at the trunk, then at the baby. "Empty, of course," she says. "Are you surprised?"

Mary grabs at her mother's neckerchief. Caroline swings closed the lid and shoves the trunk against the wall.

So Scarlett has left. Flown from their lives in yet another dramatic statement.

Scarlett had been nine years old when Caroline had married Isaac. The day after their wedding, she had run across the cliffs and hidden in the cave at Polperro; a protest against the woman who had dared invade her home. The woman who had dared invade the life for two she had Isaac had built after the deaths of their parents. They had spent the morning searching before Caroline had convinced Isaac his sister would return when she felt she had made her point. Scarlett had slunk home as the sun began to set and gulped down two bowls of Caroline's onion soup.

Twelve years later, Scarlett is still self-centred and impulsive. No doubt she'll return to the house in a similar way soon, tired, hungry and craving attention. Point made.

Strong willed, Isaac has always said. *A difficult life.* Caroline is tired of him making excuses for his sister. Tired of him blaming Scarlett's behaviour on her upbringing, as though every word she speaks out of place lies firmly on his shoulders.

She pulls the blanket from Scarlett's sleeping pallet and tosses it onto her own bed. The nights are growing colder. No sense it lying unused.

There is no sign of Asher Hales, either.

Caroline snorts. He'd been plain old Matthew Fielding when she had known him. A new name for a new man?

Hardly. He'd been as deceitful and manipulative when Scarlett had brought him home as he'd been the last time Caroline had seen him.

The thought of those days brings tension to her shoulders.

She has stopped talking to Mary, she realises. Can't voice this dark chunk of her past, even to non-comprehending ears. Can't hear the reality of it spoken, or have the words hang in the air. What if her daughter should somehow absorb them and know the truth of who her mother is?

This part of her life must stay locked away.

Has Scarlett left with Hales? The little fool. Has she been blinded by his good looks and honeyed words? Just as she herself had been so many years ago, Caroline thinks wryly.

She lays the baby in the cradle. Rocks it until Mary's eyes are heavy and her own thoughts have begun to still.

Asher Hales has left. She can begin to breathe.

The door clicks.

Isaac is buoyed. His lips are upturned, hands in his pockets, the way they always are when he has news to share. As though the surprise of it is hidden in his fist. He tosses dark hair from his eyes and throws her a smile.

The men have agreed to the run, Caroline can tell. They are a precious step closer to that life without midnight landings and lantern-lit trading runs. A step closer to that life without Tom Leach and his rival smuggling gang, that life of avoiding revenue men in the street. A precious step closer to that life without Charles Reuben.

She'll not bring Isaac down by telling him about Scarlett's empty trunk. She knows how it will play out. His smile will disappear, and his hands will come empty from his pockets. He will drop everything as he always does and run into the night chasing his ungrateful sister.

No. Let tonight be about looking to the future. Let Scarlett find her own way home.

"The men will come?" she asks, joining him by the hearth.

He catches hold of her fingers and tugs her towards him. His hands are rough in hers. "Ayes. They'll come for thirty percent."

"And you've a landing party?"

"I will. A small one. Only the most trustworthy of the men." He plants a kiss in her plaited hair. "We'll be out of this place soon. I swear it."

She clutches a fistful of his coat. She wants him nearer. His hands in hers and kisses in her hair have become so unfamiliar. Their marriage has become a thing of one-word responses and terse *goodnight*s. Of silent suppers and love worn thin by the pressure of their debts.

Caroline inhales deeply, taking in his familiar smell of ash soap and sea. Things will be different once Talland is behind them. She is sure of it. Once Talland is behind them, they will start again. Everything breaking them down will fall away.

But she sees the unrest behind his eyes. How well she knows that worry he is forever unable to still.

"Any sign of Scarlett?" he asks, sliding his hands from hers.

Caroline sighs inwardly. "She's angry. Probably drinking herself stupid in Polperro. She'll come home when she's ready."

"I ought to go after her."

"No."

His eyebrows shoot up at her sharpness. Caroline looks away. She regrets shattering the peace. "She's a grown woman, Isaac. Leave her."

"And if it were one of our children run off into the night? Would you tell me to leave things then?"

"She isn't one of our children. Our children are here, caught up in free trade. We need to get them out of this life. Have you forgotten the things Scarlett said to you? She accused you of leaving a man to die!" Caroline hears her own bitterness. It is not animosity she feels for Scarlett, not really. Over twelve years she has managed a reluctant, obligatory kind of love for the girl she had had little choice but to mother. She wishes her no ill luck, of course. But Isaac's mind is firmly on escape now. She will not let him be distracted by Scarlett's recklessness.

"I've not forgotten," he says, sliding off his coat.

He is staying. A small victory. Caroline touches his arm, trying for a gesture of solidarity. But he pulls away and carries his coat into the bedroom, reminding her that the wall they have built between each other is still as tall as ever.

THE LOST

The coach deposits Asher and Scarlett in Truro. Night has fallen emphatically, shadows lying thick and unyielding over the street. Water drips from awnings, plinking into the mud. The cloud bank is silver where the moon tries to push through.

Scarlett tugs her cloak around her. "How much further to Portreath?" She looks up the road. Down the road. Not at Asher.

"Several hours at least," he says. "We'll not find transport tonight. Best we look for somewhere to sleep."

She eyes him distrustfully. Does she have any idea of the path they are taking, he wonders? Is there any map in her head? Or does her knowledge of the world consist of her tiny village and that strip of sea between the Channel Islands? Her optimism may have capsized, but her naivety is still intact.

"How much coin do we have?" he asks.

She opens the pouch and lets Asher peer inside.

"Enough for a bed each," he says. He begins to walk towards the cluster of lights at the end of the street. Mud slides beneath his boots. He hears a dog bark in a distant alley.

Scarlett hurries after him. The knife is back in her hand, Asher notices uncomfortably.

"Where are you going?" she demands.

"I'm going to find us somewhere to stay. That's what you want, isn't it?"

She nods uncertainly.

"Put the knife away. No one will give us a room if they see you waving that about."

He waits by the door of the inn as she slides the blade back into her garter. She follows him to the counter.

"Two cheap beds," says Asher. He feels the sting of the words. His thirtieth birthday is far behind him and still his life is one of *two cheap beds*.

"We've beds in the back," the woman tells him. "Men beside the kitchen and women down the hall."

Asher nods faintly and reaches into the money pouch.

"No," says Scarlett. "That won't do." Her fingers dig into Asher's arm, silencing him

214

before he can speak. "One bed," she says. "And a private room."

The woman behind the counter presses her lips into a thin white line. Scarlett cuts her with hard eyes.

"One bed," the woman repeats. "Private room. A shilling a night."

Scarlett jabs Asher's arm again and he hands over the money. The woman takes a candle from beneath the counter and lights it from the lamp. She hands it to Scarlett. "Let it blow out and it'll cost you a copper for relighting."

She takes the candle wordlessly, cupping a hand around the flame.

The woman hands Asher a key. "Top floor. First door on the left."

He nods his thanks and trudges up the staircase, Scarlett close behind. "What are you playing at?" He is grateful for the woman's threat over the candle. Scarlett's preoccupation with keeping it burning has silenced her for a time. He slides the key into the lock. The room is bare, with chipped white walls and floorboards indented by a century of footsteps. A lone bed sits in the centre of the room, a washstand and side table crammed into the corner.

Scarlett sets the candle on the table and looks at Asher. "I'm sure if I were to leave you to the men's quarters you'd not be there in the morning." She drops her pack on the bed and flings a ratty bolster at him. "You'll take the floor."

She slides off her cloak and empties the water jug into the bowl on the washstand. She leans over the basin, splashes her face. Back to him, she pauses, letting water roll off her cheeks.

Asher watches.

She is a loaded pistol with a knife in her garter. The darkness in her has taken prominence. Largely his own doing, he knows. He had used her, lied to her. Worst of all, he had been the one to break the news to her that her heroic, dead father is neither of those things.

Yes, there is guilt. Asher has enough humanity left inside him to feel a little remorse. He finds himself missing sunny Scarlett. Her optimism and blind trust had been a light among the bitterness of his life.

How much is this black-eyed terror capable of? Her life has been shaken at its foundations. She has lost faith in her brother, her father. Lost faith in Asher himself. He is sure the shock of it is enough for her to take that knife from her garter and spill a man's blood. He fears the blood will be his own.

Tread carefully.

Beneath the ice, there must be a little of warm, trusting Scarlett Bailey who had risked her life to save him from a sinking ship.

How long ago? It feels like a lifetime, but can be little more than a fortnight. Two weeks that have left Asher's life upturned. Left him directionless. Hopeless.

For more than a decade, he has dreamt of finding the hidden wealth of Henry Avery. Wealth that would see him educated to become the surgeon he has always longed to be. What a cold irony that it is here in myth-drenched Cornwall he has come to realise the haul is nothing but fantasy.

Scarlett turns back from the washstand. Her eyes are large and mournful like a deer's. She is as lost and lonely as he is.

"You must be hungry," he says throatily. "We ought to eat."

They sit at a table in the corner of the tavern. The only other people in the inn are a young couple in matching blue cloaks and an old man sitting alone at the bar. A fire hisses and spits in the grate, smoke spluttering up a chimney in desperate need of sweeping.

In spite of his unease, Asher is hungry. When dishes of watery stew come to their table, he eats in large mouthfuls. Scarlett stirs her supper in disinterest.

The food settles him a little. Brings a scrap of clarity.

So, the haul he has spent half his life dreaming of is a myth. He has no means of making a living, let alone earning enough for the university degree that would see him soar up society's ranks.

Scarlett has dragged him on a mission to seek out the man he has spent the last decade longing to come face to face with. Yet now, with the knowledge that Avery's haul is a fantasy, the thought of meeting Jacob Bailey again makes something turn in his stomach.

The reality of all this is miserable, but there is something vaguely steadying about taking stock of his life this way.

Look harder. There must be more.

Yes. He has a great mind. A great intelligence.

He must find a new way forward.

He needs another way to make money. And right now, the best option he has is to turn Isaac and Scarlett Bailey over to the revenue men. Lead customs to the heart of the Talland smuggling ring and collect a sizeable reward.

An impossibility, of course, while he's stranded here halfway to Portreath. He needs to get back to the south coast. Scarlett will sleep deeply tonight, he is sure. He will take her coin pouch, her knife. Find transport back to Polperro and the waiting revenue men.

He tries not to think of who else he will find when he slides back into the village.

Caroline had been in his thoughts almost constantly in the years he had been away from England. Each day he would find a different memory of her: coyly sipping brandy, teasing him with a hitch of her skirts, working his sharp mind with strings of probing questions.

She had been a shrewd seventeen-year-old when they had first met. He, less than three years older. They'd both been lodging in the creaking rooms above the Three Pilchards in Polperro. He had followed a trail of paltry fishing jobs to Cornwall and become entangled in free trade. Entangled in a world of tarred coats and fishwives. He had not expected to find a sharp-witted girl from London hiding among them.

He had fallen in love hard and fast. The life of greatness he imagined for himself suddenly had a woman in it. He saw himself in a lecture theatre, scrawling feverishly. Saw himself in the coffee houses, debating the merits of animism, convincing doubting minds of the soul's power over the human body. He saw himself performing dissections as an overflowing theatre held their breath. And he saw himself leaving the Barber Surgeon's Hall for a great Fitzrovia mansion. Saw Caroline there in rose-coloured silk and satin that sighed when she walked.

It was a perfect life that awaited him, once that money was in his hands.

His perfect life had not included conviction for assault, of course. It had not included indentured servitude in New England, or a decade of exile.

Each day of his sentence, he had dreamt of returning to her. But with each passing week, month, year, it seemed more and more impossible. Somehow, he would resurrect his life, yes, but he began to doubt that Caroline would be a part of it. Though he had tried to convince himself otherwise, he has always known her love for him had been tentative. A part of him knew she would not wait. There would be no new memories to replace the ones worn thin by time. She would be that shrewd girl of seventeen to him forever.

But then, there she was, crammed into that creaking cottage, Isaac Bailey's children dangling from her and the light gone from her eyes.

Asher couldn't make sense of it. How, after all that had happened, had she ended up in Talland as Isaac's wife?

She had known him at once. He had seen the blaze of recognition in her eyes the moment Scarlett had led him into the cottage.

He'd said not a thing to her, of course. How could he with Isaac or Scarlett or some snotty-nosed child lurking around every corner?

Even if he could have managed a word, Asher could tell Caroline had closed down. She refused to look at him. Left the room whenever he was about.

He understood, of course. What a reminder he must have been. A reminder of her most regrettable deeds. Her darkest secrets.

How much would have fallen if Asher had opened his mouth?

Scarlett forces down a miniscule mouthful of stew. "When we get to Portreath," she says, "what do we do?"

"You're the one who brought us here. You tell me."

A look of uncertainty passes across her face.

He has no way to help her find her father. The letter is all that was guiding him and that is in her hands now. She must have known his uselessness when she held that knife to his middle and ordered him to take her to Portreath.

She is not bringing him for knowledge. That much is obvious. She is bringing him for protection. Her world is tiny and uninformed. She needs someone to guide her. And right now, miserable, cowardly Asher Hales is all she has.

Being her chaperone, he realises, is right now keeping him safe.

"There was a man who sailed with your father and I," he says, "who took his earnings and built a life in Portreath. Perhaps we can seek him out for lodgings." When Scarlett doesn't reply, he says: "I wondered if perhaps it was why Jacob chose to escape there. The allure of a familiar face. A friend."

He glances out the window. Rain is splattering the glass. A halo of light glitters around the street lamp.

"You want to escape," says Scarlett.

"Of course."

"Why? I thought this was what you wanted. To go to Portreath with me and find my father. Have him tell you where Avery hid his riches."

"There are no riches," says Asher.

"I don't understand why you're suddenly so certain of that."

"Of course you understand. Sometimes you just awaken and realise the lies have fallen away."

He sees shadows beneath Scarlett's eyes. "You could run," she says after a moment. "Right now. I couldn't catch you."

"I've no money." His eyes drift instinctively to the faint bulge in her bodice where she has buried the pouch of coins. A tiny sum earned from selling smuggled lace. But enough to get him back to Polperro.

Scarlett tugs her shawl across her chest. She pushes her bowl towards him. "You may as well finish it."

He brings the spoon to his lips. "I don't know why there has to be such animosity between us," he says, encouraged by her gift of the leftover stew. "We are both victims. We've both been deceived by Jacob. He left me alone on the beach with the man he murdered. Left you and your brother to carry his debts."

Scarlett doesn't reply. She watches Asher eat. When he has swallowed the last mouthful, she stands abruptly. "We're going upstairs. I need to sleep."

Yes. Sleep, thinks Asher. And he will run.

But when they get to the room, Scarlett pulls a length of rope from her pack and uses it to tie his wrists to the leg of the bed. The knife flashes between her fingers as she knots and binds, as though it has grown a part of her.

Asher watches the blade glint in the candlelight. A swing of his arm and he could knock it from her hands. Knock her to the floor. But mistime the action and she'll have the blade between his ribs in a second. The thought of the pain makes his stomach contract as though he has been struck.

She has knotted the rope tightly. It digs into the skin on his wrists. The humiliation of it makes his insides burn.

Scarlett climbs into the bed and covers herself with the blanket before unlacing her skirts and stays. She blows out the candle and falls asleep quickly.

Asher sits up against the leg of the bed; the only comfortable position he can manage. A glow from the street lamps pushes through flimsy grey curtains. He hears rain patter the roof.

He looks over his shoulder at Scarlett. In sleep, her steely expression is gone. She looks younger, more vulnerable. The heartbroken girl who had curled up against him after Bobby Carter had died.

A thread of dark hair hangs across one eye. Lips parted, skin pale.

He had never felt a great attraction to that hair, that skin, those parted lips. He had just felt a great attraction to the way Scarlett had made him feel worthy. Made him feel better than the rest. She had looked upon him and seen the great man he longed to be. Scarlett Bailey had been a precious thing.

But now her eyes are clouded with anger and she sees him as nothing more than a liar and a coward. Sees him no differently to the rest of the world. And so, it will be a joy to throw her to the revenue men. A joy to take the stand against the woman who has bound him, trapped him, stripped away the last of his self-worth. He will watch that once precious thing be wrapped in chains.

She opens her eyes. Watches Asher without speaking.

"What will you do?" he asks. "If you find Jacob?"

Scarlett doesn't speak at once. "I'll not find him. Because he's dead."

That's what this is journey is about? Proving Asher wrong? Proving the world is as it should be? A cross-county journey to bring sunny Scarlett back?

He waits.

"I don't know what I will do," she says after a moment. "I just want him to see me. I want him to know that I'm aware of what he did to us." Her voice is thick with sleep. "And you?"

He laughs coldly, yanks against the restraints. "I'm not here by choice."

"Jacob tried to pin the murder he committed on you. Don't you want revenge?"

"Is that what you want? You want me to take revenge against your father?"

She rolls over, her back to him. "It doesn't matter," she mumbles. "He's already dead."

"Humour me. We find Jacob alive and well. You discover he abandoned you and your brother in the face of his enormous debt. I put a pistol to his head. Do you stop me?"

"No," she says to the dark. "I don't."

SACRED THINGS

Flora is glad for the morning light. Her sleep had been punctuated by dead men and demons. Eyes in the dark and shadows that breathe.

Things she had believed belonged only in fantasy and folklore. But now she is not so sure. Now the solidity of her world is frayed at the edges.

She climbs from the bed and splashes her face at the washstand. The cold water sluices away the last of her nightmares. Pushing back the curtain, she finds a dull, low sun. An empty street. Behind a fringe of trees, the sea is still and purple.

She peeks into her daughter's bedroom. Bessie is breathing deeply and rhythmically, sleeping off what Flora hopes is the last of her illness.

Time to enter the parlour. She has put it off for two days.

She opens the door slowly and draws in her breath. The room is strewn with broken glass, jars shattered across the floor. The chest that had held her mother's herbs and charms lies upended in the middle of the room. A chair is overturned, and dishes lie in pieces beside the leg of the table.

Flora's stomach tightens. The room is a cold reminder of how she had been turned upon by the villagers she had grown up amongst. She is glad her mother is not here to see the way these things she'd held as sacred have been flung so callously around the inn.

Glass crunches beneath her boots. The mob have left some things intact. Her mother's adder stone ring. A watch ball bundled in a cloth. By miracle, the black glass hand mirror. She places scattered herbs back into their pouches and slides everything unbroken into the chest. She latches the lid.

Lock these things away. Don't go near them again.

But she feels an odd reluctance to imprison the trunk back in her mother's room where she had found it. Yes, this venture into the craft had been a dangerous one, but what if it had been the craft that had saved Bessie's life? In desperation, Flora had turned to healing stones and whispered incantations over her sick daughter. The next morning, Bessie had been well. A coincidence? Perhaps. But it now seems far too arrogant to discount the possibility of magic.

Flora runs a finger over the surface of the chest. It is worn soft and smooth by decades of her mother's touch. She can't turn away, she realises. She can't forget. She is the healing woman's daughter. If there is even an ounce of legitimacy to these whispered rhymes, it is up to her to find it.

She takes the chest to her own bedroom and sits it beside the washstand.

"Mammik?" Bessie's voice sounds down the hall as Flora is sweeping up the last of the broken jars. She finds her daughter sitting up in bed, tugging at the sheets. "I want to get up."

Flora presses a hand to Bessie's forehead. Cool and dry. Relief floods her.

They sit in the parlour eating porridge in front of a flickering fire. The sun pushes through the windows and burns away the last of the bitterness lingering in the room.

Bessie touches a finger to the strapping on Flora's forearm. "What happened?"

Flora pushes away memories of men dragging her from the inn, of their vicious accusations. Pushes away memories of broken glass and fire and Tom Leach's knife blade. *Bleed the witch.*

"Nothing, *cheel-vean*," she tells Bessie. "Eat your breakfast."

A knock at the door.

Flora finds Charles Reuben on her doorstep. He is dressed in an embroidered waistcoat and pleated blue justacorps, a powdered wig on his head. A black and white dog circles his ankles, entangling him in its rope leash. Flora can't hold back a smile.

"I heard your daughter was unwell," he says. "I thought to see how she is."

"She is much better. Thank you." The dog hurls itself at Flora, pawing at her knees. She bends to scratch its ears.

Reuben clears his throat. "About the dog… I've little time to care for the poor thing. I wondered if perhaps Bessie might do a far better job. If she cares to, of course."

Flora hesitates. The two sides of Reuben make her wary. Beneath this guise of caring, he is the ruthless businessman who has made Isaac and Scarlett's lives hell. Still, he has shown Flora nothing but generosity. She can offer him civility in return.

"I'm sure she will love it." She pauses. "Bess is upstairs. Perhaps you might like to give her the dog yourself."

Reuben smiles. "I would like that very much."

Bessie is sitting cross-legged on the couch, her porridge bowl in her lap. The dog strains against the rope when he sees her. She scrambles from the couch and dives onto her knees in front of the dog, ruffling his fur in a fit of giggles.

"He's after a new home, Miss Kelly," says Reuben. "Would you be so kind?"

Flora goes to the kitchen and hangs the kettle over the range.

She hears: "Take him outside twice a day for a good run."

"Oh yes sir. Of course."

Flora hears the tap of claws and Bessie's excited shrieks. She spoons tea into the pot. What would Isaac think if he came to the inn to find Charles Reuben and his dog lounging around her parlour?

Foolish thoughts. It's a pot of tea, not a marriage proposal. Courtesy, not betrayal.

She carries the tea tray into the sitting room. The dog is on the couch beside Bessie, lapping up the remains of her porridge.

Flora hands Reuben a steaming cup. "It seems he has made himself at home."

Reuben smiles. "I'm glad." He sips slowly. "I hear Isaac Bailey and his men are reopening the tunnel."

Flora says nothing. Reuben will find out the smuggling tunnel is complete, of course, when the men use it to land the goods from the next run. But she knows it best that he remains ignorant while Isaac loads the contraband from his own venture later that week.

"It has been reopened," she says shortly. "But Isaac tells me it will not be finished for several weeks or more."

"Perhaps you might allow me to see it sometime."

Flora lets her teacup clink against its saucer. "I'd prefer if we spoke of something else, Mr Reuben. I don't wish to discuss the tunnel in front of my daughter."

Reuben nods. He takes another mouthful of tea. "When do you plan to reopen the inn?"

"The windows need fixing."

"Perhaps I could—"

"It's all right," Flora says quickly. "Isaac has already offered to help me. I'll reopen once they're done."

He lowers his voice. "You know we no longer have the protection of the authorities. You risk a visit from the excisemen."

Flora picks up the porridge bowls and hands them to Bessie. "Take these to the kitchen, *cheel-vean*. Give the dog a little water."

Bessie disappears down the hallway, the dog's claws tapping on the floorboards as he scurries after her.

Flora turns back to Reuben. "I have the correct licences," she says.

"One of which is counterfeit."

"I trust you can be relied upon to keep that to yourself."

He sighs. "I regret helping you obtain that liquor licence. Operating with it is trouble."

"Your concern is noted," says Flora. "But I've made up my mind."

He smiles slightly. "You have a determination in you, Mrs Kelly. You remind me of my wife."

"Your wife? I was unaware—"

"I buried her a lifetime ago. With my son. Smallpox took them both."

She meets his eyes. "I'm sorry. Truly."

Reuben walks slowly across the parlour, cup and saucer in hand. He eyes the mantel with its clutter of chipped vases and wax-encrusted candleholders. "I often think of you and your daughter alone in this old place."

Flora shifts uncomfortably. "We are rarely alone, Mr Reuben. This is a public house."

"I worry for you."

"You've no need."

He rubs his freshly shorn chin. "I wish you would reconsider using this forged licence.

Run the place as an alehouse."

"Is that why you're here?" Flora asks stiffly. "To talk me out of using the licence?"

"No. I came to offer Bessie my dog."

"You'll lose business," she says after a moment, "if I stop buying liquor from you."

Reuben puts down his cup and meets her eyes. "It's not my business I'm concerned about."

PORTREATH

The light has drained from the day when they arrive in Portreath, the air damp with mist and sea. Wind whips across the water, tunnelling through Asher's buttonholes and stinging his ears.

Revenge, Scarlett had said.

She is wrong. Finding Jacob had never been about revenge. Asher is too old and wise for that. Finding Jacob had been about locating the money and realising his own dreams. Revenge was nothing but a pleasing by-product of the search.

But now he sees the haul is a myth, he has no desire to ever lay eyes on Jacob Bailey again.

Jacob will want revenge of his own. The things Asher had done to him after Albert Davey's death are worthy of revenge, he knows. He had been willing to risk Jacob's wrath when there had been a mountain of silver to uncover. But now he would rather sink into the earth than face the man again.

A part of him appreciates the irony. Asher had groomed and swayed Scarlett to lead him to her father. Now here she is dragging him towards Jacob with a knife to his chest.

Scarlett climbs from the coach and stands at the edge of the road, letting her boots sink into the sludge. She wraps her arms around herself. Her shoulders are hunched, head drooped. In her mud-brown skirts she seems to blend into the bleakness. A duffel bag dangles from her shoulder. "I'm sorry," she mumbles. "This was a mistake. I shouldn't have brought us here. We ought to leave." She fumbles in her pocket for the money pouch.

Asher snorts. No point looking in there. They'd spent the last of the coins securing a ride from Truro.

He begins to walk towards the quay. There will be a tavern close to the water, he is sure. He prays someone in the inn will be able to point him in the direction of his former crewmate. Prays the man will remember him, offer them a bed. His safety from Scarlett's knife blade depends on it.

They walk towards the harbour. Fishing boats knock and sway within the walls of the quay. Sea spray arches and spits as the ocean tries to push its way in. Further out in the bay, two sailing vessels are silhouetted in the last of the light.

Scarlett's eyes dart as she walks. They've travelled, what? Fifty miles? Done nothing more than cross the county. The cobbled lanes of Portreath have much in common with Polperro, yet she is as jittery and uncertain as if she'd been deposited in deepest Africa. Out of her familiar surroundings, she is like a scared cat backed into a corner. Her shoulder bumps against Asher's arm.

Nestled between the cliffs and the quay, a crooked tavern looks to be leaning against the rock. The roof is low and flat, its whitewashed walls peeling. Asher is sure the place will collapse with the next gust of wind.

"Stay here," he tells Scarlett.

She shakes her head. "You're not leaving my sight." Words of fear, not threat.

Asher elbows his way inside. The tavern is a tangle of voices and laughter, wood smoke and tobacco, cursing and breaking glass. Someone bangs loudly on a table. Rugged beams hang low, barely clearing heads. The place reeks of ale and unwashed bodies. Asher's skin prickles.

He makes his way towards the bar, Scarlett treading on his heels. She is the only woman in the place, and heads turn as she passes.

Visiting an old friend, Asher tells the innkeeper.

The man's name?

He hesitates. Richard… What? The name escapes him. He's done his best to push his days of sailing with Jacob and his crew away. He clenches his fist. He'll be damned if he'll blow his cover on account of a bad memory.

"Richard Acton," he says finally, clutching at a faint recollection.

The innkeeper's face falls. "I'm sorry, man. Richard Acton is dead."

"Dead?" Asher tries for a look of grief. Finds himself mourning only his own security. "His widow?" he asks.

"Battery Hill. Third house from the point."

And Asher leads Scarlett out of the tavern, freshly confident he has bought himself a few nights of safety. He will toss a little sympathy towards Mrs Acton and spin a pitiable tale of how the years slide away. For a moment, the churning in his stomach is still. Because if there's one thing he is good at, it is spinning a pitiable tale.

The Actons' house towers above them; a sprawling stone expanse of windows and chimneys. From the front gate they can see down to the quay and over the endless grey plain of the ocean. Scarlett takes it in, wide-eyed and silent.

"The trade was good to him," Asher tells her. There will be plenty he could take from this mansion. Riches he could pocket. Coin to get him back to Polperro and the revenue men.

No. He is not a petty thief. There's a nobility to exposing smugglers, to outing those on the wrong side of the law. He'll not lower himself to their level. He couldn't live with the shame.

"We're leaving," Scarlett says suddenly. She tugs Asher's arm, but he doesn't move.

"Scarlett, come on now. You're exhausted and emotional. There'll be a bed for you here. A hot supper. You need not have anything to do with anyone." His voice hardens. He has the upper hand now. "We're not going marching into the dark with no money and nowhere to sleep." He knocks on the door before she can respond.

When the housemaid answers, he speaks in the silky voice he has perfected. "I'm an old crewmate of Mr Acton. I'm here to see his wife. Pay my respects." And into the house they go.

They wait in a parlour glittering with gilded mirrors and finely embroidered armchairs. A bookshelf stretches from floor to carved ceiling, clutching leather bound volumes that look as if they would crumble if anyone tried to read them. A fire roars in the grate, making Asher's cheeks flush. He looks at Scarlett. She is out of place among such finery, with her patched skirts and tangled tar pit of hair. Still, his gold-rimmed reflection is hardly a picture either after two days stuffed into the coach between bales of wet wool and a night at the foot of Scarlett's bed.

Mrs Acton shuffles into the room. She is dressed in a shapeless black mourning gown, grey hair ghosting around her face. Her cloudy eyes light at the sight of guests.

Asher is confident. He can win here. This woman will bend to his charms. "Mrs Acton." He takes her feathery hand. "I'm so sorry for your loss. Richard was a dear friend to me. A great mentor. I'm deeply saddened to hear of his passing."

The old woman's voice is muted and gentle. He has to lean close to make out her words. *Thank you for your kindness.*

A pleasure to meet you.

He nods politely at the appropriate places, tosses out false names when the woman asks. He has his story ready. He and Scarlett, brother and sister. The old woman will find them separate rooms. Surely Scarlett will not dare shatter the ruse by creeping into his bedroom to rope him to the floor.

And then before he can say more, he feels her hand at his arm. She sidles against him, digs her fingers hard into his flesh.

"Mrs Acton," she says, honey in her voice, "perhaps you might be so good as to put my husband and I up for the night."

THE DARK

Ready the ship, away from Reuben's eyes. Away from the eyes of Reuben's men.

From Polperro harbour, Isaac can see through the trees to the roof of Reuben's sprawling house on the hill. He cannot see the windows.

Good. He will not be seen from inside the mansion.

Food is loaded onto the lugger. Water. Grappling hooks and rope in case the landing goes awry and they are forced to slip the tubs into the sea.

Cleaning the ship, Isaac will say, if Reuben or his men come looking. Taking care of the vessel entrusted to him. Nothing untoward here.

Tonight they will slide out of the harbour in silence. Isaac realises he is excited. Excited at the deception, at the thought of escape. He has obeyed orders for far too long. Breaking away makes the blood charge hot through his veins.

He dismisses his men. Be back here tonight. Midnight. Silent and ready.

He paces the harbour. Looks through the dark for any sign of the riding officers. Any sign of Scarlett.

Damn her.

He was done with her, he'd told himself, as she had shot accusations at him with a poisonous tongue. But of course, he can no more be done with her than he can be done with one of his children. Not knowing where she is makes him uneasy. She is a firecracker at the best of times. When last he had seen her, she'd been a powder keg waiting to explode.

At the cottage, Caroline is pacing as the baby fusses on her shoulder.

"Has Scarlett returned?" Isaac asks.

"Were you expecting her to?"

Perhaps a part of him had. This is far from the first time his sister has disappeared. Her wild temper has her storming from the house on a regular basis. She and Isaac have fought about everything from bedtimes to potential husbands. But a night's sleep or a mouthful of whisky and she is back to her sunny self. This time feels different.

"I ought to go and look for her."

Caroline plugs a bottle of gripe water into Mary's mouth. "How? You've no idea where to start."

"I can't just do nothing. She could be in danger. She disappeared the same time as that bastard Asher Hales. I don't trust him an inch."

"She's not in danger. She's just being her usual dramatic self."

"You don't know that."

Caroline disappears into the bedroom and lays the baby in the cradle. She pulls the door closed and takes the bottle to the kitchen. "You've a run to make, Isaac. You need to put your mind to it." Her voice sparks. "I'll not lose this chance because of Scarlett."

"What if something's happened to her?"

Caroline marches into Scarlett's bedroom and flings open the storage chest. The lid thuds against the wall. "Her things are gone, Isaac. Nothing has happened to her. She left on her own accord. She left because she doesn't want to be here. And nor do I."

He looks at the empty chest. Is he angry at Scarlett for leaving unannounced, or relieved she has not been taken against her will? His thoughts are cluttered. All he is sure of is his anger at his wife. "How long have you known this?" His voice begins to rise.

She doesn't answer.

"How long?"

Caroline turns away. "Get on the ship, Isaac," she mumbles. "Please. Get us out of this life."

He waits for her to look back at him. Waits for an apology he is sure will not be forthcoming.

Finally, he says: "If Reuben asks after me—"

"You've taken the ship for careening," says Caroline. "Yes. I know."

He wraps his scarf around his neck and tucks the ends into his coat. When Caroline finally looks up, her face is sunken with regret. She kisses his cheek, holding her lips against his stubbled jaw for a moment. "Be safe."

Isaac gives a short nod and steps out into the street. Light glows through the windows of the Mariner's Arms.

He pushes open the door. A fire roars in the grate, and the sudden change in temperature makes his cheeks burn. Ankers of brandy are lined up along the shelves. He sits at the bar, glancing at the forged liquor licence hanging on the wall. The printer Flora had hired to create it had done a good job. Neat, professional type-setting, a believable replica seal. Nonetheless, the sight of it makes him uneasy.

"Run the place as an alehouse," he had told her, the day he had gone to the inn to fix the broken windows. She had given a dismissive laugh. Told him not to worry for her. All he had been expecting.

She sets a cup of brandy on the bar in front of him. "You're still here."

He sips slowly. "We'll leave at midnight."

"Has Scarlett returned?"

Isaac shakes her head. "I'm worried for her. I think she's with Asher Hales."

Flora smiles. "Then it's Asher Hales you ought to be worried for." There is colour in her cheeks and a shine in her eyes. In spite of his discomfort over the licence, Isaac is glad to see the inn reopen.

She takes a seashell from her collection on the shelf and hands it to him. "Here. It will bring you good luck. Keep you away from Reuben's eyes."

Isaac smiles, running a finger over its silvery surface. He slides it into his pocket. "We could use a little good luck."

Flora takes a half-drunk glass from the bar and empties it into the trough. She wipes her hands on her apron. "I'll leave the cellar unlocked for you."

"No. We'll land in Polperro. Store the goods in the cave."

"Don't be foolish," she says. "You'll use the tunnel."

"I don't want you involved. You've enough to deal with. And there's no telling what Reuben will do if he catches us."

Flora plants a hand on her hip. "I'm not afraid of Reuben. And landing on the eastern beach is far safer than hiding your goods beneath his nose in Polperro." Her blue eyes are piercing. "Am I wrong?"

"No," says Isaac. "But—"

She leans close. Isaac smells brandy and spices on her. "You dug that tunnel. You and my husband. And I know Jack would lose his mind to know you weren't planning on using it to deceive Reuben."

He gives a short laugh. "You're not wrong about that either."

"Of course I'm not." She drops her voice. "Reuben asked about the tunnel. I told him it would not be finished for a time."

"And he believed you?"

"Of course."

Isaac smiles. "You've become a fine liar."

"Well." Her fingers edge toward the cuff of his coat. "I can manage a few lies if it will help you get away. Help you have the life you deserve."

And here is the thought Isaac has been pushing aside since his plans for escape had begun to take shape: leaving Talland will mean leaving Flora. She has always been a part of his life. The pale-haired beauty in the tavern on the hill. He had pulled carts with her, chased balls and hoops, celebrated becoming a husband, a wife, father, mother. Had held her tightly in their shared grief. Isaac can't imagine her not being a part of his life.

But the more contraband he carries into her cellar, the closer the day will come that he leaves her. He knows once he escapes Talland he will never be able to return.

The thought leaves him cold.

She pulls her hand away as though suddenly aware of it. "Tell the lander you'll be coming into Talland. The cellar will be unlocked. Have yourselves a drink when you're done."

Sleep is impossible. Scarlett lies in an enormous wool and feather bed far more luxurious than the lumpy straw pallet she is accustomed to sleeping on. And she stares wide-eyed at the ceiling.

That evening she had sat through a supper of leathery mutton, listening to Asher regale Mrs Acton with tales of their fictitious marriage. How easily the lies rolled off his tongue, she had thought. She'd forced down a few bites of meat, unsure if it was the pretence of being his wife, or the thought of finding her father that had stolen her appetite.

The food sits heavily in her stomach. She glances down at Asher. He is asleep on the floor, wrists tied to the foot of the bed.

She longs suddenly for the salt-stained hills of Talland. Longs for her sheltered lie of a life where her brother can do no wrong and her father is heroic and gone.

It had been a mistake coming here; a thing she had barely thought through. She had been too angry to look at her brother and so desperate to confront her father that she had not stopped to consider whether she could handle such a thing. Now she is here, she aches for her old, outdated beliefs.

She slides from the bed. Tiptoes past Asher and peers out the window into the mist-streaked courtyard.

It will take her days to get back to Talland on foot. Days of traversing bleak, unknown country. No money for food or shelter.

Beyond the courtyard, a lamp flickers above the door of the stables. Yes. A horse.

She fumbles in the dark for her clothes. She laces her stays crookedly and cannot find one of her garters, but she doesn't care. She takes her pack and tiptoes down the stairs. Out into the stables.

The lamp casts orange light across the hay-lined stalls. Three horses watch with giant eyes. Scarlett slides a saddle from the hook on the wall. Wind gusts beneath the door, making the lamp flicker. She tightens the saddle around the smallest of the horses and swings herself onto its back. She unhooks the lantern and begins to ride the steep hill out of town. Up, up, up. The lights of the village disappear quickly. She can't see the ocean, but hears it writhe and churn against the black rock. A different coast to her own. A different sea. It is wilder here. The lantern flickers, useless against the night. Where is she going? She can barely make out the road.

In the pulsing dark, she can feel them; the spirits of the hills dancing their invisible dance. Her ears strain. Is that their high-pitched laughter on the edge of the darkness? She can't be sure beneath the roar of the sea.

The spirits will take a lonely traveller; Scarlett knows the stories. Disorient him and make him giddy until he has lost all thoughts of where home lies.

And perhaps, Scarlett thinks, perhaps they have her. Because the land has become a maze. She has no sense of the lay of these inky purple hills.

Even if she could find her way back to Talland, what is there for her but outdated stories and broken relationships? Leaving Portreath won't restore her ignorance. It won't restore her trust in Isaac, or in Asher. It won't return her father to his watery grave. She needs the truth. If Jacob is in Portreath, she needs to know. Needs to confront him. She cannot live a life built on lies and tainted memories.

Rage flies up at her from nowhere. She feels herself fling the lantern without the thought entering her head. Glass shatters; the sound dull against the grassy trail.

With the sudden, violent blackness, her anger vanishes, replaced by shock and fear. She cannot see her hand in front of her face.

The dark has always calmed her, comforted her. But this dark is vast and endless. Inescapable. This is dark that hides burial chambers and runaways and a thrashing, untamed sea. Scarlett hears a murmur of panic escape her. So this is what it is to be afraid of the dark.

The back of her neck prickles with sweat, despite the bitter cold. A few flimsy stars push through the cloud bank; all she has to show her up from down.

She reaches for the horse's mane. Runs a hand through the wiry hair to calm herself. She presses her chest against the animal's thick neck. She needs warmth. Needs to feel another pulse, another being's breath. She feels like the last person left on earth.

The world has become dark and unidentifiable. She has broken away from her family, her home. Fled across the country with a man she no longer trusts. The spirits in the hills could take her now and who would ever know? Perhaps no one would even care.

No one is coming for her. The dark is hers to navigate alone.

THE LIGHT

The morning, Scarlett is sure, will never arrive. Her eyes try to make sense of the darkness. They strain to see the horse she is leaning against, the owl she hears hooting above her head. She tries to decipher the shifting shadows, tries to pull reality from the tangle of her imagination. How many hours has she been here on the hills, her fingers stiff and cold around the horse's reins? Far too many hours to fit into one night, she is sure.

But at last, in a small miracle, the sun does come. It is pale and cold, but it brings light. Exhausted, she takes the horse back to the stables and slips soundlessly into the house. Asher is still asleep when she kicks off her boots and climbs into bed. She is grateful for it.

She wakes several hours later to him rattling the bed frame.

"You can't leave me here all day, Scarlett! I'm not a damn animal."

Reluctantly, she climbs out of bed and unties him. He glances at the rumpled skirts she had slept in.

"You tried to leave." A faint smile turns his lips. "How far did you get without me?"

Scarlett grits her teeth.

Asher relieves himself at the chamber pot. "Mrs Acton will want to know why we didn't come to eat this morning."

"I'm sure you'll talk your way around it." She wrangles her hair into a thick plait and pins it at her neck. Her few hours of sleep have done little to energise her. And being back at the house has not eased her loneliness. She watches Asher rinse his cheeks at the washstand. Water runs down his sharp jaw. Scarlett remembers herself tracing a finger across it, his skin silky, freshly shaven. She is glad, of course, to have awakened to Asher's true nature, but there is something oddly comforting about the memory. A reminder that once she had been far more connected to the people around her than the Wild has made her now.

"Did you ever love me?" she asks suddenly.

Asher combs his fingers through his fair hair. He pulls on his coat. "No. Does that surprise you?"

No, it is no surprise, but his blatant honesty stings. "Did you care for me? Was I ever anything more than a means to finding my father?" She wills herself to stop speaking. She does not want affection from Asher Hales. But she is afraid of drowning alone in the darkness and she will reach out a hand to whoever is closest.

"I cared for you, yes," he says. "You saved my life. I've not forgotten that."

She can see what he is doing. Trying to work his way beneath her frozen shell and secure his safety from the knife at her knee. She has spent enough time around him to become adept at identifying his manipulation. But she needs something to cling to. A raft in the great expanse of the Wild. She hears herself say: "And do you care for me still?"

"I should like to," Asher says pointedly. "But when you are like this, it is a difficult thing."

She watches him lace his boots. There is a faint tremor in his hands, she notices. Beneath his neatly tied hair, the muscles in his neck are rigid.

In all the time he had been in Talland, Asher had never spoken of his family, Scarlett realises. Never spoken of another soul who might have stirred in him something close to affection. And as far as she could tell, no one had come looking for him after his ship had catapulted onto their shore. Asher Hales, Scarlett thinks, is just as lonely as she is. Had he drawn close to her only so he might hunt down Avery's haul? Or had he too needed a raft to cling to?

"Have you ever been in love?" she asks suddenly.

Asher doesn't look at her. "Yes," he says after a moment.

Scarlett feels a strange rush of jealousy. Jealousy towards the woman, no. Jealousy towards Asher himself. She wants to experience love. "Who?" she asks.

He clears his throat. "If you want to leave, we shall. I'm sure we can talk Mrs Acton into giving us a horse or two."

"We're not leaving," she says, forcing steadiness into her voice. "I need to find Jacob."

She walks towards the tavern with the knife at her knee and her hand at Asher's elbow. A grey pall of an evening has settled over the village, mist turning the street lamps into hazy globes of flame. Scarlett pushes her way inside. The front room is noisy and thick with the smell of tallow and pipe smoke. A tall man bumps her elbow, his ale spilling down the front of her skirt. Dampness soaks through a hole in her boot. She shoves her way to the bar, glancing edgily over her shoulder to ensure Asher is still close.

"Jacob Bailey," she says to the innkeeper. "Do you know him?"

Jacob Bailey?, she wants him to say. *That poor fellow is long dead.* Or, even better; *never heard of such a man.*

But instead, he says: "Jacob, ayes. Of course."

Her legs weaken. The man is lying, he has to be. In league with Asher and whoever had written that cursed letter. All part of some twisted game. "Where?" she manages. "Where can I find him?"

The innkeeper scratches his bristly chin. "Lives in that shithole on the northern hill."

Scarlett tries to swallow, but her mouth is dry. Around her, the tavern swims. "The northern hill?"

"Ayes. Make your way out of town. Jacob's is the first cottage you'll come to." His prickly face is suddenly close to hers. "You all right there, maid? Get a shot of brandy into you. Yours for a penny."

Scarlett stumbles away from him, seeking Asher out among the crowd. She has lost sight of him in the sea of sailors' slops and naval uniforms. Faces leer at her; salty beards and pocked cheeks. She looks around dizzily, searching for the door.

A hand is suddenly around her arm. "Steady there, maid."

She looks up. The man's face is lined and leathery. His red velvet justacorps is bare in places, powder on his shoulders from a threadbare white wig. There is an unsettling tattiness to him.

"This is no place for a woman to be alone," he tells Scarlett in a strange, breathy voice.

She looks at his hand, still tight around her upper arm. "Let go of me."

"You don't look well." He takes a glass from the table and presses it into her hand. "Drink this. It'll help."

She looks down at the amber liquid.

"It's brandy. Go on. It'll settle you."

The liquor has a rich, floral scent to it. "This isn't brandy," she coughs.

"Of course it is. Armagnac. Drink up. You'll feel better for it." He presses his hand into the small of her back. Spidery fingers work their way up her spine.

She drops the glass and shoves her way into the street. She leans over the edge of the quay and splashes her face. The seawater is icy, bracing. It brings back a scrap of clarity.

She straightens. Asher is gone. How could she have let such a thing happen? She ought to have left him tethered to the bed where there was no chance of him breaking free. But the thought of entering the tavern on her own had made something twist inside her. Outside of the world she knows, Scarlett has begun to see that she too is a coward.

She hunches by the tavern wall, trying to push away the lingering dizziness. She knows Asher plans to turn her and Isaac over to customs. If he makes it to Polperro without her brother's knowledge, the revenue men will be at their door. For all her anger at Isaac, the thought of him in danger makes panic rise within her.

She tries to steady her thoughts. Asher has no money. No means to make it back. Not yet at least. She has a little time. Time to push Asher Hales to the back of her mind and focus on other, more immediate issues.

The cottage on the northern hill.

She swallows heavily. Stands. Begins to walk towards the edge of the village. Women push past her clutching baskets of fish. A blue and gold carriage waits at the edge of the harbour, the horse nosing Scarlett as she passes.

As she climbs the hill, stillness takes over. Portreath becomes a flicker of light at the water's edge.

Ahead is the tiny cottage, lit only by the moon. It stands a few yards back from the road, rising from tangled gorse and blackberry bushes; a mess of leaning walls and thatching.

Scarlett stares for a moment, breathless from the climb. She had wanted the cottage to be a lie, as she had wanted Jacob to be a lie. She presses her forehead to a lightless window. The dark is too thick to see inside. Abandoned? Yes, it could certainly be abandoned.

Wind whips through her hair, carrying the smell of sea and damp earth. She hears a distant peal of laughter rise from the village.

The undergrowth crackles. Scarlett starts, darting away from the window and hiding in a tangle of trees. She holds her breath. A fox darts across the path and she lets herself breathe.

An abandoned cottage, she tells herself. Owned by a dead man.

A SAFE PATH

With Isaac and his men at sea, the Mariner's Arms is quiet. A cluster of old men sit by the fire, the hiss and crackle of burning logs punctuating their conversation.

Two riding officers arrive, order ales. Since the night of Bobby Carter's death, the revenue men have been a fixture in the area. Flora is glad when they leave.

Late in the evening, a man comes alone to the inn. He has been to her tavern before, Flora is sure. A man from Tom Leach's crew.

He sidles to the bar and takes off his knitted cap. His hair is knotted and colourless, his eyes dark beads in leathery, pitted cheeks. He smells of sweat and old salt.

"You work with Tom Leach," Flora says tautly. "You're not welcome here."

The man climbs onto a stool and tosses his cap onto the bar.

"Your pistol," says Flora. "Give it to me. All weapons to be turned in at the door. House rules."

He snorts. "Since when?"

She folds her arms.

"Don't got no weapons." He eyes the ankers lined up along the shelf. "Last time I were here we was all winking at the kettle."

Flora says nothing.

"You've a licence then. Hard to get your hands on, I hear. Expensive."

"Business is doing well," she says icily.

The man looks around the empty inn. "Don't look to be doing so well. Where's Isaac Bailey and his men? They just made a run for Reuben last week. They can't be at sea again."

"At home, I assume." Flora folds her arms. "Did Leach send you?"

The man shrugs.

She glares at him. "Are you a fool, or are you just acting as one? What does he want? Why has he sent you?"

There can be no good behind the man's visit. Isaac had sent Leach's cutter to the bottom of the river. She is sure he will want retribution.

236

"He says he's keeping an eye on things," the man tells Flora. "He don't trust none of you. And I'd say he's right not to."

Flora snorts. "Why, because Isaac and his men aren't here? Do you think them a pack of drunkards?"

He chuckles. "Perhaps."

"Why does Leach not come and see me himself?"

"He says you're a witch. He's afraid you'll set the devil on him."

Flora hides a smile.

"Perhaps I'll tell him," the man says slowly, "that Bailey and his men all seem to be missing." He twists his cap into a fat woollen sausage, a crooked smile turning the corner of his lips. "I'm sure Tom would like to know what they're up to."

Flora glances around the tavern. The other customers have left. "I don't know what you're implying," she says coldly, "but whatever it is, I'm sure you're wrong. Now leave. You're mistaken if you think you'll get served in my tavern."

The man considers her, then climbs from his stool and disappears.

The inn is quiet again.

Flora locks the door. She checks the cellar is open and the entrance to the tunnel clear. Then she climbs upstairs.

She opens the bedroom door and peers in at the children. Bessie and Gabriel breathe deeply, backs to each other in Bessie's bed. Mary sleeps in a basket on the floor, tiny pink arms stretched above her head.

Flora finds Caroline in the parlour. She had brought her children to the inn while the tavern's doors were open. Put them to bed so she might go to the cliffs and guide the men home.

Caroline's desperation for escape is glaring. Flora can't remember the last time she had seen her stand on the cliffs with a signalling lantern. In the early days, perhaps, before Gabriel and Bessie. A time of flowing liquor and sunrises.

There is a need in Caroline, Flora sees, to involve herself in Isaac's plans. To oversee the creation of their new life. At the sight of her in the parlour with a lamp in her hand, Flora feels a tinge of nostalgia; half pleasant, half tainted with sorrow.

She has missed Caroline. Still misses her now, though they stand a foot apart. Misses her friendship, her quick-witted, grounded conversation. Her rationality amongst a sea of believers.

Caroline had pulled away after Jack's death, when Flora had needed her the most. She had needed someone to speak to, someone to fill the new silence, the sudden emptiness. Had needed someone who would allow her to fall apart and not make her feel weak.

But Caroline had been unable to look her in the eye. She had been wracked by her own guilt, Flora is sure. A feeling that Isaac had been responsible for the tunnel's collapse.

Flora has never felt such a thing. Never sought to pin blame. It had been nothing but an horrific accident— one that had been as hard on Isaac as it had been on her, she is sure.

She smiles at Caroline, trying for a fragment of the warmth that had once existed between them.

"You'll stay with the children?" Caroline's fingers tense around the handle of the lantern.

Flora nods. "Of course. Go. The men will be back soon."

And Caroline disappears out of the inn, out towards the cliffs with the lantern in her hand. A lantern to alert the men of a safe path to the eastern beach. A safe path to the tunnel beneath the Mariner's Arms.

Flora paces, full of restless energy. A distant, long-ago feeling she remembers from nights waiting for Jack to return home on a ship full of liquor.

Bessie's dog scampers in from the kitchen and circles her legs. She glances at the clock on the hearth. Just past midnight. A sliver of moonlight peeks through a gap in the curtains. Flora pours herself a glass of brandy and drinks it by the window. A dark shadow of birds glides past the glass.

So Tom Leach believes her a witch. He has threatened her over it in the past. And yet it seems his fears are keeping him from the Mariner's Arms. Perhaps his fears are keeping Flora safe.

She puts down her glass and goes to the room that had once been her mother's. Sprigs of mallow leaves and yarrow hang drying from a string she had stretched across the room. She touches one of the fragile fronds.

Not yet dry. Leave them another day.

She stares at the bundles hanging from the ceiling. She had been adamant this would not be her life. She would not surround herself with healing herbs. And yet the sight of the bundled stems begins to settle a restlessness that has existed in her for longer than she has been aware of.

She goes to her bedroom and pulls the black mirror from the chest. She sits cross-legged on the bed and holds the glass face down in her lap. Through the ajar door she can hear the children's deep breathing and the husky snores of the dog.

The room feels vast around her.

A room for two. It had been her grandparents' room. Her parents'. Hers and Jack's. She feels a stab of deep loneliness.

She turns over the mirror. Sees her own faint reflection; pale hair falling in pieces over her cheeks, stark against the dark of the mirror. Sees the soft contours of her face in the glass.

Flora sees she is becoming her mother.

She hears in her head:

Watch, cheel-vean. *Patience.*

And she watches. Is patient.

Because no longer can she brush away her mother's craft as a fairy tale. No longer can she pretend to be so knowing, so wise. The more she sees, the less she understands.

She watches the glass. And there are images. Men running in the dark. Where is she seeing them? In her mind's eye? In the glass? She is unsure. Is this anything more than imagination?

Quiet. Stop thinking. Let the images come.

Horses. Guns. A man in blue lies sprawled on his back, staring blankly at the night sky.

The cellar stairs creak loudly. Flora throws the mirror on the bed, a strange tightening in her chest. Another creak of the stairs. It is too early to be Isaac and his crew, surely. The dog scampers and barks.

She hurries down to the bar. The cellar door is hanging open.

And Flora thinks of dead men walking the lightless tunnel.

She hates that this is where her thoughts go now. Hates that her mind grabs first at superstitious tales. Hates that she cannot have healing herbs without having ghosts as well.

She stops at the top of the cellar stairs. Silence now. Even the mice are still.

The quiet had bothered her the most after her husband had died. Somehow, the silence had seemed more profound when she knew she'd not be woken by his footsteps on the stairs at dawn after a run.

She steps into the cellar. As a girl, she had been afraid of the inn's creaks and shadows. Her imagination had populated the empty rooms with a colourful cast of fairies and knockers. Shadowy spirits hiding beneath the beds.

She feels that old childhood fear pushing at the edges of her rationality. She is suddenly acutely conscious of the expanse of the building around her; the upstairs rooms filled with the belongings of her dead family, the empty bar, the cluttered cellar, the lightless tunnel reaching for the sea.

And she longs suddenly for the simplicity of childhood. If only she could believe the noise from the tunnel to be the doing of fairies and knockers. Because this cellar, this tunnel, is no longer the hideout of imaginary beings, it is the site of her husband's sudden and horrific death.

She does not believe in ghosts. And yet, since Isaac had prised the tunnel open, she has felt herself drawn towards it. Felt herself making for the dark, searching for what might hide within. Searching for the boundaries of the world she has trained herself to know.

The lamplight falls on a tiny figure at the mouth of the tunnel.

"Bessie?" calls Flora.

Her daughter mumbles unintelligibly.

The lantern Flora has lit for the men sways as a draught sighs through the tunnel. Shadows flicker over broken furniture.

Bessie is standing in her nightshift, staring into the dark passage. "Tasik," she says.

Flora's breath catches. She touches her daughter's shoulder. Bessie starts, whirls around.

"What are you doing down here, *cheel-vean*?"

Bessie looks at her mother with bewildered eyes. "I don't know."

Flora kisses the side of her head, trying to slow her own racing heart. "You must have come down here in your sleep." She takes her daughter's hand. "Let's go back upstairs."

And with Bessie in bed, Flora finds herself back in the cellar, shining the lantern into the mouth of the tunnel. She hears Bessie's voice in her head.

Tasik.

My father.

Flora hears herself say: "Jack, are you there?" Her arms prickle. She is afraid, she realises. Afraid of what? Her husband?

No. Afraid she might find proof. Afraid she might see or hear something that might tilt her world to the point of no return.

Silence, she thinks. Let there be silence.

For all she would give for another minute with Jack, she can think of little worse than hearing his voice echoing through the tunnel's twists and turns.

But there is not silence. There are footsteps. Faint voices and the thud of barrels. Flora exhales sharply at the solidity of the sounds.

The noise grows louder, accompanied by streams of orange light.

Here are the men, spilling from the tunnel with dusty cheeks and windswept hair. A barrage of footsteps; the landing party and the crew, chuckling, demanding whisky.

"Whisky, ayes," she tells them. "It's waiting for you upstairs."

John Baker plants a bristly kiss on her cheek. "Bless you, Flora."

Isaac is the last man out. "We've left the ankers in the tunnel. Better way they're hidden there than have them sitting in your cellar." He rolls the empty barrels across the room to hide the tunnel's entrance.

Impulsively, Flora throws her arms around his neck. His hands slide around her waist, holding her to him. She can smell the sea on his skin.

"What's happened?" he asks, his voice muffled by her hair. "Are you all right?"

"Nothing's happened. Glad you're back safe is all." Suddenly embarrassed, she tries to pull away, but Isaac keeps her close.

"You'd tell me, wouldn't you?" he says in Cornish. "If you weren't all right?"

She can't remember the last time she heard him speak their language. English, always, for Caroline's benefit.

He steps back and looks her in the eye. "Flora? Would you tell me?"

"*Heb mar*," she says. "Of course." Her voice feels stuck in her throat.

"Good."

She unhooks the lantern from above the stairs. "He's a good thing then, your agent?"

"Seems it, ayes."

She thinks to tell him of the visit Leach's crewmate had paid her. No, she decides, she will not bring him down. Instead, she says: "I'm glad. You'll have escaped this place before you know it."

Isaac says nothing.

"You don't seem so taken with the idea."

"I'll miss you, is all."

Flora's throat tightens. She has not let herself feel anything other than happiness for Isaac at the thought of his escape. She will miss him too, of course. Deeply, desperately. Cannot bring herself to think how it will feel to walk past his cottage and see it empty. To open the inn's doors and know he will not be striding in for a drink. She cannot allow herself such selfish thoughts.

But Isaac's admission brings a heaviness to her chest. His escape will be final, absolute.

She knows once he leaves Talland they will never see each other again.

Unable to look at him, she lets her gaze drift upwards to the footsteps thudding above their heads. The landing party's footsteps. Caroline's footsteps.

Flora manages a nod. *Yes, I'll miss you too.* She knows it does not need to be spoken.

But things must change. Isaac must break free. Their past in Talland must become nothing more than memory.

INDIRECTION

After escaping Scarlett, Asher manages a few hours of sleep in the doorway of the cobbler. He wakes with an ache in his back and his skin itching with filth.

Look where his life has taken him. He hasn't felt this worthless and low since his days of servitude in New England.

He makes his way towards the harbour, stretching his neck from side to side as he walks. He kneels at the edge of the sea and splashes his face. The chill of the water wakes him, but leaves his skin sticky. He feels the patchy beginnings of a beard.

He tucks in his dirty shirt. Perhaps this dishevelled, earthy look will make him seem more amenable to physical labour.

He asks at the fishing port. No work available. Tries three farms on the hill before finding a man willing to hire him to muck out his stables.

Asher rubs his jaw. "When will you pay me?"

"End of the week."

Something about the farmer sets Asher on edge. Perhaps the constant shifting of his eyes, or the way his long fingers ripple as though they've a life of their own. The man's breeches are riddled with holes, his coat encrusted with dirt. What a sorry thing, Asher thinks, that he might take orders from such a creature.

His thoughts are an endless rattle of paranoia. Each man he has passed, he has thought to be Jacob Bailey. He needs to leave this place as soon as possible.

He takes the position.

The farm is a miserable patchwork of fields on the edge of the village. The house is bare and has with far too much in common with the barn for Asher's liking. The sleeping quarters smell vaguely of animals and the tin roof rattles when the wind blows. As far as Asher can tell, he is the only employee.

Pay in a week. He can manage to shovel shit and avoid Scarlett for a week. And when the money is in his pocket, he will return to Talland, via the Polperro customs house. What a pleasure it will be to watch from the cliff as the revenue men swoop.

His pockets will finally be full when he will go to that cottage door.

I'm sorry, he will tell Caroline. And he will mean it. Because once they had sat by the fireside with their legs intertwined and planned a better life. Once, he had looked over his brandy glass and told her he loved her. Once, he had thought that returning to England would mean returning to her.

I'm sorry, Callie, he will say, as the revenue men haul away her husband and tear that creaking cottage to pieces. *I'm sorry you couldn't see me for the man I was always destined to be. I'm sorry for your most terrible of choices.*

"My husband is unwell," Scarlett tells Mrs Acton at breakfast. "No, there's no need to disturb him. He's sleeping."

She takes a bowl of porridge upstairs to the bedroom.

"Are you sure I can't fetch the healer?" the old woman calls after her.

Scarlett forces a smile. "That won't be necessary. He'll be up and out of bed tomorrow, I'm sure of it."

And she would be up and out of the house tomorrow. This ruse, she is sure, will not last another day.

She empties the porridge out the window and paces across the bedroom. Damn Asher Hales to Hell. If she ever sees him again, she will tear out his eyes.

She leaves the house hurriedly. She has no money. Nowhere to go. No sense of where home lies among this vast expanse of hill and sea.

She has always hated being a burden to her brother. Before things had fallen apart between them, she had tried to please him, tried to prove her worth, her helpfulness. But the truth of it is heavy on her shoulders. Without Isaac, she is lost.

She walks towards the water. The edges of the beach are hemmed by jagged cliffs, rock islets rising from the waves. Venture closer and she is sure she will find a coastline pocked with caves and grottos; a warren of dark hiding places.

And Scarlett realises she is not lost. Her world may have been turned upside down, the sea on the wrong side of her, but she is still deep in a world of free trade. Pace this beach at midnight and she is sure she will see a flash of blue from a signalling pistol. See a line of boats sliding through the moonlight.

Stay or go, she needs money. She cannot sew, can barely cook and clean. Her writing is messy and her reading slow. But slip a signalling lantern in her hand and she'll see a trader safely to shore.

Her world.

How best to infiltrate the Portreath ring? Watch the beach and wait? No. It might be weeks before a run is scheduled. She needs to find the men involved. Convince them to slide a little of their wealth into her hands.

She eyes the inn leaning against the cliff. No doubt the traders spend their time in such a place. She will return tonight.

She begins to walk faster along the beach. One end to the other, her boots sinking in the sand. She is directionless still for now, but buoyed by her plan.

By the time the tavern opens in the late afternoon, her stomach is rumbling and her hands are numb with cold. She doesn't look about her as she enters. Doesn't want to know it if the man with the powdered wig is here.

The smile on the innkeeper's face tells her he recognises her.

"D'you find him, then?" he asks. "Jacob?"

She leans across the bar to speak under her breath. "Who runs the trade here?"

"There is no trade."

Scarlett stares him down.

After a moment, he says: "Why are you asking?"

"I need money."

The innkeeper chuckles. "There are other ways a girl like you can earn a few shillings."

Scarlett flushes. Feeling the man's eyes on her, she yanks her cloak closed. "I want work with the smugglers. Hawking. Or a lookout. Whatever they need."

"You want work?" A man's voice behind her.

Scarlett whirls around. The man is young; no more than a few years older than her. Hair the colour of dark coffee hangs over one eye in waves. He is dressed in sand-coloured breeches and a blue broadcloth coat. His arms are folded across his chest.

Scarlett swallows. "Ayes. Hawking. Or—"

"Or a lookout. Yes. I heard you." He eyes her, considering. His lips twitch. "Come with me."

He leads her to the back room of the inn. The tables are crooked and scratched, the fire unlit. The room smells of tobacco and piss. Scarlett shivers.

"You're cold," says the man.

"I'm all right." She eyes him curiously. Is a man so young the leader of their syndicate? She thinks of creaky old Charles Reuben. The man in front of her is slim and muscular, his face unlined and flushed with youth. Perhaps his father had led the ring.

"Is there work?" she asks, her voice trapped in her throat. She pulls back her cloak to reveal the pockets stitched on the inside. "I know what I'm doing. I've been running goods since I were seven years old. Never been caught."

The man digs his hands into the pockets of his coat. "There's no work. We don't need more hands. Stay away from this place."

She raises her eyebrows. "Then why bring me back here?"

"Best to keep our business away from the ears of the landlord."

Impulsively, Scarlett takes a step closer. She can smell musk soap on him. "You could always use more hands." She keeps her voice low. Meets his eyes. "More hands make things easier. Faster."

His lips part.

"You've a landing party full of fisherman, I'm sure," she says. "Men who are clumsy when you take them off a ship. I'm fast and I'm quiet. And I'll do it for cheap."

"You seem quite knowledgeable on such things."

"Does that surprise you?"

"And quite persistent." The man tilts his head, considering. The intensity of his gaze makes Scarlett's cheeks hot.

"Why should I trust you?" he asks after a moment.

She manages a smile. "I don't trust you either. But I'm sure we can do this without a great deal of trust. What are you paying your landing party for delivery? Ten percent? I'll do it for five. And I'll do it twice as fast."

The man rubs the dark stubble on his jaw.

She takes another step towards him; close enough for her skirt to graze the edge of his boots. Close enough to see the slatey blue grey of his eyes. She sees him swallow heavily and feels a faint flicker of satisfaction. His landing party, she is sure, does not elicit such a reaction from him.

"What do you say?"

"Very well," he says finally, huskily. "You'll meet me on the beach tomorrow night. There's a stash of tobacco needs delivering. Consider it a trial."

Scarlett smiles crookedly, looking up at him until she sees a twitch in the corner of his lips. "Tomorrow night," she agrees. "You'll not be disappointed."

THE REALM OF FAIRY TALES

Flora wakes thinking of Jack. She reaches a hand out of her blankets and feels for his tobacco box that sits on her nightstand. She holds it close, running her fingers over its worn wooden engravings. She feels a swell of love. And for the first time, a grief that is gentle, not breathtakingly sharp. For the first time, when she thinks of Jack, there is a smile on her lips instead of pain in her chest. She is surprised by it.

She dresses and goes to the drawer in the parlour for a ring of keys.

Three former guest rooms line the hall, each clutching the belongings of her departed family. Her mother's room cleared, for better or worse. The next of the untouched shrines; her husband's.

Time now, yes. Time for Jack to live on through his daughter, through memories of their life together. Not in a locked and darkened room. And not through ghostly memories of his death.

With the morning light, Flora sees her behaviour in the tunnel had been foolish. Sees the dark's ability to take away reason.

She slides the key into the lock.

Time now, yes, but her stomach still turns as she pushes open the door. She goes first to the window. Pushes back the curtains and wrenches it open. A stream of cold air blows in.

The wardrobe is open a crack. Flora had sent Scarlett inside to find clothing for Asher Hales, the night he had washed up upon their shore.

Inside the cupboard, she finds Jack's breeches, long sailor's trousers, a woollen waistcoat. Everything is hanging neatly, creaseless and buttoned.

Two days after his death, she had torn his things from the wardrobe in their bedroom to be hidden away in here. Hanging his clothing so carefully had felt like the last thing she could ever do for her husband. The pain of it had been a crushing weight she was sure she would never crawl out from. She had never imagined her grief might work itself into this soft, delicate thing that is pushing around inside her chest.

She slides a shirt from the hanger and squeezes it between her fingers. The linen is patchy and thin. It smells of mildew and moths; a reminder it has been many days and nights that her husband has been gone.

Many days and nights since she had watched Jack's eyes crinkle when her mother had spoken of her craft.

And even longer since Flora had sat opposite him at the supper table and lied. "No," she had said, her head overflowing with herbal remedies and incantations. "I know nothing of it. I've never gone near such things."

Why had she felt a need to hide it? Fear of mockery? No. She knows Jack would have accepted whatever eccentricities she had dropped at his feet.

The lies had come from her own inability to accept her roots. Her embarrassment at the superstitious haze that hung over her family's inn.

She had been ashamed at how small her world was. She'd not left Cornwall until the age of twenty, when Jack had taken her east to show his new wife off to his family. And Flora was determined not to be paraded as an ignorant west country simpleton. She would not be pigeonholed as the Cornish girl with sandy boots and a head full of magic rhymes.

I've never gone near such things.

The floor creaks. Bessie stands in the doorway in her nightshift. "Tasik's room," she says.

The dog scampers inside, nose to the floor. Flora folds the shirt and sits it on the bed. "Bessie, take your dog. He's getting under my feet."

"*She*, Mammik. It's a girl dog."

"I don't think so, Bess."

"It is. I named her Molly."

Flora smiles.

Bessie scoops the dog into her arms. "The room," she says. "It smells like him."

Yes, Flora can smell it too. That faint scent of pipe smoke and boot polish beneath the dust and damp of two lightless years.

She piles the clothing on the bed, pushing past the faint ache in her chest. She needs to do this. Needs to release the past before she ends up chasing more shadows into the dark.

"Bessie," she says carefully. "You were in the tunnel last night. Do you remember?"

Her daughter looks at her quizzically. Shakes her head.

"You were talking to someone. You don't remember who?"

"No."

Flora places the wearable clothing in a trunk for the charity collection. She takes Jack's books from the shelf. Sifts through the pile to find his favourites and puts them aside for the bookshelf in the parlour. The rest she places into the trunk. She takes a silver compass from the shelf and slides it into her pocket. "A dream," she tells Bessie. "Nothing more, I'm sure."

She needs it to be nothing more.

She latches the trunk and carries it into the hallway. A waft of drying mallow leaves comes from the room that had once been her mother's.

This venture with the mirror, with healing herbs, she would never have done if Jack had been alive. She would have lived by her husband's beliefs, the way she had lived by her mother's before she had married. As a child, it had just been assumed she would one day take over the role of village healer. A thing she had never thought to question. The first pangs of doubt she'd felt as a teenager had come as a shock. What if there was no truth to magic? What if she had grown up believing in fairy tales? At first, she could not believe she had even dared think such blasphemous thoughts.

She had only just begun to explore the edges of her own beliefs when Jack had bowled into her life, sending healing charms to the realm of fairy tales.

Flora looks at the two cleared rooms, doors swinging open, side by side. She had loved them both so dearly; her husband, her mother. Loves so blinding she had taken their beliefs and made them her own.

She would give her life to see either of them again. And yet she can't help but think who she might begin to be without them.

A RUNNING OF ERRANDS

The tunnel is filled with brandy ankers. Now Isaac needs buyers. A new impatience is stirring inside him.

"Get your coat," he tells his son. "We'll have you a sailing lesson."

Gabriel's eyes light. He pulls on his coat and bounds out of the house.

They'll sail to Fowey. A larger village, outside of Reuben's control. They'll buy food from the market and pitch from the ship chandler and this will seem nothing more than a running of errands. But Isaac's eyes will be open, his ears alert for the right buyers, the right businesses, the men with money itching to be spent.

Gabriel runs excitedly along the cliff path, reaching the harbour and bouncing onto the lugger ahead of his father. "High tide," he announces. "Westerly wind."

Isaac smiles. "Good."

He is glad his son has taken to the sea. The sea is changeable and challenging but it makes the world accessible. A life on the ocean will show Gabriel new lands, new lives. A world far greater than this oppressive pocket of Cornwall.

The sun is streaking the clouds as they slide from the harbour. Isaac stands on the edge of the foredeck, letting Gabriel take the wheel. The lugger settles into a steady rhythm. He points to a strip of pale sand between jagged rock. "See there. Lantic Bay."

"Is it a landing beach? A hiding place?"

For all he has tried to keep his son blind to it, Isaac knows Gabriel is coming to see the world through smuggler's eyes. The caves are hideouts, the lugger a running vessel, the men in blue and gold, mortal enemies. Impossible, Isaac has realised, to keep his boy shielded from a thing so embedded in the landscape.

"Not a landing beach. A sheltered bay. Safe water. A sailor ought to know his coast."

But this will not be his son's coast, of course. They will be gone from this place soon. Gabriel's coast will be a puzzle of new coves and Mary will take her first steps in a house without smuggled tea beneath the beds.

Isaac squints as sun reflects off the water, turning the sea translucent blue. "There'll be new places to sail soon," he says. "The Irish Sea perhaps. Or the Scottish Islands. Does that excite you?"

Gabriel nods, smiles his father's smile. Isaac reaches over his shoulder to steady the wheel as it lurches on the swell. He tells stories of his own travels; the turquoise seas of Spain and the fragrant syrup air of the East Indies.

"The East Indies are a long way from Talland," Gabriel says.

"Ayes."

"How far?"

"Near ten thousand miles. Four months at sea or more."

Gabriel says nothing, just looks out across the water. Wondering, perhaps what he might see, if he stayed on the lugger and let the sea carry him for four months or more.

Isaac brings the lugger into Fowey harbour. A large cutter sways on the river, its hull and bare masts painted black.

It is a ghost ship, Isaac is sure. A phantom of the cutter he himself had sent to the bottom of the river.

They are close to Tom Leach's trading territory. Polruan lies on the other side of the river.

There has been a rivalry between the two smuggling rings for as long as Isaac can remember, but there is a new intensity to it now. He can't deny it is part of what had drawn him to Fowey. There is something pleasant about stealing Leach's business as he buys his family's freedom.

Leach is loading a dinghy with unmarked crates. Isaac hurries past, a protective hand on the back of Gabriel's neck.

"Good afternoon to you too, Bailey," calls Leach.

Isaac keeps walking.

"Who is that, Tasik?"

"No one of any importance."

Gabriel looks back over his shoulder. "His ship is black. Is he a pirate?"

"Something like that."

"It's a fine ship, ayes?" Leach calls, leaping from the dinghy and jogging along the harbour to catch them.

Gabriel squints. Gives a faint nod.

"My old cutter, she met with foul play." He looks sideways at Isaac. "This one, she's better. Bigger. Holds more men. More cargo."

More men? Is Leach seeking to expand his syndicate? No doubt he seeks to steal business from the Talland free traders. Let Leach and Reuben fight amongst themselves, Isaac thinks. Whichever man loses, it will be a fine thing.

Leach rubs his dirty beard. "What are you doing in these parts, Bailey?"

"That's no business of yours."

"This is our river. What happens on it is my business. And whatever you're up to, I'm sure it's untoward."

"Untoward," Isaac snorts. "You're a fine one to speak of such things. I'm giving my son a sailing lesson. Nothing more."

Leach chuckles. Turns to Gabriel. "You taking over your grandfather's debts, boy?"

"No," he says, "I'm going to go sail in the Irish Sea or the Scottish Islands or—"

Isaac's fingers tighten around Gabriel's shoulder. He stops talking hurriedly.

Leach smiles to himself.

Isaac ushers his son away from the harbour. The back of his neck prickles. He slides a handful of coins from his pocket and hands them to Gabriel. "I need you to go to the market."

The boy's shoulders fall. "I want to come to the ship chandlers." He looks at Isaac pleadingly.

"The market first. Your mother wants currants and cinnamon. She's to make you heavy cake."

Gabriel's eyes light. "Heavy cake?"

Isaac ushers him towards the market. "I'll meet you at the chandlers when you're done."

"Where are you going?"

"I've someone to see."

Isaac watches Gabriel disappear into the winding streets.

He'll try The Ship, The Well House. A quick word to the innkeeper.

Fine brandy. A good price.

And then he'll hurry back to the market and take Gabriel to the ship chandlers for the pitch. An innocent domestic errand. His son will know this to be nothing more.

He goes to The Well House. He's drunk in the place before. Knows the innkeeper a friendly man with an eye for a good deal.

He is blunt, deliberate. "I've a shipment of brandy looking for a buyer." He brings a vial of liquor from his pocket and plants it on the bar. The innkeeper; a broad-shouldered man in his forties, uncorks it. Inhales.

"Cognac," Isaac tells him. "Fine stuff."

The innkeeper takes a swig. Nods approvingly. "How much you got?"

"Forty ankers. I'll do you a good price. What's Leach charging you?"

The innkeeper eyes him. "How do you know I'm buying from Tom Leach?"

Isaac shrugs. "He trades out of Polruan. It makes sense."

The innkeeper considers. "I'll take twenty ankers. Pay you a pound apiece."

Isaac hesitates. The price is low. He'd been hoping for more. But agree to a pound and he'll secure the sale. He nods. "A pound apiece. But I'll not make the delivery here. You're too close to the customs station. I'll bring them to Lansallos Cove in two days' time. Meet me there."

The innkeeper chuckles. "Had to be a catch at such a price."

Isaac leans forward. "This is a good deal, man. You just bring a wagon. My men will load it for you, cover it. Nothing for you to do but ride home again."

The innkeeper nods finally. "Very well. Lansallos Cove. Twenty ankers at a pound apiece."

Isaac nods. Gives the man's hand a firm shake.

The sun is staining the water as they make their way back to Talland.

Gabriel looks towards the orange horizon. "Tasik," he says, "where is Aunt Scarlett?"

Isaac doesn't answer at once. He's managed to push his sister to the back of his mind, a place she has not been since before he had taken her from the children's home. There is something liberating about washing his hands of her plight. He'd said little to Gabriel to explain her absence. Can't blame him for his curiosity.

"Aunt Scarlett needs a little time away," he hears himself say. And suddenly she is back in the forefront of his mind, jostling his son and daughter for space.

Twenty ankers at a pound apiece is a good start. Two tickets out of Cornwall. Perhaps three. Sell the second half of the haul at a higher price and he'll have enough for his family to leave. Once the money is in their hands, he knows Caroline won't wait. Won't sit around waiting for Reuben to catch them.

Won't sit around waiting for Scarlett to show herself.

Another successful sale and Talland will be a memory. Isaac follows Gabriel's gaze towards the horizon. Wills his sister to come home before there is no home for her to return to.

THE TOBACCO CAVE

Scarlett spends the day walking Portreath; memorising the maze of alleys and the indented footprints worn across the cliffs. She takes in the location of the customs station, finds huers' watch houses on the cliffs that might provide cover for the riding officers. Making a delivery in this foreign place will be a challenge, but she is determined to succeed.

When the light has faded to nothing, she waits on the beach. The sea rolls and pushes at the edge of the cliffs. White water glows at the base of the rock stacks. The last of the fishing boats slide back into the quay, their lights bobbing in a moonlit sky.

Scarlett touches the knife at her knee. There is something comforting about the feel of it against her stockings.

She turns as lamplight spills over the beach. The young man from the tavern comes towards her, his footsteps sighing in the wet sand.

Scarlett stands, her heart quickening. "You're alone."

Wind blows the messy waves of his hair back from his face. Light flickers on the sharp line of his jaw. "The rest of the party will be here shortly. You're early. The men are rarely on time."

"Where do you need me to go?"

"There's a farm at North Cliffs. You'll find the man's name on his gate. Williamson."

Scarlett nods, feeling a swell of relief. She knows the place. She will make the delivery easily. Quick and silent. "And I'll be paid?"

He nods, his eyes meeting hers. "As promised."

She gives him a faint smile. Tonight, she will have money from the traders in her hands. She will be able to afford a bed away from Mrs Acton's. Or a coach ride home.

Thoughts of her father push their way inside her head. She shakes them away hurriedly. There is no place for him here now. No place for him here, ever.

The man nods towards a cave hidden in the cliffs. "You'll make your delivery now. The men will make theirs when they arrive." He leads her through the shallow water. The sea swells around her ankles, filling her boots.

The man shines the lamp into the chasm. A wooden chest sits at the back, protected from the tide. He points towards it. "The tobacco is in the top."

Scarlett steps inside and opens the lid. A fragrant, wrapped package sits above larger bundles she guesses are silk or lace. She takes the tobacco and slides it into her cloak. The light disappears suddenly as the man steps out of the cave. Scarlett stumbles back to the beach. And her mouth goes dry.

He stands at the edge of the water with a pistol in his hand. She freezes, several feet away, the sea knotting her skirts around her calves.

He raises his weapon. "Give me the tobacco."

"You don't work with the traders," Scarlett says bitterly. "You work with the revenue men."

The man keeps the pistol trained on her. "The tobacco."

She tosses it on the sand. "A fine cover. Are you proud of yourself?"

"No. Not really."

"Good. Nor should you be."

He picks up the tobacco and slides it into his pocket. "What's your name?"

She sighs and trudges out of the water. "Scarlett Bailey." She swallows heavily.

A criminal, just like her father.

But if this scheming revenue officer knows anything of Jacob, he does not let on.

"This way, Miss Bailey," he says, gesturing to the top of the beach with the nose of the pistol.

"I'm not going anywhere with you."

"Never been caught, you say. It shows. Here's how things are. You will come with me to the customs station or I am well within my rights to use force."

His calm, even voice is infuriating. Scarlett clenches her hands into fists inside her cloak. He has a pistol. Let the Wild out here and she'll end up with a bullet in her chest.

He leads her up the beach towards the lamp-lit building close to the harbour. Her palms prickle. In all her years in the trade, she has never truly considered what it might be like to be caught. There have been close calls, for certain; the riding officers the night of Bobby's death, the revenue cutter Asher had sent on their trail. From each, she had walked away with little more than a racing heart.

But now, with a pistol at her shoulder and a riding officer's breath hot on her neck, a prison cell feels frighteningly close. Her legs are unsteady beneath her.

He pushes open the door. And in she goes to the customs house, her feet sliding in wet boots as she walks the gloomy stone corridor. Wooden doors line each side.

The officer leads her into a small room and gestures to a chair at the table. The room smells of old pipe smoke and boot polish.

He sits opposite her, their eyes meeting. She wants to strike him. Wants to snatch that pistol from his hand and pull the trigger. She clenches her teeth until the violent thoughts recede.

"You took the tobacco from here and planted it," she says bitterly. "You set me up."

He nods. "Yes. I'm sorry."

"No you're not."

He eyes her curiously. "You're not from these parts, are you. If you were, I'm sure our paths would have crossed before. Have you come to Portreath to engage in smuggling?"

"You heard what I told the innkeeper. I just need the money."

"Why?"

"To get home."

"Where is home?"

Scarlett shifts uncomfortably. She does not like how closely he is looking at her. What might he see?

"Why the interrogation?" she snaps. "Why not save us both the trouble and just arrest me?"

"I'm not going to arrest you."

She eyes him curiously. "You're not?"

"No. I lied to you. Misled you. It would hardly be the decent thing to do."

Scarlett snorts. "I didn't think you people were bothered with decency."

"Besides," he says, pushing past her comment, "I'd have to pay for the trial out of my own pocket if I were to take you to court. It's better for both of us that I let you go with a warning." He keeps his face even. "I meant it when I said you ought to leave this place, Miss Bailey. And you certainly shouldn't be involving yourself with the smugglers on this coast."

"I'm not afraid of smugglers."

"I can see that. And it may well be your downfall. Violence among smuggling gangs has been on the rise recently. And the men running the ring here are also involved in illegal impressment."

Scarlett raises her eyebrows. "So I'm to fear they'll throw the king's shilling into my ale and cart me off to serve the navy?" She gives a cold laugh. "I don't think so." She knots her hands into her cloak. "If you know who these men are and what they're doing, why not arrest them?"

"I've no proof," he says simply. "But I know they're dangerous. I'm sure you believe you can handle them, but they would have no issue with taking advantage of a young woman like you."

Anger prickles the back of her neck. She has spent her life around free traders. Can hold her own against men like Tom Leach. She doesn't need this man's misguided protection. She just needs money in her pocket.

"You don't know me," she hisses. "You don't know what I can handle." She hears a tremor in her voice. Curses herself for it. But the thought of being alone and penniless is a weight upon her shoulders. "May I leave?" she asks icily.

The officer nods. "Find another way to earn the money you need, Miss Bailey. If I catch you anywhere near the tavern again, I will happily pay for that trial."

THE PAUPER'S BOY

Isaac and Will Francis crouch in the tunnel, a pool of lamplight spilling over the ankers in front of them. A barrel of water sits beside the liquor, ready to dilute the over-proofed spirits.

One part water, four parts brandy. Isaac is careful to ensure his shipment matches that in the vial he had given the innkeeper at the Well House. One part water, four parts brandy. A profitable mix and one that will not sear the throats off its drinkers.

When the brandy is diluted and ready for shipment, they climb upstairs for a celebratory drink.

"You know this is dangerous, ayes?" says Will, sitting beside him at the bar. "Leach won't appreciate you taking his business."

"All the more reason to do it." Isaac empties his brandy, orders another. He gulps from the second glass, seeking the bliss of drunkenness. His mind races with thoughts of secret smuggling runs, then charges into thoughts of Flora.

He swallows hurriedly. These thoughts are the deadly ones. The ones that most need drowning in moonshine.

His mind is full of her. When he closes his eyes, he sees nothing but blonde hair, freckled skin, deep sea blue eyes.

She has been there always, hovering on the edge of his consciousness. Ever since their days of paddling in their underclothes while one of their mothers watched from the beach.

Why does he think of her now with such intensity? Is it the thought of leaving? The knowledge that when he finally escapes Talland, he will leave her here among the liquor and lamplight and never see her again?

She has always been a few rungs above him on the social ladder; his family elbow-to-elbow in their cottage while hers lost themselves in the echoing passages of the Mariner's Arms.

He'd thought of marrying her once, when he'd returned from sea as a young man. When he had first imagined himself breaking free of Reuben's shackles, it was Flora beside him in the escape vessel. But he'd had nothing to offer her. It had been no secret that her mother had looked down on him, believed him unworthy. He was nothing but the pauper's boy who'd once flashed her his arse while his mother's back was turned.

And then there was Caroline. Then there was Jack. His attraction to Flora had been pushed to the background. Buried under years of friendship and marriage to a woman who has no family to judge him.

He realises he is watching her. Christ, how long has he kept this up? Has Will noticed?

A scrappy black and white dog scurries down from upstairs and follows her to the hearth.

"Is that Reuben's dog?" Isaac demands, sliding from his stool.

Flora glances over her shoulder at him as she tosses another log onto the fire. "He says he can't care for him any longer. He thought Bess might like him." She folds her arms. "Don't give me that look, Isaac. It's just a dog."

"Reuben has eyes on you."

"Don't be ridiculous." She looks sideways at him. "Besides, what business of yours is it if a man has eyes on me?"

Isaac feels a fire inside him. She is testing him, he is sure. Then unsure. She and the moonshine are messing with his head.

"Reuben is dangerous," he says.

"I suspect he may say the same thing about you."

Isaac feels his legs sway beneath him. "Flora…"

She plants a hand on her hip. "Yes?"

He takes her arm, squeezes. Realises he is using it to stay upright. He feels a stray strand of her hair tickle his cheek. "Just be careful. I couldn't bear to see anything happen to you."

She pulls her eyes away.

He tilts his cup towards her. "May I have another?"

She takes it from him, a firm hand on his arm easing him away from her. "You've had enough, Isaac." Her voice is clipped. "Go home and see your wife."

THIEVES AND LIARS

When Scarlett wakes, Mrs Acton's house is quiet. After her sparring with the riding officer, she had crept in through the servants' entrance and stolen an apple from the kitchen to calm her raging stomach. This morning she must leave. Her ruse, she is sure, has been shattered beyond recognition.

She slides from the bed and dresses soundlessly, giving a final, longing glance to the palatial bed. When in her life will she ever sleep on something so luxurious again? Tonight she will probably be cowering beneath a bridge, fairy-led on that great expanse of moorland.

Her boots and stockings are still damp from her venture into the cave and the smell of sea hangs about her. Her coin pouch is empty.

She creeps downstairs. She can hear movement in the kitchen; the clatter of pots, two women murmuring. She smells the fire and the salty tang of fish.

She hurries away from the kitchen, tiptoeing down a long hallway. Three doors on either side. Silence behind each one.

She slips inside the first room. A bookshelf lines one wall; a great oak desk against another. She pulls back the dusty roll-top. It squeaks and sticks from disuse. A nib pen rests in a pot of dried ink. Beside it sit a gutted candle and a silver letter opener that may be worth a few shillings.

She keeps looking. The top drawer of the desk holds an array of documents and faded letters. In the second, a jar of black ink and pounce pot sit beside an embroidered handkerchief.

The third drawer rattles as it opens. The coins are loose at the bottom. Scarlett counts four pounds. Far more than she has ever had in her hand before.

She takes the handkerchief and wraps the coins carefully. Looks away as she slips the package inside her stays. She can't watch herself become a thief.

How she had scorned Isaac when she had caught him with Reuben's stolen tea. But desperation, she sees now, is a powerful motivator. How easy it is to cross that line from noble free trader to common thief. And what, really, can be expected of either of them?

She knows now who their father is. She and Isaac both have a criminal's blood in them. What choice do they have but to follow in his path?

She hurries from the house. The coins make a faint bulge in her bodice, slightly below her collarbone. She covers it with her shawl.

At the top of the hill, the town stretches out before her, awakening in the grey dawn. Boats slide soundlessly from the harbour. Scarlett presses a hand over the coins. Enough to leave this place. Enough to go anywhere she desires.

But she can't leave. Not yet.

She needs to see that cottage again. She knows, of course, it is not abandoned. And she needs her father to know that she knows.

She approaches the house from the back, not daring to knock on the door. She peers tentatively through the window. This time, in the pale daylight, she can make out a table and chair, a cooking pot hanging over the hearth. The house is still. Perhaps her father had left at dawn on one of the fishing boats she had watched from the hill. Or perhaps he has been out all night, filling that cave with contraband.

She rattles the window. Locked. She grabs a rock and flings it through the glass. Unlatches the window and swings her legs over the sill.

The cottage smells of tallow and wood smoke. An empty bowl sits on the table, streaked with the hardened remains of porridge. On the shelf above the hearth is a half-burned candle in a simple brass holder. Beside it sits a jar of rust-coloured dust Scarlett assumes to be witch powder. A similar jar had sat above the fireplace when she was a child; an ineffective plea to keep ill luck away from her family.

This is the cottage of a poor man. Her father had not found Henry Avery's haul.

Her father is alive.

The smoke rising from the log in the grate burns away any doubt.

Scarlett drops to the floor and hugs her knees. Tears escape down her cheeks.

She had grown up thinking her father a hero. A brave adventurer who had died fighting the sea.

But Jacob Bailey is a living, breathing coward who had lied and betrayed and killed. Who had abandoned his family in the face of his debt.

Scarlett thinks of her mother. It had taken her months to accept that Jacob would not be coming home. Half a year had passed before she had requested a memorial stone be placed in the churchyard.

The sickness had fallen over her as though she had willed it. Scarlett watched as her pink cheeks yellowed, her black hair turned grey and the lively brown eyes became cloudy and distant. Her mother had always fought back against all life had thrown at her, but with her husband gone, her will to recover had disappeared. Less than a month after standing at the memorial stone and praying for her father's lost remains, Scarlett had watched her mother's coffin be lowered into the ground.

Her anger flares. She flings the bowl from the table. Snatches at the jar of witch powder and hurls it across the hut. It smashes and spills against the flagstones. The Wild flares inside her; more bitter and angry than she has ever felt. She watches herself overturn the table, hears herself screech, feels shards of glass against her cheek as she hurls a tin cup through the window.

How can this be her father? This bastard of a man who has saddled his own children with his unpayable debts? Abandoned his wife to poverty and grief.

She wants him to be dead. Fish-eaten dust at the bottom of the sea. Wants him to be nothing but a string of tainted childhood memories.

Exhaustion overtakes her. She closes her eyes and breathes deeply, sitting among the shattered pieces of her father's new life. She cannot find calm, but the urge to destroy the house has begun to fade.

She waits, letting the day slip away. She knows she needs to find a bed for the night, but she cannot leave without her father seeing her.

She paces in front of the cottage with her arms wrapped around herself. The waiting helps her adjust to the new reality. Her father the hero is dead. In his place, her father the killer, the deceiver, the liar. This new reality makes far more sense. She is not the daughter of a hero, she thinks, running a hand over the stolen coins pressed against her ribs.

In the late afternoon she sees him. He walks the overgrown path towards the cottage, hands dug into his pockets and shoulders hunched. The hair poking beneath his knitted cap has greyed and thinned, his face become leathery with sea air. But this is the man who had carried her on his shoulders and told her bedtime stories of Henry Avery's treasure. The man who had built castles with her on the beach at Talland Bay.

She walks slowly towards him, heart racing, unsure what she will do. Fury wells inside her, blurring the edges of her vision. Her mouth is dry; the tirade she had spent hours rehearsing suddenly forgotten. She wills him to speak. He stands before her on the path, the blackberry bush knocking against him as the wind skims through it.

Finally, Scarlett says: "How could you leave us?"

Jacob pauses. Frowns. There is a hardness in his eyes she does not remember. "I'm sorry, maid," he says, "whoever you think I am, you're mistaken."

Something tightens around her lungs. She feels a sudden flicker of doubt. Has her feverish search led her to the wrong man? Has she destroyed the house of a stranger? No. These eyes, these hands, that voice; they are all there in her memories. All there in pieces.

She had been a girl of five when last he had seen her. But she is his daughter. She had assumed that would be enough for him to know her in a crowd. She has her mother's face, Isaac had told her. And she has her brother's eyes, her brother's dark hair. Jacob's own rage simmering within her. The thought of not being known to him had never entered her mind. She swallows the tears in her throat.

"Asher Hales brought me here," she says finally, pinning her eyes on him so he might not turn away. "Perhaps you knew him by another name. But you'll remember him, I'm sure. You left him alone on the beach with a murdered man."

She watches Jacob's face for any reaction, any glimmer of recognition.

"I'm sorry," he says again, his colourless lips twisting into a faint smile of pity. "You have the wrong man."

THE MAN IN BLUE AND BRASS

Her father does not enter his cottage. Perhaps he sees the broken windows and the upturned table. Perhaps he wants to get as far away from Scarlett as possible.

He turns and walks back the way he came, not giving her another look.

She feels a sharp pain in her throat. Of all the scenarios she had imagined, this had not been one of them. She forces her tears away. She will not cry for this man. Will not cry for her false memories of him, for his lonely, miserable life.

But she finds herself following him. Back down the hill towards the water. She watches him enter the harbour tavern.

This place is the hideout of smugglers and illegal impressers. How can she be surprised to find him here, shoulder to shoulder with men she had been warned away from? Perhaps the riding officer had meant to warn her away from Jacob Bailey. He would have been right to do it.

She peers through the window of the tavern. Jacob slides a coin across the counter and carries a tankard of ale into the back room. He disappears from sight.

Scarlett makes her way around the side of the building, searching for another window so she might peer into the room. Catch sight of the men who inhabit her father's life now.

She looks through the glass. Why? Is she seeking to vindicate him? Find men clustered and plotting, her father not among them?

No. It's far too late for that. She is not trying to vindicate him, she realises. She is trying to condemn him. She wants to peer through the window to that cluster of men and see Jacob in the centre with the king's shilling in his hand. See him march from the tavern with a drugged and beaten man tossed over his shoulder, ready to be thrown onto a naval ship. She wants to pile up the black marks against his name, so she might feel no guilt when she leaves this place and pretends him dead. Feel no guilt when she kicks at that hollow farce of a memorial stone.

She feels a hand around the top of her arm. Whirls around to find the young riding officer. "Don't touch me," she hisses.

He lets his hand fall. "I told you to stay away. The men in this place are dangerous."

"I've spent my life around dangerous men. And it's taught me none of them can be trusted. Especially not those of you in blue and brass."

His eyes are close to hers. "Do you wish I arrest you, Miss Bailey?"

"Arrest me?" she snaps. "For what? I didn't bring in those goods you hid on the beach. I didn't sell them. The only thing you saw me do was pick up a packet of tobacco."

"And put it in your cloak," he reminds her. "That's enough to arrest you for theft."

She narrows her eyes. "You're a bastard."

"Of course I am. I'm paid a pittance to fight a war I've no chance of winning."

"You're a fool to have involved yourself in such a thing. Every man in this county has his hands in free trade."

"That doesn't make it right."

She snorts.

"Just go," he tells her, the hard edge disappearing from his voice. "Please. I don't want to see anything happen to you."

His sudden kindness brings fresh tears to her eyes. She blinks them away hurriedly and begins to walk from the tavern. Mrs Acton's coins slide about inside her stays. They will buy her a bed for the night, but she is too scared of being discovered a thief. If she is to buy herself a bed, it cannot be here in Portreath.

She glances up at the hills behind the village. Dusk has fallen, turning them deep purple with shadow. Dangerous and otherworldly, alive with spirits. They stretch into the night and seem to go on forever.

"Where are you going?" the officer asks.

"It's none of your business." She feels her tears threatening.

"Do you have somewhere to go? A bed for the night?"

"Of course I have a bed," she says, trying for sharpness but managing no more than a choked whisper. Wind tunnels in from the sea and tugs at her skirts.

"Is there someone here for you?" he asks. "A friend? Family?"

At the thought of family, Scarlett's tears spill. She longs suddenly for that cottage on the hill in Talland. Longs for the way it had been before she had proclaimed her brother a thief and a liar. She longs to sit around the table eating Caroline's flavourless broth, stirring up Isaac and listening to a stream of Gabriel's jabber. She longs for the time when Jacob Bailey had been a memory.

She swipes hurriedly at her tears.

"Come with me," the officer says gently.

Scarlett hesitates. This man has sworn an oath to cleanse the country of free trade. He had watched her slide smuggled tobacco into her cloak. But the night is thickening, and the hills are crawling with spirits. If anyone from Mrs Acton's household sees her, they will string her up for theft.

There is little to do but follow him.

They wind through the streets towards a cluster of crooked stone houses. Some are leaning so sharply they seem to be holding each other up. The officer stops at the cottage on the corner.

"This is your house?" Scarlett asks throatily.

He nods. "In part, at least. I rent the room at the back." He leads her down the side of the building to a small door at the rear. "It's not much. But you're cold. And there's a fire. A kettle."

Scarlett wrings her cloak around her hands.

"You don't trust me," he says.

"Can you blame me?"

"I suppose not." He slides a key from his pocket and unlocks the door. "Do as you wish." He steps inside. The house is small and cramped, the single room cluttered with a table and two chairs. A narrow bed sits against one wall. The place smells faintly of musk soap.

Scarlett stays planted in the doorway. "I don't even know your name."

He looks over his shoulder at her. "It's Jamie. Jamie McCulley." He goes to the hearth and tosses a handful of kindling into the grate. Strikes the tinderbox.

Scarlett closes her eyes. She doesn't want to be this bitter, untrusting person. She wants her old optimism. Wants the sun that shone over everything until Asher Hales and his cursed letter had barrelled into her life.

She steps inside the cottage.

Is this her most foolish act of all? Walking willingly into the home of a riding officer?

Jamie looks up from the hearth where a tiny flame has begun to lick the wood. "Close the door. That wind's got a right chill to it."

The door closes with a heavy click. Scarlett looks about her. Despite its size, the house is clean and tidy, pots stacked neatly on a shelf beside jars of oatmeal and potted meat. A blue and gold riding officer's jacket hangs on a hook beside the door.

Scarlett swallows heavily. She looks back at Jamie, trying to see behind his eyes. Can she trust this decency? He has already trapped her once.

He unwinds his scarf and slides off his coat. Holds out a hand. "Your cloak?"

Scarlett shakes her head. She cannot stay long. Cannot make herself comfortable here in the home of a revenue man. A mouthful of tea to warm her and then she will be gone.

Jamie hangs the kettle on the hook above the fire. He goes to the shelf and returns with bread and cheese. Breaks a piece from the loaf and hands it to Scarlett. She kneels by the hearth, holding her frozen fingers close to the flames.

She chews slowly. The events of the day have stolen her appetite, but she had best force down a few mouthfuls if she is going to make it out of Portreath tonight.

In her mind's eye, she sees the blank look in her father's eyes.

You have the wrong man.

She blinks hard, trying to force him from her thoughts. She hates how much their meeting has rattled her.

The stool squeaks behind her. Jamie cuts a piece of cheese and pops it into his mouth. He holds the knife out to her. She shakes her head. Her eyes fix on the small leather-bound book on the shelf beside the food jars. She has heard the riding officers keep journals of their exploits. Has Jamie kept his own records of seized liquor and chases in the night? He catches her looking and she pulls her eyes away hurriedly.

"Why smuggling?" he asks.

Why smuggling? She has never been asked such a thing. Why smuggling? Why air? Why sleep? There has never been any other option.

"It's all I know," she mumbles, not looking at him. The shame of it hits her hard. She had grown up believing the words spouted by her father and the other men in the village. Smuggling was the noblest of trades. A trade that brought power back to the people. But with Jamie's eyes on her, the life she has built does not seem quite so noble.

Smuggling and theft. All she knows.

A thin line of steam begins to rise from the kettle. Jamie pours the tea into two mugs and hands one to her. She wraps her hands around it, feeling heat seep through the tin. "My father was a smuggler," she says. "I had little choice but to follow his path."

"Your father is dead?"

She stares into her mug. "Ayes," she says finally. "My father is dead." She hears her voice waver. What is this? Is she to mourn the man all over again? Why should she feel sad? This is the way it has always been.

My father is dead has not elicited grief from her for many years. Yet now her chest is aching and her tears are threatening to return.

She takes a gulp of tea.

"Why were you alone at the tavern tonight?" she asks, desperate to change the subject. "Riding officers don't work alone. And they don't spend their nights lurking about in ale houses."

Jamie doesn't speak at once. "Unofficial business," he says after a moment.

"The press gang."

He nods.

"How do you hope to stop them? A riding officer has no power over the navy."

"The gang is operating illegally," says Jamie. "They're thugs hired by the magistrate and are working without a press warrant. They're taking the money intended for the impressed sailors and keeping it for themselves. The navy has little involvement before they ship the poor bastards off to war."

"How do you know all this?"

"Speculation," he admits. "My brother was one of the men taken. I'm sure of it. He disappeared from the harbour tavern several months ago."

Scarlett's eyes meet his in a moment of sympathy. But she says: "How do you know your brother did not just stumble drunkenly into the sea?"

Jamie flinches slightly and Scarlett regrets her words.

"My brother worked for the revenue service like me," he tells her. "He long suspected the traders on this coast were involved in more than smuggling. He witnessed a rendezvous between the naval officers and the magistrate. Saw the magistrate speaking with the men we suspect are smugglers on more than one occasion."

"You think your local magistrate is crooked?"

He gives a humourless laugh. "My colleagues and I have brought five men before the court for smuggling this year. Each has had their case thrown out. We've begun taking men to trial in Saint Ives."

Scarlett realises she is staring. She stands abruptly. Jamie's words have reminded her that they are ingrained on opposite sides of the law. "I wish you luck," she says.

He frowns. "Where are you going?"

"I need to get home to Talland."

"You're leaving tonight? How? There's no coach out of here for three days."

"I'll walk," she says, pushing aside thoughts of the black-ink hills. She will walk those hills and slide past the spirits and go back to being that woman who is not afraid of the dark.

"It's many days' walk," says Jamie. "You'll get home far quicker if you wait for the coach."

"I need to leave now."

"What's the urgency?"

But of course, she can tell him nothing of the urgency. Not of the stolen coins inside her bodice, or the man on his way to Talland to turn her family in for smuggling.

Instead, she admits: "I've nowhere to sleep." Her shoulders sink.

Jamie stands, reaching for his uniform. "You'll sleep here. I've a watch tonight. I'll be out until early morning. I can sleep a few hours at the customs station when I return."

"No," Scarlett says instinctively. "I couldn't."

He wraps a faded blue scarf around his neck. "Trust me or don't. The choice is yours. But the place will be empty and it'll be far warmer here than out on those hills." He buttons the coat and nods towards the cheese sitting on the table. "Finish it if you wish."

Scarlett glances out the window at the thick dark. Looks back at the fire and the bed. She draws in her breath and manages a faint nod. "I'll be out by dawn."

MEN OF WAR

Isaac borrows a wagon from the Millers' farm to make the delivery. He waits until the Mariner's Arms has closed for the night before climbing into the tunnel with John Baker and Will Francis. They carry out the ankers and load them into the wagon, hiding the goods beneath a layer of kelp. And up through the dark they go, following the ribbon of a road towards Lansallos.

The cliffs above the cove are blue-black and bare. Below them, the beach is empty. Isaac is jittery with anticipation. He had told Caroline of the sale. Seen her excitement. Enough for two tickets, he had told her. A ticket out of Reuben's life for each of their children.

They wait in the dark, the lantern circling in the wind and making shadows pitch. An invisible sea sighs in the cove.

"You sure he's a good thing?" Baker asks. "This innkeeper?"

Isaac turns up the collar of his coat against the cold. "He wants a cheap sale." But there is a discomfort in him he is unable to shake. This new immorality makes him feel alive, but it also makes him wary. He slides a hand into his pocket, feeling the cold metal of his pistol. He cocks and uncocks the trigger.

Light moves across the clifftops. A second wagon clatters towards them.

"Thought you weren't going to show," Isaac tells the innkeeper with a crooked smile.

The man chuckles. "Pound an anker? Course I'm going to show."

Isaac climbs from the wagon and pulls aside the kelp. He and the men load the brandy into the innkeeper's cart.

"Twenty pounds," he says, once the ankers are loaded.

The innkeeper hands him the money. "Why such a good price?"

Isaac squeezes the coins between his fingers. A ticket for Gabriel. A ticket for Mary. "I'm paying you to keep your mouth shut. Not a word to Tom Leach about who sold you this brandy."

The innkeeper doesn't return his smile. "It weren't me who said a word," he says. "But perhaps Leach already knows."

"Why do you say that?"

"He came to the inn the very same evening as you. Brandy for sale, he said. I told him I weren't interested."

Isaac curses under his breath. Had Leach followed him to The Well House? "Did you tell him you already had a sale?"

"Didn't say a thing. Like I told you. But the man's no fool."

No fool indeed. Isaac is the one who had behaved rashly; scrabbling for a sale with Leach breathing down his neck. His stomach clenches.

He watches the innkeeper climb back into the wagon and disappear into the dark. He waits. Beneath the constant roar of the sea, an owl coos.

Isaac squints. Is the dark moving? His eyes strain and clutch at the shadows. He had been careful to ensure they had not been followed on the journey from Talland. But if Leach were to come to Lansallos, he would have approached from Polruan. Would have followed the innkeeper.

Isaac has sunk Leach's ship, undercut his business. And Leach is not a man who will let such things slide.

There is little to do but return to Talland.

The lantern at the front of the wagon sends an arc of light swaying across the hills. It moves over the horse's slender back, picking out shapes on either side of the road.

Something moves in the light. There, to the left of the wagon. A fox? Or something more? Isaac swallows, his mouth dry. He snaps the reins and the horse quickens its pace. The wagon pitches as the road spirals upwards. Beside him, Will Francis looks edgily over his shoulder.

More movement. This time, too big to be an animal. A pistol shot explodes in the blackness. It flies into the side of the wagon, wood splintering. The horse charges.

The path is narrow. Keep on at this speed and they risk pitching over the cliff edge. But nor can they slow. The men firing at them will be on horseback. They will be far quicker than the wagon.

Isaac looks over his shoulder at the dark expanse of the hills. They can lose themselves in the blackness. He touches the pistol in his pocket. The thought of firing back makes his stomach swirl.

A second bullet flies into the wheel of the wagon. Isaac stops the horse and douses the lantern, plunging them into blackness. The three men scramble out, burying themselves in the banks of furze lining the road. Another bullet flies into the night.

There is movement around him. His eyes adjusting to the dark, or his imagination? He sees the inky shape of a man, pistol trained on Will.

A shot shatters the momentary stillness. The man in the darkness falls.

Isaac realises he has his pistol out. He feels heat go through him. Is it his bullet in the man's chest? He doesn't remember firing. But his gun is hot. Empty. He hears Will breathe hard.

Isaac lies flat to the ground, feeling his heart thump against the earth. Feeling the vibration of hooves.

"Put your weapons down!"

Riding officers.

They shine their lamp through the dark. The white light illuminates the face of Tom Leach.

Leach fires. A riding officer falls from his horse. His lamp shatters on the earth and the blackness returns. A thunder of hooves as his horse charges up the hill. Has the second officer escaped? Is he waiting in the dark? Can he see which man pulled the trigger?

A second shot from Leach. The spark from the pistol lights the night. Another body falls.

From his hiding place, Isaac sees Leach slide from his horse and stand over the riding officers' bodies.

"Dead," he tells his men. "We need to leave."

"What about Bailey?"

Leach's response is inaudible. He leaps onto his horse and charges away from the lifeless men.

Isaac peers into the faint moonlight. Baker is on his knees behind the wagon. He grips his side, worms of blood trickling through his fingers.

"Christ," Isaac hisses, "can you stand?"

Baker nods. He climbs slowly to his feet, leaning heavily on Isaac. Will hurries towards them. Baker groans and curses as he stumbles into the wagon, his blood leaving dark streaks down the front of Isaac's greatcoat.

Isaac climbs into the box seat. He snaps the reins and the horse charges up the narrow path. Baker groans as they rattle through a ditch.

Isaac grits his teeth. The nearest surgeon is in Plymouth, a day's ride away. Logic tells him the horse will never make it if they keep up at this speed. But it feels foolish to slow the wagon with an injured man inside. The jolting rattles his body, his thoughts. He sees the man in the darkness fall. Feels the gun hot in his hand.

Sweat prickles his forehead. A man is dead on account of him.

A man who would have killed Will had he not acted first.

There is no place in this life for morality, for sentiment. No place for a man unwilling to pull the trigger.

Will climbs into the box seat beside him. "The wound is deep. He's losing too much blood. We've got to get him help."

"We'll take him to the inn," Isaac hears himself say. "Flora can help him. Give him something for the pain at least."

What is he doing? He doesn't want Flora any deeper in her mother's craft after the way the villagers had come after her last week. But the groans from the back of the wagon are turning his stomach.

The lights of Talland break the horizon.

Isaac's head is still swimming when he thumps on the door of the Mariner's Arms.

"Isaac. What's happened?" Flora tugs a pale blue shawl around her. She is barefoot in her nightshift, long blonde hair spilling over her shoulders. Her eyes fall to the bloodstains splattered across his coat. "Are you hurt?"

"John Baker's been shot. I'm afraid he'll not make it to Plymouth."

A look of uncertainty passes across her eyes and Isaac regrets coming. But she says: "Where is he?"

"In the wagon outside."

She nods towards the hearth. A log glows orange in the grate. "Stoke the fire." She runs upstairs, returning moments later with the kettle and a handful of small, dark leaves. She crushes the fronds into a cup and hangs the kettle above the fire. Her eyes are hard and determined.

"Take a little brandy," she tells Isaac. "Give it to him for the pain."

Steam begins to curl from the kettle. She pours the boiling water over the leaves.

Isaac follows her out to the wagon. John Baker's wife has been fetched and is sitting beside her husband, his bloodstained hand in hers. Soundless tears run down her cheeks. Will sits at Baker's other side, his coat pressed to the wound above his hip.

Isaac hands Will the cup of brandy. "Give him this."

Flora climbs across the blood-splattered kelp. She eases Will's hand away and lifts Baker's blackened shirt. "I need more light."

Isaac unhooks the lantern from the front of the wagon and kneels behind her, feeling the heat of the lamp against his cheek.

She pulls the leaves from the cup and lays them carefully over the wound. Baker shifts and sighs. She presses a fresh cloth to his hip, gesturing to his wife to hold it in place.

"The yarrow will slow the bleeding," she says. "But you've got to get him to a surgeon as soon as possible."

Mrs Baker gives a sob of thanks.

Isaac and Flora climb from the wagon and watch as it disappears up the hill. They walk wordlessly back to the inn. Flora lets out a long breath.

"You did a fine job," Isaac says, pressing a hand to her shoulder.

Flora manages a small smile. She empties the kettle into the trough behind the bar and scrubs the blood from her hands. "Will you stay a moment?" Her eyes are pleading; voicing that loneliness he knows she would never allow herself to admit to. She pours two cups of brandy and presses one into his hand, not waiting for his response.

These are the times he feels for her the most; this time of night when the inn has closed and her daughter sleeps and the empty rooms gape around her. No, he thinks, he does not want to be alone either.

He slides off his bloodstained coat and tosses it over one of the stools. He takes a long sip, the liquor steadying him a little. Flora sits by the hearth, her shawl sliding from one shoulder. Firelight flickers on her cheek, making her pale hair shine. Isaac sits beside her, drawing his knees to his chest. When had he last seen her like this; barefoot, with hair tumbling down her back? Not since they were children, tearing across the rim of the water, the beach seeming as though it would go on forever.

She brings her cup to her lips and watches the fire. Isaac feels her eyes drift to him. "Was Leach involved?" she asks finally, her question shattering the stillness.

He takes another mouthful of brandy. Nods. "He and his men ambushed us on the way back from Lansallos."

"How did he know you were there?"

"He must have seen me at The Well House. Suspected things perhaps. Followed the innkeeper."

"One of Leach's men came to the inn the night you were in Guernsey," Flora tells him, staring into her cup. "Prying. Asking after you. I thought little of it at the time. But I ought to have told you."

Isaac touches her bare wrist. Her skin is hot.

"The riding officers showed themselves," he says. "The two of them were killed."

Flora exhales sharply. "Killed by who? Leach?"

"Ayes." As he speaks of dead men, his heart begins to thunder again. A fresh wave of dizziness rips through him. He is suddenly far too hot to sit by the fire. He stands, stumbles. His empty cup clatters against the flagstones. Flora leaps to her feet and takes his arm.

"There's something else, ayes? Tell me what."

He closes his eyes. "One of Leach's men is dead. I fear it was me who shot him."

For a moment, Flora doesn't speak. The fire pops loudly.

"You shot a man who was firing at you?" she says finally. "And what were you to have done? Stand by and let him kill you?"

He opens his eyes. Shadows dance in the firelight, making everything unsteady. She presses her hands to his cheeks. "You did what you had to do," she says. "To survive. I don't know what I would have done if it had been you lying in that wagon tonight. And I don't know what I would have done if you'd gone to make that delivery and never come home."

Her hands slide from his face and grip the laces of his shirt. The spicy scent of yarrow hangs about her, tinged with soap and brandy. He can feel the heat of her body through her thin nightshift. The linen clings to the curves of her hips.

He swallows. "It's late. I ought to leave." He turns for the door, but Flora keeps her hands clenched around his collar. She tugs him back to her.

And he stops thinking. Kisses her hard. She will pull away, of course. She has not given up on goodness the way he has. But she is pushing her body against his, clutching fistfuls of his shirt. She is sighing into his mouth as his hand slides beneath her shift. She is in his hair, inside his breeches, a dizzying blur of white skin and roaming lips.

And then they are no longer standing; the fire-warmed flagstones hot beneath their bodies. She has lost her shawl. When? Isaac has no thought of it. Her narrow fingers are pulling his shirt over his head, seeking the sparse curls of hair on his chest. The flames heat his cheeks, his neck, his back. His skin is blazing.

Stop, he thinks distantly. *Stop*.

But the thought is pushed out by Flora's mouth against his. Her willingness to pull her shift to her waist. Her hot hands tug his body to hers.

He is inside her before his conscience catches him. What use is there trying for morality? He has blood on his hands now. There is no point seeking decency, so he may as well seek happiness, however fleeting and lustful, however driven by stress and brandy and men lying lifeless on the road.

He opens his eyes when he feels her still beneath him. Her hair is spilling over the flagstones like fallen snow. Their eyes meet. Where do they go from here? Do they retreat to silence, to the old pattern of friendship, to never speaking of this night again? Never speaking of it and never speaking of it and never speaking of it until it is over and forgotten and gone?

He sees shards of green in her eyes, the faint powder of freckles on her cheeks. Feels her ragged breath against his chin. He lowers himself to her, kisses her lips and the hollow curve of her throat. Her pulse vibrates against his mouth. He doesn't want this to be forgotten and gone. He wants it to have just begun.

Flora pushes him back and sits suddenly. Her eyes are wide and anxious, as though she has snapped out of a spell and caught sight of what they have done.

Isaac reaches for his shirt. "I'm sorry. I'll leave. I—"

She clamps a hand over his, stilling him.

"Riding officers were killed," she says. "A man in blue staring at the sky." She hugs her knees. "I saw it in my mother's mirror."

"That's impossible," Isaac says, without thinking. *That's impossible* is an instinctive reaction to years of Scarlett's ghost stories. He regrets saying it to Flora. He pushes her hair aside and holds his lips to her neck. "You don't believe in such things. You never have."

She says: "I'm not sure that's true."

"Of course it's true. You've always had a rational mind."

Why is he so eager for her to be wrong? Why such desperation for a solid, unbending world?

He needs the reliability of it, Isaac realises. He can't have the solidity of his world upturned by images in a black mirror. His life is shifting around him. He is watched by a man who will kill him if he discovers his deception, is flooded with desire for a woman who is not his wife. His sister has vanished, and he will tear across the world in search of a new home. Take rationality out of his life and he fears he may drown.

STORY-TELLERS

Three days until Asher is paid. Three days until he escapes this filthy, menial job of mucking out another man's stables.

For four days, he has barely ventured from the farm in case he crosses paths with Jacob or Scarlett. The week has been a mindless blur of shovelling, hauling and hoeing. The place has left him with the incessant feeling of bugs crawling beneath his skin. There is a chill inside him he fears he will never warm from.

He longs to wash, to shave, to change his clothes. Three days, he tells himself. Three days and he will be free. Three days and he will be on the road to the Polperro customs house. Out will come his tales of false-bottomed luggers and smuggling tunnels.

Forgive me, Callie, I loved you once.

It is late afternoon. He carries the sack of feed to the stables for the horses. An hour or two before the work day is done. He will eat gruel. Sleep. Spend a few blissful hours lost in his dreams.

They come for him before his mind can make sense of it. The sack is knocked from his arms, grain spilling. He flails, trying to reach the shovel. The hands around his arms are vice-like, his feet almost lifted from the ground. His head is held, something pungent and vicious poured down his throat. He coughs, splutters. Hands are clamped over his mouth and nose, forcing him to swallow. The world blurs and there is dark.

The lugger lurches back towards Polperro harbour, deck shimmering with baskets of pilchards. Isaac blinks hard, grateful for the sudden wall of spray that flies over the gunwale, washing away his exhaustion.

He had stumbled back to the cottage long after midnight with Baker's blood on his greatcoat and Flora's scent on his hands. Had slept would could barely have been an hour before dawn had pushed through the windows and he'd stumbled in a daze to the fishing port.

He rubs his eyes and watches from the foredeck as the village grows larger.

The harbour is busy. People are milling about by the water's edge, restless as bugs in a jar. This is the way of this village, Isaac knows. When shots are fired, or ghosts walk the hills, the people flock together and work themselves into nightmares, seeking out answers from whichever poor soul they feel can provide them. The vicar, the healer, the leader of the smuggling ring.

For all their midnight landings and whispered plots, Isaac knows his role in the syndicate is a poorly kept secret.

He had said nothing about the previous night to the fishing crew. Played down the absence of both John Baker and Will Francis.

An illness, yes. Spreading? Most likely.

Deadly?

In his mind, he heard Baker groan as his blood stained kelp and straw. Had he survived the wagon ride to Plymouth? Survived the barber surgeon's bullet extractor? Isaac knows it unlikely.

He looks back towards the harbour. No doubt the riding officers' bodies have been found. An investigation has begun. The villagers will have questions, Isaac is sure. And they will come to him.

But he must remain silent. Ignorant. He must walk through that crowd with his head down. No one can know the real reason for John Baker's absence. No one can know he and Isaac were riding the roads of Lansallos last night.

Not Reuben, not the authorities.

There will be dragoons at the cottage door later, Isaac is sure. Trailed by wolf-eyed riding officers, keen for a rare conviction. Rival smuggling gangs suspected. Isaac knows the revenue service believes him involved in free trade. They'd have him condemned if it weren't for lack of proof. He had best keep his story short and straight.

Children pour from the charity school in a flurry of giggles and chatter. Flora peers through the chaos of blue smocks and bonnets for her daughter. She wills Bessie to hurry.

She had gone about her day as though nothing had happened. Comb and pin her hair and pretend she had not tended to Baker's gunshot wound. Make porridge and pretend she had not asked Isaac to stay. Walk Bessie to school and pretend she had not seen the conflict in her mirror.

She feels eyes on her as she waits by the church. The maid from the vicarage walks past on her way to the market. Two fishermen eye her as they stride towards the cliff path. She sees Caroline on the other side of the street, waiting for her son. Flora turns away hurriedly. It feels as if they know it all.

Witch. Charlatan.

Adulterer.

In a moment of brandy and firelight, her conscience had left her. She has always prided herself on her strength, but with Isaac's breath on her skin, she'd abandoned her resolve. She has become one of those whispering, red-faced women who had appeared so regularly at her mother's door. Shilling for a course of Queen Anne's Lace to prevent an unwanted child. Flora's skin burns at the thought; a heady mix of desire and shame.

Bessie shrieks with laughter as she flies out of the gate with one of her friends. Her cheeks are flushed, her blonde hair a spidery mess, escaping out the sides of her bonnet. Barely a trace of her illness left, Flora thinks. Her mind is a tangle. Healing stones and yarrow leaves, magic mirrors and the allure of a married man.

Bessie's hand in hers, she hurries towards the cliff path. A crowd has gathered at the harbour; villagers chattering nervously by the water's edge. She sees Isaac's lugger sliding towards the docks. And there is Charles Reuben striding down the hill towards the commotion.

No doubt word of the murders has spread. Flora quickens her pace. She wants the silent safety of her inn.

Before she reaches the cliff path, she hears the rap of hooves behind her. Hears: "Good afternoon, Mrs Kelly."

She curses under her breath. "Go on ahead," she tells Bessie. "Wait for me at the top of the hill."

She turns reluctantly. The two riding officers are familiar. One old, one young. Polished buttons, polished boots. Shorn chins and red noses. They had been drinking at the Mariner's Arms the night Isaac had been to Guernsey.

"Good afternoon," Flora says stiffly.

The men swing themselves from their horses. Boots thud dully on the earth.

"How is business?" the older officer asks.

"Fine, thank you very much." Flora eyes the crowd. Caroline and her children are making their way towards the harbour. The fishing boats knock against their moorings. Women from the pilchard palace elbow their way through the crowd, trying to retrieve the baskets from the decks of the lugger.

"Two riding officers were killed close to Lansallos Cove last night," the officer tells Flora. "We assume the shootings were the work of a smuggling gang."

"I see. How dreadful." She grits her teeth. Deflects their questions.

Who was at your tavern last night?

Did you see anything unusual?

Has there been any trouble of late?

"There's been no trouble," she says shortly.

"I hope you'll be watchful. Violence among trading gangs is becoming increasingly common. This is not a good time for a woman to be running a business alone."

She gives a wry smile. "Then I suppose I ought to close my doors until I find myself a husband."

The officer pushes past her iciness. "Perhaps you've heard talk among the men who frequent your tavern. Heard of plans, perhaps, or rivalries."

A clamour of voices floats up from the harbour. "I'm sure the men involved in this conflict have far more sense than to let their plans be overheard by the innkeeper."

The officer tugs at his reins as the horse shifts restlessly. He meets Flora's eyes in an attempt at camaraderie. "If you're afraid of speaking out against these men, we can offer you protection. It is of utmost importance that an arrest is made over these murders. The smugglers involved need to be made an example of, in order to put an end to this rising violence."

She gives a short smile. "I don't need protection against the smugglers. Thank you."

The officer considers her a moment. He swaps a glance with his colleague. Lowers his voice. "We can also offer protection against the excisemen." He looks at her pointedly. "Should you require it."

Flora swallows heavily. Protection from the excisemen is an alluring prospect. Protection against the forged licence on her wall. But all she knows of the conflict she had learned from Isaac. She cannot give the officers information without revealing her sources. "I don't need protection from the excisemen either," she says, forcing a smile. "I have nothing to hide."

Isaac strides through the crowd with his head down, ignoring the questions being flung at him from every side.

What do you know?

What did you see?

Caroline shivers. It unnerves her how quickly gossip spreads in this place.

"A word, Mr Bailey?" Isaac looks up at the sound of Reuben's voice.

Caroline hands the baby to Gabriel and ushers him off to play on the beach. She elbows her way towards the two men. Up close, she sees shadows of sleeplessness on Isaac's cheeks. Sees that flicker behind his eyes that warns her his patience is thin. He glances sideways at her.

"Mrs Bailey," Reuben says smoothly, "you needn't bother yourself with our business."

"My husband's business is my business."

Reuben looks at Isaac, who nods for him to begin. She is glad he has not dismissed her.

"You've heard of the conflict in Lansallos, I assume?" Reuben says finally. "Two riding officers were murdered." His gaze is firmly fixed on Isaac, as though Caroline weren't there.

"I've heard."

"The authorities assume a conflict between rival trading gangs."

Isaac says nothing. He had been tight-lipped with her too, Caroline thinks. Had told her only the bare outline of the story. The riding officers killed by Tom Leach as they intercepted the conflict between the two gangs. John Baker shot. She wonders what details

Isaac had left out. Wonders if he would have said anything at all had she not been waiting by the fire when he walked into the cottage carrying a blood-splattered greatcoat.

"Do you know anything of it?" asks Reuben.

"Why would I know anything of it?" Isaac says brusquely.

"You and your men will be suspects. Customs already have their eyes on you."

Caroline sees Isaac's jaw tense. She wills him to keep calm. Anger will not convince Reuben of his innocence. Nor will it convince the revenue men.

"I had nothing to do with what happened last night," he says. "I was at home with my family."

Reuben's eyes shift, as though trying to determine if he is telling the truth. Caroline feels something turn over in her stomach.

"What business would the men and I have had in Lansallos? Our next run isn't for a month."

"No," Reuben says. "It's not." He makes a noise in his throat. Weighted silence hangs between them. An old woman pushes through the crowd towards Isaac, then darts away as she catches sight of Reuben.

"Why are you still here?" Isaac snaps. "I've told you I know nothing."

"I'm still here," Reuben says tersely, "because I'm not sure I believe you."

He snorts. "Fourteen years of loyalty and this is how you repay me? They're saying two riding officers were shot at close range. Do you truly think me capable of such a thing?"

Reuben stands close. The creases in his face are deep. He is growing old. He has no heir, Caroline thinks distantly. If he were to die, her family would be free.

"I'm not entirely sure what you're capable of," he tells Isaac. "I don't know how much of your father is in you."

"What exactly does that mean?" Isaac turns to leave, but Reuben clamps a firm hand over his forearm, preventing him from leaving. Isaac yanks his arm free. "You've no power, Reuben. Without Bobby Carter's protection you'll answer to the law like the rest of us. What will you do? Shoot me? Risk hanging for murder?"

Caroline grits her teeth. She tries to catch his eye. *Stop.*

Reuben's cheeks redden with anger. "You're a fool to be so brash, Bailey. You're a man with much to lose."

"Go to hell," Isaac spits. He turns abruptly and marches towards the path back to Talland. Caroline calls hurriedly for Gabriel and chases her husband up onto the cliffs.

She is breathless by the time she reaches him. Wind tears at their hair and clothing, sends bracken and blackberry bushes bending towards the sea. She wants to lace her fingers through his and tell him to be calm. She wants to take his arm, smooth his hair, kiss his cheek. But she does none of these things.

Half way home, Isaac says: "Do you think he knows?" He doesn't look at her.

Caroline doesn't answer at once. She quickens her pace to walk beside him. "Perhaps." The response feels stupid, but it is all she can think of to say. She is glad Isaac has not shut her out. "Is there anything you might have done to make him suspicious?"

He shakes his head slightly. "We were careful. Discreet."

"Yes, well, somehow Tom Leach found out you were in Lansallos. It's possible Reuben did too." She wonders again what had happened on those cliffs. There are things her husband is keeping from her, of that she is sure. But she knows better than to hound him while there is fire behind his eyes. Instead, she says: "You said we had enough for two tickets."

Leaving Talland has never been more pressing. With Reuben on one side and Asher Hales and his secrets on the other, Caroline is sure she will crumble unless they escape this place soon.

"Two tickets, ayes," Isaac says finally. "But selling the rest of the brandy will be difficult. The riding officers will be all over the area. And I can't sell to The Well House. Leach obviously knows I've been dealing with the innkeeper."

"Then you need to find another buyer. Perhaps head east? Away from Leach."

"It will take time. We need to be patient."

"We don't have the luxury of patience," Caroline snaps, her own anxiety tearing free.

"We can't start behaving rashly at the first hint of trouble." Isaac doesn't look at her. He says again: "We need to be patient."

And here are the doubts Caroline has been refusing to let take hold. Doubts she can no longer ignore. For all Isaac's talk of breaking free of Reuben, there is something holding him to Talland, something stealing his urgency and dampening his desire for escape.

Scarlett perhaps. Yes, Caroline understands. She doesn't like it, but she understands. When they leave this place, they will tell no one where they are going. Will never speak of it aloud in case Reuben's men are listening. Talland will be a place they can never return to. And if they leave before Scarlett comes home, she knows Isaac and his sister might never be reunited.

IMPRESSMENT

Scarlett curls up on her bed in her boots and cloak and lets her eyes drift closed. She had left Jamie's cottage at dawn, determined to be gone before he returned from his watch. She had pushed her trust for him far enough. Best now that they forget each other.

In the rising sun she had walked out of Portreath, following the road the coach had taken. There were villages this way, she remembered. Villages filled with dust covered miners who spent their days digging treasures from the hills. Follow the road, she told herself, as the clouds closed in over the sun. Follow the road and the spirits in the hills would not lead her astray.

She had reached Redruth by mid-morning and found an inn on the edge of the village.

A bed for two nights. She slid the stolen coins across the counter, keeping her eyes as blank and innocent as when she encountered riding officers while running goods up Talland Hill.

And so, a bed. A small victory. In two days, the coach will leave for the south coast and she can go back to believing her father is gone. She runs a finger absentmindedly over the coins. Where else could they take her? What else might she see? She thinks of the colourful world of Isaac's travel stories. Thinks of palaces and mountains and men speaking in other tongues. She tries to imagine herself immersed in such a world. She can't do it, she realises. Isaac's stories are all she has to build the image on. She cannot imagine mountains or palaces. Can't see herself immersed in anything but free trade.

She kicks off her boots and lies back on the bed. Orange light is pushing through the curtains, the night drawing nearer. Another woman enters the room, clutching a faded saddle bag to her chest. She goes to the bed beside Scarlett's and takes off her cloak. Scarlett checks her shawl is covering the bulge of the coins.

Jamie McCulley is in her head.

Jamie who had made her tea and slept on a chair at the customs house so she might have a safe night's rest.

No, these thoughts are dangerous. He has brass buttons and a riding officer's journal and friends in high places.

Jamie who had led her into the cave and set her up for smuggling. Neat, preachy, *that doesn't make it right* Jamie.

Good. This is safer.

But what does it matter? She has left Portreath. When the carriage comes it will take her further and further from that tidy little room at the back of the stone cottage.

Where is he, she wonders? What is he doing? Is he prowling the harbour tavern, searching for the hideout of the press gang? Galloping along the clifftops in a flurry of blue and gold?

And are there men in that tavern by the cliffs tossing back tainted liquor, unaware they are about to be hauled off to war?

Scarlett's mind goes to a man in a white wig, pushing a glass of scented brandy into her hand. *Armagnac*, he had told her. But she knows the smell of Armagnac. And it was not what had been in the glass.

Is the man in the wig one of the impressers?

He had trailed and touched and crooned over her. If she were to bend to his advances, could she pull information from him? Could she catch the press gang mid-operation as Jamie has been unable to do?

No. Such a thing is dangerous. Foolish. This is someone else's battle. Besides, she has already left Portreath.

She thinks of Jamie and his vanished brother. Thinks of his hot eyes as he had told her of his desire to catch out the impressers. She sits abruptly. Someone else's battle, yes, but she does not want him to fight it alone.

The other woman peers at her from over the washstand. Scarlett pulls on her boots and cloak and leaves the inn before she changes her mind.

The light is draining quickly. She walks fast, eyes on the path. Follow the road and she will be safe. She will not be fairy-led by the spirits haunting these hills.

The sky is icy pink beneath the clouds. The engine house of the mine is silhouetted on a distant hill. She crosses a peak and the sea unfolds below her. Portreath is close. She winds her way down into the village, wind lashing her hair against her cheeks. Gulls swoop and screech, then are carried back towards the clouds on a sudden updraught of air.

Scarlett hurries towards the tavern. In the early evening, the place is quiet. Peering through the window, she sees the innkeeper leaning on the bar. He is chatting to a fisherman in an enormous tarred coat. No sign of the man in the wig.

No sign of Jacob.

Ought she wait for wigged man to appear? There is no guarantee, of course, that he will come tonight.

She needs to explore the tavern. How are the impressers taking the drugged men to the navy? What is Jamie missing?

Never mind that the man with the wig is not here. There are other men inside she can get close to. Other men she can persuade to tell her their secrets.

She takes off her shortgown and crams it into her pocket. She unpins her hair, letting it spill over her shoulders in sea-hardened waves. Tightens the laces of her bodice and tugs her stomacher low.

She prays her father is not inside to see her.

What does it matter? Her father has no idea who she is.

Blood thumping, she shoves her way inside the tavern. The front room is busy, noisy. Heads turn as she enters. The innkeeper catches her eye and beckons with a grimy finger.

"You best watch yourself, maid," he says as she draws closer. "If you're looking for the traders again, now's not the time to do it." He nods towards two uniformed men drinking in the corner. "Customs are paying us a visit."

"I'm not here for the traders," she says brusquely. "Like you said, there are other ways a girl can earn a few shillings." She tries to force away the colour she feels rising in her cheeks. She is doing this for Jamie, she tells herself.

The innkeeper chuckles, eying the swell of her breasts at the top of her stays. "Indeed there are." He leans over the bar. "I have money."

Scarlett shakes off her revulsion. "You also got a tavern to run."

He grins. "Perhaps you come back for me later."

She flashes him a sickly smile and makes her way into the back room. It is darker here. Colder. A few men sit at the tables, glasses in front of them and pipes in their hands. A curtain of smoke hangs over them. Their conversation is low, punctuated by bursts of gravelly laughter.

She feels eyes on her. Her mouth is suddenly dry. She edges hesitantly towards one of the tables. Before she reaches it, she hears a voice close to her ear.

"Not seen you in here before."

The man is barely taller than her. His cheeks are pink, stomach straining against the buttons of his worn blue waistcoat. His grey streaked hair is tied back messily. He stands close to her, swaying slightly.

Scarlett forces a smile. "You got money?"

"Of course."

"Good." She glances around the room at the other men. Now she has been claimed, their attentions have returned to their conversations. "Outside," she murmurs.

The man nods, making his way towards the front of the tavern. Scarlett grabs his arm.

"We can't go out the front door," she says, her fingers kneading his arm. "There's a man in there I turned down. Didn't like the look of him."

He grins. "And you like the look of me?"

"Very much." She gives him a syrupy smile. Ignores the skin prickling at the back of her neck.

He reaches brashly for her hand, sliding sausage fingers between hers. "The least we can do for the poor fellow is say goodbye."

She sidles closer to him, her skirts brushing over his boots. "Is that what you're here for? To bother yourself with other men?" She gives him doe eyes. "Or to bother yourself with me?"

One corner of his lips turns up as he considers her. "There's no other way out."

She smiles coyly. "Ayes there is." Her heart is drumming. "I know what goes on in this place. I'm sure you do too."

The man hesitates. After a moment, he gives a faint nod. Leads her towards the enormous stone hearth. No fire in the grate. No wood. No ash.

He steps over the grate and turns, disappearing from view. Scarlett bunches her skirts in her fist and follows him into the fireplace. To the side of the grate, a narrow hole has been beaten into the stone. Through it, she can hear the sigh of the sea.

She squeezes out of the hole, finding herself on a narrow path between the wall of the tavern and the cliff face. Clever, she thinks. The tavern is built in such a way it looks to be leaning against the rock. No one would ever know a path ran behind it.

In the splintered moonlight, the man is little more than an inky shape. He comes towards her, pressing her back against the rock. His stale breath is hot against her cheek. Seized with panic, Scarlett fumbles beneath her skirts for the knife. The man's fingers dive beneath her petticoat, squeezing the bare flesh above her stockings and making sickness rise in her throat. She yanks the blade from her garter and holds it to his throat. His hands fall.

"What is this?" he hisses.

Scarlett feels her breath come thick and fast. She has not thought this through. Unless she cuts the man's throat, he will come after her. He will go back to the tavern and spread word that the press gang's passage has been discovered. What choice does she have but to kill him?

The knife trembles in her fist. She does not want to be a killer. Does not want to leave a dead man in her wake, the way her father had done.

She does not want to be Jacob.

"What do you want?" the man spits. "Money?"

She hesitates. He cannot know she has any interest in the press gang. Before she can speak, he says:

"I've coins in my pocket. Let me get to them." His hand edges towards his pocket, her knife still hard against his throat.

Scarlett drives her knee into his groin and runs, leaving him hissing and cursing behind her. She tears through the narrow chasm between the rock and the tavern, then follows the path up a winding hill. Hidden by darkness at the top of the cliff is the blue and gold carriage she had seen the night Asher had escaped. There are no windows in the coach, she realises. How had she not noticed this the last time she had seen it?

She edges towards it. In the near darkness, she sees the box seat is empty. She moves silently towards the carriage and opens the door, willing herself not to make a sound. A crumpled figure lies on the floor. Asher. Her breath catches at the sight of him. He is sprawled on his side, taking short, shallow breaths. His hair is matted and tangled with straw. His eyes are closed, but he shows no sign of injury.

Scarlett kneels over him, rocking his shoulder. "Asher."

No response.

She presses her fingers to his neck. His pulse is fast. She leans close, trying to catch the scent of tainted brandy on his breath. The sweet waft of hay lining the floor of the carriage masks everything else.

Footsteps come towards the coach. Scarlett shifts, trying to bury herself in the shadows. The carriage creaks as men climb into the box seat.

"Go," someone calls to the driver.

"We can't. The judge wants two men."

"Can't find anyone else tonight," says the first voice. "Customs are in the tavern. One's the best we can do. Take him to the stables."

And the coach begins to move. Asher stirs and groans.

"Quiet," she hisses.

"Scarlett?" He doesn't open his eyes. "Help me."

The carriage stops. Scarlett presses an ear to the side of the coach, trying to catch hold of any sound that might give away their location. The sigh of the sea is gone. An owl coos. Footsteps. She wriggles beneath the bench.

The door creaks open and lamplight falls across Asher's face. Scarlett sees the legs of the men that climb into the carriage and grab his limp body. Hears him groan as he is hauled into the night.

The door slams and she lets herself breathe.

When the footsteps have faded, she slips out of the carriage. In the darkness, it is hard to make out her surroundings, but light glows beneath the doorway of a large, weather-beaten outbuilding. A cart shed? She hears mumbled voices. Men. They swing closed a heavy wooden door at the front of the building.

Where had they found Asher? Is he too to be thrown onto a naval ship and carted off to war? A fitting punishment for abandoning her, she thinks wryly. A fitting punishment for seeking to turn her and Isaac over to the revenue men.

There is a crack beneath the door of the cart shed. She presses herself to the muddy ground. She can see boots moving. How many men? Five perhaps? Six? Is the magistrate among them, paying the impressers for their services? Are there men from the navy here, come to collect their new recruit? The boots are ragged. None that look to belong to a magistrate, or naval officers.

Scarlett hears more footfalls. This time, they are sloshing through the mud outside the shed. Coming towards her. She scrambles to her feet and begins to run, her boots sliding in the mud. And a thick arm is around her waist, the man's other hand over her mouth to stop her scream escaping.

ABANDONMENT

Scarlett kicks wildly. She thrashes against her captor, trying to see his face. He flings her onto the ground outside the stables. Pain shoots up her side.

"Who in hell are you?" he hisses, his bearded face looming over her.

"I'm no one. I saw nothing. I—" She tries to stand, but the man pulls a pistol. Cocks the trigger. And in a sudden flash of movement, he falls, a fist slamming into the side of his head.

Jacob stands over the motionless body. "Run, Scarlett."

She stares at him, frozen.

His eyes flash. "Go!"

She scrambles to her feet and races towards the lights of the village. There are footsteps behind her. Heavy, growing closer. She keeps running. Hears him call her name. Lungs blazing, she stops running and lets him catch her.

"You knew who I was."

Jacob lowers his eyes. "Of course." He is breathless. "You're the image of your mother."

Her anger flares. A thousand questions well up inside her. She feels hot and cold at once. The Wild beats around inside her, making her head and heart pound.

Before she can order her thoughts, Jacob says: "You can't be anywhere near this place. It's not safe."

Scarlett doesn't move. "Why did you pretend not to know me?"

He snatches her arm and begins to walk further down the hill, leading her away from the press gang's hideout.

"Let go of me!" She thrashes against him.

He lets his hand fall, but keeps walking. "These men will kill you if they find you. Your seeing them has compromised their secrecy."

"I shouldn't be surprised to find you with your hands in such things," she spits. "Is this where free trade takes you now? To impressment? Taking blood money from a crooked magistrate?"

Jacob keeps walking. And stops. They are at his cottage with its overgrown front path. She has walked the entire way beside him, Scarlett realises.

"I'll answer all your questions," he says, unlocking the door. "I'll tell you whatever you want to know. But I'll not do it in the street. I can't risk those men finding you."

In spite of herself, Scarlett follows him inside. Jacob lights the lamp and sets it on the mantel. He has cleaned some of the mess she had made. The shattered jar of witch powder has been swept up, the broken windows patched with rags. She feels a fleeting stab of guilt. Jacob gestures to a stool beside the table.

Scarlett sits hesitantly. Her father drags a storage trunk across the room and perches on the edge, facing her. His face is leathery beneath his beard; lines where there had not been lines, hollows in his once round cheeks. He is a strange phantom copy of the father she had known.

She feels his eyes on her, taking her in. Her skirts are caked in mud, her hair windswept and tangled. She is still without her shortjacket, she realises sickly, her breasts straining against her overtight stays. She yanks closed her cloak.

"What were you doing at the cart house?" he asks. "Was it me you were looking for? Or the man you call Asher Hales?"

She pins him with cold eyes. "I'm the one asking the questions."

Jacob looks down. "I'm a coward," he says. "That's why I pretended not to know you. You caught me by surprise. It was all I could think to do." His voice is thin. He does not sound the way she remembers.

She balls her hands into angry fists. "You're more than a coward."

He nods slowly. "How did you find me? Was it Asher Hales?"

Scarlett pushes past his question. "The press gang has him. Was that your doing?"

"He found work on a farm owned by one of the men in the gang. The man told me he'd hired a new worker. After you came to my cottage and told me Hales was in Portreath, I became suspicious."

"So it was your doing."

"He'll not be taken to the navy. Not yet at least. Not until he knows I'm the one responsible for his capture. I need him to know that."

Scarlett snorts. "Was it not enough for you to leave him on the beach with a murdered man?"

Jacob looks at his hands. "I want to explain to you about that night on the beach, Scarlett."

"You think I care one scrap about that night on the beach? You left us! We thought you dead!" Her voice rattles. "Your lies killed Mamm. She thought you had drowned and it broke her heart. And—"

"Your mother is dead?" Jacob interrupts.

Scarlett feels a sudden pain in her throat. For a long time, neither of them speak. Outside the cottage something rustles in the grass.

"I'm sorry, my girl," Jacob says finally. "More than you could know."

She shakes her head. "How can you say you're sorry when you're out here doing what you're doing? Pretending Isaac and I don't exist? Do you have any idea of the life you left for us?" She stands abruptly. "Leave me alone. I don't want a thing to do with you."

"Then why did you come to Portreath?"

Her heated reply falls short. "It was a mistake," she says finally, her voice catching. She swallows, determined not to cry in front of him.

Jacob stands and reaches for her arm again. This time, she lets him take it. His fingers are gentle against her bare wrist.

"What can I do?"

She stares at her feet. "You can come back to Talland and tell Charles Reuben you're alive. Tell him the debt belongs to you and not to Isaac."

Jacob looks down. "I can't go back to Talland. I'm sorry."

She pulls away. "Why not?"

"It's complicated."

"Why?"

"Because I'm a coward. I can't face Reuben. And I can't face your brother."

"That's not so complicated," Scarlett hisses, pulling open the door.

"You can't go back out there."

"No one has followed us."

"You don't know that. The men—"

"The men are dangerous, ayes. Are you not one of them? Are you not a part of the press gang? Why should I believe I'm any safer here with you?"

Jacob frowns. "Scarlett, please. I—"

"You've made it quite clear you want nothing to do with us," she snaps. "And you'll have your wish. I've spent most of my life believing you dead. I'll have no trouble convincing myself this is still the case."

She leaves the cottage without looking back. Perhaps there are men following her. Perhaps they have pistols in their hands, ready to put a bullet in her brain for finding their cart shed and their prisoner and their passage behind the inn. But she doesn't care.

She walks until she reaches Jamie's cottage.

"I know where the press gang is operating," she says when he opens the door.

He ushers her inside. "Did you go to the tavern again?" Scarlett hears a flicker of impatience in his voice.

She plants her hands on her hips. "Do you wish to know where the gang is operating or not?"

He nods. "Tell me."

And so she tells him of the drug-infused brandy, of the windowless carriage and the man in the powdered wig. Tells him of the passage through the fireplace and the cart shed on the hill where sailors are handed to the magistrate and sold on to the navy.

She says nothing of Asher Hales, or her father.

"How do you know all this?" Jamie asks.

She doesn't reply.

After a moment, he nods resignedly. "I'm glad you're safe."

Scarlett shivers. She crouches by the hearth and stares into the flames. And for the first time, she begins to see that the life she has built is a dangerous one. She thinks of the knife at her knee and the wolf eyes of Tom Leach and the lightless paths through the hills she has been running since she was a child.

Violence on the rise, Jamie had told her. Yes, she had heard of conflicts across the country. Had caught hold of stories passed between Isaac and his crew. The Hawkhurst Gang in the east. The riding officers strung up for murder last month while defending themselves in Looe. And yet somehow, she has managed to remain blind to the brutality of smuggling, even while rage at Leach and his men made her blood hot and her thoughts wild.

She hugs her knees.

"Was there a prisoner?" Jamie asks. "In the barn?"

She nods. A prisoner, yes. An anonymous, nameless prisoner.

"What will you do?" she asks. "Now you know where the press gang is operating? Do you have the authority to arrest them?"

Jamie begins to pace. "I have the authority to arrest them for smuggling."

"What do you mean? Those men weren't smuggling."

"No. But I can make it look as though they were. Seized contraband is brought into the customs station regularly. I can sneak out a haul and hide it at the cart shed." He looks at her with hot eyes. "When we know the gang is in there, I'll tell the other officers I've received a tip-off. They'll find the contraband and make the arrest."

Make the arrest. Arrest her murderer of a father.

Scarlett leans back against the leg of the table. "I always knew the revenue service was crooked."

Jamie chuckles, catching the short smile in the corner of her lips. "Those men deserve all that comes to them."

Guilt at her abandonment of Asher gnaws at the back of her mind. He would not be thrown onto a naval ship tonight, her father had told her. What worse fate did the press gang have in mind for him? Perhaps she ought to tell Jamie. Perhaps they ought to try and rescue him.

No. She had risked her life for him once and look where it has led her. To hell with him. He can find his own way out of the press gang's grasp.

She pushes away her guilt. Asher Hales is not worth guilt.

Jamie slides a stool to the fire and sits close to her. "How did you know?" he asks again. "I'll not be angry. I just want to know. I've been trying to catch those men out for months. I knew the impressed men were disappearing from the tavern, but it was the naval officers themselves taking them to the ships. I knew there had to be a place where the gang kept the men before handing them over. A place where they could liaise with the magistrate and collect their earnings."

"One of the men gave me a glass of brandy when I went to the inn that first night. There were something not right about it. A strange smell… I remembered what you said about the impressed men being drugged and…"

"But the hole in the fireplace," he pushes. "How did you find it?"

Scarlett avoids his eyes. "Someone showed it to me."

"Showed it to you?"

She hesitates, then looks at him with a wry smile. "It seems some men become quite trusting when they think a girl is going to lift her skirts." Her cheeks blaze.

Jamie starts to chuckle, making her laugh too.

"I thought you looked a little different," he says, trying far too hard to keep his eyes averted from her chest.

Scarlett takes her shortjacket from her pocket and slides it on hurriedly.

He touches her shoulder. "Stay here tonight."

"You have a watch?"

"No. But I can sleep on the floor."

"I couldn't."

"Why? Because it wouldn't be proper, or you don't want to risk another night in a riding officer's clutches?"

"Both."

He sighs slightly. "I thought we were past such distrust."

How she longs to be past it. How she longs to look into someone's eyes without trying to sift the truth from the lies.

"You know," Jamie tells her, poking at the fire, "I'm risking a lot by trusting you too."

"Why?"

"You've seen my journal. You could easily have read it when you were here alone last night. Could have sold my secrets to the Portreath traders."

"Then you're a fool to trust me."

"Perhaps." He presses a warm hand to her forearm. Scarlett feels something move in her chest. "Stay. You may not believe it, but I can assure you you're much safer here with me than out on the hills."

She hesitates. Her legs are aching with exhaustion, her mind craving the relief of sleep. Her bed in Redruth feels half the world away. "I'll take the floor," she says. "I insist."

Jamie pulls the blanket from the bed and hands it to her. "Then you'll take this at least."

"Do you have another?"

"I have my coat." He kicks off his boots and curls up on the sleeping pallet, pulling his broadcloth coat over his body. He rolls over and blows out the lamp. Scarlett lays the blanket by the hearth and cocoons herself in it. The fire is warm against her cheek. She turns, finds herself watching Jamie. The coat barely covers him; his knees pulled to his chest and his stockinged feet uncovered.

Scarlett stands. She slides the cloak from her shoulders and slips it over his body. He looks up. Smiles. Catches her eye in the glow of the flames.

She returns his smile faintly, then crawls back to her blanket beside the hearth. She lets her heart slow. Lets the crackle and sigh of the fire still her feverish thoughts. The flames die away and soon the only sound in the room is the in and out of breath. And how calming it is, Scarlett realises, to hear this riding officer's breathing rise and fall beside her own.

FLOWERS AND FIRE

The light is good here in Jack's room. In the day, the sun fills it, unlike the constant shadows that lie over so much of the inn. This is a better place for drying herbs. Flora goes to her mother's room and takes down the strings of plants. She ties them to the handle of the wardrobe in Jack's room and stretches them upwards towards the mantel. The sun has sunk now, and a fire is crackling in the grate. Below, the inn is quiet. Today is a day of rest.

These rooms had been guest chambers in the days when Flora's grandfather had run the Mariner's Arms. She had always planned to use them for the same purpose. But perhaps not. Perhaps in her inn they might have a different use.

Word has begun to spread that there are healing herbs drying in the village tavern. There have been people at the door, seeking cures for aches and coughs and pains. Men at the bar asking for tonics along with their liquor. Being of use, Flora is coming to realise, is a fine thing.

The floor creaks as Bessie appears in the doorway.

"Why are you out of bed, *cheel-vean*? It's late."

Bessie pokes at the flower fronds gently. In the golden light they are silhouettes, their spider leg shadows dancing over the walls. "I want to watch."

Flora makes her way along the line of hanging plants, touching the leaves, testing their dryness. What would Jack think if he could see her? She pushes the thought away. It doesn't matter. Jack is not here. Not in this room, not in this house, not in the tunnel. She hands the dried leaves to Bessie.

Careful now. Gentle. She hears her mother's words come from her mouth.

She brings the chest from the corner and opens the lid. Kneeling together in the red-yellow light, she and Bessie place them into pouches.

"What's this one? And this one?"

Flora tells her daughter the names of each. Mallow, angelica, yarrow.

Bessie lifts the black mirror from the chest. "What's this?"

Flora hesitates. "Your *mamm-wynn* used to say it was a magic mirror. She used it to try and see the future."

Bessie's blue eyes light. "See the future? Can you really do that, Mammik?"

Of course not, Flora would have said a month ago. *A mirror cannot tell the future.*

Instead: "I don't know."

Bessie peers into it.

"What do you see?"

"Just myself. And the flowers and the fire."

Flora smiles. She is glad Bessie has her father's rationality.

Jack feels suddenly close. What has triggered it? This faint regret over the scent of yarrow replacing his tobacco and brandy smell? Or is it the guilt she feels when she thinks of Isaac's hands running over her skin? Guilt at lifting the covers of their marriage bed and letting another man slide beneath.

"Bedtime," she tells Bessie, suddenly flustered.

With her daughter in bed, Flora is restless. There are accounts to do, but her mind is far too preoccupied. She walks through the still bar, her boots beating a rhythm on the flagstones. She has the mirror in her hand, she realises. Why has she brought it with her?

Her collection of seashells sits on the shelf above the cups. She takes down the shell Isaac had found for her in the cave, running her thumb over its pearly surface.

She cannot let herself fall for this man. No good can come of it.

Cannot fall for this man.

But she knows the futility of trying to talk herself out of it. She had fallen for Isaac Bailey when they were children building castles in the sand.

She and Jack had never spoken about what would happen if one of them were to die. That was a conversation for the old, the sick. They had been far too young and lovestruck to consider their own mortality.

Flora is sure Jack would want her to find happiness again. She is not yet two and thirty. With luck, she has far too many years ahead of her to spend walking alone through empty rooms.

So in another life, she is sure Jack would be happy to see her with Isaac. But in this life, Isaac has Caroline. He has children and debts and he must leave Talland.

And so: *what are you thinking?*, she can hear Jack say. *What are you thinking?*, as loud and clear as if he were looking over her shoulder at the shell in her hands.

She feels the pull of the tunnel. With the looking glass in hand, she walks down into the darkness, running a hand along the wall to keep her bearings.

What are you thinking?

What is drawing her down here? What does she truly expect to find? She does not believe the dead will walk.

But nor had she believed in healing incantations. Had not believed tomorrow could be seen in the mirror.

Why are you losing hold of who you once were?

But is she losing herself or finding herself? She can't be sure.

She looks into the mirror. Searching for what?

Everything feels hazy; her beliefs, her sense of self, where this world ends and another begins. She wants clarity, she realises. Wants answers. And she will look anywhere to find them.

The tunnel is dark, the mirror dark. Nothing to see but black rock walls. Light bounces suddenly off the surface of the glass, filling the tunnel with a sudden hot glow.

"Flora?" Isaac's voice snaps her back to reality. He looks down at the mirror. "What are you doing?"

What *is* she doing?

He takes her hand and walks with her back towards the inn. When they are out of the cellar, he takes the mirror and sits it face down on a table. He pulls her towards him, his lips crashing against hers.

Flora digs her hands into his hair, returning his kiss. It's a joy, she realises, to be here in the present, in this solid, earthly world. A joy to feel a man's breath on her skin, to feel herself touched in ways she hasn't been for two years. It's a joy to feel her body ache and burn, reminding her that she is bright among the living.

Upstairs, silent, dark. The sigh of clothing against the floor. No dead men in the looking glass, no one walking the tunnel. The rest of the inn is still. She hears only his sharp intake of breath and her muffled murmurs against his shoulder as the pleasure of it mixes with pain.

Soon he will be gone. And she knows it is his leaving that has brought them here. His leaving is what has allowed this to happen. Because soon he will be gone and the secret of this will disappear, die.

She lies with her head to his chest, his heart drumming close to her ear. She can see nothing but the inky outlines of their bodies. The dark makes it easy to hide. To forget and ignore the world hunting and panting around them.

A knock at the door and reality clatters back sharply.

"Flora Kelly?" A man's voice. Unfamiliar. "Open the door."

She fumbles in the blackness, snatching her shift from the floor. The bed creaks as Isaac sits, lighting the lamp.

"Let me answer it," he says, pulling on his breeches.

Flora laces her bodice with jittery fingers. "Don't be mad. No one can know you're here."

She hurries downstairs, heart thumping. Opens the door to find the excisemen.

She is detached from her body when they go to the wall and pull down the liquor licence. She watches them break the glass, pore over the contents, pry at the seal.

She hears the words.

Under arrest.

Can't register their meaning.

Forgery.

She feels the officers' hands around the tops of her arms. Her head swims.

Isaac's voice at the bottom of the stairs. "Get your damn hands off her."

Flora tries to pull away. "No need to manhandle me like an animal."

"I'm coming with you," says Isaac, buttoning his coat.

"No. You need to stay with Bessie." She glances at the looking glass teetering on the edge of the table. "And lock the mirror away."

WARFARE

The excisemen lead Flora to the wagon waiting outside the inn. One of the officers pulls open the door. "Inside."

She bundles her skirts in her fist and climbs into the cart. She sits on the dirty boards and hugs her knees to her chest. The carriage rattles up the hill, the lights of the Mariner's Arms disappearing into the darkness.

Flora's stomach turns over.

She will breathe. She will stay calm. Fear will accomplish nothing.

The wagon stops abruptly, jolting her forward. She hears the footsteps of the excisemen come towards her. The door opens and she climbs out into the night. They have arrived at the Polperro customs house. The men lead her into a small room with a wooden table in the centre. They sit on one side, nodding to a stool opposite.

"Sit."

She does. Her mouth is dry. "May I have some water?"

He pours a cup from the jug on the desk. Flora gulps it down. The water is preserved with rum and leaves a bitter taste in her throat.

"Who printed the licence for you, Mrs Kelly?"

She raises her eyebrows. "That's what you want? To take down a dishonest printer?"

"I suggest you be a little more cooperative. As it stands, you're facing charges of forgery and selling liquor without a licence. If you're found guilty, you'll likely face imprisonment. Perhaps transportation."

The thought of it makes heat flood her body. But she meets the officer's eyes, forcing steadiness into her voice. "A Cornish jury will not convict their own."

"Are you certain of that? Certain enough to risk incarceration? Risk losing your daughter?"

She swallows heavily. Certain? No. But she will not let them see her unease. "You know I'm guilty," she says. "You know my licence is forged. Why are you questioning me? Why not just take me before the magistrate?"

The officers exchange glances and she feels something shift inside her.

The first officer leans towards her. "You know of the murders that occurred in Lansallos recently, I'm sure."

She nods.

"The local riding officers tell me you have so far been unhelpful in their investigation."

"You're in league with them, are you? I suppose I ought not be surprised."

His eyes harden at her sharp tone. "We know well there's a smuggling syndicate operating out of Talland. A thing the revenue service is most eager to prove." He pours his own cup of water and takes a casual sip. "Isaac Bailey was at your inn tonight."

"Is such a thing a crime?"

The officer's lips turn up. "That entirely depends on what he was doing there." His chair creaks. "But adultery laws are of little interest to us. They are a matter for your own conscience."

Flora keeps her gaze steady, despite the fire in her cheeks. "Let's not bother ourselves with each other's consciences."

The officer folds his arms. "Was Isaac Bailey involved in the murders?"

"I've no idea. Why are you asking me? Don't you have an innkeeper in Lansallos you might threaten?"

"We've come to you because you're the one with the counterfeit licence," the officer says sharply.

Flora swallows.

"It is important for not only the men of the preventative service but also the safety of the villagers that we put an end to this increase in gang violence. As the murders took place so close to Talland, we have every reason to believe Isaac Bailey and the other smugglers in his syndicate were involved."

"It seems you've made up your mind," says Flora.

"Yes. But we need a witness. Someone willing to stand up in court and condemn these men."

"A witness?" She laughs coldly. "You know I wasn't in Lansallos the night of the murders. I was in Talland running my inn."

The officer doesn't reply at once. "You'll tell the court you witnessed the shootings."

Flora sits back in her chair. "I suppose I shouldn't be surprised by your corruption."

"You are in no position to be self-righteous, Mrs Kelly. You have knowingly broken several laws."

Flora lowers her eyes. The man is right, of course. "Who told you about my licence?" she asks.

"What makes you think anyone told us?"

She smiles wryly. "You knew all along, I suppose."

"We suspected as much. You were offered the chance to help the revenue service. Had you done so, we would never have come looking."

Flora wraps her arms around herself. How foolish she has been, rushing into reopening with the forged licence, risking her and Bessie's safety. She had been desperate to keep the Mariner's Arms open, just as Jack would have wanted. But Jack, of course, would not have wanted this.

The officer leans towards her. "We want this warfare between smuggling gangs stopped. So much so we would be willing to overlook an innkeeper with a counterfeit liquor licence."

"Isaac Bailey is a friend," Flora says sharply. "If you think I will turn him in to free myself, you are mistaken."

"Take her to the lockup," one officer tells the other. "Let her think it over in there for the night."

And she is dragged from the customs house with vice-like hands at the top of her arms.

The lockup is a tiny stone hovel on the edge of the green. The stocks stand beside it, stained with blood and dinted by stones. The officer pulls a ring of keys from his pocket and unlocks the door. There is nothing inside but a narrow wooden bench. The floor is strewn with mud and filth.

Flora steps inside before the officer puts a hand to her. She swallows hard, the stench of human waste turning her stomach. She presses her palm hard against the wall, determined not to show her fear. She shivers violently, wishing for a shawl or cloak.

"I trust you understand the situation, Mrs Kelly," the officer tells her, moonlight shafting over his face as he pulls on the door. "Keep silent and you'll face the magistrate. Name names and you'll go free."

MEETING

The morning light burns through Asher's eyelids and makes his head pound. He blinks tentatively. His mouth is dry. He can smell hay and earth. Is he on the farm? His blurry eyes see men's boots.

He tries to sit. His whole body is an ache. He slumps wearily against the wall. This is not the farm. To one side of him sits a blue and gold carriage, its windows covered. He is in someone's cart shed.

This is not the farm, but the man coming towards him is the farmer. His eyes are darting and his fingers dance. He is wearing the same patched waistcoat he has been since Asher had met him.

"What do you want?" Asher spits.

The farmer chuckles. "Took him long enough to come out of it."

Asher tries to move, tries to see who the man is speaking to. A wall of pain slams him as he turns his head. He blinks hard. "What did you give me?"

"Just a little opium."

"Opium?"

Just a little opium would not have left him unconscious all night. He remembers the burn of the brandy they had forced down his throat. The liquor combined with the drug would have made for a lethal combination. He ought to be dead. Cold sweat prickles his skin and he lurches to one side, retching into the hay.

As he moves, he sees the other man. A man he recognises at once.

Jacob Bailey steps close. Leans over him. His breath is hot and stale against his cheek. Asher's stomach rolls.

Jacob hauls him to his feet, then shoves him down again. Asher lands hard on his side, pain shooting through him and dizziness seesawing the world.

This is not the meeting Asher had imagined when he had stood on the deck of the *Avalon* and watched Cornwall crawl towards him. Not the meeting he had imagined when he had cajoled and courted Scarlett to lead him to her father. In the meeting with Jacob Asher had imagined, he had been the one with the power. He would raise a pistol, give a victorious smile. *Tell me how to find the hidden wealth of Henry Avery.*

But there is no wealth and no pistol and no power. Just pain in his side and hay beneath his head. Opium in his blood and sickness in his throat.

Yes, Jacob had wronged him, but the things Asher had done in retaliation were far worse. A fist to his stomach and his breath leaves him. He gasps, coughs. Jacob strikes him again. Again. Blood runs hot and salty down his throat.

He will die, Asher thinks. Today is the day he will die. Terror seizes him. He has always been fascinated by death. But it is not so intriguing, he realises, when the death coming towards him is his own.

The farmer pulls Jacob away. "Leave the man in one piece or the judge won't pay."

Asher rolls onto his knees. Coughs out a line of spittle and blood.

Jacob produces a pistol from his coat. He leans over Asher, breathing heavily. Dirt is streaked along one weathered cheek. The wildness in his eyes suggests he has no intention of leaving Asher in one piece. "You brought my daughter here. Why?"

Asher coughs, pain shooting through his side. "She found you then. A pleasant reunion, I'm sure."

Jacob shoves the nose of the pistol into Asher's neck.

He inhales sharply at the pain. "You'll kill me then? To protect Scarlett from me? Believe me, you have things the wrong way around."

"I'm not going to kill you," says Jacob. "You're worth more to me alive than dead. The navy pays well for a man with sea legs."

Asher feels fresh heat course through him. The world feels colourless and unsteady. He stands, stumbles. He feels the farmer's hands around the tops of his arms. He tries to struggle against them, but his muscles are weak with opium and fear. If he is not to die here, he will die with a touch rod in his hand, fighting for a country who had cast him from her shore.

Jacob stands close, pressing the gun to Asher's stomach. "It will be a great thing when a Spanish bullet takes you down. I don't want a thing more to do with you, or that hedge whore of yours."

Asher begins to laugh slowly, humourlesly. A Spanish bullet, he realises, is worth it, just to be the one to deliver the news. "That hedge whore has married your son."

BURIED TREASURE

The gun teeters in Jacob's hand. "You're lying," he says finally. "My son would not be so foolish as to go near that witch."

"Caroline," Asher says tautly. "Her name is Caroline. And no. I'm not lying. As much as I wish I were."

Jacob looks at the farmer. "Leave us. I'll take him to the judge when I'm done with him."

And the two men are alone. Jacob begins to pace. Asher eyes the doorway. Eyes the pistol. He will never make it. The opium is still playing with his legs.

"Why are you here with Scarlett?" Jacob asks after a long silence.

Asher wipes the blood trickling from his lip. "Because your dear daughter put a knife to me. Forced me to help her find you."

"You're a liar."

"I am a liar," says Asher. "But I'm telling the truth about this. Scarlett has your blood running through her. How can you be surprised she has a violent side?"

Jacob turns away.

"She's an anger in her like I've never seen," Asher continues, relishing the man's discomfort. "I'll warrant she gets that from you. Was it that wild anger that drove you to kill Albert Davey when he told you Avery's haul was a myth?"

Jacob doesn't look at him. "It's no myth."

"Of course it is."

"Believe what you like."

Asher shifts. Dare he try and believe again? A faint flicker of hope sparks inside him, quelled suddenly by the pistol hanging from Jacob's fist. Pain begins to pulse behind his eyes. "Why kill Davey?" he asks finally.

"Because I needed his money. What choice did I have but to kill him?" Jacob speaks plainly, without emotion.

What had he been thinking, Asher wonders, involving himself with such a man all those years ago? Little wonder his life has taken the course it has. But he is unable to push aside his curiosity. The pull of Avery's haul has taunted him for far too long for him to turn away now.

"Davey told you where the haul was hidden?"

Jacob nods faintly.

"Then why did you not claim it?"

"You know why." When he turns back to face Asher, Jacob's eyes are hard. "I've heard enough from you. It will be a great pleasure to sell you off to the navy after all you've cost me." He raises the pistol, nods towards the door. "Walk."

"We both want the same thing," Asher says hurriedly. "We both want Caroline away from Isaac."

His words are ones of desperation, but he is surprised to find he believes them. He would leave Talland, he had told Caroline, the morning he had returned from Isaac's trading run to Guernsey. He would leave her to her miserable life of patched skirts and broken windows. Would leave her to watch as her husband was strung up for smuggling. She would become nothing more to him than a memory.

But he sees now, somewhere not so deep inside, he had had no intention of leaving her. Caroline is as important to his perfect life as Avery's money.

He had tried to convince himself he could have the life of his dreams without her in it. Fill the hole she had left with a dazzling career and a string of beautiful women. But now she is back in his life, he sees he can do no such thing. As hard as he has tried to ignore it, he knows the passion he'd felt for her when they were young is still raging inside him.

He watches Jacob pace across the cart shed. "We've wanted the same thing in the past," he tells Asher tautly. "But it seems we are unable to cooperate."

Unable to cooperate indeed. But Asher hears the roar of cannon fire, feels a touch rod in his hand. Smoke in his eyes, a watery grave.

"We can cooperate," he says, his voice thin with desperation. "We will go back to Talland and I'll bring Caroline to you. She'll not risk Isaac finding out what she did. She'll have no choice but to leave."

Jacob gives a snort of humourless laughter. "With you?"

Asher swallows. In the nearby stables, a horse sighs noisily.

"If I see her, I will kill her. Not hand her over to you so she can run away and live happily."

The knot in Asher's stomach tightens. Is this fear for Caroline? Or for himself? Jacob will have a bullet for each of them, he has no doubt. But his only hope of escaping the navy is to convince him they must return to Talland together.

"Kill her?" he says, forcing steadiness into his voice. "And do you expect Isaac will allow you back into his life if you burst into the village and murder his wife?"

Jacob doesn't look at him. "I'm quite sure I have no place in Isaac's life."

Asher sees Caroline with Jacob's bullet in her chest. Sees blood snake and pool across her body. Sees her eyes become glassy. He coughs down a fresh wave of sickness.

He cannot let himself be impressed. Cannot let Jacob take him to the magistrate. He will die and so will she. Convincing Jacob to ally with him is all the hope he has.

"You are so certain Isaac will turn you away?" says Asher. "Even if he knows the true reason you left?" He knows he is playing a dangerous game. Isaac Bailey is a hard man to read. There is no way of knowing how he would react if he were to find out the truth of why his father left. Does Isaac have it in him to kill those who have wronged him? Perhaps he would be safer fighting the Spanish, Asher thinks sickly.

Jacob paces across the shed. "I don't need you to get Caroline out of Isaac's life. Scarlett is in Portreath. I'll tell her everything. When she returns to Talland with that knowledge, Caroline will have no choice but to leave."

And another wave of fear comes. Scarlett knowing the true reason her father abandoned his family, Asher realises, is far worse than Isaac knowing. Scarlett is gunpowder hovering inches from a flame.

He forces out a chuckle. "And you think she will just believe you?"

"Why shouldn't she?"

"Because she despises you," Asher hisses. "She would happily see you dead and she'll not believe a word that comes from you."

"And if it came from you?"

"Then there is even less chance of her believing it."

Jacob folds his hands behind his head. "Where can I find her?"

"I've no idea."

"Don't lie to me! You're the one who brought her here."

"And I've been lying unconscious in this cursed shed since yesterday. I've no idea what's become of Scarlett."

For a long time, Jacob doesn't speak. Asher's heart thuds. "You need me," he says desperately. "You want rid of Caroline, I need to be involved. You know I'm right."

Jacob grabs Asher's arm and shoves him forward. Pins the pistol into his spine. "Walk."

And Asher walks on unsteady legs out of the cart shed and down a winding hill. The sea stretches out beneath him, beating ceaselessly at stacks of black rock.

They walk until they reach a tiny shack a few yards back from the road. Jacob unlocks the door and shoves Asher inside. He forces him onto a stool and uses a length of rope to bind his wrists and ankles.

Jacob makes for the door without speaking.

Is he going to seek out his daughter? Tell her his real reasons for leaving Talland? If Scarlett believes his story, Asher is of no value. He will be thrown onto a naval vessel and Jacob Bailey will have his revenge.

He prays Scarlett's untrusting side is still intact.

WITNESSES

"Two minutes." The excise officer opens the door of the lockup, letting Isaac inside. Flora leaps to her feet, squinting in the sudden, muted sunlight. The door slams and the dark returns abruptly.

"Bessie. Is she—"

"She's safe. She's with us." Isaac pulls her into his arms. "You're frozen," he says, feeling her shiver against him. He slides off his coat and pulls it over her shoulders. "Did they hurt you?"

She shakes her head. Pulls the coat tighter around her. "They want me to name names. Tell them I witnessed the murders." Her breath plumes in a silver cloud. "They suspect you, Isaac. But they've no proof. No witnesses." She rubs her eyes. "I'm surprised they let you see me."

"And if you turn me over to them? They'll free you?"

She gives him a withering look. "You know I'd never think of it."

Isaac begins to pace, his thoughts charging. He'd not managed an hour of sleep. His boots slide through the muck on the floor of the lockup. "Tell them you saw Leach kill the riding officers."

Flora looks at her feet. "I couldn't."

"Leach killed those men," Isaac hisses. "I saw him do it."

"Yes, but I did not."

He lets out his breath in frustration. He lifts Flora's arm, where the cut from Leach's knife is still strapped tightly. "Have you forgotten what he did to you? You owe the bastard no loyalty!"

"I'll not lower myself to his level."

"Not even to save yourself?"

She turns away, her jaw clenched and her eyes hard. Isaac burns with a thorny mix of frustration and respect. "You've lied to the revenue men before," he reminds her.

"A few petty lies are one thing. Turning a man in for murder is quite another." She wraps her arms around herself. "They can take me to trial. I'll not be found guilty by a magistrate who has drunk at my inn. The Cornish protect their own."

"You cannot possibly know that! The revenue men may well have had a word in the magistrate's ear."

"Perhaps. But I'll not stand up in court and claim to have witnessed something I didn't see." Her voice is thick with exhaustion. "You may have given up on morality, Isaac, but I haven't."

He exhales in frustration. "Ayes, Flora, you're a damn picture of morality, with your forged licence and your smuggled liquor and…"

"The married man in my bed?"

Isaac sighs. He drops onto the bench and tugs her down beside him. He laces his fingers through hers and holds her hand against his chest to warm it. "You can't count on a lenient magistrate. The authorities want someone to pin the murders on. They want to make a point to other trading gangs. Give them what they want. Please."

She stares into the darkness, not speaking. He wonders what she is thinking.

The door creaks. "Time," the officer says curtly.

Isaac turns back to Flora and drops his voice. "Think of Bessie. Where would she be without you?" He squeezes her hand. "Where would *I* be without you?"

She lets out her breath, pulling her fingers from his. "Where would you be? You will be far from Talland with your wife and children, Isaac. That is where you will be." She slips his tarred fishing coat from her shoulders. "Take it."

"Don't be foolish. You're shivering."

"And what will you wear?" She drops her voice. "That greatcoat covered in John Baker's blood?"

The officer gestures for Isaac to leave. He takes the coat reluctantly and stands outside the lockup, simmering with frustration.

Reuben's mansion blots the hill. Just the sight of it makes Isaac angry. But Reuben will be another voice trying to talk Flora towards reason.

He climbs up to the house and knocks on the door. "I need to speak with Reuben urgently," he tells the maid. She ushers him inside and disappears down the hall.

After a moment, Reuben appears from the parlour. He is in his shirtsleeves, his head bald without its customary white wig.

"Mr Bailey," he says stiffly. "I'm surprised to see you here." His voice is curt and clipped.

"Flora needs your help."

The hardness in Reuben's eyes vanishes. "What's happened?"

Isaac tells him of the excisemen's visit, tells him of the arrest.

Reuben exhales. "I should never have helped her obtain that licence."

Isaac says nothing. As much as he longs to blame Reuben, he knows Flora would have gotten her hands on a licence with or without his help. "They've offered her freedom if she names the traders involved in the murders." He must tread carefully. Reuben cannot know of his involvement. "They've asked her to lie to the magistrate in order to put an end to the warfare between traders."

"I take it she will not agree."

"She's stubborn. Trying to cling to a little morality."

Reuben gives a short chuckle. "Aren't we all." He rubs his chin. "You believe Tom Leach and his men were involved?"

Isaac nods. "Flora knows this. But she'll not turn him in. She'll not condemn a man on hearsay."

Reuben lets out his breath. "Her decency is misplaced as far as Leach is concerned."

"She's counting on a lenient magistrate in Polperro," Isaac tells him. "She's telling herself she'll not be convicted by a man who has drunk at her inn."

Reuben reaches for a greatcoat hanging on a hook beside the door. "Then she needs to believe she will face a magistrate from outside these parts."

Flora is surprised to see Reuben enter the lockup. "How did you know I was here?"

"Your friend Mr Bailey told me."

She shivers. "Did he have you come here and convince me to turn Tom Leach in?"

"I've come on my own accord, Mrs Kelly. I do not act on Isaac Bailey's bidding." Reuben stands in the doorway, eying the filth-covered floor. He reaches into his pocket and hands her an apple. "Here. I thought you may be hungry."

"Thank you." Flora's stomach is rolling. She is not sure if it is hunger or fear.

Reuben stays with his back pressed to the door. "As you may know, I am well acquainted with this town's magistrate. When I heard of your arrest, I sought him out. The revenue service are always quick to take a prisoner to trial. I wanted to know when you will be facing the court."

She stiffens. "And?"

"And he knows nothing of your case. From this I could only assume he would not be the one overseeing the trial. I spoke to the men who arrested you at the inn last night. And I'm afraid my suspicions are correct. They plan to take you to trial in Exeter."

She feels suddenly hot and dizzy. "What?" she manages.

"Your trial is important to them," says Reuben. "They don't want a biased magistrate."

She begins to pace. "They don't care about my trial. They just want to pressure me into lying about witnessing the murders."

"Yes. That's exactly why your trial is important to them."

A line of sweat runs down her back. "When?"

"They plan to take you to Exeter tomorrow morning."

Flora sits, her legs weakening. She stares at the strip of light pushing beneath the door. The constant darkness is tangling her thoughts.

"I'm sure I need not tell you, you cannot rely on leniency from a magistrate outside of Cornwall," says Reuben. "And I'm sure the revenue men have made you aware of the penalties for forgery."

She nods faintly. Imprisonment. Transportation. She will be torn from her life, her home, her inn strung with flowers.

She will be torn from her daughter.

What will happen to Bessie? The children's home? Is she to grow up among orphans because her mother pretended she had morals?

She can't let such a thing happen.

She will do this for her daughter, she tells herself. Will do it for Bessie. Yes, she can find a justification for immorality. A validation for lies in the witness stand. There is always a justification if you look hard enough.

"Tell the officers I wish to see them," she says, avoiding Reuben's eyes. Her voice comes out sounding like someone else.

"I'll do that," he says. She catches a faint smile in the corner of his lips.

She is pacing the lockup when they arrive.

"Yes, Mrs Kelly? Is there something you wish to tell us?"

She draws in her breath and lifts her chin. Forces a steadiness into her voice. "I saw Tom Leach kill the riding officers in Lansallos."

RETRIBUTION

The windowless carriage sits at the top of the hill. Light flickers in the tavern below.

Scarlett waits at the edge of the quay for Jamie. He needs to hurry if they are to plant the contraband in the cart shed tonight. The moment the press gang seize their target, the carriage will be on the move and their chance will be lost.

She turns abruptly at the sound of footsteps. Jamie is in uniform, ready for his watch later that night. His hands are dug into the pockets of his coat, wind blowing dark waves of hair back from his face. Scarlett is not sure if she is comforted or unnerved by a man striding towards her with brass buckles on his boots. He grins at the sight of her and she finds herself returning his smile.

She looks back at the tavern as muffled laughter sounds through the windows. "The innkeeper must know what's going on this place."

Jamie turns up the collar of his coat. "No doubt he gets a cut in exchange for his silence." He pulls a package from his pocket and hands it to Scarlett. "Put it in your cloak." There is a crooked smile in the corner of his lips.

"What is it?"

He grins. "Tobacco." He gestures to his own overflowing pockets. "I've jewels and lace. Anything bigger was too difficult to get out of the customs store without being seen." He nudges her shoulder. "I thought you'd like the tobacco. Old time's sake and all."

Scarlett hesitates.

Jamie's smile disappears. "Truly? You doubt me?"

She swallows hard. No. If she is to walk into a trap, she will do it in pursuit of her old, trusting self. She slides the tobacco into her pocket. "Of course not." Her voice is trapped in her throat.

Jamie touches her elbow. "Show me how to find the cart shed."

The house in front of the shed is dark. A lamp swings in the breeze above the front door, but the windows are lightless. Scarlett slips through the gate and leads Jamie towards the cart shed. He heaves open the thick wooden door and slips inside. Shoves the bundles of lace and jewels behind a shelf stacked with oil tins.

"What will you tell your colleagues?" Scarlett asks, handing him the tobacco. "Will you admit you set the men up?"

"Never. I'd be strung up myself. I'll just tell them I have my suspicions about the place. Request assistance with a raid."

"And if they discover the contraband came from Customs House?"

"Then the press gang will be charged with theft of government property." He turns to face her. "I'm sure you don't think well of me. You've seen more than one of my underhand tactics." She hears a flicker of light in his voice.

"You're doing this for your brother," says Scarlett. "I understand." After a moment, she says: "I'd do the same." She feels a sudden, desperate urge to see Isaac. She longs to tell him all she has uncovered. Longs to tell him of the press gang and the cottage on the hill and the almost-regret in Jacob's voice. She cannot carry the weight of it alone.

She and Isaac had parted on terrible terms, but he will worry for her, of course. He always has. She can't shake her concern over him either. When last she had seen him, he had been sinking ships and speaking of escape. She hopes he is keeping his new recklessness out of Reuben's sight.

She follows Jamie from the shed. He goes to the front of the property and sits with his back against the stone fence surrounding the house. "You don't need to be here," he tells her.

She sits beside him. "I want to be." She needs to be a part of this, she realises. Needs to see Jacob punished. To Jamie, she says: "You could use the company."

He smiles. "This must feel like a betrayal to you. Working with the revenue men." There is playfulness in his voice and Scarlett knows he does not mean her to feel shame. She feels it anyway.

"It's the right thing to do," she says, hugging her knees.

Jamie raises his dark eyebrows. "I'm sure there are many who would disagree with you. I'll lose my job if anyone finds out what I've done."

"The right path is not always so clear," says Scarlett.

Jamie murmurs something soft, unintelligible. Hair blows across his eyes. Their breath is silver in front of them, disappearing into the thick of the night. And Scarlett begins to remember the power the darkness has over her; its ability to banish the Wild and bring a little peace. She feels the churning inside her begin to still.

What a strange thing, she thinks, that she might feel such calm as she sits beside a riding officer waiting to string up her father.

The right path is not always so clear.

Jamie shifts beside her, his shoulder knocking against hers. The contact sends an unexpected rush of energy down her arm. She pushes it away. Tomorrow the coach will leave for Talland and Jamie McCulley will become a memory.

"Right thing to do or not," he says, "I know you risked a lot to help me." He presses his gloved hand to her wrist. "I'm grateful." His fingers move against her arm and the fluttering inside her intensifies. She wants to slide closer. Wants to feel his hand move past her wrist. Under her cloak. Wants to feel those gloved fingers on her neck, her cheek, her lips. She realises she is holding her breath.

She feels him trying to catch her eye.

She has made mistakes around men before. Most notably, in the form of Asher Hales. She has let herself fall hard, fast and foolish. Mistakes.

Jamie would certainly be a mistake. But his hand is warm and restless, and the carriage will leave tomorrow. In the morning he will be a memory.

She turns to face him. His nose is close to hers. And his hand is sliding up her arm, beneath her cloak, slow and gentle and curious. Scarlett hears her breath catch.

The noise comes first. A rhythmic rattle as the windowless carriage pelts up the road.

Jamie pulls his hand away and leaps to his feet. "I'm going for the other officers. I'll take you back to my cottage on the way."

"No. You need to get the others as quickly as you can. I can make my own way back."

He hesitates. "All right. But promise me you'll go straight to the cottage."

Scarlett squints as the carriage draws closer. She can see her father in the box seat. She nods. Watches Jamie disappear into the dark.

Light spills from the front of the carriage and sways over the road. Scarlett hides behind the stone fence, keeping her head down as the coach rolls through the gates towards the cart shed.

She dares to look up. She will leave, yes. She has promised Jamie. But she can't take her eyes from her father. He climbs from the box seat and opens the carriage door. He tilts his head to stretch his neck, the way Scarlett remembers him doing when she was a child. Three men jump from the coach and haul out a limp body. Carry it towards the stables. And Scarlett walks deliberately towards the carriage. She wants Jacob to see her. Wants him to know, when the riding officers appear and haul him away, that she has had her retribution.

He catches sight of her as he is latching closed the carriage door. "You always were a brave thing," he says. "If more than a little foolish." She expects an eruption, but he gives a small smile and says: "I'm glad I found you." He puts a firm hand to the back of her neck and walks her towards the gate. "You need to leave. Asher Hales is not here. There are only men who would happily kill you."

Scarlett swallows heavily. Yes, she needs to pretend she is here to save Asher, or Jamie's plans will be ruined.

"Where is he?" she asks Jacob. "What have you done with him?"

"Don't waste your time worrying over that man. He's not worth it." He walks her towards the front gate. No, Jacob cannot leave. The riding officers will be here soon. She can't let him walk free.

"I need to speak with you," she says.

His fingers soften against the back of her neck. "Not here, Scarlett. It's too dangerous. I've told you before."

"Here," she says sharply. "Or nowhere."

Jacob sighs. Nods. He stands by the gate, one side of his face lit by the lamp above the front door. He looks at her expectantly. And so Scarlett asks him that which has been bubbling inside her since she first read Asher's letter.

"Did you ever truly love us?"

She hears a sound come from Jacob's throat. He stares out at the dark expanse of moorland beyond the house. His eyes are glassy. "I know you have no reason to believe me. But things are not as straightforward as you think. Everything I did was for you."

"You're right," Scarlett says coldly. "I don't believe you."

He sighs. "Isaac's wife. Tell me about her."

"Why?" When her father doesn't reply, Scarlett says: "She loves him. She loves him enough to have married into the debt you saddled us with. She loves him enough to settle for a life of poverty."

"And how does she treat you?"

Scarlett shrugs. "We will never be close. But she has always done right by me." She looks at him pointedly. "She was the closest I had to a mother. Perhaps I have not always been so grateful." She frowns. "Why do you care about Caroline?"

"I just want to know of your lives." Jacob looks distant. "Are there children?"

She lets out her breath. "If you want to know of our lives, you know how to find us."

"Tell me, Scarlett! Are there children?"

"Yes," she says tautly. "Two."

For a long time, Jacob doesn't speak. Scarlett glances sideways at him. What is he thinking?

"And you," he says after a moment. "Are you surviving?"

She laughs coldly. "Surviving? Ayes. I get by with what little scraps Reuben decides to toss my way."

"That's not what I meant." Jacob turns to look at her. His eyes glow in the hot light. "I've a great anger inside me, Scarlett. An anger that makes me lose control. An anger that scares me." He swallows. "I know it's in you too."

She looks at her hands, unnerved by the intensity of his gaze. "You don't know a thing about me." She can feel Jacob's eyes on her. Refuses to look at him.

"When I became a father," he says, "I grew terrified of passing this anger on. I didn't want my sons and daughters to suffer as I had. I never saw it in any of my other children. But then you came along. And I watched that anger rear up inside you. I saw the darkness I feel within me show itself in your eyes."

Scarlett shifts uncomfortably.

"I let it take me over," Jacob says, "and I killed a man. I killed him because I wanted to steal from him. I was lucky I didn't hang for it. I don't want the same thing to happen to you."

Scarlett doesn't speak. She wants to, she realises. Wants to speak to the only person in the world who will understand. She wants to ask him if he too feels detached from his body when the Wild takes hold. Wants to know if the dark brings him peace. Wants to know if he has ever felt the anger take prominence, the way it has done for her these past few days. But she doesn't want to allow him in. Doesn't want him inside her head. He doesn't deserve it.

She feels him work his fingers through her hair, the way he had done when she was a child. The way he had done to calm her when the Wild seized her.

Tears well behind her eyes. The father she had thought she had lost is standing before her with his hands in her hair. How is it that she feels only bitterness? She pushes away a tear as it escapes down her cheek. "You left us with a debt we can never hope to repay," she says finally. "And it's your anger you're sorry for passing on to me?"

Hooves thunder suddenly up the path, along with a spear of light. Three horses charge through the gates, Jamie on one of them. He stops abruptly at the sight of Jacob and Scarlett, leaving the other officers to make for the cart shed.

He climbs from the horse and looks at Scarlett. "Why are you still here?"

Jacob eyes Jamie's uniform, then looks back at his daughter. "I can't be surprised at this, I suppose," he says, his voice strangely empty of emotion. "After all I've done to you."

Scarlett says nothing.

"You'll truly see your own father strung up?"

Her throat is tight. There would be a feeling of satisfaction when the riding officers came, she had been sure. But there is none of that. Just guilt. How dare he make her feel guilty after everything else he has done? She meets his eyes boldly.

"Go," Jamie tells Jacob.

Scarlett whirls around to face him. "What?"

"Quickly. Before the other officers find you."

Scarlett feels her father's eyes on her. She turns her back. And she hears his footsteps disappear out of the gate and thud down the hill. Hears her father run back into memory. She forces away the pain in her throat.

"Is that why you came to Portreath?" Jamie asks after a moment. "To find your father?"

Scarlett's tears spill and she swipes at them angrily. "Why did you let him go? He may have been the one who took your brother."

"You would have come to regret it if he was arrested because of you."

Damn Jamie and his decency. Damn him for shining a light on her failings.

"Don't pretend to know me," she hisses. "Or anything about my father." She feels hot and unsteady as she forces the rage to stay inside. Jamie cannot see the Wild. Not now. Not ever. From the cart shed, she hears the shouts of the revenue men. "Go inside," she tells him sharply. "Go and do your job."

She feels calmer by the time she makes it back to the village. She climbs up Battery Hill, stopping outside Mrs Acton's house. She reaches into her stays and pulls out the coins. What freedom this money would bring her. How much of the world she could see. But there is already far too much of Jacob in her. She does not want his greed too.

She sets the coins on the front step, still wrapped in the embroidered handkerchief. Mrs Acton will know who had taken them, she is sure. But at least she might begin to make amends.

She walks back down the hill. A thin line of dawn is pushing away the dark.

She has nothing now. Her only way back to Talland is to walk. But she would rather have nothing than carry pieces of her father inside her.

TRAVELLERS

Jacob throws open the door of his cottage. He is a violent stench of sweat and animals.

"You were right," he says, his fingers working at the knots binding Asher to the stool. "My daughter will not believe a word that comes from me." He pulls him to his feet. Slides the gun from his pocket. He is flustered. Angry. A mess.

"I cannot just walk up to my son's house and knock on the door. He'll cast me out before I manage a word." He jabs his pistol into Asher's spine and shoves him towards the door. "You will come back to Talland will me. Tell Caroline I wish to see her."

Scarlett's legs are already aching when she returns to Jamie's lodgings. Her eyes are heavy with sleeplessness. She has not yet even walked the hill out of the village. How distant Talland feels.

He opens the door before she knocks. He is still in his uniform shirt and breeches. "Where have you been? I was worried for you. I thought you were angry with me for letting your father go."

She doesn't look at him. "May I please have a little bread?"

He ushers her inside. Takes a loaf from the shelf and wraps it in a cloth. "You told me your father was dead," he says gently. "Why?"

Scarlett stares at her feet. "Because I wanted him to be." She blinks away her tears. "I know it a dreadful thing to say."

Jamie presses the loaf into her hand. "Stay a while. Rest. The coach doesn't leave for a few hours."

"I'm not taking the coach. I…" She draws in her breath. "I don't have my money anymore." She catches his eye for a moment and he nods silently. She is grateful he does not ask questions. She holds the wrapped loaf to her chest. "Thank you. For everything." She turns towards the door before he can respond. She knows if he tries hard enough he could convince her stay. She can't let such a thing happen.

She swallows a little of the bread, then sets out towards the hills. In the morning sun they shine and shimmer. The grass ripples as the wind skims through it. She must keep her wits about her as she walks.

She hears the rhythmic clop of hooves.

"Scarlett," says Jamie, "you can't walk all the way to Talland."

She looks up at him. He is wearing his broadcloth coat and long black riding boots, a scarf knotted at his neck. A bag is strapped to the saddle.

"You own a horse?" she asks throatily.

He smiles. "Yes. I'm a riding officer."

She begins to walk again. "Go home, please."

"Get on the horse."

Scarlett shakes her head. She can think of few worse ideas than taking a revenue man home with her.

"When we get to Talland, I'll turn around and come straight back, I swear it. I just want to see you there safely."

She squeezes her eyes closed. How desperately she wants someone to travel with. Someone to help her negotiate the maze of paths and hills and spirit-riddled streams.

But it cannot be this man.

She shakes her head.

"Why not?"

"Because of what I am. Because of what my family is. Turn us in and you would eat well for a year." As she speaks, she hears her own bitterness, her own doubt. She wants nothing more than to trust him. But the Wild refuses to release her. She puts her head down and quickens her pace. Jamie walks the horse beside her.

"My job is to patrol the coast between Portreath and Saint Ives. What happens in Talland is outside my jurisdiction."

Scarlett thinks of the false bottom in Isaac's lugger. Thinks of the tunnel snaking through the hill beneath the Mariner's Arms. "And I am to trust you not to hand over our secrets to your colleagues on the south coast?"

"Yes," Jamie says firmly. "You are to trust me."

Scarlett lets out her breath. "I want to," she says. "Truly. I want to trust you so badly."

"Well," he says, "the thing is, you can't stop me from riding all the way to Talland beside you. But if I'm to keep on at a walking pace, it will take far longer. So you may as well get on the horse."

Scarlett grits her teeth. Then, finally, she nods, letting Jamie pull her into the saddle. Feels the restlessness inside her begin to still at the warmth of his body pressed against hers.

EVIL SPIRITS

"I'm glad to see you," Reuben tells Flora. "Glad to see you free. You made the right decision."

Flora shifts edgily. Being inside Reuben's mansion makes her uncomfortable at the best of times. "My conscience thinks otherwise."

Reuben takes the pipe from his mouth and gestures to an armchair. "Tom Leach is not worth a guilty conscience, my dear."

Flora remains standing in the middle of Reuben's garish gold-rimmed parlour. She does not remove her cloak or woollen bonnet. "Some time ago you said you would buy my liquor back from me. Does that offer still stand?"

Reuben pulls himself from the chair. "You wish to sell your liquor?"

"What choice do I have? The excisemen know my licence was forged. I've no option but to operate as an alehouse."

He takes a step towards her. "Are you sure you'll not sit? Have a little tea? You're on edge. I can tell."

Flora grits her teeth. She has not slept. After the excisemen had released her, she had gone home and scrubbed herself clean. Set off to Reuben's the moment she was dressed. She wants nothing more than to make the necessary arrangements and be done with it. But being rude to Reuben will not help her cause.

She sits reluctant. Reuben gives a self-satisfied smile and calls for the tea. He sits his pipe in an ash tray.

"The liquor," Flora says stiffly, "will you buy it back or not?"

"Of course. You know I'm a man of my word."

She gives a nod of thanks. "Will you have your men collect it? Five ankers are still unopened."

"The men will be there tonight. Perhaps I might join them. See how the tunnel is progressing."

Flora thinks of Isaac's brandy hidden in a bend of the passage. "There's been little

312

progress," she says hurriedly. "There's nothing to see."

Reuben rubs his chin. "I'm sorry," he says after a moment. "I know the Mariner's Arms is very dear to you. I know you feel running the place as an alehouse will put you at a disadvantage against the inns in Polperro. But I'm sure you'll manage to keep it afloat. You've a passion for the place. And you're putting every penny towards purchasing a legitimate licence, I'm sure."

Reuben's condescension makes her want to shove his pipe in his eye. "Yes, well. Pennies can be few and far between."

He opens his mouth to speak, then pauses, his colourless lips parted. He laces his thick fingers across his middle. When he speaks, his voice has lost a little of its pretentiousness. "I could make a good life for you and your daughter, Mrs Kelly."

Flora's eyebrows shoot upwards. "I'm perfectly capable of providing for my daughter." Her voice comes out sharper than she had intended.

"Thanks to my generosity."

"You wish repayment for your assistance?"

"No," he says hurriedly. "Forgive me. I—"

Flora stands. Eyes the door.

"I didn't help you expecting anything in return," Reuben says hurriedly. "I merely…" He climbs from his chair to look her in the eye. "You and I, we've both lost a great deal." He swallows, shifting his weight between his brass-buckled feet. "I care for you, Flora. Very much. I would like the chance to show you."

The maid brings the tea tray into the room and sets it on the table. It clatters loudly in the silence.

"I'm sorry," Flora says, "Bess and I are happy as we are." A faint stab of remorse twists inside her. She has never seen this fragility in Reuben's eyes before.

He waits for the maid to leave, then steps closer, cupping her elbow. "A woman ought to have a man in her life. For security." She shifts uncomfortably and he removes his hand. "What would you do should the villagers turn on you again as they did recently?"

"I shall manage without you, as I did last time. I'm sorry Mr Reuben, I owe you no explanation."

"Very well." His cheeks are flushed. "You can expect my men this evening to collect the remaining ankers. I'll have payment for you once they are received."

Flora nods faintly. "Thank you."

He clears his throat. "The tea. Will you stay for a cup?"

"I don't think so." She hurries towards the door.

"Isaac Bailey is a married man, Mrs Kelly," Reuben says suddenly.

She feels a blaze in her cheeks. "This has nothing to do with Isaac," she snaps, keeping her back to him. She stops walking. Turns slowly. "The excisemen asked me why I had changed my mind," she says. "Why I decided to save myself by turning Leach in." She had planned not to raise the issue. But Reuben's mention of Isaac has stirred up her anger. "They seemed rather vague when I told them I did not want to be taken to trial in Exeter. They seemed to have little idea what I was speaking of."

Reuben fills a tea cup and brings it slowly to his lips.

"You lied to me," says Flora.

"That is quite an accusation."

She stares him down. "Are you saying I'm mistaken?"

Reuben smiles, but the warmth has disappeared from his eyes. The cup clinks loudly as he sets it back on the saucer. "I'm saying it is unwise to accuse those who clearly have your best interests at heart."

Her encounter with Reuben does not help Flora's sleeplessness. Her body is exhausted after a night shivering in the lockup, but her mind refuses to still.

The kitchen is filled with the sickly scents of apples and nutmeg. A pot of spiced ale bubbles on the range. Flora stirs it, tastes. It is far too sweet and lacking intensity.

Underwhelming.

An hour earlier, Reuben's men had taken the ankers of brandy from her cellar. If the Mariner's Arms is to survive as an alehouse, she'd best make lambswool a damn sight better than this. She tosses in a random handful of ginger.

There is a knock at the door. She stiffens. Visitors make her wary these days. She sets the pot on the table and makes her way downstairs. Peering through the keyhole, she sees the riding officers who had questioned her in Polperro the day after the shootings.

They will be bringing news of Tom Leach, she is sure. That afternoon, the officers had ridden to Polruan to bring in Leach for the murders. In two days' time, she will stand before the magistrate and lie. Send Leach to the scaffold to save herself.

Bessie, she thinks, *she is doing it for Bessie.*

But she knows the truth of it is far more complex. She is doing it for Bessie, yes, but she is also doing it to spare herself the prison cell she deserves.

The riding officers do not tell her of the trial. Instead they tell her of Leach's escape. Tell her of how he had hidden himself in the alleys of Polruan and vanished into the hills. Evaded capture.

"Evaded capture?" Flora repeats.

"Yes. I'm sorry, Mrs Kelly. We're doing everything we can to find him."

"Does he know I was the one who turned him in?"

"No. But I suggest you be watchful nonetheless."

She nods, strangely unaffected by the news. She isn't afraid of Tom Leach, she realises, because he is afraid of her.

When the riding officers are gone, she unwinds the strapping around the gash on her wrist. The cut is pink and raw, but healing well beneath the poultice of ground ivy. It will leave her with a scar, but it will be one that reminds her that she need not be afraid. Leach believes her inn is filled with black magic. Play up such a thing and he will never again venture through the door. Besides, she thinks, he has no way of knowing she was the one who had turned him in. His suspicions will go elsewhere.

Isaac, Flora realises, is the one who needs to be watchful.

She goes to the street, locking the door behind her and cocooning Bessie in the inn.

Candlelight flickers in the window of Isaac's cottage. She feels a strange flush of nerves as she knocks on the door.

Adulterer.

Intruder.

He looks surprised to see her. Despite the late hour, he is still dressed in his breeches and boots. His lips part, as though debating whether to invite her inside. Flora stays planted in the doorway.

"Leach is on the run," she says, before he can speak. "The riding officers went for him this afternoon. He got away."

He frowns. "What? How could they let such a thing happen? After you—"

Flora fixes him with hard eyes.

Don't.

She can't bear to hear the truth of it spoken.

Caroline appears from the bedroom, tugging a shawl around her shoulders. She is barefoot in her nightshift, her hair in a long plait down her back. Flora can't look at her.

"You and Bess ought to stay with us," Isaac tells her. "You're not safe in the inn."

She holds back an incredulous laugh. What is he thinking? "Leach doesn't know it was me who turned him in. He's far more likely to blame you. I came to warn you."

"She's right," says Caroline. "You're the one he'll suspect, Isaac. And it seems he would have had no issue with killing you in Lansallos." A tremor runs through her voice.

She and Caroline fear the same thing, Flora realises. They are both terrified of losing Isaac to Leach's bullet. And these, she thinks, are fears she has no right to have. These fears ought to be Caroline's alone.

Isaac glances between them. He must know, of course, that they share these unspoken thoughts.

Flora tries to catch his eye. She wants reassurance from him. Wants him to tell her that he will be safe and careful and that she need not fear losing him. But these fears, of course, are for Caroline, not her.

Isaac touches his wife's shoulder.

"I've got to go," Flora says hurriedly. "I left Bessie alone. I just thought you ought to know…"

As she is walking back to the inn, she hears him call after her.

She whirls around. "Go back inside. Caroline is no fool. She'll suspect something."

He reaches for her arm. "Please don't go back to the inn," he says breathlessly. "I hate the thought of you and Bess alone in that place."

She keeps striding down the hill. "Bess and I are just fine."

"Leach has come after you before."

"I'm not afraid of Leach."

"How can you say that after what he did to you on the beach?"

"That's exactly why I'm not afraid of him. He believes me a witch. He's too scared to come near me."

"Stay with us," Isaac says again. "You and Bess can take Scarlett's room."

She gives a cold laugh. "You can't be serious."

"Caroline doesn't know a thing. No one does."

Flora exhales sharply. She unlocks the front door. Isaac follows her inside. He grabs her waist and pulls her to him. Their faces are cold from a night on the edge of winter. He kisses her impulsively.

Flora tenses. She wants nothing more than to take him upstairs to that sanctuary at the top of the inn and feel his body against hers. She wants to lie in that thick dark and hear his breath in her ear. Wants to lie in his arms and feel the warmth of him. And then, she thinks, then she would finally sleep.

But she would wake and the rest of the world would come charging back. There would be Caroline and Leach and guilt and *adulterer*.

She turns away. "Stop. I can't. This isn't right, Isaac. I can't walk past your family in the street. I can't look Caroline in the eye. And what if the village were to find out about us? I've already had them turn on me once."

"I'd make sure everyone knew it wasn't your doing."

"It's always the woman's doing," she says bitterly.

Isaac runs his fingers down her cheek. "I can't just walk away and leave you here. Not with Leach on the run."

"I'm not afraid of Leach," she says again.

"You ought to be."

Sudden anger wells up inside her. "No," she says sharply, "you cannot tell me how I am to feel. What I ought to think. You cannot force me into acting the way you wish!"

Isaac frowns. "What are you—"

"Were you in on Reuben's lie?" she demands. "Was it your idea to have him tell me I'd be taken to trial outside of Cornwall?"

He rubs his eyes. "How did you know?"

"Does it matter?"

He begins to pace, hands folded behind his head. "I had to do something! You were going to face incarceration. And for what? To protect Leach against conviction for murders I saw him commit!"

"It was my decision to make, Isaac! How dare you try and manipulate me! And to work with Reuben, of all people!"

"Ayes, I was willing to work with Reuben. Does that not tell you how desperate I was to protect you?"

"I don't need your protection," she hisses.

He shakes his head in frustration. "Why can't you accept help? Even from me?"

"Because I don't want you to look at me with pity. I don't want to be that poor, helpless widow who can't save herself."

"Is that truly how you think I see you?" Isaac exhales sharply. "You're infuriating. You're so damn infuriating. I don't pity you, Flora. You're not the kind of woman who needs pity. The way I feel about you, I—"

"No," she says abruptly. "You can't say it. You can't." He cannot speak of love, then vanish across the ocean with his wife. She lowers her eyes, her heart pounding and her skin hot. "Please," she says throatily. "Just go."

Isaac's breath is hot against her ear. "You want this like I do. I know it."

"Yes. I do. But we cannot have it." She looks down. "Go back to your family. You've plans to make. Plans that are far more important now Leach has escaped."

She wants him on a boat out of Talland as quickly as possible. Wants he and his family gone. Yes, there will be an ache in her chest when she walks past his empty house, but it will be far easier than walking past he and Caroline in the street. "You need to leave," she tells him. "I'm sorry."

His footsteps sigh across the flagstones. The door closes with a creak and thud. Flora feels something sink inside her.

She goes upstairs to her mother's chest and reaches to the bottom for the bundle of cloth. She takes it out carefully and unwraps a globe of dark green glass. The watch ball. She lifts it by its rope hanger and watches it glow in the light of her candle. The ball had hung above the front door when she was a child. Protection against evil spirits.

She carries it downstairs to the bar. The hook on which it had once hung is still there, cobwebbed and rusting above the front door. She hangs it, then steps back to watch it sway in the draughty tavern. There is something calming about seeing it back where it had once been.

Who had taken it down? She does not remember. Her father? Her husband?

Had she removed it herself?

Who had decided the Mariner's Arms no longer needed protecting from evil spirits?

Evil spirits? Perhaps she believes. But she knows Leach will look at such a thing and see black magic swinging on a rope. Knows the sight of such a thing will prevent him from setting foot in her inn.

And the rest of the village? Will they look at her and see the village charmer? Come to her for magic rhymes and potions against the dark?

So be it.

The thought of it begins to dull the ache left by Isaac.

She will be *witch*.

But she will not be *adulterer*.

She runs a finger over the cloudy glass of the watch ball. Goes back to the kitchen to finish the lambswool.

SECRETS

Asher is restless and sick as the coach rattles towards Talland. He doesn't want Caroline to see him like this. His shirt is a patchwork of stains and stenches, his skin discoloured with grime. She is supposed to look at him and see greatness. Not this miserable excuse for a man.

He knows the way it will play out. Caroline's eyes will flare and harden when she sees him, as they had the day he had walked into that cottage behind Scarlett. There will be bitter words and empty threats and she will tell him he has no place in her life.

He had had no place, perhaps, in the miserable grind she had built with Isaac, but Asher is returning with news that will upturn her world. This time he is returning with Jacob Bailey. The wall she has built around her secrets is trembling on its foundations.

Asher had first heard of Henry Avery's haul on a smuggling voyage to Guernsey. Had heard of the riches from Albert Davey, the man Jacob would gun down on the landing beach so he might get his hands to a little of the lost silver.

The moment Davey had spoken of the wealth, the path to Asher's dream life had begun to reveal itself. At last he would have a way of making it to university. A way of becoming a surgeon. Of becoming a great, respected man. At last, he would have a way of becoming better than the rest.

He and Jacob sat together in the tavern and made plans to uncover the haul. Their ideas were underhand and immoral, Asher knew, but immorality was a small price to pay in exchange for greatness.

The plans were kept a secret, of course, from everyone but the woman he loved.

He and Caroline had never spoken of their feelings, but Asher's love burned hot and sure. He wanted to wake every day beside her, ensconced in a lavish curtained bed. But he feared her feelings for him did not burn as brightly. How could he expect otherwise when he filled his days hauling fishing nets and came home smelling of bilge water?

Hearing his plans would change everything. He would tell her of the places his brilliant mind would take him, tell her of the lavish life he had planned. And she would come to love him as he loved her.

He was hot with desire as he climbed the stairs to her room. Tonight, she would see beyond his fishing boots and oiled coat to the man he truly was.

When she opened the door, he slid a hand around her waist and pressed his lips to hers.

She put an arm out, preventing him from entering her room. "If I were to let you in, what would I have to offer my husband?" No anger in her voice. Just challenge.

Asher returned her faint smile. "What does a man have to do to become your husband?"

"Are you asking for my hand?"

His heart pounded. "Do you wish it?"

Caroline tilted her head, her eyes glittering in the lamplight. "I'm yet to be convinced by you."

"Let me inside," said Asher. "There's a secret I wish to share with you."

Caroline gave a short laugh. "Does that line work for you often?"

His eyes hardened. "Trust me. You will want to hear this. This is what will convince you that I am worthy of your hand."

And so she lowered her arm. Let him inside.

They sat on the floor by the hearth with glasses in their hands and legs intertwined. In the flickering light, he told her of Avery's lost wealth. Told her of his crewmate who had produced a piece of silver from his pocket the night their ship was becalmed in the Channel. Told her of his plans to find the haul and the glittering life he would make for them.

He'd marry her then, Asher said. Then and only then, so she might be wed to a respectable surgeon and not a sea-stained pauper.

Instead of the smile Asher had been expecting, Caroline frowned. "You've no idea how to find this silver. You've not a thing to go on but the ravings of an old man. This is a just a child's treasure hunt." Firelight made the brandy in her glass glow the colour of autumn leaves. "I thought you more intelligent than that."

"It's far more than a child's treasure hunt," Asher hissed. "It's real. And we will find it. The old man, Davey, he has no need for it."

"We? Who is *we*? You and I?"

"The man's name is Jacob. We make the Guernsey runs together. He has means to get the information from Davey. He's promised me a share of the fortune if I help him."

"Means? He will threaten the man into telling him?" Her voice was even and controlled. Was she angry? Critical? Intrigued? Asher couldn't tell. He hated that he couldn't read her.

She sat with her back against the foot of the bed, staring into the fire. The dance of the flames accentuated the fine curves of her cheekbones. A ghost of a smile appeared on her lips. Asher knelt over her suddenly.

"I need to find this money," he said fervently. "I need to be far more than a lowly fisherman. I need to learn. To study. I'm destined for so much more than this, Callie. I've always known it. You know it too. You'd not be here otherwise." He pushed a dark strand of hair behind her ear. "I've never had a way to get there before. But now I do. I'm going to make a great life for myself. For us. You'll want for nothing."

Caroline smiled faintly. Asher had known he would have to work hard to make her see their future. But she had caught a faint glimpse of it. He could tell by the shine in her eyes.

"A fine house in London," he said, seizing the momentum. "A lady's maid of your own. Roast lamb for supper. Silk skirts and lace bonnets."

She raised her neat eyebrows. "These are quite some promises. I'm not entirely sure you can deliver."

Asher dove forward and kissed her. Tasted brandy on her tongue. "I can deliver," he said, full of certainty. "You'll have all those things. And everything else you desire. We'll have the life we have always wanted."

The carriage reaches Polperro.

Asher and Jacob begin the walk towards Talland; a silent march across the cliffs in which time falls away. Jacob makes for the landing beach. A cold irony, Asher thinks, for the man to lead him to this place.

Jacob presses his back against the jagged shards of rock on the edge of the beach. Asher remembers hiding in the same place, the night he had been wrecked. He can still see the dark bones of his ship beneath the surface.

Jacob's eyes are glassy. He has not been here for sixteen years. What is he thinking? Is he seeing his children build castles on the sand? Or watching Albert Davey's blood stain the thin thread of the river?

"Bring her here." His voice is thin, but dark with theat.

Asher nods. Begins to walk towards the cottage.

What is he doing, taking Caroline to this man? Can he truly trust him not to put a bullet in her chest? Not to put a bullet in his own chest?

He could run now. Run back over the cliffs towards Polperro and turn the Baileys in for smuggling. But do that and he will lose Caroline forever. His only chance of being with her is to take her to Jacob. Convince her to escape the past by rebuilding her life with him. Building that life they had dreamed of as they'd sat drinking brandy by the fire so many years ago.

He knocks on her door. His heart is speeding. He watches a look of horror fall over her face as she answers. She takes in the stains on his clothing, the bruises he can feel swelling at his cheekbones.

"What do you want?" she hisses. A stained apron is knotted around her waist, the skirts beneath it a misery of grey and white patching. She looks past Asher into the street. "Where's Scarlett?"

"I've no idea."

"She's not with you?"

"No. But—"

"Get away from my house." The door swings towards him.

"Caroline—" He puts a hand out, stopping the door from closing. "You need to come with me."

He sees a flicker of pity in her eyes which stings more than her anger. "What happened to you?"

He reaches for her arm, the tightness of his grip preventing her from pulling away. "Callie, listen to me." He looks into her eyes, trying to find that shrewd girl of seventeen. He sees only ice. "You need to come. Jacob is in Talland."

THE LIFE WE HAVE ALWAYS WANTED

The life we have always wanted, he said. Over and over; *the life we have always wanted*. Caroline had no idea what the life she had always wanted looked like. She had never allowed herself to dream.

She had not known her mother. Her father was dead before her fifteenth birthday. But Caroline considered herself luckier than so many of her fellow Londoners. She had a good job as a lady's maid, food on her table and a roof over her head. Alone, yes, but what did *alone* matter, as long as she was alive?

Her mistress, a bent and withered woman of seventy, had a weakness in her heart. *The sea air*, her doctor said. And so it was. The household would move to Cornwall, where the sea worked its way into everything.

To Caroline, the west country was so distant it may as well have been another land. But what was keeping her in London beyond her parents' graves? Cornwall was a distant land, but it was one with work. Security. Perhaps a future.

When the old woman died before a year was through, Caroline found the place had worked its way beneath her skin. She took a job as a wealthy couple's daily and found a room above the Three Pilchards. A room on the other side of the corridor from Matthew Fielding, the man who would come to call himself Asher Hales.

It was curiosity that drew her towards him. He was a fisherman—she had seen him return with the fleet many times—but he walked with his shoulders back and his chin lifted, as though he were a man of status. He drank red wine instead of mahogany. Spoke of medical advancements and the merits of slavery, refusing to acknowledge the superstitious garble coming from the local men around him.

He told her of foreign silver hauled from a recent pirate raid. She would have assumed it a myth had it come from anyone else. And he began to convince her that the life she had always wanted was a life of luxury at his side, paid for with stolen riches.

She had never known love. She supposed this was it. Matthew Fielding made her mind travel to new places and her body heat. Yes, love.

The soldiers came to the Three Pilchards early in the morning. A murder on the beach in Talland, they said. A dragoon had been assaulted. A young man in custody.

Her young man.

She couldn't bring herself to sit through his trial. Didn't know why. Was she too distraught? Perhaps. Or perhaps she wanted to distance herself from the whole affair.

The man she told herself she loved had sliced open the arm of a British soldier as he was hauled away from Albert Davey's dying body. Of the assault, he had little choice but to plead guilty. But he took no responsibility for Davey's murder.

Caroline was unsure whether to believe him. She knew Albert Davey held the secrets of Henry Avery's lost wealth. She knew there was every chance the jury would find Mathew Fielding guilty of murder. And if that happened, she did not want the crowd to look across the courtroom at her and see the woman who had talked herself into loving a killer.

She sat outside the courthouse and listened as the verdict spilled out of gossiping mouths.

Innocent of murder.

Guilty of assault.

Matthew Fielding would be spared the hangman but would spend the next decade a prisoner.

Caroline felt nothing.

The news came that he had been purchased by a land owner in the colonies. He would be shipped off to New England to serve his sentence as an indentured servant. A season's journey away.

The day before he was due to leave, she ventured to the prison at Launceston Castle. She walked the stone steps down to the jail, her skirts in her fist and her heart drumming. The stench of sweat and waste rose up to meet her, tightening her throat and turning her stomach. Her shoes clicked loudly against stone, announcing her arrival. She tried to tiptoe. Already, she regretted coming.

Five pairs of eyes turned to look at her as she approached the cell. Men mumbled, called, cursed. Matthew hissed at them to be silent. He stepped up to the bars. His hair hung loose on his shoulders, his chin patchy with the beginnings of a beard. Behind his eyes, she saw a new intensity. The darkness of them made her wary.

Caroline looked down. She knew that after she left the castle, she would never see him again. For the best, yes, she knew, but she did not want this wild-eyed creature to be the way she remembered him. Perhaps what she felt for him had not been love, but it had been as close as she had ever known.

He reached through the bars and lifted her chin, forcing her to look at him. "This is Jacob's doing," he hissed. "All of it."

Caroline thought to argue. Matthew Fielding had been convicted of assault. Surely no one's fault but his own. She said nothing. If he needed to blame another, let him.

"Jacob needs to be punished. I need you to make sure there's some sense of justice in this miserable world." His eyes glowed. Caroline could tell he had spent his days in the castle planning, plotting.

She knew him well. Knew he would do all he could do avoid conflict, but would plan and manipulate from dark corners. Spread trouble anonymously.

"Jacob has ruined my life," he said. "We need to ruin his."

He told her of his plan, detailed and precise. A plan she would carry out while he was tossed about by the sea and carried to another world.

No, she thought to say. *I'll not be a part of this. I'll not be a part of your revenge.*

But there was something about this man; something about the unsteady blaze in his eyes, the way he still held his chin high, even though he was dressed in rags. Something that made Caroline listen to every word of his plan, even though she knew she was being manipulated.

He looked her in the eye and said: "I know you'll do this for me. I'm all you have in the world."

Some logical part of her knew this was not true. Take Matthew Fielding out of her life and she was left with friends, work, home and a far simpler existence. But with his prison-hardened eyes on hers, she saw only loneliness. She saw empty nights alone in her room, countless hours of scrubbing dishes as she tried to scratch together a living. Saw a loveless life of spinsterhood now the man who wanted to marry her was to be shipped across the world.

"Yes," she said. "You are all I have in the world."

"We are to be torn apart by this man. Do you not want to see him punished?"

Caroline said: "Of course."

First, she was to seek out a man from Jacob's smuggling crew. A man who showed his captain no loyalty. An easy thing to find, Matthew had assured her. Jacob had near killed his crew two years earlier, overloading their ship on account of his greed and rolling it in the middle of the Channel.

"Edward Baker," Matthew said. "He has a wife and son in Talland. They say Edward fought with Jacob about overloading the ship. Edward told him it was dangerous, but Jacob pulled rank. Took the ship out anyway and near killed all his men. Edward's had a hatred for his captain ever since."

Caroline asked after Baker the next night at the tavern. The fishing boats had returned from sea and the inn overflowed.

"I hear you want rid of your captain." She had dressed in her best yellow skirts and pinned flowers in her hair in place of a cap. Ordered wine instead of her usual mahogany. She wasn't sure why. Was she trying to seem less of a troublemaker?

Edward Baker looked her up and down. "You're right," he said finally, curiously. "I don't trust my captain an inch. We'll all end up dead if we're to keep sailing with him." He shoved a pipe between his teeth. "How do you know these things? Who are you?"

Caroline was afraid the man might turn away when she mentioned Matthew Fielding's name, but he just grunted and blew a line of smoke at her. "I'm listening, girl," he said. "Whatever you got to say, I'm listening."

She tossed back a mouthful of wine to steel herself. "You want Jacob out of Talland.

Out of your lives."

"Ayes. The man's a murderer. No doubt in my mind who killed poor Mr Davey. And I nearly died on account of Jacob's greed."

"I want him gone too. He ruined the life of the man I love."

There was a crooked smile in the corner of Edward's mouth. Caroline could tell he was yet to take her seriously.

"And how exactly do you plan to be rid of him?" he asked, a flicker of humour in his voice.

"He has a family."

"Ayes. A wife. Young daughter."

"And he would put their safety and happiness before his own?"

Edward lowered his pipe. "What are you suggesting?"

Caroline's hand tensed around the stem of her glass. It was not just about avenging Matthew anymore. It was about showing Edward Baker she was serious. Proving she was more than just talk. "Where can I find Jacob's wife?"

Edward tapped a finger against his bristly chin, considering her. Finally, he said: "The pilchard palace. Meet me by the harbour tomorrow afternoon and I'll show you who she is."

Jacob's wife was a slightly built woman who Caroline guessed could be no older than forty. Her striped blue skirts were faded beneath a grimy apron, a bulk of black hair knotted at her neck. She walked along the harbour with one of the other women, fish baskets clamped to their hips and their free hands flying in animated conversation. Jacob's wife tossed back her head and laughed, her dark eyes alight and warm.

Caroline watched from the other side of the harbour. Her stomach turned over. She wouldn't hurt the woman, she reminded herself. Not as long as Jacob did as he was told.

"She works here every day," said Edward. "In the afternoon, she collects her daughter from the charity school and they walk the cliff path back to Talland."

Caroline swallowed. "How old is the daughter?"

"A little one. Four, perhaps five."

She squeezed her eyes closed.

"Wait a while and she'll go for her. You'll see her."

"I don't need to see the girl," Caroline said hurriedly. She turned away, unable to watch Jacob's wife any longer. "The rest of the crew," she said, trying to force confidence into her words, "can we expect their loyalty? Or will they support Jacob?"

"I don't know," Edward admitted. "But it don't matter. Best we keep this whole business to ourselves in case there are men in the crew still loyal to their captain. Jacob don't need to know it's only the two of us involved. We'll tell him we have the rest of the men on side. He'll have no way of knowing us lying."

The following night, they went to the Three Pilchards for Jacob. Edward nodded towards a man sitting alone at the bar. He wore a blue knitted cap and dirty hide coat, his hands wrapped around a tankard. Caroline watched him from the doorway.

What had she been expecting? A burly, tattooed monster with black eyes and sharp teeth? This was just a man.

She imagined him on the beach with a pistol in his hand. Imagined him pressing his crewmate for information on the lost silver. Imagined him pulling the trigger and leaving Matthew alone on the beach with the bleeding body at his feet.

Good. Now this was easier.

Caroline slid onto the stool beside him, Edward hovering at her shoulder.

Jacob peered at her. A shag of grey streaked hair hung over one eye. "Who are you?"

"I'm the woman who loves Matthew Fielding."

He shifted uncomfortably, then managed a faint smile. "You're better off without him, maid."

"You've destroyed his life," she said. "And mine."

Jacob snorted into his ale. "The man was convicted of assault. How is such a thing my doing?"

Caroline narrowed her eyes. The man's dismissiveness made her neck prickle with anger. The harder she looked at him, the easier it was to imagine him with a murder weapon in his hand. For the first time since she had left Matthew in the castle, she began to believe she was doing the right thing.

"Go home, girl," said Jacob. "Get yourself a good night's sleep and you'll soon forget the bastard."

Anger flared inside her. She slid from her stool and stood close. "You destroyed our lives," she hissed. "And so we will destroy yours."

He chuckled. "You will, ayes? How will you do that?"

There again; that doubt. That flippant look in a man's eyes that said she was nothing but a triviality. "Your wife and daughter walk the cliff path back to Talland each afternoon," she said icily. "They make themselves easy targets up there in the open."

Jacob's eyes flashed. Something in them sent a shiver through her. Yes, she thought, Matthew was right. This man needed to be punished. And she had his attention.

"You will leave this place," she told him. "Tonight. You will be alone, just as Matthew Fielding is. And if you don't, we'll be waiting for your family the next time they try and cross the cliffs."

Jacob snorted. "You think I'd leave my wife and child on the empty threats of some jilted girl?" She heard the waver of uncertainty in his voice. Was buoyed by it.

"You think these empty threats? You took the man I love away from me."

"Matthew Fielding committed his own crimes. I had nothing to do with it."

"You left him on the beach with the man you killed!"

Jacob sucked in his breath at her raised voice. He glanced hurriedly around the noisy tavern. Caroline didn't take her eyes from his.

Jacob slid from his stool and stood close to her. He stank of sweat and sea. "Go near my wife and daughter and I will kill you."

"Kill her," said Edward, "and your crew won't let you live."

Jacob looked at him for the first time. Colour was rising in his cheeks. Caroline saw his fist clench around his tankard. "Ten years as your captain and this is what I get in return?"

"Do you truly expect loyalty? You near killed us all when you lost Reuben's cutter. And now our crewmate turns up murdered on the beach?"

"I didn't kill that man," Jacob hissed.

"We're not fools," Edward said blackly. "If you were willing to kill Davey, how do we know you'd not do the same to us? You'll leave. And you'll not come back. Leave our lives. Leave the syndicate. And if you even think of returning, know your crew will be watching for you. Watching for your wife and daughter when they make their way back along those cliffs."

Jacob clenched his jaw until it shook. "You're lying."

"Can you be sure of that?"

Jacob lurched suddenly at Edward. The two men clattered into the table, the tankard of ale splattering over the floor. Caroline stumbled backwards, pulling a knife from her pocket. She held it close to Jacob's chest. The feel of it in her hand made sickness rise in her throat. But the thing was almost done. She could not let him see her uncertainty now. Her fist tightened around the handle. "You know what you need to do."

Jacob gripped the edge of the table. His breath was hard and fast. "Let me see them one last time," he said finally. "Let me leave in the morning."

The ache in his voice made Caroline look away. She wanted suddenly to tell him to stay. Tell him it was all a mistake. She had not loved Matthew Fielding enough for this. But things had gone too far.

"You'll leave in the morning," she said.

"What are you doing?" Edward hissed at her. "He bloody well leaves tonight."

Caroline couldn't look at him. "You'll leave in the morning," she told Jacob again. "You'll see your family one last time."

"We'll be watching your house," said Edward. "Making sure you and your family don't try and escape in the night. In the morning you'll take the dory out. Let them believe you drowned."

The next night, Caroline sat in her room and penned the letter.

Jacob is no longer in Talland…

She wrote slowly, carefully. The writing came out looking like someone else's. Good. She didn't want to be this person. This bitter, lovelorn woman who mourned manipulative men and destroyed lives. Perhaps Jacob had been right about Matthew Fielding. With him gone, she felt none of the loneliness he had predicted. Just a dull sense of relief. Perhaps he was a man who could be forgotten. Perhaps the flickering thing Caroline had uninformedly called love could be left in the past.

She leant close to the page as the candle hissed and spat.

He left this place in his fishing boat, the village believing him drowned.

Matthew would want to know everything, of course. He would want to know of the way they had hunted down Jacob's wife at the pilchard palace and how Caroline had pulled a knife from her pocket to end it all. But she had no desire to spell out the details. Had no desire to go back there, to put to paper a record of the things she had done. And so, the briefest of letters. The bare facts.

Jacob gone. Punished.

She left the letter unsigned, unable to see her name scrawled at the bottom of such atrocities. She sent it to Matthew's uncle in Bristol, as he had instructed. He would send for it, he'd told her, the moment he returned to England.

A strange thing, Caroline thought, sending the letter away, knowing it would not be read for a decade or more. By then, this whole sorry business would be a distant memory. If Matthew wanted to hunt down that phantom treasure, let him. But she would not let it consume her the way it had consumed him.

The life she had always wanted was hazy. She only knew it wasn't this.

"You're lying," Caroline tells Asher. "Jacob wouldn't dare come back." She hears the thinness of her voice, the desperation in her words. She has always been terrified that he might one day return.

"I'm not lying," says Asher.

She shoves hard against his chest, knocking him into the doorframe. "You went looking for him," she hisses. "You went looking for him because you still believe in that fairy tale of a treasure hunt."

He reaches a grimy hand towards her shoulder. His face is discoloured with bruising, his lip split and swollen. Does he truly mean to comfort her? She pushes his hand away. "I hoped your time in New England would be enough for you to forget all this."

"And forget you?"

"Yes." She doesn't look at him. "And forget me."

"I was not the one who went looking. It was Scarlett. I was an unwilling participant in the whole mess."

"You told Scarlett Jacob is alive?" Her legs feel suddenly weak beneath her. Her world is on the verge of toppling. "Does my husband know?"

"No," Asher says tautly. "Your husband doesn't know. But Jacob is quite desperate to speak with you. I suggest you come with me before he decides he would rather have words with his son."

Caroline goes to the cradle. Mary is clucking and kicking, her smock tangled at her waist. Her eyes light when she sees her mother. Caroline feels a sudden pain in her chest. There is so much Jacob could take from her. She feels trapped in the worst of her dreams.

She scoops Mary from the crib and places her in her basket. She follows Asher out of the cottage. The day is dark, threatening rain. Wind bends the trees and whips the sea into white peaks. Their footsteps crunch rhythmically. Where is he taking her?

"You call yourself a wise man," she tells him bitterly. "And yet you're still chasing this myth."

"You believed," Asher reminds her.

"I was a fool. And barely more than a child. You're a sad, resentful man who has hung his desperate dreams on a fairy tale."

"Can you not see the same resentment in yourself?"

The truth of it makes something tighten in Caroline's chest.

"Not that I blame you, given the life Isaac Bailey has provided you with."

She laughs humourlessly. "You think the resentment in me is Isaac's doing? No. This is guilt. This is the pressure of hiding the truth of what we did from my family." Her voice catches as a sudden rush of tears tightens her throat. She forces them away. "None of this is Isaac's fault. I love him."

Asher looks over his shoulder and gives her a faint, infuriating smile. His battered lip is fat and purple. "I'm sure you did, once. What else would have led you to do such a foolish thing as marrying Jacob's son?"

She feels him trying to catch her eye. Doesn't let him. Revulsion swells inside her. How could she have done the things she had done out of love for this man? The revulsion twists into self-hatred.

"Did you know it at the time, Caroline? Did you know who you were marrying? Did you know who his father was?"

"Of course not," she hisses. "I didn't even know Jacob had a son."

Isaac Bailey was everything Matthew Fielding was not. Isaac was honest, upfront. He had told her of his debt to Reuben the day they had met. A brutal thing, of course, but somehow, the fact that he had been so open about it had made it easier to carry.

The day she'd met Isaac in the Ship Inn, he'd been standing at the bar in his fishing boots, his hair windswept and his skin smelling of the sea. He was living the simple fisherman's life Matthew Fielding had been so desperate to escape. But a simple fisherman's life, Caroline had realised as they sat together in the inn, their knees edging closer to each other's, was all she needed. The day she met Isaac, the need for silk and satin Matthew had planted within her had fallen away.

Matthew Fielding's proposal at her bedroom door had been desperate and needy, full of plots and plans and empty promises. When Isaac had asked for her hand, there had been no talk of wealth, or luxury. But nor had she had any doubts. The joy of it was enough to push Matthew to the back of her mind and take Jacob with him. She was sure she would never see either of them again.

Her new husband rarely spoke of his father. There had been little love between them, Caroline could tell.

The father, the man responsible for the smuggling runs and the strain. A nameless, long dead man she knew no more of. Cared to know no more of. Isaac's father had piled them with debt. His memory had little place in their lives.

It had been no great revelation. No plate-smashing, gasping realisation on Caroline's part. In casual supper-time conversation, the father had been named—*Jacob*.

She sat at the table, letting the pieces float their way together.

Jacob who had died at sea.

Gone without a trace.

Her breathing quickened as she looked across the table at Scarlett.

Jacob with the young daughter.

Caroline excused herself and rushed to the bedroom. She lay on top of the bedclothes, her head swimming and her skin hot.

She thought of running. But Isaac's child was stirring inside her. And he had also stirred within her a love far deeper than the miserable flicker she had felt for Matthew Fielding. Life as Isaac's wife had brought her far more joy than the games she'd played chasing chests of buried silver.

She closed her eyes and tried to breathe. Edward Baker had died less than a year after they had sent Jacob away. No one else in the village knew what they had done. She could bury the past. Forget. Make it as though it had never happened. Never think of it and never think of it and never think of it until it was over and forgotten and gone.

Isaac came to the bedroom. Found her on her back, staring at the ceiling. He leant over her. Touched her forehead, her cheek, the swell of her stomach.

She caught the laces of his shirt and tugged him into a kiss. She would bury her secrets deep. Push that dark shadow of her past away.

For years she has tried to forget. Tried to believe what Isaac and Scarlett believe; that Jacob is dead and gone. She had convinced herself it was a likely possibility; an old man with no money, no family. It was likely that death would find him.

But there he stands, motionless on the landing beach, looking out across the sea he had disappeared on. Death has not found him.

Why has he dared return? He has seen through her empty threats, no doubt. But why now?

She realises then that he knows. Asher has told him the woman who had forced him to abandon his family is married to his son. She swallows, forcing away a violent wall of sickness.

She takes slow, careful steps towards him. Sets the baby's basket at her feet. Asher has disappeared. She is not surprised.

Coward.

She looks up at Jacob. She has never forgotten his face. And yet she had seen not a flicker of him in Isaac when she had met him in the Ship Inn. The resemblance is there, of course. It is there if you know to look. And never before has she known to look.

At the sight of Jacob, she is the pliable seventeen-year-old she had been the last time she had seen him, a wine glass in her fist to give her courage. She lifts Mary to her chest, needing her daughter's closeness. Her little hand is soft against her neck.

"Put her in the basket," Jacob says stiffly. "I can't look at her."

Caroline finds her voice. "She's your granddaughter."

"She's a reminder of my son's mistakes."

Caroline keeps the baby tight against her chest.

"Put her in the basket." Something in Jacob's voice chills her. She lays the baby in the carrier. Mary screeches in protest.

Jacob bends slowly, looming over the basket. He lowers his head until it is close to Mary's tear-stained face.

Caroline's heart thuds. "Get away from her."

Jacob tilts his head. "Do you think I will hurt her? Do you think I have it in me?"

"I don't know."

Mary shrieks louder and beats her fists into the air.

"I know you want to punish me," says Caroline. "But please don't hurt my child. I'm begging you."

Jacob gives a short laugh. "You've a nerve asking such a thing, after all you've done to my family."

"I would never have hurt Scarlett, I swear it."

Mary's tears stop momentarily as he presses a grimy finger to her chin. Her dark eyes widen.

"Asher Hales is just a sad, lonely man. But you have so much to lose. You're a fool to have stayed in this place."

"Please." Caroline's voice wavers. "Think of Isaac. She's his daughter."

Jacob stands. He is close; too close. Hot breath on her skin. His face is lined and weathered beneath the grey mess of his beard. "I often wondered if you were telling the truth," he says. "Whether you truly had my entire crew ready to kill for you if I dared come back. I could never have risked such a thing, of course. But I always dreamed of returning. Let the years pass and my crew forget. Or die. And then I would come back for Scarlett and Isaac. Free them from Charles Reuben." He watches the sea rise and fall. The ribs of the shipwreck poke between the dark peaks of water. "I was sure you'd no longer be here. And even if you were, I knew there'd be no one looking out for someone like you. I could put a bullet in your chest and there would be no one to stop me." He gives a short, humourless laugh. "And yet it seems the man looking out for you is my own son."

His words sound distant. Caroline hears her heart racing in her ears. Surely she is to die here on the landing beach in the shadow of Albert Davey. Jacob has dreamt of killing her for sixteen years and he will do it here, now, in front of her daughter. And then? And then he will go to Isaac and tell him everything. He will tell him the real reason he left his family and she will be dead and gone. She will have no way of ever telling her husband how deeply, desperately sorry she is.

She waits for the gun to appear.

Jacob stares her down. There is no gun.

Finally, she dares to ask: "What are you going to do to me?"

A crooked smile appears in the corner of his lips. She can see how much he is enjoying this game; toying with her while her baby wails at her feet. He reaches into his coat and Caroline stops breathing. But Jacob's hands stay in his pockets, as though he has a secret hidden in his fist.

He says: "I'm going to tell you where Henry Avery hid his haul."

HILLS OF SILVER

"Do you think me a fool?" Caroline says shakily. "You expect me to believe this? If the haul is where you say it is, why did you not claim it?"

"Do you really need to ask that?" Jacob tells her. "How could I have risked returning to Talland to uncover it? How could I have risked you and Edward Baker killing my wife and daughter?"

Hearing him speak the words is brutal. A reminder that, no matter how hard she has tried to forget, the past cannot be changed.

She is not a killer. Just the feel of that knife in her hand had made her skin prickle with sweat. She would never have raised a finger against Scarlett or her mother. But of course, Jacob had not known this. He had had no room for risk.

Caroline thinks of him bending over Mary's basket, his dirty finger pressed to her chin. No room for risk.

She wraps her arms around herself as icy wind tunnels in from the sea. "Why tell me this? Why me of all people?"

"I know when I left, my debts to Reuben were passed on to my son." Jacob laughs humourlessly. "What a difficult thing that must be for you."

The muscles in her shoulders tighten. She feels hot and sick. "So you'll tell me where the haul is hidden so we can pay off Reuben's debt?"

Jacob snorts. "No. I'm telling you where it is because I know there's a desperation in you to make your life better. That was what drew you to Matthew Fielding, ayes? Didn't he promise you a better life once he found that money? A life of wealth and luxury?"

Caroline stares at the colourless sand. She can't look at Jacob. Can't look at Mary, thrashing in the basket, begging to be held.

"I'm giving you a way to have that life you longed for." He takes a step towards her. Caroline shuffles backwards uncomfortably. "And yet what will happen if you go to your husband with an armful of foreign silver? He will ask questions. He will want to know how you found it. And you will be forced to admit to him what you did. Wife or no, do you really think Isaac will allow you to remain under his roof knowing all this?"

She lets out her breath. "And what of my children? Would you have them grow up motherless or would you have me take them from their father?"

"That is your decision." He glances down at Mary. "Truly, I care little what happens to those children."

Caroline plucks the baby from the basket and holds her tight against her chest. She smooths her hair until her tears begin to ease. "You are heartless," she tells Jacob, peering at him over the top of Mary's head.

"Do you truly expect otherwise after all you've put me through?"

"And do you truly expect me to believe this business about Avery's haul is not a trap?"

"It's not a trap. I want you out of my son's life. Away from my family. I'm offering you priceless information. Take the money. Have that comfortable life you've been denied."

"Without my husband."

"You've a marriage built on lies."

Caroline feels the ache of it in her chest. "So you will turn down your chance at that money for the good of your family."

"My need for that money has only ever been for the good of my family. I used to think what they needed most was for me to pay off my debts to Reuben. But it is far more pressing to get you away from Isaac."

"I love Isaac," she hisses. "And he loves me." But beneath her words, she feels a tug of doubt. "Why do this?" she asks. "Why not just kill me?"

Jacob folds his arms. "Because against his better judgement, my son chose to make you his wife. If I were to kill you, I would lose any chance of him ever allowing me back into his life." He sighs. "I know he'd not believe it if I simply told him what you did. He'll not believe a word that comes from me. Nor will my daughter. She thinks I abandoned her."

Caroline feels him trying to catch her eye.

"I know what you're thinking. You'll make up a lie about how you found the money." His voice drops. "It won't work. It will not be easy to get to. No one will ever believe you just stumbled upon it. Only a person who knows where to look would have any chance of finding it." He leans close. "A person who has been told a secret."

Caroline looks away uncomfortably. She knows he is right. "I don't want that money," she coughs. "I don't need it."

She thinks of Isaac's ankers hidden in the tunnel. Thinks of Leach's escape.

It is not safe for her family in Talland. Can Jacob tell *I don't need the money* is the biggest of lies?

They will find another way out. Isaac is on the road right now finding new buyers. She will not follow Jacob's directions towards what can be nothing but trouble.

She lays Mary back in the basket. "I'm sorry," she says, her voice thin. "I'm so sorry for everything. I would take it back if I could." She draws in her breath and meets his eyes. "But I will not do what you're asking. I cannot leave my family."

He grabs her shoulders and slams her hard against the rock. A cry of fear escapes her as pain jolts down her spine.

Jacob holds her against the cliff. "You'll do as I wish," he hisses. "You have too much to lose to disobey me." He shoots a glance at Mary.

"No," Caroline says shakily. "You're doing this for Isaac. You wouldn't hurt his child." She shakes her head. *You wouldn't, you wouldn't.*

"Can you be sure of that?"

She pulls her eyes from his.

"No. You can't. Just as I couldn't be sure you didn't have my entire crew on hand, ready to hunt down Scarlett." He keeps a firm hand against her shoulder, the rock cold and hard against her spine.

"This is how it feels," he hisses, the threads of his beard tickling her cheek. "This is what it's like to have no choice but to leave."

Caroline lets herself into the cottage. She lowers Mary's basket to the floor and her legs give way beneath her. A sudden, violent sob wells up inside her and echoes around the still house.

No choice but to leave.

Jacob had left the beach without saying more. Does he truly mean to come for Mary? If she stays in Talland, how long will it be before he breaks down the door and spills all her secrets? The uncertainty of it is terrifying.

Caroline looks over at the baby. She has fallen asleep in the basket, her chest rising and falling beneath the blanket. Her tiny lips are parted, long lashes dark against her pale skin. Caroline squeezes her eyes closed. It hurts too much to look at her.

She hears footsteps outside the house. She scrambles to her feet as Asher passes the window. There are few people she wants to see less, but he knows far too much about her past to let him slide off into the village.

She wipes her eyes hurriedly. Lets him inside before he knocks. "Where is Jacob?"

"I talked him out of asking for a room at the Mariner's Arms. Told him it was best he keep his distance. He's gone to Polperro to find a room at the Ship."

Caroline swallows heavily. The Ship Inn is a tavern populated by the fishing fleet. Would Isaac recognise his father if he stumbled across him in a crowded room?

She presses a hand to her mouth to stop another sob escaping.

Asher touches her shoulder. "Oh, Callie."

She shoves him away. "The smell of you turns my stomach. As does the sight of you."

Something passes across his eyes. "You know," he says after a moment.

She flinches. "Know what?"

"Have we not had enough of games?" He lifts his chin. "Jacob knows where Avery's haul is. And so do you."

"Avery's haul is a myth. That's all I know of it."

Asher smiles slightly. "You've always been a terrible liar. But a fine keeper of secrets."

She looks away.

His fingers slide around her elbow. "Jacob told me you know. Tell me where it is. We can have that life we dreamed of."

Caroline exhales sharply. "Do you honestly think that's what I want? I've made a life!

One without you in it."

He waves an arm around the cottage, with its rickety table and threadbare curtains, the smoke-stained bricks above the fireplace. "This sorry life? This is what you have made? I could give you so much more than this."

She feels a sudden urge to strike him. "You cannot give me anything! You have nothing." She stands close to his beaten, discoloured face. "You are nothing."

She sees the faint quiver of his jaw. This is the way to break him down, she knows. Chip away at his fragile sense of self-worth.

"That is not true," he hisses. "You know it's not. I've a life of greatness ahead of me. I'll be a fine surgeon one day." And she is that foolish girl with brandy in her hand, leaning close to hear him blather about vast, unreachable dreams. Listening to him plan out the details of the life she had always wanted.

"No," she spits. "No you won't. You'll never be anything more than the filthy, desperate fool you are now." She turns away, unable to look at him. The sight of Asher Hales reminds her of all the worst parts of herself.

He grabs her arm, yanking her towards him. His eyes are flashing. "Where is the money?"

Caroline lets out her breath. "Jacob told you I know where the haul is because he wants us to destroy each other. Can't you see that? He didn't need to tell me. Threatening my daughter would have been enough. But he wants this. He wants you and I tearing each other apart over money we will never get our hands to."

"Why will we not get our hands to it?" he demands. "Where is it?"

Caroline hesitates. If she tells him what she knows, will he take the money and leave without her? She can't be sure. Perhaps it's worth the risk.

She opens her mouth to speak, but something stops her. That money will get her family away from Reuben. Away from Tom Leach. It will bring them safety, security, a life without debt. If there is even a scrap of a chance she can get her hands to it without Isaac asking questions, she needs to try.

Asher digs his fingers into her bare forearm. "You know how long I've dreamt of finding that wealth," he hisses. "You know what it means to me."

"You think it will make you a good man. A worthy man. But you and I, we'll never be good or worthy. Look at what we did to Jacob's family."

"Jacob deserved all he got."

"Perhaps. But what about Isaac and Scarlett? What about their mother? Did they deserve it?"

"Love has made you soft," Asher says bitterly.

Caroline pulls her arm away. "Leave." She stares at the floor. In the basket beside her feet, Mary sighs in her sleep.

Caroline hears Asher breathe close to her ear. "I know everything about the Talland smuggling ring," he says finally. "And I will go to Customs House and tell them all of it. See Isaac and Scarlett in the hands of the authorities."

Caroline swallows heavily. Forces herself not to react.

"Or you will tell me where the haul is. And you will leave this place with me once we find it."

No. She will not let him trap her. Will not let him win. This man is smart. A plotter. Manipulator. But she can match him.

"Leave with you?" she repeats, her voice controlled and even. "Is that truly what you want?"

He presses grimy fingers to her cheek. Lifts a loose piece of hair from her face and tucks it behind her ear.

Chin lifted. Shoulders back.

Look at him, she thinks, bruised and bloodied, grappling at the shadow of the man he longs to be. The entire time she has known him, he has been lost in a dream.

When I become the man I am destined to be…

Their life would begin then.

You'll love me when I become the man I am destined to be.

Sixteen years later, he is still clinging to the same beliefs. She can see it in the desperate shine of his eyes. He will find the haul. He will become that great surgeon. And she will come to see he is a better man than her husband. She will see he is the man she ought to have chosen. The man she ought to love.

She sits at the table and clasps her hands. "I need time."

"How much time do you think you have? Jacob has been waiting to punish you for the past sixteen years."

Caroline swallows a wave of sickness. "I will bring the money to you tomorrow night," she says. "And we will leave."

His fingers run over the bare skin on the back of her neck. "Where is it hidden?"

She flinches. "You don't need to know. But I will have it for you."

"Tonight," he says.

"No. It's not enough time."

His voice hardens. "Tonight, or I tell customs of the smuggling tunnel. Of the false bottom on your husband's ship."

Caroline sucks in her breath. "I'll not go without my children."

"Very well. Bring them. Meet me at the Ship Inn. We will leave at midnight."

"No." Her memories of the Ship are of Isaac at the bar in his fishing boots. She will not have them tainted by Asher Hales. "I'll meet you at the harbour."

THE MAN WITH THE LOST DREAMS

The stream of customers into the Mariner's Arms is steady, despite the miserable emptiness of the liquor shelves. Flora wonders if the fishermen who charge in and toss back tankards of spiced ale are doing it purely in an act of solidarity towards her. Either way, she is grateful.

She is surprised when Isaac slips through the door. She doesn't want him in the inn. Doesn't want him in the village. Just the sight of him makes her heart jump and ache. It will be far easier when he is gone. Far easier and far more difficult.

He leans against the bar, gives her apologetic eyes. "I'll not stay. I just wanted to make sure you were all right." His voice is low, secretive. The sound of it makes something stir inside her.

She gives him a small smile. "Everything is fine."

He nods at the watch ball swaying above the door. "Protection against evil spirits?"

"Or evil men."

"Do you truly think this will keep Leach away?" Curiosity in his voice, not criticism.

Flora concentrates on wiping the counter top, unable to look him in the eye. "Leach is a superstitious man. He fears magic. And he believes I can wield it."

"And you?" says Isaac. "Is that what you believe?"

She scrubs harder. "I believe I dismissed my mother's craft too quickly." The admission makes colour rise in her cheeks. She stops. Isaac is not the person to discuss such things with. He has seen too much of the world to give any weight to Cornish superstition. But she has also seen too much to cast it aside.

"This change in you," he says carefully, "it happened when we opened the tunnel. Are you thinking of Jack? Do you think he—"

"It's not about Jack," she says, too quickly. "Jack is gone. There's nothing more to it." She feels Isaac trying to catch her eye. Doesn't let him. "Besides," she says, "it doesn't matter what I believe. It matters what Leach believes. And I'm sure his fears will be enough to keep him away."

Isaac presses a hand to her wrist, forcing her to look at him. "I hope you're right."

He pulls his hand away as the door creaks.

Will Francis.

Isaac whirls around to face him. "What happened to John? Is he–"

"He's alive," says Will, sliding onto a stool at the bar. "Resting at home. Barber surgeon took the ball out. Managed to keep him alive."

Isaac exhales sharply. "Thank Christ." He claps Will on the shoulder. "You're a good man to have brought him back safely."

Will smiles at Flora. "It were your doing, Mrs Kelly. The yarrow you gave John kept him alive til we got to Plymouth."

His words fill her with a pride she had not been expecting. She fills two glasses of ale and places them on the bar. "Here. All I can offer, I'm afraid. But you'll drink to John nonetheless."

Will grins, tossing a mop of fair hair from his eyes. "Not hiding anything under the bar for us then?"

"Wouldn't dare. I've gotten to know the excisemen a little too well in your absence. Unless you want to climb into the tunnel and help yourself to Isaac's brandy, there's little I can do."

Isaac takes the glass and, finally, the stool at the bar. "I found a buyer in Bodmin," he tells them. "An innkeeper willing to take the rest of the brandy. Forty pounds for the lot."

Flora's eyebrows shoot up. "Forty pounds? That will give you enough to leave."

Isaac nods. He takes a long mouthful of ale, not looking at her.

She had wanted this, she reminds herself. Things will be easier once he is gone. Never mind the knot that has lodged itself in her stomach. She had wanted this.

"I'm glad for you," says Will. "That bastard Reuben will have to find someone else to make him his fortune."

"As am I," says Flora. Is her voice too bright? Too flat? Why is she having such trouble speaking normally? She squeezes her cloth between her fingers. Bends her head to catch his glance. "Tell your wife."

Isaac nods. "I will."

The cottage is quiet, the children asleep. Rain patters against the window.

Caroline can't handle the stillness. Stillness gives her too much room to think. She wants Isaac home, Mary fussing, Gabriel leaping about the house in mud-caked boots. And yet the thought of seeing any of them is a deep, unplaceable ache.

She paces. Finds herself gnawing a thumbnail; a nervous habit she had left behind in childhood.

They would leave tonight, she had told Asher. Told him words he had wanted to hear. Words that would get him out of her house, her life, however fleetingly. Words she had never intended to see through.

But perhaps it's best she truly does leave. Disappear from Isaac's life before he finds out what she has done. Agree to Asher's demands before he goes to the revenue men with everything he knows.

But what of the children? She can't bear to leave them. Can't bear to take them from their father. And the money? It would see her family far away from this place. See new clothes for her children, boots without holes. Nights without hunger and forced smuggling runs.

But Jacob is right, damn him to hell. Uncover those riches and she will face questions. There is no way she can claim to just have stumbled upon the money. Isaac will question and probe and her most dreadful of deeds will spill into the open.

The door clicks and creaks. She stops pacing as Isaac enters. She hovers awkwardly, gripping the edge of the table.

He frowns. "Are you all right?"

"Of course." Her heart is pounding. Can he see the secrets behind her eyes?

He comes towards her, a smile curling the edge of his lips. A buyer in Bodmin, he tells her. He will make the sale in two days' time. Forty pounds in their pocket. Enough to leave.

Caroline closes her eyes. This is the news she has longed for. How she wishes she could be happy. But there are mere hours before midnight and still she has no idea what she will tell Asher.

"I thought you'd be happier," says Isaac, hanging his damp coat over a chair.

She touches his cheek. "I am happy. You've done so well." He can he tell her smile is forced, she is sure. After twelve years together, they know every shift and nuance of each other's faces. Know how to read even the subtlest of expressions. But lately, they have also come to an unspoken agreement not to ask questions. A silent accord that their marriage will survive better if they keep their thoughts to themselves. He will come home late from the inn and she will ask nothing. She, harbour a fierce grudge against the man from the wreck and he will ask nothing. It is a brutal, lonely thing, but a thing Caroline is glad of now. If Isaac were to find out what she is hiding, she knows there would be a look on his face she had never seen before.

"Perhaps you might start to ready the house," he tells her. "Clear the shelves and the like…"

Ready the house.

Their escape is finally in reach.

To hell with the money. It doesn't matter. Leave the wealth to Jacob and Asher. Let them fight over it, destroy each other over it. She can live with holey boots, live with supperless nights. She will eat stale bread every day for the rest of her life if only she will be free of this place, safe with her husband and children.

She kisses Isaac impulsively. Tastes the rain on his lips. "Ready the house," she says. "Yes, I'll do that."

He smiles stiffly. "Will you come to bed?"

"In a while. I'm not tired."

He falls asleep quickly, his heavy breathing sounding beneath the bedroom door.

Caroline sits by the dying fire. The last embers shift and crackle.

Less than an hour until midnight. Soon, Asher Hales will be waiting for her at the harbour.

And the answer comes. Manipulative. Underhand. What better way to trap such a man?

She goes to the bedroom. Hanging inside the wardrobe is Isaac's greatcoat, stained with John Baker's blood. She takes it back to the kitchen and slides on her cloak.

"Mammik?" She freezes at the sound of Gabriel's voice. His dark head appears around the door of the children's bedroom. "What are you doing?"

"Nothing, my darling. Just cleaning Tasik's coat." A tremor in her voice, though she knows, at eight years old, her boy is too young to think her words anything other than truth. Too young to believe his mother capable of lies and deceit. She doesn't deserve this unconditional trust.

He chews the sleeve of his nightshirt. "Why are you wearing your cloak?"

"I'm cold, is all." She kisses the side of his head. "Go back to bed."

She waits for his footsteps to patter back to the bedroom. Waits for silence.

The coat in her arms, she slips out of the cottage.

Asher is waiting at the edge of the harbour. He has washed his face and tied back his hair, but he wears the same dirt-encrusted shirt and breeches. The glow of the street lamps accentuates the bruises on his cheeks.

He eyes her. "Where are your children?"

"At home in bed." Caroline shivers, pulling Isaac's coat close to her body. A misting rain is cold against her cheeks. The sea clops against the harbour walls.

Asher looks down at the greatcoat. "What is that?"

She meets his eyes. "Your coat. Stained with the blood of the two riding officers murdered in Lansallos last week."

He glares. "That coat belongs to your husband."

"Can you prove that?"

"Prove it?" he snorts. "To who?"

"To the revenue men. The magistrate."

"What are you talking about?"

Caroline's heart is speeding. "You try and turn Isaac and Scarlett over to the revenue men and I will be right behind you with this. Evidence of your involvement in the riding officers' murders."

Asher's eyes flash. He opens his mouth to speak, but Caroline continues. She hears her voice grow stronger. "The revenue men have proven they're desperate to make an arrest. Make a point to other smuggling gangs. They care little whether or not they're convicting the right man."

Asher forces a cold laugh. "That will never work." Uncertainty in his voice. "You've nothing but your word."

"And your bloodstained coat. It's far more than Flora had to convict Tom Leach. And yet the authorities are more than willing to have her take the stand."

Asher's jaw tightens. Caroline feels a flicker of satisfaction. "You're a man with a criminal past," she says. "A man with an unsolved murder hanging about him. A fine suspect to pin a crime on." She clenches her fingers around the coat. There is something pleasant about reminding him of these things. Reminding him of how far he is from the man he longs to be. "Flora doesn't have it in her to lie before a court," she says. "When they catch Tom Leach, she'll crumble in the witness stand and the revenue men will have nothing. But you can be sure that I will have no difficulty standing before a jury and claiming I saw you return to our cottage the night of the murder, dressed in this."

For a long time, Asher says nothing. A peal of laughter rises from the Three Pilchards. "You are a manipulative witch."

Caroline smiles crookedly. "I must have learned such things from you."

She turns to leave. Asher grabs her arm. When she looks back at him, his steely façade has given way to desperation. "I have nothing," he hisses. "No money for food, or clothing. Nowhere to sleep. I lost everything I had when I was wrecked upon that cursed beach." He grips her cloak, pulling her close. "You have to help me." She turns her head, repulsed by the stink of him. "Give me a little of the money."

"I don't have the money," she says. "I don't care about it."

Asher pulls on the edges of her cloak. Fixes her with wild, glowing eyes. She has seen this look before. Seen it when he'd stood before her in Launceston Castle and told her of his plan to destroy Jacob Bailey. "You're planning to leave," he says suddenly.

She shakes her head. Asher can know nothing of her plans. She can't trust him not to tell Jacob.

"You are. I know it. You're not foolish enough to stay here and risk Jacob hurting your children." He pulls her close, his nose grazing hers. "You have a way out, don't you."

Caroline shoves him away and begins to walk back to Talland. She waits for him to follow, but there is nothing but stillness as she charges up the dark path. She is bristling with nervous energy. She pulls Isaac's coat tight against her chest to steady herself.

In the morning, she will ready the house. Pack the last twelve years into travelling trunks so they may start again.

Their way out is hazy and unformed. But they have no choice but to succeed.

Asher watches until the tiny figure of her is lost on the darkness of the hill. His legs give way beneath him. He sits at the edge of the harbour, hopelessness welling inside him. Water kicks up from the edge of the moorings, splashing his legs and stinging his eyes.

Caroline is right. His dreams of greatness will only ever be dreams. The realisation is brutal, vicious. He doesn't believe any more. He puts his head to his knees. What else is there to do?

"That was Isaac Bailey's wife," says a voice behind him.

Asher turns. Looks up. The man standing over him is tall and thin, his greatcoat dirty and far too large. His hair and beard are streaked with grey. Skin hangs in pockets beneath his eyes. Asher knows this man. Tom Leach, the trader with the black ship.

"What is she doing out here with you so late at night?"

"That's no business of yours."

Leach chuckles. "It's a sorry day when a woman brings you to your knees."

Asher turns away. He watches shadows move across the surface of the water. Somewhere in the darkness, a gull lets out a mournful cry.

Why is Leach here, Asher wonders distantly. If Caroline is to be believed, the witch in the inn had turned him in for murder. Why has he returned to Talland when the shadow of the scaffold hangs over him? Asher lets the thought peter out. He doesn't care.

"You're a sad and sorry man, aren't you," Leach chuckles.

"I'm a great man," Asher says flatly. "You've no idea of the things that await me."

"And yet here you are on your knees, staring desperately after another man's wife."

The truth of it is a deep ache within him. Asher Hales has never felt further from greatness.

"The Baileys are planning to leave?" asks Leach.

Asher nods faintly, not looking at him.

"That can't happen. Isaac Bailey does not just get to go free. Not when he's sent the authorities after me."

Asher thinks to tell Leach it was the witch who had condemned him. But no. Let him blame Isaac. He looks up at the dark figure standing over him. They are both sad and sorry men, Asher realises. He has far more in common with this outlaw than he does with the surgeons and scientists he longs to walk among.

Leach holds out a hand to haul Asher from the ground. "Tell me what you know."

WALKING IN THE DARK

The sky is white with morning light when Scarlett and Jamie reach Talland. From the top of the hill, the sea stretches out endlessly, a glassy lake after the heaving ocean on the north coast. Red and grey roof tops are speckled between the trees, the church spire a silhouette on the cliff.

Scarlett stays motionless, feeling the horse breathe beneath her. The view is achingly familiar. Everything has shifted, yet this place is constant, unchanging.

"I can walk the rest of the way," she tells Jamie. "There's no need to come down into the village."

His chest is pressed against her back, his arms reaching around her as he grips the reins. She has grown accustomed to the feel of it. She doesn't want to slide from the saddle and confront the real world. But the journey is over. She must face Isaac and Jamie must leave.

"I need to rest the horse before I return to Portreath." His voice is close to her ear.

"Will you make it back for the press gang's trial?" she asks.

"I hope so."

"What will happen to them? The hangman?"

"More likely, they'll be forced into the navy themselves." She hears a smile in his voice. "It seems a just thing." He dismounts and offers her a hand as she slides from the horse. He keeps her fingers in his for a moment. "I'll find lodgings in Polperro tonight. Come and see me in the morning. I'll not leave until I've said goodbye."

Scarlett nods. Manages a faint smile. She doesn't want *goodbye*. But brass-buttoned Jamie cannot stay.

He kisses her cheek. "Good luck."

She watches him leave. And she begins to walk down the hill.

There is the cottage. Home, but it makes her stomach roll.

She will go inside and ask forgiveness for the distrust she had had in Isaac. Forgiveness for running away. She will tell her brother all she has discovered. She has come back to Talland so she might do these things. But something stops her. A sudden fear.

Perhaps Isaac will not forgive her for the things she had said to him. Perhaps he will not forgive her for racing unannounced into the world and upturning the lie they had both known to be truth. Perhaps the door will be closed on her and she will be forced to carry the knowledge of who their father is alone.

And then what? She can't live a life without her brother in it. Isaac has been more of a father to her than Jacob ever was.

She keeps walking. Past the cottage. Through the creaking gate of the churchyard. She weaves through the crooked headstones until she stands among her family's graves.

She kneels at her mother's headstone. Runs a finger across the weathered letters. Had her mother known the truth of who Jacob was? Had she seen something beneath his eyes that might have shown her the kind of man she had married? Or had she been blinded by love, the way Scarlett had been?

Beside her mother; two brothers. *Robert, Michael.* When Scarlett thinks of these names, she remembers hands lifting her high in the air, peals of boyish laughter. But perhaps these hands, this laughter belongs to Isaac. Her memories are faint and fragile.

Three that had been and gone before her time. Just names. *August, Elizabeth, Emily.*

And the memorial stone for her father.

It had made her happy, once, to think that Jacob was not down there in the earth with the others. That he might be freer than the black-eyed things the rest of her family had become.

She turns away. She can't bear to look at the memorial, tainting the resting place of her mother and siblings. She leaves the cemetery. She cannot go home. Not yet. She cannot face Isaac with such restlessness beneath her skin.

Someone is in the cellar. Someone earthly, real. Someone who has crawled into the tunnel from its mouth on the eastern beach.

Flora hears movement from behind the locked door, far too heavy to be mice. Far too solid to be the walking of the dead. The dog yaps and scrabbles against the door.

She takes a knife from behind the bar and slowly turns the key. The dog charges into the dark mass of the cellar. The morning light in the bar does little to light the shadows.

Flora lowers herself onto the top step, hearing it creak beneath her. She lights the lamp at the top of the staircase and slides it from its hook. The beam skims over broken furniture, ankers of ale, the barrels stacked across the mouth of the tunnel. Have they been moved? Impossible to tell.

The dog is weaving between the furniture, nose to the floor. He stops trotting. Pricks up his ears. There is silence now. Nothing but the irregular breath of the lantern flame.

Had she been wrong? The sounds had been so real. Perhaps she has spent too long staring into the black mirror. Is the line between this world and the next beginning to blur?

A knock at the front door startles her. She blows out the lamp and locks the cellar. Finds Scarlett on her doorstep.

Flora pulls her into a tight embrace. She is glad to see her. Glad she is safe. Glad for the steadying arms around her. With another person in the bar, her excursion to the cellar suddenly seems foolish. With another person in the bar, it is easy to blame her imagination.

She steps back, holding Scarlett at arm's length. "Where have you been?" she asks, in a faintly scolding voice usually reserved for Bessie.

Scarlett opens her mouth to speak. Says nothing. Her dark hair is windblown, her eyes large and sombre.

"You'll tell me when you're ready, ayes?"

Scarlett nods. "Can I come in?"

"Of course." Flora ushers her inside. She glances at the pack slung over Scarlett's shoulder. "You've not been home."

She shakes her head slightly.

"Isaac is worried for you," says Flora.

Scarlett squeezes her eyes closed. "I can't face him. Not yet. I said such terrible things to him. I'm so afraid he'll not forgive me."

Flora pulls her into her arms again. Is she trying to comfort Scarlett or herself? She can't be sure.

Tea. Yes. It will steady them both. She takes Scarlett's arm and walks with her upstairs.

Flora goes to the kitchen and hangs the kettle over the range. She hears the floorboards creak beneath Scarlett's feet. Hears her chatter with Bessie in the room full of flowers.

"Angelica," says Bessie. "Mallow leaves. Yarrow."

Flora finds them both at the window, staring down into the street.

"There's men here, Mammik." Bessie doesn't turn.

"It's Reuben," Scarlett says darkly. "And his footmen."

Flora puts the tea cups on the side table. A knock rattles the front door. A second knock without pause. The dog barks and scratches.

"Mrs Kelly?" calls Reuben. "Open the door please." There is a thinly-veiled anger in his voice Flora has not heard before.

She ushers Bessie towards her bedroom. "Reuben has been asking to see the tunnel," she tells Scarlett. "I told him it wasn't finished so Isaac could hide his brandy ankers in there. But I'm afraid he's come to see it himself."

"Brandy ankers?" Scarlett repeats. "Isaac made a run of his own?"

"Ayes. He means to leave as soon as he's sold them."

Scarlett sucks in her breath. "I need to see him."

Another thump on the door.

Scarlett hurries down the stairs. "I'll go to the tunnel," she tells Flora. "Hide the brandy on the beach."

Flora nods. Opens the cellar door for Scarlett and locks it behind her. She answers Reuben's fourth knock, giving him her warmest smile.

"The tunnel," he says darkly. "I hear it is finished."

Two footmen stand behind him. Their hair is windswept, dust streaking their coats. And Flora feels something tighten in her chest.

Footsteps in the tunnel. Footsteps in the cellar. Reuben had had his footmen sail around the point and enter the tunnel from the beach. Catch her in her lies.

"I wish to see it," he says.

"I'm afraid now is not a good time."

"Why not?" Reuben strides into the house, trailed by his men.

Flora feels a sudden surge of anger. "Surely these men do not need to charge into my home this way," she says, managing a little of her own sharpness. "This feels very threatening, Mr Reuben."

He hesitates. Finally, he nods. "Wait for me outside," he tells the men. The door slams as they leave. Reuben strides towards the cellar.

"I've just made a pot of tea," Flora says hurriedly. She can hear the strain in her voice. "Perhaps you would like a cup?"

Reuben nods at the cellar. "Unlock the door please."

If she refuses? Surely he will not hurt her. But her refusal will arouse his suspicion. She needs to take him down there. A slow, careful walk through the dark that might give Scarlett time to slide the ankers onto the beach.

She slides the key into the cellar door. In and out, in and out. She jiggles it in the lock. "I'm sorry. This door, it catches dreadfully." She glances at Reuben. Sees the thin smile on his face. She eases open the door and takes the lantern hanging at the top of the cellar stairs. She fumbles with the tinderbox and lights it carefully.

Had Reuben's men found the ankers when they had crept through the tunnel? And if they had, would they have had any thought as to what they were?

She leads Reuben into the passage. Takes slow, careful steps. And the light falls on the barrels of brandy sitting at a bend in the tunnel. Scarlett has managed to move less than half.

Flora tries to slide past them, hoping the ankers might hide themselves in the shadows. But Reuben stops walking.

"What are these?"

Flora hears Scarlett breathe in the darkness behind her.

"Are you hiding contraband?" Reuben demands.

"Of course not. They belong to me. I hid them after the excisemen found my licence."

"Do you think me a fool?" She has never heard Reuben raise his voice before. "I bought your liquor back from you not two days ago."

She holds the lamp close to his face, making him squint in the hot light. "And do you imagine you are the only man I conduct business with? Where would I be if the revenue men were to uncover your operation?"

He eyes her. "Who else did you buy from?"

"That's no business of yours."

Reuben snatches the lamp. He bends, shining the light over the surface of the barrels. He makes a noise from the back of his throat. "You're hiding contraband," he says again. "For who? Isaac Bailey?"

"You're mistaken."

He looks at her closely. The flickering light accentuates his deep frown. "I see," he says, but Flora can hear the disbelief in his voice. There is something else there too. Disappointment?

She can see this through his eyes. He has done nothing but support her since she had first spoken of opening the Mariner's Arms. And she has given him lies in return. His eyes are cold and unforgiving. Flora sees she can no longer count on protection from Charles Reuben. Can no longer count on his amnesty.

Silence hangs between them.

Reuben shifts his weight and Flora flinches.

He will not hurt her, surely. She tells herself again.

He will not hurt her.

"I'd best go," he says finally, shortly. "My men are waiting."

Flora stiffens. Perhaps Reuben will not hurt her, but she knows his men will have no issue with such a thing. Reuben will direct them as a general directs his troops and they will obediently go after whichever fool has dared to cross him.

He begins to walk slowly from the tunnel, his footsteps crunching on the earth.

Scarlett presses her back hard against the wall, her face turned from the light in Reuben's hand. Finally, he and Flora are gone. Dark falls over the tunnel.

She has to get to Isaac. Tell him Reuben has found the brandy.

Trailing a hand along the wall to keep her bearings, she runs towards the thin shaft of light at the end of the tunnel. She clambers through the split in the rock and her boots sink into sand. The beach is hemmed by purple-black slate, the rock extending into the water like jagged walls. The only way back to the village is through the sea and around the point.

Gripping her skirts in her fist, Scarlett runs into the water. Waves swell around her waist, the current knocking her from her feet as the cold tightens around her lungs. The rocks are slippery beneath her boots. Barnacles tear the skin from her hands. Half-swimming, half-climbing, she scrambles around the point until she reaches the landing beach.

She hunches, exhausted, and squeezes the seawater from her skirts. Gulping down her breath, she hurries up the sand towards the cottage.

The door is locked. She rattles it, thumps loudly. "Isaac?"

Silence.

She knocks again. "Is anyone there?"

Moth wings patter against the glass. Scarlett hears her heart thudding in her ears.

She will not panic. Isaac is out fishing. Caroline has taken Gabriel to school.

No. Today is Friday. The charity school is closed.

She goes to the window. Peers through the murky glass into Isaac and Caroline's bedroom. The wardrobe door hangs open. Empty.

Her stomach knots.

The next window. The kitchen shelves are bare. Stray pots are strewn across the floor. Beside them, a trunk is overturned, clothes lying in a heap. Has someone else been here? Or have they just left in a hurry? She cannot tell. She only knows this is the house of people who do not plan to return.

She shivers in her wet clothes.

Had Isaac felt Reuben breathing down his neck? Have her accusations towards her brother been enough to make him leave without her? She glances again at the pots and clothing flung across the kitchen. Perhaps he had had no choice.

Her throat tightens. She needs to get to the harbour. Needs to look for the lugger. The fishermen at least will know if Isaac has left.

She hurries towards the cliff path.

FRAGILE LIGHT

At the back of a cave beaten into the Polperro cliffs, the light is hatched and fragile. With each exhalation of the sea, the tide grazes the rim of the rock, washing away the footprints that lead down from the edge of the beach.

Caroline kneels with her spine pressed to the back of the cave, one hand full of Mary, the other tight around Gabriel's arm. The light is hatched and fragile, but peer into the cave at the right angle and she knows they will be seen.

They were to have their escape. A thing she and Isaac have been speaking of since the first days of their marriage. Once, escape had been a wild fantasy, whispered of beneath the bedclothes in the same breath as French champagne and voyages around the world. Later, a desperately longed for dream. And finally, since Isaac had found the new buyer in Bodmin, escape had begun to feel tangible.

But their escape was not supposed to be like this.

"Tonight," Isaac had said that morning, sitting on the edge of the bed. Caroline had slept little, still jittery from her clash with Asher Hales. "I'm to go to Bodmin. Make the sale. The moment I get back to the cottage, we leave. We'll have one of the men take us to Fowey from the eastern beach. Find passage out of Cornwall from there."

And Caroline had let herself grip a little tighter to that elusive life of freedom. A life free of Asher and Jacob and all their secrets.

She knelt, her eyes level with her husband's, her knees pressing against his thigh. She wanted to feel his hands in her hair, his lips on hers. Wanted the distance between them to disappear.

It didn't matter, she told herself. It didn't matter that his eyes were lowered and his arms folded stiffly across his chest. Once they had left this place, he would let her in. Once Talland was a memory, they would find each other again.

She kissed his cheek. "I'll ready the house as you asked."

When he had left for the fishing port, she dressed hurriedly and pulled the trunk from beneath the bed. She tossed in her few pieces of clothing, along with Isaac's spare shirt and breeches. She went to the kitchen. Emptied the shelves of pots and candles and wiped them free of dust. She took the fish kettle from above the fire and scooped the ash from the grate. Let there be no trace of them left in the cottage. Let there be nothing for Jacob or Asher to find if either of them were to come looking.

The knock at the door was violent, insistent. Two of Reuben's footmen pushed past her into the house.

"Where is your husband?"

And with the footman's fierce words, fear blazed down Caroline's spine. Reuben knew of Isaac's run. There could be no doubt.

She glared at the men, not speaking.

They eyed the bare shelves, the packed trunk. "Planning to leave are you?" One reached into the chest and flung two of the pots across the kitchen. They clattered loudly against the table leg. "Escaping?" He overturned the trunk, kicking the clothes across the floor.

"Get out of my house," hissed Caroline. A fist to her stomach. She doubled over, gasping for breath.

Gabriel rushed from the bedroom in his nightshirt. "Mammik!"

"Get back in your room," Caroline coughed. "Stay with Mary."

One of the men snatched a fistful of her hair, forcing her to look at him. "Where is your husband?"

"He's not here."

They charged into the bedroom, searching. Then they threw open the door to the children's room. Gabriel's fingers were tight around the rim of the cradle, his cheeks wet with tears. Caroline ushered him behind her and stood protectively in front of the crib.

"Tell us where your husband is."

"Where do you think he is? He's at sea. Trying to make a living seeing the bastard you work for has taken everything we have."

And the men were gone.

Caroline bent over the crib, trying to find the breath that had been knocked from her. The muscles in her stomach were throbbing. She threw open the wardrobe and tossed out Gabriel's coat and breeches. She knelt, clutching his shoulders. "Get dressed. Quickly. We need to leave."

They would not beat Reuben's men to Polperro. The thugs would make for the harbour and wait for Isaac to return. Perhaps even sail out to meet him.

But there could be no staying here. Reuben knew of Isaac's plans for certain, and he would want him punished.

Caroline hurried to the bedroom and pulled out the pouch of money Isaac had hidden beneath the mattress. It wasn't enough. Not even close. But somehow they would find a way.

Would Reuben's men be waiting outside the house? Watching her the way they had once watched Isaac and Scarlett try to slip out from beneath Reuben's eyes?

She had to risk it. How to get to Polperro? The cliff path would be quicker, but it would leave them exposed. Take them past Reuben's mansion. Too dangerous. The path through Killigarth was longer, but they would be hidden among houses and trees. They could wind down towards the harbour in the shadow of the hills.

She threw on her cloak and bonnet. In the children's room, Gabriel was lacing his boots, his eyes wide and fearful. She yanked his hair into a tail, pulled him from the floor and knotted a scarf around his neck.

Money. Warm clothes. Mary in blankets, scooped from the cradle. She rushed from the house without looking back.

As she approached the water, Caroline could see the masts of the lugger silhouetted at the edge of the bay. But there, at the other end of the harbour, was Will Francis, roping one of the fishing dories to the moorings. She hurried towards him, hot and breathless. Felt her skin prickling beneath her shift.

Will looked up in surprise. "Mrs Bailey?"

"I have to get to Isaac," she said. "Reuben's men are after him. They know of the run. We need to leave."

His face darkened. He began to unwind the boat's moorings. "I'll go for him."

"Reuben's men will be watching for the lugger," said Caroline.

Will nodded. "I'll bring him back in the dory." He pointed towards the black rock face that slid sharply onto the beach. "In there. There's a cave where we hide the contraband. You see it?"

She nodded.

"Hide in there. You'll not be seen from the land." He glanced at the children; both staring up at him with enormous brown eyes. "You need help getting there?"

"I can manage," said Caroline. "Just fetch my husband. Please."

Isaac doesn't speak as the dory cuts through the swell. He glances over his shoulder at the cave where his family is hiding. Glances at the harbour for any sign of Reuben and his men.

He had heard Will's words only distantly as he had rowed towards the lugger.

Your family.

Reuben.

He knows.

For a moment, the world had lost its colour. Distantly, Isaac heard Will say: "Get in the boat."

And then he was rowing, rowing, tearing oars through the water until his arms burned.

He has no thought of how they will escape this place without tickets on a passenger ship. Walls of cliffs on either side of the village. Reuben will expect them to leave by sea. There will be men watching the harbour. Men watching the roads in and out of town.

Isaac leaps from the boat the moment it bumps against the moorings. And he stops. On the harbour's edge stands the traders' banker, the most loyal of Reuben's men. Their eyes meet.

He cannot go to the cave. Cannot lead the banker to where his family is hiding.

The banker's hand goes to his pocket.

A weapon there, yes. Message received.

Fourteen years ago, Isaac had stood on the beach and had this man hold a pistol to his head. The banker had threatened to shoot if he had tried to leave Talland.

Empty threats, Isaac had thought at the time. But with seven-year-old Scarlett clinging to his hand, there had been little room for risk.

He feels his own pistol against his hip.

The banker won't shoot. Not here in the middle of the village. He may be loyal to Reuben, but surely he'll not put his head in a noose for another man's cause.

Follow him to the cave, however, and they will be hidden from the authorities. Isaac will find out just how empty the banker's threats are.

He begins to walk. Step, step, step. Up the hill. Away from the cave, away from his family. Footsteps behind him. Isaac glances over his shoulder. The banker has his pistol out.

"How did he know?" Isaac asks darkly.

"He found the ankers you hid in the tunnel."

"Reuben went to the inn?" What of Flora? Isaac slides his hand into his pocket. Wraps his fingers around the pistol.

"Don't," says the banker.

Isaac turns slowly. Wind lashes his hair across his eyes. He brings his hand slowly from his pocket. The banker's shot is frantic, uncontrolled. It flies over Isaac's shoulder and splinters the cold air. Isaac whips out his pistol, hands shaking with the sudden rush of energy. The banker's pistol is empty. Isaac could shoot. Run to the cave and find his family. There would be one less man trying to block their escape.

But he thinks of the dizziness that had seized him when he had pulled the trigger on Leach's crewmate. In his mind's eye, he sees the dead man fall. Feels the hot weight of it in his stomach. A line of sweat runs down his back.

"Go," he tells the banker. "Get out of here."

The banker climbs to his feet, eyes not leaving the pistol. Isaac holds out his hand. "Give me your weapon."

The banker hands it to him slowly. Begins to walk. When he reaches the top of the hill, he turns. Calls down to Isaac, his words carrying on the wind.

"You go to your family. We'll go for the witch who helped you hide your goods."

LIGHTLESSNESS

Isaac finds them in the cave. Caroline is kneeling in the sand, her back pressed to the wet black rock, an arm tight around each of the children. The sight of them alive and unharmed brings a sound of relief from the back of Isaac's throat. And he is on his knees beside them, feeling the children's soft hair against his cheek. Caroline latches an arm around his neck and pulls him towards her.

"I have the money from beneath the mattress," she says, her voice close to his ear. "We can make it around the point on foot. Get Will to bring the dory to us."

Her plan is a good one. The best they have. Isaac feels a sudden, unexpected swell of love for his wife. The guilt he has been ignoring rears up inside him. A part of him wants nothing more than to take his family and run around that point, into the dory, into the bay. A part of him wants nothing more than to sail away from this life and hope it will lead him back to the woman he married. But there are men heading for the Mariner's Arms to punish Flora for helping him. The thought of her in danger makes sickness rise in his throat. He presses his palms to Caroline's cheeks. "Go," he says. "Take the children around the point. I'll send Will to find you."

"What about you?"

He can't look at her. "Reuben's men are going after Flora. They want to punish her for hiding the ankers. I have to go and help her. I'm sorry."

Caroline's eyes flash. "No," she says. "No, Isaac. We need to leave right now."

"And if Flora and Bess were to be killed because we just ran away and left them?"

Caroline inhales at his sharpness. He feels her eyes boring into him. But she gives a faint nod. "Hurry back," she says huskily. "Please."

Isaac nods. "Go. Take the children."

"No. We're staying here. We'll not leave without you."

Guilt, more guilt. He kisses her forehead. "I'll be back as fast as I can."

Caroline snatches his arm as he turns to leave. "Don't take the cliff path," she says. "There's nowhere to hide."

Isaac nods. Runs from the cave and up the inland path.

From the top of the cliff, Scarlett can see the lugger; a tiny shape in the morning haze. Is Isaac out fishing? Or has he taken his family and left?

She crouches, gulps for breath. Her legs are aching and her lungs burn.

And she sees him.

No. He ought to have been thrown into the hold of a naval ship. Ought to be eating hard tack half way to the Caribbean war.

But no, Asher is here on the clifftop, eyes distant, as though he has come to imagine himself in a place far better than this.

His face is blue and yellow with bruising, his shirt grimy with old, brown blood. The strand of hair hanging loose from his queue is coiled and stiff with sea. He turns away when he sees her charging towards him.

"Was this your doing?" she cries. "Did you go to the revenue men? Is that why my family has left?"

He glances at her wet clothes. "What are you talking about, Scarlett?" His voice is tired. There is a new hunch to his shoulders. A new droop to his chin. The glassiness in his eyes makes her wary. What, she wonders, is a proud man like Asher Hales capable of when his world begins to crumble?

"Did you see my brother's ship leave?" she asks.

He squints. "He left, yes. With the fishing fleet. This morning."

"With the fishing fleet? Did it seem as though he were coming back?"

Asher chuckles. "Here you are wanting my help again."

Scarlett's anger flares. "Tell me what you saw, Asher! I need to know if my family has left."

He stares out at the tiny shape of the lugger. "She is leaving, yes. And taking with her all she knows."

"What? Who are you talking about? Caroline?"

"Yes. Caroline. She is leaving."

"Where is she? Where is Isaac? Have you seen them?"

"She knows," Asher says distantly. "She knows how to find the money."

"What are you talking about? What money? Avery's money?"

He nods.

Scarlett tugs at her hair in frustration. "You're making no sense, Asher. What happened to you?" She knows the answer, of course. Jacob is what had happened. "How did you get away from the press gang?" she asks, her eyes falling to the beads of blood staining the front of his shirt.

Asher snorts. "Through no help of yours."

"What happened to my father?"

"Do you care?"

"No." She narrows her eyes. "You're here to turn us in. That's why you've come back, ayes?"

"They're in the cave," he says suddenly, pointing down to Polperro and the columns of rock on the edge of the beach. "Your family. I saw them."

"My family is in the cave?"

"Yes."

"Why?"

"I don't know." Weariness in his voice. "They're hiding. But you need to go there. Tell her she can't leave."

Scarlett stares at him. Tries to see behind the blank façade of his eyes. She has been foolish enough to trust him before. If she were to walk into that cave she could be easily trapped. Trapped by revenue officers. Trapped by Reuben and his men. Perhaps trapped by Asher himself. She has no idea what he is capable of.

But the cottage has been emptied. It is clear her family will not be returning. What choice does she have but to go to the cave? What choice does she have but to trust?

The light is hatched and fragile. With each exhalation of the sea, the tide grazes the rim of the cave, washing away Isaac's footprints that lead back to the edge of the beach.

Caroline can't shake her anger at his leaving. With rational eyes, she knows he is right to do it. They cannot leave Flora and Bess to face Reuben's men alone. But there is no room for rationality. Only fear and impatience. Anger that burns beneath her skin. She can't help but wonder where Isaac's loyalties lie.

She tries to slow her breathing. The children can sense her fear, she is sure. Mary is wriggling in her arms, mewling, grappling at the hem of her cloak. Gabriel is a barrage of questions.

What are we doing?

What's happening?

Where is Tasik going?

A sudden change in the rhythm of the water, as though legs are moving through the shallows. Caroline holds her breath. Pins hard eyes on Gabriel to silence him.

Is someone there?

Instinct tells her to run; leave this cave, this village, this land where her secrets hang so thick in the air. What had she been thinking, building a life here, upon the ghosts of her most regretful of deeds? Jacob is right. She had been a fool to stay.

The noise comes again. Legs sighing through the water. This time there can be no doubt.

It could be any of them, Caroline realises. Asher coming for money. Jacob and Reuben for retribution. Tom Leach hunting and seeking the voice who had turned him in.

Gabriel knots his fingers in her skirts. In the light spilling through the narrow opening, she sees his eyes are wide and fearful.

Mary whines against her shoulder. Caroline smooths her hair, rubs her cheek, her back. *Quiet now. Quiet.*

A shadow passes over the mouth of the cave.

One way in. One way out.

Caroline looks over her shoulder. Beside her, the chasm extends into a narrow, lightless passage. She cannot hope to fit inside it. But her children will. She hands Mary to Gabriel. "Take her," she whispers. "Get as far back as you can."

Gabriel murmurs in fear. "What about you?"

She kisses his cheek. "Go on. Hurry. Be brave."

He nods wordlessly and wriggles into the passage. Mary stares back over his shoulder, her face crumpled and tearful. Caroline stares into her daughter's eyes until they vanish into the dark.

THE DROWNED MAN'S CAVE

The cave is close. Scarlett tries to peer into it from the edge of the beach. She sees nothing but rock and dark.

How many times had she sat on this beach as a child, telling stories with Bobby Carter of the drowned smuggler haunting the cave?

"Step inside," he had dared her. "Are you scared?"

Her stomach knots as she edges towards the slit in the rock. She longs for ghost stories. Tales of drowned sailors. Longs for the ethereal and intangible.

There is a shape inside the cave. A figure, lying on the sand.

Caroline.

Scarlett hurries inside and drops to her knees. She reaches fingers towards Caroline's neck. Her pulse is fast. Alive. A line of blood runs down the side of her head. Scarlett gives her shoulder a gentle shake. Caroline stirs. Her eyelids flutter.

A murmur in the darkness. Scarlett turns abruptly. Gabriel is crouching in the narrow passage at the back of the cave, eyes swollen with tears. His arms are tight around his sister. Scarlett hurries towards them, pulls Gabriel into her arms. Can he feel her heart thumping against her ribs? He mumbles in fear against her wet shoulder. Scarlett plants a kiss in his hair.

"Did you see who did this?" she whispers. "Is someone here?" The cave is small. There is no one else in here with them. But the rest of the cliff is rugged and sliced with hiding places. Is whoever attacked Caroline still hiding in the dark?

Gabriel shakes his head against her chest. "Mammik told me to hide." His fingers dig into her neck. She hears herself whisper calming words she doesn't believe.

It's all right.

Don't be afraid.

She feels Gabriel stiffen. He pulls free from her arms and points a shaking finger into the blackness.

A noise from behind her. Movement on the edge of her vision. A half-swallowed cry from Gabriel. For a fleeting moment, she feels the air around her move.

And then there is pain.

And then there is black.

The Mariner's Arms is quiet. The street is quiet. Isaac hears the wings of a bird beat above his head. It feels as though the village is holding its breath, waiting for Reuben to strike.

He knocks. His heart is drumming. He had taken the inland path as Caroline had asked; a longer journey than the exposed ribbon over the cliffs. What if he is too late?

He sighs in relief when Flora pulls open the door.

"You're still here," she says. "You need to leave. Reuben, he found—"

"Get Bessie," Isaac tells her, "and come with me. Quickly."

She stays planted in the doorway, the green globe of the watch ball circling, circling above her head. "Did Scarlett find you?"

"What?"

"She was here when Reuben found the ankers. She went to your cottage to warn you."

Isaac exhales sharply. "We'll find her." He tugs Flora's hand. "You can't stay here." He tells her of the smugglers' banker and the threats he had made. Tells her of the way he had disappeared over the cliffs towards the inn. And he sees that infuriating hardness fall over Flora's eyes. That infuriatingly admirable stubbornness he has come to know so well.

She pulls her hand free. "I'm not leaving. I'll not be scared from my home."

"What about Bessie?" Isaac gestures wildly at the watch ball. "You mean to protect her with this? Magic is not going to save you, Flora. You used to know that. It won't save you from Reuben and it won't save you from Leach."

Her jaw tightens. He expects an eruption, but she grips his shoulders to still him. "No one is here, Isaac. No one is coming for me. Whatever the banker told you was a lie."

He stands motionless for a moment. Has he been a fool to leave his family in the cave? Has he fallen for empty threats, so Reuben might put a stop to their escape? His hike back to Talland will have given Reuben time to block the roads out of Polperro. Given him time to station men at the mouth of the harbour. Isaac sucks in his breath. "Christ. I need to leave."

"Yes," says Flora, her eyes on his. "You must."

And so this is the end, he realises. The end of sneaking down the tunnel to see her, the end of fire and brandy and hot stones beneath them, the end of this thing that had left him lit up inside the way he hadn't been for years.

For the best. He can't hope to fix things with Caroline while he is drawn to the light from the inn on the hill.

He can't say it. Can't handle the finality of *goodbye*. So he takes her face in his hands and pushes his lips hard against hers.

Flora pulls away abruptly at the sound of footsteps behind them. "Caroline—" She starts to say, but she is silenced by the coldness in his wife's eyes.

Isaac watches a look of wild anger pass across Caroline's face, but it is replaced quickly by a different horror. She looks past Flora, her eyes meeting Isaac's in desperation. Her words are a garble, beads of dried blood clinging to her cheek.

Scarlett, she says. And *men.* And then she speaks with sudden, sickening clarity.

"The children. They've been taken."

BOOK THREE

WILD LIGHT

DREAMING

Her fevered dreams are like this: drowned sailors and haunted hills and the shadows of giants screeching at the sky. She is back in the cave, hearing the sea behind her, feeling herself fall.

Scarlett cries out. The sound sends the sea and the cave away, but the world is still as dark as a barrow. She tries to sit. Her head is thundering. The blackness makes everything unsteady.

Footsteps come towards her.

"Scarlett?" It is Flora's voice. She feels hands on her shoulders, easing her downwards. "Stay still."

"Where am I?" Scarlett's breath is loud in her ears. Fast. Frantic. She gulps down air. Feels as though she is drowning.

"You're at the inn," says Flora.

Pain sears Scarlett's head as she moves on the pillow. She remembers it distantly; the footsteps in the sand behind her, the sudden, splintering blow to the back of her skull. "Light the lamp," she coughs. "I can't see."

Sounds break through the desperate rattle of her breath. Birds. Hooves in the street. The muffled sigh of the sea. There is a strange warmth on her cheek that must be fire or sun.

She reaches into the dark. "Light the lamp," she says desperately. "Please. Light the lamp at once."

She feels Flora's hands at the tops of her arms.

"Lie down, Scarlett," she is saying. "Lie down." Somehow she sounds both close and far away.

"Light the lamp," Scarlett says again. But her voice is faint and fading. There is pain in her head and an invisible sun on her cheek. She lets herself sink back into the bed, lets Flora smooth the blankets she has entangled in her terror. And the fear that engulfs her is hot and sharp as she blinks and blinks again and still she sees nothing.

ENEMIES

The blood is like ink in the sand. Isaac can't pull his gaze from it.

His sister's blood? His wife's?

His infant daughter's?

He and Caroline have spent hours tearing through Polperro, searching for their missing children. Racing from the pilchard palace to shops and houses, questioning, hunting for someone with knowledge. Anyone who might have heard the cry of a child, or seen a man entering the cave with a weapon in his hand.

Their fruitless search has brought them back to this thread of beach inside the cliff where blood is staining the sand.

"Tell me what you saw," Isaac says, for at least the third time.

Caroline's answer is the same. After Reuben's men had stormed their cottage, she had raced to Polperro, desperate to escape the village. Had sheltered in the cave on the beach while Will Francis rowed out to fetch Isaac from the lugger.

But she had not been hidden. She had seen shadows come towards the cave. Heard footsteps in the water. One person. Perhaps more. She had pushed Mary into Gabriel's arms. Watched as her children disappeared into the narrow passage at the back of the cave.

She had been struck from behind, her eyes locked with Mary's. Had awoken to find Scarlett unconscious on the sand beside her and the children gone.

Behind her tears, Caroline's eyes are critical. Isaac had left them. Left his family in the cave to go for Flora.

He had truly believed her in danger, he reminds himself. Had truly believed the smugglers' banker would kill her for helping to deceive Reuben. But it does nothing to ease his guilt.

"Perhaps Gabriel ran," he says, desperately trying to make himself believe it. "Perhaps they're hiding somewhere." But he knows his crimes have left him surrounded by enemies. Knows it far more likely his children have been taken. He folds his hands behind his head.

"The revenue men have eyes all over this village. Perhaps they saw something. We ought to ask at Customs House."

Caroline gnaws her thumbnail. "The revenue men have their eyes on you. If we tell them about the children they'll start digging into our life. Is that what you want?"

Isaac paces the thin curve of the beach, letting the sea wash over his boots. "I don't care what they find. I just care about getting the children back."

"*I* care what they find." Caroline's voice rattles. "I can't lose you too."

Isaac opens his mouth to speak. Says nothing. He doesn't deserve her loyalty.

"Bring the revenue men into this and you'll put Scarlett in danger," she reminds him. "And Flora." Her voice is clipped.

Caroline is right, of course. The revenue men are waiting for an excuse to pry, to dig. And if Isaac falls he will take half the village down with him. There can be no going to the authorities. This is theirs to carry alone.

Caroline turns to look back at the village. Clouds lie on top of the hills, drawing the light from the day. "We ought to go to Reuben again," she says.

Charles Reuben's had been the first door they had pounded on. Had been told by his housekeeper the man was unavailable. A sign of his guilt, surely.

Isaac gives Caroline's shoulders a gentle squeeze. "I'll go to Reuben. You go home. Rest. You've been hurt."

She shrugs out of his grasp. "How could I rest? I need to keep looking. There are people in this village we've not spoken to."

After a moment, Isaac says: "Be careful. Please."

She nods faintly. Turns to leave.

"Caroline. Wait." He reaches into the water, wetting the cuff of his shirt. He wipes gently at the line of dried blood streaking the side of her face. He leaves his fingers against her cheek for a moment. It makes his chest ache.

Caroline pushes past him and makes her way into the village.

Isaac strides up the path towards Reuben's mansion. And for the first time, he feels it. That wild rage that takes hold of his sister, that had taken hold of his father. That rage in their blood. He feels it writhe inside him, trying to force its way out. It quickens his heart and makes his skin burn, despite the icy sting of the wind.

He must keep calm. If Reuben has the children he must bend to his requests. This is not a time to lose control.

He draws in a long, slow breath, trying to still his rage. And he understands, fleetingly, what it is like to be Scarlett. Feels what it is like to have that anger batter around inside. A faint glimpse inside the head of the fiery, willful sister he had scooped from the rim of the sea.

He had found her in the cave, blood running from the back of her head and turning the water pink.

Dead, he had thought. Their last words to each other ones of bitterness and anger.

But no, a faint pulse. Breath tickling the back of his hand.

Isaac pulled her from the water's edge as the tide surged towards her. Her blood vanished into the tarred black sleeve of his coat.

For a moment, he stood motionless, frozen with the unbearable horror of it.

Scarlett, Gabriel, Mary. The dried blood at the side of Caroline's head. He felt the weight of his sister in his arms, felt the weight of the situation pressing down on him. It was suddenly hard to breathe.

"Isaac," Caroline said in a half voice. It drew him out of his daze.

He looked up. There were people at the harbour. Two women rolling a barrel past the door of the pilchard palace. Will Francis roping the dory to the quay. Isaac carried Scarlett towards him. Will leapt from the boat at the sight of them.

"Take her to Flora."

Isaac knows nothing of what has happened to his sister. How long has it been since he had watched Will carry her over the cliffs? Three hours? Four? Perhaps more.

He has no thought of whether Scarlett is still alive.

He pounds on Reuben's door, throwing his rage into the brass knocker until he feels it will break with the force of it. But when the maid answers, he finds himself eerily calm. Anger will not pull answers from Reuben. Anger will not help him find his children.

He follows the maid into the parlour and waits for Reuben to appear. He paces, hands folded behind his head. His boots click rhythmically on the polished boards. Distant sounds come from within the house; laughter and the clink of knives against plates. The smell of roasting meat turns his stomach.

Charles Reuben enters the parlour, his lips pressed into thin white line. He is dressed in a gold-threaded waistcoat and pristine tailed white wig. He looks at Isaac as though he were a stray dog who had weaselled its way through the door. "Bold of you to come to me," he says. "Are you here to make your apologies? I trust you've realised what will happen if you betray me again."

"Where are they?" Isaac asks evenly.

Reuben folds his arms across his thick middle. "Where are who?"

Isaac feels a line of sweat run down his back at the effort of remaining calm. "Let's not play games."

"I've guests, Mr Bailey. And you are taking up my valuable time. Believe me, I'm in no mood to play games either."

Isaac clenches his teeth. "Someone has taken my children," he says. "And attacked my wife and sister."

Reuben hums. "It seems your deceitfulness has bought you a number of enemies."

Isaac lifts a glass ashtray from the side table. He needs something in his hands, something to tense his fingers around, something to channel this anxiety into.

"I don't have your children," says Reuben.

No, this is too easy. He will not just turn away at Reuben's word. Isaac's fingers tighten around the ashtray. "You expect me to believe you had no part in this?"

Reuben meets his eyes. "I am a good and decent man, Mr Bailey. I don't lie. You know that. I've never been anything but honest with you."

"You had your men come after my family this morning," says Isaac. "And you sent the banker after me and my seven-year-old sister. Had him hold a gun to our heads."

"Because you were trying to avoid paying debts that are legally and rightfully yours."

Isaac draws in a long breath, trying to slow his heart. "I will stay here," he hisses. "I will stay here and run goods for you for the rest of my life. Just let my children go."

"Yes," Reuben says evenly. "You will stay here and run goods for me until every penny of your father's debt is paid off, because that is what a decent man would do." He runs a finger over the top of an armchair. "But I do not have your children."

Isaac hurls the ashtray. It shatters on the floorboards with a satisfying crash. Glittering shards escape across the room and settle beneath the clavichord.

A tiny smile appears in the corner of Reuben's lips. "You have much of your father in you, Mr Bailey. It's taken me some time to see it."

Caroline catches a glimpse of herself in the window of the Ship Inn. Her eyes are underlined with shadow, her hair tangled down her back. Blood stains the edges of her cap. She pulls it from her head and bundles it into her fist. Rakes her fingers through her knotted hair.

Looking like a madwoman will not help her cause.

She rattles the door of the tavern. Locked. Inside, she sees the innkeeper wiping a cloth along the bar. She raps loudly on the window. The innkeeper shoos her away.

"We're closed," he calls, his voice muffled through the glass.

Caroline knocks again, louder.

Finally, the man pulls the door open a crack. "What do you want?"

"I need to speak with you," she says breathlessly. "Please. It's very important."

With a sigh, the innkeeper steps back, letting her inside.

The tavern is quiet. Dust motes dance in a shaft of sun that highlights the deep scratches on the tabletops. The innkeeper looks expectantly at Caroline.

"Did you have a man take a room here last night?" she asks, pinning him with eyes that tell him she wants answers, not questions. If Asher Hales is to be believed, Jacob Bailey had asked for a room here after he had confronted her on the beach yesterday. But then, Asher Hales is not a man to be believed. She cannot pretend to be surprised when the innkeeper says:

"No ma'am. Just our regular lodgers in last night."

Caroline goes to the Three Pilchards. There is a sickening symmetry to it. She steps through the door with her bloodied cap in her hand, more lost and undone than she had been that night sixteen years ago when she had walked into this place and told Jacob to abandon his family. And here she stands, looking for the man again.

She approaches the bar slowly. Clears her throat. "I'm searching for a man who is staying at your inn."

The innkeeper lifts a leather-bound ledger from beneath the counter. "Name?"

Caroline watches him flick through the pages. "He'll not have given you his real name. But he would have come to you last night."

"I weren't working here last night. My brother was. Can't help you without a name."

She reaches over the counter and plants a hand in the middle of the book to stop him closing it. "Someone has taken my children. And this man may know something." She smacks her palm against the pages, making the innkeeper start. "Last night. Who was here?"

He narrows his eyes, then after a moment, looks back at the ledger. "Room two," he tells her finally. "A man come in yesterday afternoon."

Caroline feels a sudden thumping behind her eyes. She manages a nod of thanks.

She makes her way upstairs on shaky legs and pounds on the door of room two. Nothing but silence. She can't pretend to be surprised.

Each minute that passes, she is more and more certain that Jacob is the one who has taken her children. He will want her to suffer as he had suffered. Will want her scared, desperate, ready to spill her secrets. Of course he is not here waiting for her.

She presses her eye to the keyhole. Sees nothing but rumpled bed clothes and a bare, scratched table. She makes her way down the hall, peering through the keyholes into the other rooms. More rumpled bedclothes. More empty tables. A woollen bonnet in one room. A riding officer's jacket in another.

Nothing to hint at the whereabouts of Jacob and her children. Nothing to suggest that the world might not be carrying on as though nothing at all has happened.

She gnaws on her thumbnail until the skin around it is red and raw. She sinks to the floor in the hallway outside Jacob's empty room and brings her knees to her chest.

Jacob wants her to leave Talland. Leave Isaac. He had made threats against Mary. But surely he knows she will not leave without knowing her children are safe?

She will do anything to save them. Will tell Isaac her every secret if it will see Mary and Gabriel safely returned. That's what Jacob wants isn't it? For her to look into her husband's eyes and tell him of how she had torn apart his family? She knows the only way Isaac will believe such things are if they come from her own mouth.

But she needs Jacob's word. Her son and daughter in exchange for her secrets. She will not destroy her marriage if it will not give her back her children.

She lets her eyes close. In her mind's eye she sees Gabriel creeping into the passage at the back of the cave. Sees Jacob leaning over Mary's basket. Sees Isaac with his lips against Flora's.

She opens her eyes. Blinks hard and swallows the sickness in her throat.

The stairs creak and she leaps to her feet, pressing a hand to the wall as dizziness cows her.

"You're still here?" the innkeeper demands. "You can't just wait around on the floor all day. What will my customers think?"

"Customers," Caroline snaps. "You've got no customers. I've not seen a soul."

The innkeeper jabs a finger towards the staircase and she makes her way out of the inn, the ache in her chest intensifying.

Jacob Bailey, she realises sickly, will be found when he wants to be.

THE GOOD AND DECENT MAN

Scarlett hears footsteps coming closer. Her fingers tighten around the edge of the blankets. How terrifying the sound is now she cannot see who is approaching.

"Who's there?"

"It's me, Scarlett."

Tears spill suddenly down her cheeks. She is so glad to hear Isaac's voice.

The bed moves beneath his weight. His arms slide around her, pulling her close. She feels his hair tickle her nose, feels his bristly chin against her ear. He smells of salt and sweat and ash soap.

The muscles in his arms are tense. She can tell something is very wrong.

The memories swing at her suddenly.

Isaac had been planning to escape. Had made a run to Guernsey without Reuben's knowledge. Bought liquor from an agent of his own.

Scarlett remembers trying to hide the contraband from Reuben. Remembers racing home to find the cottage empty. Remembers Asher Hales sending her to the beach in Polperro.

They're in the cave, he had told her. *Your family. I saw them.*

She had found Caroline lying motionless on the sand, blood running from the side of her head.

"Caroline," she says suddenly. "Is she—"

"She's all right. You're not to worry yourself over her."

"Then what?"

There is silence for a moment. Finally, Isaac says:

"Gabriel and Mary are missing. They've been taken by whoever attacked you."

Scarlett feels suddenly hot and sick. The pain in her head intensifies. She opens her mouth to speak, but what is there to say? Her stomach knots.

"Do you remember seeing anything?" Isaac asks. "Before…" His hands are tight around her wrists, steadying her or himself, Scarlett is unsure.

And she is back in that cave, seeing the water sweep through shafts of white light.

Watching blood run over Caroline's hair, watching Gabriel's arms reach towards her in fear. These cannot be the last things her eyes ever see.

Movement. Yes, there had been movement behind her. She had seen it fleetingly on the edge of her vision.

"They struck me from behind," she says. "I didn't turn in time to see who it was. I'm sorry."

How useless her words are.

"Reuben found your ankers in the tunnel," she tells Isaac. "Was he the reason Caroline was hiding in the cave? Do you think he took the children to stop you from leaving?"

"Scarlett, I don't want you involved. You need to rest. I only asked in case there was anything you remembered."

"Don't keep things from me," she says, pulling herself into sitting. "Not now. I couldn't bear it."

Isaac doesn't speak at once. "I confronted Reuben," he says finally. "He claims to know nothing."

"He's lying."

"Perhaps."

"I saw the look in his eyes when he found those ankers," says Scarlett. "He was angry enough for this. And he's always been willing to do anything to stop us from leaving."

She had been seven years old the night they had tried to escape. She remembers walking across the beach with Isaac, picking their way in moonlight towards the path on the cliff. Remembers the glow of the lantern spilling over the beach, illuminating the gun in the banker's hand.

Run, Isaac had told her, his big hand clasping hers. But even as a child she had known. Had known Reuben's men would not hesitate to shoot.

Nor would they hesitate to take Gabriel and Mary. Would see it a fitting punishment for Isaac's betrayal.

"I'm sorry," she says suddenly. "For all I said. For the things I accused you of. I'm so sorry. I—"

Isaac brushes the hair from her eyes, the way he used to do when she was a child. "It doesn't matter," he says. "None of it matters. Not anymore."

Finally, Scarlett agrees to rest. Isaac watches as she curls up on her side, moving carefully on the pillow to avoid the swelling at the back of her head.

She closes her eyes. Isaac is glad of it. Her drifting, unfocused gaze has made knots of his stomach. Scarlett had been his to protect. Gabriel and Mary, his to protect. And look how he has failed them.

He makes his way into the hallway, closing the door gently behind him.

Where is Flora? He knows it best, of course, that he disappear out of the inn without speaking with her. But he doesn't want that. Doesn't want to disappear. Doesn't want her to disappear.

He hears the clatter of glasses in the bar. She has taken everything from the shelves and is polishing the wood with beeswax. She wears an apron over faded, rose-coloured skirts, her blonde hair in a messy knot at her neck.

She squeezes the polishing rag between her fingers. At once there is everything and nothing to say.

"Any word?" she asks.

Isaac shakes his head. "Reuben denies everything." His eyes drift to the bare shelves.

Flora follows his gaze. "It's a trivial thing to do, I know. But I couldn't bear to keep still."

Isaac gives her a small smile. He remembers this about her. In the weeks after her husband had died, he had called on her each day. Would find her cleaning windows or blacking the hearths, or hemming and re-hemming every item of clothing her daughter owned.

I couldn't bear to keep still, she'd told him.

"Are you sure Scarlett is all right here?" he asks.

"Of course. She'll stay as long as she needs."

"Do you think this will be permanent?" His voice comes out husky.

Flora sighs, tugging at the rag. "I've no way of knowing. I'm sorry." She comes out from behind the bar and presses a gentle hand to his elbow. In spite of himself, Isaac feels his insides heat. His desire for her is still there, poorly hidden, simmering inches beneath the surface. He tries to will it away.

"This isn't your fault," she says. "None of it is your fault."

He doesn't reply. How can he stop believing this his fault? Had he not run back to Talland for Flora, none of it would ever have happened.

"I'd best go," he says.

Flora nods, pulling her hand away. "You'll be in my prayers. You and the children."

When Isaac returns to the cottage, the windows are dark. Caroline has not returned.

He had wanted her to be home. Had wanted to tend to her a little before he went back out to search. Make a fire for her to rest in front of. Tea to warm her.

A fire and tea, of course, will not make up for his betrayal. But perhaps they might begin to show her how deeply he still cares.

He steps inside. Immediately, the silence hits him. An awful, thick stillness without the chattering of a baby or a little boy's footsteps or Scarlett's sassy asides.

How desperately he had wanted to leave this life behind. But now, to sit around the kitchen table with his family, planning the next run to Guernsey feels like the greatest of unreachable joys.

He lights a lamp and his breath leaves him. At his feet lies their upturned travelling chest. Pots and pans are on their sides by the hearth. Clothes have been flung across the cottage. A shirt has found its way into the fire grate, underskirts lying beneath the table.

Had Reuben's men done this?

Behind the scattered clothes and pots, the house is spotless. The shelves are bare and dusted, the grate empty of ash, the wash stand polished and dried. Caroline had readied the house for their escape. Exactly what had happened to make her run?

I'm a good and decent man, Reuben had told him.

Lies, every word. There is no decency to Charles Reuben. No goodness. Are Gabriel and Mary hidden somewhere in the passages of that great sprawling mansion? Had they heard the laughter around Reuben's dinner table that afternoon? Had they been close enough to hear their father's voice?

For all Reuben's denial, Isaac can't get past the thought that he and his men are responsible for the kidnapping. Punishment for his daring to double cross him, as his father had done so many years ago.

How far would Reuben go? Surely his business brain would not seek to kill Isaac's children. They are the ones who will carry the debt when he dies. The thought is both sickening and faintly comforting.

He gathers the clothes from the floor and throws them back in the wardrobe. Closes the door to the empty nursery so his wife might be saved from looking inside. He sets the pots back on the shelf. The sight of them reminds him that neither he or Caroline have eaten all day. He has no appetite, but he knows a little supper will do them both good.

He takes the lamp to the garden and pulls a few potatoes from the damp earth. Carries them inside and lights the fire.

The door creaks open. Caroline collapses into a chair at the kitchen table. "What did Reuben say?"

"He denies everything. Claims himself a good and decent man."

She stares into the flames, a curtain of dark hair falling over one eye. "And you've only just returned?"

Isaac wipes his muddy hands on his breeches. "I went to see Scarlett."

"You went to the inn." Her voice is cold.

"To see my sister."

For a moment, Caroline doesn't speak. "How is she?" she asks finally.

Isaac feels a heaviness in his stomach. He can't bear to speak the words. *Blow to the head. Blinded.*

"Alive," he manages. "Scarlett is alive."

Caroline pulls her shawl around her shoulders, edging her chair closer to the fire. She looks up at Isaac with watery eyes. "What now?" she asks. "How are we supposed to just carry on?"

He crouches beside her, covering her hand with his. She is stiff, unresponsive.

He has no answer for her. Has no thought of how to make this better. And so he says: "I'm sorry."

Caroline pulls her hand out from beneath his.

"I know it'll not fix anything. And I know it won't help us find the children. But I truly believed she was in danger. That's the only reason I went back."

Caroline is silent for a long time. "A good wife ought to turn her back on such things," she says finally.

Isaac closes his eyes. Guilt tightens his insides. He goes to the table for the potatoes.

"Don't bother," says Caroline. "I couldn't eat."

No. Nor could he.

"Try to sleep," he tells her huskily. "You need it." He sees the fire reflected in her glistening eyes.

"How could I sleep?"

"You need to try. I'll go back out. Look for the banker. He may know something."

Caroline shakes her head.

Isaac presses a firm hand to her shoulder. "Go and rest. I wish it. As your husband."

She snorts. "You wish it," she repeats coldly. "As my husband." The chair squeals noisily as she stands. She disappears into the bedroom without another word.

INCANTATIONS

Scarlett wakes and the images that had lit up her dreams are gone. This is the second time she has woken to darkness and the shock of it is still raw. She touches the swelling at the back of her head. There is something vaguely steadying about the pain. It anchors her to the world she cannot see.

The darkness is deep and wide, littered with pricks of phantom light, too tiny, too imperceptible to be anything but her eyes struggling to make sense of their new futility. She forces herself to breathe slow and deep. She cannot let herself feel anger at whoever had done this to her. The dark has always been able to send her anger away, but how will it be now dark is all she has? If the Wild traps her here, there may be no way of ever getting out.

Inhale. She smells the enchanting scent of drying herbs. Smells the evidence of that healing woman's life Flora had sworn would not be hers.

Scarlett runs a hand over the wall beside the bed, feeling stone worn smooth. She needs to place herself in this world, in this room that had been the village charmer's. She feels the rough grain of the blanket, the globes of the bedposts, the cloying warmth of the pillow.

At the foot of the bed, she finds a pile of coarse wool. Her cloak?

She runs a finger over the hem, following it up over lines of hooks and buttons. Yes, she remembers. She had been at the inn before she had been attacked. Had been speaking with Bessie in the room full of flowers. She had left her cloak draped over a chair.

She digs a hand into the pocket. The letter Asher Hales had given her is there. The letter that had told her Jacob Bailey had abandoned his family. She does not take it out. Best that cursed thing stays hidden.

She tosses the cloak back over the foot of the bed. She cannot just lie here and hope. Cannot just pray for the light, or for the safe return of her brother's children. She had been the last one to see them. Had held them in her arms while their mother lay unconscious at her feet.

She tries to think. Tries to remember.

Air moving against her cheek. She had been struck from behind. Had had no chance to see who was in the cave with them. But there must be something in her memories; some sound, some smell, some hint at who had been there.

Think. Remember.

But there is nothing. Nothing to remember beyond the white hot pain that had taken her sight away.

The dark shifts and sways around her. Where is Flora? Scarlett needs to not be alone.

The rooms around her are quiet. She hears a table groan as it is pushed along the floor in the tavern below.

She climbs out of bed. Runs a hand along the wall until she reaches the doorway. She knows the inn well. This is the first guestroom. That way is the parlour. And here; the top of the stairs. She feels the floor fall away beneath the tips of her toes.

"Scarlett—" Flora's voice is sharp. "Stay there."

No. She feels the stair rail beneath her hand, worn smooth, just as she remembers. There is something faintly comforting about it. The world she knows is still here. Slowly, carefully, she steps down into the bar. The familiar scent of beeswax polish rises to meet her. Her hand slides off the end of the bannister.

"You ought to be resting," says Flora. She pushes aside Scarlett's hair to inspect the gash on the back of her head.

No, she ought to be out there helping Isaac and Caroline find their children. Ought to be out there punishing whoever had attacked her.

The pale sun on her cheek tells her it is morning. A full day since she had arrived from Portreath and walked down the hill into Talland.

She ought to be in Polperro, saying goodbye to the man who had brought her home.

Jamie will know nothing, of course, of all that has happened. He will know nothing of the attack in the cave or the missing children or the eternal darkness that has fallen over her. He will just see that she has not come to say goodbye. He will think his role in the revenue service has been enough to turn her away.

Her throat tightens.

"At least sit down," says Flora, leading her to a chair.

Scarlett sits. A shawl is tossed around her shoulders. Never in her life has she felt so useless.

This cannot be forever.

"You can help me, can't you, Flora? You know how to fix this, ayes? You know what to do."

Flora doesn't answer at once. Her silence makes Scarlett's stomach roll.

"Answer me," she says, sharper than she had intended. "You can help me, can't you."

And Flora says: "Of course."

Of course, she'd said. *Of course I can help.*

When Scarlett goes back to bed to rest, Flora finds herself pacing the room that had once been Jack's. Leaves are strung up across the mantle to dry, filling the place with the scent of the moors. She runs a finger along them, feeling their damp, velvety softness.

Of course I can help.

What else was there to say? How could she have admitted she has no idea where to begin?

Her head is full of tonics and incantations. Cures for coughs and colds, snake-bites and scurvy. Charms for luck and to keep the devil at bay.

But a cure for lost sight? Flora is not even sure such a thing is possible.

Her mother would have believed it was. Her mother had believed everything could be cured with concoctions and prayer and whispered incantations. But for all the steps Flora has taken to immerse herself in the world of the craft, her faith is precarious at best.

She empties the contents of her mother's chest onto the floor. There are pouches of angelica and mallow and lengths of hangman's rope. The black mirror, wrapped in a cloth so it might hide its secrets. There is little that will be of any help to Scarlett.

Had her mother felt this same uselessness, Flora wonders? Had she held herself responsible each time her incantations had failed to save a life?

Her mother had not been a good healer. All the faith in the world had not stopped men dying with her charms in their hands. Flora had grown more critical of the craft each time another body was lowered into their churchyard.

But there is no time now for criticism or doubt.

She tries to think. Tries to sift through her memories for any charm that might be of use.

Crowfoot, the kenning herb, for ulcers of the eyes.

It won't work. She feels it inside her.

But she has trained herself to offer cures with conviction. And she knows Scarlett is a believer. She will trust the crowfoot can bring back the light. And that, Flora is sure, has to be worth something.

She puts everything back into the chest and goes out to the hallway. She will try with the crowfoot when Scarlett has had a little more rest.

Two of the old guestrooms opened. Flora has sifted through the belongings of her mother, her husband. Only one more room to open. She can't remember the last time she had seen its door unlocked.

Her father had been a merchant sailor who had spent months on end at sea. In his long absences, she and her mother had lost themselves in a world of fragrant, bubbling teas and mirrors.

His death had been a sudden thing, a week after Flora's ninth birthday. Her most vivid memories of the man are of him lying dead on the floor in that locked-up room. One moment he had been replacing a loose floorboard, the next, lying on his back, staring at the rugged beams of the roof. Flora remembers crouching beside his body, eyes fixed on the pale threads of hair beneath the open laces of his shirt. She had tried to imagine the still heart that lay beneath.

It had been after her father's burial, she supposes, that her mother had locked the door.

Had she hidden his things away in there to try and stem her grief?

After her father's death, Flora's life had gone on much the way it had when he'd been alive. There will be little sentimentality when she opens that door. None of the gentle grief she had felt when she had sifted through her mother and husband's things. Just a vague sense of pity for a man she had barely known.

But there is a reluctance in her, nonetheless.

She is opening these rooms so she can put guests inside them. This has been her plan from the very beginning. But the closer she gets to such a thing, the more uncomfortable it makes her.

She will open the tavern to the people of Talland, yes. But the top floors of the inn have always been her home. She had been born in these rooms. Had stitched her wedding dress, become a mother. It feels wrong to let strangers traipse their way through such precious memories.

But she has little choice. Because now, with the shelves bare of liquor and the excisemen's eyes on her, the Mariner's Arms is nothing but a languishing alehouse. Soon, the men who have bought her lambswool in an act of charity will have a thirst for rum and brandy she'll not be able to satisfy. Her only hope of survival is to fill the place with overnight guests. Have strangers' footsteps echoing down her halls.

Sighing to herself, she pulls the ring of keys from the drawer in the parlour. She carries it back to the locked room.

Which key?

Each jams in the lock and refuses to turn. Flora tries once more, then makes her way back to the parlour and tosses the keys into the drawer.

She tried, she tells herself. What more is there to do?

RUINS

She is not coming.

Jamie has waited throughout the morning. He has done so many circuits of Polperro he'll be seeing these whitewashed cottages in his dreams. It is well past noon. His horse is growing restless at being saddled and unridden.

Winter is close and dusk will come early. He needs to leave now if he is to make it to Truro before dark.

He has been here far longer than he intended. Had promised Scarlett he would return to Portreath the moment he knew she had made it home safely. Promised her he would turn his back. Not peek beneath the surface into her life of smuggling.

Resting the horse, he had told her, as an explanation for his staying. Resting the horse and himself. There had been an element of truth to it. He and Scarlett had ridden across the county in less than two days. They had spent a night in a Truro inn, Jamie kept awake by the snoring of eight other men in the dormitory around him. By the time they had reached Talland, he had been craving sleep. But there had also been a reluctance in him to leave her.

He'd spent the night at the Three Pilchards, close to Polperro harbour. Had stared at the ceiling until dawn, listening to ratlines clatter in the dark. He can count on one hand the hours of sleep he's had since Scarlett Bailey had barrelled into his life.

He'd lay there with his thoughts full of her. He knew well how foolish this was. He was an officer of the revenue service. She, the woman he had caught with her hands in a chest of smuggled tobacco. He ought never have ridden to Talland with her. Ought to have given her money for a coach ride home and wished her the best of luck. A far more sensible course of action. But sense, Jamie is coming to realise, is something he seems to have in short supply of late.

And so, today, she has not come. Today, she has been wiser than him. She has seen it is best to end this now, before he becomes anything more than the man who had seen her home.

There is a dull ache in his chest as he swings himself onto his horse. For the best.

He tells himself again. *For the best.*

He begins to ride. Suddenly he wants nothing more than to be gone from this place. He wants to be back in Portreath, patrolling the cliffs on horseback while the sea curls beneath him. He wants windblown hair and rain-soaked clothes, wants the thunder of hooves rattling his body. He wants to hide in watch houses to catch smugglers in the act, wants to comb the cliffs to find the men hiding beneath.

And this is what she is, he reminds himself, as Polperro slips into the valley. Scarlett Bailey is the woman willing to run smuggled tobacco to the men on the hills. She is midnight landings and silent deliveries and the secret language of the signalling lanterns. Reminding himself makes this easier. She is all the things he has committed himself to eradicating.

The last patches of blue disappear from the sky as he follows the road into rusty moorland. A cold wind swirls, catching hold of the ends of his scarf.

He will head west, make for the river. Follow it north until he finds the road to Truro. He will retrace the journey he and Scarlett had made from Portreath; a windswept trek past tors and barrows and ice-flecked streams.

She'd spent most of the ride talking. Her reluctance to have him accompany her home was gone before Portreath had vanished behind the hills.

"What's your horse's name?" she'd asked.

He said: "Scarlett."

She laughed. "You're making that up." She looked over her shoulder at him. "Are you making that up?"

Yes, he said, he was making it up. He told her of how he'd purchased the horse from a Portreath farmer and had named her Arrow, for the markings on her flank. He told her of teaching himself to ride on his grandfather's farm, of the enormous black horse in his *sira-wynn*'s stables that had terrified him when he was a boy.

She had chattered about her years in the children's home, and the excitement she had felt when her brother had appeared to take her back to Talland. She told him of her niece and nephew and her cottage on the hill. Days pressing and salting at the pilchard palace, nights serving ale at the village tavern.

She leant back against his chest and Jamie felt his heart quicken.

Later, she told him of the letter she had been given, claiming her father had been hiding in Portreath.

He knew of her father, of course, the bastard who'd been up to his eyes in illegal impressment. When she'd begun to speak of him, Jamie had found himself changing the subject.

They had talked for two days without drawing breath, yet had managed to dance around enormous chunks of their lives. He knew nothing of how deep she and her family was in the world of smuggling. And he'd told her no details of his appointment to the revenue service two years earlier. Told her nothing of the patrols, the watches, the trials he had been involved in to see smuggling syndicates unravelled and free traders carted off in chains.

There'd been an unspoken understanding between them. Topics too difficult to raise. A bridge too fragile to cross.

The roads are empty and thick with mud. The river slices the earth, silver and sighing.

Jamie crosses the bridge. Sees the skeleton of a castle blotting the sky. The ruins are otherworldly in the half light. He turns up the collar of his coat, shivering as he rides past.

He and his brother had been raised by their grandmother, a woman with an endless supply of ghostly tales and legends. She had believed the stories unquestionably, had told them in whispers while the fire hissed and rain pattered against the glass. His earliest memories are of curling up beneath the bedclothes listening to tales of haunted ruins. Relics populated by grey ladies and silent, vanishing monks.

Jamie looks up at the castle shell. It is round and low, built on a faint rise of the earth. One side of the grey stone wall is little more than rubble. There is a prickly energy to the place, as though fragments of the past still linger.

He continues riding. Such places have always unnerved him.

At the edge of his vision, he sees something move in the ruins. He stops the horse. Looks again at the castle. Such places have always unnerved him, but they also hold his curiosity.

He waits. Hears the wings of a gull beat above his head. And there it is again, clearer this time. A flash of movement within the keep. He sees a man with dark hair tangled around his shoulders. Jamie sees only the back of his head as he darts through the shadows. The figure is gone so quickly he is unsure whether he had seen anything at all.

He takes the horse closer. Watches the animal for any reaction, any sense of the otherworldly. The horse turns up its ears. And a sound comes on the wind. The cry of a baby.

Jamie almost laughs. In the ghost stories his grandmother had told, there was always the cry of a baby.

He waits. There is no more crying. There is no sound at all, but the distant burble of the river. It had been nothing but his imagination, surely.

He ought to ride away. The place makes the hair on the back of his neck stand on end.

But as he turns to leave, he hears murmuring. Men's voices.

Jamie hesitates. He has hunted down free traders in graveyards, found ankers stored in coffins, hauled contraband out of empty wells.

He knows an abandoned castle is a fine place for smugglers to hide their goods.

The thing about this life, Jamie had come to realise when he'd first begun to patrol the coast, was that it was impossible to stop looking. Stop suspecting, stop doubting, stop guessing. This journey was supposed to be about nothing more than seeing Scarlett home safely. And yet he has his uniform and journal in his saddle bag, his pistol in his pocket. How can he stop looking in a place where smuggling is as natural as breathing?

He glances again at the castle.

He had promised Scarlett he would ride away and not ask questions. Had not imagined keeping his word would be so difficult.

So here are his choices: approach the castle and uncover a potential smugglers' haul.

Or ride away, keeping his promise to a woman who had not seen fit to say goodbye.

Ride away. A promise is a promise.

If there are smugglers in the castle they may well be a part of the Baileys' syndicate.

The shot comes before he has a chance to move. It flies over his shoulder and sends his horse bolting across the moor. He grapples with the reins to avoid being thrown. When the horse begins to calm, he gently slows her, fumbling in his pocket for the pistol. Riding away from murmuring men is one thing, but to hell if he'll turn his back when there are shots flying over his shoulder.

He climbs from the saddle, lowering himself slowly to the ground to avoid making a sound. He glances around him. There is nowhere to tether the horse, but the bent skeleton of a tree. He loops the reins around a gnarled grey branch, hoping it will hold.

He draws in his breath, pushing his dark hair out of his eyes. The castle rises ahead of him. To his left, the gate that had once held the drawbridge gapes.

He cannot enter this way. The shooter will be expecting it.

He follows the wall until he finds a place dilapidated enough for him to climb through.

Inside is silent. The castle roof is long-vanished and clouds hang low over the crumbling ruins. Jamie's breath makes a cloud in front of him.

He grips his gun. His heart is thudding. The footsteps, the fleeting image of the man, the crying child, they had felt otherworldly. But the gunshot— that had been real.

He walks carefully, silently, keeping to the patches of grass that poke between the stone.

He can smell horses. Where are they hidden? There are plenty of rooms still intact enough for a man to hide his animal.

He finds them in the shell of the great hall. Two dark grey horses, shifting restlessly in the shadows. They are saddled, their reins looped to an outward-jutting piece of stone. There is no sign of any contraband.

Jamie continues along the edge of the courtyard until he is back at the hole through which he had entered.

There is nothing. Not a sound from this world, or another. No sign of men, or smuggled goods. Whoever had been here has left.

He makes his way out of the hole in the castle wall and across the indent left by the long-empty moat. The men have not taken their horses. They cannot be far. But the light is beginning to drain and shadows lie thick over the moor. He sees no sign of movement, beyond his horse silhouetted in the distance. The tree branch to which he had tied her lies broken on the ground.

He walks slowly towards the horse, crooning and murmuring to keep her from bolting. He lurches for the reins and runs a hand down the velvety plane of her nose.

Then he goes back to the castle. Waits for the men to return for their horses.

He sits in the saddle for two hours or more. There is no one.

He shivers. He is exhausted and shaken. Will not make it to Truro by dark. It would be foolish, he knows, to ride any further north tonight. Best he return to Polperro.

He hesitates. He had promised Scarlett he would not stay.

But whatever had been between them is over and done. Surely she cannot begrudge him a safe night's sleep.

He tugs on the reins and heads back towards the village.

THE DOMAIN OF DESPERATE MEN

"I heard about the children," Martha Francis says, appearing at the cottage door with an elaborately wrapped saffron cake. "I'm so dreadfully sorry."

Caroline doesn't look up from the carrots she is slicing. Eating is the last thing she feels like doing, but she and Isaac have agreed to force down a little supper. She knows they will need to keep up their strength if they are to continue searching at the rate they have been. She has spent the day questioning villagers in Killigarth and her eyes are heavy with exhaustion.

Isaac gives Martha a nod of thanks, gesturing for her to enter.

Caroline grits her teeth. Eating is the last thing she feels like doing, closely followed by indulging Martha Francis. Her knife slams rhythmically into the chopping board. A slice of carrot flies across the kitchen.

Martha sets the cake on the table. "You need to go to the forest," she says fervently. "You need to go after them."

Caroline looks up. "What? Go after who?"

"The piskeys, of course. The fairies." Martha turns to Isaac. "You know this was their doing, don't you?"

Caroline feels something sink inside her. The brief moment of hope gives way to anger. She puts down the knife and closes her eyes.

Isaac ushers the old woman back towards the door. "Martha, please. It's not a good time."

"You know I'm right, Isaac," she says, winding her apron around a gnarled finger. "I know you've not forgotten everything your mother taught you. You know there are spirits out there we ought to be afraid of. Spirits that are more than capable of taking your children."

"I've not forgotten," Isaac says, impatience on the edge of his voice. "I just think our time could be better spent looking elsewhere."

Martha sighs, shaking her head in frustration. She looks over Isaac's shoulder at Caroline. "You ought to have pinned her to the crib."

Caroline's eyes flash. "What?"

"Young Mary. You ought to have pinned her nightgown to the crib. It's what I used to do with my Will. Only way to stop the fairy folk from taking them."

Caroline charges out from behind the table. "Get out!" she cries. "Get out of my house with these ridiculous stories!" She slams the door as Martha bustles over the doorstep. The thud of it rattles her insides. She chews her thumbnail. "She's blaming me," she says, beginning to pace in front of the hearth. "She thinks me a bad mother."

Isaac takes her shoulders and holds her against him. "No one is blaming you."

"Did you not hear her? I ought to have pinned Mary's nightgown…"

"Ignore her. She obviously doesn't know the full story."

Caroline shrugs out of his grip. "I'm done with this place," she says bitterly. "I'm done living among people who cannot see sense." Once, she had welcomed these tales. They had brought a flicker of magic to a life that had been devoid of anything close. What harm would it do, she had thought, to imagine for a moment that piskeys danced on rooftops and giants walked the earth. But the allure of myths and fairy tales had worn thin many years ago.

Isaac plays with the lacy edge of the cloth wrapped around the saffron cake. "It's just how these people are," he says gently. "These stories are how they cope. How they make sense of the world."

Caroline throws the carrots into the pot and hangs it over the stove. "These stories are not going to help us find our children."

With supper forced down, Isaac goes back out to search. Caroline stands in the doorway and watches him leave. Wind stings her cheeks and thrashes her skirts around her legs. Bends the trees towards the sea.

She stays motionless for a long time. She cannot go back inside. The emptiness of the place is stifling. Go inside and she will find herself staring at the door of the nursery, thinking of the disused bed, the rumpled blankets, the empty cradle swaying in the draught.

Go inside and she will find herself staring into the room she shares with her husband. She will wonder how many nights he has lain beside her, wishing he were somewhere else.

She had had her suspicions, of course. Had told herself they would amount to nothing. She had not wanted to believe her husband capable of such things.

But how can she be angry when her betrayal is so much worse? How many nights does she have left to lie beside him before her secrets unravel completely?

The pain, the anger, the fear of it is too much.

A figure moves through the darkness.

Jacob Bailey is striding down the hill towards the cottage. Caroline races towards him. There is a tirade on her lips, but Jacob speaks first.

"Why are you still here?"

"Do you honestly think this is the way to get me to leave?" she cries. "Do you expect me to disappear from this place without knowing my children are safe?" She hurries inside, away from the prying eyes of the village. Slams the door behind Jacob.

His eyes dart around the cottage, taking it in. This had been his home too, Caroline remembers. He had sat at her table, made fires in her hearth, slept in her bed.

She sinks into a chair and rubs her eyes in resigned exhaustion. "Tell him," she coughs. "Tell Isaac everything. I just want my children back. They can't suffer for my mistakes." She hears the waver in her voice. She doesn't care. Let Jacob win.

He hovers over her, a frown deepening the creases in his leathery brow. "Something has happened to your children?"

Surprise in his voice?

No, he is playing with her. He is the one who has done this, Caroline is sure. He has done it to punish her, to force her to leave. To put her through the same pain she had inflicted on him.

"Just tell me where they are," she says. "Please."

But something has softened in Jacob's face. His lips are pursed beneath the grey mess of his beard. "What happened?" he asks.

Caroline sees something in his eyes. Something she has seen in her husband's eyes. That desperation to protect his family. This, she remembers, is the man who had exiled himself to save his wife and daughter's lives.

The realisation swings at her suddenly. Whoever had taken the children had attacked Scarlett to do it. Jacob Bailey would kill a man in cold blood and set up another to take the blame. He would steal, he would lie, and he would risk his crewmates' lives for his own gain.

But he would not harm the daughter he had done everything to protect.

"It wasn't you," she says.

"Of course not."

Caroline begins to gnaw on her thumbnail. "I believed you," she says. "On the beach. I believed you when you said you'd hurt Mary."

Jacob turns away. "She's Isaac's child. I'd never lay a finger on her."

Caroline's thoughts race. She had been sure Jacob was responsible. She had watched Isaac charge up Reuben's front path and been certain he would find nothing. She is not sure whether this revelation makes her terrified or relieved. But Jacob Bailey is not the only one seeking to bring her down. He is not the only man she wishes she had never met. How much can she continue to hide when her children's lives are in danger?

She pins Jacob with cold eyes. "Where is Asher Hales?"

This feels like the greatest of mistakes. The domain of desperate men.

Asher crouches at the edge of the river and scoops a handful of murky water into his mouth. He winces, tasting mud. The light has faded and the trees around him are thick silhouettes. He has planted a lamp in the muck of the riverbank, and the water ripples orange in the glow of the flame.

He looks up at the sound of approaching hooves. Tom Leach is in the saddle, leading a second horse by the reins. They are fine grey mares, stolen from a farm on the outskirts of Polperro.

They were to hide, Leach had said, in the ruins of Restormel Castle. He had been sheltering there alone since he had run from Polruan and the authorities almost a week earlier.

The castle had been a good place to shelter. Silent and ghostly, surrounded by nothing but empty moorland. Cover from the wind and river water to drink.

But this afternoon Leach had seen a man approaching. Shots had been fired. The silence and safety of the castle broken.

Involving himself with this reckless man, Asher sees now, had been the greatest of mistakes.

But two nights ago he had sat at the edge of Polperro harbour and watched Caroline walk back over the hill to Isaac. The woman he loved was to leave this place with her husband, taking with her the knowledge of how to find Henry Avery's haul. Money Asher had spent half his life searching for.

He had been on the verge of giving up. His dreams of becoming a wealthy, educated surgeon felt unreachable. Caroline was right. He'd never be anything more than a desperate fool.

And then there was Tom Leach, standing over him at the edge of the harbour. Asher had seen something of a kindred spirit. Lost men. Shunned and scorned.

Leach had asked questions and Asher had found himself answering. Had spilled all he knew about Caroline's desire to leave Talland.

Leach paced. "When?" he asked. And: "How do they mean to get past Reuben?"

To each; *I don't know.*

Asher knew he had nothing. No reliable information. No way to stop Caroline from disappearing. No way to resurrect his glittering future, his longed-for dreams.

"They can't leave," Leach said, staring across the anchorage to the dark shape of Isaac's lugger. "I'll not let it happen." He kept staring. He was making plans, Asher could tell.

"You're a wanted man," he told Leach finally, more to fill the silence than anything else. "Why are you here?" But as he spoke, he began to see.

Two riding officers had been killed in Lansallos. Tom Leach the prime suspect. He had returned to this place to punish Isaac for turning him over to the authorities. He was making plans to stop the Baileys from escaping. And Asher Hales needed to be a part of them.

"Tell me what you're planning," he said. "I can help you." He pressed his shoulders back, lifted his chin. He knew he looked a sorry creature; his face bruised and swollen, his clothes grimy and splattered with old blood. But he wanted Leach to see the man he was beneath. Wanted him to see that Asher Hales was a fine person with whom to share a secret.

"Their children," Leach said finally. "We'll take them."

Asher swallowed. He didn't know he had been expecting, but it wasn't this.

Take Caroline's children? Did he have it in him to deliver such brutality? A big part of him doubted it. But he saw the brilliance of the plan. With Caroline's children beneath his arms, he would have power. He would speak and she would listen. Be swayed. Manipulated.

She would tell him where Henry Avery's money was hidden. And she would leave this place on his arm, to build the life they had planned. She would have no choice. No leverage. Her children for her secrets.

Asher managed a small nod.

Leach raked long fingers through his beard. "In the morning," he said, "when Isaac has gone to sea, you'll go to the cottage and take the children from their mother. Bring them here. I'll have a boat waiting."

Me? Asher thought to say. *No. I couldn't...* He wanted to be involved, yes. But he didn't want to be the one with blood on his hands.

But he saw the pistol tucked in Leach's pocket. Saw the wildness in his eyes. This man was a killer. If the tales were to be believed, he had murdered two revenue officers at close range. He could not let this man anywhere near Caroline.

And so over the cliff path to Talland Asher walked, a man following orders. He hated the way such a thing felt. And yet he was so drained and weary, that acting on his own accord had begun to feel like an impossibility. He had been making plans for more than half his life. Had never seen any of them become reality. Why not let someone else carry the burden for once?

When he reached Talland, the village was still blanketed in darkness. He sat on the edge of the road, staring up at the Baileys' lightless cottage.

He ought to act now. Force open the window and take the children from their beds. What was the alternative? Take them in broad daylight from beneath Caroline's nose? Such a thing would require force, violence.

He couldn't. What kind of man would raise a hand to the woman he loved?

Act now.

His legs were heavy with reluctance, his thoughts sluggish and dull.

He sat staring at the cottage until dawn. He watched Isaac leave for the fishing port, watched farmers wheel carts of vegetables over the hill towards the market.

Watched Scarlett appear from the top of the hill.

Asher scrambled from the road and hid himself in the copse of trees opposite the cottage.

She stopped outside the front door, knotting her fingers together. Then she walked back down the road towards the church.

Enough hesitating. It had to be now.

Asher stepped out from his hiding place and crept closer to the cottage. Through the window, he could see Caroline racing across the house, shoving clothes into a trunk that sat in the middle of the kitchen.

How was he to go about this? He had no weapon with which to threaten her. Even if he had, she knew him well enough to know he would never have the courage to use it.

And here came men striding up the hill from the direction of the Mariner's Arms. Men

Asher had seen before. Men working for Charles Reuben.

He watched as they forced their way into the cottage.

Muffled shouts. Crashes and thuds. And as quickly as they had arrived, the men were gone.

Out they came from the house; Caroline and the children. They were dressed for travel, a chaos of cloaks and scarves and hats. Had disappeared over the cliff path before Asher could make sense of it.

He followed.

At the top of the hill he stopped and looked down into the village. There was Caroline, hurrying towards the cliff-rimmed harbour. Behind the jagged wall of rock, Asher knew Tom Leach was waiting with his stolen dory.

It had been more than an hour since Isaac had left for the fishing port. How long would it be before Leach declared Asher a failure and went after the children himself?

Caroline waded through the shallow water on the edge of the beach, a hand around her son's wrist, the baby pinned against her hip. She ushered the boy into the cave. What was she doing? Seeking shelter from Reuben and his men? This, Asher felt certain, was not the secret, underhand escape Isaac and Caroline had planned.

He ought to go to her, he thought distantly. Ought to tell her that Leach was waiting on the sea. Ought to tell her the cave she was sheltering in was not by safe water.

But go to Caroline and he would open himself up to Leach's wrath. The thought of being on the wrong side of that animal was terrifying.

He sat on the edge of the cliff and watched the dizzying roll of the sea. Let Isaac fight Tom Leach. No doubt they had been working towards it for years.

He let his eyes grow glassy. Let the sea blur. Was this guilt he was feeling? Self-loathing? His thoughts were tangled.

Once his mind had been so sharp. He'd questioned and analysed and worked tirelessly to unravel the riddles of the world around him. He'd studied every inch of the human body, inside and out, had hypothesised on the intangible magic of the soul. Asher Hales had been a man destined to make his imprint on the world.

He laughed aloud. That man had been beaten out of existence.

Here was Scarlett again, charging towards him, yanking him out of his stupor.

"Was this your doing?" she cried. "Did you go to the revenue men? Is that why my family has left?"

She was a mess; her clothes dripping with seawater, skirts tangled around her legs. Dark threads of hair clung to her flushed cheeks.

"What are you talking about, Scarlett?"

"Did you see my brother's ship leave?" she asked, her voice strained and desperate.

"He left, yes. With the fishing fleet. This morning."

"With the fishing fleet? Did it seem as though he were coming back?"

Asher laughed humourlessly. "Here you are wanting my help again." To hell with her. He would not let himself be threatened by Scarlett Bailey any longer.

"Tell me what you saw, Asher! I need to know if my family has left!"

How like her father she was, with her flashing eyes and violent temper. Could she see the resemblance?

He let out an enormous sigh and looked back out across the sea. "She is leaving, yes. And taking with her all she knows."

"What?" Scarlett demanded. "Who are you talking about? Caroline?"

"She knows," he said distantly. "She knows how to find the money."

"What are you talking about? What money? Avery's money?"

Asher nodded faintly. He was dimly aware that this secret was not his to reveal. Dimly aware of how much Caroline's life would unravel if he kept speaking. But if her life were to unravel, she would have nowhere to turn but to him.

Scarlett, in her frantic state was unable to catch hold of the threads he was dangling. "You're making no sense, Asher," she snapped, looking at him as though he were a madman.

Little Scarlett Bailey with a knife at her knee. Let her go to Leach. Let her try and stop him. It would be a fine thing to see.

"They're in the cave," he told her. "Your family. I saw them."

Asher feels himself tense as Leach slides from the horse. It had been a welcome respite to have him return to the castle for the animals. It is a difficult thing to relax, Asher is coming to realise, when in the company of Tom Leach.

He glances over his shoulder at the children. They are asleep on the ratty saddle blanket he had tossed on the ground, the boy on his side, the baby curled up against his stomach. They are a mess of grimy clothes and tangled hair, suffused with the stench of river muck and shit.

Leach lashes the horses to a tree. He glances at the children, then at Asher. "Kill them."

Asher looks down. The easiest option, perhaps. And, he sees now, it was what Leach had intended to do from the beginning. What better punishment for Isaac Bailey?

In the end, Asher had followed Scarlett down to the cave. At the end of all this, there would be Caroline, and there would be money. Go through with this brutal plan and it would lead him to the life he had always wanted.

He stood at the mouth of the cave and held his breath. Caroline lay on the sand with a line of blood running from the side of her head. Sickness rose in Asher's throat. He wanted to kneel at her side, help her awaken and promise her everything would be all right. But Leach stood less than a foot away, a long metal creeping pole in his hand.

Scarlett was crouching at the back of the cave, speaking under her breath to the children. Asher watched as Leach raised the pole and swung; a fierce blow to the back of Scarlett's head. The crack filled the cave and brought a sound from Asher's throat.

Scarlett fell close to his feet. Leach yanked the children out from the gap in the rock, a hand over the boy's mouth to muffle his screams. He shoved them at Asher. At the kicking, shrieking weight of them in his arms, the reality of what they were doing swung at him. But it was too late to turn back. The thing was done.

He clamped a hand over the boy's mouth, unsure what else to do.

Leach marched from the cave without looking back. "The boat is waiting around the point."

"Kill them," Leach says again. He tosses Asher the pistol. It feels heavy in his hands.

Asher looks down at the gun. He has no food for them. No shelter now their hideout at the castle has been discovered. The brandy bottle he has been using to drug them both into a stupor is dangerously close to empty.

"They're precious leverage," he tells Leach. "Without them, we have nothing."

The baby sighs and murmurs in her sleep. Asher feels a tug of regret. The mewling of Caroline's daughter was supposed to come from the nursery in their grand Belgravia townhouse, not some filthy saddle blanket here at the end of the earth.

He needs to get to her. Tell her the children are safe and will be back in her arms the moment she agrees to his wishes.

But just how safe are they? Leach's pistol is loaded. The situation, Asher is beginning to realise, is slipping from his control. Perhaps it had never been in his control.

He flings the gun back towards Leach. It thuds heavily on the earth.

"Take them then," Leach says dismissively. "You want to keep them alive, you do it somewhere else."

Asher glances at the children. They cannot spend another night out in the cold. They might never wake from their sleep.

But where is he to go? He has no money, no food, no clean clothes. He is as much of an outcast as Leach.

"Your house in Polruan," he says suddenly. "Let me use it."

Leach snorts. "You're not using my house."

"Why not?"

"Because my wife is in it. And I don't want her dealing with the likes of you."

Asher snorts. If Leach's wife has any wit to her she will have run the moment her husband had disappeared. Gone some place he could never find her.

But he says nothing. Because when Leach speaks of his wife there is a look in his eyes Asher has not seen before. A look that is almost concern, almost affection.

Asher climbs to his feet. His boots sink into the mud on the edge of the river. "Let me take the children there, just for the night. I can tell her you're safe. Alive." Would the woman care, he wonders? But he says: "She's worried for you, I'm sure."

Leach looks at him without speaking. Finally, he gives a short nod. He picks up his pistol and tucks it back in his pocket.

Asher hunches over the boy and shakes his shoulder. He blinks, then his dark eyes widen, as though remembering where he is.

"Get up," says Asher. "We're leaving."

The boy scrambles to his feet. Stumbles. There is still brandy in his blood. "Where are we going?"

"Somewhere you'll be warm."

Asher looks down at the baby, unsure quite what to do with her. The boy plucks her from the ground and holds her tight against his chest. She gives Asher a slow, brown-eyed blink, then stuffs her mouth full of her brother's hair.

Asher swallows heavily and gestures towards the horse.

Leach pulls the remains of the brandy from the pack. "Go to Caroline Bailey and I'll kill you." He tilts the bottle, watching its contents run up the side of the glass. "She and her husband can't know their children are alive. Let them suffer."

Asher says nothing. He hauls the boy onto the horse, then climbs into the saddle behind him. Gabriel grips the pommel with one hand, his other arm wrapped around his squalling sister.

Asher rides by moonlight, out of the thick forest and onto the muddy road that will take them to the coast. The boy's head turns from side to side as they walk. He is sharp-eyed, quick. Asher is not surprised by it. He is half Caroline.

He goads the horse into a canter, to quell any thoughts of escape.

Gabriel looks over his shoulder at Asher. The boy recognises him from the days he had spent at their cottage, he can tell.

"Aunt Scarlett says you almost drowned."

The mention of Scarlett brings a faint tug to Asher's chest. She had saved his life. And in return, he had led her into the cave where Leach and his creeping pole had been waiting.

"What is it like?" asks Gabriel, looking out over the dark plain of the sea. "Being shipwrecked? Did you hear the voices in the wind? Did they call your name? Did you think you were going to die?"

The night is thick by the time they reach Polruan, sparse stars speckling the cloud bank. Asher leads the horse through the winding streets, following the directions Leach had given.

The baby has begun to cry again, fraying Asher's nerves. He hauls the children from the horse and knocks on the door of Leach's cottage. It is answered by a young woman in a patched grey dress and apron. Strands of orange hair peek out from beneath her cap, grazing a soft, freckled face. Her blue eyes are enormous.

"You're Tom Leach's wife?" Asher asks in surprise. "Jane?" He had been expecting someone older, someone harsher, someone with the same ferocity in her eyes as her husband.

She eyes him warily, then looks at the children. The boy is staring up at her, the baby a grizzling, kicking mess.

"Who are you?" Jane asks Asher.

"Your husband sent me."

"You've seen Tom? Is he safe? Where is he?"

Truly? Such concern for the man? Such innocent, wide-eyed worry? What has Tom Leach ever done to deserve such things?

"He's safe," Asher tells the woman. "For now."

"Where is he?" she presses. When Asher doesn't answer, she twists a finger around the edge of her apron. "Are these your children?"

Doesn't she know better than to ask questions? Doesn't she know who her husband is?

Asher nudges Gabriel into the house. "Tom wants you to take care of them," he lies.

She nods stiffly, then kneels so she is eye level with the boy. He looks at her distrustfully, his arms tightening around the baby.

"Is this your sister?" Jane asks gently.

He nods.

"May I take her?"

He hesitates. "She's scared."

"I know." Jane's voice is soft, despite Mary's wailing. "Let me help."

Finally, Gabriel loosens his grip and lets Jane lift the baby into her arms. She rubs Mary's back and speaks to Gabriel in words Asher can't hear. Then she ushers him into another room.

Asher hovers in the doorway, feeling an intruder. Not knowing what else to do, he steps inside. A fire is crackling in the hearth, underskirts hanging over the guard to dry. A single plate sits in the middle of the table, scattered with breadcrumbs.

Asher goes to the fire. He reaches over the guard and holds his hands close to the flames. He feels chilled to the core.

When the children return, their faces have been wiped clean, the twigs and grass combed from their dark hair. The baby smells far less eye-wateringly foul.

Jane bustles around the kitchen with Mary on her hip, pulling bread from the shelf and filling a saucepan with milk. She hangs the pot over the fire and places a plate of bread and cheese in front of Gabriel. She smooths his hair. Murmurs more unintelligible words.

Finally, she looks back at Asher. "And who exactly are you?" she asks.

He says: "Matthew Fielding." It feels fitting to give his old, tarnished name. Asher Hales was supposed to be a new name for a new man. And he has never felt further from that man.

Jane watches Gabriel stuff the cheese into his mouth. He's had nothing but a few scraps of stale bread in days, Asher realises, feeling a faint stab of guilt.

"Tom took these children?" Jane asks under her breath. "Why?"

Asher finds himself tugging at the laces of his shirt. A nervous habit that had developed around the time he had begun to involve himself with Tom Leach. He forces his hands into his lap. "He wants revenge against the man he believes turned him in for murder."

Jane's jaw tightens. Her eyes move over him, scrutinising. Then, as though she has decided he is not worth the attention, she goes to the hearth and pours the milk into two tin cups. She passes one to Gabriel. Sits the baby on her lap and drizzles the warm liquid into her mouth.

Asher glances about him for any evidence of other children. He sees nothing.

He eyes the plate of bread and cheese. He is hungry too. But asking to be fed feels like a step too far.

Tomorrow he will go to Caroline. Put an end to this. To hell with what Tom Leach wants. He has followed the man's orders too long already.

The thought of going against Leach's wishes makes Asher edgy. Nervous. But Tom

Leach is a wanted man. He has no leverage. He has nothing. Asher will get what he wants from this whole sorry exercise. Somehow, he will wrangle his life back onto the course it ought to have taken.

The chair squeaks noisily as he takes a seat at the table. Gabriel shoots him a distrusting look, then turns back to his food.

"Tomorrow," Asher tells him, his voice coming out softer than he had intended. "Tomorrow you'll see your mother."

THE GIRL WITH LIGHT FINGERS

Jamie comes downstairs from his room at the Three Pilchards. His legs are weighted and his eyes heavy. He holds up a hand to shield his eyes from a violent spear of morning light. He orders strong coffee and sits at the bar with his hands wrapped around the mug.

At the other end of the counter, sits a man he recognises. Jamie had sent him away from the press gang's cart shed before the riding officers had made their arrests. Scarlett's father is staring out the window, sipping from a shallow tin cup.

Why is he here? Has he come after his daughter?

Jamie knows he ought to walk away. Scarlett has made it clear there is to be nothing more between them. What good will it do to approach her criminal of a father? But he has been kept awake by thoughts of Scarlett Bailey for too many nights now for him to walk away. He tosses back the last of his coffee and approaches the man.

He eyes Jamie warily. "You. What are you doing in this place?"

So the man remembers him. Remembers the way he had sent his fellow riding officers into the cart shed to take down the press gang.

Jamie says: "I thought to see your daughter home safely."

Scarlett's father brings his cup to his lips. "You and my daughter are not a good match. Leave her be. Leave my family be."

"I know what your family is."

"Then you'll understand it's not personal when I ask you to stay away."

Staying away, Jamie is coming to realise, is proving far more difficult than he had anticipated. "Do you know where she is?"

The man sighs heavily. "Scarlett wants nothing to do with me, as you well know. I got no idea where she is." He leans forward, pinning Jamie with hard eyes. "Listen boy," he says, "my family is in enough trouble without them getting involved with people like you."

"Trouble? What kind of trouble?"

He snorts. "I'm not in the habit of sharing my problems with the preventative service."

Jamie nods, only half listening. He looks through the window of the tavern. The path winds up over the cliffs towards Talland.

And before the thought is properly formed, he is riding that path, higher and higher, towards that cluster of red roofs, towards that church on the hill.

He weaves his way down into Talland. At the bend in the road sits the village tavern. Mariner's Arms, says the wooden sign above the door. Jamie remembers the place from Scarlett's stories. He will ask here. Hope someone can point him in the right direction.

If Scarlett and her family are in trouble, he needs to know.

She wakes to the feeling that she is not alone.

"Scarlett?"

It is Jamie's voice, but this is not possible. Jamie has ridden back to Portreath. He had waited for her in Polperro and she had not come to say goodbye.

She reaches for him anyway. Finds his arm, solid and warm. A noise comes from the back of her throat. Solid and warm and real. She grips tighter.

"You came looking for me."

"Why does that surprise you?" His voice is low and gentle.

Why? Because she had not seen fit to say goodbye? Yes, but there is more. She had not expected to find Jamie at her bedside because she had walked into the trap he had laid for the Portreath smugglers. She had sat in his cottage with stolen coins in her bodice. She has made a life doing everything he is trying to put an end to.

But he is here. Making her heart and breath quicken, as they had done each time his body jolted against hers on the journey from Portreath. Her heart and her breath, it seems, have little regard for who he is and what she has done.

She pulls herself from the pillow, ignoring the ache in her head. She wraps her arms around his neck and pulls him close. His hands feel solid and wide against the side of her ribs.

"I'm so sorry this happened to you," he says.

What is there to say? What is there to be done?

Scarlett doesn't answer. She presses her cheek into his shoulder, feeling the coarse thread of his coat.

"Your father," he says after a moment. "He's in Polperro. Did you know it?"

Scarlett lets out her breath. No, he can't be here. Not among all this lightless chaos. She can't manage Jacob being here too. She waits for the anger at her father for following her. But it doesn't come, as though the Wild knows there is no room for it here now.

"What can I do?" Jamie asks.

Scarlett hesitates. Everything that needs doing cannot be done by a man who has sworn an oath to the revenue service. Whichever of her brother's enemies has taken the children, he is deep in free trade. Deeply entrenched in a world Jamie cannot be privy to.

In spite of it, she wants him here.

There is Gabriel and Mary and Reuben and Jacob. This unyielding, inescapable sightlessness. But right now there is Jamie. His arms around her and his hot breath on her neck. She wants to reach through the dark and touch every line of him.

But he has already seen far too much of the unlawfulness in her.

"Leave," she says, forcing herself out of his arms. "That's what you need to do."

"What?" The bed shifts, but he doesn't stand. For a fleeting second, Scarlett is glad she can't see his face. His voice has hardened. "I thought you trusted me."

"It's not about trust."

"Then why?"

How does she say it? How does she make sense of it? She needs Jamie to leave, because if he stays he will see all the dishonest, deceitful things her family does. How long will it be before he comes to despise her?

She feels him stand. Hears his footsteps move across the floor.

"Is that truly what you want?" he asks.

Scarlett doesn't reply. The floor creaks on the opposite side of the room.

She throws back the blanket and slides out of bed. Her nightshift is thin. Barely reaches past her knees. She feels exposed. Indecent.

Where is the shawl Flora had tossed over her yesterday?

She fumbles on the chair beside the bed until her fingers touch the soft wool. She knots it around her shoulders.

Across the room, she hears Jamie breathe.

There are no footfalls. He is not coming to her. He is letting her find him. She is grateful for it.

This time there is no wall, no stair rail to guide her. Walking through the room is like finding her way through space.

Her outstretched fingers find Jamie's chest. She presses her palm hard against him.

How must she look to him, she wonders, with her vacant, useless eyes swimming through the dark? She lowers her head so he can't see her face. Feels his palm against her cheek. His fingers are rough and warm.

"Look at me," he says.

And she does. Turns to face him, lifts her eyes to his. And in her mind she sees him, the sharp jaw, the messy waves of hair, eyes the colour of winter sea. The image of him takes the tension from her shoulders and replaces it with a gentle fluttering in her stomach.

She wants to stay here forever, with her hand pressed to his heart, feeling the rhythmic thud of his pulse beneath her fingers. Life against life.

"Tell me what's happened," he says. "Tell me everything."

And of course, she cannot stay here forever. She cannot, even for a moment, pretend the world is as it should be.

"My niece and nephew are missing," she tells him. "They've been taken by whoever attacked me."

She hears Jamie's sharp intake of breath. Feels him shift beneath her.

"I may know where to look."

OLD SILENCE

Flora hands her clothing, one piece at a time. She waits patiently as Scarlett navigates the chaos of invisible buttons and laces.

The thick woollen stockings are her own; Scarlett recognises the darning on the heels and toes, the ribboned garters her own. Both have been washed and smell of soap instead of sea.

The petticoats are unfamiliar, as are the soft woollen skirts. Her own clothes are bloodstained, she imagines. Sea-stained, mud-stained. Perhaps beyond repair.

The bodice feels strange beneath her fingers. Flora's hand covers her own, guiding the lacing from one eyelet to the next, until Scarlett is bound tightly into the stays.

"Will you pin my hair?" she asks. She is going nowhere but her own cottage, but she feels the need to make herself presentable. She can't be this sorry, bed-ridden thing any longer.

She feels a brush tug through the thick snarls of her hair.

Flora is careful to avoid the gash on the back of Scarlett's head. "I assume," she says, light in her voice, "you might eventually tell me who this man is who came to my door in a panic, desperate to find you."

Scarlett feels a small smile in the corner of her lips. And then she thinks of Jamie waiting for her in the bar downstairs, pacing unwittingly above the smuggling tunnel. What would Flora think if she knew she had let a riding officer wander through her inn? Scarlett trusts Jamie, yes, but she knows she cannot expect everyone else to.

And so she tells Flora only vague outlines of the story; a man she had met on her travels, the man who had accompanied her home.

Flora slides the last pin into Scarlett's hair. "I'm pleased for you."

Scarlett presses against her skirts to feel her empty garter. "My knife. Where is it?" It must have been with her when Will had brought her to the inn.

"What do you need a knife for?" asks Flora.

Scarlett knows it is foolish. But the thought of stepping sightless into the world is terrifying. She has grown accustomed to the feel of having a knife at her knee. Has grown accustomed to the security of it.

"Do you have it?" she presses.

After a moment, Flora says: "Yes. In the kitchen."

And Scarlett speaks in a voice that clearly says she does not want to be judged. "May I have it?"

And so this is morning, shrouded in darkness. She hears the sea, hears the sob of the gulls, hears wind bend the trees. The air is cool against her cheeks. It smells of salt and washed up weed.

Scarlett's steps are tentative, and she grips Jamie's arm tightly. But she knows this road well, she realises, this path that winds up to her cottage from the Mariner's Arms. She begins to walk faster.

"This way," she says. "Past the bell house." She needs to get to Isaac. Tell him all Jamie had told her about the crying baby in the castle. She is suddenly hot with urgency. "My cottage," she says. "It's the one by the bend. With the red chimney. Do you see it?"

"Yes."

"Is anyone there?"

"There's a light in the window."

Her fingers knead his arm. "Please don't say anything to my brother about our father. He doesn't know Jacob is alive."

"Is it not a thing you ought to tell him?"

Scarlett says nothing. She wants to tell Isaac. Needs his help to shoulder the load. But it cannot be now. "He's too much to deal with," she tells Jamie. "He doesn't need to know a thing about Jacob while his children are missing."

"I'll not say a word."

A sudden thought seizes her. She runs her fingers down the front of Jamie's coat. "What are you wearing?"

"You mean, am I dressed as the enemy?" She hears a smile in his voice. "No."

"Good. Best you don't say anything about that either."

She knocks lightly on the cottage door.

"Scarlett?"

She is glad to hear Isaac's voice. "I wasn't sure you'd be here," she says. "I thought you'd be out looking."

"Only came back for a little sleep." She can hear the strain in his voice. Wishes she could take it away.

"This is Jamie," says Scarlett. "He has information."

"Information?" She hears Caroline come towards them.

"I passed the ruins of Restormel Castle yesterday," Jamie tells them. "There were men hiding inside. Men who fired at me." He pauses, as though suddenly hesitant. "They fired at me after I heard a baby crying."

Scarlett hears a sharp intake of breath from Caroline.

Isaac says: "I'll go to the Millers' for the horse."

He and Jamie leave, plunging the cottage into silence. Scarlett sits on the floor beside the hearth, hugging her knees to her chest. How desperately she wants to be out there with them.

A chair creaks noisily, reminding her she is not alone. Caroline doesn't speak.

It has always been this way between the two of them. There is no chatter. No small talk. When they are alone, there is little to do but be silent.

But things are different now. The disappearance of Gabriel and Mary is an ache in Scarlett's chest. She can barely imagine how it must feel for their mother. A part of her wants to throw her arms around Caroline and tell her everything will be all right. But this is not the way things are between them. This is not the way things have ever been.

"We'll find them," she says instead. "I know it."

Caroline doesn't speak at once. "I'm sorry," she says after a moment. "You shouldn't have been caught up in all of this."

"If it were Reuben's doing, he has as much against me as he does Isaac."

"You believe it was Reuben?"

Scarlett curls her fingers around her knees. "It makes sense. He found the ankers in the tunnel. Knew you were trying to escape."

Caroline doesn't reply. Scarlett hears her leap to her feet and hurry across the room.

"Stay here," she says.

"Where are you going?"

"To fetch more wood. The fire's almost burned out." The door swings open, letting a blast of cold air into the house. It slams heavily, a sound Scarlett feels in her chest.

She hears murmured voices. Who is Caroline speaking to? Scarlett cannot make out her words, but can tell she is angry.

The second voice comes again. A man's voice. It is faint, but familiar. Are her overworked senses playing tricks? Or is Asher Hales outside their house?

Scarlett stands. A hand out in front of her, she edges across the cottage. She clatters into the corner of the table, rattling the chairs. Pain shoots down her leg and she curses under her breath.

The voices stop abruptly.

"What are you doing?" Caroline demands, bringing another gust of wind inside with her.

"What are *you* doing?" Scarlett grips the edge of the table. She feels strangely unsteady, as though she were standing on a ship in the middle of a wild ocean.

"I told you, I was fetching more wood." Caroline locks the door and returns to the kitchen. Scarlett can tell there is no wood.

"Is Asher Hales outside?" she asks, trying to keep her voice even.

"Asher Hales? Of course not. What possible reason would he have to come here?" Without seeing Caroline's face, it is difficult to tell if she is lying.

Scarlett sits at the table. A log shifts noisily in the grate. "Asher told me to go to the cave," she says finally. "He told me you were hiding in there. I wasn't sure whether to trust him. I decided I had no choice." She touches the raw patches on her palms. She had torn the skin on the rocks when she had swum around the point to reach the landing beach.

"I've been telling you for weeks not to trust that man." Caroline's voice is cold.

"He couldn't have been the one who attacked you," says Scarlett. "He was on the cliffs with me."

"But he could have followed you into the cave. He could have taken the children."

"You believe it was him," says Scarlett. "You don't think it was Reuben. Why? Why would you suspect him?"

"Because I don't trust him."

"No. You never have. Why not?"

Caroline gives a cold laugh. "Do you truly need to ask that, Scarlett? You just said yourself, the man led you into the cave where you were attacked and blinded."

"Why have you never trusted him?" Scarlett hears her voice rise. The more Caroline speaks, the more certain she feels that it had been Asher outside the house. "Why did you have such hatred for him the minute I brought him through that door?"

"I suppose some people are just a better judge of character than others."

Scarlett clasps her hands together, tighter. She feels suddenly, intensely vulnerable. Caroline could come at her and she would have no thought of it.

She shakes the thought away. Foolishness. Surely this is nothing more than her racing, panicked imagination. Caroline is family. How many nights have they sat opposite each other at the supper table? Scarlett knows she would never hurt her.

But something has shifted. Intangible, but she can feel it. It as though something that has been in place for years has suddenly been dislodged.

"You don't need to be here," Isaac tells Jamie. He is riding a horse borrowed from a neighbouring farm. Climbs the steep hill a little too quickly. "I know how to find Restormel Castle. There's no need to put yourself in danger."

Jamie shakes his head. "There were men firing from the ruins. You ought not be there alone."

Isaac looks over his shoulder and gives him a short nod of thanks.

Up, up they wind. The path is narrow; trees on one side, sheer cliffs on the other. Isaac's eyes are fixed firmly on the brown mire of the road.

He has questions surely, about this man who had arrived on his doorstep with Scarlett's arm in his, claiming to know the whereabouts of his missing children. Jamie is glad he doesn't ask them. Scarlett has sworn him to secrecy on far too many issues. Best they ride in silence.

At last the hill peaks and an expanse of farmland stretches out before them. They goad the horses into a gallop. Jamie feels the vibration of hooves against earth deep inside his body. Wind stings his cheeks, sweeps the hair from his eyes. His ears burn with cold.

By afternoon, the castle is on the horizon; a dark shape in the shadows of the purple-green moorland.

They slide from the horses, tying their reins to the twisted trunk of the tree. Jamie feels that familiar edginess as they approach the ruins. He grips his pistol.

They enter through the main gate and weave through the battered shell of the keep.

The ruins are silent. No footsteps, no gunshots. No cries of a child. The place smells of earth and old, cold stone.

Their footsteps echo. Neither of them speak, as though they are afraid shattering the stillness will cause the building to crumble. Shadows shift as the cloud bank thickens, making the muscles in Jamie's neck tighten.

Too quickly, they arrive back at the gate. They have circled the castle. Found nothing.

Isaac calls for his son. His voice disappears into the emptiness. He exhales sharply and leans back against the rugged wall.

Jamie looks sideways at him. There is plenty of Scarlett in him; the sharp coal-chunk eyes, the dark, unruly hair, the steely set of his jaw. Jamie has no trouble imaging this man sliding a shipment of liquor beneath the revenue men's noses.

He knows that had he looked at Isaac Bailey a week ago, he would have seen nothing but a thief. But perhaps the line between right and wrong is not always so clear. However entrenched in smuggling Scarlett and her brother are, they surely don't deserve to have their children taken or their sight stolen.

"I'm sorry," he tells Isaac. "They must have left after I caught them here."

"The man who was firing at you. You didn't see his face?"

"No. But there was something. So quick I can't be sure of it." Jamie hesitates. This doesn't feel the place for ghost stories. "Long dark hair. A man."

And Isaac begins to run, out through the ruins and across the plain towards the horses. Jamie charges after him.

"Where are you going?"

Isaac is breathless as he swings himself onto the horse. "I know who's taken my children."

The old silence takes over.

Scarlett concentrates hard, trying to follow Caroline's every movement, trying to place her within the cottage. Her head begins to ache.

"Are you hungry?" Caroline asks finally.

Scarlett shakes her head. Her stomach is churning. Churning at the fear of Jamie and Isaac riding the moors. Churning at this new distrust of her sister-in-law.

"Here." Caroline pushes a glass into Scarlett's hand. She smells the hot tang of brandy.

"Are you trying to drug me?" she blurts.

Caroline doesn't speak at once. "I thought it might help you relax a little," she says. "God knows we could all use it."

Scarlett wraps her hands around the glass. Perhaps she is being foolish. Perhaps her imagination is racing in the dark and she is seeing danger where it does not exist.

She sips the brandy. Feels it slide warm down her throat. At the taste of it, she is back downing drinks after a run, back helping herself to the liquor kettle after a night's work at the Mariner's Arms. Things she fears she will never do again.

The silence is too much. Scarlett empties her glass and stands, feeling her way towards her bedroom. "Tell Isaac to fetch me," she says, "the minute he returns."

"I didn't expect you to keep me waiting," Asher says, when Caroline finally emerges from the house.

"What choice did I have?" Her voice is sharp and low. "Did you want Scarlett to hear everything?"

"Where is she?"

"Sleeping." Her eyes meet his.

Asher flinches under her scrutiny. The bruises on his face are yellowing, his hair stiff as straw. He had managed to find clean clothes at Leach's house, but the shirt is straining across his muscular shoulders and the sleeves of the coat dangle past his hands. There is little more degrading, Asher has realised, than wearing another man's clothes.

"Where are they?" Caroline's eyes are fierce, her voice wavering.

"I can't tell you that now."

She flies at him suddenly, her fists slamming into his chest. Asher's feet stay planted on the ground. He had been expecting such an attack.

A sob escapes her, and she covers her mouth. "You want Avery's money," she says finally.

"Of course."

Caroline blinks back her tears.

Asher feels something tighten in his chest. He could ease her sorrow, of course. Could take her to Polruan and show her where her children are lying, shoulder-to-shoulder on that pile of blankets Jane Leach had set up in front of the hearth.

He could make her happy, like he has always wanted to do.

He could do that, yes. But Asher knows he won't. It must be like this. Caroline has become manipulative, underhand. The only way to win is to play her game.

She shakes her head. "I don't know how to get to the money."

"Then I suggest you find a way."

She looks at the ground for a long time.

Asher feels nervous. Caroline is smart. She has trapped him before. He knows he must be on his guard around her. It was what had made him fall in love with her in the first place.

She has always made him think. Challenged him. Never allowed him to become complacent.

But when she finally speaks, what she says is: "I will leave with you right now. Just take me to my children. And then we will go anywhere you choose." Resignation in her voice. "That's what you want, isn't it? To make a life with me, just as we used to talk about?"

Asher hesitates. He wants to leave this place with her, yes, but he needs Henry Avery's silver too badly to just walk away. "We can't have that life without the money," he says. "Without it we have nothing. What are we but paupers?"

"You will find another way to make the money you need," she says. "You're an intelligent man. The most intelligent I've ever known."

The words are heat inside him. Asher is dimly aware she is telling him only what he wants to hear. But he can't make himself care. Her praise tugs him back from the brink of self-hatred. Her praise reminds him of his great potential.

But he must not let himself fall for these honeyed words. "Why should I believe you?" he says. "You told me before you'd leave with me. And you led me into a trap. Threatened to frame me for the riding officers' murders."

"Why should you believe me?" Caroline repeats. "Because you have my children! Do you truly think I'd do anything to put them in danger?"

"I need the money," says Asher.

"And I need my children." Silence hangs between them. Finally, Caroline asks: "Who attacked me? And Scarlett? I know it wasn't you. You're not capable of such a thing."

At the top of her cheek, Asher sees the angry red gash, the purple floret of bruising; evidence of Leach's attack. "I'm sorry. I never meant for you to be hurt." He hears his voice waver with a sudden rush of emotion.

Caroline presses her hand to his cheek. The unexpectedness of the gesture makes Asher's breath catch. At the feel of her skin against his, he is a young man again, overflowing with love and lust.

"Please," she says. "You loved me once. Perhaps you still do."

She is close to him, her breath hot against his nose and her fingers moving along his cheekbone. She is tugging the years away, taking him back to that ambitious man he used to be. How he wants to be that man again.

At the back of his mind, his common sense is roiling. She is playing him. This is love for her children, not love for him. But Asher wills that voice into silence.

She wraps her fingers around the laces of his shirt and pulls him towards her. Touches her lips to his.

And here comes his drive, his optimism, his dreams. Everything that had been sucked away by his conviction, his poverty, his shipwreck. Everything the Baileys had taken from him.

When Caroline pulls away, her eyes are glistening. "Take me to my children," she says. "And we will leave."

She is right. He is an intelligent man. He will find another way to make that money.

And he will have Caroline by his side as he does so.

He nods slowly. "Get your things."

Caroline slips back into the cottage, leaving Asher waiting on the edge of the road. She creeps past Scarlett's door and into her own bedroom. Takes her cloak from the hook on the wall and slides it on. She feels strangely detached from her body. It has to be this way, she supposes. Let herself feel and she will crumble.

She runs a finger over the coarse thread of Isaac's pillow, swallowing the pain in her throat.

This will be the end. She will never lie in this bed beside her husband again. She will go with Asher Hales. There can be no more tricks or traps or manipulation. Not with her children's lives in danger. She will go with him as he wishes. And when his need for the money inevitably resurfaces, she will tell him all he wants to know.

Caroline's throat tightens. No, she will not cry. There is no time, no place for tears.

She pulls closed the door of her bedroom. Goes to the nursery. She has not been inside since her children were taken. She brings in no lamp or candle, unable to look too closely at its emptiness. But in the long, dusky shadows, she sees Gabriel's nightshirt, tossed on the floor in their desperation to escape Reuben's men. Toy soldiers are lined up on the floor by the foot of his bed, poised and silent. They have missed the battle.

What will the children need? They had been dressed for escape; Gabriel in his coat and scarf, Mary swathed in blankets. But she needs to take something for them, something that might help them feel close as she follows Asher away from her husband. Something to remind her that these sacrifices will be worth it.

She takes Gabriel's sap whistle and a rag doll for Mary. Stuffs them both into the pocket of her cloak and closes the door quickly.

Here is the reality she has been avoiding. She is to take them from their father.

She wishes she could tell herself she has no choice in the matter, but she knows it is not the case. She could disappear with Asher Hales and send Gabriel and Mary home.

But she cannot do it. If she is to vanish from this life, she cannot do it alone.

She will have her children and Isaac will have his pleasures at the inn on the hill.

She slips silently out the front door. She has left no note, no explanation. Let Isaac wonder, guessing at irreconcilable anger and secret love affairs. Nothing he imagines will be worse than the truth. He can never know she was the one who had forced his father to abandon his family.

Asher has a horse waiting, its reins looped to a tree close to the cottage. "Where are your things?" he asks.

"I have all I need," says Caroline. She has brought nothing but the toys and the clothes she is wearing. Why? Taking her things will raise Isaac's suspicions, of course. Does she want to be far away before he discovers she is gone? Prevent him from coming after her?

Or it is more that this does not yet feel real? She will need no more than the clothes on her back because tonight, she will be home in her cottage.

Asher gestures to the horse. "I'm sorry. I've only one. We'll have to ride together." He does not sound sorry.

He offers his hand to help her mount, but she turns away and swings herself into the saddle. It has been many years since she has ridden, and she grips the pommel with white knuckles.

"You never used to ride astride," says Asher. He smiles close to her ear. "When did you stop caring about decency?"

Caroline bites back her retort. Asher Hales cannot see her animosity towards him. He needs to believe their love can be rekindled. Her children's safety depends on it.

The afternoon is grey as they ride the hill out of Talland. Rain spills over the cliffs, turning the dark ribbon of the road to mud.

Caroline can feel the heat of Asher's body. The nearness of him is uncomfortably familiar.

She wants to hate him. And a big part of her does. But she knows, of course, that she is not without blame. For years she has feared the repercussions of the things she has done. She has always taught her son to take responsibility for his actions. And she will do the same. To walk away from her life like this is the punishment she deserves.

Dusk turns the sea and sky purple. Wind cuts through Caroline's wet clothes, making her shiver violently.

They wind their way down into a tiny lamplit village. The river stretches out beneath them, silvery in the half light.

Asher stops the horse outside a small cottage behind the blockhouse. The walls are made of mismatched stone, the roof missing several tiles. One window is patched with a piece of colourless cloth.

Asher slides from the horse and offers a hand to Caroline. She leaps out of the saddle and charges towards the door.

"Whose house is this?" She peers through the grimy window. Can make out little but inky shapes inside.

"You don't need to know." Asher loops the reins to a nearby trough. He knocks on the door. "Jane," he calls, his voice low. "Let me in."

"Who is Jane?" Caroline hisses. "Who has my children?"

There is no response. Not from Asher, not from inside the house. Caroline pounds on the door again. "Who owns this house?" she demands. "Who are you working with? Tell me!"

Asher looks away. "Tom Leach."

"No," Caroline coughs. "No. Please tell me you're lying." Dizziness swings over her and she hunches, trying to gulp down her breath. She tears at the rag covering the window. Reaches through the jagged glass beneath it until her fingers touch the door latch. She pulls it open and races into the house. "Gabriel?" she calls. "Gabriel, are you here? Mary?" She charges through the cottage. Finds nothing but dark spaces.

A light flares in the kitchen.

Asher has a lamp in his hand, its flickering glow falling on a pile of rumpled blankets by the hearth. "They were here," he says.

Caroline reaches down and presses her fingers to the blankets. She feels her throat tighten, the whistle and rag doll heavy in her pocket. She sinks to her knees. She clutches at the blankets, trying to catch hold of any scrap of her children; a fragment of their warmth, a waft of their scent, a stray strand of hair.

"I'm sorry." Asher's voice is cracked. "Leach and his wife have taken them."

REPRIEVE

Caroline sits on the floor of Tom Leach's kitchen, holding her knees to her chest. Beside her, the logs in the grate are cold and black. Rain splatters against the glass. The flame in the lantern spits and vanishes.

Her feelings for Asher creep a little closer to hatred. But she cannot let herself feel it entirely. Hate him and she will be alone in this.

She ought to have known better than to trust Asher Hales to keep his word. This man has never been anything more than talk.

In the faint glow of the street lamp she sees him staring into the grate. He has knotted the laces of his shirt around one of finger.

"What does Leach want?" Her voice rattles. "The money?"

"Leach doesn't know about the money," he says distantly. "He just wants to punish your husband."

"Punish him? For what?"

"For turning him over to the authorities for murder."

"What?" Caroline cries. "That was not my husband's doing. It was Flora Kelly's." Rage flares inside her, hot and fierce. She cannot feel hate for Asher, Caroline realises, but she can damn well feel it for Flora.

She hears horses approaching the house. She leaps to her feet and peers through the window. There is Isaac, trailed by the man Scarlett had brought home.

Why are they here? She cannot make sense of it. But she doesn't care. She had never thought she would see her husband again.

She races out the door and throws her arms around his neck. For a fleeting second, that image of he and Flora together is gone. None of it matters. She just needs him close. His arms slide around her waist. And for a moment, Caroline lets herself breathe.

He steps back. "Why are you here?" He looks at her, then at Asher, who has stumbled into the street, unsteady as a drunkard. "Why are you with *him*?" Isaac lurches forward in anger, but Caroline grips his arms, holding him back.

"Mr Hales came to the cottage after you and Jamie left. Said he had information. He told me Leach had the children. But they're not here."

Isaac looks distrustfully at Asher. "How did you know it was Leach?"

"I saw him do it. I was on the cliffs at the time. I saw him go into the cave."

Caroline feels Isaac's arms tense beneath her fingers.

"You saw him take our children? Attack my wife and sister? And you didn't do a thing to stop it?"

Asher shrugs. "I was on the cliffs. There was nothing I could have done."

Isaac grabs the collar of Asher's shirt and shoves him hard against the wall.

"Isaac, please." Caroline tries to force her way between the two men. "Stop." She plants a firm hand to her husband's chest. Feels his heart thundering. "Stop."

Isaac glares at Asher. "Why did you only think to tell us this now?"

Asher snorts. "Because I suspected I'd get a response such as this one."

Caroline turns to Isaac. "You knew it was Leach. How?"

He doesn't take his eyes from Asher. "Jamie saw him at the castle."

Caroline glances at Jamie; this tangled-haired boy who had appeared on their doorstep. The sight of him makes her think of Scarlett alone in the cottage. Alone in the cottage with far too many things to ponder.

Perhaps Scarlett could be convinced that it had not been Asher outside the door that afternoon. But it doesn't change the most brutal of facts. Scarlett knows her father is alive. And it will only be a matter of time before she tells Isaac.

If she hasn't done so already.

But Scarlett, for now, is a concern Caroline does not have room for. What Isaac's sister knows is inconsequential, as long as the children are in danger.

"Scarlett's alone at the cottage," she says, her hand still pressed against Isaac's chest. "Someone ought to go and check on her."

She feels a faint stab of guilt at having left Scarlett alone. But what choice had she had?

"I'll go back for her," Jamie says, his eyes darting towards Isaac as though seeking permission.

Isaac nods wordlessly. He watches Jamie leave, then swings himself onto his horse. "I'm going to the harbour to look for Leach's cutter."

Caroline nods. "I'll follow you. But I need to tidy the place first. I don't want anyone knowing we were here."

She stands in the doorway, watching the horse disappear around the corner.

Asher steps past her into the house. "I was wrong about you. You've become quite a liar."

Caroline turns away uncomfortably. She pulls the rag back down over the broken window and winds the edge of the fabric over the nails it had been attached to. "Tell Leach about the money. Tell him I know how to get to it. He can have it in exchange for my children's safe return."

Asher's lip curls. "That money is for you and I." He fades out as he speaks, as though he is coming to realise his worthlessness. He looks out the window into the dark street. There is little to see but a faint circle of lamplight. "I don't know where Leach is," he says finally.

"Find him."

He takes a step towards her. "If I tell Leach you know how to find the money, all your secrets will come out. It will destroy your marriage."

Caroline looks away. Asher is right of course. Jacob Bailey had been the one to tell her of the haul. And if she speaks of what she knows, the truth of all she had done to Jacob will spill out with it. But she has no choice. Her children cannot die to keep her secrets.

"Find him," she says again. "Please." She marches towards the door, desperate to go after Isaac. What would she have done, she finds herself wondering, had Asher led her to the children tonight? Would she truly have ridden out of her husband's life? Taken his children away without him ever knowing they were safe? Would she have had it in her? Even Jacob had had the chance to say goodbye.

Asher snatches her arm. "Where are you going?"

"I'm going to find my husband."

His eyes flash. "You are to leave with me. We had an agreement."

She gives an incredulous laugh. "An agreement? An agreement is worthless if you cannot keep your word!" She yanks out of his grip. "You were unable to bring my children to me. You are full of lies, just as you have always been."

She sees the tremor of anger in his jaw. "That is not true," he hisses.

"Then prove me wrong. Find Leach. Tell him about the money. And get my children back."

A faint thread of moonlight makes the river shine. Beneath the dark water of the anchorage lies Leach's old cutter. Isaac had sent it there himself. But there is no sign of Leach's new ship. He is not surprised.

He sits atop the horse, feeling the animal breathe beneath him.

He has a name, at least. Knows which of these bastards they are looking for. But the thought brings little comfort. How can it when his children's lives are in the hands of a man with no morals?

He turns at the sound of footsteps. Caroline is trudging towards the harbour, her arms wrapped around herself and her shoulders drooped. The hem of her skirts is dark with mud. The weariness Isaac feels is etched in her face.

"His ship's not here," he tells her.

She nods, coming to stand beside the horse. She takes a rag doll from her pocket and runs a finger over its tattered face.

"I'll take the lugger out at first light," he tells her. "Search the coast."

Tears spill suddenly down her cheeks. She wipes them away with her palm.

Isaac reaches down and tentatively brushes the hair from her eyes. "Let's go home. There's no point us staying here. He's not coming back."

For a moment, Caroline doesn't speak. Finally, she nods and lets him pull her into the saddle. Her body sinks wearily against his.

He keeps his arms tight around her as they climb the hill out of the village. The rain has eased, but the roads are still slippery. He is careful not to push the horse.

Caroline's body is heavy against his. He presses his head into the crook of her neck. Every inch of her is achingly familiar; the strand of hair by her ear that never stays tucked beneath her bonnet, the coarseness of her damp cloak, her faint musky scent. That familiarity is an anchor.

"Please forgive me," he says, his words muffled by her hair. "What happened with Flora… it was a mistake. My loyalty ought to have been to you and the children. And I promise now it will be. Always."

At the mention of Flora, he feels her stiffen. But after a moment she sinks back into him. Covers his hand with hers.

A reprieve, Isaac thinks. A tiny flicker of optimism that he has not destroyed things between them forever.

He can't do this alone. Can't carry the weight of this. He knows Caroline can't either. They need each other.

"We'll be gone from this place soon," he says finally. "You and I and the children. I swear it." He presses a kiss into the cold skin on her neck. Can feel her trembling.

"I'm so afraid that will never be." Caroline's voice is distant and broken. Isaac feels it twist inside him.

"It will," he says. "We're going to find them. We have to believe that."

Caroline is silent for a long time. She leans into him, digs her fingers into his arm, gripping a fistful of his coat as though she were afraid to let him go. Then suddenly, sharply, she shuffles forward in the saddle.

"Do you love her?" she asks.

Isaac lets out his breath. "Caroline—"

"Just tell me." Her back is rigid, her eyes fixed on the road in front of them.

"You're my wife," he says. "That's all that matters."

Scarlett wakes from a sleep she had not intended to fall into. The world around her feels distorted. This is not the inn.

She panics, thrashes on her sleeping pallet. Her bed, she realises. She had fallen asleep here waiting for Isaac and Jamie to return. The thought calms her a little.

Around her, the silence is thick.

"Caroline?" Her voice disappears into the stillness. She is alone.

Outside, an owl coos. Night. How many hours has she slept? How long until morning? What does it matter? Morning or night, the light is not coming.

She runs a hand along the side of her sleeping pallet, along the bedside table, over the cold stump of the candlestick. Slowly, the familiarity of the room returns to her.

She had been alone in the darkness like this the day her mother had died. She had woken in the night to find her mother's raspy breathing silenced. Had gone to the room beside her own and found her staring motionless at the ceiling. Her chest did not rise or fall. Her fingers did not twitch. The illness she had promised would be a passing thing had claimed her in the night.

Scarlett had been five years old. She had crawled beneath her parents' bed and curled up in the dark. The light would come, she had thought. The light would come and make that chest rise and those fingers twitch. But when the light had come, it had shown every line and shadow on the colourless face that had once been her mother. Scarlett had run from the cottage on unsteady legs and belted on the door of her neighbour, Martha Francis.

And from out of the dark comes another memory. Her father bending over her bed, before the sun had risen. A kiss on her forehead, his cheeks wet. He had disappeared that day, and the village had believed him drowned.

He had known then that he would not be returning to Talland. Had believed he would never see her again.

She had forgotten those tears, that gentle kiss. Tears, surely, of man who had not wanted to leave.

A knock at the door.

"Scarlett?" It is Jamie's voice. She climbs hurriedly out of bed and makes her way across the cottage, traversing the gauntlet of chairs and tables and fire screens. She pulls open the door. The feel of Jamie's hands on her shoulders is steadying. The darkness feels easier to navigate.

"What's happened?" she asks. "Where are the children? Where's Caroline?"

The news is sickening. Tom Leach, says Jamie. Taken the children in an act of retaliation.

Scarlett lets out her breath. She had hoped for it to be Reuben. He at least operates under the illusion of decency. She sinks to the floor, hopelessness welling inside her.

So Leach was the one who had attacked her. The man who had cornered her in the cave and condemned her to this eternal dark. The Wild is there at her edges, threatening to tear itself free. And then Jamie sits beside her, sliding an arm around her shoulder and pulling her close.

Concentrate on the feel of him, she thinks. Concentrate on that warmth, on the pressure of his fingers against her arm. Concentrate on the smell of him; that faint scent of musk soap and horses and salty air. She breathes long and deep until the anger begins to fade.

She hears herself ask: "Where is my father?"

"At the inn in Polperro. Do you wish to see him? I think he would be glad of it."

Scarlett remembers herself suddenly. "No," she says. "I don't wish to see him. I want him gone from this place. If you see him, tell him to go back to Portreath." But a hint of regret lingers inside her.

What can I do, Jacob had asked, as she had stood in his cottage on the hill in Portreath.

Come back to Talland, she had said. Come back to Talland and save us from this life.

And here is he is.

She shakes the thoughts of her father away. There is no room for him in her head. No room for him in her life.

Suddenly she wants nothing more than to be out of this cottage where memories hang so thick in the air. She climbs to her feet and reaches for Jamie's arm. "Will you take me back to the inn?"

LOCKED DOORS

"Crowfoot," Flora tells Scarlett. "For illnesses of the eyes."

Flora has learnt to speak with confidence when she proffers cures to the other villagers. But today she can manage nothing more than thin uncertainty.

She is sure Scarlett sees the flaws in this soft-spoken attempt at a cure. She knows her blindness has been caused by a blow to the head and not an illness of the eyes.

But Scarlett says: "A cure?" There is too much hope in her voice.

Flora's stomach shifts uncomfortably. She takes Scarlett's arm and leads her to the bed.

Scarlett leans back, shifting the pillows beneath her to ease the pressure on the back of her head. Flora soaks a cloth in the water seeped with crowfoot. She wrings it out and places it gently over Scarlett's closed eyes. Water runs down her cheeks, leaving damp circles on the sheets.

Scarlett shifts suddenly, slightly. "What was that sound?"

The inn must be a warren of noises for her heightened hearing. As it changes shape with the weather, the Mariner's Arms rattles and groans like a ship at sea.

"It's an old place," says Flora. "The noises used to scare me as a girl." She allows herself a faint smile. "Sometimes they scare me still."

Scarlett brings a hand to her face, her fingers working across the damp cloth. "You must open your doors again," she says. "I'll not have you lose business because of me."

Flora sighs. "I'll not get by serving second-rate lambswool. And I can't risk selling liquor without a licence again."

"Plenty of taverns manage to survive as alehouses," says Scarlett.

"If they're taking storage money from smugglers on the side." Flora smiles wryly. "Perhaps I ought to have asked Reuben for a cut in exchange for his men using the tunnel."

There is no chance of such a thing now, of course. Whatever trust had existed between she and Charles Reuben had vanished the moment he had found Isaac's brandy ankers in the tunnel. "The only way I'll survive is to put guests up here."

"Would that be so bad?"

Flora doesn't answer. The more she thinks of it, the less she likes the idea. After all that has happened these past weeks, she has little faith in the goodness of strangers. "It's no matter," she says. "I can't find the key for the last room. I couldn't open it even if I wanted to." Carefully, she lifts the cloth. Scarlett keeps her eyes closed for a moment, as though afraid to open them. Flora's heart thuds. She needs this to work almost as badly as Scarlett does.

But when Scarlett opens her eyes, she lets out a heavy sigh. Her jaw trembles and she screws her eyes closed again, as though desperate not to let her tears escape.

Flora presses a hand over hers and squeezes. "Be patient. It may work yet." She is telling herself as much as she is Scarlett, she realises. There is a sick feeling in the pit of her stomach.

Scarlett sits abruptly. "Where are my boots?"

Flora gathers them from the floor and hands them to her. "Where are you going?"

Scarlett pulls them on, tying the laces with violent, angry movements. "I don't know. But I can't just sit around all day and hope." She climbs from the bed. "The keys," she says suddenly. "Can I try them?"

"If you wish."

Flora goes to the parlour for the keyring. She hands it to Scarlett, leading her down the passage towards the door of the third guestroom.

Scarlett presses an ear to the keyhole. "There's mice in there."

"I'm not surprised. It's been locked up since I was a child."

Scarlett begins to try the keys, shoving each one forcefully into the lock. The door will not open, Flora is sure. She has tried each of the keys at least three times.

She makes her way back towards the bedroom. Best she get rid of the crowfoot. Best not leave the scent to linger, reminding Scarlett of its failure.

She turns at a sudden thud. Sees Scarlett ramming her shoulder against the locked door. As Flora opens her mouth to speak, Scarlett kicks hard, the door flying open and pieces of the lock splattering over the floor.

"I'm sorry," she says, not sounding sorry in the slightest.

Flora hurries towards the room. The wood around the lock is splintered and rotting. Inside is dark, thick wooden blinds closed across the window. It smells musty and old. Forgotten.

Flora pulls back the threadbare curtains. The windows beneath are thick with grime. Little of the pale daylight makes its way through. She goes to the parlour and returns with the lamp.

"What's in here?" Scarlett asks.

The floor creaks loudly beneath Flora's boots. She had expected the room to be filled with her father's things. Locked chests and overflowing wardrobes, like she had found in the other two guestrooms. But there is no furniture here. Nothing but empty shadows. A threadbare rug is nailed to the floor. A mouse darts past Flora's boots and vanishes into a hole in the corner of the room.

She trails a hand along the wall. Feels a faint indentation beneath her fingers. She holds up the lamp.

Letters have been carved into the stone with a rough hand. They are arranged in a square, spelling unintelligible words. Flora has seen this arrangement of letters before. Her mother had written it on parchment to hang around her patients' necks. A charm against evil. A spell for the light.

She shivers violently, wrapping her arms around herself. The room is bitterly cold. Its unexpected emptiness makes her feel unsettled, as though she has spent her life living in a place she had not known at all.

"Flora?" Scarlett pushes. "What do you see?"

Lying on its side behind the door, she notices a small glass bottle, its contents dried and brown. She grabs it from the floor and slides it into her pocket. Makes her way into the hallway, ushering Scarlett out ahead of her. "Nothing," she says. "It's empty."

THE DEMONS OF BRIDLES LANE

In the afternoon, Flora feels herself drawn back to the third guestroom. She runs her fingers across the letters carved into the wall. Had her mother done this?

She pulls out the bottle and looks at it again. She has kept it in her pocket all day. It feels the safest place for it.

Dried blood inside, she is sure.

This arrangement of letters, this bottle of blood, Flora knows them charms against black magic. Charms to keep demons and dark spirits away from the living. Her mother had always believed such things necessary. She had sworn by her scrawled incantations, her witch bottles and watch balls. Had distributed charms for luck to the villagers each spring.

But there is something about these hastily scrawled letters that sends a chill through Flora's body. They speak of fear, of desperation. What had frightened her mother enough to take a knife to the wall of the house? Was it the reason she had locked the room up?

It doesn't matter, Flora tells herself. Her mother is at rest. She has been lying in her grave for more than three years. Whatever had frightened her is long gone.

But somehow it does matter. It matters because the thought of her mother in terror is one Flora cannot bear. And it matters because the Mariner's Arms is home. And if her mother had seen something within its walls that had scared her enough to barricade one of the rooms, Flora needs to know of it. In case whatever had scared her is not long gone.

She glances out the window. The sun is setting, and the sky is orange. People are filing out of the church. Flora squints. A baptism, perhaps. Yes, she remembers. The Millers' new baby. She had given skullcap to the midwife.

The vicar stands by the gate in his black robes, clasping the hands of his parishioners as they leave.

Impulsively, Flora grabs her cloak.

Bessie chases her down the stairs, her dog at her heels. "Where are you going, Mammik? Can I come?" She is out the door before Flora can respond.

By the time they reach the church, Reverend Dodge has returned to the vestry. Flora stands outside, watching Bessie tear across the grass with the dog. She feels strangely reluctant to enter.

At the sight of her, Dodge appears in the doorway. A smug smile turns his lips. He looks as though he has been waiting for this moment. Waiting for the witch from the inn to come to him, begging for him to cleanse her soul.

"Mrs Kelly," he says. "I'm glad to see you here." He gestures for her to enter. "You can come in, I assure you. The Lord will not strike you down." He laughs thinly.

Flora does not.

She steps inside, suddenly cold. The last time she had been in the churchyard, she had watched George Gibson leap to his death. The last time she had been in the churchyard, she had watched figures move in the darkness. Seen things she does not believe in.

She looks up at the angular ceiling, looks at the coloured light straining through the windows above the altar. She hears Bessie call for the dog.

"Is something troubling you?" Dodge asks.

Flora hesitates. For a moment, she considers leaving.

Forgive me Father, this was all a mistake...

But she says: "I opened one of my guestrooms. And I found things in there that... unnerved me. There was an arrangement of letters carved into the wall. An arrangement my mother used to banish dark spirits."

Dodge hums.

"You know something of it," says Flora.

"Perhaps. Your mother called me to the inn many years ago. Back when you were just a child. She asked for my help cleansing the place. Exorcising it, as it were. I did as she asked, but it did not satisfy her. She asked me to return to the room and bless it on many occasions."

No. This is all far too familiar. She will not be drawn into another conversation with the vicar about the ghosts walking among them.

But she finds herself asking: "What did my mother believe she saw?"

"Demons," Dodge says plainly. "I told her she could expect little else, given her forays into black magic."

"Black magic," Flora hisses. "Please, Father, this is most offensive. My mother was just a healer, as you well know. She only ever did the things she did to try and help people." Anger bubbles beneath her skin. How foolish she has been to look to Dodge for help. She ought to have known he would come back to her with *demons* and *black magic*.

He smooths his dark robes. "You came to me for answers, Mrs Kelly. I'm simply doing my best to provide them."

Flora grits her teeth. Could there be an inch of truth to the vicar's words? Though she does not believe demons walk the halls of the Mariner's Arms, she knows well her mother may have. But black magic? Surely not. Her mother had been a good woman. Had turned to charms and incantations to find cures, to lift curses. She had never been one to lay them. Dodge suggesting she had involved herself in harmful black magic feels like the greatest of insults.

Flora heaves open the door of the church. Bessie is picking at the ferns by the fence, close to where Flora had once seen a shape move in the shadows. The dog is weaving between the headstones, nose to the ground.

As she makes to leave, Dodge says: "Scarlett Bailey. How is she faring?"

"As well as can be expected. I'm doing all I can."

Dodge murmurs in response. "I worry for that girl. She has always been troubled." He runs a finger along the top of a pew. "It is hardly surprising, I suppose. Her parents didn't see fit to baptise her until she was more than a year old."

Yes, Flora has heard this. Two of Scarlett's siblings had gone to their graves days after their baptisms. An omen, of course. An omen of the worst kind. Jacob Bailey and his wife had not brought their youngest child before the vicar until she had seen out the deadly first year.

Flora feels a flicker of anger on Scarlett's behalf. "Jacob Bailey was very superstitious," she tells Dodge. "But that doesn't mean his daughter is troubled."

Dodge gives her a look that clearly tells her he is tired of her dissent. Who is this witch to step inside his church and question him? Fall into line or be swept up by the devil.

"She will be in my prayers," he says.

Flora regrets coming. "Thank you for your help," she tells him stiffly.

Dodge smiles without warmth. "I hope we will see you here on Sunday."

She gives a short nod and makes her way across the churchyard, her boots sinking into the damp earth. It feels as though the ground is trying to swallow her alive.

There, by the edge of the path is her mother's grave. A withered bunch of heather sits against the headstone. She ought to replace it. But she feels Dodge's eyes burning into the back of her. She calls for Bessie and hurries through the gate.

UNGODLY THINGS

It is past midnight when Isaac brings the lugger back into Polperro harbour.

The revenue men are waiting. Customs officers board the ship, raking through the hold in search of hidden contraband.

Isaac is in no mood for the interrogation. He has spent almost twenty-four hours searching the coast with Jamie and Will Francis. They are exhausted, frustrated. Have found no sign of Leach's black ship.

Isaac is not surprised by the revenue men's attentions. They have had their eyes firmly fixed on the place for weeks; desperate to find the scrap of evidence that might take down the Talland trading ring.

After a painfully slow and thorough search, the officers climb back to the deck. One gives Isaac a curt, wordless nod. The other two climb back to the harbour without so much as glancing at him. Their frustration at finding an empty hold is poorly hidden.

Will stares after the revenue men as they march back towards Customs House. "We'll go out looking again in the morning," he says. "First thing."

Isaac gives a nod of thanks to the two men. He is grateful for their selflessness.

He knows little of this man Scarlett had brought back to Talland with her. The few attempts Isaac had made at conversation with Jamie had been met with tight-lipped, insubstantial answers. Isaac hadn't pushed the issue. He'd not been in the mood for speaking either.

"Go home," he tells them. "Get a little sleep."

Will nods. "You ought to do the same."

Isaac watches the men leave; Jamie to the Three Pilchards and Will over the cliff towards Talland. He checks the moorings, then climbs from the ship and begins to walk towards the cliff path.

He hears footsteps behind him. Turns to see Reuben approaching the dock.

"I was beginning to think my ship had been stolen."

Isaac keeps walking.

"I require your services," Reuben says, keeping pace beside him. "I've word an East

India merchant will be sitting at anchor outside the mouth of the river tomorrow night. A shipment of cognac and Burgundy wine. I've arranged for a purchase to be made."

"Go to hell," Isaac spits. "My children are missing. I'm not trading for you."

"Has there been any word of them?" Reuben asks dutifully.

Isaac grits his teeth. "Tom Leach has them."

"I see." Reuben's voice is calm and even, as though they were speaking of the day's catch. "Then you will be searching the area around Polruan, I assume. Taking the lugger towards the Fowey river." Isaac catches the faint smile on the edge of his lips. "You'll meet the merchant, as I've arranged."

"And what will you do if I deny you? There's nothing more for you to take from me."

Reuben smiles thinly. "That is not entirely true, is it, Mr Bailey."

Isaac closes his eyes. Reuben is right of course. That bastard of a banker who acts on his superior's whim would not hesitate to hurt Scarlett or Caroline or Flora.

"Tomorrow night," says Reuben. "The mouth of the river."

Isaac quickens his pace. "I heard you the first time."

He sees little of the path in the faint moonlight. He is glad for the darkness. Concentrating on walking the cliffs stops his mind from straying to darker places.

From the top of the hill, he can see down into the village. A lamp is glowing in a window of the Mariner's Arms.

He doesn't mean to think of her. He knows how wrong it is for there to be anything in his mind other than his family. But she is there in his thoughts, where she has always been. The more he tries not to think of her, the more she fills his head.

Flora doesn't speak when she finds him on her doorstep. The green glass watch ball sways above her head as wind gusts through the open door. He pulls her into his arms. He needs the feel of her, the warmth of her. Needs her gentle voice, her intoxicating earth and brandy scent.

She pushes the door closed, without releasing her grip on him. Her fingers knot themselves in his hair. "What can I do?"

Isaac doesn't answer. *This. Just this.*

He wants to lose himself in that room at the top of the inn, wants to escape the nightmare his life has become. Wants to forget it all, never mind how fleetingly.

"You can't be here," Flora says, her voice low.

He knows this, of course. Knows that if anyone were to see them entwined like this, Flora would be shunned by the village for disregarding a man's marriage vows. And never mind the village, his sister is upstairs. Scarlett of all people can never know. He couldn't bear for her to discover he has betrayed his family like this.

And yet feeling Flora in his arms is the only thing that has slowed his heart in the four days his children have been gone.

He tries to take all of her in, running his hands over her arms, her hair, her skirts. She presses herself against him, as though willing to be taken.

He wants her lips, her skin, her ragged breath against his ear. But no. He cannot be this man. Cannot do this to Caroline.

Flora steps back. "You ought to leave, Isaac."

She is right, of course. And he hates that she is right.

He leaves without another word.

The Mariner's Arms has its shadows, but it has been many years since the place has stopped Flora from sleeping.

Perhaps it is not this empty guestroom that is causing her sleeplessness. Perhaps it is the ghost of himself that Isaac has left behind.

The inn is silent; Scarlett and Bessie sleeping. It must be close to dawn. Flora is glad when the dog scampers down the passage, the tapping of his claws breaking the stillness. He stops at the doorway of the guestroom. Flora crouches, calls to him. He stays planted in the doorway, ears pricked up and whiskers twitching.

She looks down at the rug nailed to the floor. It is worn through to its thin reed matting, with just a few sparse patches left of its original blue and green. Flora remembers her father arriving home from a merchant voyage with it rolled up on his shoulder. Remembers him unfurling it over the parlour floor, turquoise as a piece of the sea. She had spent hours crawling back and forth across it, entranced by the softness of it beneath her palms.

How has it ended up here, neglected and forgotten?

She grabs a corner and yanks hard, until the nail holding it to the floor flies free. Another corner, another, another until the rug lies curled up in the centre of the room.

There is something beneath it.

She pulls the rug away and crouches, holding the lamp close to the floorboards. A scratching in the wood. A faint circle, hemmed with carved symbols she cannot make out.

She knows this, like she knows the letters on the wall. A magic circle, for the conjuring of spirits. Her stomach lurches.

Her forays into black magic…

"No Mamm," Flora says, aloud. "What did you do?"

Black magic, her mother had taught her, was a dangerous, powerful thing. A thing never to be spoken of. A thing far too dangerous to go near. It had the power to end life, the power to change the past and future, the power to call up spirits.

Her mother had been terrified of demons and ghosts. As far as she was concerned, they were frightening, undeniable things woven into the fabric of life. What could have led her to dabble with such things?

Little wonder she had been scared enough to hack the letters into the wall. Little wonder she had filled the bottle with drops of her own blood. Flora knows the enchantment. A drop of blood from the bewitched to set the darkness at rest.

Why does this bother her so, she wonders? She doesn't believe in such things. Why does she care that her mother had played at the edges of something ungodly?

It bothers her, she realises, because she has begun to shape her own life around the craft her mother had lived by. A craft she believed was intended to help, never to harm. What else had the village charmer seen fit to do? How much of her craft had she kept hidden from prying eyes?

And it bothers her the most that Dodge was right. Bothers her that the vicar had known more about the village healer and her craft than her own daughter had.

The rap of the brass knocker yanks Flora from her thoughts. She hurries downstairs, half hoping for Isaac, half hoping for anyone else.

She finds Caroline on her doorstep.

Flora feels a violent stab of guilt. There ought to have been apologies, a shamefaced explanation at the very least. In light of all that has happened, Flora had felt it best to stay away. But now such a thing feels like the greatest act of cowardice.

"I'm sorry," she says, before Caroline can speak. "I don't expect forgiveness. I just—"

"I'm not interested in your apologies. I need your help."

"My help?"

Caroline tugs her cloak tighter around her body. "Everyone says you have your mother's skills." The sharpness in her voice has been replaced with uncertainty.

Flora looks down. "I really don't—"

"Believe me, I wouldn't come to you if I weren't desperate. But Tom Leach has my children. I'm willing to try anything."

"Tom Leach?"

Scarlett had said nothing of this when she had returned to the inn last night. Nor had Isaac mentioned it when he had appeared on her doorstep earlier. No doubt they had both sought to protect Flora from her own guilt. Caroline clearly has no such sensibilities.

"He's taken them because he believes Isaac was the one who turned him over to the revenue men," she says pointedly.

"I'll go to him at once. I'll tell him it was me."

"And put your own child in danger?" Caroline's knuckles whiten around the hem of her cloak. "We've no idea where he is. Isaac has spent all day looking for him."

"I'm sorry," says Flora. "More than you could know."

Caroline looks up at the watch ball. "I've been in this place long enough to know the stories. Magic mirrors that show you hidden things."

Flora's stomach turns over.

"You have one."

She nods slightly.

"Could it show you where Tom Leach is hiding?"

Flora swallows. She doubts, of course. Doubts herself, doubts the mirror. But her uncertainty had not helped Scarlett and it will not help Caroline. Or her children.

She steps aside and gestures to the staircase. "Upstairs."

Flora perches on the edge of an armchair in the parlour, the black mirror across her lap. Caroline sits in the chair opposite, arms folded tightly, eyes fixed to the floor.

Flora tightens her grip on the handle of the mirror. How desperately she wants to be of use.

She had seen the murder of the riding officers in the glass, she reminds herself. Had seen dead men on the road, as clearly as if they had been lying on the floor beside her.

What had she been doing to bring about such a vision?

She closes her eyes momentarily, willing her thudding heart to still. She blinks, then lets her eyes relax as she stares into the dark surface.

She sees her own face, sees the dance of the candles behind her. But she needs more. Needs an image in the glass. A glimpse of Tom Leach, or the children, or anything that might begin to atone for the crime she committed when she took another woman's husband to her bed.

There is nothing to see but her own distorted reflection.

"I'm sorry," she mumbles. "I wish I could be of more use. I really do."

For a long time, Caroline says nothing. She stares into the fire, winding a stray strand of hair around her finger. "Did you pin her nightgown?" she asks distantly.

"What?"

"Bessie. Did you pin her nightgown to the crib? To stop the fairy folk from taking her?"

Flora reaches out and presses a hand to Caroline's wrist.

She pulls away sharply and leaps to her feet. "I don't know why I came. You can't help me." She turns and rushes down the stairs, disappearing into the dark tavern.

Caroline throws open the front door of the inn. What had she been thinking? She is not a woman who believes in magic.

She stops suddenly, looking over her shoulder into the empty bar. The key to the cellar is in the lock.

She lets the front door close heavily, then creeps towards it.

She lights the lamp at the top of the stairs and climbs down into the shadows. Broken chairs lie scattered over the cellar floor, ale ankers piled up in one corner. Larger barrels are stacked up against the wall.

Shoving one aside, Caroline sees she is standing at the mouth of the tunnel. The passage into the rock is smaller, tighter than she had expected. The sight of it is unsettling. She has never liked the idea of Isaac traipsing through the centre of the cliff. She likes it even less now she sees how narrow and black it is. An easy place, she thinks, for a man to die. She slides the barrel back into place.

Holding the lamp close, she runs a hand across the cellar wall. And she finds what she is looking for. Finds what Jacob Bailey had led her towards. An irregularity in the bricks.

Jacob had not been playing her. He had not been lying. Here is a place where the wall has been broken into. A place where the bricks have been removed, then carefully replaced.

A perfect hiding place for foreign silver.

A BLACK SHIP

Asher wakes from a broken sleep on the floor of Tom Leach's kitchen. It is still dark, but he feels as though he has slept several hours.

The door clicks open. "Mr Fielding? Are you there?" It is the voice of Jane Leach.

He scrambles to his feet. Jane is breathless and flushed, strands of red hair plastered to her freckled cheeks. Muddy skirts cling to her boots. "I couldn't stop him," she says, gulping down her breath. "He came in the morning, after you'd left. He believed you were planning to give them back to their mother. Said he couldn't let such a thing happen."

"Where are they?" Asher asks. "Did he—"

"They're alive," says Jane. "I begged him not to hurt them. I went with him because I was so afraid of what he might do."

"Where is he now?"

"He's on his ship. He thinks I'm sleeping. I managed to get out without him noticing." She winds the edge of her cloak around her finger. "I can take you to where he's moored. But we've got to hurry."

Asher pulls on his coat and follows Jane out of the house. The dawn is pearly and purple, the streets glistening after a sprinkling of rain.

What is he doing? Why is he walking in the direction of Tom Leach? The man could kill him in a second. Is likely to do so if he discovers Asher has been to Caroline.

But there is something about those children that is pulling him towards them. Is it the fact that they have Caroline's blood running through them? Or is it his own regret at having done what he has? His last lingering scraps of decency?

Asher follows Jane up the hill out of the village. She leads him along the narrow path worn into the top of the cliffs. Her head is drooped, her shoulders hunched. She looks over her shoulder at him. "You don't seem like a man who would do such a thing."

And what do I seem like, Asher thinks to ask? What kind of man do I appear to be? If one was to glance at him, would they see any scrap of that life he so longs for? Is there even a ghost of that man left inside him? He is sickened by how far he has fallen.

He thinks of who he had been before he had returned to Cornwall. He had been the man who could see the beauty, the mysteries of the human form. The man one episode away from catching the soul in its escape from the body. One episode away from great scientific discovery.

Now he is a man whose dreams lie in pieces. A man who has taken the wrong path.

"It's gone too far," he admits, his voice low.

"Yes," Jane says dully. "When you involve yourself with Tom, this is usually the way things end up."

She gives him a wry smile that doesn't reach her eyes. She is older than Asher had first thought; past thirty, perhaps. Still far younger than her husband. A caring, gentle woman. How had she ended up sharing Tom Leach's bed?

"He was not always the way he is," she says, as though reading his thoughts. She watches her feet as she walks. "We had children of our own once. Three boys. Influenza took them all in a winter. Tom weren't the same after that."

Asher wraps his arms around himself to keep out the wind. "So he will kill another man's children to make up for his own loss?"

"No," says Jane. "He will kill another man's children to see his own sense of justice done."

"Down here," she says finally. The path veers down the rugged slope of the cliff. Asher plants a hand into the grassy bank to steady himself. His boots crunch into the pebbles at the bottom.

Leach's cutter sways on heaving grey water, its black masts barely visible between the folds of the cliff. Jane's boots crunch across the shore towards the dory she had left on the beach.

Asher shoves the boat into the water. It sighs noisily through the pebbles. He looks over his shoulder at Jane. "You could leave now," he tells her. "Be free of him. What life can he give you as a wanted man?"

She picks at the dirt beneath her fingernails. "No. He's my husband." More picking. More dirt. A swell of sea washes over her boots.

Asher feels a pang of curiosity. Had her husband held her as they had buried their children, he wonders? Had they wrapped themselves in each other's arms in an attempt to ease their grief? He finds it hard to imagine Tom Leach capable of such things. What does this woman see in him that is so meticulously hidden from the rest of the world?

Jane knots her skirts above her knees and wades through the water. She climbs into the dory, making it lurch wildly. Asher jumps in after her and begins to row.

He watches the beach grow distant. Can feel the cutter looming behind him. When the shadow of the ship falls over them, he lifts the oars and lets the dory drift. He reaches out a hand to stop the boat knocking against the hull. Above their heads, the cutter is quiet.

"You ought to go aboard first," he tells Jane. "Get back to your bunk before he notices you gone."

"The children are in hold," she whispers. "You've got to get them off the ship. I'll try and get Tom into the cabin so you can go in through the saloon." She reaches for the ladder and pulls herself onto the rungs.

Asher waits until she has disappeared over the gunwale, then uses the mooring rope to attach the dory to the ladder. He climbs onto the ship, feeling it sway with the tide.

The deck is still and dark. Ratlines clatter above his head as wind whips up the water. He pulls the hatch open a crack. Peers into the saloon. He sees no one. Murmured voices come from inside the cabin.

Asher hurries down the ladder and slips into the hold. It is dark, full of inky shapes. He waits on the ladder as his eyes adjust to the lightlessness. He cannot see the children.

Above his head, the voices grow louder. Leach has emerged from the cabin and is marching across the saloon.

"Did you go to the authorities then?" he demands. "Did you tell them where I'm hiding? Do you want to see your own husband on the scaffold?"

"No," Jane coughs. "Of course not. I didn't go anywhere."

Asher hears a thud, then her muffled cry of fear.

In the hold beneath him, the baby begins to shriek. Asher slides down the ladder into the dark, feeling his way between water kegs and lines. He sees Gabriel on his knees, crawling towards his sister.

Leach rips open the hatch, letting a stream of light into the hold. Asher darts forward and pulls Gabriel back into the shadows. He feels him trembling.

Jane pushes past Leach and scrambles down the ladder. "Let me take her," she says. "I'll calm her down." She grabs Mary from the floor, her eyes gliding over Asher and Gabriel. The baby held tightly to her chest, she makes her way out of the hold.

"How long are you planning on mothering these scraps for?" Leach demands.

Jane's response is fiery. "As long as I need to. I'll not let you harm them."

Asher releases his hold on the boy. "Can you row a dory?"

Gabriel nods.

"Good. The boat is tied to the bottom of the ladder. You've got to go. Now, while they're in the cabin. Follow the coast and it will take you back to Talland."

Gabriel's eyes are wide with fear. "What about Mary?"

"We'll not get her out now. Not without Leach seeing. You've got to go. Tell your parents where the ship is."

The boy shakes his head. "I have to get Mary."

Asher grits his teeth. "I will get her," he says sharply. "You've got to get off this ship. Or you're both going to die."

"No!" he hears Jane cry. "Please, Tom. You can't!"

Gabriel rushes towards the hatch. Asher grabs his arm, yanking him back. He scrambles out ahead of the boy. Leach is marching up the ladder to the deck, Mary tucked beneath his arm. She is shrieking. Jane is shrieking. Tears are flooding both their faces. Jane grabs her husband's arm, trying to pull him from the ladder.

"Please Tom!" she cries. "Please!"

Leach shakes her off.

Asher races up the ladder after them. Jane is a flurry of desperate hands, clutching at her husband's coat, trying to pull the baby from his grip. Leach pushes past her, making for the gunwale. For a moment, Asher's vision swims. There is the sea. And Caroline's daughter. The child will die, and it will be his fault. He will lose any hope he might have had of a life with the woman he loves.

"Don't," he says suddenly.

Leach whirls around in surprise.

"Her mother. She knows things. Knows how to find a fortune."

"What are you talking about? How did you find me?" Leach turns to glare at Jane. He shoves her away as she makes another desperate lurch for the baby.

"There's money hidden somewhere in Talland," says Asher. "And Caroline Bailey knows how to find it. But if you kill her daughter you'll have no way of bargaining with her."

He hears the faint creak of the hatch. He steps back, back again, trying to draw Leach across the ship. Trying to give Gabriel a chance to disappear behind them.

Leach takes a step towards him, the baby shrieking and thrashing beneath his arm. "Why should I believe this?"

"Is it not worth taking the risk that I might be lying?"

Behind Leach and Jane, Gabriel slips out of the hatch on soundless feet. He climbs over the gunwale and onto the ladder.

"A haul of silver," says Asher, "brought to Cornwall by Henry Avery."

"And how does Bailey's wife know about this?" Leach's eyes are distrusting, but Asher can see he has his attention. He shoves Mary back into Jane's arms and Asher lets himself breathe.

"Someone told her of it," he says. "Her father-in-law."

Out of the corner of his eye he sees the dory slide away from the ship and begin to move across the sea.

LOYALTIES

Scarlett wakes to the sound of footsteps in the room she had kicked open. It is early, she guesses. The air is cold, and the street quiet. The groan of the floorboards is all she can hear. She climbs out of bed and makes her way to the guestroom.

"Flora? Is that you?"

"Ayes. Are you all right?" Her voice is tired.

The musty smell is strong, though not as pungent as it had been the day before. Scarlett runs her hand along the wall, trying to see the room through her fingertips. It is cold inside. "Have you slept?" she asks Flora.

"Not really."

"What have you been doing?"

Flora sighs heavily. "Trying to use the mirror."

"The black mirror?" Scarlett kneels beside her. Her fingers move across the floor and brush the cold glass. "You've been trying to use this all night?"

"My mother used to say it worked best for her when she'd not slept."

"What do you hope to see? The children?"

Flora doesn't answer at once. "Caroline came to see me last night," she says finally.

Scarlett sits up. "What did she want? Did she say anything to you? About Asher Hales?"

"Asher Hales? No. She just asked for my help finding the children. But I wasn't able to give it."

There is a knock at the door. Flora climbs to her feet, her footsteps disappearing out of the room and down the stairs.

Scarlett stays kneeling on the floor. She lifts the glass, imagines herself looking into it. Images flow through her mind: sea, ships, her father. Just her imagination? Or can the dark glass penetrate her unseeing eyes?

"Scarlett—"

Flora's voice makes her start. She lowers the mirror, feeling foolish.

"Jamie is downstairs. He wishes to see you."

Scarlett leaps to her feet and hurries down into the bar.

"It's early," says Jamie. "I know. I just—"

"It's all right. I'm glad you're here."

"Your father came to me at the inn yesterday," he says. "Asking if I knew anything about the children. He's very worried for them. And for you."

Scarlett sighs heavily. She doesn't want Jacob here. It is only a matter of time before he crosses paths with Isaac. She is not sure her brother could handle walking past their dead father in the street.

"He doesn't have the right to worry for us," she tells Jamie. But she can hear the weariness in her voice. She is tired of anger. Tired of rage. Tired of the darkness that lies coiled inside her. How can she deal with the darkness within when she has nothing but darkness without?

"He wants to see you," says Jamie, his hand against her wrist. "Perhaps you might let him?"

And so it is to be like this. Lawful, decent Jamie is to play peacemaker between she and Jacob. She feels hot with frustration. Jamie knows well the things her father had been involved in. He had taken down his press gang himself. Why is he so eager for them to reconcile?

But she finds herself saying: "Tell him I will meet him on the beach."

"Is he there?" she asks. Her boots sink into the wet sand of the landing beach, a fine mist of sea cold against her cheeks.

"I'm here, Scarlett," Jacob says, before Jamie can answer. "What can I do?"

Leave, she thinks to say.

But something stops her. Is it the fact that Jacob is here, come to Talland as she had asked? Or is it the memory of his wet cheeks, as he had bent to kiss her goodbye?

No, she will not let herself be swayed by hazy recollections. Jacob Bailey is a murderer. He had taken down a man in the very place they are standing.

She had asked Jacob to meet her here on the landing beach, so he might be forced to remember the things he had done. But had she asked him to meet her here, so she might also not forget?

Why had she agreed to meet him in the first place?

"You can't do anything," she tells him. "There's nothing to be done."

"I want to help find whoever did this to you. And I want to help Isaac find his children."

"Isaac doesn't know you're alive."

"You've not told him." His voice is flat.

Scarlett says nothing.

"Why not?"

"Do you truly think he would care to know? After you disappeared and left him to pay your debts?"

Though she doesn't want to admit it, Scarlett knows there is also a part of her that wants to keep Jacob a secret. If Isaac were to know, the decision of whether to allow their father back into their lives would no longer be hers alone. She needs that control.

"I want to help," Jacob says firmly.

"It's too late for that. You made it clear a long time ago where your loyalties lie."

"My loyalties lie with you, Scarlett," he says. "They always have. I—"

"How can you say that? After all this? Everything that's happened to me, and to Isaac's children, it's all because of you! It's your fault we got caught up in this life! It's your fault we've had anything to do with Reuben or Tom Leach or this smuggling ring! I want nothing more to do with you. And I know Isaac would say the same." She turns abruptly, stumbling up the beach. Feels a hand around her arm.

"He wants to help you, Scarlett." Jamie speaks softly. "Let him."

Anger boils inside her. She yanks her arm away. "My father is a smuggler and a murderer, Jamie." Her voice is loud. She hopes Jacob can hear. "He was a part of the press gang who took your brother. He is everything you despise. Why do you have such trouble understanding that I don't want him in my life?"

"Just hear him out. You needn't do anything more."

She can't pretend to be surprised by his response. Decent, upstanding Jamie. He makes her feel like a terrible person.

She shoves hard against his chest. Feels him stumble backwards with the shock of it.

And she starts to run, her legs pumping, energised by the Wild. Beneath her feet, the path rises in the same narrow ribbon it has for her entire life. She hears the sea thrash and sigh against the rock. There is a strange thrill at knowing the earth could disappear from beneath her feet at any moment. It makes her feel alive.

She feels her hair lash against her cheeks, hears Jamie call after her. She keeps running. His footsteps, his shouting grows closer. And his arms are suddenly around her, squeezing her tightly, holding her still. She thrashes against him.

"Stop," he says breathlessly. "Stop. You'll fall."

Forced into stillness by his firm grip, she stops writhing and gulps down her breath. Her blood is hot. She can feel it thumping behind her eyes. The Wild is tangling her thoughts, making firecrackers of phantom light dance across her vision. She has little recollection of what she had said to her father.

How does she stop this anger? How does she free herself? The dark is all around her, powerless to take the Wild away. The dark has always brought her peace, but all she craves is the light.

She closes her eyes. It does nothing of course, but perhaps for a moment she can convince herself that the darkness is a choice. She lets herself fall into the great expanse of it. That endless void that steals her anger. Her heart begins to slow, and she sinks to the ground, suddenly exhausted. The damp earth soaks through her skirts. She brings her knees to her chest. The Wild has slunk away. But it is too late. Jamie has seen.

Tears spill down her cheeks. "I never wanted you to see this side of me."

She hears the long grass rustle as he sits. For a long time, he doesn't speak. Scarlett feels his hair tickle her cheek. A fine rain has begun to fall, and she lifts her face to the sky.

"Why does your father make you so angry?" he asks finally.

Scarlett grabs a fistful of his coat, needing him closer. "He left us," she says. "He left us to carry his debts. Left my mother to die of grief. Nothing he does can take that back." She turns to face the sea. Imagines it beneath her; grey and white and shifting. She takes a long breath, trying to find calm. "I wish you hadn't told him about the children," she says finally.

Jamie hesitates. "I didn't. He was the one who told me his family was in trouble. It was why I came back to Talland to look for you."

Scarlett frowns. "How else would he have known?"

"I don't know." Jamie squeezes her shoulder. "This is a small village. Word spreads. You know how things are."

"Are you sure you said nothing?"

"I'm certain."

Jamie leaps suddenly to his feet. He speaks fast, frantic.

A dory, he is saying, rowed by a child.

A child with dark hair? Yes.

"It's Gabriel," says Scarlett. "It must be." She feels Jamie yank on her hand as he begins to run down the path. She hurries after him.

The sea is rough, he tells her as they run. Gabriel will need help to land.

And in her mind's eye Scarlett sees that little boat lurch as the sea does its best to tear it away from their shore.

Jamie scrambles onto the rocks at the edge of the beach. The current has caught hold of the boat and is sweeping it past the narrow pocket of sand and shale. From here he can see around the point to a second crescent of rock-hemmed beach. The boat is see-sawing on the swell. He tears at the buttons of his jacket, then stops. Another figure is moving through the water. Scarlett's father. He has left his coat on the sand and is swimming towards the dory.

"What's happening?" Scarlett pushes.

"Your father," Jamie tells her. "He's swum out to the boat. He's helping Gabriel bring it in. They'll land on the beach around the point." He wonders if Jacob knows the boy is his grandson.

Jamie takes a step higher up the wall of rock. Behind the half-moon beach, the cliffs rise steep and dark. The only way back to the village is over the rocks and through the sea.

"Go to the cottage," Scarlett tells him. "Tell Isaac and Caroline that Gabriel is at the inn."

"The inn?" Jamie repeats. "What do you mean? He's landing on the beach."

"Don't ask questions," Scarlett says sharply. "Just get them."

"What about you?"

"I can find my way there."

"Are you sure?"

"Yes." Urgency in her voice. "Go. Quickly."

Jamie looks back over his shoulder. Sees the boy and the old man stumble up the beach and vanish into the cliff.

He goes to the cottage. Catches Isaac on the path, heading for the harbour.

"The inn," he says. "Gabriel is at the inn."

"What?" Isaac doesn't wait for Jamie to respond. He returns to the cottage for his wife, then they are charging down the hill towards the tavern.

Jamie follows. Scarlett has made it to the inn and is thumping on the door.

"He came in on the dory," she tells her brother. "Made it to the eastern beach."

No mention of their father, Jamie notices.

Flora opens the door, a dog yapping around her ankles. Caroline pushes past her and opens the cellar door. As she does so, the boy stumbles out, his dark hair windswept and tangled. He lets out a choked cry and throws his arms around his mother.

"Mary," says Caroline, gripping his grimy cheeks in her hands. "Where's Mary?"

Gabriel sniffs. "She's still in the place. On the boat."

Jamie stands with his back to the wall. He feels an intruder.

He hears Scarlett call his name.

"I'm here," he says, reaching for her arm.

She stands with her shoulder pressed to his. She is calm now; the rage drawn away. He is coming to recognise this about her; the way her moods rise and fall like sea. Still, he had not been prepared for the violent squall that had torn through her on the cliffs.

"Is he here?" she asks under her breath. "My father?"

"No."

Jacob has stayed hidden. Perhaps Scarlett's outburst on the beach has shown him such a thing is for the best.

Jamie glances at the open door of the cellar. And he finds himself walking towards it. Is he looking for Jacob? Or does he want to see what else is down there?

Perhaps a little of both.

He climbs down the stairs, squinting in the dark. Barrels are stacked up along the wall. Two are lying on their sides, as though they have been shoved out of place. Behind them, the rock gapes. His curiosity getting the better of him, he peers into the hole. He sees shoring timbers, and then darkness as the passage vanishes into the cliff.

He had known this, he reminds himself. He had known from the beginning what he was taking Scarlett home to. But the sight of the smuggling tunnel reminds him of all they have been unable to speak about. That bridge they are unable to cross.

What is he doing here in Talland? He has a comfortable home in Portreath, honourable work. Honourable work he is jeopardising each day he stays in this place. He had told his commanding officer he would be away no more than four days. Two days to Talland, two days back to Portreath. He had not counted on entangling himself in the nets of these smugglers.

But how can he leave? How can he ride away when Scarlett's world is falling down around her? Despite the smuggling tunnel and her light fingers and the pocket stitched on the inside of her cloak, she has made him feel things he has never felt before.

He is not sure he could ride away now, even if he wanted to.

He hears the stairs creak.

"Your father's not here," he says.

Scarlett nods slowly. She turns away, as though doing so might prevent him from seeing too much. Prevent him from seeing her shame. There is so much of her she doesn't want him to see, he realises.

She feels her way towards the mouth of the tunnel.

"Are you there?" she calls softly.

But there is silence. Nothing but the sea sighing distantly through the rock.

BRUTAL MEN

"The man from the wreck told me I had to leave without Mary." Gabriel's words are muffled against his mother's shoulder. "He said if I didn't we'd both die."

Caroline sits close to the fire with Gabriel in her lap, his long legs on either side of her and his arms curled around her neck.

Isaac crouches beside them. "You had to go," he says gently, a hand pressed to Gabriel's back. "You had no choice."

His son looks at him with tired and frightened eyes. Isaac takes a long breath. Does he feel violent relief that Gabriel is safe? Or terror at the thought of precious, uncomprehending Mary alone in the hands of Tom Leach? Uncomprehending, he supposes, is something of a blessing.

"Where is the man from the wreck now?" he asks Gabriel.

"I don't know. He just told me I had to leave."

"Tell me again," says Caroline. "Anything you remember. Anything you saw when you got off the ship."

"I don't know. I only remember the sea. And the cliffs."

"Which cliffs, Gabriel?" Caroline pushes. "Where?"

"I don't know."

She rakes her hands through his tangled hair. "Please, my darling. You have to think harder."

Gabriel shakes his head violently. Buries his eyes in Caroline's neck.

Isaac touches her shoulder. "He's exhausted. He needs to rest."

She nods wordlessly. She carries Gabriel into his bedroom and lays him gently on the bed. He is asleep in minutes.

Isaac watches from the doorway. His eyes fall to the empty cradle. "What do you suppose Hales was doing on Leach's ship?"

Caroline laces her fingers through her son's. "It doesn't matter. He helped Gabriel get to safety. That's all that's important."

"Of course it matters! They must have been working together. Hales knew how to find

Leach's ship. Knew how to find his house." He folds his arms behind his head, his thoughts charging. "But if he were working with Leach, why would he have come to see you last night? Why help Gabriel escape?"

For a long time, Caroline doesn't speak. "Perhaps he had a change of heart," she says finally. Her voice is cold, as though she is angry Isaac has dared to ask these questions. "Perhaps he doesn't have it in him to be that brutal man he was hoping to be."

When Scarlett climbs back up to the bar, everything is quiet. Isaac and Caroline have taken Gabriel home. Flora has disappeared upstairs. But Jamie; he is still here.

She stands with her back pressed against the front door. She does not know what to think. Does not know how to feel. Gabriel is safe. Mary is still missing. Jamie has looked into the smuggling tunnel.

His footsteps come towards her.

"I'm sorry," she says instinctively. Sorry for what? Sorry for who her father is? Sorry for helping her brother pay off their debts? Sorry for not fighting harder when Charles Reuben had first slipped a tobacco rasp into her hand and told her to run it up the hill beneath the riding officers' noses? She doesn't know. She just wishes she were a better person.

"I knew what I was bringing you home to," says Jamie. He is close, his voice making something warm in her chest. He takes a step and he is closer still, his breath tickling her nose.

Scarlett's fingers tense around her skirts. "You ought to…" She can't get the words out.

Leave. Before you see the knife in my skirts. Before you see more of the darkness in me than you already have.

How can he stay? How can he see?

She is not gripping her skirts anymore, she realises. She is gripping the sea-hardened edges of his coat.

He doesn't leave. Instead, he presses a kiss into her lips that makes her murmur with its suddenness. His stubble grazes her, hot and sharp. And her lips part beneath his, wanting more of him.

It is at once both gentle and forceful. And it makes her see the glaring imperfections of every other kiss she has ever had.

Too soon, he pulls away. Her pulse is fast and her skin is hot. And this thing has just become infinitely more difficult.

"Why did you do that?" she demands, her fists still tight around the hems of his jacket. "Why didn't you leave?"

His palm is pressed to her cheek, warm and rough and scented with sea. "I can't leave." She hears a smile in his voice. "You're blocking the door."

She tugs him closer, unsure what else to do. She just knows she wants him near.

The brass knocker beats against the door. Scarlett is grateful for the interruption. Grateful for something to take her attention from the terrifying race of her heart.

She clicks open the door.

"The dory," Isaac says, marching inside. "Which way did it come from? Which way was Gabriel rowing?"

"I saw it coming around the point," says Jamie. "He must have come from the west."

"From Polruan." Isaac begins to pace.

Scarlett follows the sound. Left to right, left to right. "Can he tell you anything about where he was when he left the ship?" she asks.

"Nothing of any use."

"Leach must be close," says Scarlett. "Gabriel couldn't have rowed far on his own."

"Leach would have moved the moment he discovered Gabriel had escaped." Isaac keeps pacing. "Gone back towards Polruan, perhaps. He knows the river better than anyone."

"That may be," says Scarlett, "but you're far more intelligent. Wherever he is, you'll find him. I know you will." And when they do? How far will Leach go for retribution? The thought is too horrible to follow far.

She hears footsteps come down the stairs.

"Any word?" Flora asks. "Was Gabriel able to tell you anything?"

"He says Asher Hales helped him escape. He and Leach must have been working together. I don't know how else Hales would have known how to find the ship."

Scarlett opens her mouth to speak. Isaac needs to know, surely, that Asher had paid a visit to their cottage that night. But what if she is wrong? What if she had misheard? Everything has been unsteady since her sight had been taken away. Her hearing is strangely heightened, and she is not certain she can trust it.

Isaac says: "Reuben wants me to meet a merchant on the river tonight."

Scarlett's shoulders stiffen. She is glad Isaac is confiding in her. But she cannot bear to imagine what thoughts are charging through Jamie's head.

"You ought to make the run. We need to keep Reuben on side." Her words are short and sharp. Conversation over. But Isaac says:

"You're right." He stops pacing. "I could use an extra pair of hands," he says to Jamie. "If you—"

"No." Scarlett's heart leaps into her throat. "No, Isaac, he can't."

"It's all right, Scarlett," says Jamie. "If—"

"No," she says, louder. She grips Jamie's arm. "You should go back to Polperro. Please."

He hesitates. "If you need me I'll be at the inn," he says after a moment.

Scarlett nods stiffly. She chews her lip, listening to his footsteps disappear.

"What was that about?" asks Isaac.

"He's not a sailor," Scarlett garbles. "He'll be of no use to you."

"He was of fine use when I went looking for Leach yesterday. Managed to find his feet."

"You can't take him!" she cries. "You can't." She drops her voice suddenly. "Promise me, Isaac."

"All right. All right. Calm yourself." He presses a hand to her shoulder, ushering her inside. "Let me see you upstairs."

Scarlett lets him walk her up the staircase. How she hates being chaperoned like this. She has become more of a burden to her family than she has ever been. But Isaac's nearness is steadying.

"You're going out searching?" she asks.

"Ayes." The parlour door squeaks as Isaac pushes it open. He ushers her inside. "Will's going to meet me at the harbour."

"Be safe," Scarlett murmurs. "Please." She wraps her arms around his neck and squeezes. The thought of her brother going charging after Tom Leach is terrifying. But she knows he has no choice.

She listens to him leave. Listens to the floorboards creak beneath his feet. Two sets of footsteps.

"Is Gabriel well?" Flora asks Isaac. They are in the hallway. At the top of the stairs perhaps. Flora's voice is hushed.

"He's exhausted and scared," he tells her. "But unharmed."

After a long pause, Flora says: "This is my doing. Leach has Mary because of me. I should never have turned him over to the authorities."

Scarlett cannot catch Isaac's response, but his voice is soft and gentle.

She creeps across the parlour, each footstep carefully placed so as not to make a sound. She presses an ear to the door.

"Please be careful," says Flora. "I couldn't bear to lose you."

Scarlett feels an intruder. This is not a conversation between friends. This is a conversation between two who care for each other deeply, desperately. Their half-whispered words are loving and secretive.

What is she not seeing, Scarlett wonders? Loving looks, gentle hands? Has their lifetime of friendship become something more?

Perhaps Caroline is not the only one hiding things.

PRECIOUS INFORMATION

Caroline hears footsteps. She climbs from Gabriel's bed and goes to the kitchen, pulling the nursery door closed behind her.

Isaac has returned from the inn. Caroline's heart thuds. She is terrified each time he speaks with his sister. There is so much Scarlett could tell him.

Gabriel had rowed from the west, he says. From the direction of Polruan. The direction of the river.

He tells her nothing else.

If Scarlett truly knows their father is alive, why has she not told her brother? Caroline has no thought of it, but she is slightly buoyed by the silence. Whatever her reasons, it seems Scarlett wants to keep this vital piece of knowledge to herself.

Isaac takes his scarf from the back of a chair and bundles it around his neck. "Will's agreed to meet me at the harbour," he tells Caroline. "I'll set sail the moment he arrives."

She nods. Takes the poker and jabs at the fire. Sparks fly up the chimney.

Isaac needs to know about Avery's money. If he finds Tom Leach's ship tonight, that information might be his only leverage to keep the man from harming their daughter.

Asher Hales had promised to tell Leach of the haul. But Asher Hales cannot be trusted.

That precious information may be all that is keeping Mary alive. It cannot be left in the hands of a liar.

Isaac picks up the woollen gloves he had left on the hearth to dry. He stuffs them into the pocket of his coat.

Caroline draws in her breath. She must tell him.

Now.

That precious piece of information that could keep their daughter alive.

That precious piece of information that will see their marriage in pieces.

It must be done.

She looks up at him. Feels suddenly dizzy. She grips the edge of the table. Isaac presses a steadying hand to her arm.

How can she do it? How can she face the interrogation that will surely follow? How can she bear to see that look of hate in her husband's eyes when he learns Jacob had been the one to tell her of the money?

It must be done.

"If you find Leach…" she begins. The words catch in her throat.

"I will find Leach," Isaac says firmly. "I'll not come back until I do." He grips her cheeks in his hands. "I'm going to bring Mary home. I swear it." He holds his lips against her forehead for a moment. Then he turns and marches from the house.

Caroline stumbles to the doorway. *Call after him*, she thinks. He needs to know. But by the time she finds her voice, he has already disappeared up the hill.

She goes back to Gabriel's bedside. Sits with her fingers laced through his. He is still sleeping deeply.

Her heart is fast. What kind of mother is she? How could she have been so selfish and cowardly when her own child's life is in danger? She closes her eyes as a tide of self-hatred sweeps over her.

She leaps to her feet at a knock at the door. Lets Asher inside hurriedly.

"Where is Mary?" she demands.

He is dressed the same ill-fitting clothes he had been the last time she had seen him. The long sleeves of his coat are folded ridiculously over his hands, his shirt stretched tight across his shoulders. His hair is tied back neatly.

He peers into the bedroom at Gabriel. "I'm glad he made it back safely."

"Where is Mary?" Caroline says again, her voice rising.

Asher raises his eyebrows. "This is all the thanks I get for helping your son escape?"

"Thanks? You were the one who took him in the first place!"

"No. That was Tom Leach."

At the mention of Leach's name, Caroline's throat tightens. She pulls closed the nursery door and lowers her voice. "Did you tell him of the money?"

Asher nods.

A strange sort of relief floods her.

"He's given you two days. You'll meet him at The Ship. You give him the money and he will give you your daughter."

Caroline presses a hand over her mouth to stop a sob escaping. Two days. The money will be near impossible to get to in such a short amount of time. But she must find a way. She sinks into a chair at the table, her legs suddenly unsteady.

"Where is it?" Asher asks.

Caroline stares at the floor. She does not want him to know. Does not want Asher Hales to be the man with whom she is sharing this secret. But she cannot do this alone. And there is no one else she can ask. "It's in the Mariner's Arms. In the wall of the cellar."

Asher's lips part. "The wall of the cellar?"

She nods. "There are bricks out of place close to the opening of the smuggling tunnel. You can see where the wall has been broken into."

"Why is it there?" The excitement in Asher's voice is thinly veiled.

"Jacob said Davey paid Flora's father to hide it in the inn. He was too scared to keep it in his own house. I suppose he was afraid of men coming after him." She stands, and begins to pace. "Tell Leach what I just told you. The haul's whereabouts in exchange for my daughter."

"Leach wants the money. Not just information."

"This is priceless information," Caroline hisses. "How can I get to that money?"

"You can get to it," says Asher. "You just can't get to it without telling people what you know."

Caroline's thoughts are racing. He is right. She can get to it. She must. There can be no other way.

She stands close to Asher. Looks into his eyes. She knows he still loves her. And she must use that. "I need your help," she says. "I need a boat. I need you to take me to the eastern beach tonight. Around to the mouth of the tunnel."

THE HEALING WELL

Scarlett appears at the door of the kitchen. The place is a chaos of potent scents; apples and nutmeg, ginger and cinnamon. "Lambswool?" she asks Flora.

"I hope so." Flora tosses the fruit into a pot of simmering ale. "The last batch was something of a disaster." She is jittery after the morning's events. Had needed something to keep herself occupied. When she had returned home after taking Bessie to school, she had gone straight to the kitchen and set the pot to boil.

"I'm glad of it," says Scarlett. "I was worried you were thinking to not reopen the inn."

Flora doesn't answer. The thought had crossed her mind. The Mariner's Arms has given her anxious nights, has led her to the lock-up. Letting the place fall into disrepair had felt fleetingly appealing. But she has worked far too hard to let the inn slide through her fingers.

She stirs the pot, then glances over her shoulder at Scarlett. "Are you all right?" she asks. "Is there something you need?"

"The well at Saint Cleer," says Scarlett. "Will you take me?"

They take a carriage from Polperro. The morning is misty and damp, the sun a perfect circle glowing behind the clouds.

They share the coach with three others; an elderly couple Flora has seen selling eggs at the market and a man in a tarred fishing coat who cracks his jaw with disturbing regularity.

Scarlett sits with her eyes turned to the window. A force of habit? Or is she trying to picture the world that is passing her by? Is she seeing the neatly trimmed hedges and the vast sweep of the moor? Does she see the engine houses of the tin mines blotting the purple-grey landscape?

At Liskeard they leave the coach and pay a farmer to take them to Saint Cleer.

Flora has given little credence to the stories of holy wells. They would be a fine thing to believe in, of course, these sacred springs that dot the country and bring back lost health and fortune. But she has always needed more than fervently spoken words in order to believe. She knows proof is something the desperate mind rarely bothers to seek.

But she has seen images in dark glass, has watched stones and rhymes heal her daughter. Perhaps there is magic in the water of the well.

Either way, it is not up to her to make such decisions on Scarlett's behalf.

Flora knows she is the one who ought to have suggested they make this journey. She has come to realise her mother's craft is something she needs in her life. Has come to realise the village healer is something she needs to be. But the things she had found in her mother's room have rattled her to the core.

She has doubts. Scepticism. And now she has begun to question the very decency of this thing she is beginning to build her life around.

She has trained herself to speak with conviction. But the people of Talland need a healer who truly believes. A healer who can swear by her cures, without fearing she is crossing some boundary into darkness. Without belief, without faith, what is she but a charlatan?

Believing in the magic of healing wells opens up far too many possibilities. If there is magic in the world, it means there is far more power in her mother's chest than Flora had first believed. It means she has the ability to see tomorrow, and all the responsibilities that come with that. It means there is the possibility that hastily scrawled circle on the guestroom floor has the power to conjure up something unwanted. And it means there is the chance her husband does not lie quiet in his grave.

Flora knows that if she is to be a successful healer, she needs to embrace this world, understand it; the light and the dark. She is not sure she has the courage. Nor is she sure she has the skills. She has not helped Scarlett, has not helped Caroline. The only place the craft has led her of late has been to discover things about her mother she does not want to know.

She shifts uncomfortably as the farmer's wagon lurches over a rut in the road.

Scarlett says: "How long have you been sharing my brother's bed?"

Flora feels suddenly, foolishly hot. "It's finished," she says. "That's all that matters." The words leave a hollowness inside her. She picks at a scrap of beeswax beneath her fingernail.

"You love him." Scarlett's tone is matter-of-fact, not accusatory.

Flora looks out the window. The spire of Saint Cleer's church is cutting into the cloud bank. "What does that matter?" she says finally.

Scarlett reaches out and loops her hand through Flora's arm.

They sit in silence until the wagon clatters to a halt.

Hemmed by vast moorland and ancient stones, the village of Saint Cleer seems to straddle this world and another. Wind ripples the grass, vivid green between stone cottages and curving mud-black roads. Clouds hang low, threatening to open.

The farmer points down the street. "The well's on the corner. Past the village green." He glances at Scarlett. "You need help getting there?"

"I can manage," she says brusquely. She clenches her jaw with determination.

Flora's stomach tightens. Scarlett has too much faith. There is a belief in her, Flora knows, that when they make the journey home, she will be seeing those engine houses for real. How far will she fall if the water fails her?

The well sits among the grass on the edge of the narrow street, presided over by unkempt trees and a worn Celtic cross. With Scarlett gripping her arm, Flora steps carefully over the low stone fence, aware she is navigating for both of them.

The path to the water is well worn. The sick and desperate have been coming here for centuries, Flora knows. People have knelt on this bank seeking cures for black death, cures for the sweating sickness. Madmen have been dipped beneath the water in hope it might restore their sanity.

Flora has been here once before, as a young girl, when her mother had accompanied one of the villagers to the well to seek relief from consumption. Had the water worked that day? Flora had never thought to question it.

The air is still, cold. All she can hear is the murmuring echo of water against stone.

Scarlett draws in her breath. "Take me to the edge."

Scarlett kneels on the wet grass and reaches down into the water. She hears it bubbling, moving beneath her.

She needs to believe. She has become afraid of the dark. Has become afraid she'll not survive it.

She reaches into the well and cups a handful of water, bringing it to her face. She lets the drops run down her cheeks. She holds her breath, waiting for the light, the clouds, the crooked spire of the church.

She sees nothing. Below her, the water keeps moving. Keeps bubbling.

Is this a sign the well has failed? Do the sick who touch this water emerge instantly healed? Do madmen step from the bowsenning pool with their senses intact?

Why has it forsaken her? Is she not a good enough person? Has a lifetime of smuggling and light fingers rendered her immune to the healing water? Has she gone too far into the dark to ever be pulled back?

She reaches for her bonnet. Her throat tightens, but she will not cry.

To cry is to admit defeat.

In the carriage, she says aloud: "The water will work. I know it will. Perhaps it will just take time." She hears the waver in her voice. Forces it away.

"Yes," says Flora. "Perhaps."

The cart wheels hiss as they carve through the mud. Scarlett grips the edge of the bench to keep her balance. That pain in her throat is there again, her tears close to spilling. She swallows and swallows, forcing the pain and the tears away.

Flora says: "You have a man who cares for you very much."

Scarlett knows she is only speaking of such things to distract her. But the mention of Jamie makes something flare inside her. The feeling is half pleasant, half terrifying. And entirely unfamiliar.

Involuntarily, she brings a hand to her mouth, feeling the place his lips had touched hers. A kiss after seeing the Wild, after seeing the smuggling tunnel.

What had he been thinking? Why had he not ridden away?

She had learned so much of him on their journey from Portreath. A childhood of farming and folk tales and summers in the sea. She knows he hates spiders, knows he drinks mahogany. Knows he'd happily eat taddago pies for every meal. And yet she knows not a thing of his work, beyond the glimpses she had seen in Portreath. What had driven him to fight smuggling? Has he faced men willing to kill to keep their hauls hidden? How many free traders has he seen imprisoned, transported, impressed?

Each time their conversation had veered in that direction, they had pulled it back to safer ground. Scarlett is acutely aware they are keeping things from each other. Hiding away the parts of their lives that make them incompatible.

She winds her shawl around her finger. The edge is damp with well water.

"You're worried," says Flora, "of having a future with him if your sight does not return."

"Is that what you think? That my sight will not return?" She tries to keep her voice steady.

"I don't know, Scarlett. I'm sorry."

Flora's bluntness is a fist to the stomach, but Scarlett is grateful for her honesty. She tugs her shawl tight around her shoulders.

"Jamie is a riding officer," she blurts.

And this, she realises, is the way to shoot a conversation dead. She understands the silence, of course. Jamie had walked through Flora's inn. He had climbed into the cellar and seen the tunnel.

Jamie could have them all before the magistrate.

"I see," says Flora, after far too long. "And can we…"

"We can trust him," Scarlett says shortly. She entangles her hands tighter in her shawl. Flora's silence tells her what she has known in the back of her mind all along; that she and Jamie are anything but well-matched. "I shouldn't have said anything," she mumbles. "But I just needed to tell someone."

"He seems a good man," says Flora, finding her voice. "Truly. You ought to keep him close."

Scarlett allows herself a faint smile. Flora's words are reassuring. Because ill-matched or not, she desperately does not want Jamie to ride away. Just how insurmountable, she finds herself wondering, can their differences be?

"Will you take me to the Three Pilchards?" she asks. "I need to see him."

CONFESSION

Jamie sits in the corner of the tavern, his officer's journal on the table in front of him. He records the details of the shooting in the castle ruins, and of Tom Leach's fleeting image through the hole in the keep. Records the search for the man he had undertaken in Isaac Bailey's lugger.

He looks up to find Scarlett standing over him. She is wearing her cloak and woollen bonnet, her pale blue skirts streaked with mud. She smells of earth and water.

"Jamie?" she says. "Are you there?"

He touches her hand. "How did you find me?"

"Flora brought me here." She sits beside him, her fingers grazing the notebook. "Is that your journal?"

He closes the book. "Yes."

"Am I in there?" she asks. "Did you write of the thieving woman from Talland you trapped on the beach?"

Jamie smiles. "No. I assumed you didn't want such a thing on record."

"Take me up to your room," she says suddenly.

He swallows. "I can't, Scarlett." He keeps his voice low. "People will talk. They'll think badly of you."

More to the point, if he has her in his room, his control will likely slip through his fingers. And that would make this far more complicated than it already is.

"The people in this place know the kind of person I am." Scarlett winds her shawl around her hands. "Please. I just need to speak with you. About things it would be dangerous for stray ears to overhear."

Jamie does not want to speak. Speaking is far too difficult. There can be no more avoiding the issues they have been dancing around.

A big part of him longs for her. Wants nothing more than to whisk her up to his room and feel her move beneath him. Wants nothing more than to wake every morning beside her. But can they truly have a life together when it feels necessary to hide so much from each other?

Smuggling is not a choice, she had told him. A thing she had been forced into by her father. And yet when he had caught her on the beach in Portreath, she'd not been acting on her father's bidding. She had been acting for no one but herself. Had turned to smuggling as a means of making money. She had grabbed at a dishonest solution, instead of trying to earn herself an honest wage.

There was a part of him that had wanted to string her up for it. Wanted to show her there was no place for smugglers on his scrap of Cornwall's coast. And by right, he ought to have done it. There are few riding officers foolish enough to turn down the chance at a conviction. But there are also few riding officers foolish enough to lose their head over a woman with smuggled tobacco in her cloak.

He cannot stay here at the inn forever. One day soon he will be forced to make a decision. Commit or ride away.

He takes her upstairs. Unlocks the door and guides her inside. The room is small and cramped, with a narrow bed against one wall and a table and single chair in the corner. He leads Scarlett to the bed, then sits opposite her on the chair. Her knees are an inch from his. He can feel the heat rising from her body.

She takes off her bonnet and sits it on the bed beside her. Beneath it, her hair is a windswept snarl. She folds her hands in her lap. Inhales. "My brother conducts free trading runs for the syndicate boss to pay off our father's debts," she says. "He added a false bottom to his lugger so he can slide smuggled goods beneath the revenue men's noses. He uses the tunnel beneath the Mariner's Arms to bring them in from the beach." Her voice drops a little. "We are all involved. I run the goods to buyers, and carry the signalling lantern. Flora stores the contraband in her cellar. Caroline has adulterated smuggled tea and sold it to unsuspecting buyers. And half the village is in Isaac's landing party."

Jamie doesn't speak at once. This should infuriate him, of course. He has spent countless nights intercepting deliveries, has lost friends to smugglers' bullets. But he is grateful for her honesty, her openness.

He reaches for her hand. He closes his eyes, wanting to experience this as she is. The warmth of their skin pressing against each other's, the steady thud of his heart.

He opens his eyes. Her hand looks small and fragile in his. He knows it an illusion. There is little fragility to this woman.

He tells her. Tells her of his training, the careful planning of his patrols, the oath he had sworn at Customs House. He tells her of the letters passed along the coast between officers, and of the way the army so often refuses to assist with their raids. He tells her of his desire to see the country cleansed of the dishonest blight that has seized it.

"Why?" she asks. "Why such hatred for free trade? Did smugglers steal from you? Kill your family? What?"

"No." He shifts uncomfortably. She has been honest with him, and he will do the same for her. "I despise it because it's wrong, Scarlett. That's all. It's dishonest and wrong."

"Yes," she says after a moment. "I know it is." She tries to slide her hand from his, but he doesn't release his grip.

"Why are you still here?" she asks. "You've been away from Portreath for more than four days. Your commanding officer will not be happy."

"No. But how can I leave without knowing your brother's children are safe? How can I just ride away?"

"That's why you're here? Because you want to help my brother find his children?"

Jamie says: "It's far more than that."

And suddenly she is standing over him, her knees threaded between his, strands of her hair tickling his cheek. Her hands are sliding over his shoulders, his chest, feeling the shape of him. Her lips finds his. She is forceful, possessive. Seems to care little where such a thing might lead.

This is far too dangerous.

"Scarlett," he manages, desire thickening his voice, "we can't. I'll not take you before you're married."

His words drop heavily into the silence.

How has this conversation brought them here?

Scarlett is young, strong-willed and clever. Despite all that has befallen her, Jamie is sure she soon will marry. Soon there will be a man waking each morning beside her. And he will have to decide if he is brave enough, strong enough for that man to be him.

She slides out of his arms and sits back on the edge of the bed. Knots her fingers together. "And if Isaac finds Mary? If he brings her home safely? What will you do then? Will you go back to Portreath?"

For several moments, he says nothing. He does not want to leave. But a part of him is afraid to stay. How can he hold a position in the revenue service and have a future with this woman?

"Do you wish you'd stayed in Portreath?" she asks.

"No." He does not need to think.

And then he sees. If he does not take his chance to be the man who wakes up beside her, it will be someone else. And Jamie realises how desperately he does not want that to be the case.

He takes her face in his hands, directs her gaze.

Here. Look at me.

"If Isaac finds Mary, then yes, I will leave," he tells her. "I love my job. I want to return to it."

No, not *want*. *Need* to return to it.

He is aware of what he is really saying. *I need to fight this life you have built. I need to punish those who do what you do.*

He is aware of what he is really saying, and he is aware of the absurdity of it. Because what he says next is: "But I would like nothing more than for you to come back to Portreath with me."

I would like you to come back to Portreath with me and watch as I do these things. I would like you to come back to Portreath and listen as I relay stories of midnight patrols and hard-fought court cases. I want to sit at the supper table beside you and tell you every moment of every day.

Absurdity of course. But how desperately he wants a life in which he returns to his cottage each night to find her in it.

Scarlett makes a noise in her throat. Is this happiness? Disappointment? He can't read her. She stands suddenly and wraps her arms around his neck, pushing her body hard against his. "The healing well failed," she says. "My sight might never return." Her voice is muffled by his hair.

"I don't care." He'd had no thought of it. Her blindness is the smallest of the divides they will have to cross.

He is asking a lot of her, he knows. Asking her to leave her family, her home. Asking her to leave behind the world she knows. And for what? To be a riding officer in trade-drenched Cornwall is no easy thing. There is constant distrust, constant whispers behind his back. There is the curse of looking at everyone and wondering what they are hiding. There are the conversations that stop when he and his colleagues walk into taverns. There are friends who tell him only half truths.

A life by his side will not be easy.

If Scarlett is to turn him down, he will not blame her. But he needs her to know how he feels.

No need for an answer now, he tells her, pushing her tangled hair behind her ears. The future is so hazy, so uncertain, that to answer now would be impossible. But he is glad there is to be no more hiding.

He kisses her gently. "I'll take you back to the inn."

"Not yet," says Scarlett. "Just let me stay a while."

He lays back on the bed and pulls her down with him. Her hand slides over his chest, coming to rest above the place his heart is drumming. She rests her head against his shoulder. And he closes his eyes against the last threads of daylight that are filtering into the room.

GHOSTS IN SHADOWS

"What's wrong, Mammik?" Bessie asks, as she and Flora walk back over the cliffs from the charity school. Smears of pink sky push through the thick bank of cloud. Wind whips their hair against their cheeks.

Flora slides an arm around her daughter's shoulder. "I'm sorry, *cheel-vean*." She has been distracted since returning from Saint Cleer that afternoon. In truth, she has been distracted since Scarlett had kicked open the guestroom. Has found herself raking through memories of her mother, analysing, overthinking.

She takes Bessie's hand and keeps walking past the inn.

"Where are we going?"

"We're going visiting." Flora knocks on Martha Francis's door.

Martha opens the door a crack, her face breaking into a smile at the sight of them. She ushers them inside, pressing wrinkled hands to Bessie's cheeks and planting a wet kiss on her forehead.

"Mammik said we're going visiting," Bessie announces.

"Visiting? I see." Martha looks past her at Flora. "Is everything all right?"

Flora manages a faint smile. She feels suddenly foolish. Has she really let the carving on the floor rattle her so much?

But she needs to know what her mother had been doing in that guestroom. And she needs to know why. Perhaps Martha will not have the answers. But Flora can think of no one else to ask.

Martha plants Bessie by the hearth with a cup of milk and an enormous slice of saffron cake. She hangs the kettle over the fire and nods for Flora to sit.

Flora perches on the edge of a chair at the kitchen table. Edgily, she picks at the wax on the rim of the candleholder. "You knew my mother well, ayes?"

Martha smiles. "Yes, of course. Meg and I were dear friends."

"You came to her for help a lot, didn't you. For charms and the like."

Another nod.

Flora watches Bessie break the end off her cake and cram it into her mouth. "You trusted

450

her then? You trusted the charms she gave you?" The words feel bitter on her tongue. Feel like a betrayal. Is she truly asking such things about her mother? The woman she remembers as being nothing but caring and selfless?

Martha doesn't speak at once. "What's brought this on, Flora?" she asks gently.

Flora sighs. "I opened up one of the guestrooms in the inn. And I found some things inside. Things my mother warned me away from when I was a child." She sucks in her breath. "Things the vicar would class as black magic."

"Ah." Martha looks unsurprised.

"You know something of it."

Martha spoons tea into the pot. "You know what your mother was like, *cheel-vean*. You know easily she got carried away. You've a much more level head on your shoulders than she ever did."

Flora manages a pale smile. She is not sure this is true.

"Meg saw something in her black mirror one day," says Martha, the teaspoon dangling from her fingers. "Something that terrified her."

"Something in the mirror?" Flora repeats. "What was it?"

"She wouldn't say. But whatever it was, she were desperate not to see it come true. Told me she were doing her best to reverse what she had seen. Said she knew an enchantment that could stop it happening."

"Counter-sorcery."

"Ayes, I suppose that's what it were."

Flora sighs. "I thought her wiser than that."

"Don't think ill of her," Martha says gently. "It was a difficult time for her. She'd just lost your father. She wasn't thinking clearly. She made a mistake, is all. And she knew it too."

"What do you mean?"

Martha's voice becomes low and conspiratorial. "Poor woman scared herself silly. She were convinced she were seeing things. Ghosts and demons hiding in that room where she made the enchantment."

Flora leans back in her chair. She thinks of her mother walking through the inn, her husband dead, her daughter asleep; in that dark, lonely place Flora herself has been far too many times. How easy it is, she knows, to let imagination get the better of you in such a place.

She pictures her mother staring into the mirror, her eyes distant, her pale hair falling over her shoulders. Her mother had believed staunchly in the power of the dark glass. Had trusted that tomorrow would appear beneath its surface. What had she seen to rattle her so much? What had been so dreadful she had sought to reverse it by venturing into dark enchantments and counter-sorcery?

In her mind's eye, Flora sees her mother driving a knife across the wall of the guestroom. She imagines her face contorted in fear, as her grieving, terrified mind found demons in the empty shadows of the inn. Imagines her locking the door of the tainted room and throwing away the key.

Flora rubs her eyes. The creaking passages of the inn, she knows well, have the power to take away rationality. How she wishes she could hold her mother, just for a moment, and tell her not to let her feverish mind carry her away.

"The black magic," she says. "She did it only to try and change what she saw? There was no other reason? There was nothing spiteful about it?" She looks into her hands. "She was not seeking to punish anyone? Lay a curse?"

Martha takes the kettle from the hook above the fire and pours boiling water into the teapot. "Of course not," she says gently. "You know who your mother was, Flora. You know she only ever used the craft to help people. Never to harm them."

Yes. Of course. Flora feels a stab of guilt that she has dared think otherwise. Her mother had been the most devoted of healers. Had always done all she could to help the people of Talland. Perhaps her work had angered the vicar, but Flora has come to realise that such a thing is easily done.

That evening, she goes to the churchyard with a bunch of heather in her hand. She takes the withered stems from her mother's grave and lays fresh flowers in their place.

HIDING PLACES

Isaac grips the wheel of the lugger. The wind is cold against his cheeks, but he is blazing inside. They are slicing through the sea towards the mouth of the river. The silhouette of the merchant ship peeks out of the gloom.

They had spent the morning combing the coast, tracing the outlines of beaches that appear and vanish with the tide. When there had been no sign of Leach's ship, they had made their way onto the river, squeezing the lugger down tree-lined narrows and tight, muddy offshoots.

And now, Reuben's rendezvous. Ten cases of cognac and Burgundy wine to be stored beneath the bulkheads.

Isaac is furious at the interruption. But he cannot risk Reuben's anger. Cannot risk making any more enemies.

Will stands beside him on the foredeck, turning up the collar of his coat against the wind. The sun has slipped into the water, leaving only cloud-drenched moonlight. "I've told the landing party to be ready on the eastern beach," he says. "They'll take the goods into the tunnel."

"Forget the landing party. I'm not going back until I have Mary."

"I know," says Will. "I know. But what if we find her after we've made this exchange? We can't bring the lugger back to port full of contraband. We'll be stuck at sea until we can get word to the landing party. Best they're ready and waiting."

Will is right, of course. The revenue men are watching Talland far too closely for them to be haphazard with their landings. The last time Customs had inspected the ship, they had been dangerously close to uncovering the false bottom in the hold.

"I'll go aboard," says Will, as they draw closer to the merchant.

"You don't have to—"

"You're a mess, Isaac. Better way I make the transaction. You stay here and help me get the goods aboard." He is lowering the dory before Isaac can argue. Climbs down the ladder and steps into the boat.

453

Isaac stands at the wheel, feeling the lugger shift on the waves. He looks over his shoulder towards the blue mouth of the river. The water is dark and silky, curling away towards the hills.

His stomach turns over. Leach will have discovered Gabriel's escape by now, surely. Will he have taken his anger out on Mary? At the thought, he feels suddenly, violently ill. He closes his eyes and tries to breathe.

His knuckles whiten around the wheel. The moment the lugger is loaded, he will head back onto the river; a warren of murky tributaries and dark snarls. That black ship must be hiding in there somewhere. And he is not leaving this place until he finds it.

In the darkness, Caroline can make out the inky shape of Asher on the landing beach. He paces, arms wrapped around himself to keep out the cold. A dory sits at the edge of the water, waves slapping against its hull.

Caroline looks back over her shoulder at the village. She has left Martha Francis watching over Gabriel. Had hated to leave him. But what choice does she have?

"The boat," she says. "How did you get it? Did you steal it from the harbour?"

"No. I purchased it." Asher snorts. "Of course I stole it."

Caroline holds out the pick she had found among Isaac's gardening tools. "Will this work?"

Asher takes the pick. "It ought to break down the wall, yes. But I don't know how you expect to do this without anyone hearing you. You'd best hope the inn is empty."

Caroline swallows heavily. Before she had come to the beach, she had ventured down the hill to the Mariner's Arms. A lamp had been flickering in one of the windows. Flora and Bessie will be there for certain. And Scarlett?

Caroline steps into the boat. If she is to be discovered, so be it. "Just take me around the point."

Asher shoves hard against the dory and it slides through the sand, gliding onto the surface of the sea. He climbs over the gunwale and sits opposite Caroline. She turns her head to avoid meeting his eyes.

She will find the money tonight. She has no choice but to do so.

But as she had spent the day piecing together her plans to unearth the silver, she had also pieced together her plans to let Asher Hales carry the blame.

It was Asher who had discovered the hiding place, she will tell Isaac, when he demands to know how she came to know of these riches. Had discovered its whereabouts on his journey to Portreath. Gleaned the information from an unnamed man. And she had threatened him, she will say. Threatened a cowardly man into giving up his knowledge.

She sickens herself with these lies. But lies are far less painful than the truth. The thought of Isaac looking into her eyes and seeing who she really is sickens her to the core.

A cold breeze skims across the water, splintering the reflection of the moon. Caroline pulls her cloak tighter around her. Her breath is silver as it rises into the night.

Asher pulls on the oars. The dory slides soundlessly around the point. And there is the eastern beach. Though she has been in Talland for more than a decade, it is the first time Caroline has seen it.

Asher rows towards the shore, leaping into the water and shoving the boat up the sand. He offers his hand to help her climb from the boat. Ignoring him, she clutches her skirts in her fist and steps into the shallow water, exhaling sharply at the coldness of the sea.

She trudges up the beach, squinting to make out the contours of the rock face ahead of them. The mouth of the tunnel is invisible in the dark. She trails a hand across the cliff, stopping when she feels it fall away beneath her fingers.

"Here." She crouches low, her skirts in her fist. As she steps into the rock, the pale moonlight vanishes, leaving her in impenetrable blackness. It is a sudden, disorienting sensation. She presses a hand against the wall to guide her. Asher is close behind; his footsteps crunching, his breath fast. Caroline feels the earth gather in her throat.

And then there is no more rock, just the smooth wooden plane of the barrels blocking the tunnel entrance. She throws her body weight against them, making them groan along the floor.

She steps into the cellar or the Mariner's Arms.

"There's a lantern by the stairs," Asher tells her under his breath.

Little point him being so silent, Caroline thinks wryly, feeling her way through the darkness. The moment they slam the pick into the wall of the cellar, they will be heard. Flora will come, perhaps Scarlett. She must have her story ready.

Asher will deny it all, of course. He will argue, and he will hurl accusations. Caroline can only hope there is enough lingering trust in Flora and Scarlett for them to believe her over him.

She finds the lamp, lighting it with a trembling hand. She carries it across the cellar, holding it up to the wall beside the tunnel. The flame is hot against her cheek.

"Here," she tells Asher. "The bricks have been replaced. It looks as though there's something behind them."

He nods silently, his eyes wide. He has been searching for this wealth almost half his life. And here he stands before its hiding place.

He will not get his hand on a single coin.

Every scrap of this haul must go to Leach to spare her baby's life.

What will Asher Hales do if they discover the money tonight? Caroline knows he is selfish, fixated on his dreams. Knows there is every chance he will take the silver and run. Does he love her enough to put Mary's life ahead of his own? She doubts it.

But she needs him. Needs him to strike the rock, just as she had needed him to row the boat around the point. To this whole sorry operation, Asher Hales is frustratingly necessary.

Caroline holds up the lamp and nods towards the wall. "Do it."

Flora rifles through the chaos of the kitchen cupboard until she finds a ream of shagreen at the bottom. She runs a finger over the coarse animal hide. It will do well for smoothing away the carvings in the guestroom.

She rubs the shagreen over the wall, beginning to smooth down the letters. A part of her regrets planing away this scrap of her mother. But these letters must be erased. Like it or not, she must open this place to guests soon, just as she must do with her mother's room, Jack's room.

When Isaac has found Mary, she tells herself. When Scarlett is healed. Then she will open the tavern doors again. Then she will open these rooms. She will hire workers. Men and women to run the bar. And she will dedicate herself to caring for her guests. The Mariner's Arms will be a place she can be proud of. A place Jack would have been proud of. She feels a swell of determination.

The black mirror is leaning up against the wall where Scarlett had left it.

And in the corner of her eye, Flora sees it.

Firelight in the glass.

She has seen this many times; flames dancing over the black surface of the mirror. But now a chill runs through her. Because this is no reflection. The fireplace in this room has sat cold and disused for more than twenty years.

She lifts the mirror, unable to pull her eyes from it. She looks closer. And she realises exactly what she is seeing.

She tosses the mirror in shock. It shatters on the floor, black glass spraying across the room, lodging in the indents of her mother's magic circle. Flora steps backwards, stumbling hard into the wall.

And she stops. Feels the floorboards bend beneath her feet. She looks down. Here in this corner, the boards are a darker colour than the rest of the room. There are large gaps between them and she can feel a cold draught gusting through. She goes to the parlour for the fire poker. Shoves the tip of it in the gap between the boards and wrenches hard. One snaps loudly, revealing a dark recess beneath the floor.

She stops. Is there noise below her as well?

She waits. Yes, a crashing, a splintering in the cellar, two storeys beneath her feet. At the end of the passage, Bessie's dog barks.

Flora draws in her breath. Is she to let herself fall for this again? This trickery of the tunnel? Crashing, splintering; yes, she had heard that the day Jack had died. These sounds are nothing more than her memory playing tricks. She tries to push the noise away.

She shoves the poker between the floorboards again. Another falls away. She shines the lamp into the space beneath the floor. Mice scurry into dark corners, escaping the sudden beam of light. Bessie's dog races into the room, yapping, circling, trying to push his way past her.

In the space beneath the floorboards is a cloth bag. Flora shines the light over it, wary of its contents. In her time, her mother had packaged all manner of things into bags;

hangman's rope and earth from a grave, fingernails and blackened animal hearts. She cannot tell what is inside.

She reaches down and lifts it carefully. It is small, no bigger than an apple. Heavy. She opens the bag and inhales sharply. Silver. It glitters faintly in the lamplight.

A mythical treasure. A thing Flora had not believed in. So much of her world, she is coming to realise, is made up of things she does not believe in.

She sets the floorboards back over the hole and takes the bag into the parlour. She sits on the edge of the armchair to inspect the coins more closely. They are rough-hewn silver, foreign characters imprinting surfaces worn smooth. The bag is heavy in her lap.

And there is more thumping, more splintering. If these sounds are otherworldly, this other world is coming far too close. Flora know Isaac's landing party will soon be arriving on the beach, ready to bring the latest haul through the tunnel. But this is not the sound of the landing party.

Clutching the bag of silver, she makes her way down into the cellar. Lamplight flickers at the bottom of the stairs.

And there is Caroline, sitting amongst the broken furniture. A dust-covered pick lies on the floor. Beside the mouth of the tunnel, the brick wall of the cellar has been hacked at, revealing an empty cavity carved into the rock.

Flora stares.

She had been certain she knew every inch of the inn. Knew every passage, every brick, every corner, every shadow. But how foreign this place seems now, with its carvings and cavities and its treasures beneath the floor. She feels oddly betrayed.

Caroline doesn't look at her. "It was supposed to be here. I was to give it to Leach. In exchange for Mary's life." She stands shakily. "But it's a myth. It's all a lie."

The steps creak beneath Flora's feet. "It's not a myth." She holds out the pouch.

Caroline stares at it for a moment. She takes it and peeks inside, her lips parting with shock. "It was supposed to be in the cellar wall. That's where your father put it."

"How do you know that?"

Caroline doesn't answer.

"You came looking for it. How did you know it was in my inn? Who told you?"

Caroline tries to step past. Tries to reach the door.

No, she is not leaving. Not like this. Not without answers.

Flora's hand shoots out and grabs her wrist. There is no trust between them, of course. How can there be? There is no trust, but there is this shimmering silver secret.

"Who else knows of this?" Flora asks sharply. "Who else can I expect to find treasure hunting in my cellar?"

"No one."

"How did you learn of this? Who told you it was here?" It is not just about her and Bessie's safety, Flora realises. She needs to know who these people are who understand the Mariner's Arms better than she does. Needs to know how they had come to learn of this secret. This silver that had shown itself to her at the very moment Caroline had gone looking. The inn, it seems, had wanted to give up its secrets tonight.

Flora feels her hand tighten involuntarily around Caroline's wrist. "Tell me. I need to know."

Caroline pulls away sharply. "You don't need to know a thing." She stands close to Flora, her eyes flashing. "You'll tell no one. Do you understand?" She slips the pouch inside her cloak. "After all you've done to me, you will keep this to yourself."

A THING OF RETRIBUTION

The river narrows. There are trees and dark, trees and dark. A sliver of a moon shines off the water.

"Down here," says Isaac.

The lugger is sliding silently through the water, sails trimmed to catch the faint breath of wind.

Will shines the lantern down the thin corridor of water. "It's too narrow. We'll barely make it through. There's no way Leach would have managed to take the cutter this way."

"Down here," Isaac says again. "I'm sure of it."

He turns the wheel, feeling the hull grind against mud. He wills the lugger to keep moving, exhaling in relief as it rides the faint swell.

Down the tributary. Trees and dark.

And ahead of them is Leach's cutter. With its masts and hull painted black, it is little more than a shadow, anchored in the centre of the river.

What Isaac feels is not entirely relief. Not entirely anticipation. Right now, he has hope that his daughter is alive. And he knows climbing aboard the ship could see that hope torn away forever.

He looks to Will. Wordlessly, they furl the sails, leaving the lugger to drift. Isaac uncoils the mooring ropes. He will secure the ship to one of the trees lining the river. Drop anchor here and the noise is bound to attract Leach's attention.

With the lugger secured, Isaac pockets his pistol and blows out the lamp. Light glows through the porthole of Leach's ship, picking out the gnarled trees at the edge of the river.

Isaac leaps from the ladder, landing in the shallow water close to the bank. He waits for Will to follow.

They trace the curve of the river, the water sighing around them with each laboured footstep. And they reach the black hull of the cutter. Isaac takes his pistol from his pocket, holding it above the waterline. He begins to wade towards the ladder. Water bubbles around his chest, the cold tightening his lungs. Will grabs his shoulder, holding him back.

"You can't just go charging onto the ship. You know Leach won't hesitate to shoot."

But what plan can be made? Without knowing the layout of the ship, they are just fumbling in the dark. Isaac's earlier reluctance has given way to urgency. He needs to get aboard the cutter as quickly as possible. There is no time for thought. No time to make plans.

He climbs the ladder and swings his legs over the gunwale, bringing streams of dark water with him. The deck is silent. The smell of pipe smoke hangs in the air, tinged with the murky breath of the river.

There is a hatch on the raised foredeck. Leading down to the saloon, Isaac guesses. It is tightly closed. He presses an ear to it. Through it he hears nothing.

A second hatch at the other end of the ship. It is open a crack and Isaac sees a faint light blinking beneath. He makes his way towards it and peeks through the gap. He sees a redheaded woman move beneath the hatch. He cannot tell if she is alone.

Tom Leach's wife. Jane. Isaac has seen the woman before. Seen her fawning over her husband at their cottage in Polruan.

He pulls on the hatch, cursing as it groans beneath his hands.

Jane looks up, swallowing a gasp of shock. Her eyes widen, but she doesn't speak. Doesn't scream. Does nothing to alert her husband.

Isaac lowers himself into the cabin. Jane watches silently, with her back pressed to the door.

Isaac's eyes dart around the room. He sees a tiny shape in the corner of the bunk, covered with a thin grey blanket. Motionless. He feels dizziness sweep over him. Is she sleeping? He is suddenly afraid to take a step. Afraid to go to her.

"Who are you?" Jane whispers.

Isaac steps towards the bunk. "I'm her father." He pulls back the blanket and sees the dark mop of Mary's hair. She lies on her front with her knees tucked beneath her, a fist curled beside her cheek. Isaac presses a soft hand to her back. He feels her body rise and fall with breath. The relief is so great he hears a sound come from his throat. He scoops her carefully from the bunk. It feels important not to wake her. To keep her blind to all that is happening. He closes his eyes for a moment, feeling the warmth of her as she burrows against his thudding chest.

When he looks back at Jane, there is a faint smile at the edge of her lips. "I did my best to care for her," she whispers. "Keep her fed and warm."

Isaac gives a short nod. It doesn't feel right to thank her. "Where is your husband?" he asks under his breath.

"In the saloon. He has his weapon."

Isaac glances up at the hatch. He cannot climb back through with Mary in his arms. He will need to hand her back to Leach's wife. And he is not sure how far he can trust her.

Pistol in hand, he steps out into the saloon. Leach is sitting at the table, a pipe in one hand and a gun in the other. His pistol is trained on Will, who stands in the doorway, countering Leach's weapon with his own.

Isaac walks slowly towards him, eying the hatch leading back to the deck. On the edge of his vision, he sees Jane emerge from the cabin.

"Why?" he asks.

Leach sets his pipe in a bent tin ashtray. "It was a thing of retribution. But it's about so much more than that now."

"What are you talking about?"

Leach leans back against the bulkhead. "Your daughter for the silver your wife knows how to find."

"Don't involve my wife in this." Isaac feels Mary wriggle against his side. Feels her little hands clutch at his coat hem.

The corner of Leach's lips turn up. "You don't know," he says after a moment. "You don't know about that silver. But your father did."

"My father has been dead for years." Isaac's fingers tighten around his pistol. One bullet, he thinks, and the man would be dead. Retribution for his children, for his sister.

But how can he pull the trigger with Mary beneath his arm? She will not understand, of course, but she will see. She will hear. She will witness her father take another man's life. A part of her will carry it with her always.

Leach stands up from the table. "A haul of silver," he says. "Come to this place on a pirate ship. Hidden in your village. And your wife knows how to find it."

The claim makes Isaac feel strangely unsteady. But he shakes his head. A lie, of course. He and Caroline have lived in poverty their entire lives. If she had known such a thing, she would never have kept it from him.

His finger shifts on the trigger. No, he tells himself. Tom Leach is not worth the guilt that will follow. He does not want to leave a trail of blood behind him. He just wants to get his daughter home. Leach is outnumbered. Disadvantaged. Isaac steps towards the hatch.

Leach lurches suddenly and snatches his wife's arm. Yanks her in front of him and holds the pistol to her head. "Leave and I'll kill her."

"Go," Jane tells Isaac. "He'll not do it. I know he won't."

He can't risk it. Whatever faith this woman has in her husband's decency, Isaac does not share it. He glances at Will. They both have their guns firmly fixed on Leach. Beneath Isaac's arm, Mary shifts and whines.

In a sudden flash of movement, Will grabs the lantern hanging above the door and flings it across the cabin. The flame disappears, plunging the ship into darkness. Will rams a fist into the side of Leach's head. He stumbles forward into the table.

Isaac grabs Jane's wrist. "Come with us."

"No." She pulls free of his grip. "I can't."

"He'll kill you for letting me get to Mary."

"He won't. I trust him. I do."

Leach is climbing slowly to his feet. If his wife wants to face her husband's wrath, Isaac realises, he has no choice but to let her.

CLIFFTOPS

Scarlett can feel a strange restlessness to the place as Jamie walks her back over the hill to Talland. It is night now; she can tell by the emptiness of the streets, by the icy edge to the wind. She knows the landing party will be lining the cliffs and beaches, waiting, hoping for the return of Isaac's lugger.

Despite their earlier candidness, Scarlett wants Jamie back in Polperro before he catches sight of any of it. Him knowing how deeply she and her family are involved with smuggling is one thing. Him witnessing the whole event is quite another.

They reach the front door of the Mariner's Arms.

"You ought to get back," says Scarlett.

"Shall I see you upstairs?"

"I can manage." She feels in her pocket for the key Flora had given her.

Jamie holds her close, his lips to hers. Jamie who wants to take her back to Portreath. A thing she can't even begin to fathom right now.

She listens to his footsteps disappear. Stands in the doorway. The restlessness is within her, she realises. Disquiet brought about by her uselessness. She ought to be up on those cliffs with a signalling lantern, watching for Isaac's lugger.

How can she just sit at home and wait?

She calls up the stairs to Flora. She is going to the cottage. No, no I don't need help. Jamie is here.

She starts to walk. Feels the ground slope upwards. She finds the gate of the churchyard. She pushes hard and hears it creak beneath her hands.

She walks with her arm outstretched. Feels the smooth headstones graze her fingers. There is her mother, her brothers, her sisters. There is Jacob's memorial under which nothing but earth lies.

She stops walking. Listens. Is that the sigh of footsteps through the mud? Is the landing party here?

"Is someone there?" she calls, her voice low.

"Miss Bailey?"

She reaches a hand towards the voice. Makes contact with a man's thick chest.

"Who's there?"

"It's me. Ned Arthur."

Yes, Scarlett knows the man. A farmer from Isaac's landing party. A man with arms like tree trunks and a face so rough he looks unfinished. "You need help?" he asks. "What are you doing here?"

"Take me to the cliff," says Scarlett. "Tell me what's happening."

Arthur takes her arm and leads her across the churchyard. She feels the wind rush up from the sea and lash her hair about her cheeks. They are close to the edge of the cliff.

"No sign of your brother's ship yet," says Arthur.

"Is he to land on the eastern beach? Use the tunnel?"

"Ayes. We'll make our way down there when we see the ship." For several moments he says nothing. Then his gravelly voice makes Scarlett start. "There's a light at the edge of the bay. The revenue men are watching."

Asher huddles at the end of the tunnel, listening for any sounds from the cellar. He hears nothing. If Caroline and the witch are speaking, their voices are being swallowed by the rock.

He had tried to warn her. Pick to rock and this would no longer be their secret. He had not been surprised to hear the witch's footsteps. Just surprised it had taken her so long to find them.

At the sound of footsteps, Asher had grabbed Caroline's arm and tried to pull her into the tunnel. She yanked away. She had to find the money, she told him. Had to save Mary. It didn't matter if Flora found them.

Asher looked back at the gaping hole they had made beside the tunnel entrance. There was an empty space behind the bricks. A perfect hiding place. But it was shatteringly, sickeningly empty. "The money's not here," he said. "Jacob lied to you."

"No. It must be here. It must be. I have to find it."

Asher looked at the dust and splintered brick scattered around his feet.

There was no money. Caroline was just blind with desperation.

Jacob had been playing with them both. Punishment for all they had done to him. And yet Asher had not seen it. He had been mad enough to try and believe again.

The witch's footsteps were coming closer.

He would not let himself be seen here. Couldn't bear for anyone to know he had been so foolish as to trust the ravings of Jacob Bailey.

He grabbed Caroline's hand again. "We need to leave."

She glared fiercely. "Do as you wish. I don't care." Such coldness in her eyes, her words.

And for the first time in days, Asher saw with clarity. Saw he could not pretend any longer. He was nothing to her. Never would be. Perhaps he never had been.

What hope did they have of a future?

And so he turned. Began to walk back through the tunnel. Let Caroline try and explain herself when the witch found her in the cellar with bricks around her feet. Let her admit she had fallen for Jacob's lies.

He can feel cold threads of air sighing in from the beach. His boots sink into the sand as he breaks through the mouth of the tunnel and trudges towards the sea. He will not stay here and be reminded that he had fallen again for the myth of Avery's haul. Will not be reminded that his love is unrequited.

He sees the lights of a ship at the edge of the bay. Too large to be Isaac Bailey's lugger. A revenue cutter perhaps? It is close enough to row out to.

To hell with Avery's money. There are other ways to make his fortune. He will approach the revenue vessel and tell Customs all they want to know. Reward money in exchange for his knowledge. An anonymous informant, of course.

With a swell of fresh determination, Asher shoves the dory into the sea.

"I see the lugger," Ned Arthur reports. "Coming around the point."

Scarlett's heart begins to thunder. She knows Isaac would not be returning without Mary. Dare she hope for good news? "Where is the revenue ship?"

"On the edge of the bay."

Isaac will be prepared for this, Scarlett tells herself. Customs have been watching the harbour for weeks. There is no element of surprise to their attack. The lugger is faster, and Isaac has been outrunning revenue men for almost half his life. Still, their presence makes her uneasy.

She hears the distant clatter of hooves. "Who's there?" she whispers. "Riding officers?"

"I don't know." Arthur's voice is close to her ear. "It's too dark to tell."

The sound of hooves comes closer. Drumming, echoing, approaching the bell house from the top of Bridles Lane. Scarlett hears movement around her; footsteps sighing through the grass. How many of the landing party are here in the cemetery?

"We've got to hide," Arthur hisses.

He begins to run through the churchyard, tugging Scarlett along behind him. She stumbles awkwardly, disoriented by the sudden movement.

And she loses her grip on his arm. Has he pulled away or has she let go on her own accord, aware she is slowing him down? She cannot be sure. She only knows she is alone.

The sound of hooves has stopped. Are the riding officers here, prowling through the churchyard?

She knows she cannot speak, cannot call out, in case someone should hear her. She takes a long breath to steady herself. She reaches around her, trying to place herself within the churchyard. She has seen the place almost every day of her life. And yet fear is blurring the details. Her fingers graze the tops of gravestones. They are far too small to hide behind.

Somewhere in the distance, she can hear footsteps sighing through the wet grass. Do they belong to the landing party or the riding officers?

She needs to make for the church. She knows the revenue men will not hesitate to search it— they have had their eyes on the place since the night of Bobby Carter's death— but there will be places inside she can hide. Behind the pulpit, under the pews, beneath the table in the vicar's vestry.

She trails a hand over the graves until she finds the path. She follows it towards the church and pushes on the heavy door. It opens with a groan.

Inside smells of incense and candle wax. A familiar scent of funerals and marriages and sleep-deprived Sundays. She knows this building. She can find her way.

She edges towards the pulpit and crouches in the dark.

BURNING LIGHT

The church door creaks open. Scarlett holds her breath and presses her back hard against the pulpit. She hears footsteps. Two men. Perhaps three.

Sharp, clean footsteps. Riding officers' boots.

She has no thought of how dark it is. She can smell the waxy trail of extinguished candles, but if there is even one flame left burning, if there is even a thread of moonlight shafting over her face, it could lead the riding officers straight to her.

She presses her eyes against her knees, trying to keep her face hidden. Trying to let her dark hair cloak her.

The footsteps come closer. Scarlett presses a hand against her mouth to silence her noisy breathing.

Closer they come. Closer still.

And then more distant. The door creaks open and the footsteps fade. The clop of hooves vanishes up the lane.

She knows the revenue men will not go far. They will prowl Bridles Lane, watching the beaches, waiting for their chance to catch the Talland smugglers with their hands full of French wine.

Scarlett stands shakily, gripping the edge of the pulpit to keep her balance. She feels her way to the door of the church and heaves it open. Cold air blows against her cheeks.

"Mr Arthur?" Her whisper is swallowed quickly by the night. She waits.

Silence.

Has the landing party dispersed? Scarlett can't be sure. But if they truly have left, there will be no one to alert Isaac of the riding officers' presence. No one to warn him not to land in Talland.

She needs to find the signalling lantern. Needs to find a bundle of furze to set alight.

She makes her way outside.

A headstone, another, another. And then the row of graves stops. Ahead of her, Scarlett knows, is the thin strip of earth on which she has stood so many times with a signalling lamp. Beyond that; cliffs and sea.

She feels for the headstone at the furthest end of the churchyard. It belongs to Elizabeth Hodge, Martha Francis's mother. Behind it, the lantern is hidden. Scarlett reaches down, letting out her breath in relief as her fingers touch the cold metal. Beside it sits the tinderbox and a bundle of dried furze. The riding officers had not found it.

Slowly, she begins to walk towards the cliff edge. Each footstep is slow and tentative, testing the ground ahead of her before she edges forward.

The darkness seems to be moving, shifting, rolling like sea. She kneels dizzily. Finds the ground solid beneath her.

She strikes the tinderbox. And there is light.

A flicker, a pin prick, piercing the darkness. But it is enough to steal the air from her lungs.

The blackness returns. Hurriedly, she strikes the flint again. The charcloth flares. Yes, light. Bigger this time, bolder. Orange and yellow and hot in front of her eyes. The beauty of it makes her cry out.

She holds up the tinderbox with shaking hands. She sees nothing but the erratic dance of the flame, but right now, that flame is enough. She lights the dried fronds of the furze.

And she sees more; sees white peaks as the sea breaks against the cliff, sees the inky shape of the church. Sees the jagged stone teeth of the graves, their images blurring and sharpening.

She holds up the burning furze towards the dark shape of the lugger. This path is not safe, the flame tells her brother. The riding officers are watching.

Scarlett stamps out the furze as it burns down towards her fingers. With the fire out, the darkness has returned and she can see little.

She panics. Have her eyes failed her again, or is this just the thickness of the night? She holds the tinderbox to the wick of the lamp, exhaling in relief as shapes appear out of the darkness.

Isaac will take the lugger to Polperro. He will slip the tubs into the sea and land his most precious of cargoes. She needs to be there. Needs to help him find a safe path, away from the riding officers' eyes.

With the mast lamp doused, the lugger is suspended in blackness. But every curve and crag of these cliffs is familiar. The pale moonlight is enough to show Isaac the way.

His skin is hot, despite the bitter cold. His heart has not slowed since they had left Leach's cutter.

Now the children are safe, they must try and escape again. They have little money, but somehow they will find a way. There is no other option. Leach will come for his family, for certain. He will come for retribution, for that phantom silver. But he will not be foolish enough to come tonight, Isaac is sure, not with the revenue men circling like sharks.

Isaac had not been surprised to see the customs ship patrolling the entrance of the bay.

No doubt they have been watching the harbour. Have been waiting patiently for his return.

A flame on the cliffs in Talland. He cannot land on the eastern beach as planned. He will have to make for Polperro. Slide the lugger between the shards of cliff and land around the point.

He is prepared for this, he reminds himself. He has landed in Polperro many times. And he knows the lugger well enough to outrun the revenue men. But never before has he tried such a thing with his daughter sleeping below deck.

He sees another shape riding the inky sea. A dory, moving steadily towards the customs ship. Isaac squints. He can't make out who is aboard. He turns to Will, who is standing at the wheel.

"The spying glass." He holds it to his eye. There is just one man in the dory. Isaac feels a faint flicker of relief. The revenue men, he knows, never work alone. He looks back through the glass. In the darkness the figure is hazy, but familiar. This is Asher Hales.

Isaac's fist clenches around the neck of the spying glass. His relief disappears.

Hales is heading straight for the revenue cutter.

The bastard has done his best to expose the Talland ring. Has sent the revenue men after them before. No doubt he is seeking to do the same thing now.

"Come about," Isaac hisses to Will. "We need to catch him."

Asher Hales knows far too many of their secrets to let him climb aboard that ship.

Scarlett's steps are unsteady on the cliff path. It feels as though her eyes are remembering how to see. She walks as far from the edge as possible, her fingers clutching the heather on the rim of the path to keep her afloat. Her other hand is tight around the handle of the unlit lantern.

She hurries towards the harbour, the steep path pulling her into a run. She will make for the point on the other side of the village. Signal to Isaac from there.

But there is Jamie, standing at the edge of the anchorage, his eyes following the light of the revenue cutter as it moves across the water.

Look at him with his messy waves of hair and his worn broadcloth coat. Look at the fine curve of his chin and the ropey muscles in his hands. He is everything she remembers.

She flings her arms around his neck.

"You see me," he says into her hair. The lantern bumps against his side. He steps back. Eyes it.

She sees him. And what does he see?

He has seen her running over the clifftops with a signalling lantern in her hand. No doubt he has seen the riding officers charging through the village. That's why he is here at the harbour, Scarlett is sure. To see if these traders will entrap themselves in the revenue men's net.

Does he wish for such a thing to happen?

This man, with his riding officer's journal and his brass buttoned coat, has a hatred for smuggling.

I despise it because it's wrong, he'd told her. *Dishonest and wrong.*

If he watches her signal from the clifftops, how long will it be before he despises her too?

"Go back to the inn," she says. "Please."

"Go back to the inn?" he repeats. "And hide away from all that's happening?" His voice is calm and even as always, but Scarlett hears a hint of tension beneath.

"Please," she says, her voice wavering. "Isaac has Mary. I need to help him get ashore." She lowers her eyes. "And I don't want you to see the things I do."

Isaac grips the gunwale. They are close to the revenue ship. Far too close. But they need to reach Asher's dory. They cannot let the bastard get aboard the cutter. Out will come their secrets, and everything will fall. Hales will implicate Scarlett, will implicate Flora. Customs will find Will on the lugger and the landing party on the beach. Isaac knows he will not be the only one to face the court.

He eases the lugger towards the dory, cutting across the path of the revenue cutter.

A bullet flies over their bow. They are in range of the customs ship.

And from this, Isaac knows there will be only one outcome. The lugger will be captured.

This knowledge brings a strange sense of calm. He wants Reuben's ship to be caught, Isaac realises. He wants this lugger, with smuggled liquor hidden its bulkheads, to fall into the hands of the revenue men. Wants the ship to be torn apart, wants her pieces to be sold at auction.

Isaac looks down at Asher's boat. They are close. If they launched their own dory, he and Will could row out to meet him.

And so he fills their lifeboat with mooring ropes and spare balls and powder. Fills it with the things he will need to make Asher Hales compliant.

He runs below deck for Mary. He has strapped her to the mattress with a mooring rope to stop her crawling from the bunk. Is glad she has managed to sleep through the whole ordeal. He pulls her free of the rope. Slips off his coat and wraps her in its bulk.

He climbs back onto deck and helps Will wind the davits, lowering the dory into the sea. And down the ladder towards the lifeboat he climbs, leaving the ship that has been in his care for more than fourteen years. What a joy it is to abandon her here, in the path of the revenue men.

Will takes the oars and pulls away from the lugger, hidden by the thick of the night. Isaac glances edgily across the sea. The revenue cutter to his left. Asher Hales to his right. He has his pistol in one hand, his daughter in the other.

Never again, he thinks. When all this is over, his children will never see him with a weapon again.

Asher has seen them coming. He has changed course. Away from the revenue men, towards the open water.

Isaac lifts his gun. "Stop."

At the sight of the pistol, Asher stops rowing. Isaac smiles wryly to himself.

Coward.

Will lifts the oars and lets their gunwale collide with Asher's The two boats groan and thud against each other. Will and Isaac climb into Asher's dory. They yank him to his feet, making the boat tilt wildly. Water spills over the gunwale.

Isaac keeps his gun steady. For not the first time that night, he wishes he had it in him to pull the trigger. Asher Hales no longer in their lives is an enticing prospect.

Will binds Asher's wrists with mooring rope and shoves him to his knees. "What will we do with him?"

They cannot let him go. He knows too much.

Perhaps they can imprison him in Flora's cellar. Bind his wrists and ankles so he has no chance of escape. No chance of turning them in.

Isaac looks over his shoulder at the drifting lugger. When Reuben discovers his ship has been captured, he will be at the cottage door, of course. Demanding an explanation. Demanding repayment.

It doesn't matter. Isaac has his children. Once the revenue men have turned their backs, he and his family will find a way to leave.

He watches the lugger career across the path of the customs vessel.

Let them catch her. Let them think her a ghost ship.

Go back to the inn, Scarlett had said. Jamie feels hot and restless. He wishes he were able to do as she had asked. Wishes he were able to turn away from all that is unfolding. But he needs to watch. He is as ingrained in this world as Scarlett is.

He stands outside the inn and looks over the water. The two ships are close together. But there is something strange about the way the lugger is moving; a drunken dance, her sails limp and windless.

There is no one aboard. Jamie is sure of it. Isaac has left the ship to fall into the hands of the authorities. A deliberate act, no doubt. Has he escaped in their lifeboat? Does he have his daughter?

Jamie can just make out Scarlett's tiny figure at the top of the cliff.

She has seen the strange motion of the lugger, he is sure. She will know her brother is no longer aboard. Will know he is trying to land.

She has set a light flickering on the point. What is she telling Isaac? Jamie rubs his eyes. How many nights has he spent squinting into the dark, trying to determine the language of lanterns on the cliffs?

Whatever the meaning, it doesn't matter. Scarlett is not safe. She is hidden from the revenue men riding the roads of Talland, but has made herself a beacon for those who will be coming from the west. The riding officers will have banded together to hem in the pocket of coast they suspect is seeing action.

Scarlett must know this, surely. She has spent her life outrunning the revenue men. But she is acting rashly, desperate to get her brother, her niece, safely ashore.

Hell. She will trap herself up there.

Her brother will land safely, but the riding officers will take her instead.

Jamie curses under his breath. He had promised her he would not involve himself in her corner of the trade. But it is far too late for that.

He runs into the inn and snatches the saddle bag holding his pistol and powder. Hurries to the stables for his horse.

REVENUE MEN

Jamie rides towards the lantern Scarlett has set flickering on the cliff.

He cannot see her in the pale orange light. There is nothing around but coarse scrub and she has hidden herself well. She is sickeningly good at this.

"Scarlett," he hisses.

She appears from behind him. He cannot even tell where she had been hiding.

Her eyes are wide. "Why are you—"

"Get on the horse," Jamie hisses. "Now."

She moves to douse the lantern, but he yanks her away. "Leave it burning. Let the officers come this way." He grabs her arm and pulls her into the saddle behind him.

Inky plains of farmland stretch out ahead. Beyond that? He has no thought. But they cannot ride the path. Officers will be approaching from either side, drawn to the signal fire on top of the cliff.

He digs his heels in, goading the horse into a gallop. Scarlett's arms tighten around him.

Hooves thunder across the farmland, the horse leaping the thin threads of the streams. Jamie's heart is thundering. His cheeks burn in the cold air. He dares a glance over his shoulder. He hears hoof falls, fast and rhythmic. They are growing steadily louder.

Had they seen Scarlett on the cliff? Would they recognise her if they were to find her on the back of his horse?

He hears her sharp intake of breath beside his ear. Her arms tighten around his waist.

"Let me off," she says breathlessly. "Let them catch me. They can't see you with me. They'll find out who you are. You'll lose everything."

Jamie keeps riding.

He knows she is right. If he is found in league with these smugglers he will have nothing to return home to but a prison cell. There is too much corruption in the revenue service for the courts to make light of it.

He pushes the thought away.

Ahead of them, the farmland gives way to trees and tangled scrub. The branches are too low-hanging to ride through. He skirts the edge of the woodland, cutting into the trees as they thin slightly. Moonlight shafts through the bare branches.

When they break into the open again, the lights of a village are flickering ahead of them. Jamie slows the horse to a walk. "Where are we?"

"We're in Killigarth." Scarlett's breath is hot and fast against his ear. "Do you think we lost them?"

Jamie listens. He hears the murmur of a stream. Hears soft, distant footsteps. He hears no horses. "I think so."

"I've got to get back to Polperro," says Scarlett. "I've got to help Isaac." She points to a narrow path snaking up the incline. "That's Talland Hill. It will take us back to the village."

Jamie tugs on the reins and begins the descent. The road is narrow and slippery. Clouds billow across the moon.

And here comes the thunder of hooves again. Talland Hill, Jamie realises, will lead them into the village, but it will also lead them into the revenue men's path.

"Hide," he hisses. "I'll draw them away."

Scarlett leaps from the horse and buries herself in the undergrowth.

Jamie rides back up the hill towards Killigarth. He fires his pistol. The sound splinters the cold night, eliciting a screech from somewhere in the village. He reaches into his saddle bag and pulls out his riding officer's jacket, along with his peasant knife.

He flicks open the blade and swipes it across his palm. Lets the blood run over the white trimming on the edges of the coat. He climbs from the horse and tramples the jacket into the dirt. Reloads the pistol. Another shot to bring the riding officers closer.

He waves them down. "You've men patrolling out here?"

The officer nods. "We do."

Jamie holds out the jacket. "I found this on the road. Looks as though a man has been injured."

The officer takes the coat, inspects the bloodstains. "Where did you find this?"

Jamie points towards the hills, away from Scarlett, away from her brother's landing. He keeps his other hand hidden behind his back, a seam of blood trickling between his fingers and spilling onto the earth.

The dory grinds through the shallow water, thudding against the rock. They are hidden from the revenue men by a dark curtain of cliff. From here, they can climb ashore and wade around the point to the beach.

Isaac glances up at the clifftop. The signal flame has disappeared, leaving only starlight above them. He holds Mary tightly and climbs from the boat, leaving the dory to be carried away on the tide.

Will shoves his pistol into Asher's back, forcing him to walk. His hands are tightly bound behind him.

"Make a sound," Will hisses, "and I'll shoot you."

Asher snorts. "And what fate do you have in store for me if I remain quiet? Something similar, I assume."

They wind their way past the harbour and up onto the cliffs. Mary is wide-eyed and alert, peeking out from beneath the folds of Isaac's coat. She follows the men with a sharp gaze that is more than a little Caroline.

As they wind their way onto the cliffs, Isaac says: "You helped Tom Leach take my children. Why?"

Asher doesn't look at him. "I helped your son escape. I risked my life for him."

Isaac pushes past his excuses. "What have I done to you that's so damn terrible?"

Asher snorts. "It's not about you."

And here is that unsteadying hot-then-coldness. Isaac thinks of Leach's words.

Your daughter for the silver your wife knows how to find.

He tries to force the thought from his mind. Leach is a madman. A liar. Asher Hales is little better. And yet he finds himself asking:

"Is it about my wife? And this haul of silver?"

"There is no silver," Asher says bitterly.

Isaac grits his teeth. "What of Caroline? Does this involve her?"

Asher gives a cold laugh. "Why are you asking me? Why not ask your wife? Or your father?"

Isaac feels the words cut into him. He does not look back at Asher. Cannot let him see the uncertainty in his face. Cannot let him see the way his words have rattled him. He lifts Mary higher onto his shoulder. To hell with Hales, with Leach, with their lies. He will not walk into these traps they are laying. He has far more important things to concern himself with.

"Take Hales to the Mariner's Arms," he tells Will. "Tell Flora all that's happened." He glances down at the baby. "I've got to get Mary home."

SPLINTERING

Caroline cannot bear this waiting. The night is so still she can hear the sea sighing against the beach. Can hear Gabriel breathing through his closed bedroom door. Hears drops of old rain plinking from the roof.

She glances at the fish kettle in which she has hidden the silver. No one will find it there. Not even her husband.

If Isaac has not returned in two days' time, she will take the money to The Ship and give it to Tom Leach. And she will spend her life wondering whether Flora Kelly feels guilty enough to keep silent. There is something bitterly cruel about it, Caroline thinks. Having her most destructive secrets in the hands of the woman who had lain with her husband.

But then there are footsteps. The creak of the door. And there is Isaac with their daughter in his arms.

Caroline cries out, rushes to them. She snatches Mary, holds her tight, tighter, against her thumping chest.

She throws an arm around Isaac, pulls him into her, her arm latched around his neck. His hand slides to the small of her back. It is an habitual gesture, but there is no warmth to it. Caroline feels something tighten in her stomach.

It doesn't matter. Mary is here, safe, bright-eyed. Pawing at her mother's neckerchief and speaking indecipherable words.

Caroline sinks to the floor beside the hearth. She can't get her daughter close enough. Finally, she looks up at Isaac. Tears are blurring her vision. "Where did you find her?"

"On the river."

"Does Leach know you have her?"

He nods.

Caroline's eyes drift to the fish kettle. They have their children. They have the silver. And she has a story concocted that will place the blame at Asher's feet. It will be easy enough for Isaac to believe. After all, Asher Hales had been one of the men who had taken their children.

They have their chance. They must take it now, before any of the people holding her secrets see fit to open their mouth. She reaches up for Isaac's hand. "Let's leave," she says. "Right now."

"We can't leave tonight. Customs are about. They've seized Reuben's lugger. They'll be expecting me to run. If they catch us on the road, they'll see it as an admission of guilt."

There is coldness in his voice. Caroline's chest tightens. What does he know? Has Scarlett spilled the news about their father? Told Isaac of how Asher had been whispering to his wife in the street?

Caroline climbs to her feet. She pulls Isaac close, Mary squeezed between them. Perhaps if she holds him tight enough, wishes hard enough, she will take things back to that secretive, sheltered place they had been before Asher Hales had washed up upon their shore.

Mary and Gabriel are safe. How desperately she had longed for this. Just for now, let her curl up beside her family, with her husband and children in her arms. Just for now. Before everything crumbles.

She stands close to Isaac, trying to inhale every breath of him. She presses a hand to his arm, memorising the feel of him beneath her. Just for now. Let them lie in the dark together and let his coldness fade away.

"You need to rest," she tells him. "You've not slept properly in days." She brushes the hair from his face. Looks into his eyes. She cannot read him. For the first time in their marriage, he feels like a stranger.

After a moment, he takes a step back. "Go to bed," he says stiffly. "I'll wait up a while. Make sure there's no trouble."

Scarlett waits by the door of the stables. She hears Jamie's footsteps inside, hears a metallic rattle as he returns the saddle to its hook.

Her chest aches. She cannot bear to face him.

Finally, he steps outside. Scarlett takes his hand in both of hers. In the flickering light of the lamp above the door, she can see the neckcloth knotted around his palm. Sees the specks of crimson beneath.

"You need to leave," she says, her voice coming out as little more than a whisper. "I'll not have you dragged down by me."

For a long time, Jamie doesn't speak. Doesn't look at her. "Why did you have to get involved in this life?" he asks finally.

Scarlett swallows the pain in her throat. It is a question for Jacob, not for her. She has never had a choice. But this does not feel like a time for excuses.

How desperately she wants to turn her back on this world. How desperately she wants to ride back to Portreath with Jamie's arms around her and live a life without Charles Reuben in it.

Tears prick her eyes and she blinks them away hurriedly. "I can't leave my family," she manages. "I can't leave Isaac to carry our father's debts alone."

"I know," Jamie says softly. "I know."

He pulls her into him. Holds her wordlessly for a long time. Scarlett keeps her arms clamped around his waist. She presses her head into his neck.

She can't bring herself to let go. Because when she does, it will be the end. Jamie deserves far better than her.

Finally, he steps back. "I want to stay until I know your family is safe," he says. "If Isaac has Mary, Leach is bound to retaliate."

"No," Scarlett says firmly. "You need to leave tonight. Please." She can't bear for him to be here any longer.

After a moment, he nods. "If that's what you wish."

She swallows hard, forcing her tears away.

He opens his mouth to speak.

"No," Scarlett says hurriedly. "Don't tell me goodbye. I couldn't bear it."

Jamie draws in his breath. Nods wordlessly and steps back into the stables.

And Scarlett puts her head down and walks, unable to watch him go.

DEBTS

Scarlett sits on the point, listening the sea clop against the rock. She shivers violently. Tugs her cloak tighter around her body.

She wishes she could feel joy. Gabriel and Mary are safe. She can see the world around her again. But it does not push aside the ache deep within her.

A part of her has always known she and Jamie was an impossibility. She had tried to convince herself otherwise, tried to believe their feelings for each other were enough to overcome their differences. But they are firmly planted on opposite sides of the law. Being with her will only bring him down.

She feels watched. For a moment she is afraid to turn around. Who is there? Leach? Reuben? The authorities? But no. It is her father watching her from the edge of the beach. He steps carefully across the rocks and sits at her side. Scarlett shifts uncomfortably.

"You see me," he says.

She nods. Turns away so he can't catch her eye.

"I watched the ships come in," he says. "What's happened? Is Isaac safe?"

Scarlett nods. "Ayes. And so are the children."

And out come the obligatory responses. I'm so glad, thank the Lord, tonight we can sleep… Things Jacob Bailey, who had abandoned his children, has no right to say. Scarlett grits her teeth, swallowing her anger.

"What will you do?" he asks.

She hugs her knees. "I don't know. If we try to leave this place again, Reuben's men will be watching. I don't know if we can take that risk." She looks squarely at her father. This is his chance, she thinks. If he wants to earn his way back into their lives, this is it. This is his opportunity to go to Reuben, show him he is alive. Tell him the debt belongs to him and not to his son.

Jacob doesn't speak. Just nods slowly. "Reuben is a dangerous man," he says. And then no more. Nothing to suggest he might do as Scarlett had hoped. Nothing to suggest he might be willing to shoulder the debt that is rightfully his. The back of her neck prickles with anger.

"Please leave," she says shortly. "I don't want you here." She turns away, making it clear the conversation is over.

Jacob stands. On the edge of her vision, Scarlett sees him nod. And then he is gone.

Finally, she climbs to her feet. She trudges across the beach, chased by the edge of the tide.

As she makes her way back into the village, she sees her father walking alone through the empty street. His chin is lifted, and his steps are long and fast. He climbs the hill towards Reuben's house.

Scarlett finds herself following.

Jacob slides through the gate and makes his way to the back of the property, hidden in the shadow of the house. He weaves through the dark garden and finds the door leading to the servants' quarters. He reaches into his pocket. Pulls out, what? A tool? Scarlett cannot make it out. Jacob shoves it into the lock and wrenches until the door pops open. He disappears inside.

Scarlett runs across the grass and slips into the house. She follows the servants' passage past rows of rough-hewn wooden doors, some with rhythmic snores coming from behind them. She passes the kitchen with its lingering scent of roast meat, passes the laundry that smells of wet clothes.

The door leading up to the mansion is hanging open. Scarlett climbs the stairs. And she is in Reuben's lavish entrance hall. She has not been inside since she was a child. The house is bathed in darkness, lit only by the moon pushing through the curtains. She can make out the inky shape of the grand staircase, the spidery arms of the brass chandelier. There is a strange familiarity to it, as though it has been days since she had last been inside, rather than years.

Jacob, it seems, also remembers the place well. Scarlett can see his figure at the top of the stairs. He disappears into the passage towards what she guesses are bedrooms.

Scarlett begins to climb.

At the top of the staircase she looks about her. The passage stretches out in either direction, the hall thick with the lingering scent of melted wax.

A creak of the floorboards to her left. The door to one of the bedchambers hangs open a crack. Scarlett creeps down the passage and peeks into the room. Reuben is lying on his back on a wide, curtained bed, breathing deeply in sleep. Jacob stands at his bedside, a knife in his hand.

Scarlett holds her breath, unable to move.

She watches as Jacob presses his blade into Reuben's neck. Why does she say nothing? Why is she simply letting this happen? Blood fountains from the wound, black in the faint light. Scarlett watches it run over Reuben's shoulder and pool on the floor.

She cannot tell if he wakes. Does he see the face of his killer? Or does he slip away from this life without so much as an exhalation?

Scarlett covers her mouth, feeling her own cry well up from her throat. She had known, before this, that her father had killed. Countless times, she had pictured him on the landing beach, pulling the trigger on Albert Davey. And yet it had remained a distant, intangible thing.

There is no distance to this. Nothing intangible. This is far too real. For all the gratitude she has for the return of her sight, Scarlett wishes she had not had to witness this.

She wants him to know. Wants him to know that she is here, and she has seen.

She steps into the room. Jacob is standing over the body, staring at the silky pool of blood, as though he is afraid Reuben might be suddenly resurrected.

Scarlett takes another step towards the stained bed. Her heart is thumping. Reuben's eyes are glassy. She is sure she can see surprise in them.

Jacob turns. Doesn't speak at once. He glances down at the knife in his hand. "You saw me," he says.

Scarlett doesn't respond. She knows there is no need. She keeps walking, closer and closer to the body. He is gone, this man who has held her family prisoner for so much of her life. She needs to see. Needs to be certain. It doesn't feel real.

She looks down. His blood is on her boots, on the hems of her skirts.

This house is full of workers. Men and women who could wake at any time. They will find her here with a body before her and blood on her skirts.

And she will not go to the scaffold for Jacob Bailey's crimes.

She turns abruptly and hurries from the house. And as she marches through the narrow streets towards the cliff path, she realises. The murder had been carefully planned. Jacob had known what he needed to pick the lock, had known the location of the servants' entrance, had known which door had led to Reuben's bedroom.

He had been planning this, she sees, since he had arrived in Polperro. And for how long before that?

She is aware of him walking behind her. She doesn't stop. Doesn't turn.

He says: "I just wanted you and Isaac to be free of him."

"And this is how you thought to do it?"

Jacob had blamed the anger inside him for the murder of Albert Davey. The Wild had seized him and taken away all reason.

But this had not been wild anger. This had been cold-blooded and calculated. Murder for his own gain. Just as Davey's had been.

Jacob reaches for Scarlett's arm to stop her leaving. "You're free of him now. You and Isaac ought to go and live your lives. Get away from this place."

Scarlett thinks of Jamie. Thinks to tell him they are free. Thinks to tell him she has a chance to build a life without free trade in it.

And then she looks down. Sees the blood staining her skirts. Feels the Wild inside her, dormant, but waiting. And she feels her father's blood pulsing in her veins. Killer's blood.

Was it truly Reuben who had drawn her into a life of crime? Or had that tendency been lying inside her all along? Perhaps she had had no choice in the matter. Perhaps this is just who she is.

She cannot go to Jamie with blood staining her skirts. He is far too good for that. He is far too good for a wife who stands by and watches a man die.

"You ought to go back to Talland," says Jacob. "Someone will find the body soon."

There is sadness in his voice, as though he knows he has lost whatever fragile chance at reconciliation he might have had.

He is right to be sad. Scarlett does not want this man in her life. Does not want this reminder of what impulses might lie inside her, coiled up beside the Wild.

But there are pieces that do not sit right.

"You told me once that everything you'd done was for me." She doesn't look at him. "What did you mean by that?"

Jacob sighs heavily. "It doesn't matter. It's too late for any of this. It's best I just go. You're far better off without me."

"The night you left you were upset. I remember you crying. Why?"

He looks at the ground for a long time. Finally, he meets her eyes. "Because I believed I was never going to see you again."

"That was your choice."

"Well." He glances back at Reuben's mansion. "We all make bad choices."

She doesn't speak.

"Go, Scarlett," he says.

She gives a faint nod. And up she walks, over the cliff. The path is lit only by the moon, but after days of darkness, it feels as bright as morning. Her steps are crooked with weariness, with emotion, with lingering flashes of dizziness.

She stumbles down the hill into Talland and lets herself into the cottage.

Isaac is asleep, sitting up against the wall. A half-burned log splinters in the gate. He opens his eyes as Scarlett stumbles towards him.

He sees it all, she realises. Sees the blood on her skirts, the anguish in her face, sees her eyes dart around the cottage as though they are taking it in for the first time.

She drops to her knees beside him. "Isaac," she says, her voice splintering, "our father is alive."

TRUTHS AND LIES

She tells him everything. Tells him of Asher's letter and the murder of Albert Davey. Tells him of Portreath; of Jacob's press gang and Jamie's brass buttons. The way the light had returned as she had stood on the cliff. And she tells him of the pool of blood that now lies at the side of Charles Reuben's bed.

Isaac listens without speaking. By the time she has finished, there are tears pouring down her face, but Scarlett feels a weight lifted from her shoulders. Isaac slides an arm around her, pulling her into him. With the two of them sitting alone in front of the fire, it feels suddenly as though she is back in her childhood; a time that has come to feel far more distant than it truly is.

"I wish you'd told me earlier," Isaac says gently. "You didn't have to carry all this alone."

His eyes are glassy, underlined with shadows of exhaustion. A faint frown creases the bridge of his nose.

"What are you thinking?" she asks.

He lets out his breath. "I don't know, Scarlett. I don't even know where to begin."

She turns to look at the stripe of dawn light pushing through the curtains. "I think he's gone back to Portreath," she says. Gone back to that cottage on the hill. Gone before men on horses come seeking Reuben's killer.

Isaac looks into the fire. He makes no effort to move, to catch sight of his father, to chase him over the hills. She has made the right decision, Scarlett thinks, in letting Jacob go.

They will have a new life outside of Talland, and their father will have no place in it.

Isaac squeezes her shoulder. "Go and change your clothes. Gabriel will be up soon and I don't want him to see the blood."

She nods, climbing to her feet and making her way to her bedroom. The stained skirts belong to Flora, she realises. The blood has soaked through the sky blue wool, blackening it in patches. Scarlett climbs out of them, kicking them into the corner of her room. She cannot bear to look at them. Can't bear to look at that bloody reminder of all her family is.

Isaac stands outside the house, the blue-grey morning lightening around him. His thoughts are tangled with exhaustion. How is he to make sense of all he has learned?

Jacob, alive. He is shocked, of course, but Scarlett's news is strangely easy to accept. His father had always been one to put himself first. One who had sought wealth with little regard for decency. For him to have saddled his children with his debts is far from implausible.

Jacob will not be waiting in Polperro for a coach. With Reuben's blood on his hands he will have little choice but to leave on foot. Get as far from the place as possible before the body is discovered.

He cannot have gotten far.

Isaac goes to the Millers' farm for the horse. Up over the clifftop he rides, watching the sun break over the horizon. He sees the lugger at the edge of the anchorage. Today the revenue men will take her to Looe for auction. The ship will be broken up, her parts sold to the highest bidder. Isaac wishes he could watch. There would be a great sense of satisfaction to seeing that ship in pieces.

He keeps riding. Out of Polperro, onto the narrow road winding northwards towards Portreath. He knows he will not be able to ride too far. Knows the revenue men will be watching.

In the pearly light, he sees a man walking alone on the road. His shoulders are hunched, his grey hair loose at his neck. He watches his feet as he walks. Isaac can only see the back of his head, but he knows the man is his father.

He stops the horse. For a moment, he considers turning around. What does he have to say to this man? Why has he come? To see for himself, he supposes.

He takes the horse closer. Jacob turns.

Isaac stares at his father. He is older, of course, but there is something achingly familiar about him. Something that tells Isaac that Jacob Bailey is the same dangerous, hard-edged man he had been sixteen years ago.

Jacob digs his hands into his pockets. It is too late. Isaac has already seen the blood staining his fingers.

"You've come to see if it were true then?" Jacob asks finally.

"Something like that." What does he really want? Why has he ridden so impulsively across the clifftops to catch sight of the father he had never wanted in his life?

Jacob sniffs. "When I left, I—"

"Don't." Isaac shakes his head. "Scarlett's already told me all I need to know."

Jacob lowers his eyes. "I see."

Isaac's hands tighten around the reins. He regrets coming. "Why return?" he asks finally. "After all this time?"

Jacob looks at the ground. "I thought perhaps I could put things right."

"Put things right? By killing Charles Reuben?"

"You'd expect no less from me, surely." There is a hint of bitterness in his voice.

"And who do you imagine they'll suspect?" asks Isaac. "Who do you suppose they'll pin the murder on? No one has a better motive for killing Reuben than me."

Jacob looks down at his ragged cloth shoes. "Take your family and leave, Isaac. Have the life you ought to have had."

Yes, he ought to leave. What is stopping him?

"Why are you really here?" Jacob asks after a moment. "Is it because you have questions for me?"

Isaac feels his muscles tighten. This, of course, is the real reason he had bolted up the hills on a borrowed horse. Because he has questions he is unable to ignore. Because the last time he had looked into his wife's eyes he had seen a stranger. He has begun to doubt the woman who has been his anchor for the past twelve years. And it feels as though the earth is shifting beneath him.

"What do you know of her?" he asks. "Caroline."

Jacob eyes him. He is looking closely. Too closely. Then he pulls his bloodstained hands from his pocket and stares down at them. After a long time, he says: "All that happened to me was my own doing. There's little point dwelling on the past."

For a second, Isaac doubts himself. He has always known his father a criminal. And now he has shown himself as so much more than a petty smuggler. He is a killer. The man who had abandoned his family. Is he really coming to this man for the truth about his wife? Is he really seeking answers to questions Tom Leach had planted in his mind? Surely he owes Caroline more than this.

"You're right," he tells Jacob. "There's little point dwelling on the past." Little point standing here with a man he has never trusted. He tugs on the reins and begins to ride back to Talland.

"Where have you been?" Caroline pushes, racing out of the cottage to meet him. Her hair has been combed and pinned neatly for the first time in days.

Isaac feels strangely reluctant to tell her any of this. Reluctant to tell her of his meeting with Jacob, or of the things he and Scarlett had spoken of that morning. What does this mean? Surely *my father is alive* is not something a man keeps from his wife.

He ignores her question. "Did the children sleep soundly?" he asks, grappling for something that might break the tense silence. The children at least, are common ground.

And Caroline is speaking, yes a part of him hears her. But he cannot fathom what she is saying. Because he sees the smugglers' banker striding up the path towards them, a pistol in his hand.

FAITHFUL MEN

Isaac hurries into the house and locks the door behind Caroline. "Take the children to the nursery. Stay close to the floor."

Scarlett appears from her bedroom. "What's happening?"

A gunshot flies through the window. Isaac feels shards of glass against his cheek. Caroline swallows a scream and slams the nursery door.

"Who is it?" Scarlett breathes hard, pressing her back against the wall.

The banker, Isaac tells her. Come to punish them for Reuben's murder.

He glances at the bedroom. He had tucked his pistol beneath the mattress when he had returned home last night.

Scarlett is closest.

"My pistol," he whispers. "Beneath the bed."

She nods silently. Disappears into the bedroom and returns with the gun. She slides it along the floor towards him.

A second shot flies through the window.

The banker is calling to them; angry garbled words. Isaac hears *coward* and *killer*. Behind the nursery door, Mary shrieks.

He squeezes the pistol. How many times has he found himself here? His life in danger and feeling unable to shoot?

Scarlett reaches for the fire poker. "Bring him inside."

Knuckles white around his gun, Isaac opens the door. He steps back to let the banker into the house.

"You killed Charles Reuben," he says, his gun held out in front of him.

This man, with his untidy grey queue and bristled chin looks just as he has for the past fourteen years. Soulless. Blank. The look of a man who acts on another's bidding.

"Do you have proof of that?" Isaac asks tautly. He takes a step backwards, drawing the banker further into the house.

"Proof?" the banker spits. "I don't need proof. Every man in this village knows you wanted Reuben out of your life."

"You're right," says Isaac. "I did."

Scarlett moves suddenly, thrashing the poker at the banker's head. He drops heavily to the floor, his gun spilling across the kitchen.

Isaac stands over him. The man's eyes flutter and his fingers curl. Isaac finds himself lifting his pistol. He has to do this. If he doesn't shoot, there will be another man after them. Another man to take his children, to shoot through his windows, to hold a debt over his family. He feels his finger shift on the trigger.

"Don't Isaac, please," Scarlett coughs. "You can't shoot him. You can't be like our father."

Isaac hesitates.

He had never wanted to be like Jacob. Had only followed his path out of necessity.

But he has a choice now.

Are Mary and Gabriel to face each other twenty years from now, and whisper to each other, *you can't be like our father?*

He lowers the gun.

Scarlett catches his eye and gives him a faint nod. He takes the banker's gun from the floor and tucks it into his pocket.

Caroline emerges from the bedroom with Mary on her hip. She looks down at the body. "Is he—"

"He's alive," says Isaac. "And he'll not be down for much longer. We can't stay here." His thoughts are charging. Where are they to go? They have no escape plan in place. Polperro harbour is still full of revenue men, preparing the lugger for auction.

"What does he want?" Caroline's voice is thin. "Why has he come for us?"

"Reuben is dead," Isaac says shortly. "Murdered."

"Murdered? By who?"

But he is marching into the bedroom, pulling the trunk out from under the bed. Anything to avoid the question. Anything to avoid mentioning his father. "Pack your things," he tells her.

Caroline unlatches the trunk and begins to throw their clothes inside it, the baby still clamped to her side. There is a hardness in her eyes. She has done this before, of course. Has packed up their life this way, only for Tom Leach to tear the children from her arms.

"Do you think more men will come for us?" Scarlett asks from her bedroom.

Isaac goes back to the kitchen and stares down at the banker. "I suppose now we'll find out how many of Reuben's men are loyal to him." He takes the trunk from Caroline as she drags it out of the bedroom. He sets it beside the door. "We'll go to the inn," he says. "We'll be hidden there. If more of Reuben's men come looking, they'll not be able to find us."

Caroline presses her lips into a thin white line. But she nods wordlessly.

Isaac reaches beneath the mattress and pulls out the pouch of coins. They will shelter in the Mariner's Arms until nightfall. He will find someone to bring a boat to the landing beach. Perhaps they can make their way east towards Looe. Away from Tom Leach. Away from Reuben's men. Away from the authorities.

In the dark they will be invisible.

Scarlett is waiting in the kitchen. She has a bag slung over her shoulder and her cloak hooked closed. She stands over the groaning body of the banker with a knife in her hand. Isaac meets her eyes.

They have tried this before. Tried to disappear from this place, only to face the banker's pistol.

This time there will be no failing. No returning. When he steps from this cottage, he knows it will be for the last time.

Isaac ushers his family out into the street and pulls the door closed heavily. He sees Scarlett glance at the house, but he doesn't look back.

Let this place be forgotten. The memories within it are tainted.

He wants to have faith in his wife. Wants to believe there are no secrets between them. Wants to believe Tom Leach and Asher Hales are nothing more than madmen. Wants to believe his wife has never set eyes on his father. But the doubt has been planted. It is there, undeniable, crawling beneath his skin. And it has discoloured the memories of the life they have shared.

He tucks the trunk beneath his arm and presses a hand to Gabriel's shoulder, pulling him close in an attempt to reassure him. They wind their way down the road until they reach the Mariner's Arms. Isaac pounds on the door.

"We need to hide."

Flora doesn't ask questions. She hurries them inside, locking the door after them. Above their heads, the watch ball sways in the draught. Through the silent tavern they walk, climbing the stairs to the parlour.

And they wait for the dark.

TRUST

Asher sits in the cellar with his back against the bottom step. His wrists are bound. Ankles bound. What a sorry creature he is.

Again he is a prisoner here in this dank, miserable place. The realisation is a brutal one.

This time, the tunnel is open; a black mouth vanishing into the rock. A second hole gapes beside it. In the lamplight, he sees the cavity Caroline had discovered behind the bricks. A fine place for hiding silver. And an even finer place for a lie.

Asher stares at the broken wall for a long time.

He knows for certain things won't work out the way they had the last time he was cowering down here, a shipwrecked sailor with mystery around him. Scarlett Bailey will not walk down the stairs with a wash bowl and razor in her hands and lovingly sponge away the filth. She will not primp and preen him and stare lovingly into his eyes.

No. Asher Hales is quite certain he will not leave this place alive.

Flora slips back inside the inn. She has made arrangements. At nightfall, Will Francis will be waiting on the beach, ready to steal Isaac and his family away from Talland.

She stands for a moment in the empty bar, reluctant to go upstairs and face Caroline. Reluctant to tell Isaac that tonight he will leave. It can be the only way, of course. But the thought of him disappearing is an ache inside her.

Dust dances in the faint streaks of sunlight. Glasses are lined up along the shelves, logs piled beside the cold hearth. Everything smells of beeswax polish.

Tomorrow night she will reopen the inn. Tomorrow night, when Isaac is gone. She will have something to put her mind to. A part of her longs to see the tavern's doors unlocked again.

But beneath her feet is Asher Hales. He cannot be released. He will run to the revenue men and lead them to the tunnel. Customs will be at her door within the hour.

What is she to do? Keep him a prisoner in her cellar forever? No. How can she run a tavern with a man tied up beneath her patrons' feet?

He cannot remain a prisoner indefinitely. Nor can he be released. Though she has done her best not to think of it, Flora knows the truth.

To avoid facing the courts, one of them must kill Asher Hales.

She makes her way upstairs and clicks open the door of the parlour. The room is grey and thick with shadow; the curtains pulled closed to keep out prying eyes. The logs in the grate sit cold, no smoke rising from the chimney. Perhaps no one is watching the inn, but a seemingly empty building will raise less suspicion.

Gabriel and Bessie are on their knees by the hearth, attempting to throw knucklebones in a gauntlet of dog's paws and Mary's curious fingers.

Flora can't look at Caroline, perched on the edge of the couch, gnawing her thumbnail. Can't look at Isaac, pacing by the covered window. And so she looks at Scarlett.

"The boat will be ready at nightfall," she says. "Will Francis will be waiting on the eastern beach."

"Thank you." Isaac pulls the curtain back an inch and peers through the window. "Any sign of the banker? Or any of Reuben's footmen?"

Flora shakes her head. "Not that I could tell."

"Good."

"The banker saw us leave the cottage," says Scarlett, picking listlessly at the waxy candleholder on the mantle. "He'll be watching. Waiting."

Isaac nods. "With luck he'll think we've already left."

Flora leaves them in the parlour and goes to Jack's room. She runs a finger over the mallow fronds hanging across the mantle. They are not completely dry, but she needs something to put her mind to. She carefully unthreads the stems and sets them on the table. She will crush and jar them, then mix with lard for bruising.

She hears the floor creak. She knows instinctively that Isaac is behind her. Can sense him, feel him. For a moment, she is afraid to turn around.

"I saw the damage to the cellar wall when I went to check on Hales," he says after a moment. "What happened?"

Flora keeps her back to him. She keeps unthreading the leaves. What had happened to the cellar wall, she feels certain, is a secret that would see Caroline and Isaac's marriage torn apart. It is not her secret to tell.

However much she might wish to.

She feels his hands on her; firm against her shoulders. He is close. Too close. His breath is hot against her ear, his voice resonating within her.

"Flora," he says, "please tell me."

No. It is not her place.

"Look at me," he says.

And like an obedient child, she does, turning to look up at him, his nose inches from hers. In his eyes she sees distress, sees anxiety, sees questions.

"Was Caroline involved?" he presses. "Did she come here looking for something?"

Flora closes her eyes.

"Did she come looking for money? For Henry Avery's silver?"

"Caroline is in the next room," Flora says finally. "Why are you asking me these things? Why not ask her?"

Isaac doesn't answer at once. His fingers tighten around her shoulders, then work their way downwards until they reach the bare skin on her forearms.

"Because I trust you," he says after a moment. "And I don't trust her."

Flora forces herself away. Forces herself to ignore the tug of desire that gathers at the feel of his skin against hers. Never mind who Isaac trusts and distrusts. Come tonight he will be gone.

I trust you. And I don't trust her.

He had intended for her to hear this, Caroline has no doubt. Had heard her in the hallway, perhaps. Had known she would follow him as he trailed Flora like a doting pet.

Isaac steps from the guestroom, finding her in the passage. Yes, she has seen. Yes, she has heard. Her husband has no trust in her because he knows she was the one who had gone searching for Avery's haul. He knows she has been keeping secrets.

Caroline feels herself beginning to tremble. This is it, she realises. This is the moment she has been dreading since she had first learned who Isaac's father was. This is the moment she hovers on the edge of the cliff and struggles to pull herself back. This is the moment she can no longer outrun her past.

Jacob Bailey has won. They have reached the scenario he had engineered when he'd told her to go treasure hunting in the walls of the Mariner's Arms. The wealth unearthed. Isaac asking questions. She, with nowhere to turn but outworn lies. This is everything Jacob wants.

I trust you. And I don't trust her.

Isaac returns to the parlour without a word. He too is dreading the confrontation, Caroline can tell. He is dreading the truth he is edging closer and closer to. The truth of who his wife is and what she has done.

He leaves the door ajar. Caroline cannot bring herself to look through it. She can't look at any of them; not Mary chewing on her rag doll, or Gabriel chasing the dog. Not her husband who has learned she cannot be trusted. If she looks at any of them, she will not go.

She doesn't look at the coats slung over the back of the chairs or the knucklebones scattered across the floor or anything that might remind her of the life she had once had.

She goes to the guestroom, where Flora is untying the piece of twine hanging from the mantle. She does not let herself think. Does not let the tears that are tightening her throat become anything more than a faint pain. She closes the door behind her.

Flora looks up in surprise. Her lips part. Is she to speak? Is she to cobble together some miserable apology for breathing down the neck of another woman's husband?

Caroline couldn't bear it. She reaches into her pocket and hands her the pouch of silver she had taken from the kettle that morning. "Take it. Help my family get away."

Flora stares at the money. "What?"

Caroline grits her teeth. Must she spell things out?

Her secrets are far too close to the surface. Stay here in Talland and they will spill. The decision is brutal, but it has been made. There are things that Isaac can never know. Things her children cannot know. She would rather be alone than have her family learn who she truly is.

"I need to leave," she tells Flora. "And so do you." She keeps her eyes down. "If Tom Leach learns the money is in your inn he will come looking."

"Tom Leach won't come to this place," says Flora. "He's too afraid."

Caroline gives a cold, humourless laugh. "Do you truly believe that? There was a fortune hidden in your walls."

"Then give it to him." Flora holds out the pouch. "As you planned to do before Mary was rescued. Keep him out of our lives."

No. Isaac and the children must use this money to leave Talland. They must disappear before Jacob finds them and tells them the truth of why he left. Isaac has doubts and suspicions, but doubt is far better than knowing for certain the things his wife has done.

"I don't want Leach to have the money," she tells Flora sharply. "I want Isaac to have it. I want my family to have the life they deserve." Caroline feels her tears threatening. She blinks them away. She cannot fall apart. Not here. Not now. "Isaac loves you," she says, her voice cracking. "Give him a good life. Make him happy."

Flora's fingers tighten around the pouch of money. "And what of your children?"

At the thought of the children, Caroline's tears spill. "They can't know," she says. "They can't know any of it. And if I stay here, they will see who I truly am." It is suddenly hard to breathe.

Her children will be safe, she tells herself. Loved. They will have their father, their aunt. And they will know their mother as a good woman, not as a liar who seeks revenge. It is better this way. If she stays, they will be forced to watch as their father grows to hate their mother. They will be forced to hear of what she did to tear their family apart. They will grow up in a house full of bitterness and anger. Her children deserve better than that.

Pain seizes her throat. "You don't need to understand," she tells Flora. "You just need to do what I'm asking."

She turns away and pulls open the door. It must be now, before she changes her mind.

WILD

Down the stairs she goes, her eyes fixed on the door ahead. She cannot bear to think of anything else. Just that door. Just look. Just walk.

Caroline steps out into the street. She begins the long, steep trudge up the hill. None of this feels real.

Tonight she will tuck Gabriel into bed, will sing a lullaby to Mary, will fall asleep in Isaac's arms.

She needs to let herself believe this fantasy. If she thinks of how alone she will truly be tonight, she will not keep walking.

She hears footsteps behind her. No, she doesn't want footsteps. Does not want to be followed. Is it Flora with the money in her hands, pretending she wants her to stay? Or has Isaac seen her leave? Is he following her out of duty? She can't bear for it to be either of them.

"You're leaving?"

Caroline turns. She had not been expecting Scarlett. And she had not been expecting this bitterness in her voice. The sound of it makes Caroline's blood cold.

"Is it because of this?" Scarlett has a knife in one hand. A crumpled page in the other.

It takes a moment for Caroline to realise what it is. But when she does, her chest lurches.

'Jacob has left Talland.'

There is her carefully formed handwriting, crafted to look like someone else's. A record of all the dreadful things she has done. How long has Scarlett had this letter in her pocket? How long has she known?

"This is your handwriting," she says finally.

Caroline's throat tightens. "You can't be out here. Reuben's men may see you."

Scarlett shakes the letter at her. "What did you do?"

Caroline doesn't speak.

"Tell me!" cries Scarlett.

Yes, Caroline thinks, she owes her this. Owes her the truth. And so she meets Scarlett's

492

eyes and says: "I forced your father to leave Talland." Her voice wavers, but she forces herself to continue. "I had Edward Baker show me who your mother was. He told me of how she brought you back across the cliffs on your way home from school. I told Jacob we were watching you. Said he was to leave the village. I told him his crew would kill you and your mother if he dared come back." She swallows heavily. "I told him he was to take the dory out and let the village believe he had drowned." The words are bitter on her lips. But she needs to keep speaking. Needs to tell Scarlett everything. Perhaps doing so will purge this poison from her body. Or perhaps she is just afraid of the silence that will follow. "Edward Baker followed him out to sea. Forced Jacob to tell him where he was going. We wanted to know he would do us no harm. Wanted to know he was truly gone."

Scarlett doesn't speak. Not for a long time. She just stands outside the inn with the knife in one hand and the letter in the other, the wind blowing her hair across furious eyes.

She is scared of her, Caroline realises. She has seen the intensity of the anger inside Scarlett. Knows there is no certainty that she will not die for this.

She longs to turn away. Look down. Look at the sea. Look anywhere but at Scarlett. But to do such a thing feels wrong. Feels as though she is shying away from all she has done. She holds Scarlett's gaze. Waits for the eruption. Perhaps, she waits to die.

"Why?" Scarlett asks finally.

"I thought I was doing it for love. I just did as he asked. I was a fool."

"He," Scarlett repeats. "Asher Hales."

Caroline nods.

Scarlett scrunches up the letter and shoves it back in her cloak pocket. "And now you are to walk away? Leave your children, just as you forced him to do?"

Caroline swallows the violent pain in her throat. "You know I have no choice."

"You're right," says Scarlett. "You don't."

Tears escape down Caroline's cheeks and she pushes them away. "They'll need you," she says. "Gabriel and Mary. And Isaac."

There is only silence.

"I'm so sorry, Scarlett," Caroline says finally. "More than you could know."

Still, Scarlett says nothing. Her dark eyes are unflinching, her knuckles white around the handle of the knife.

"Isaac cannot know any of this," Caroline coughs. "It will kill him. You know it will." She meets Scarlett's eyes pleadingly. "If you love your brother, you will keep this to yourself. Please. I'm begging you." She knows she has no right to ask. But she does it anyway. She needs to believe that when she leaves this place, she will take the worst of her secrets with her.

Scarlett turns. Lets herself back into the inn without another word.

Scarlett goes to the cellar. From the top of the staircase, she looks down on Asher Hales.

He is slumped against the top step, his wrists and ankles bound in mooring rope.

A prisoner. He deserves no better.

Scarlett realises she has the knife in her hand. She had not had any thought of it. Had she been holding it the whole time, she wonders? Had she been standing in the parlour watching the children play jacks, with a knife in her hand and blood on her boots? Had she been holding the knife to her chest like this as she had listened to Caroline's confession?

How many times had she stared at that letter and not seen the truth of who had written it? How many times had she been fooled by Caroline's carefully disguised hand? But this morning she had seen with fresh eyes.

Shock? Perhaps not as much as she ought to have felt. Because there had been Asher Hales outside their house. Caroline had been guarding secrets.

Guarding *this* secret.

Scarlett lights the lamp and pulls the cellar door closed behind her. Asher watches.

So it is like this. Her father had left his family on account of this man. Her mother had died of grief as a result of the things he had set in motion. He is a plotter. Manipulator. A man who uses his silky voice and handsome face to have others do his work. Strange, Scarlett thinks distantly, that a man with such talents might end up a prisoner.

She had been foolish enough to fall for him. But she sees now that she had not been the only one to do so.

She imagines Caroline hunched over her writing desk, scrawling this letter to the man she had loved. Thinks of the anger in her eyes when Asher had first arrived at their cottage. It hadn't been a look of anger at all, Scarlett realises. It had been a look of fear.

The man from the wreck had carried Caroline's darkest secrets ashore.

Scarlett kneels slowly beside Asher. He glances down at the knife, then looks up at her with shadowed eyes.

Before she knows what she is doing, Scarlett has the blade against his throat. "You forced my father to leave us."

"What are you talking about?" His voice is defiant, but something is passing across his face. Something that makes his jaw move and his eyes lose focus. Fear.

This coward.

"Don't lie to me," Scarlett hisses. "I saved your life."

"And now you will kill me?"

She stares at him. What would it be like, she wonders, to push that blade into his throat?

"Do it then," Asher says tiredly. "I'd expect no less from Jacob's daughter." His voice is hollow and empty. He is a man who has given up. A man with nothing to live for.

It would be easy. Draw the knife across his throat. Drag the body out through the tunnel and toss it into the sea. Cold and calculated, just like Jacob's murder of Reuben.

So be it. Asher Hales cannot be let free. One of them will have to kill him. And who better than her? She already has the darkness in her. Sooner or later, it will see her with blood on hands. Why fight it?

"Tell me the truth," she says. "Admit what you did."

She presses the blade into his throat. A tiny seam of blood appears on his pale skin.

"All right," he hisses. "Yes. I wanted Jacob gone. He deserved to be punished after framing me for murder."

Scarlett grits her teeth until pain shoots through her jaw.

"Do you wish you had let me die on that wreck?" Asher asks. "Do you wish I had let you go on believing a lie?"

She squeezes her eyes closed. A part of her longs for it more than anything. Longs for her heroic, dead father who had never killed a man. Longs for Caroline to be nothing more than the woman her brother had met at the tavern. The lies are much easier to carry than this betrayal.

She watches a thin trail of blood run onto the collar of Asher's shirt.

Her mind is cluttered. The only thought she can make sense of is this:

Asher Hales deserves to be punished. He deserves to die.

He deserves to have her push that blade deeper into his skin. Deeper and deeper until the blood runs out of him and he is sitting upright no more. The thought makes Scarlett hot with anticipation.

How right she was to send Jamie away.

There are footsteps. Someone is coming through the tunnel.

Out of the corner of her eye, Scarlett sees her father. Her father who had been forced to leave his family by Caroline and Asher Hales.

Why is he here? She can't make sense of it. He had killed Charles Reuben. He ought to be running.

She looks at Jacob, not removing the knife from Asher's throat. Ought she see him differently with this new information? Those tears she remembers from the night he had left had been the tears of a man forced from his home.

But when she looks at her father, all she sees is him driving his knife into Reuben's throat. The sight of it had sickened her. And here she is about to do the very same thing.

No. She will not kill Asher Hales. The thought is clearer than any others she has managed today.

She will not be like Jacob. She will not let the Wild win.

She inhales. And she is in control, she realises. With the clarity of her thoughts, the darkness inside her has loosened its grip.

She lowers the knife. Sets it on the floor.

And she sees that her father has not come through the tunnel alone.

There is Tom Leach, carrying a pistol, carrying a pick. His skin is dark and grimy, his beard a ragged mess.

Scarlett has never feared him before. But she sees now just what he is capable of. The man had blinded her, kidnapped the children, all for his own retribution. He has a gun in his hand, and no morals.

Scarlett eyes the knife she has placed on the floor.

"Don't," says Leach.

She looks questioningly at Jacob. Why are they together?

"I'm sorry, Scarlett," he says. "I came back to Talland to find you. I wanted to help you get away. But he found me outside your cottage. Said he knew I could find the money. He forced me to show him where it was hidden."

Scarlett's thoughts knock together. So Jacob had known the hiding place of the haul, just as Asher Hales had believed. How had Leach come to know of the money? How had he known who Jacob was? Seeing the man outside their cottage, she supposes, would have made it easy to guess. There is plenty of her in her father. Plenty of Isaac too.

Jacob had come back for them. Even with Reuben's blood staining his hands. He had come to help them get away. Scarlett knows Isaac had gone after their father that morning. Had something passed between them to make Jacob return?

She steps backwards towards the stairs. Leach trains his pistol on her. She clenches her teeth and fixes him with hard eyes.

"Untie me," says Asher. "I don't know how many people are upstairs. And if you leave me here, you'll be fighting them alone."

Leach runs his hand over the hole in the wall.

"It's not there," says Asher. "Any fool can see that." He glares at Jacob. "The man is lying to you. He's been lying to all of us."

Leach raps his knuckles against the rock. "Perhaps whoever went looking did not dig far enough." Finally, he makes his way across the cellar and unties the ropes binding Asher's wrists and ankles.

Asher stands slowly, rubbing the raw skin on his arms. He takes the knife from the floor and, with a smile on the edge of his lips, presses it hard to Scarlett's throat.

BLACK MAGIC

Flora turns away from the window. She does not want to see Caroline as she trudges up the hill.

She ought to go after her, she knows. Ought to send Isaac after her. But something stops her. Is it the knowledge that Caroline does not want to be followed? Perhaps.

Perhaps it is something else.

Flora sits with her back against the wall, her skirts pooling around her. She feels the weight of the silver in her pocket. Feels the solidity of this thing she had for so many years believed a myth.

She cannot take the money, of course. Cannot leave this place as Caroline had asked. The inn is her life. She will give the money to Isaac. But she can do no more. The Mariner's Arms has been in her family for generations. She will not see it turn to dust on her watch.

This place is home. Never mind the black magic in the guestroom and the creaks in the night. This place is home.

The door opens. Isaac frowns at the sight of her on the floor. "Has something happened?"

She reaches into her pocket. Dumps the pouch of silver on the floor. A coin spills out and rolls across the room.

Isaac stares. "Where did this—"

"Caroline wants you to have it."

His lips part, but he doesn't speak. Perhaps finding an answer to this is far too difficult. He stares out the window. He must see her, surely, climbing the hill, disappearing from their lives. What is he thinking?

Flora pulls her knees to her chest. "You ought to go after her," she says finally.

"She found it in the cellar," says Isaac. It is not a question.

"I found the money," Flora admits. "By accident. It was hidden beneath the floor of the guestroom. I gave it to Caroline. She was to give it to Leach in exchange for Mary's life."

Isaac stares out the window. "You found it," he says, "but she was looking for it.

497

Someone told her she would find it here. My father."

"Your father?"

Isaac says nothing.

"Whoever told her was wrong," Flora says finally. "Perhaps it was once in the cellar, but my father must have seen fit to move it. I don't know why."

Isaac turns away from the window. He sits beside her, his shoulder pressing against hers. "When I was a boy, I used to get out of bed in the night and watch the landing party come up the road. Carry their ankers into the inn. It stopped after your father died. After that, Jacob used the cave in Polperro to hide the goods."

Flora lets out her breath. "I knew nothing of it." What had gone on beneath her as a child, as she had slept upstairs in the inn? Were the creaks and thuds in her nightmares the footsteps of smugglers? "You think that's why my father moved the money upstairs? Because he was afraid the revenue men might search the cellar for contraband?"

"It's possible."

It is possible, of course. No doubt smugglers have been hiding their goods in the Mariner's Arms for as long as it has stood on this hill. The Mariner's Arms, Flora is coming to realise, is a place that knows how to keep secrets.

And the realisation comes. "The hole in the cellar wall. If it was dug by my father..." She inhales sharply. "If it was there when you and Jack were building the tunnel..." She fades out, unable to voice the words.

Isaac nods. "Ayes. It would have weakened the rock. It could have caused the tunnel to collapse."

Flora closes her eyes. She feels suddenly ill. And for a strange, drawn-out second, it feels as though the building is shifting around her. Feels as though all the death and darkness the place has seen is seeping from the walls.

Isaac presses a hand over hers. She wants to lace her fingers through his, wants to pull him closer. Wants him as a barrier between the inn and herself. But he pulls away too quickly. Climbs to his feet. "I need to go after her."

And Flora says: "Of course."

His footsteps are rhythmic as he makes his way towards the front door of the inn.

He does not know what he will say to her. Does not even know where to begin. He only knows that going after his wife is a duty. He cannot let her walk away.

Perhaps there is a part of him that wants to do so. But how will he look his children in the eye and tell them he let their mother leave?

He hears voices in the cellar. Men. And the sudden crack of pick against rock. The sound resonates through his body.

He slides his hand into the pocket of his coat, feels the cold metal of his pistol. He glances at the front door. Glances at the cellar. And he walks towards the thumping, the splintering, the men hiding beneath the inn.

He opens the cellar door a crack. And there is Tom Leach, heaving a pick into the wall. He is carving deep into the rock beneath, straying into the edge of the tunnel. Dirt rains over him, darkening his bare forearms and cheeks. And there is Scarlett, there is their father. Jacob is standing with his back pressed to the wall, arms folded across his chest. What is he doing here? Is he working with Leach? Isaac knows he cannot put it past him.

Asher stands with an arm clamped around Scarlett's front, a knife held to her neck. Isaac sees her eyes dart to him. She looks away hurriedly.

His hand tightens around his pistol. How long will it be before Leach realises the money is no longer in the wall?

He curses silently. He has been foolish. Had assumed Leach neither brave nor foolish enough to return to Talland while the revenue men are prowling. And he had been naïve enough to believe Flora when she'd assured him Leach was too afraid to enter the Mariner's Arms.

He wants to shoot. Desperately, urgently wants to shoot. Damn the consequences or the guilt. He just wants to see Leach dead. But he is outnumbered. Act rashly and Asher will have that knife in Scarlett's throat.

"Dead men walk that tunnel," Scarlett tells Leach. "Perhaps you'll disturb them." She is infuriatingly brazen. Isaac wills her to stay quiet.

Leach looks over his shoulder to glare at her. His eyes glow in the dusty pits of his cheeks.

"I told you," says Asher. "I told you it's not there."

Leach hurls the pick across the cellar. It clatters into a pile of broken chairs and sends shards of wood flying. He marches up to Scarlett. "Where is it?"

She gives him steely eyes, Asher's knife still hard against her throat. "Why are you asking me?"

Isaac watches his father move silently across the cellar. Behind Leach's back. Out of Asher's eyeline. He disappears into the tunnel.

Scarlett's gaze doesn't falter. "It's a myth," she tells Leach.

"It's no myth. Your brother's wife, she knew of it. Knew how to get to it."

Isaac feels a tug in his chest. He forces himself to focus.

"My brother's wife has left," says Scarlett. "Perhaps she's taken the money with her."

Leach pulls his pistol.

Isaac lifts his gun higher. He tries to align the barrel with Leach's head. Here at the top of the stairs, the angle is wrong. He will need to step down into the cellar. He holds his breath and pushes on the door. The hinges creak noisily.

He hears Leach's shot, feels the burn above his elbow. And somehow Scarlett is at his side, gripping his shoulder, calling his name.

She runs a hand over the worn timber of the door frame. The wood has splintered where the bullet has lodged inside. "The bullet is in the wall," she says. "It's just grazed you."

The pain is disorienting, and she sounds far away. The bullet is in the wall, he tells himself. It does little to help the burn, but it does slow the racing of his heart. He grips his arm, watching beads of blood drizzle out between his fingers.

Flora is waiting in the tavern. Ready. The gunshot rattles her. She runs down into the cellar. Lets out her breath at the sight of the blood staining the arm of Isaac's shirt. She looks past him at Asher and Leach.

She is ready, she reminds herself. Caroline had warned her these men would come.

"You want the money," she says, standing at the top of the cellar stairs and looking down at them. The lantern in her hand makes shadows on their faces. She steps back as they approach. The two men climb the stairs, their pistol and knife keeping Isaac and Scarlett at bay.

Leach shoves his way to the front. Behind him, Asher Hales waits, watches.

Leach's eyes dart as he steps into the bar. Flora has made it a frightening place, just for him. The watch ball hanging above the stairs, the bottle of dried blood on the counter. In the dim light, it is easy to believe the Mariner's Arms is a place of ghosts and demons and all those things her mother had feared. Leach is afraid of this place, Flora knows. Perhaps she is a little afraid of this place too.

"Do you have it, witch?" he hisses.

Flora nods.

His eyes flash. She knows he wants to come after her. Wants to strike her, knock her down. But what might such a thing cause? He believes her capable of calling the devil and sending ships to the ocean floor. Think of what she could do to a mortal like him.

She climbs the stairs. Can hear their footsteps behind her, heavy and rhythmic.

Leach turns his pistol to Asher, warning him to stay back. And Asher stays, because he is a coward.

Flora leads Leach past her mother's room, past Jack's room, into the third guestroom. Shards of the black mirror crunch beneath her boots.

Leach steps inside uncertainly. She sees his eyes move over the half-planed letters carved into the wall, over the filthy rug, over the loose floorboard that had hidden the silver.

There is a great power to this, Flora realises. A great power to this craft her mother had made her life. Is it magic? Perhaps. After all, the healing water had brought back Scarlett's sight. Perhaps it is magic, but perhaps it is more about manipulation. Perhaps the power lies in taking a man's fear and making him believe.

She will not lose sight of her rationality, her reason. But she cannot discount the craft entirely. Because her mother's black mirror, Flora has come to realise, is far more than just a parlour trick. She has seen men's deaths in that dark glass. And she has seen fire rip through her inn, burning it to the ground.

"Where is the money?" Leach demands. He holds the gun out in front of him. Flora knows it is empty. He had fired at Isaac. Had not had time to reload.

She nods towards the loose floorboards. "Under there."

Leach eyes her hesitantly. He goes to the corner of the room. Prises up the boards.

And there is nothing, of course. The silver is heavy in Flora's pocket.

Her heart is thumping. How will all this happen, she wonders? The details in the glass have been unclear. But she is suddenly, deathly certain that tomorrow, she will not be reopening the Mariner's Arms.

She pulls aside the rug. Sets the lantern on the floor, its flame lighting the indents of the circle.

Leach looks back at her. With the light beneath him, his face is strangely shadowed. He looks old and worn. "Where is the money, witch?" he demands. And then he looks down. Looks down at the rough-hewn circle with which Flora's mother had sought to change the images in the glass. The circle she had believed was full of dark magic. The circle she believed had unleashed demons into her home.

Leach stares at his boots. They have inched across the outer edge of the ring. "What is this?" The malice in his voice has given way to terror.

And Flora has no thought of where her answer comes from. The words escape on their own accord. "A man who steps inside the circle," she says calmly, "is a man destined to die."

She sees the flame come at her as Leach grabs the lantern and hurls it in horror. The lamp flies past her and splinters against the window.

Leach rushes from the room.

And Flora turns to watch the flames climbing their way up the curtains. They tear through the dry, dusty fabric and race towards the thick beams of the roof. She feels the smoke in her throat, in her eyes. But the sight of it is mesmerising. She cannot look away.

She glances down at the circle. Black magic? Or just a trick of the mind? Either way, it had been a frighteningly easy line to cross.

She feels a firm hand around her arm. She turns, expecting Isaac. But Asher Hales is standing close, his breath hot and stale against her cheek. He seems to barely notice the fire.

"The money," he hisses. "Where is it?"

Flora digs into her pocket and pulls out the coin pouch.

Asher stares. "No. That cannot be all of it."

She looks him squarely in the eye. "This is all of it. It's just one man's share."

His lip curls. "Give it to me."

This money is not intended for men like Asher Hales. This money is intended for Isaac to build his new life. But Asher has Scarlett's knife in his hand. Smoke is pushing into the passage and flames are climbing the rafters. Soon this place will crumble.

Flora hears Isaac calling her name. They need to leave. Need to get their children out safely. She cannot stay and fight Asher Hales.

And so she upends the bag of silver into the room, kicking the coins in the direction of the flames. Asher shoves her away and darts towards them, dropping desperately onto his hands and knees.

Isaac grabs Flora's arm and pulls her from the burning room. A cloth is knotted around his upper arm, an ink stain of blood darkening the fabric. "Quickly," he says. "We need to leave."

Bessie darts out of the parlour and runs towards Jack's room. Flames are beginning to lick the doorframe. Flora snatches her arm, yanking her back as a wall of heat slams them.

Is this, she wonders fleetingly, what her mother had sought to reverse? Had she seen a snowy-haired girl in her mirror, dashing through the burning rooms of the Mariner's Arms? She will never know, of course, not for certain. But today she has begun to understand the allure of black magic.

"Downstairs," Flora tells her daughter sharply. "Quickly."

Bessie grips her dog, her eyes full of tears. "What about all the flowers?"

Yes, the flowers will burn in their pouches and pockets. They will burn along with her mother's chest. The lambswool will bubble and the polished shelves will splinter away. The fire will take the room in which she had been born, in which she had stitched her wedding dress, become a mother.

It will take the floorboards that had hidden the silver. Take the cellar stairs worn thin by smugglers' boots. It will blacken the tunnel in which Jack had died.

Tomorrow, this place will be a cold stone shell. The rain and the wind will beat it down until there is nothing left.

Flora cannot bring herself to feel sorrow. Cannot bring herself to feel anger. Because she knows, somewhere deep inside, that Tom Leach has brought her exactly what she had wanted.

Leave through the front door and Reuben's men will find them. They must go through the tunnel and wait on the beach for dark. Wait for Will Francis to appear in that boat that will take them away from Talland.

Isaac opens the cellar door, letting smoke billow in from the bar. He slams it hurriedly behind them.

Dust is raining down over the tunnel opening, the wall to one side a gaping mess. Bricks and earth are strewn over the floor, along with Leach's discarded pick.

Step carefully.

Isaac takes the lamp from above the stairs. He hands it to Flora for lighting. She shines the lantern into the tunnel and clutches her daughter's hand. And in they go, Flora and Bessie first, Scarlett with Mary in her arms. Isaac hunches and steps into the passage, a hand pressed to Gabriel's shoulder.

Something is not right. He hears that groan of shoring timber, that strange raspy breath of the rock. Sounds he has heard so many times in his sleep.

He grabs a fistful of Gabriel's coat and throws him back towards the cellar. He hollers for Scarlett, for Flora.

They have heard it too; that groan above their heads. Have felt the trickle of stone against their cheeks. There is no time for thinking, only for running.

The rock roars as it falls. Earth spills from above as the hacked-at shoring timbers splinter beneath the weight. And it is all sickeningly familiar as Isaac scrambles forward, breathless, and lands hard on his hands and knees on the floor of the cellar. Pain shoots through his arm. He clambers away from the opening, shielding his son. There is dust and smoke and rock and noise.

And then it is over. As sudden and incomprehensible as it had been the first time.

For a second he is afraid to open his eyes. He hears Mary shriek wildly. Feels Gabriel crawl out from beneath him. And he looks.

There is Gabriel and Mary and Scarlett. But there is no one else.

Scarlett clamps a hand over her mouth to stop a violent sob.

For a moment, Isaac is frozen, staring into the black pile of debris where the tunnel had once been.

None of this is real, of course. How can it be? It is too quick, too sudden, too brutal. In a moment the cellar door will open and Flora will find him, her daughter hovering at her side. He feels himself grapple at the image of it, trying desperately to make it real.

He calls her name. And there is nothing. Just Mary whining into Scarlett's shoulder and a distant crash from the inn above their heads.

Scarlett's voice is hushed and broken as she says: "We need to leave."

THE ESCAPING SOUL

Flames are curling around the bannister, pushing their way into the bar.

"The door at the back is blocked," Scarlett says breathlessly. "We need to go out through the front."

Isaac tries to focus. Tries to push aside the violent pain in his chest. He cannot think. Not now. He has to get his family to safety.

There will be men waiting outside, he is sure, waiting to punish them for Reuben's murder. Men that will have been alerted to their presence by the smoke streaming from the Mariner's Arms. But they have no choice but to go this way.

Villagers have gathered at the edge of the road, watching, murmuring. Martha Francis is hurrying towards them. Isaac cannot look at her. Cannot bear to answer her questions. Cannot bring himself to put to words all that has happened. If he speaks of it he will crumble.

He sees Ned Arthur on the other side of the road. "The banker," says Isaac. "Have you seen him?"

Arthur's eyes are on the flames pouring out the upstairs windows. "Saw him on the beach. You think he's there waiting for you?"

Isaac glances past him. If the banker is waiting on the beach, there will no doubt be more of Reuben's men prowling Bridles Lane. They will not have their escape easily.

He looks up at the church spire cutting through the trees. "The bell house," he says, catching Scarlett's eye.

Where else is there to go?

Asher Hales hurries down the staircase, landing heavily on his knees on the floor of the tavern. His lungs are burning and water streams from his eyes. His shirt is damp with sweat. But none of that matters. Because Henry Avery's haul is in his pocket.

He hears a crowd outside the door. He cannot go this way. No one can see him. What if they are somehow able to see the treasure he is carrying? Too many people know of this money. Too many greedy, untrustworthy people.

He snatches a poker from beside the fireplace and smashes one of the narrow windows at the side of the inn. He scrambles out of it, falling to his knees and coughing the smoke from his lungs. After a few moments, he stands dizzily, drawing down long breaths of air. He begins to walk.

For a few yards, he follows the stream carved into the hill behind the inn. And when he is sure he is alone, he pulls the pouch from his pocket. Stares into it. He shifts the bag from one hand to the other. It is real. It is here. It is his.

He smiles a real smile. When was the last time he had done such a thing?

There are other things in the pouch too. Shards of black glass he had scooped from the floor in his desperation to reach the silver. He lifts one out and turns it over in his hand. Then he tosses it into the stream, letting the water carry it towards the sea. He hears a distant roar as the Mariner's Arms spills its insides.

And he begins to walk. Up the hill he will go, away from Talland, away from Cornwall. East, then east and east again, until he reaches London.

He is beginning to remember himself. Beginning to remember who Asher Hales was always supposed to be. A pioneer. A man of science. A man who is better than the rest.

Tom Leach stands ahead of him on the path. Asher can't help but laugh. Poor, foolish Tom Leach who had turned away from a fortune because of a woman's trickery.

There is a gun in his hand.

Asher glances at it. He knows he ought to be afraid. He is always afraid. But somehow, this new-found wealth has given him courage. He takes Scarlett's knife from his pocket.

"Why have you come looking for trouble?" he asks Leach. "Don't you know you're going to die? You stepped inside the witch's circle." The words are so foolish he almost laughs, but he sees the terror in Leach's eyes.

"The money. Give it to me." Leach raises his pistol. There is a tremor in his hand. He has a gun and Asher only a knife, but it is Leach who is afraid.

Can a man bring about his own death, Asher finds himself wondering? Can the mind convince the body to die? A fascinating concept.

Leach's shot is wild with terror. It flies over Asher's shoulder. And before he can think of what he is doing, Asher has his knife in Leach's throat. Wine-dark blood fountains over his fingers.

What a feeling of power.

Leach falls across the thick muck of the path, animalistic rasps coming from his throat. And Asher's heart begins to speed. This is the moment he has been chasing his entire adult life. The moment of death. The escape of the soul.

He almost laughs. For years he has been trying to witness this moment. And in the end, all he needed was to kill a man himself. How simple. How achingly perfect.

He watches. Leans close to the body. He cannot miss a thing.

Look; twitching of the arms and legs. The departing soul causing movement as it escapes. Watch as the eyes turn to glass; a sign that the body is now no more than a shell. He looks upwards. Can the soul be seen?

There, above the body. A shifting of the air. So subtle it is almost imperceptible. But Asher is certain. The soul escaping. If they were in darkness, he is certain, the escaping life force would shine like the corpse lights as it moves away from the body. Perhaps such a thing could be measured. Recorded. Extensively researched.

For a long time, Asher sits beside Leach's still form.

He will go to London and present these ideas in the coffee houses. Share them among his fellow students, his fellow surgeons, his fellow inquiring minds.

He takes the pistol from Leach's motionless hand. Reaches into his coat pocket for the powder flask and balls. He opens the chamber and pours the powder in carefully.

Soon, Asher Hales will be a great man. And Caroline Bailey will realise it. She will crawl from the wreckage of her life and come to him. This money in his pocket will see him to greatness. Fame. It will be easy for Caroline to find him. Because he will be the man who shines like the brightest of stars.

The church is empty but for a woman praying close to the altar. Sunlight spears the coloured window, but does little to light the nave. The smell of smoke hangs in the air, clinging to their clothing, their hair, the sky.

Scarlett goes to the window and tries to peer through. Tries to catch a glimpse of the banker.

He had been waiting for her and Isaac on the beach, back when she was a child. Fourteen years later, he is still waiting. There has to be an end to it.

Isaac follows her into the churchyard. They peer down at the beach. There he is, the tiny figure of the banker, pacing the sand, watching, waiting.

"Stay low," Isaac hisses, pushing her to the ground. "Don't let him see you."

Scarlett lies on her front at the edge of the rock face, feeling the wind rush up to meet her.

The banker will find them if they take the cliff path. Will find them if they try and leave by sea, now the eastern beach is inaccessible. He will surely have stationed men at the top of Bridles Lane.

Why such loyalty to Reuben, Scarlett wonders? Even after his death?

She sucks in her breath. There is a boat on the edge of the bay, moving steadily towards them. She squints. Her vision feels cloudy, unreliable. "Can you see who it is?"

"Ayes," says Isaac. "It's Jacob."

They watch in silence. Watch him slide through the water towards them, slowly, silently, behind the eyes of the banker. Watch him come to help them escape, as he had returned to Talland to do.

Isaac looks over the edge of the cliff. "We've got to climb down."

Scarlett's eyes follow his. The rock is rugged and dark. Vertical, no. But not far from it. Waves beat relentlessly up against the base.

"It's climbable," says Isaac.

She wants to believe him. Wants to believe they have a means of escape. But the rocks are slippery with sea mist and rain. She knows, beneath his coat, the sleeve of Isaac's shirt is darkening with blood.

"You've been hurt," she says. "How can you climb?"

He squeezes her shoulder, and climbs to his feet. "We've no choice."

Scarlett searches the church. There is no rope. Nothing that will help them scale the rock. But they are hidden in a curve of the cliff. From here the banker will not see them.

And so, they will climb.

Isaac and Scarlett take the children out to the graveyard. They pass the headstones of their family, pass their father's memorial. They pass the grave of Martha's mother behind which the signalling lanterns hide.

Scarlett takes Mary from Isaac. The bullet is in the wall, she reminds herself, with flames on all sides. Still, he cannot climb the cliffs with a child beneath his arm.

"Let me take her down," she says.

Isaac unwinds the scarf from around his neck. He ties it tightly around Scarlett's front, latching Mary to her back.

Scarlett tucks up her skirts. They have to go. Now. Before Reuben's men see Jacob in the bay. She peers over the edge at the sea thrashing the headland. Mary's legs curl around her waist.

And they climb because they have no choice. Rock slides beneath their boots, sending earth raining into the sea. Scarlett's knuckles whiten as she grips the slippery crag. One step, she tells herself. Then another, another. Like walking the clifftop in the dark. To the side of her, Isaac and Gabriel are climbing slowly, steadily. She sees them speak to each other, their words lost beneath the roar of the sea.

Scarlett's boots touch the rocks at the base of the cliff. A swell of sea rolls towards her, tugging at her ankles, trying to pull her off balance. She dares to glance over her shoulder. Jacob is close. His boat is bumping and grinding against the rock. The water is too shallow for him to come any closer.

Scarlett times her run across the rocks with the inhalation of the sea. Mary wriggles and bleats, trying to escape the confines of the tightly knotted scarf.

Jacob reaches out a hand and helps her into the boat.

With five people aboard, the dory sits low in the water, the swell pushing over the gunwale. They keep close to the cliffs, away from the eyes of the banker.

Isaac takes off his coat and snatches an oar from his father. He begins to row.

"You've been hurt," says Jacob.

Isaac shakes his head dismissively, though Scarlett can see beads of sweat glistening on his forehead. The dory tilts on the swell. They pull away from the cliff, towards the open water.

Jacob looks at Scarlett. He nods towards the pocket of his coat. "In there."

She reaches inside. Finds a large key.

"My cottage in Portreath," says Jacob. "You'll be safe there."

"What about you?"

"I've no one after me," he says. "The two of you will need it more."

Is she to say *come with us*? Is she to invite him back into their lives? She can't bring herself to do it. Even after all she has learnt, Jacob Bailey is still the man with blood on his hands. He is everything she does not want to become.

She doesn't speak. Just nods silently and slips the key into her pocket.

Asher stands at the edge of the cliff.

He looks at the pistol. Looks down at the boat.

He has one shot.

Who is this bullet for? Scarlett Bailey, who had drawn his blood? Isaac, who had taken the woman he loves and made her his wife?

No, each would be a waste.

What a potent thing it is to be a man strong enough to take a life. He feels dizzy with the power of it. And this power ought not be wasted.

This bullet is for one man and one man alone.

SILENCE

He is alive. And then he is gone.

The shot comes from the clifftops. Finds Jacob's chest. There is barely a sound, and not a hint of warning. Jacob's body falls backwards, the oar sliding from his hands. His death is sudden and still and silent.

Scarlett holds her breath. She waits for the next gunshot. Waits to die. But there is only quiet. Only the water lapping at the side of the boat.

And so Jacob Bailey is dead. Scarlett has gotten what she had wished for in the darkest, most bitter moments of the Wild.

She looks down at her father's face. He is expressionless, blank, the breeze moving the unruly grey thatch of his hair. She reaches over and closes his eyes.

She looks at her brother. His eyes are fixed to the bloom of blood spreading across Jacob's chest. Scarlett looks up at the clifftop. There is no one there. Whoever had pulled the trigger is gone.

Isaac clears his throat. "Help me." His voice is husky.

Scarlett nods. They will send Jacob's body to the sea floor, back to the place it has always been.

She pulls Mary around to her front. Unties the scarf and hands the baby to Gabriel. The children watch with wide, silent eyes.

Scarlett reaches an arm beneath her father's body. She feels the weight of him, feels his fading warmth. She and Isaac lift him over the gunwale. And down his body goes into the waiting sea.

Scarlett feels an unbidden swell of emotion. She covers her mouth, forcing her sob back inside. It doesn't feel right to break this stillness. Tears blur her vision. Are they tears for Flora and Bessie, or tears for her father? She blinks them away hurriedly. She cannot allow herself to crumble. Not here. Not now. Not until they are safe.

She presses a hand to her chest as a striking, physical pain wells up inside her. She leans over the gunwale and watches the last shadow of her father disappear. "He didn't want to leave us," she says. "He was forced to."

Isaac turns to look at her. "By who?" There is a thinness to his voice and she can tell he is afraid of the answer.

Scarlett reaches into her pocket for the letter. She screws it into her fist. Slips it over the edge to follow Jacob's body to the sea floor. "Asher Hales."

She shuffles onto the bench and takes up the seat left empty by her father. Begins to pull the oar through the water. The patch of sea beneath which Jacob lies becomes lost in the enormity of the ocean.

"The eastern beach." Isaac's voice is caught in his throat. "We need to check."

Scarlett nods wordlessly. She presses a hand over her brother's and squeezes tightly.

They row in silence, the oars sighing through the sea. Scarlett is desperate to make it around the headland, desperate to leave Talland and the banker and the invisible shooter behind. Desperate to leave Jacob's circle of sea and the funnel of smoke above the Mariner's Arms.

But she cannot bear to look as they round the point to the eastern beach. Cannot bear to have this tiny flicker of hope torn away.

She doesn't look over her shoulder. Can't manage even the briefest of glances at the beach beyond the tunnel.

Isaac leaps into the shallow water.

Still Scarlett can't look. Her heart is pounding.

"Flora and Bess," she says. "Are they there? Are they safe?"

Gabriel is on his feet, watching the beach, making the boat tilt and the baby squeal. And he is garbling, *ayes Aunt Scarlett, they are there, they are safe.*

She dares to turn. Sees Isaac in the water, thrashing towards the shore. Sees Flora and Bessie at the edge of the sand, the dark mouth of the tunnel behind them. The dog is running in circles around the narrow curve of the beach.

Scarlett hears a cry of relief escape her. The gratitude makes her body hot and tired and achy and alive; all these things at once. She watches Isaac take Flora in his arms. And Scarlett brings the boat closer, closer until the oars graze the bottom of the sea.

Flora lifts Bessie into the boat, then lets Isaac help her inside. And then they are rowing again, around the point, beneath the plume of smoke that is palling the village.

Isaac takes one hand from the oar. He slides his fingers through Flora's. And Scarlett can tell by the look in his eyes that he can't bring himself to let go.

TOMORROW

"Ground ivy," says Flora. "It will help it heal." She pins the strapping around Isaac's arm and carefully pulls down his shirtsleeve. Her fingers ghost over his skin.

He gives her a smile. "Thank you." Slightly rigid, slightly stilted. Things have shifted. Everything is different.

Flora holds his gaze for a moment, then sweeps the last scraps of ivy from the table and tosses them into the fire. She goes to the sleeping pallet in the corner of the room where Bessie is curled up on her side, the dog snoring at her feet.

Jacob's cottage is tiny, crowded with them all inside.

When they had arrived here, two days after escaping Talland, Isaac had found himself oddly drawn to the tin cups, the bowls, the candle holders lining the shelves. Had found himself peeking into the storage chest and feeling the coat, the mittens, the worn woollen cap that lay inside. He couldn't make sense of why. Was it grief for his father that had him rifling through his things? Curiosity? All he had learned about Jacob's disappearance had him questioning who the man had truly been.

He had found a stash of money in a jar beside the flour. No fortune, but enough for those elusive tickets out of Cornwall.

This is not the way he had imagined his escape. Caroline had always pushed so strongly for their freedom. It doesn't feel right to be doing this without her. But just how real, he wonders now, were any of the plans he and his wife had made? Just how real had any of their life been?

There is bitterness in his throat at the thought of all he has learned. And there are questions he feels sure he will never know the answers to. Questions he is not sure he wants answered.

He does not know what to think. Does not know what it is he is feeling. Is it grief, or anger or betrayal or sorrow? Perhaps it is all these things at once.

But he will keep moving. Tomorrow, they will take a coach to Penzance and find the ship that will carry them north, away from a life of free trade. Perhaps he is feeling grief and anger and betrayal and sorrow, but he is also feeling hope.

He tosses another log on the fire, sending sparks shooting up the chimney.

Gabriel is asleep by the hearth, curled up on his side with a hand splayed out in front of him. Isaac sits. Presses a hand to his son's shoulder, feeling his body rise and fall with breath.

On the other side of the room, he hears them murmuring, Flora and Bessie, whispering to each other in their hushed and musical way. He dares to glance across the room at them; their matching faces, their pressed-together knees, the cascades of silver-blonde hair.

There is a part of him, of course, that wants to go to her. That part of him that had longed for more when her fingers had grazed his forearm. That part of him that had been as excited as a child when she'd said, *yes Isaac, I will climb on that ship beside you.*

But everything is different. Strange. Dizzying. Being with Flora is no longer about escape, about vanishing fleetingly from the strain of the world around them. The moment he walks across the room and takes her in his arms, it will make this real.

Right now, there is the shadow of Caroline. There is their hazy, unformed future and there are answers to find to his son's impossible questions. He cannot allow himself to think of that warmth she leaves inside him. Cannot allow himself to think of how it feels to hold her in the dark.

So for now, he will just think of how calming it is to hear her breathe in the night. Will think of the heart-splitting gratitude he had felt when he had found her safe at the end of the tunnel. Will think of how glad he is that she will be there when he wakes.

In the morning, Scarlett walks with them into the village.

"You will write, ayes?" she asks. "The very moment you're settled?"

Isaac smiles. "The very moment."

She knots her fingers in her shawl. There is the carriage, on the edge of the village green. There is the coachman, heaving trunks onto the roof and tying them with rope. The sight of it makes this real.

"And the children?" she asks. "You'll manage?" There is guilt in her for leaving them. Leaving Isaac with only pieces of the truth. Guilt at leaving him to build a new life in the wake of the things he has learned. After all the years she has spent longing to be a help to her brother, is she truly to leave him now, when he needs her the most?

"You've to make your own life, Scarlett," he says firmly. "I'll not have you lose that chance because of me." He squeezes her shoulders. "Besides, we'll not be alone."

No, she thinks, a faint smile on her lips. They will not be alone. The thought of it leaves a warmth inside her.

She throws her arms around Isaac's neck, her throat tightening.

How is she to do this; live a life without her brother to anchor her? The thought of it is far too overwhelming. But she knows it is time to do so. She cannot stay latched to him forever.

She steps back, swiping at the tears she is unable to contain.

"Are you certain?" Isaac asks, his hand still around her wrist.

She nods. Her throat, her chest are aching, but yes. Certain. "I'll see you again, ayes?" she says, her voice wavering. "Promise me I'll see you again."

"Of course." Scarlett can tell he is trying for lightness, but she hears the emotion thickening his words. He kisses her cheek. "Of course you'll see us again. You'll see us again before you know it."

And so she watches as they climb aboard the coach that will take them to the harbour in Penzance. Watches as the carriage gets smaller and smaller until there is nothing but hills and sky.

She stands outside Jamie's cottage for a long time. She is a mess. She has no bonnet, no comb, no clean clothes. But she also has no weapon. She has no idea what has become of her knife. But she doesn't want it. Perhaps she doesn't need it. Perhaps she can be a person who is in control.

She wants to be someone without blood on her boots or a blade at her knee. And if she knocks on Jamie's door, she will have to keep this promise to herself and be just that.

Perhaps he will turn her away. Perhaps he has already seen too much. Perhaps she ought to have climbed into the carriage with Isaac and Flora.

She knocks. And there is nothing but silence. It does little to ease the thundering in her chest.

For a moment she thinks of leaving. Thinks to walk back up the hill to that lonely cottage where her father had spent so much of his life.

No. She does not want to be Jacob.

Rain begins to spill. It streams across the cobbles and turns the edges of the road to mud. Scarlett presses her back against Jamie's door. Water runs from the thin edge of the awnings and drizzles down her neck.

It is dusk when she sees him. He is in his neat blue uniform, hands dug into his pockets and a scarf bound tight at his neck. Water drips from the ends of his hair.

At the sight of her, he stops striding. Smiles.

"I'm glad you're happy to see me," she says throatily.

He pulls a key from his pocket and slides it into the lock. "I'm happy to see my lodgings. It's a good night to be inside." He chuckles at Scarlett's uncertain expression. Puts a hand to her shoulder to usher her into the house. "I'm happy to see you too. Very happy."

They stand opposite each other, letting pools of silver water gather at their feet. With Jamie's eyes on hers, Scarlett's carefully rehearsed words become a tangled mess.

"It's cold," she manages.

Jamie takes the tinderbox from the shelf and crouches to light the fire. When he looks back at her, one side of his face is lit with the glow of the gathering flames.

"My father is dead," she says.

He stands. "Scarlett, I'm sorry, I—"

"I'm not telling you for your sympathy. I'm telling you because…" She fades out. How does she put into words this new control she feels inside her? This belief that, on the day of her father's death, the Wild's hold on her had died too? How does she explain the way she had felt the anger release her when she had lowered that knife from Asher's throat?

The Wild is still there, of course. She knows it has not left her. It is in her blood, it never will. But she will not let it take her to the dark places it had taken her father. She will not let it put a dead man at her feet.

She says: "I was wrong to let you leave."

She feels painfully vulnerable. Knows there is every chance Jamie could shake his head and send her away.

He steps close and takes her hands. Runs a finger over the curve of her thumbnail. "I have nothing to give you," he says after a moment. "I don't even have an oven."

Scarlett smiles slightly. "What need do we have for an oven?"

His grip on her hands tightens. "I'm out until dawn several nights a week. And I'm terrible in the mornings."

She raises her eyebrows. "Are you trying to turn me away?"

"No." He presses a hand to her cheek. "No. I just want you to know what this life will be."

Yes, she sees a glimpse of this life. She sees herself walking through the village to distrustful whispers as the smugglers do their best to keep their secrets away from her ears. She sees herself battle to keep her anger inside. And she sees nights of lying alone in the dark, terrified that Jamie might entangle himself with men as ruthless as Tom Leach.

She sees this imperfect life and she wants it anyway.

She kneels by the edge of the hearth. Jamie sits beside her, his wet shoulder pressing against hers. Steam curls from their clothes, hot and white in the firelight.

"Does this mean you're staying?" he asks.

Scarlett smiles to herself. She has much to tell him. Tales of collapsing tunnels and burning inns. The stray bullet that had flown from the clifftops. There is Reuben's murder and the silver beneath the floor and the smugglers' banker pacing the beach. She wants to tell him it all. Every piece.

She holds her hands to the fire. Stares into the light.

By now, the ship will have left Penzance harbour, taking her brother northward towards islands and snow. By now, she is sure, the Mariner's Arms is nothing but a shell, and Charles Reuben is deep in the earth of their churchyard.

And just beyond, in the inky blue of the bay, a man lies on the floor of the sea. From the top of the cliff his memorial stone watches, having waited almost two decades for him to arrive.

HISTORICAL NOTE ON THE WEST COUNTRY TRILOGY

When Richard Dodge became the vicar of Talland Church in 1713, he quickly developed something of a reputation. Dodge became famous across the county as a ghost and demon hunter, known for his ability to cast restless souls away from the land of the living. He conducted regular exorcisms in Bridles Lane (also spelled Bridals Lane) and was sought out by everyone from parishioners to fellow clergymen when the supernatural ventured a little too near.

Dodge's most famous feat took place in 1725, when he was approached by Mr Gryllis, a rector in nearby Lanreath to lay the ghosts of headless horses several villagers had seen on the moors. Dodge supposedly caught sight of these ghostly horses, only to discover they pulled a carriage transporting the devil himself. Dodge proceeded to exorcise the moor, causing the spectral carriage to be pulled back to Hell. Records of this event exist in Talland Church's archives to this day.

Though we can surmise Dodge's exorcisms were a cover for local smuggling activities— of which the vicar would have undoubtedly received a cut— his demon-filled sermons would have been readily believed by the superstitious population of eighteenth-century Talland.

Richard Dodge remained vicar of the parish until 1746, when he died at the age of ninety-three. His body is buried at the top end of the churchyard, close to where the cemetery gives way to the sea.

There are many theories surrounding the haul of Henry Avery, widely acknowledged as one of the most prosperous pirates in history. His looting of the treasure ship *Gunsway* in 1695 remains the biggest single pirate raid ever recorded, with the haul totalling approximately $100 million in today's currency.

One of the most enduring theories suggests Avery hid his wealth in the cliffs of south Cornwall. A letter supposedly written by Avery to a close friend detailed three chests of jewels and gold buried close to Lizard Point. So convincing was this piece of evidence that, in 1779, three men from Saint Michael's Mount embarked on a two-year treasure hunt, hacking into the cliffs at the south-west tip of the county. The hunt came to an end when one of Avery's descendants told the men his ancestor had died penniless in Barnstable, north Devon.

While there is no evidence to suggest any of Henry Avery's haul ever made its way to Talland, seventeenth century pirates' articles dictated that any takings be distributed fairly between the captain and ship's hands. As a result, numerous shares of the *Gunsway's* haul would no doubt have found their way back to England in the possession of Avery's crew.

All incantations and healing charms, from the bags of good luck Meg gives her visitors in *Moonshine (Prequel)* to the fire-warmed stones for the child's-cough (whooping cough) Flora uses in *Bridles Lane*, are based on ancient Cornish healing lore. The arrangement of letters on the wall of the guestroom in *Wild Light* is known at the Sator Square:

S A T O R
A R E P O
T E N E T
O P E R A
R O T A S

Utilised extensively throughout Cornwall as a charm against black magic, the square was also used as far back as the first century, having been discovered on ancient Roman drinking vessels and carved into columns in the buried ruins of Pompeii and Herculaneum. Its function in Roman times remains unclear.

To this day, practitioners of herbal lore and ancient Cornish witchcraft can be found around the county.

ABOUT THE AUTHOR

Johanna Craven is an Australian-born author, composer, pianist and terrible folk fiddler. She currently divides her time between London and Melbourne. Her more questionable hobbies include ghost hunting, meditative dance and pretending to be a competitor on The Amazing Race when travelling abroad.

Find out more at johannacraven.com.

Printed in Great Britain
by Amazon

48553691R00299